For Craig
With thanks and all
good wishes Judith
21-6-13

Root and Branch

Judith Whitworth

Also available in Kindle version on Amazon.

ISBN: 1483915824

ISBN-13: 978-1483915821

ACKNOWLEDGMENTS

Evelyn Bacharach, for information on early Jewish poetry.
Doris Leverington-Ellicott, for part of the Catholic Mass.
Craig Ferguson, for helping me with this computer.
My late, youngest son, Frederikos Tripos, for listening.

CONTENTS

CHAPTER ONE

ADINA

Bread! That was what it was. Sweet, rich-smelling bread. Good white flour bread, made with cinnamon, maybe a little honey and sesame seeds. Just like the special breads they had at home for feast days. Adina lifted her head and breathed in the tantalizing smell deeply. It was the first time she had smelt anything like it since she left home, oh but such a delicious smell. Her mouth watered.

An early morning breeze, capricious, wandering, had stealthily swirled through the normally fetid streets of the city. Through the narrow lanes, over the rooftops and courtyards, then into the great market square, where the girl now stood.

Tears pressed out of her eyes, so she shut them tightly. No tears, she had decided that very firmly right at the beginning, they did no good anyway. Despite herself, a tear did squeeze from a lid and splashed down her cheek. Unthinking, she raised a hand to brush it away, which was checked by the chain on her wrist. She had forgotten the chain.

"It is just for show Adina," said the Eunuch kindly. "They, the buyers, like to see a lovely girl so tied." He had stopped abruptly, aware that he had already said too much, and liking her, did not want to frighten her. For she had been an easy one to break in, few new slaves were as sensible. Quiet, clever, kind, she had surprisingly eased his lot considerably and he would be sorry to see her go. Without being aware of it, he had delayed with her sale. He had, for some strange reason unconsciously kept her too long, but with the big holiday approaching, he knew the master would take no more excuses.

He had bought fine brass chains for the girl, just to show she was special, symbolic bonds as it were. Indeed, shining and new, they did look more like jewels than prisoner's chains against the thin gauze of her tunic.

"I am to stand out there wearing that!" her face grew crimson. The sheer tunic had been handed to her by the old woman, yet she wore the coarse old shift, refusing to change out of it.

"You must!" the Eunuch sounded gruff and she understood there must have been a disagreement between him and the master. He was obviously a valued and trusted slave, yet feelings or modesty were not part of the business.

So there she stood shivering in the dawn cool, wearing a cobweb.

Adina concentrated on the smell of bread, then, as usual, let her mind wander. When she had finally realized that she would never go home, she had decided to think deeply of her life, her childhood, her home, her parents. Everything. She needed to recall and impress all her memories firmly in her mind, so that, whatever the future held, she could lose herself in the precious thoughts of the past.

The wayward breeze brushed at her skimpy robe, which caused her to shiver again. She had been shocked at being so shamefully clad, yet quickly discovered that if she bent ever so slightly forward, the thin cloth would not peak on her nipples. What a disgrace, that she, daughter of an important and wealthy man, should be paraded for sale, wearing almost nothing. If only her father knew. If only he would ride up now on his fine Arab horse and take her home.

Enough, enough. Those thoughts only bring tears. No tears. Another slid unbidden down her face but this time she let it, remembering the chains.

"Are you alright?" The smooth voice of the Eunuch sounded just below and behind her. He had been watching her with regret, saw the tear, felt her pain, and his own.

She did not answer. Well what could she say? Was she alright? Yet she knew from the past weeks, indeed months, that he meant kindly.

"Can I get you something?" the voice said again.

This time she was alerted.

"Yes," she turned slightly to see him. "I smell wonderful bread, I'd like some." And watched him walk swiftly away, just a little surprised.

Daylight was almost with them, a glint of sun, reflected on some glass or metal high on the southern ramparts of the city wall. Without moving her head, she tried to observe this place where she and the other slaves awaited their fate.

They had been placed on the southern side of the square, so, according to the Eunuch, they would have some shade from the row of dusty trees during the day. For it wouldn't do to have them fainting in front of prospective buyers. To her left stood the other slaves but unlike her, they were cruelly shackled. Her eyes rested on the little boys and her heart ached for them. So young, so like her younger brothers, what a terrible thing had befallen them, and now they were to be sold. Yes terrible, for such young things to be in so hopeless a position. She coughed lightly to alert them, and was rewarded with smiles.

"Remember all that I told you, my dearlings," she called quietly, trying to throw her voice to them. "Everything, yes?" to which they nodded earnestly. There was a stir from the line beyond them, as all the others heard her too, and gratefully smiled.

This last slave trader, a big man in the business obviously, fat and lazy, had collected the cream from far and wide to sell here in this great city. She had seen him twice. Once weeks ago when she had been dumped, almost smothered in a huge sack at his feet, then last night. He must have had good reports of her from the Eunuch that she was no trouble, for he had even spoken kindly to her. Of course, he hoped she would bring him a good price. To her knowledge, she was the only green eyed, auburn haired, fair-skinned virgin for sale, of their group anyway.

A great sigh caused her whole body to shudder, so she leaned against the wooden bar behind her on which she was chained.

How, had it happened? Why, had it happened? She forced her mind back yet again to her home and everything of the catastrophe of what - six months ago?

At fifteen, she had been considered almost a woman. So, in the women's quarters, she was one of them, and her mother's new pregnancy was freely spoken of. The previous one, before the birth of her youngest brother, she had still been considered too young and talk of it had still been taboo. Of course she was well aware of what was happening, but never included in the woman talk. Silence fell, and the women bowed their heads over their work when she came in. This time, they had included her, even joked that it would be her turn next, for her mother stated flatly, easing her discomfort, this was definitely the last child she would bear.

It had, she realized vaguely, been a poor pregnancy. Her mother had been very sick for months, something which worried the women, for since Adina, her first, the five following pregnancies, all boys, had been totally trouble-free.

"I am hoping," her mother had said many times, resting as usual, always exhausted with her sickness, "that this will be a girl again, for I was just so with you. I do hope so. A companion for my old age, for you will be married soon, and how I shall miss you." The sweetest smile.

Nothing had been arranged yet, but there was talk, and Adina knew that with her two grandmothers and her mother, a good choice would be made. Her father might think it was he who made the decisions, but they all knew that he did not. It was generally known amongst the women and slaves, that the two older mistresses of the house were all-powerful. Clever, scheming and plotting women, they knew every little thing about their households, and their family. They were good mistresses too, if their slaves had the sense to toe the line at all times. Thanks to heaven, her mother had laughingly said many a time, they were also united and better than real sisters, fast friends. Their one ambition in life was to ensure the wellbeing of their son, daughter and their children.

It was they, so many years before, who had arranged her parent's marriage. Two great houses, landowners and sound business men, with only one child each, it might have meant disaster. Yet with the planning of the two women, that one marriage had been fortuitous, fertile and very successful. She, Adina, the firstborn, had been named for those two tough grandmothers. Adara and Nina resulted in Adina. Fair-skinned, with a golden glow and soft green eyes from Adara, and from Nina, magnificent, deep red hair. Everyone was happy. Then came the five boys, Drabo, Miert, Scion, Crayer and Daron. Their lands and trade had flourished. The two older boys were already travelling with their father and his managers to learn the business. The younger ones were more often than not at the farm, riding, hunting, playing war games, and learning the arts necessary to the sons of wealthy families.

The town where they had their house was just on the edge of the desert, but near the sea, so what breezes there were penetrated the specially made wind slits and shutters. Adina had loved her home and the shady courtyards full of plant life, the fountains playing. The constant rich smells which came from the kitchens intermingling with the scent of jasmine and, yes often, horse manure. It was a busy place, run mostly by her father's mother, whose home it had been on her marriage. Her own mother, beautiful and gentle, had been a great catch. Despite all the forebodings of ill luck, she had bred a fine family. Jealousy, her grandmother, Nina had explained. Human weakness wished bad luck on them, yet not only were they a fine couple, it had been a love match. Tenderly she brushed the red tresses, lovingly, hair so like her own, but remembering the tangles of her own girlhood, brushing more kindly than the nursemaids did.

Her father was very often away on business and often as embassy for the court. When she did see him, she was just a little in awe of him, for he was a big man, dark, and burnt from the sun, his hair a red black, if such a colour could be so described. Yet he was proud of his firstborn; with the promise of delicate beauty as her mother, she was also clever. It had been with some surprise when he learned that she could read and write. An accident, claimed the scribe, who was employed to tutor his sons, trying to hide his pride in his best pupil. Yet it was no accident that he also taught her Latin when the boys were out at their war games. What joy to fill her eager mind, which like a sponge soaked up everything he taught her, as well as languages, such a relief from their bastard of a tongue. He claimed that she had just picked it up, by observing her brothers. Having been bitterly disappointed at her birth, even suggesting she be exposed, her father had been ashamed. A son was what he wanted, not a girl. It was probably the last time his mother had forgotten herself and swiped him across the head. For she had been a tough mother, determined that her one chick should grow into a fine rooster. Expose one of their own, even if a girl? Certainly not! They were not peasants. What a wicked thought.

"Do not be stupid!" she again raised her hand, but only for show. "See this beauty? The same as her mother, so fair, so fine." And her voice thickened with a hint of emotion. "I think she will have my hair!" Holding the little thing to the light, turning it this way and that, so that the smudge of a fiery glow could be clearly seen. "There will be plenty of boys, just you see." And so there were.

The last year or so, when her father did see her, he narrowed his eyes and observed her beauty, mulling over in his mind who he should give her to in marriage. It would have to be to an important and wealthy man, advantageous, for she was lovely, and being his only girl, would have a fine dowry. Other people married their daughters younger, but not they. It never occurred to Adina that the reason was their wealth, there was no need. The summer had dragged on relentlessly, fading the surroundings, bleaching even the palm trees which towered above the courtyards and as happened very rarely, even the fountains fell to a trickle. Despite the expense, they sprinkled water on the flat roof every night to cool the hot floor stones and sat up there, hoping for a breeze. Little burners were set under the couches from which drifted aromatic smoke, to keep away the mosquitoes. Perhaps her mother would take up a small harp and sing softly, then tiring, would hand it to Adina. The maids brought up light meals and cold sherbets which they took without enthusiasm. While her mother's belly grew, she herself seemed to shrink, her eyes huge and often feverish. This time she was afraid, why, she herself could not explain, for she had birthed quite easily before. A cloud of fear blacked out the future which no amount of persuasion could dismiss.

The two grandmothers fluttered and tended to the tired woman, their anxiety kept for others who were ever stung by uncalled for reprimands. To the last kitchen slaves, every member of the household caught the worry, so voices were hushed, work was done swiftly and quietly. Everyone tried to be invisible. Yet Adina felt so close to her mother the last days, trying to anticipate her needs, running to fetch and carry, sitting near with her sewing, singing, or just being as quiet as a mouse.

Her father was away more than usual. He hated illness, hated to see his beautiful wife so faded and unattractive. Adina had learned much of men, and the wily skills of women during those months. Several times she had watched secretly through a shutter, how her grandmother sorted through a basket in the store room, her fingers trailing in indecision over the contents. Then, she saw the gift being slipped into the hand of her father, who would pretend he had bought it specially to give to his wife on his rare visits. It always worked, her mother's pleasure was well worth the lie. Adina looked at her tough grandmother with new eyes, growing aware in leaps and bounds, of the power of women.

Even the birth was bad, long, drawn out; it seemed nothing would help the pain. Silent, Adina watched her mother fight the screams which tried to escape her cracked lips. Only village women screamed. It was their only time of glory, for, poor things, no one ever listened to them at any other time.

Her father was sent for, and having drunk too much wine, was deeply asleep when at last, the baby girl was born.

Beautiful, chubby, like a three-month-old-child despite her long birth, they all gazed in awe. Another green eyed, red-haired little beauty lay serenely in a grandmother's arms. The women were ecstatic, clapping their hands and singing their songs of joy, disregarding the master who groaned hearing it, his head splitting from the excesses of his drinking.

Her mother seemed to glow with renewed energy and, reaching out, her smile so tender for this last child, she cradled her.

"She is just like you were at birth, my Adina," she said, her voice filled with love, "Just somewhat fatter." So they all laughed with relief, glad, oh so glad it was over.

That night the two grandmothers ceremoniously took the new daughter to show the father. His head, still hurting, for he really was not a heavy drinker normally, caused him to grumble at the intrusion and he merely squinted at the sleeping bundle.

"Leave it here awhile," he ordered, "I have guests coming, they must see her."

So they did, surprised, returning to the new mother with comforting sweet words as to the pride and joy the father had for his new daughter, wanting to show her to his friends.

The rest she barely knew, for she, like everyone, was tired and had gone to sleep in the room she shared with her grandmothers. Meanwhile, the house was quiet, leaving them in charge. Happy all was well and trusting no one else, they would be taking it in turns to care for the new mother and babe. Having slept well, Adina looked at the window and saw a streak of dawn, so she closed her eyes again.

The first thing she knew about the tragedy, was the screaming. Frightful, endless, wordless, on and on. She had shaken herself out of a nightmare to find it was real. It seemed that every throat in the house was open, screaming as if they were being murdered. Over the next ghastly day, it all came out in fits and starts between tears and tearing hair.

Happy, light of body once again, her mother had slipped down the stairs to see her husband. He was alone again, his friends having left. He was very drunk, having started again to try to cure the searing pain in his head. He watched her half-seeing with bloodshot eyes as she looked around the room for her newborn daughter.

"I've sent it away," he announced, his words slurred. "I did not want another daughter, so I had it disposed of."

Adina could only guess at the terrible scene. Her mother twisting her robe in her hands, weak from her pregnancy, the heat, a long birth, white faced, unbelieving.

"But she was so beautiful, like our Adina, a companion for my old age, when Adina gets married." Wringing her hands, beseeching. Dragging at his hands, trying to re-kindle the love they had had. "Please, please, my husband, let me have her."

Oh the noise of the woman, oh his head. He hit out, sending her reeling, the first time in their years together had he struck her.

"Go off woman, leave me. She is gone. I did not want another daughter. Who will find her dowry? Go now, and be satisfied with what you have. Leave me!" Pushing at the clinging hands, a picture of guilt, angry, hurting, he glowered. Knowing in the mists of his mind that he had committed a great sin, and that the all-powerful women in his life would never, ever, forgive, or let him forget it.

Silently, she had gone back to the roof where her mother waited. No word was spoken, only her empty hands were held out as staring at the night sky, tears poured from her eyes. Shocked, unbelieving, the older woman had raced, found her sister-in-life, and together they had descended like the furies upon the son. So began the search.

"Will you take something to drink?" Later, love and pity in their very breath, the women tried to comfort the grieving mother as they bound her breasts.

"Just some fruit," she replied almost too calmly, "I am a little dry. Better not drink too much if I am to stop the milk." So practical, always the perfect girl, they accepted her words numbly while they wondered at her.

The bowl of fruit was brought, a small knife to cut it and a bowl of water to rinse her hands afterwards. In sorrow they changed her soiled cloths silently, washing her down, cooling her exhausted body.

"I am cold," she said. So thinking that she was in shock, they brought soft blankets and covered her tenderly. At last exhausted, they slept, the three women. The stars bright above them, glinting through the roof of vines, soft, salt-laden breeze rustling the dry palm fronds.

It appeared in the dawn, that she still slept, so they went down to the kitchens as usual, to give orders, to make up a tray, and returned just as the sun rose. Putting the tray down on the side table, Adara noticed flies buzzing around her daughter and frowned. They must change the cloths again, bathe her, and put on fresh clothes. Perhaps she was bleeding heavily.

The truth took moments to sink into their paralysed minds as they began to draw off the bed covers. Both women touched the stiff form, drew back the blankets, and saw the knife still clutched in blood-stained fingers. Blood, everywhere, blood, soaked in the bed clothes, blood dark and stiffening.

So the screaming began, like in a place of torture, on and on, driving every soul in the house frantic, then up to the roof, horror, disbelief. Adina stood in her shift, gazing at the open mouths, the streaming eyes, the hands clutching, cradling, till Mina, her old nurse, drew her away.

"She died in childbirth you hear?" Mina hissed as she shoved her out. "You saw nothing, understand?" Then in the privacy of the bedroom, took the girl in her arms and wept also.

They buried her the next day as was correct. Lying on the bier, she had looked marble white, so beautiful in death, if possible more lovely than in life. As the men carried her out of the gates, Adina standing on the highest roof, had strained to see the last of her mother.

"You are to go to the farm," her grandmothers instructed her curtly. Their shock and sorrow had left them almost as cold and lifeless as their beloved daughter.

"Tell your brothers as kindly as you can, just that she and the baby died in childbed. They have heard of it before, it is better they do not know the truth for now. No doubt they will learn of it eventually."

By the time the funeral was over, the mourners properly entertained and departed, they were all prepared to leave and dusk was falling. Only ten miles along well-known roads, the journey would not take long in the cool of the night. It would be better to leave that house, she realized, now just a house of sorrow. In her shock, she considered her father for a moment, then dismissed him, he who had, it was whispered, been the cause of all the trouble.

They left the place without farewells, she and the old groom on ponies, Mina on a donkey, while a mule carried their luggage. The grandmothers had hurriedly got everything together, a welcome task in their fog of misery. Led by the groom, covered in their all-enveloping burkas, they left the streets and pressed on into the country. Along the way, Adina learnt the whole ugly tale, for Mina, beside herself, rocked and wailed endlessly. Mina had been nurse to all of them and far more than a slave, for she had been nurse to her mother also. Loving, wise, very old but wiry and surprisingly fit, she always amused them by speeding about the huge, rambling house with amazing agility.

"Is it bad being a slave?" the young Adina had asked years before, sitting on the lap, stroking the beloved face of her nurse.

"It was at first my angel," she had replied absently, trying to untangle the beautiful hair of her charge.

"And now?" the curious child had pressed, for only recently, there had been a new slave who had wept all the time, and had tried to run away, and so had been beaten by the gateman.

"I was from a poor family my love, so who knows what my life would have been if I had not been bought by your grandfather. Of course by the time I reached the slave market, I was broken, not a virgin many times over, so almost worthless. Yes," she had stopped, her unseeing gaze picturing the scene of her salvation, "I was lucky," and kissed her roundly. "You are my family now."

Now as they plodded along, it was Adina who spoke words of comfort, leaning down, caressing, her own sorrow superseded by the need to give strength to this very old, much-loved friend. Every mile which passed brought fresh bursts of sorrow from the old one. As the darkness surrounded them, silence fell too. There was little moon these days and it was not up yet.

Where they went wrong, she never could guess, but the old groom, exhausted by the tumultuous day, when no one had taken a siesta, must have nodded off. For they had wandered far from the road, deep into the desert, till the beasts, weary too, not knowing where they were going, had just stopped.

"Wake up, wake up!" Adina shook the groom. It was hopeless, they were surely lost, the old man shattered and useless. Realizing that she must take charge, Adina found some bushes nearby and settled the weeping Mina under them, first spreading a rug on the coarse gravel, a linen sheet over to protect them from the dew.

It had been the linen sheet she learned later, which had given them away.

"I went over to see what it was," the boy said in his coarse accent, his breath as foul as his camels. "So I found you," a great grin creasing his face. "You are mine too, because it was I who found you. My brothers can have the beasts and goods."

"Be careful with her," whispered the terrified Mina. "She is the daughter of a great man; he will reward you generously when you return us safe to his home." But the brothers, three squat, coarse fellows, would hear none of it.

"We will not return you anywhere you silly old woman. We will get such a good price for her, and the animals and goods, far more than he will reward us. Are you mad? Old fool!" and spat copiously into the dust. On and on she pleaded as the morning light showed how seriously they were lost. There was no house, road, or familiar landmark in sight.

"Let me go back, and you keep the girl with the groom. I will bring money, I promise, lots and lots of money. My mistresses, her two grandmothers, will give you all you want."

The three men heard yet just laughed, happily going through the bags of food, slicing the smoked meat, the sweet breads and wine and drooling, fighting like dogs over it. The little lost party watched on hopelessly, till suddenly the old groom, understanding his terrible crime of neglect, leapt to his feet and flew at them with a knife. Of course this did no good and only caused an uproar, and merely left him dying in moments, spread-eagled and bleeding on the sand, a mass of knife wounds.

Now Mina understood completely the hopelessness of their situation. Beckoning the boy, she urged him closer by whispering.

"Listen to me young man," she began, searching for the clever words to calm him, to catch all his attention. "My young mistress is not only beautiful, she is a virgin! What a price you will get for her. Now I think that you are more clever than your brothers, aren't you? So if you are going to make good money by selling her, make sure she remains intact." She pressed a finger to the side of her nose and gave the boy a crafty wink. "Whatever you do, make very sure that they do not use her! Do not use her yourself, for believe me, her price will halve, for the slave masters always know if a girl is pure."

"How?" he demanded. His attention caught, he bent to hear the old woman. He had listened, understood and decided suddenly. "I'm off," he called to his brothers, startling them from their slumber after gluttony, "this girl is mine. You can keep the rest."

Pulling the burka well over Adina, he humped her on his camel. Trying to see Mina, fluttering her hands through the thick folds of cloth, she just caught a glimpse of the beloved old face as they raced away. Thankfully, she didn't see what happened next, what in their anger they did to the old woman. Indeed, this at least she was spared, for she never did know. Poor Mina, praying to her childhood gods that her words to the young bandit would keep her beloved child safe, barely felt the agony as they jested with her until death.

Adina had passed from hand to filthy hand for what had seemed years. Yet watching the seasons, she thought it must be only months. She was always hungry and the food offered was uneatable. The windowless cellars where she was pushed to sleep were crowded and verminous. She was filthy and her head itched. It was all unbelievable, and she waited daily to be rescued and taken home. Gradually, she stopped listening for her father's horse, his furious voice, and wondered why? Finally, the unspeakable prisons, the disgusting creatures who guarded her, smoothed out with the Eunuch. She had been bathed in the communal bathhouse, yet another stealthy oiled finger had ascertained her virginity, feeling restriction, hastily withdrawn and now, she at least felt clean and almost human again.

"If you inform my father, he will richly reward you," she had pressed the Eunuch to listen, little knowing how many times he had heard such words before. At least this time, he shrewdly guessed, it was the truth. But he had his own life to think of, or at least half of it, and his plans. He would not jeopardise anything to prevent his own escape, for of course, he too, was a slave.

"Listen to me please. Put your past life behind you as if it had never been. It is gone, lost. But you still have many years before you, think of them, how do you want them? Will you fight all the way, to be passed from man to man to be used, and abused. When they are done with you, when you are old, will you be cleaning the latrines, sweeping after the pigs? Or will you be wise, and concentrate on my words, which are spoken in kindness. You see Adina, I have been where you are now, worse, something you will not suffer. They took my manhood." She winced and looked away from his tortured face.

"Pretend it is a game, play it. Be refined, then they might treat you well. Be gentle and good, and you will not get beaten. Be a hypocrite whenever necessary, do not show your fears, your joys, any feeling. Be clever, an enigma, as I am. Who knows, you may even find a master who will return you to your family, if," he raised his voice, "you are only good."

It was hard at first, but it helped. She began to take an interest in her fellow slaves, all, like she, waiting for a buyer. They came and went, they wept or were mute. As if they were brothers and sisters, she comforted them and demanded salves from the Eunuch for their sores. Eventually the old woman who provided their poor meals, began to notice her and spoil her with little treats, for here was unexpected help in a poor job.

The two big black eunuch brothers who were their guards watched, did not speak, for they had no tongues, but always expected a bid for escape. When two little brothers, not twins but near enough to look like it, were castrated, they watched as she stole into their cell at night, kissed them and bathed their faces as she sang them to sleep.

"Try not to touch your wounds dearlings," she implored. "They will go bad, and you will die. Many do die you know, sweetings, so hear me now, listen to Adina," and wiped the tearful faces again. "If you do not try to touch yourself, they will untie your hands." So eventually, the poor little things listened and obeyed and their wounds healed. After that, they let her take the few quiet slaves into the courtyard to walk, play knucklebones and see the sky. It was a relief when they put her in a tiny cell on her own, so she would not be molested. The Eunuch had been right. He was clever. He who spoke many tongues, had lost his manhood, yet like her was a slave, albeit with much trust and freedom.

She had been escorted, well-covered, to the baths the night before. While she entered, the black brothers sat about waiting outside, idly throwing dice as they so often did. The old woman unpacked her poor little bath basket of soaps, sponges and oil and set to work. The luxury of it, the baths, the steam, the scents, the bracing scrub and massage the two women gave her made her tingle and feel alive. They gave her fragrant tea and tiny almond cakes, as if she was a lady customer, not a slave. Totally languid and relaxed, she was suddenly alerted to her position. Why was she here? Why the good bath, the treats? Horror filled her. She was going to be sold tomorrow, some big feast day they had spoken about. The quiet, organized if dull life in the slave master's cellars was almost over. They had given her something light in the tea to calm her. She had slept then, while the two old hags, long-time friends, sat and gossiped quietly nearby. When she woke, still drowsy, she wanted to thank the old one, not unlike Mina, for being kind to her.

"I will ask my father to buy you a fine worked-copper bath box," she heard a strange voice. Not hers surely? Her father? "He," she hesitated, "will bring you a hammam box." They looked at her surprised, what was she talking about? A fine bath box indeed! They looked so astonished, their eyes round with surprise.

Then the funny side of it hit her. She had offered to give the old one an expensive gift. Oh dear. She a slave, to be sold on the morrow, without one tiny coin to her name, not even her robe her own. Poor fool that she was, she had, in her father's name offered a fine bath box to the old woman. Quietly at first, she began to laugh, then it held her, so she rocked, and the laughter, bursting up grew, like a wave grows, larger, larger. Totally hysterical, wild, terribly loud in the echoing baths, her laughter ricochet about the damp walls, causing the women to panic. The cries of alarm, the laughter, echoing and weird, attracted all the other women who came, wide eyed to stare, some of them weeping in sympathy at the crazy scene.

Alerted outside, the two eunuchs listened shocked, dropped their dice and ran inside, till they found the source of noise. By now, every woman in the baths had gathered. Aghast, they stared, helpless, moaning or just open-mouthed, till one matron, mother of daughters, lifted her hand and landed a good slap firmly across Adina's face. Silence. The eunuchs came to first, and seizing their chance swept up the girl, rolled her in whatever cloths came to hand, bundled her over a shoulder and ran home.

"What happened?" asked the Eunuch, stunned by the wild rush. "What happened?" By now Adina was sobbing quietly, all laughter gone.

"She said she would ask her father to buy me a fine bath box," wailed the old woman, somehow touched, equally upset by the strange turn of events.

They put a cold compress on her cheek which was very red, the Eunuch all the while visibly trembling.

"Will she be alright tomorrow?" he kept repeating, then in another language told the old woman to quickly brew up some sleeping tea. They watched over her during the night, changing the cold cloth to her face, fanning her or covering her with a light cloth in the cold early hours. Exhausted from tears, the bath and the tea, she knew nothing of their care.

"Here is your bread my lady." The voice interrupted her thoughts, and she felt a warm bread slip into her hand. A slight smile acknowledged the gift. Bending carefully, she popped a piece into her mouth. It tasted good. So very slowly, she tore up little pieces and ate it, working it around her mouth as if it would be her last meal. It would have been nice to share it with the little boys, but they were too far away.

The Eunuch looked carefully at the slightly swollen cheek. It would pass. He went from one to the other of his slaves, adjusting chains, offering a jug of water, encouraging them. Oh what a dreadful world they lived in.

The sun was well up by now and many people, the poor and servants doing their daily shopping, passed by. She did what the Eunuch had suggested and stared ahead, refusing to be drawn to look or react to any person. He had told her to be aloof, so she was aloof and fixed her eyes on a flowering weed growing out of a crack on a high wall before her.

Twice, coarse men stood before her, examined her and made a play of guessing her price, but the Eunuch was soon after them, so they moved off.

A tug at her hem made her frown. Again, a tugging. Despite herself, she looked down. A tiny, very ugly old woman, barely as tall as the platform on which she stood gazed up at her. Adina smiled, the faintest little smile in acknowledgement. Then her hand was drawn down by the chain, her fingers, tightly closed were prized open, and something was pressed in.

Chickpeas, salted chick peas! Which she liked. Quickly she gave the tiny woman another fleeting smile and bent to pop one in her mouth.

"Never bite on chick peas." Mina had always scolded. "One day you will break your teeth on a too-hard one and you will be sorry."

Would little kindnesses always make her sad? Must she always drag these memories from her past to cause the tears to form? A drop fell on the sheer stuff of her tunic, and dried almost immediately. The tiny woman hurried away at astonishing speed.

The Eunuch came by now and again, either with buyers or offering water, for it was getting very hot, the sun in the mid heaven. The brothers followed and did the undoing of chains and leading sold slaves away. Adina moved her gaze to stare at a tiny stone window in the ramparts and tried to put her mind through it, into the coolness inside. A plump man and wife bought the little boys and she managed to wave quietly at them, throwing them a smile of encouragement. For the couple did look kindly and might feed the children properly.

The empty marketplace of the dawn was by mid-morning full and very noisy. Hawkers called out, trying to out-yell each other. Donkeys brayed and hens squawked. From her platform, Adina had a good view over the crowds. A line of loaded camels passed by and later, went off without their burdens. The noise and smells were familiar, yet it felt to the girl as if she were in another world. For she had never been right in a great market on market day before, it just was not done.

The hours passed and Adina began to feel tired. The Eunuch brought her some dates and water which helped a little. He was disappointed no one decent had made an offer for her. There had been several foolish tryers, but, using their familiar code, he had advised the slave master to wait. This girl was special. They must not be in a hurry; it was for him a matter of faith, he would insist that they wait for the right buyer.

Adina began to feel more than tired and now was hungry and thirsty too. Bunching her toes on the rough boards of the platform she stood on, she swallowed. With the heat came foul smells. It occurred to her that dozens, maybe hundreds of other poor innocents had stood right there where she was. The heat had caused the stink of old urine to rise from the boards, so she realized that those before her had wetted as they stood. Had it been from fear or just the need? Thinking of it now, she felt a fullness in her bladder and her heart began pounding with distress. Where was the Eunuch? How much longer would she have to stand there? Surely someone wanted to buy her.

He came just as the crowds were thinning, the day hot, everyone wanting to go home for food and sleep. A tall horse sidled up to the stand, and for a moment Adina thought it was her father, then closed her eyes tight to shut out the stranger.

Relieved, the Eunuch unlocked her chains, dropped a cotton robe over her head and led her to the slave master's house. Blinded from the sun, she took moments to appreciate the dim courtyard, not so very different from the one at home. Understanding her needs, the old woman led her to a privy nearby, and tidied her up muttering kindly before leading her back to sit on a stone step by a small pool. There was man talk and she recognized the banter of bargaining. Glasses clinked, but aloof, she straightened her back, and enjoyed the cool.

The Eunuch drew close behind her and spoke very quietly in her ear.

"Look at him straight in the eye Adina, do not fear him for this is a good man," he fussed as he muttered around her, tweaking her robe straight. "He is a physician, I do not know if he speaks your tongue, but he is a good and clever man. I am happy for you Adina."

A soft burka was flung over her head and she was led out. The old woman and the Eunuch hovered by the door as a pony was brought forward. Unseen hands helped her. The two black eunuchs, eyes sad that she was going, lifted her up bodily, caressing her on the way, making soft sounds from their throats which she understood was their farewell. The old woman put her hand to her lips.

"Go with God. Remember to do what I have told you," said the Eunuch and, "I will try to see you again and how you are getting along." Softly spoken words just for her, which steadied her pounding heart. She found that she was trembling and gripped the pommel of the saddle to try to stop. They had been kind in their way. They had become familiar. With a lurch, the pony was lead off through the narrow streets, to a new life.

It was like being born again. A great stone gateway led into a luxuriant green courtyard onto a maze of corridors and dim rooms. Kind hands undressed and bathed her. Then she was led to a cool, dark room and gently pushed onto a low couch. Fragrant tea and honey cakes were brought. Again, she felt an oiled finger probing, and swiftly withdrawn. For the first time in months, Adina did not feel afraid. All life had gone from her, all courage had drained through her fingers, her toes, her eyes and her mouth. She just did not care about anything anymore, so numbly she awaited her fate. Let them use her as they wished. Somewhere from nearby she could hear the tumble of a fountain and listening to it, shut her eyes and turning her head to the wall, she slept.

CHAPTER TWO

KAREEN'ALA

The man sat cross-legged on the floor, the tray of food before him and unaware that he was being watched, concentrated vigorously on stuffing his mouth. Having observed him for a full moment, Kareen'ala quietly shut the tiny window, and frowned to herself. Then, with some considerable noise, she marched into the room, both her maid servant and the house eunuch close behind her. Scrambling to his feet, the messenger swallowed and cleared his throat bowing at the same time.

"Well." She was a stern mistress, even hard, but it was well known that if you did your work and watched your manners, she was quite the best.

"Well," she repeated, "what message do you have for me from my son?"

For the thousandth time, she regretted that she could not read. Women did not read, or so her son told her. He would send messengers, who she never trusted to get the message right. It was quite the norm. What other reason did she need to read anyway? She sighed, then remembering why she was there, put a cold eye on the messenger who had finally swallowed and was about to speak. He had learned the message by heart. It made no sense, but then they rarely did.

"Honoured Madam," he bowed again. "My master, the honourable physician, sends you greetings and -" he stopped short seeing her stick raised.

"The message!" she almost hissed. Which so confused him, he had to sort the message out in his head with all speed.

"My honourable master says to tell you," silence, eyes to the rafters, "the perfect flower you sought, is in his hands, and that he will bring it to you before the full moon." There, it was said correctly.

She smiled, she actually smiled. The maid and eunuch glanced swiftly at her, always alert to her moods, then at each other. So it was good news! Thanks be to God.

In very little time the news had swept through the house, out into the yard, beyond into the fields, way up in the hills till at last, Harran her son, for of course everyone knew that the physician was son of the first wife, her real and only son, Harran heard. Intrigued, he slung the birds over his shoulder, whistled to the dogs, and with his falcon hooded on his wrist, he urged his horse down the hill, soon far ahead of the boy who had come to tell him.

"When is my brother coming mother?" he asked, breathless and bright eyed. He was a handsome boy, tall and strong with his father's dark hair and amber eyes. His mother smiled secretly to herself. Let him wait, he would know all in good time.

"Yes," she looked up at him from her work, "your brother is bringing me some fine plants for my garden, around the full moon." Then noticing the pheasants he still carried, she smiled her approval. "Good son, I will make some smoked paste to make patties with, for your brother enjoys good country cooking while he is away from the terrible city."

As usual, they were set to it as if they never did a day's work in their lives. Every single thing had to be taken out. Floors swept and washed, mats shaken and sprayed with herb water. Whitewash was daubed throughout, and into every nook and cranny, should there be any small creature lurking therein. She was relentless, driving them all, and it was true, herself also. Of course they would all pay for her activities, for having broken her leg, the physician far away and late to attend, it had not healed well. If she suffered, so also did they.

Without exception, they were all in awe of the physician. He was a great man, important, clever, rich. Everyone knew of him and his work, and in a small way, his fame and glory touched each one of them. It was useful being a slave in that house, for they could ask favours, for themselves, or for others. Without hesitation or request for payment, if they went to him, he never turned them away. Knowing that the mistress was also very proud of her stepson, they asked, and she would generally, if she thought the case serious enough, seek help on their behalf.

The tempo of the place became ever more frantic as the days passed. Every part, be it house, courtyard, henhouse, tower, slaves quarters, stables, gardens, everywhere was swept and polished. For this is how the great man liked it.

"Dirt," he told them sternly, "dirt is the cause of most illness."

Of course they did not believe it. Well dirt was a part of life, no one could escape dirt. Yet it was true that their household had fewer illnesses than most, and so if he said they must be clean, they would be clean.

Kareen'ala finished sorting the cooking herbs and swept the husks into a pot to be thrown on the brazier. She was excited, he had found the perfect flower the messenger had said. She wondered what she would look like? How she would be? If only she could persuade her own young son to love and wed her, even if without a dowry? It would not be the first time a wife had come to this house empty-handed, didn't she know? If it worked, then she would continue to be the mistress.

There were, anyway, no decent young girls that she knew of for many miles around. Rough! Bandits all of them, their daughters, coarse country girls who were old by the time they were twenty. If it were not for her elder son, she knew well how their lives would be here, on the edge of the plain. With bandits in the hills, all about, waiting to rob, fire, kill, they would never have made such a good life here. But, because they had a famous physician, the best indeed, no one dared to molest them. It had gradually come about if any one of them was ill or wounded, they came to her. If she could not help them with his lotions and salves, if her own herbs failed, she sent them to the city to him. So they were left alone in peace. Many was the time when she had tugged an arrow head from a filthy, rotten back, crawling with flies, stinking. More than once she had pulled on a broken arm or leg till she heard it crack into place, then with splints, had bound it up. All due to her son, who had taught her but who was not her son, but the one who she loved far more than the son of her womb.

The place was ready, each job done twice over. Even the leaves in the garden were washed of dust, the cistern emptied, cleaned out and filled with fresh water. Aching backs, cracked hands, yet all done with a strange willingness, an anticipation.

Once again, Adina was in limbo. Not the limbo of the slave master's cellars, for this was all peace, tranquillity, softness, kindness. Each day she waited, expecting the worst. Every time the door opened to her little quarters, she stiffened, now, now it will happen. But it did not. Gradually, she came to learn the heartbeat of the house where she was so gently imprisoned. The far bell of the outer gate, quiet speech, cries of pain, words of comfort. With the ever open doors and shutters, sounds drifted about, little could be concealed. The Eunuch had said he was an important physician, and gradually, she came to believe it.

Why then was she here? Why was she kept, like a daughter of the house in luxury, soft clothes, good food, baths, whenever she wanted? Also, as a daughter, she was kept in seclusion. She suspected that something they gave her to eat or drink made her very calm. Her sleep was untroubled, and when she thought of her family, it was without sorrow.

It was dim in her quarters, for ladies should not let the sun darken their skins. The walls of the courtyard were high and the trees within, almost closed over the sky. All for coolness she knew, but even so, it was a green dimness where faces were blurred and everyone looked similar. Gentle women came to see her, alone or in twos, spoke kindly, sat, spun, or played a board game and left. They had to be of one family, for together with the drug and the dimness, they were to her eyes, as one. Except the tiny, ugly woman, who had given her chick peas while she stood in the slave market. She was her friend. It was she who oiled her after a bath, massaged her, combed her hair and made all sorts of splendid arrangements with it. Unfortunately she knew few words of their language, so they used mime, touch and gentle laughter, so very soon, she managed to communicate very well.

Occasionally, the physician came to see her. He took her out to the terrace and to the light, silently looked into her mouth, pried open her eyes, nodded, clicked. Then, one day he surprised her by speaking so she could understand. Obviously, he did not know her tongue well, but he knew enough to tell her, "Tomorrow we are going to the country to the family land, where my mother and brother live. It is a farm I suppose, but the main work is breeding horses," he smiled. "Excellent horses too, which you will see before long. You are to serve my mother who speaks your language. She is a good mistress, do not be afraid, she will be pleased with you."

But she was afraid, another new, strange place. All of her wanted to cry to him, "Let me stay here, take me, do what you will with me, but do not send me away again. I am afraid, afraid." Lying on her bed, she had refused food, to acknowledge the little woman, to play knucklebones or dice. So she supposed they had once again given her something in her drink to calm her, making her feel dull, floating, uninterested in everything.

A fine dark burka was tossed over her head and she was led into the courtyard. Hands touched hers, quiet voices bid her goodbye. Then up on a pony and away down the street into the night, the first time she had been in the city since the market day. The group rode in front, beside and behind her.

"So," she thought idly, "he paid a good price for me." It was difficult to know how long they rode, hours certainly. Once they stopped, dismounted and she was told to go behind an outcrop of rocks to relieve herself. When she returned, she saw that the horses all wore bags on their feet, and caught a flicker of fear.

The moon was up and an eerie light fell all about the land through which they rode. To her right, were distant hills, to her left stretched an endless plain. Just as dawn began to streak the sky, they came to a fork in the road. An elaborate stone well stood in the divide, water falling into a stone basin, silver in the early light.

"Come," the physician helped her down easily, as if she were a child. "We are almost home. A man goes ahead to warn them of our arrival. Some moments rest, a drink for us and the beasts. This is good water," and went to fill a cup for her.

Just then a night beast cried out, a terrible, lonely scream which made them all start. Adina felt as if her heart would burst with fear. A savage pain engulfed her, fear searing through every fibre of her body, so she fell sobbing to the earth, her body shaking uncontrollably, her breath coming in gasps. This was an evil place, of that she was sure, and nothing would stop her from believing it. That cry was a warning, an omen. Quickly she was hoisted on the pony once more and now they hurried uphill, urging on their tired beasts with heels, knees and whips.

Because of her fear, she did not see her new home as they entered, for the burka was all askew, blinding her. Unseeing, her hand held firmly, she followed, stumbling up steps, along corridors, on hollow sounding wooden boards. When the burka was gently taken off, blinking, she looked around in the dawn light. Soft hands smoothed her hair. They were in a big, beautiful room, with high ceilings and vivid rugs on the scrubbed wood floor. A vine-laden veranda was on one side covered in screens. Great pots filled with plants stood about, some ablaze with flowers which impressed her, and caused her to look about even more curiously. This was a lovely place. When the maid moved away, Adina saw an older woman standing before her smiling, smoothing her head cloth.

"What are you called my child?" in her own tongue, which so shocked Adina, she had no voice to answer. Eyes wide, she stared, then, "Adina lady." It finally came out.

"Adina," she said, nodding, "an unusual name. How came you of it?" So Adina told her of her two grandmothers, and how her name came about.

"And your mother?" stopped, seeing immediately the wave of sorrow. "Ah," she went on kindly, "perhaps your mother is dead?" To which Adina merely hung her head. "Then may I ask you, as we are to live together, if you will call me mother? For I have no daughter, and it will please me greatly."

So why not? She seemed kind. The girl raised her head, a small smile.

"Mother," she said, glad to have someone who she could understand, speak easily with, so that was that.

Once again her life became quiet with a gentle routine. She was kept in the women's quarters, yet therein free to wander about the several pleasant rooms. Through the diamond screens of the verandas, she saw a great vista of fields stretching into the horizon, and watched the distant farmers busy about their work as tiny ants. Often those first days, she heard, then saw, groups of horsemen riding out, falcons on their wrists, their huge hunting dogs running behind. She was alerted by a yell, a curious yammering cry, which seemed to goad the horses on. As she watched them chase the small game across the dry land far below, she heard the cry, and had to smile. When she asked about it, she was answered with a laugh. This it seemed, was how the family summoned their beasts and had for all time.

Her mistress, who she unhesitatingly called mother, seemed to be a busy woman. For the first few days, she rarely saw her. Slaves came and went, brought food, water for bathing, small tasks for her to do, spinning, sewing. Silently, they stood with their hands outstretched bearing her tasks. When she accepted them, they seemed pleased, always smiling tentatively at her. For this one was special, they had been told and certainly she was very beautiful. She was to therefore be treated with great consideration and kindness. As she was lovely as well as gentle, it was easy.

A commotion alerted her one day, but try as she did, she could see little from the lattice. There was much noise, shouting, horses stamping about, all of which was later explained. The physician had returned to the city.

So the boy Harran did not see Adina, indeed knew nothing of her, for a new slave was of little interest to him. What was exciting, was that he was being permitted to accompany his brother to the city. Now this, oh joy, was what he wanted.

In time, Adina learnt that the horses newly arrived from the city, always stayed, while fresh ones took their turn.

"Hence we have happy, healthy horses," laughed the mistress.

The moment the party had left, Kareen'ala drew her new daughter out of the shadows and together they left the house and explored.

"I was sorry to leave you alone your first days child, but with both sons here, this mother was very busy keeping them happy."

It was so good to be out and about. Adina felt suddenly bright and cheerful, after being confined one way and the other for many months, now she was free. Well, free to go about outside anyway. Ever conscious of her mistress's lameness, she paused here and there, sometimes holding out a hand, offering an arm, all of which was noted by the older woman, a small smile of satisfaction on her face.

The great house was built on a hillside. Large, it was two storied on the lower, south side and set in a rectangle around a fine courtyard. A handsome stone gateway, with stout doors which were locked at night, was the only entrance. The family quarters on the upper floor consisted of a string of rooms. The mistress had the largest room, which acted as a day room and where they usually ate. Through it to one side was a tiny room with only one door, where Adina slept. A store room, or large cupboard, it was filled with stacked chests, rolled carpets and bedding rolls, all full of herbs so the room was thick with the smell of them. It seemed that she was still protected.

Several more family rooms, which were closed, were strung along the south side, where the views from the veranda were magnificent. Fragrant plants were daily watered and Adina made it her job to pluck off the dead heads to encourage new flowers as she had done at home. When it was hot, the cane blinds were dropped, and the shutters on the north verandas were opened. Even on the hottest day, there was always a breeze from somewhere and Adina thought it all very clever and practical. One room deep, all the other rooms were entered from the latticed verandas all about. The whole structure seemed airy and light and she liked it.

A large, stone-lined cistern fed by a spring in the courtyard was the main source of water for the house, and there was ever constant activity about it. Waste water channelled continually along stone gutters to the garden below. The outside walls were fresh painted, a soft terracotta, and vines and flowering creepers grew with abandon even to the roof. On the south west corner of the house, which sloped steeply downhill, stood a tall, broad tower built of golden stone blocks, perched on a rocky outcrop. The area immediately below the house was a fine garden where vegetables and fruit trees grew. They walked slowly, Adina intrigued by everything, particularly the tower which rose above them.

"That was the first building here," Kareen'ala told her. "It is very old, from my husband's family, when they were bandits."

Shocked, Adina did not respond, but her eyes were round with surprise till Kareen'ala giggled. "Well they were, except no one but me admits to it now." Whenever she could, Adina went through the courtyard into the tower, climbed the rickety ladder and sat on the roof, gazing across the plain. She liked it there and being alone, for it seemed that it was rarely used except the lower levels as store rooms. Sometimes she took the little harp she had found hanging on a beam, to practise and sing to, for it reminded her of her own mother and home. Kareen'ala always knew where she was from the sweet sounds which floated down. Truly, thought Adina, she had nothing to complain of. Her mistress/mother was almost as kind as had been her own mother. Indeed, it was very like home in essence, for all the household were kind. They involved her in everything, so it was easy to help in all matters as best as she could, as she had learned at home. Any new task she worked at hard and soon mastered. Gentle praise and encouragement made her feel useful and part of the place. She soon realized that her new home was a sort of caravanserai, for travellers often came up the dusty track from the well, slept either in the courtyard, or if they were respectable, took a room. Sometimes they stayed several days to rest or exchange their horses, buy new ones or await another caravan, so to travel on in greater numbers in safety. She was very much her mistress's companion, never being included in the work of cooking or caring for these people. In busy times, the mistress always sent her to her room, and hearing the raised voice berating every member of the household, Adina happily obeyed. Despite the extra work and demanding mistress, the slaves seemed to welcome the travellers. For no doubt it made a change from daily toil, and they might receive little gifts for their service. After a few weeks, even the new language seemed to come easily to Adina till she felt as if she had been there all her life. It was all made easy because her new mother helped her, translating from her own tongue, and being young, she was quick to learn.

Weeks passed, summer waned, cool breezes told her that autumn was coming till one day, Kareen'ala took her aside and spoke gently to her.

"My younger son will return soon," she said. "He has been staying in the city with his brother. He is young, handsome and wilful, like his father, and I do not want him to see you. For then our peace will be over for he will surely lust after you, which I do not want, for you are my companion. Anyway, we will wed him to a local wife before long."

Once more she found herself confined in the women's quarters, there to spin, weave and sew and in the evenings, play the little harp. Nothing in her life had changed really, except she missed the garden, the farm, the tower. It had been new to her, not a country-bred girl, getting used to the animals, feeding the hens and seeing the little lambs and goats run to their mothers when the flocks came home. She did not see very much of the fine horses which were kept higher in the hills, except when they were exercised by the grooms. Then she pressed her face against the screen and watched in admiration as the shiny-flanked thoroughbreds pranced down to the well, fighting the bit all the way.

Kareen'ala was pleased that the girl enjoyed learning new domestic crafts. However many slaves they had, it wouldn't hurt for her to know how to make fresh cheese, cutting and hanging herbs to dry, and when Harran was away, even milking the goats. Although at the farm at home Adina had known it was done, it had never involved her. It was absorbing, being part of the household, helping in the kitchens, for with the harvest coming in, all the stores were being put up for the winter. Her grandmother had always gone to the farm to do this work at this time, but she was more a town girl, ignorant of the importance of gathering and storing. Here, storing the harvest was not only for themselves she understood, but for the son in the city. Now she paced her quarters, wishing she could go outside again and be free. Indeed, she suddenly realized, life had resumed the lazy, closed boredom of her old home.

Harran reluctantly returned to the country in a poor temper. He had enjoyed his brother's house, his aunt, his cousins. The city was filled with wondrous things to do and see, and he had even begun studying with an old slave. Reluctantly too, he had realized that his brother was and always had been, far more clever than he would ever be. There were seven years between them, for his brother had been born of another woman, who had died. For a time he had considered asking if he too could study medicine. But he soon realized that it would be far too great a work for him. He was a country boy, horses and the land would be his future. Even so, listening to his brother reading in the evenings, had at least given him the firm intention to learn to read and write.

He had been surprised and pleased when his brother had given him the slave, Shimos, his first, he even had the paper. A strange old man, he seemed almost too calm, certainly he needed to be with the lively young master. Each day, when the heat abated before night, they had their lessons. First he was put to writing with the slave dictating. Then, taking the same book, he would read the page for the morrow. When these were done satisfactorily, the bait, the reward, the old man, pulling his grey robe tight about him for he was always cold, drew out a precious book and read.

He told of great feats, brave men, beautiful women, strange lands, far oceans, and for the moment anyway, Harran was absorbed in his studies and contented.

With autumn turning into winter, it became cooler, and Adina rejoiced. A compromise was reached, that the moment Harran left to go to the land or to hunt, providing Adina had completed her tasks, she was free. This meant she usually first ran up the hill to visit all the little animals in the farmyard, to collect the eggs, or run down into the garden to cut the day's fruit and vegetables. Then, her work done, she stole off with the harp, up into the tower, there, between gazing at the ever changing scene, to practise and sing.

Kareen'ala was satisfied. The girl was a flower indeed, far more beautiful and good than she could ever imagine. The scribe was called and told to take down a letter to send to the physician, to once more thank him.

"You are hurting with the cold weather mistress," Shimos said, settling himself by her on a low chair, a board before him laden with parchment and inks.

"Yes," she moved, trying to get comfortable, "this leg. What bad luck for me, who was always so healthy, and my son, who could have put it right, too far away to heal it early."

Even so, she knew how lucky she was, with her fine home, her many good slaves, the helpful girl, and now this old scribe. Mind you, his arrival had caused some sniffing from the house eunuch, but things were beginning to settle down. As she dictated, the scribe wrote. The extra bonus was that he knew her tongue, after a fashion. As the girl knew it too, and the other servants did not, it pleased her, for she felt that it gave her some privacy.

"Shall I ask him to send you something for the pain?" Shimos asked, poking a quill into his ear. "Excuse me for saying so, but it will not harm you madam, in the autumn of your life, to indulge a little."

She eyed him, his hand poised with the pen. He was an interesting man, who must have been good-looking in his youth. As always, she wondered at his story, but it had never been her policy to pry into the background of her slaves. They had come to her as just that. Their past was theirs. Still, this one was obviously educated, or else he would not have been chosen by her clever son.

"You don't think indulging in drugs is a slippery slope then, Shimos?"

He thought for awhile, put the pen down and stretched his fingers.

"Living with pain is not clever mistress." He looked straight at her, liking her, aware that if all went well, he would stay with her till he died. If he was sensible, of course. "There are some who overdo everything. They eat too much, they drink too much, they have mad sexual appetites. Yet, a little of all those things, if in need, well, it is my belief, that after a lifetime of toil, we are, if we are able, entitled to a little comfort and self-indulgence."

She listened, just a little surprised at the long speech. But he was right of course. He was, as well she knew, far more intelligent, educated and well-born than was she.

"So why not, Shimos? Tell him I only need to have the pain eased in the evenings and for sleep."

He scratched at the parchment, sanded it and blew, then held it up and read.

"Teach me to write the word, 'mother', Shimos," she asked surprisingly. They smiled at each other.

"Well yes, and why not, a good idea," and rustled amongst the papers to find an old piece for her to work on.

Adina came in quietly on soft slippers to light the lamps, for it was dusk, and the tower had been quite cold, a wind blowing in through the slits off the hills. There was a shout from the courtyard. It was Harran calling Shimos, who got to his feet and bowed.

"Excuse me mistress, the young master calls for his lesson," and left. Adina watched the older woman struggle with the pen. "M o", she wrote.

"What are you writing, mother?" the girl asked.

"Shimos is teaching me to write my name, not, Kareen'ala but Mother, so the letter for my son will be signed properly." Shyly, she struggled on, Adina watching her. The girl then went down on her knees beside the low table, took up another pen, and wrote in large letters, mouthing the sounds.

"M - M, o - o, th - th, er – er," and sat back on her heels smiling. "There you are, if you say the sounds at the same time, it will be easier."

Kareen'ala stared first at the letters, then the girl. She was shocked.

"Can you write?" she asked, her breathless voice filled with awe. Adina nodded, suddenly aware that she might have committed a sin.

"And can you read?" her mother asked. Adina nodded again, the smile gone.

"Read this," the fresh letter was handed to her, and holding it to the light, Adina read.

My dear and honoured Son,

I send you greetings and all good wishes for your health and contentment. Here we are all well, by the grace of God, preparing for winter, the harvest in and safely stored. Your goods await the next caravan which passes, with this letter also. Your brother is learning well, and again I thank you for sending Shimos to teach him. My new daughter is as ever a joy, she cares for me and makes the light shine when the days are dim. I thank you once again, my good son and I am glad to tell you that our plans are working well.

Shimos suggests that you may send me some light substance to relieve the pain I suffer in my leg. It is always bad in cold weather and in the evening. My nights are often troubled with it. Of course, if you could bring it to me yourself, even though you are a busy man, a short visit from you would give me great happiness.

I am, Kareen'ala, your dutiful and ever loving --------.

Adina put the page down, her face puckered in a small frown.

"Does your leg really hurt so badly?" she asked kindly.

Kareen'ala smiled. What a find! A lovely girl, pure, gentle, and she could read and write. Pains forgotten for a moment, she reached across and pinched the young cheek in a kiss.

"When you get old child, it is natural to have little pains and aches. But Shimos is right, something gentle to help me sleep will be useful."

After that, the two women became even more close. Adina came to read to her mistress, and gradually explained how she had learned from her brothers' tutor, how although it had not really been approved of, her father had been proud of her. Gradually, without plan or guile, Adina's story came out, except the end. The older woman was fascinated, for it sounded such a good, rich life, she could not imagine how the child came to end up in the slave market.

When it arrived, Shimos arranged a little pipe and supplied his mistress with her drug. It helped. She felt at peace and pain free, so most evenings she took to talking with the scribe, often together with the girl. They lazed on low chairs, stools or cushions, Kareen'ala always on the couch. A brazier of charcoal was carried in at dusk, so they kept warm. If there were travellers staying, Harran and the house eunuch cared for them. Kareen'ala had decided to begin to retire from the hard work of running the place. It had come to her suddenly how lonely she had been before these two interesting slaves had come into her household. Where she had before sought out work to pass the hours, there was no longer need, for now she had gentle companionship. God is good she thought, reaching for a dried apricot.

CHAPTER THREE

HARRAN

Harran looked down proudly at his wife and daughter. The momentary disappointment that the child was not a son had gone, and now, he was merely filled with love. Adina smiled up at him, tired, happy, her wonderful deep red hair, damp from her labours was spread about on the fresh linen. The tiny head in the crook of her arm, was a strange red-black, and with his curls, not straight as Adina's.

"And with my curls and blue eyes," announced a proud Kareen'ala after further examination of this, her first real grandchild. For it was most unusual in that land to have other than brown or black eyes.

Adina had told her husband many times that she had been the firstborn, and a bitter disappointment to her father. Yet, she told him, smiling with her memories, after that came boys, and more boys. Kareen'ala was however, ecstatic, glad too that this first one was small, so although long, the birth had not been too difficult.

"Karina," whispered Adina, rejoicing at the pleasure in her mother-in-law's face. "We will call her for you, Karina," and pressed her mouth against the small brow, and resettled the stiff, tight-bound bundle in her arm, closed her eyes and slept.

Kareen'ala smiled at her son as she gently took the baby and laid it in the cradle which had also been his.

"Well done my son," she straightened up. "You have gladdened my heart."

He grinned at her, glad at her pleasure, clever sly old woman. Only a year before, he had just known that his mother had a personal slave. Young, full of dreams and life, he had kept away from the women's quarters as was correct. His brother had confided in him when he was in the city, that a bride was found. A beauty, learned and pure as a very precious jewel. So he dreamed of her, never guessing that all the time, she lived in his house, at the farm in the country.

He could not remember quite when he had become aware of her. The soft music of the harp drifted down from the tower to where he sharpened his knife on the old stone which they always used. His knife had to be ever sharp, tasks in the fields and on the hunt demanded it. But so sharp! He grinned to himself. It mesmerised him, the sweet notes of the harp, the occasional light voice that came on the breeze, so he made a point to sharpen his knife every evening. He tried asking Shimos, who although a slave, was a friend. But the scribe gave some sort of addled reply. Music practise indeed.

In the end, it was really quite simple. He merely sauntered to the tower, silently bid his hound, his constant shadow, to sit and wait, and crept carefully up the creaking ladder. With his head just above the top floor, he peered about, and for moments the darkness kept her from him. Then, eyes directed towards the sweet sound, he saw her, silhouetted against the golden evening sky.

How long he stood there he did not know. She was all beauty. The perfect nose, the flaming long hair being blown in the breeze, the soft swell of her breast against the vivid sunset. The sweetness of her music seemed to surround and embrace him.

"What is your name?" he asked, his voice shockingly loud in the quiet. She started, held the harp close to her breast and stared at him without answer. He tried again, this time using his mother's tongue, for if she were the personal slave, it could be she would answer to that.

"What is your name?"

Adina heard and understood the first time, for after months in her new home, she could speak their language well enough. She tried to see him clearly, a stranger, but not. He was surely the younger son, he who she must avoid.

"I am Adina," she replied clearly, without adding "Master", but he did not notice.

"What are you doing here?" Silence. Silly boy, what did it look like she was doing there? Adina knew all about boys, she had five brothers after all. On not getting a reply, he heaved himself up and stood tall before her.

They looked at each other mutely, then, her heart suddenly beating furiously, Adina asked quietly, "Shall I play for you?"

"Yes, and sing," came the prompt reply.

It was just all lovely, she was lovely, the way her hands plucked and stroked the strings, the way her voice rose and fell. So many of the songs she knew were love songs, it had not been her intention to play one, it simply came. Perhaps he did not understand the words, yet he understood. When it ended she rose, and as casually as she could, went to the top of the ladder.

"I must go now," she faced him, and saw how handsome he was, a mass of dark curls framing his face in the half light. "My mistress will be needing me."

So that is how it happened. Every evening he went to the tower, and there she was, breath quickening, waiting for him.

"We did it Shimos," said the happy Kareen'ala. "He wants her, that awkward boy. If we had given her to him, he would have rejected her. But, oh my little stallion, he found her himself did he? Well, better he always thinks that."

Adina was troubled. She had heard her mistress mother speak of her son's marriage and of his intended bride. It was all arranged. Looking up at him, for she was smaller than he, her soft green eyes were huge and sad.

"Harran, oh Harran, we must stop this, for your mother will be angry. She, who has been so good to me, she will send me away, sell me." Ending on an agonised note, head down.

Fiercely he gripped her shoulders, willing her to look up at him. His eyes were an unusual golden brown, unlike his mother. Face so close, Adina stared at them, fascinated.

"Never! Do you hear? She will never sell you. For I know she loves you, as a daughter, she has been so content since you came. And when she knows that I love you too, and want you?" To which she pushed him away, unbidden tears falling.

"Do not say that. If she hears, she will be angry with both of us, and surely I will be sent away."

Tenderly now, he drew her near, brushing the stray hair, so full, so rich in colour. Lifting her up, he kissed her first on her brow, then her cheeks, and then, softly for the smallest moment, then wildly, bruising her mouth savagely.

"You are mine Adina," he whispered into her hair. "Do not doubt that you will be mine and soon. I will write to my brother and you will see, he will persuade her."

Each day hung heavy on Adina who went about her tasks with such a lassitude, Kareen'ala grew anxious.

"It is puppy love mistress," hissed Shimos. "Don't you remember, the first time? The highs, the lows, not sleeping, being off your food? The sighs, the pain, the joy." He snorted to himself. "You must not notice." He was cross, for this sport was not to his liking, although he knew the mistress had her reasons. Besides, he had found himself loving the girl too, and seeing her dejection, sorrowed for her. Each evening they met. It was agony and delight. Close, their young bodies yearned, yet Adina held herself aloof still.

"I want you!" Harran ground his need harshly into her slender body. "I will ask if you can be my woman." Which started her weeping again, for she had never thought to be merely someone's woman. Her future had been to be a wife, of an important man too, and mistress of her own house.

"All day in the fields and in the hills I think of you, and dream of holding you thus."

"All day in the house and garden I think of you too, and long to hold you also."

Adina waited till she was alone in the big room where she spent much of her time. Taking the quills from their holder, she carefully shaved them to a point with the sharp little pen knife and all but one, replaced them neatly in their pot. Next she took up the small pestle and mortar and ground the dried, black berries, just a few, into a fine powder. Taking a walnut half, she tipped the powder into it, wrapped it tightly in a piece of rag and tucked it with the quill in her bodice. Checking that she was yet alone, she folded two small sheets of parchment in her breast, then went straight up to the roof of the tower.

Waiting for her with a smile, Harran took pen and paper and wrote, as poorly as he always did, begging his brother for his mother's new slave girl for his own. There were only two bad blotches. With his letter drying on the parapet, Adina took the quill and wrote neatly to her father, wherever he was. Briefly she said that although a slave, she was very well, in good health and wished to marry the son of her mistress. She begged him to write, to come to see her, or just to send her dowry. With it, she could wed, and be a wife, instead of merely being a slave and bed mate to her love. Setting it to dry beside the other, she pondered how she could get it to him.

Finding him was a vague dream, so for the moment, she placed it high on a rafter, wedged with a stone.

"Read them quickly," ordered Kareen'ala, who missed nothing. "Now!" to Shimos who carefully opened them. "Read!" she became angry, seeing his eyes skim the words, angry that she too could not read.

Shimos sighed, spread the sheets out and read them to her.

"Madam, you have what you wish, a love match. Now let them be I implore you, and send a letter to the physician, with an invitation to their wedding feast." He paused frowning, looking at Adina's page, she wrote so well compared with his clumsy pupil. "It might even be clever to ask your son to go to the slave master, to try to trace the girl's father. A dowry is always useful, I feel sure she speaks truth, everything about her tells of a good upbringing and respectable family. It can do no harm?" he ended on a query, raising his eyes.

Kareen'ala took the letters without a word and left the room giving no answer. She had to think. He was right of course, a dowry would always be handy, but say if the father wanted his daughter back? She agonised over the problem. It was unthinkable she leave them, loving her as they did. The girl was doubly theirs now.

That night, still worrying, Kareen'ala lay staring into the darkness, pulling the blankets well over her for it was truly winter now. Despite her little pipe, the camomile and willow bark tea, she could not get comfortable and tossed about while the night dragged on. A light knock alerted her. Now who was it? It could not be Adina who slept in the small room on the other side, and Harran was noisy, so it must be Shimos.

"Come," she said abruptly.

Shimos came in carrying a small lamp which he protected from the draught of the opening door with his other hand. Standing by her couch, he gave a delicate cough. Kareen'ala turned her face away, for she knew he had come to scold.

"I have been thinking," he began. The woman heaved crossly, trying to get comfortable for the cold had made her leg ache more than usual, and the drug did not seem very effective. Perhaps it was a poor batch. Thinking, that was all he seemed to do, silly man. Well who hadn't been thinking? She grunted.

"If we can find the girl's father, if we tell of your great love for her, the romance between your son and his daughter? If we can invite them to the marriage feast to see that she will not be a slave anymore, but the young mistress of a fine establishment? Perhaps that would be the clever road?" Shivering, he trailed off, trying to read her reaction in the shadows. "Of course, the main problem will be to find him," he ended quietly and to himself.

Kareen'ala lay silent, willing her mind to still, irritated by this problem and the silly man shivering at her bedside, who always thought and spoke too much.

"Oh for the love of God will you get in?" she said fiercely and swept the blankets open, "standing there with your teeth chattering!"

Shimos stood stock still. Was he hearing right? Was she inviting him into her bed?

"Get in man!" she hissed. "Am I to freeze to death while you think about it?"

With great care, Shimos set the little lamp on a small table and then eased under the blankets. Amazement gave way to heaven. Oh bliss, only another body could produce such comforting warmth.

Kareen'ala grimaced with shock. His legs were like sticks of ice. With a grunt of pain she wrapped her own plump legs about him, wincing as the cold touched her.

They lay for moments, Shimos revelling in the welcome warmth of her body yet startled and grinning broadly in the darkness. Kareen'ala breathed deeply, suffering from his chill and trying to understand what she had just done.

"Well," said Shimos, "isn't this nice? My wife and I always used to say that bed was the very best place to talk." Which caught the woman's attention, and distracted her from thinking of the improprieties of her situation.

"Were you married then Shimos?" she asked, her voice changed and mild.

They settled together more comfortably, Shimos arranging his mistress on his shoulder and placing the bedclothes snugly around her neck.

"Ah yes but indeed madam, but a hundred years ago as it were, when I was perhaps the same age as our Harran."

"Tell me," she asked, but nicely, not as the mistress giving an order, forgetting her rule never to pry into the past lives of her slaves. They lay in comfortable silence awhile, Shimos thinking of that sweet young wife, of his youth, unconsciously stroking the soft arm of his bed mate.

"She was not so unlike our girl. Not as pretty, not such bright hair, smaller, clever too. Poor angel died in childbirth, so you see, that was my marriage. Circumstances decreed that I did not marry again."

Kareen'ala heard yet half, her mind on the rhythmic stroking. It had been so long, since she had had a man in her bed. It was perhaps nearly twenty years since her husband had died. Remembering with a half smile she slowly relaxed, for he had been a ruffian, taking her with wild enthusiasm, which she had to admit, had been just what she needed then as a young thing. Somehow, idly she wondered, why no other man had entered her bed since. Perhaps her life had been too full, being mistress of such a busy establishment. Intrigued, very carefully, she slipped a hand under his clothes and between his legs and began to explore.

"Kareen'ala!" he gasped, using her name for the first time, now really startled, "madam!"

She smiled, feeling the fascinating soft folds of flesh and continued tenderly playing. Different, quite different but nice.

"So are you satisfied, you wicked woman, that I am not a eunuch?" smiling despite himself. She snuggled close.

"I am glad of that Shimos," she said softly, continuing her exploration.

"I am an old boy, madam," said Shimos faintly, fearful, despite his delight, that he may not be able to perform satisfactorily and please her.

"Oh shush," she giggled, "you might be old and useless, but I see that this little man I have in my hand, is behaving quite young and eager."

In the next room, ever awake because of her love, Adina listened to the sounds which came through the wooden partition. At first alerted, she thought there was some problem with the murmuring voices. Gradually she realized what was happening and smiled, eyes wide, covering her mouth, hugging herself in the dark. Of course she had sometimes observed her real mother, heard that special tender voice of love. Often she had seen her parents after a night together, their glow, their mutual delight. How wonderful! Now here were these two people, whom she had such an affection for, her substitute parents indeed, making love.

"I will be fit for nothing tomorrow woman," exclaimed Shimos, exhausted, satisfied and still amazed by the unexpected events.

"You never do anything anyway, my dear," replied a replete and drowsily happy Kareen'ala.

They lay together in friendship and comfort till he heard her breathe even into sleep. He thought for a mere moment about returning to his own cold couch, but decided to wait till dawn. No one would come till then, and this was very pleasant.

He lay warm for once, a long time thinking, for he was never a great sleeper. This unexpected affair might even be an advantage, if he was careful. It could also mean that she would be more pliable in permitting the search for Adina's family.

Life, oh strange and lovely life, he silently thanked the gods for allowing his last years at least to be safe and quiet. Yet, as well he knew, it was human nature to worry and grieve over something. He had been surprised to find his interest become acute over Adina, his fellow house slave. The girl was special. He sought in his heart and soul why he worried so. Perhaps she did resemble that young wife of his. There was a beautiful fragility about her which brought the man out in him, the protector. Yes, that must be it, she did have some similarities to that long lost, sweet wife. Quite different from the delicious, robust and lusty woman beside him and he grinned again.

"Is it true?" asked Harran, the following evening, alert with incredulity. She nodded, eyes shining.

"Yes I am sure of it," and held him close, breathing his man smell, his sweat from the day, the tang of beasts with whom he had been working.

"It could be," serious now, "that this will soften her?" Again Adina nodded.

"It certainly could be." Happier and filled with a new optimism, they held each other closely.

The next reliable travellers who passed through were entrusted with the important letter, also asking for a search to be made for Adina's family. It was all done quietly, for in such a household, little remained secret for long. Meanwhile, the two letters were replaced on the beam, for it wouldn't do to spoil the story yet.

A new and gentle relationship developed between mistress and scribe, yet it was discreet, a night-time friendship. On the surface at least, Shimos went about during the day in his vague old manner. The other slaves had in the beginning grumbled about the old scribe. He had seemed useless, pottering about in unusual places at odd times. Yet it appeared that he served his purpose, writing letters and keeping accounts and he never expected anything from anyone. The occasional gentleman who came with the caravans and stayed the night seemed to enjoy his company, talking or playing difficult board games. Yet his one grace was that together with Adina, he appeared to keep the mistress happy, for she was certainly more calm, and no longer harangued or had them whipped as she had done in the past.

Determined now to learn, Kareen'ala took to her room more often, calling Adina or Shimos to help her.

"She is just a little too old to learn, Adina child," whispered Shimos, "but let us encourage her to read first, if it is what she wants and at least write her name." This they did almost every day, and Kareen'ala was very content.

Every night, Shimos crept into the warm embrace of his mistress. Not that she was always demanding of his attention, she was not. Yet it was to become over the coldest nights, a haven for them both. Inevitably, as Shimos had said, it turned out to be a good place to talk.

For the first time ever, Kareen'ala told of how she had come to that place. Her trader father, his little ship, going to sea with him, with her three brothers after the death of her mother. The pirates. It seemed as if once begun, she could not stop, the need to tell all was so enormous.

"My dear," Shimos held her close. "It is past now, long gone, they will no doubt all be all dead, picked clean by the crows, their bones bleached white by the sun and sea. And here are you dear lady, alive, well, lovely, happy, mistress of all you behold!"

She did take comfort from his words and his nearness, yet on she went, only stopping sometimes to wipe a tear, or blow her nose. The brutality of their raping. The beatings, the hunger and thirst, till at last, on their way to the slave market in the city, they had stopped here. The then mistress had surprised them all with the fury of her raised voice, for she had insisted on their bonds being untied, so she could wash and lay salve on their festering wounds. They had been shut in the downstairs of the tower, but at least unbound. They had been fed good soup and given fruit. Then, oh thanks be to God, the mistress had singled her out to buy. For being large with child, she wanted a nursemaid for her little boy.

"I loved her, as the mother I had lost, Shimos. She was so good, so fine, I have ever tried to model myself on her. A good wife and mother, and always a strict but fair mistress to her slaves. And how she suffered, for she lost that next boy baby, and the next, and the next, ever growing weaker, till she died, surely of sorrow." A sob escaped her as she remembered the white face, the beseeching hands, the weak voice, "'Love him as your own sweet Kareen'ala,' putting her little son's hand in mine. Which I did, and do now, and he me, a son to be proud of. Thanks be to God." When she had recovered, she went on. "When the master took me to his bed, it seemed the most natural thing, for we were all that was left of the family, and little changed. We were never wed by a shaman or priest. Times were rough then, there were bandits and ruffians, constantly beating upon the door, in those days, this was a poor old farm. For what you see now, I have built. It was a ramshackle old place before. Only the old tower remained standing when all else fell down in an earthquake when Harran was two. That was when my man died, dead under a great piece of masonry. It was then my poor little unborn daughter slipped from me. For most of the slaves had also perished or fled, so alone I struggled to pull him free and could not."

Shimos listened sadly to her story, realizing that it was perhaps a great balm to her to speak of all those sorrows which had been locked up in her heart. Gently he caressed her, all the while murmuring words of comfort till it seemed she was empty, so at last she slept peacefully.

One could not help but see the new serenity which shone from her eyes, and which so delighted the two young lovers, they forgot their agony for a time, to rejoice.

A letter came from the city. With trembling hands Kareen'ala opened it, calling for someone to seek out Shimos and bid him come immediately.

"He agrees!" Shimos smiled widely at her. "He will come with the full moon in two months time, for just a few days to attend the feast. He has begun the search for the girl's family." They hugged each other and danced around like children, the floor boards sounding as a drum. Shimos would have liked to pick her up and swing her about but she weighed far more than he, so he was left satisfied with only the idea. The letter for Harran was taken by a slave to where the young master was breaking two colts in a meadow high above the house.

"He has written, quick my love, you read it, for you know I am hopeless."

They sat close together on the parapet of the tower, and Adina read.

"Greetings my brother, Harran. Your letter found us well, with quiet times in the city during the coolness of winter with few plagues, just coughs and sneezes. I salute your taste young man, for yes, I think that you are wise to love the beautiful and clever Adina. As our mother writes only praise of her, this will mean a peaceful house with harmony between the women. This is not always the case, as I often hear from my patients. I have taken the liberty to approach the slave master for details of Adina's origins, for such a special girl must have come from a good family."

Adina looked up, smiled, breathless with excitement and read on.

"I will extend the invitation for them, if they can be found, to come to visit us, to see for themselves that their daughter is well, happy, much loved and to become one of our family. I also told the Eunuch who works for the slave master, to tactfully suggest that if they wish to bring her dowry, I believe it will make Adina more happy. For apparently, a bride likes to have her own things."

Now this one did lift up his beloved and whirled her around, laughing, kissing, till breathless he stopped, demanding the letter be read again.

That evening, after they had eaten, Harran had asked to speak with his mother, Shimos and Adina. Like the colts he was trying to tame, he enthusiastically told them his news. Drawing Adina to his side, holding her hand unbearably tightly, he slowly read out his brother's letter. Kareen'ala and Shimos listened, both trying to appear serious, not daring to look at each other, for fear of laughing.

It was no use. Forgetting her lame leg, as a young woman, Kareen'ala jumped up from her couch and rushed to embrace first her son, then Adina. Shimos stood to the side, smiling his approval, trying not to crow. It all came out, the whole plot. The scheming, the subterfuge, first one facet came to light, then another. The young lovers were in turn incredulous, indignant and joyful. Laughter hung exquisitely in the room, radiating from one side to the other, like a rainbow.

During the next weeks, loaded mules arrived with many fine things from the brother in the city. Lengths of cloth for new robes for the women, jewels chosen by his wife, gifts for his mother and the bride. Every time a caravan passed too, there was something. They were so happy, the mother and daughter, opening, admiring, sharing. The chill days were warmly spent around a great brazier set in the centre of the room. Here they spent many hours each day sewing, planning and admiring their handwork. Extra slaves came to help, and in no time, each woman had many fine new clothes. Word came too that enquiries about where Adina had come from had been broadcast far and wide. Now there was real hope of finding her family.

The wedding was in early spring, a small yet joyful affair, for the bride had no one, no relatives to swell the guests. Once again, the whole house was freshly painted. The chests in Adina's little room were opened and splendid hangings were drawn out from between laurel and rosemary branches. Every blank space on the walls was richly covered. All the women's patient work and glorious colours were displayed for all to admire. Rugs were beaten and washed, and while they lay in the sun to dry, the floors were scrubbed with ash to a silver white.

Meanwhile, the kitchen prepared all manner of delicacies which would store. Huge tins of succulent, honey dripping cakes of all shapes and colours, sesame biscuits and sugar almond sweet meats. There was much excitement and shouting accompanying the boys who were lowered into the south side of the cistern, there to lay them shrouded in nets and out of harm's way, on the cool, dark shelves. Kids and lambs were slaughtered and hung first above fragrant smoke, then in dim store rooms, where the windows were draped in fine cloth against the flies. Fowl were plucked and marinated in herbs and spices before being smoked too. Spicy sausages were filled with finely chopped meats, thick with garlic. The preparations seemed endless, while the smells were tantalizing, driving everyone to work harder in optimism of the feast ahead.

A shaman arrived to direct the proceedings. From a mountain village, he was an incredibly, filthy old man with dark, beady eyes and a flowing yellow beard. Shimos took him to the men's wash house and wrapped him in a clean robe before putting him in the seat of honour. From under her veils, Adina watched with admiration as Shimos organized and sat by him, for the old man was not only very hard of hearing, he was very demanding.

The feasting went on for three days until late at night. Every room and balcony was turned into a bedroom. Bedding rolls were spread out at night and rolled up and stored during the day. The place was packed. The physician and his family were only a few of the guests who arrived. Somehow many had picked up the news and came, if not in friendship, then in curiosity or just for a good meal. There was music, singing, eating and drinking. Fingers dipped into great platters of the tastiest, fragrant saffron rice. Tender joints of lamb, kid and fowl were torn up and greedily relished. Maid servants brought from the city took round bowls of flower-scented water for the guests to wash their hands. All the while, Adina sat like an exquisite, richly-dressed doll, while Harran, resplendent in his wedding finery, devoured her with his eyes.

Shimos was tired. It had all been so exhausting. The old shaman however, never paused for breath and seemed to revel in the activities. Wide awake, all day and most of the night, he seemed only bent on ever speaking with him, bellowing in his ear. The last evening, when already many guests had left, they sat together in the great courtyard with a jug of wine. Shimos was worn out and knew that if he began to drink, even good manners would not prevent him from falling asleep. Pouring two brass cups with wine, he lay back on the cushions and shut his eyes.

A slave busied about the fire, drawing it up, for light and comfort as night fell, rather than for keeping the food hot.

"Why do you deny the gift?" said the shaman, suddenly, very loudly, very clearly. Shimos woke from his doze, looked at him in surprise. Gift, what gift?

"Here." The shaman held out what looked like a small nut. "Eat this. I need help, I get old. I know there is something to learn, I feel it, yes I feel it, yet it evades me." His hand outstretched trembled. "Eat!" he ordered, his fierce beady eyes willing Shimos to obey. Anything for peace, so, against his better judgment, Shimos took the nut and popped it into his mouth.

It was faintly sweet, slightly salty. He looked straight at the shaman and asked.

"What way can I help you then?" all the while pushing the gummy stuff about his mouth, not really liking it. Somewhere, long ago, he had done just this, when he was young and foolish. When? Where? He could not remember so gave up as he felt his mind part from his body.

The shaman approached, grew huge before him, then retreated far, far away. A voice which echoed came whistling about his head.

"Concentrate on the girl Adina, the bride. She is the one I think. Concentrate! Think on her."

Shimos looked about at the familiar place. He had not noticed before that it was so beautiful. The fire light flickered over the soft coloured walls and arches, making the shadows of the veranda railings quiver. The bougainvillea was a more piercing red than he remembered. Its new leaves shone in the half light, a brilliant emerald green, while the jasmine surely, was sweeter smelling than ever before.

"The girl," said a voice close by. Much as he tried to muster a vision of Adina he could see no one. He shut his eyes. Then gradually a scene appeared, a simple country view of the brown of the autumn earth and a small apple tree. He tried to concentrate. Apples! Now where had he seen, eaten apples? No answer came, however hard he searched in the mists of his memory. So he looked at the tree, sweet green leaves turning for autumn, with fruit, rosy red and shining. As he watched, one apple fell on to the bare earth. There, before his eyes it grew into a tree. Swiftly it grew, brilliant green, with colourful birds like shining jewels flitting through the branches. Other apples fell, yet they dried up, quickly changing from red to brown as they rotted back into the earth. Still the little tree grew, soon shadowing its parent which began to shrink, the leaves having fallen, it seemed to die and crumble till it too, was rotting on the earth. Still the young apple tree grew and new apples hung there, fine and rosy.

Now a river of water swiftly appeared, wave upon wave washing about its roots and trunk, bright blue and gold. Then he caught sight of a ship with white sails in the distance which curiously swept up, gathering the beautiful tree, its apples glinting like rubies in the sunlight as it sailed swiftly away.

Shimos shook his head and looked at the shaman whose face was huge, close in front of him. Such black broken teeth, like menhirs in the night he thought. Such pits, all over his skin, like middens, such moles, like camel dung with huge whiskers growing out of them. He peered into the tangled, yellow-white jungle which was the old man's beard and fought hard not to go in for surely he would get lost there and for sure there would be huge insects there, waiting for him. Back to the eyes, oh but those eyes, they could surely set fire to him.

"Do you remember the time before?" the booming voice asked, so close, it was in his head.

Before, before, before? As an echo. He only wanted to see where the pretty apple tree went, watching it sail away on the fine ship, far, far away. When he looked back to where it had stood, the river had gone, and just bare earth remained. There was nothing there, no single tree, no fallen apple to be seen. Perplexed, he turned to the shaman, his brow puckered.

"Tell me what you saw now, never mind about the time before. What did you see now, see now, see now?" The first clear words echoed, repeating again and again, fading to a whisper.

So remembering every detail, Shimos told.

"There was a single pretty little apple tree. It dropped a rosy red apple which grew, but the other apples which fell, just rotted. The new tree, very beautiful, green and lush, quickly outgrew its parent, which withered and died. Then suddenly a golden tide of water came, covering and consuming the brown earth about its roots. Then a ship with white sails came on the water and took the fine young tree which was laden with apples like rubies, and sailed far, far away." He shut his eyes again.

Now he was a bird, flying over the ship, watching it sailing on and on, till a great mist came up, and all he could see were the rubies twinkling at him like lights.

He surely must have fallen into the sea, for cold water splashed his face and crept between his lips and he felt his body cool and washed. Occasionally he heard the distant angry voice of thunder and he felt himself floating, floating through the air. Turning this way and that his body rolled and tossed in the waves so he lay and did not fight it.

When he woke, he was in his own little room and the old shaman was sitting beside him. Shimos smiled lazily at him, feeling very tired as from a great journey.

"You have the gift my friend, yet I fear your vision was not a good omen, so I stayed till you woke, despite the anger of the mistress, to tell you not, on any account, to speak of it to anyone."

Shimos frowned, trying to understand what the fellow was speaking of, hadn't he left yet? Then, like a great light, it hit him. The vision. The tree! Roughly he grasped the old man's hand.

"Tell me the meaning then if you please? For I cannot understand it."

Leaning forward to speak near Shimos' ear, the shaman for once spoke quietly.

"They are doomed, all of them, except for her first child. That one will go far away, cross the seas and make a great family. Good people. Important. Wealthy. Noble. The rest are doomed, I know not how or when. That is all I can tell you."

Shimos closed his eyes. No! his mind screamed, not Adina, not Kareen'ala? Again he reached for the brown withered hand.

"Can we do nothing?" The old one, his eyes hooded now, gently shook his head.

"Perhaps not," he said very quietly, quite unlike before. "Yet who knows? The firstborn child, that is the one to watch out for. That you can do. I think your task is there, with the first born."

The floor shuddered and a door slammed. Kareen'ala was furious. Eyes blazing, she swept in and ordered the shaman out with barely a courtesy.

"What did he give you? The old fool!" she raged sobbing, all the while bathing the white face. "And what were you to tell him, Before, he said, before? What happened in the past? Do you know this man? OH!" she sat on the bed and held his hands. "I have been so worried my dear, you have been gone, far away, for days!"

Shimos felt so tired, so weak, yet all the time he kept remembering his vision, and clung to the realness of the plump woman in his life, fearful of what was to come.

CHAPTER FOUR

DRABO

It was easy to forget the nightmares watching the joy of the newlyweds. Harran took his bride everywhere with him, be it to farm or the city. Together they rode, hawking, racing, laughing wildly at each other across the brown earth, loving life, every minute of it. While he worked with the young horses, she fondled and tamed the foals, laughing at their baby antics, her white teeth contrasting with her sunburned face, the wonderful hair, rippling and glinting. He gave her a small, very fine young mare, and loving it, she rode like the wind, as one with the beast.

"If you knew what a beautiful sight you two are!" exclaimed the happy Harran. "Your hair and her hide, the same glorious copper!" And so it was.

By September, when her belly was swelling with her first child, Adina had given up believing her father would come. Still, she was happier than she could believe and Harran was a loving and caring husband; their passion was exquisite.

They had been given new rooms which were wonderfully draped and furnished. Adina loved it all and felt great pride that she had been so endowed. Life changed, yet did not really change. They all did what they had done before, but the pattern was different. Where their love had before been intense and perfect, now it was free, out and open and she felt cherished. While Harran was her love and her mate, Kareen'ala and Shimos stood as her parents, gently attentive of her health and needs.

Seeing her difficulty in climbing up to the tower, Harran built a fine wooden stair for her. Every evening she went up there, urging all the family to join her now that access was so easy. Gazing at the brilliant night sky, there was a feeling that she had done it all before. Yet now it was she with the swelling child, not her mother, who waited and rested in the evening breeze.

As she so often did, Adina gazed down across the sun-burnt slope toward the well far below. A cloud of dust had heralded travellers, and not unusually, they had stopped to rest and drink at the well. Suddenly, she was alerted to the people below. Something, something made her heart beat faster. Laying down the little robe she was stitching, she stared in the evening light.

The party of horsemen came up the hill, and craning to see better, she caught her breath, for surely, oh surely, the tall man in front was her father? Gathering her strength she ran down, found Kareen'ala with the cook, and babbled her news.

It was not her father, but Drabo, her eldest brother. Staring at him, hands over her face, she gazed in disbelief. He had grown so. He was even taller than her father had been, and oh, so like him in every way. With a cry, "Drabo, Drabo!" she ran into his arms and held him close, sobbing as if her heart would break.

"Sister, sweet sister," her brother held her fast. "You are alive, our precious Adina, alive and well. God be praised."

After that, it was all laughter and love, and endless speaking. He was so fine her brother. So able. So well dressed, his robes of the best cloth, with fine woven borders and embroidered shirt. She was so proud to introduce him to her new family, who she realized were just as delighted and impressed with him as she.

A feast was hurriedly brought, so they sat on the roof and ate and talked till tactfully, the family left them, knowing that the siblings needed time alone.

Right from the moment they had left the house on that fateful day, Adina told of their getting lost in the desert, the robbers, the death of the groom, leaving Mina. How the boy had sold her and how she had gone from place to place, slaver to slaver, for many moons. Till at last, the nightmare over, the physician had bought her. After that, all was well, for she was brought here, to kind Kareen'ala, and meeting her son, who was now her husband and thus finding happiness.

In turn, Drabo told of how they had not known for very many days that she had disappeared. With the death and funeral of their mother, they thought she was safe at the farm till the younger brothers had arrived home and the awful truth came out. The grandmothers almost went mad in their grief. Where was she and where to search? Why had they not arrived at the farm? Where had they got to? Each one of them had blamed themselves, their grief was even more terrible. First mother, then daughter. Till weeks later, her pony was found for sale in a nearby market, and although the trader knew nothing of her abduction, he told them he had bought it from some stranger brothers. Their father had locked himself in a dark room, refusing food or comfort, almost insane with guilt and sorrow.

Again, brother and sister clung to each other in sadness and joy. A slave brought up a small brazier and sprinkled herbs over the coals, making sweet smoke against the insects. It was all so familiar.

At last, understanding that she must be lost, they had resumed their lives as best they could, never ceasing the search, wider, further, systematically and quietly. The grandmothers arranged a new wife for their father, for they had each other, and recognized surely he needed someone for comfort. They were very lucky to find a young widow without children who was beautiful and quiet, and fitted into the household serenely.

Then, Drabo holding her face in his hands, smiling, kissing her, came a real surprise. For of course the grandmothers had sent after the servant who had taken the new born baby girl, supposedly to leave it in the desert. Safely with a wet nurse, they had thought to bring her back when calm returned, when the father had regained his sanity, just in a matter of days. Yet with the mother's death, they had left the child where it was till it became obvious that the new wife was barren. Having had no child in her five year marriage, none coming with the new husband, they brought the year-old baby and wet nurse back, to great rejoicing.

"She is exactly like you, Adina," her brother held her hand, "her hair, her smile. She has brought happiness back into our house. Father is calm and loving again, and our new mother is so full of joy with the child." He paused. "It doesn't do to remember that if mother knew the baby was safe, she would not have taken her life. Now we have the little one back, and we must rejoice that we know that you are safe and happy." He bent his head to hide the tears, for men did not show weakness. "God is good. This day sister, is the happiest I can remember. I only want to leave you to race home to tell them how you are, so well, more beautiful than ever, and with such a good and loving family."

He had brought just a few things, in case it was a false alarm. All they knew was that a girl with red hair and green eyes had been sold into slavery, was here, and was seeking her family. Now that he knew it was her, they would return with her dowry, all of it. Meanwhile she unpacked the two small wooden chests and delighted in her personal treasures, old friends. Her little carved box with her combs and trinkets, her shawls and kerchiefs, in the sandal-wood chest. Last but not least, her mother's hammam box, the fine copper casket to take to the baths, filled with oils and sponges.

"My little sister?" she asked. "Will she not need this, for we have no bath here?" Yet he assured her that the new mother had many beautiful things, and the child was surely as her own, and so would never go without.

Fine gifts were given to Kareen'ala and Harran, even a cloak for Shimos, who her brother did not realize was a slave. They were happy days when he hunted with Harran, toured the land, enjoyed the excellent meals and talked endlessly. Yet all the time he was eager to leave, to take the wonderful news home. Harran had chosen a fine mare as a gift, half-sister to the beauty which Adina owned. Drabo was deeply touched by the gift and felt it would show his own family what good people Adina was now with.

"I beg a favour now brother. The Eunuch at the slave master, and the two dumb brother eunuchs, a fine money gift for them I beg you, for they were so kind, protecting me, giving me back my self-esteem. And the old woman," she smiled remembering her last hysterical night at the baths. "A money gift too, but a special gift for her, a fine hammam box, and oils, please brother." Considering for a moment what they could give to the physician, she continued. "When my dowry comes, then I will choose what to give to my brother-in-law and his family, for without them?" She stopped and raised her shoulders.

When he left, a great calmness overwhelmed Adina. Even if she never saw any of them again, she felt happy with the knowledge that all was well with them, as with her. Now she thought only of keeping calm and healthy for the coming child.

"So I will build you a bathhouse!" announced the proud Harran, fingering the fine workmanship of her copper box. He was openly impressed that his wife was, as his mother had stated, from a very fine family. "Then you can use your hammam box. We might be simple country folk, but my wife is a lady with a beautiful casket for her oils. And what use is that without a bathhouse?" Harran was very happy.

Any sorrow Adina might have felt at her brother's departure was erased by the excitement over the plans for the new bathhouse. Shimos was urged with pen and paper into discussions, as they all walked round and about the property choosing a place. It was to be small, just for the family, very fine, and built properly, of cut stone. Not too far, or too near, this was a big decision.

Finally it was decided to build it below the tower, far from the farm yet not far from the house, it would be an easy walk. Water and wood could be taken from the gardens. Waste water and ashes would go back onto the earth. By winter, it was ready, and after the birth of her daughter Karina, carrying her precious casket, Adina went with Kareen'ala for their first bath, revelling in the luxury of their own bathhouse.

Some time later, a stout man detached himself from a big party of travellers and asked to speak to Adina. Shimos and Kareen'ala sat close by, for it didn't do for a stranger to speak alone with her, a slave had run to fetch Harram.

However, they need not have worried, for with great courtesy he introduced himself as a friend of her father. From the court, he was on his way with letters, as envoy to a distant land. Then he opened his great, embroidered shoulder bag, took out a bulging linen bag and gave it into Adina's hands.

Next, he took a large leather purse which he gave to Harran.

"There, I have executed my obligation to your father. He asked me to guard it well, and to place it into your hands."

When he had gone, hands trembling, Adina opened it up, an excited Kareen'ala at her elbow. At first they had been surprised, for inside was a rather plain leather waistcoat, big and somewhat clumsy. Folded in it, were a sheaf of wrapped and tied letters, which Adina held to her breast, filled with anticipation of reading them. Exploration of the waistcoat revealed many secret pockets, craftily sewn and closed with tiny bone buttons. Now they understood why it was so heavy. With cries of delight and awe, the two women laid out the collection of jewels which had been secreted in its folds. Many Adina recognized as her own, but most were her mother's and even from her two grandmothers. Yet there were more, exquisite, rich, and gem-encrusted, rings, bracelets, necklaces and pins, all new to her. She gazed at them, eyes filling with tears, realizing that they must be wedding gifts, no doubt from all her family. Kareen'ala was impressed all over again that her daughter-in-law was obviously from a wealthy and certainly honest family.

"We will put them all back my dear daughter, for you to wear on special occasions and for your children to inherit." Yet secretly she rejoiced to know that here was boundless treasure, for who knew when black days might come again.

The girl child grew, a stringy, active little thing, ever smiling, always ready to come or go. Apart from the many slaves who vied to entertain her, she had four parents. They were her world, and she adored them equally.

When she learnt to walk, she danced on her toes, arms uplifted. Her blue eyes sparkling and her shining red-black curls dancing too, glinting in the sunlight.

During the early years, she was oblivious of the annual sorrow which fell as a cloud on her home. As she grew older however, whispers caught her active mind, so gradually she became aware of the sorrow which engulfed them. Time after time, year after year, her mother bore a son, a fine living child, who gradually faded away and died. Eyes, which had once been bright with optimism, became dull. Joy and laughter left their house. Her once beautiful mother now seemed so thin and fragile, her hair lack-lustre, her green eyes dull and faded. Try as she might, Karina failed to make them all happy again.

Gradually, she took over her mother's place to go with her father up to the farm, to first watch him with the horses, then in time, to help him with them. He watched her in turn, amused, as the little thing gritted her teeth, hung on to her pony and tried to keep up with him. It seemed as if she had a special way with the animals, for she had no fear, and this they all respected. In no time she was on her mother's mare, for Adina grew too weak to ride with her husband anymore, and her mare needed love and exercise, which Karina delighted in giving it.

Kareen'ala watched her son secretly from under her head cloth. He was a man now, sorrow lining his mouth, sadness etching his eyes. They had just returned from burying the sixth boy child, and he must go to Adina to give her comfort.

"Why?" they all asked themselves, and sometimes each other, "Why?" And Shimos took another glass of wine, trying to dismiss the apple tree from his mind.

Even the elder son had no answer for them, except to say that yes, he had seen it before. So many questions, no answers. Yet, he wondered if it was in their blood, for hadn't his own mother suffered the same? Babe after healthy babe, who had, Kareen'ala told him, just shrivelled up and died before their eyes. The same and yet? How was it that his own, good wife successfully bore healthy, living children?

Kareen'ala had made up her mind there and then. She would insist and she would win. Reason, they must understand reason. Days of raised voices followed, she was a virago and none could escape it.

"Don't you love her you great fool?" she howled at her bowed son. "Do you want to kill her?"

Then days of silence, which was almost as bad.

"I have decided," announced Kareen'ala. "Harran will take a second wife," and simply got on with it.

There had been trouble again in their district. Bandits, who masquerading as shepherds, were once again living in the hills, stealing, killing, raping and burning. It was just a matter of time before they would be attacked. So she put it round, quietly, craftily. This daughter-in-law was no use for breeding, they were searching for a fine, healthy, strong, young woman to be second wife to her son.

Hearing it, Adina weakly thought it out and agreed. Her love for Harran still burnt brightly. She believed he still loved her too. But there was anger, sorrow, a complicated jumble of emotions which seemed as a knife between them. Gone was the laughter of the past, gone their light and joyful loving. Sullen, brooding, Harran worked hard, drank hard, and took her ever more cruelly. Gone was the tenderness and passion. Now he was brutal, as if he wanted to plant a good seed in her, digging deep and furiously. Yet once again, a beautiful long limbed, serene son was born, to simply fade away, unable to cry anymore, it died before their eyes.

"No!" she raised her hands in front of herself as if to ward off evil, "not again my love, never again. Your mother is right. You must take a new wife. You need sons. Live, healthy, fine sons. Something is wrong with me, that I can only bear them, simply to die."

Eyes dull, he looked at her, his desire fading. Gone was his beautiful Adina with the copper hair and glowing skin. Before him lay a faded shadow of her, skin dry and wrinkled, dull hair, and her lovely eyes always fearful and without hope. He nodded and left the room, so at last she could let the tears fall. Why? Why?

After weeks of hordes of ruffians visiting them, Kareen'ala chose. Not that she especially liked the girl, others had certainly been more appealing. It was because of her father and brothers she chose her. They were the biggest, roughest tribe in the area. Sense, sound sense. And anyway, who could ever compete with Adina? The feast was arranged for just after shearing, when the workload was lighter, money boxes full and perhaps some rain to grow a whisper of grass on the parched hills. As the girl had no mother, Kareen'ala insisted she, together with her ancient grandmother, came to live in the women's quarters before the marriage. This would serve a double purpose, for not only could they lick the girl into shape, Harran would be refused entry for the time being, and be obliged to leave Adina alone.

"Another pregnancy would kill her," she muttered to no one in particular. "And me," she added sadly.

On the surface, the preparations were as great and as happy as the first marriage years before. But the laughter was brittle, and eyes were wary. It was not a happy house, with the master glowering and both mistresses weeping. As for the new bride, well, some mistress she would make! A rough, coarse country girl, whose features would thicken and disappear into folds of fat as soon as maybe. The slaves looked at her under their head-cloths or straw hats and only felt pity. Breeding stock she was, but little else, for she was as a wild sow to an Arab mare.

They tried, Kareen'ala and Adina, they really did. They took her giggling and reluctant to the bathhouse, soaked and scrubbed her, yet still she stank.

"Perhaps it is the food she ate mother?" suggested Adina in her own tongue. "I have never smelt any girl so bad."

With pursed mouth, Kareen'ala scrubbed on, ignoring protests from the old grandmother. Whatever it was, she would root it out for it was unbearable. No sooner was the girl bathed and in fresh clothes, than she immediately began to sweat and stink again. Yet, they were kind to her, teaching her just about everything. How to sew, helping her to make simple clothes. For, she seemed wholly ignorant in womanly ways, liking only to squat in the courtyard with the old woman, cracking pumpkin seeds between her strong teeth, and leaving the shells scattered everywhere for someone else to clear up. They washed her strong hair in various herbs and worked on it with every style. Yet she barely changed. Pouring sweet oils on her face and hands they massaged her all over, but she remained, to their eyes at least, an impossible task. While Adina felt anxiety for the girl, in her secret heart she was glad that she was not beautiful, so she hoped that Harran might not grow to love her. Torn between good sense and fear, Adina began to feel stronger. With rest and relief at not starting yet another fruitless pregnancy, her old longing for Harran grew so strong, she dreaded to see him.

"When everything is organized," Kareen'ala said, Shimos and Harran standing to attention and listening, "Adina, Karina and I will go to the tower. We will take provisions and we will lock the door, until the feast is over." They nodded in agreement. It was better that way, for there would certainly be many and drunken guests who might just cause trouble.

The bride, magnificent in her finery, gold shimmering in her robe, jewels hanging on her head, was joyfully exhibited by her family. All anger at the high-handed mistress of the house evaporated when they saw how she had turned their girl into a beauty. Through her veil she did look lovely, even Kareen'ala had to admit it. They had starved her for three weeks to lose some fluid. It had not been easy. They had kept her in the shade so that her skin lost its ruddy glow. They had really used all their arts to make her up with kohl, rouge and lapis powder and yes, they were rewarded with an almost-beautiful bride.

"I am afraid," the new bride had said tearfully clinging to Adina's hand. Adina melted. Poor girl, fear was not unknown to her, yet she was lucky, Harran was good, and she had spoken firmly to him, reminding him that the girl was still very young.

"Do not fear little sister," she had replied kindly. "Our husband is a good man, a sweet lover, he will be kind. And when you are with child, if you do not want him anymore, you can say so. Mother and I are here to help you. Do not be afraid."

"I am afraid!" Harran said to Shimos, the father-figure. "I do not desire her, ugly girl, she repels me. I shall not be able to mount her, I know it. I am afraid."

Shimos sucked the air in and nodded to himself. He had wondered about that.

"Now listen to me my boy," sharp fingers biting into Harran's arm. "You just have to make believe it is Adina, forget Nikina. Think of Adina, hold her face in your mind, remember how it was with her, and you will rise. Put away all foolish thoughts that this one is any different, really. Well she is, I know," he added quickly, "but get her with child quickly, and the deed will be done."

He did immediately. It was as if the whole household sighed with relief, so Harran crept back into the bed and arms of Adina. Happy again, giving him comfort as she could, yet she never allowed him to enter her, and so prevented the chance to conceive again.

Like a young heifer, Nikina swelled greatly and suffered no ills during her pregnancy. She was cosseted and petted, and happy with the attention, only complaining that she was not given enough food. When her time came, Kareen'ala sent for the grandmother, for if anything went wrong, she needed her there to share the blame.

They arrived, the whole clan grinning with pride and anticipation. Their noise and stink were only equalled by their constant demands for food and drink to rejoice.

It started quietly, the women clustering about giving comfort and encouragement. In no time, the screaming began, bloodcurdling, wave after wave till Harran urged the male guests to join him hunting to get far away. Why was this one making such a fuss when Adina had born all her children in utmost silence?

At the darkest time of night, with one last shriek of effort, a son was born. A plump, dark skinned, hairy boy who took over the screaming from his mother. The old grandmother took it up, uttering incantations, while Adina, her heart heavy, helped wash and settle the new mother.

It did not look like her sons. They had been long limbed and fair while this one was black haired, fat and squat, exactly like its mother's family. Even so, it looked healthy. But then, so had hers, at first.

Six days later, when tempers were frayed with the extravagant rejoicing, they held a feast, for it was obvious that this lusty son had no intention of fading away as had his half-brothers. Once on the breast, he seized upon the great dark red nipple and guzzled and puked and guzzled more.

Karina hung about closely, desperate to be near, to touch, to hold the new brother. Young though she was, she could feel the undercurrents of emotion from every side. The only ones who were happy were her new aunt and the baby. The other grandmother was, however, ferocious in her actions and had little patience with the girl-child from the first wife. So, when she thought no one was looking, she drove her away, hissing through toothless gums on any feeble pretext. Her granddaughter had succeeded where that poor, delicate first wife had not. They had the boy, a fine, strong boy too. He was what mattered.

Once again the house was filled with guests to celebrate the new son. Yet again Kareen'ala took Adina and Karina up to the tower and barred the door.

"Bring your jewels, Adina," she said in private, "nothing is safe to leave with that rabble about. I will bring food and drink for I consider that we deserve a little rest. We can stay up there even till they leave." To the young mother she said kindly, "This is your big day daughter. You must entertain your husband's guests, show them your fine son and be proud. We will retire and leave it all to you. The slaves will take care of everything, while your grandmother will mind the child. Now you must enjoy yourself after your labours."

It was a bright, clear night and the only thing which was missing was silence. For the guests were wild in their jubilation, filling the night with their bawdy singing while their women danced to sensuous country music. There was a chill in the air and Kareen'ala not only had a heavy heart, her leg was aching from the last days of toil, and in the turmoil, Shimos had forgotten to give her the little pipe. Truly, she was feeling her age with all this emotion and trouble. Perhaps now life would resume its gentle rhythm. Holding her precious granddaughter close, she pointed to the stars and told her stories, just as her father had.

"When we went on his ship, for he was a trader you know, he always steered by the stars."

Adina lay and gazed up too, listening to the kind voice and trying to ignore the noise from the courtyard which rose in gusty waves. She hoped that someone was caring for the baby, for without them there, he might be tossed about from one relative to the other. For the thousandth time, she asked herself how all this had come to pass.

Pressing her hand into the pit of her stomach she grimaced at the dull pain, then smiled. At last she had given in to him. He had been so pressing, so loving, and needing him too she had weakened and welcomed him and yes, it had been as of old, a love-making made in heaven.

As the night grew chilly, the fire in the courtyard grew higher, giving a great light. So too rose the noise, for everyone must have been very drunk. On the flat roof of the tower, the three cuddled close together under their blankets, trying to shut out the noise and trying keep warm.

Then it happened, a gentle shaking at first, like scratching a mosquito bite. Then it grew, and grew, with a great noise like a herd of beasts coming towards them, closer, closer. Kareen'ala sat up, clutching the child to her. Oh no, not again! When she tried to stand she was thrown down, so she just reached out, arms encircling, and drew the girl to her. There was only one thought, one thing to do, as the earth heaved and swayed and the sound of timbers and masonry crashed below them in the courtyard. The screams, the terrible screams rose as did the fire. Gathering up Karina, her namesake, she did the one thing she must, she must somehow protect the child.

CHAPTER FIVE

SHIMOS

Sitting just behind Harran, Shimos stifled a yawn. How much longer was this ridiculous rejoicing going on for? He absently gazed around, thinking how what was normally a large and airy courtyard, now seemed small, crowded and stifling. The heat of a huge fire in the centre pushed the crowd back under the verandas. Wherever there was a gap amongst the sprawling guests, one of the gaudy visiting women was flaunting her flesh, gyrating in a sickening manner. Shimos grimaced, such ugliness! In his early life, women kept to their quarters, not like this primitive lot. Elsewhere slaves threaded their way, doling out food, from great copper bowls and platters. There was plenty of pushing and shoving for space, but at least that was generally good natured. The stink of unwashed bodies was thick and he wrinkled his nose, absently wondering why these people smelt worse than their camels.

At least the clever Kareen'ala had skilfully relieved them of all their swords and scimitars and locked them in the tower so that any drunken brawl would be relatively harmless. Of course they still had their small knives, which were needed for eating with. Still, a small eruption of bad temper and those knives could deal out cruel punishment. He pressed his hand to his side where his own small knife lay. Old he might be, but if any man should raise his hand to young Harran, Shimos would certainly put an end to him.

Bored, he sighed deeply. Days and days of entertaining these stinking ruffians, with so much extravagant congratulations, and for what? That gross, hairy, ape-like boy child? Fruit of that smelly, unfortunate female poor Harran had been obliged to mate with, to get a son, one who would live. He closed his eyes, seeing in comparison, the fair Adina and all her newborn sons, long limbed, fair and lovely. Then, a pain in his heart, he remembered, as one after the other, pitifully shrinking before their eyes, their cries growing so thin, they seemed to beg for release from their brief lives. Trying to shut it out of his mind, he squeezed his eyes shut tight. It was no use. Finally, every one of them had been laid out, serene and beautiful in death. Why? What could the matter be that her first child should be so light, gay, strong and beautiful? And six, or was it seven! How could the gods cause those little sons to die? Again, the pain smiting his heart, he remembered the first wedding, so different from this charade. He remembered the ugly old shaman, the drug and the vision of the apple tree, and fearful but finally accepting, knew that what would be, would be. He shifted his bony buttocks, trying to get comfortable. More than anything, he would love to leave this writhing mass of sweating humanity, for the night despite being cool, the fires in the confined courtyard made it overly hot.

The wine was being brought round again. Putting his hand over his cup, Shimos indicated the other guests, so the slave moved on, picking his way through the pile of reclining bodies. At least they would all soon be sleeping and the noise would end. Yet just a few kept up the pace. The poor dancing girls still made a pretence of life, their behinds quivering to the weary squawls of the pipers. Stiff, he wondered if he could slip away without anyone noticing. Harran, who was as the son he had never had, lay on his cushions, half sideways, slobbering in drunkenness. Disgusting. Sadly, and of course, the boy could not hold his drink as well as this rough mob of new relatives.

Before the feast had begun, when the ladies had crept up to the tower, Shimos had gone down to the bathhouse and smugly prepared for his escape. Leaving his bath sheet, soaps and oils, he had set a small fire under the cauldron with the full intention of leaving the feast as soon as he decently could. There he would pass the rest of the night in peace, cleansing himself of their vile stink. Oh, but what an ordeal. Perhaps he could pretend a call of nature and slip away? Very carefully, he got up, making sure he was not noticed. As he passed the fine wooden stair to the tower which Harran had built, he considered joining his precious ladies. Then thought the better of it, for with any luck, high up there, above the racket, they may even be asleep. Slipping out of the great gateway, he drew it shut behind him and sucked in the clear night air. Slowly, for it was very dark, he pottered down the hill.

Relieved, safely at the bathhouse, he shoved the door closed and set a stone against it to keep in the warmth, and out any of the curious. Taking a light from the little furnace, he lit a lamp and carefully poured the steaming water. Gingerly, sucking in his breath at the heat, he lowered himself in. It was wonderful to sit and doze in the fine marble tub, and soak away the aches and pains of old age and of the past wearisome days.

When it came, he was dreaming, a thing he rarely did these days. His father and he were trying out a new pony with their war chariot. It was exhilarating, flying along, holding tight to the light bamboo frame, laughing into the bright summer sky. His father raised the whip and brought it down, but not on the beast's back, just to frighten it to go faster. This was no time to abuse the creature. Come the real thing, then he would use the whip or die.

The rattling and shaking grew wilder, the noise increased, and a small pebble fell from the vaulted stone ceiling into the water, splashing his face. Suddenly awake, Shimos stared into the darkness for a moment, then he knew what it was. Earthquake!

Holding tight to the sides of the bath, he crouched down in the dark, for of course, the lamp had gone out. Aware that the whole structure could come down on his head, he thought only for himself till he remembered Kareen'ala. When it had passed, he sat stock still listening. So dense were the walls of the small bathhouse, little sound penetrated. Strain as he might, he heard nothing. Wrapped in the sheet, he lay on the resting ledge and dozed. With the dawn chinking through cracks in the door, he fixed the sheet tightly about himself and struggled to open it. Yet it would not open. The earthquake had perhaps shifted the foundations so the door post had moved. Beating on it, he called till he was hoarse, yet still no one came. Repeating his calls he waited what he thought must be hours. Still no one came.

Feeling about, he gathered up what little wood there was left from the furnace. At least he had a plan now; better than beating and shouting on the door, he would burn it down. Made of good olive wood, it took time to ignite, but when it did, the fire flared up and Shimos, skin scorching, climbed once more into the now cold bath, a wet cloth over his head, and waited till it was consumed. Then taking a scoop he doused the embers, and gingerly picked his way out.

To his surprise it was dusk. He had not realized that he had spent all the day trying to free himself. Quickly he struggled up the hill, wishing that he had remembered his sandals and trying to avoid the sharp stones on the path. Pausing for breath for a moment he looked up. Despite the gathering night, he stared in disbelief at the house. For it was no more, just a pile of fallen masonry and black, smoking timbers, ragged ribs, stark against the fading sky. Then he looked at the tower and sighed with relief. At least that still stood. Heartened, bent over, he hurried on up, holding the stitch in his side.

"Kareen'ala!" he called. "Kareen'ala!" No sooner had the sound faded than three heads appeared at the top of the tower.

"Shimos, oh Shimos!" Oh the joy to hear her voice. Three voices called to him in unison, "Shimos, Shimos!" He hurried on, delight giving him strength to try to find a better vantage point.

"Are you alright my lady? My dearlings?" he called, voice full of love and hope. "Are you all alright?"

"Yes, oh yes, Shimos, and glad to hear you, for no one else is alive I fear, least no one replied to our calls all day. Oh Shimos!" and a wailing fell on his ears, and their cries rose pitifully as night shut out his sight of them.

When they silenced their cries, they spoke, shouting up and down. A plan was made, but they would have to wait till morning. Returning to the bathhouse Shimos realized his belly was totally empty, so scooping up the cold bath water, he drank copiously of it. Grimacing, drinking waste from his own body, he smiled wryly, for hadn't he drank much worse during his chequered life? It was another bad night and his sleep was fitful. He thought he felt more shakes and he was cold, the door being down and with no fire, or indeed the comforting body of his mistress.

With the dawn, he rose and winding his cloth about him, set off up the hill, feeling faint with hunger, his stomach griping. The women seemed well, greatly heartened by his presence, even laughing at him, for he was quite blackened from the fire. So they spoke of their plans, or rather what they had planned for him to do, for the staircase had burned away. They had no way to come down.

First, he must explore and see if anyone lived, and if there was any help to hand. It was soon evident there was neither. Sickened by the sight within the courtyard, he cautiously went to the stables behind the house and carefully, one by one undid a rough lot of camels and scrub ponies, letting them free. Awful creatures, camels, brought by awful guests, who wouldn't be needing them anymore. That task done, he returned to his place beneath the tower. Next, he was directed to the farm, there to feed the horses, and maybe a slave might be there? Trembling with weakness and hunger, Shimos slowly went up the slope, for it was quite a climb. Yet there too, there was no sign of life, but the animals. Crowding the gate, they gave him welcome, neighing and nickering for they were hungry and indignant, having always been well cared for. The gate into the walled paddock was firmly closed, no doubt by the last groom who must have sneaked off to the feast and his end. After what seemed an age, Shimos elbowed his way through the shoving horses to their stables, there to climb to the loft and toss down hay for them. Fortunately he had seen it done many times, or he certainly would not have known what to do. At least, he thought with relief, their water trough was fed by gravity from a spring up in the hills. He really did not think he had the energy to carry water for them all.

Next, he went to the grain store, an interesting box-like building set on polished boulders against the vermin. The falcon's great cages were placed all about in it, cleverly made of strongly woven bamboo. It was they who kept the place free of rats and mice, feeding themselves when there was no meat from hunting. Nervously over-filling their water troughs, he left them. He did not like these birds, with their sharp beaks and cruel eyes.

Remembering the little paddock where the house sheep and goats were kept, he took up a great pile of hay to take to them. Apart from being hungry, they looked well enough and those in milk each having a suckling, none needed milking. Stacking their little hay rack full, he closed their gate once more and returned to the big barn.

A hen alerted him with her enthusiastic chorus and, mind racing, he realized that the women might appreciate some eggs. Searching about, he did discover some well-stocked nests and after sucking one warm egg dry, he put the rest in the water pail on a handful of hay, and was actually pleased with himself. Farming having never been a part of his life, he thought over what he had done, and considered the next job.

It might be the best thing to leave all their gates open, for he knew they would return for water. Yes, that was it, so he did the rounds again. Animals cared for, he examined the several ladders about the buildings and chose the second tallest, because it was the lightest made. Even so, and dragging it, the water pail banging his legs, it took time to take it down to the tower. At last, with a huge effort of will, he set it up somehow, the women directing from above yet it was far too short. Oh but the disappointment of it, the shock. Silently they all gazed at the rough stone blocks and wondered if there was any way they could breach the distance. The eggs hooked on a long, forked stick to reach them, were a very poor compensation.

"Stay there where you are safe and I will go for help Kareen'ala. Do you have water?" They had not. So they tied their scarves together and lowered their jars which he filled from the spring at the well below the tower. It was late afternoon by then, yet he decided he must make a move, for he doubted his strength would last for much longer. Going down to the garden he plucked vegetables and ate them raw where he stood, his stomach growling mightily. Dressing in his finest yet blackened clothes from the bathhouse, he took also the bath sheet, and started down to the well again, there washing and drinking his fill before turning his face to the West toward the nearest village.

Two days passed, and when he did not return the women grew anxious, saved the water for the child, and sang to keep their spirits up. Not only were they worried about Shimos, a sickly foul stink of death began to rise from the ruined courtyard. Try as they did, the stink together with strange noises of scavengers filled the nights and there was no escape from it.

Adina looked carefully at the ladder propped against the tower wall. If she could tie some cloth somehow, and lower herself slowly? Surely she could get her feet on the ladder, and so go down? Perhaps some ill had befallen Shimos. The waiting was terrible. Kareen'ala was troubled. She was afraid for the much loved girl, yet, as she was light, perhaps she could go safely down? Perhaps? They waited till early on the fifth morning. Carefully covering the child so she would not wake, the two women worked to make a rope of clothes. Trembling and afraid, Adina kissed the fearful older woman and carefully went over the parapet. Digging her toes into the rough gaps between the blocks, clutching the cloth rope, she went down, slowly, bit by bit, Kareen'ala's anxious face above her in the dawn light. At last, her foot touched the top rung. Closing her eyes, Adina gradually had a hold of the wood, let go of the rope, and tentatively began her descent.

"Careful my child," hissed Kareen'ala from above, whispering an incantation to her god, yet her god did not hear. For on that steep slope, on the dry earth, the ladder was not firmly placed and shifted. Holding her breath, Adina held tight, willing it to steady, yet it began to tip and fall sideways, slowly, slowly gathering speed. In a great arc, it fell, faster and faster till the momentum threw Adina down onto the rocky slope of the tower foundations. There, so perhaps God had heard, mercifully her head hit a rock, and she knew no more. Moments after her heart had stopped, the tiny new life within her womb died also. Her lifeless, lithe, yet broken body, tumbled down the slope, bouncing lightly into the thick green cover of the garden. Stuffing her hands into her mouth, helpless, Kareen'ala tried not to scream as she watched, rocking her plump body in utter despair.

When the child woke, she had regained her composure and had the story that Adina had gone to find Shimos, and to bring help. At least in his mercy her god had hidden the body from the child, for that she had to be grateful. There had to be a way down; somehow she must save the child and take her to the city to see if her physician son had survived the disaster. There just had to be a way. Making a shelter with cloth against the sun as they had each day, they sat and played with their jewels. Kareen'ala told the child the colours, and the names of the stones, if she knew them. It was unbelievable Kareen'ala thought, here we are, draped with all these treasures, and we will soon have no food and water, and we may even die.

The next day, she spied dust from the East, and watched excited as three horsemen stopped far below at the well. Summoning her last strength, Kareen'ala screamed to attract their attention. Then she stood on the parapet and waved a sheet, so at last they saw her and started up the road.

"Help me down friends," she called. "For the love of God, help a poor woman to get off this tower." They stood below, looking up doubtfully. It looked hard, and why should they? She was nothing to them. Lowering their eyes they turned to go.

"Don't go, I beg you," she called again. "Save a poor woman I pray you. See, see!" she held up her little bag of jewels and shook it, "I can pay you friends, I have money and jewels. Just help me down!"

Muttering to each other, the men narrowed their eyes, assessing the possibility. They did not need more money or jewels, for they had done well, stripping the dead and dying along the way, their packs were full. Now they needed water, food and a clear road to get far away. Even so, a little more wouldn't hurt. They dismounted and tied their laden beasts to a shrub.

Walking around the tower, they found a higher place on the other side and carried the ladder, setting it up securely. Meanwhile Kareen'ala took her precious granddaughter into her arms.

"Listen to me my dearling," she gazed into the blue eyes, so like her own, willing the girl to attend. "I fear that these may not be good men, so I will go down first, give them my jewels, and find out. Only when I call you that it is safe to come down, will you do so." Clasping the skinny little arms she repeated herself. "Keep your mama's jewels secret, right where they are in the jacket. Never tell anyone about them, you hear? Let them think what I have is all. Now," she paused on hearing a call from the men below. "Remember, on no condition come down, unless I call you, or Shimos, or," she hesitated and covered her distress with a fierce kiss, "Adina. Or even other good people, you will surely know. Stay here till we call you, none other."

To her surprise they helped her down, the lighter one aiding her feet, one at a time, down the rough ladder. At the bottom she smiled at them, trying to subdue the fear which rose in her throat for they were evil looking men. Now, close to, their smell surrounding her, she could plainly see that. Holding out her hand with the little bag of jewels she forced herself to smile again.

"Here you are then friends, all I have, take them and my thanks too."

In the far distance, dragging himself along, Shimos came, slowly, too slowly. At times he crawled, where the stones were few, then he walked till he fell. For he was bleeding from a mass of cuts, on hands and knees, flies tormenting him and his whole body was racked with pain. At last, along the dusty road, he had seen life, a cloud of dust approaching, two animals, a great horse with a huge fair man on its back, accompanied by a tiny dark man, atop a small mule. Hands outstretched he begged them to stop, but they rode on, only thinking he was begging. In his fever of hunger, thirst and anxiety, Shimos gathered strength and ran after them. Pleading with them, clutching at their saddle bags, he quickly realized from their blank faces, that neither could understand him.

He wiped his eyes on his filthy sleeve. No question about it, his sight was going too. Blinking hard, he readjusted his vision and stared at the big man till it dawned. A foreigner! Yes, that was it. Trembling, he sought in his muddled head for the words.

"Greetings," he mumbled in Latin and repeated it louder, shouting, "Ave!" The big man looked hard at him, his irritation turning to interest. What was this then, a beggar speaking Latin?

"Ave!" he replied.

Shimos slid to the ground and held his head. He must keep going. Here was help. He had to remember.

"Ave, amice." (Greetings friend) he said as clearly as he could, the years falling away, the rich, fruity voice of their tutor eunuch ringing in his head.

The little dark man dismounted and took a flask from his saddle. Gently he took away the shaking hands and pressed it to the parched lips. Shimos drank gratefully.

"Tibi gratias do amice." (I give you thanks, friend.) He persevered, still in Latin.

Intrigued, the big man dismounted and handing his reins to the other, squatted beside the scarecrow figure. He would like to speak with the man, but the few words which had been spoken were just about all he knew in Latin. After all, what need were fancy languages to a horse master? Fishing in his pocket, he took out a few dried figs and pressed them into the old hand.

"Equos!" (Horses) he spoke urgently. Then in English, "I am looking for," reverting to Latin, "Equos!"

Shimos heard him and strangely, understood. Gaul? He thought to himself, or Hibernia? Somewhere North anyway. Then he caught his breath. The vision! A ship sailing across the sea! Now here was his chance.

As they wanted horses, he would direct them to the farm, where they would find the women and save them. Feeling faint again, he shut his eyes. The gods had not deserted them. He had filled the hay racks, surely the horses would be alive, after? He frowned. The days were a blur, yet this was at least worth a try. Sweeping the dust by his feet with his empty hand, he felt for a sharp stone and began to draw. Pointing East, he drew a road, then the well. He took particular care of that, for they must not miss the road up to the farm. Satisfied, he looked up, tapping the earth with the stone. The sun was easing in the sky and the heat abated by the minute. The big fair man looked at the map in the dust and stabbed it with a finger.

"Equi?" (Horses) he enquired again in Latin. Shimos nodded.

Well! The saints be praised. Here was someone in this God-forsaken country who not only spoke Latin, he seemed to know what he was talking about. It had been a hellish journey and all in the name of God! They had lost almost everything; so many men killed, their baggage, their tents stolen and worse, their animals. How to travel in this parched and racked land without mounts? Then the earthquake, the first, and he fervently hoped the last he would encounter in his life. Thanks to the Virgin, they had been sleeping in the open. For with dawn, riding on again, they had seen the destruction it had wrought. Town after village laid flat, with only broken, injured, pitiful people left there, milling about helplessly. And the stink of it! Oh to be in England where stink was natural and normal and not like this, of putrid decaying flesh. Whatever mad new project Lord Robert decided on next, he was determined he would not be going and would find a good excuse to stay at home.

"Go, good Tom," had said his lord. "You if anyone can find beasts to replace all we lost. Go, and we will bide here till you return." Wearily, Tom had left camp, taking only his strange assistant Dummy. He knew not where to look, where to start to look indeed, so without much hope he rode North East. For days they had travelled the dry land, yet no one had a horse for sale. Those they had seen had been worthless, bony, useless beasts, even for meat. Just one man had pointed this way, mentioning the word "water", undoubtedly the well this old one also spoke of. And horses! Hope filled his heart, the first for a long time. Emptying his pocket of figs, he pressed them into the hand and turning, leapt on his great horse.

"Vale," (farewell) in Latin, and, "thank you old man, go with God," in English. Waving to his companion he rode off, leaving Shimos gazing absently into the dust.

He sucked on a fig, and felt the taste explode in his mouth, giving him courage.

Before long the two riders came to the well, and grateful, man and beast drank deep, filling their water bags and flasks. A small road curved behind the pile of rocks above the well, and in the distance they spied a tower alongside a ruined building. Urging their beasts, the two men rode up the hill towards the buildings, their noses registering the foul, sweet, all pervading smell of death which came from it.

Hearing their clatter, Karina peeped over the parapet. Two men! A big horse and a mule. Biting her lip she considered if the smaller might be Shimos, but as they came closer, decided against it. Besides, he never rode, he said he was afraid to. Standing on tiptoe, she watched as they approached, suddenly aware that the one on the mule had seen her. Fearful, remembering her grandmother's last words, she ducked down and waited.

Tom followed the pointing arm to the top of the tower before them and nodded. So there was someone here, good. Now perhaps they would sell them horses, even though there were none in sight. He turned and gazed out over the plain, vast, and, he guessed, probably fertile after the rains. Yet now it stretched gold and brown, empty and lifeless, but then, so it was everywhere these days. Unloading the beasts, the small man made camp against the side of the tower. Then mounting his mule, he led the big horse off in search of pasture.

It was the mule, sharp little thing that she was, who scented the horses over the ridge. Taking breath, she set up her ugly roar of enquiry, to receive immediate and hearty response, which alerted the man into riding further. There they were! Dozens of horses milling about, calling anxiously, jostling and barging to see the arrivals. As had done Shimos, he struggled with the gate, went in and instinctively found the hay in the loft which he tossed down. They were very hungry he noted, they hadn't eaten recently. Shutting the gate once more, he hurried back down to the tower again.

Tom watched him approach, aware of his excitement. This human abomination had become more than useful to him, even if he was dumb. In fact, he had been as a gift from God, they had travelled together for about six months now. Their meeting, he winced remembering it, had been unusual in the extreme. Their group had come to a well and he had been hauling water up for the horses, the few they had left. Suddenly, he had felt a weight, had pulled harder and looking down, had seen the bright eyes of a creature at the end of the rope. Slowly, carefully, he had brought it up, lifting the frail body over the rim, and laid it on the grass.

Oh the wickedness of man! How could one human do that to another? It had taken some hours for the exhausted creature to sit up and mime his need for food. At least he had water and too much of that too! Handing him a piece of flat bread, he had watched as it was torn into tiny shreds, worked about the mouth for ages, and finally, was swallowed. Absently Tom had thought it a strange way of eating, but wise for a starving man perhaps. It wasn't till some days later, when the miming was beginning to irritate and he had shouted, that the poor thing had opened his mouth and pointed within. There, where there had been a tongue, was just a raw red stump where it had been cut out. Oh dear Heaven, what a terrible land they were in. What kind of people were they to do that, then throw the lad into a well where no one could hear his cries for help? Since then, in his clumsy way, he had been kind, making gruel for the lad, giving him his own little bowl and spoon, till he regained his strength. Gratitude shone from the bright eyes and growing stronger by the day, he quickly became invaluable. His intelligence was incredible, coupled with acute hearing and sharp eyes, he missed nothing. As time went on, Tom realized that he himself was the dullard, and that his new companion's wits were more than sharp.

"Tom." He had tapped his chest. "Tom." The dumb man tried, but the sound which came out was "Ong". Tom in turn called his new companion Dummy, which he accepted, without a word of course. As a shadow, Dummy stayed with the big fair man, who he quickly realized was not a lord, as were many of the others in the party, but the horse-master.

Dummy now stood breathless in front of his friend, arms waving and explicitly neighing and miming that he had found the horses, lots of them. Tiredness gone for the moment, they hurried up the hill and Tom viewed the fine herd with astonishment. Arabs and mixed, he realized, so many of them, more than enough indeed. Turning to his companion he put a big arm about the thin shoulders and beaming, hugged him.

It was night before Shimos finally reached the well. The moon was late in rising and he had strayed from the road in his weakness, wasting time, struggling to find it again. Once he heard horsemen, their loud voices drowning his cries for help. Yet he did manage to see three as they sped by? Yes, yes, three, not the two of before. Relieved that they were not the couple he had spoken with earlier, he earnestly hoped his eyes were not playing tricks.

Gratefully, he sank his face into the clear cold water of the trough. After drinking, he splashed the dust off his face and head, wondering if he would ever be clean again. Knowing that he should go on up to the tower, his courage failed him and deciding to rest a while, he crept up above the well, and leant against the rocks which were still warm from the sun. He knew he was ill, for his breathing was bad. It had all been too much these past days, and his age was telling. Always a slender man, Shimos had grown thin in his later years, despite the plentiful food of late. Now he was just bones, bruised and cut skin barely covering them. His breath rasped, and he wondered if he was dying. Listening to the wheeze and gasps from his own racked body, it came to him very slowly, that near by, someone else suffered. Like the wind, of which there was none, came a soft moaning. As a winter wind slicing through the cracks in the door, it rose and fell. Yet it was late summer, he corrected his wandering mind, and there was no wind, or indeed door.

The sound came from close by, among the jumble of great boulders, a moaning, very quiet, regular and pitiful. Intent, he stopped his own laboured breath and alert at last, realized it was another being. Crawling toward the sound in the darkness, he touched a body lying on its face. Horror filled him as his hands explored, for this body, so loved, so full of love and life was cold and sticky.

"Kareen'ala!" a thin scream, as a wild beast rent the air. As an echo, a terrible, lonely scream rose as he gathered her into his arms weeping. Once more stumbling to and from the well, he tried to give her to drink. Trickling water from his wetted robe into her mouth, he whispered endearments. Wiping her face, he kissed it, sobbing all the while. At last she seemed to understand he was there and fresh tears fell from her eyes to mingle with his. Fearful that they would be discovered, he eased her near to the cover of the rocks, then, edging into a crack, he drew her in after him, urging her gently to help if she could. It seemed well nigh impossible, yet he laboured on, his strength ebbing, his determination urging for more. Safe in their tight little cave, he cradled her in his arms, forgetful of his own weakness.

Somehow she told him, with little whispers, a few words, lips frothing, gasping for breath. For he realized, trying to soothe her, she must be gravely hurt. No matter how he tried to support her, something, perhaps a broken rib was piercing her from within.

"Shush, my dearling," he whispered. "Rest my sweet lady." But on she went, somehow determined to tell him. Adina falling. Three men. The ladder again. Her jewels. On and on. The nervous fingers weakly clutched at the rags which still hung about his body gradually stilled. He pictured it all. Not for the first time in her life, a brutal raping. This way and that, fighting over her, all three of them, drinking, laughing, cruelly using her. And when she tried to crawl away, taking her from behind, breaking her ribs with their weight, bruising her face against the bare stones. Her breath seemed to bubble out of her lips, and silently weeping, he knew that he could not help her.

Shimos had forgotten how to pray, yet the distant memory of his mother came to him, kneeling before the house altar, burning incense. Then the old shaman, the vision, flickered into his mind and eyes wide open, he remembered the child Karina on top of the tower, all alone. There was just one hope now, the two men he had met who sought to buy horses.

"Gods of my childhood," he screamed silently. "Not for me I ask, not for me!"

Now and again his exhaustion caused him to faint. Then he would waken, and making sure Kareen'ala was there, doze off again. Tomorrow he thought, yes, tomorrow, he and Kareen'ala would go and find them and all would be well. Seeking the last fig in his clothing, he tried to press it into the broken mouth of his beloved mistress but it fell, dropping into the damp earth below them.

A half moon had risen, and a single cloud scudding across the dark night sky shut it out for a moment.

Just then, a shadow passed over and paused, and a great angel of death swooped down and reached for the soul of the woman. Gently placing it with the others in a fold of its robe, it hesitated. It had been a busy time. Folding its wings, it squatted on the rocks above the well and listened to the sweet sound of water falling into the trough. Aware of the flickering soul of the man below, it waited, then, as it died, gathered it up too, and swept away.

Later, much later, a magnificent fig tree grew out of the rocks, and became famous with travellers for its sweet fruit, the fallen fruit earnestly sought out by the beasts. Yet not a living soul ever knew of how it came to be there. Or that it had been nurtured by the husks of those two loving souls, who had died there, in each others arms.

CHAPTER SIX

KARINA

Karina woke as the first light rose from the Eastern sky. Despite the plentiful covers, she had been cold, missing the warm body of her grandmother. She could not remember how many days she had been on top of the tower, yet today, she was sure, she would go down. Lying quietly, she listened, there was no sound. Rising from her pile of blankets, she squatted over a drain in the corner, then quickly got back under the covers. Despite her sleep, she felt tired, hungry and frightened.

At the foot of the tower, Dummy too was aware that morning was near, and he sought in his mind why he felt a niggle of excitement. Something new was happening, but what? Suddenly he remembered the horses and grinned broadly. What a find! Today they would arrange to buy the horses, round them up, and start back to the great camp of the foreign lords. Jumping out of his blanket, he began the day with his usual efficiency, and carrying two water bottles, ran down to the well below to wash himself and fill them. A quick survey the night before had shown him a running channel from the great ruined house behind the tower, but the water was fouled, obviously something dead lay in it, for even the mule had refused to drink. Making a small fire, he set the pot on to heat. Tom, his benefactor, always liked to start the day with a big pot of hot herb tea. Not, he thought wryly, that he had many herbs left, but perhaps with help from the people in the tower, he could find some. He cast his eyes upwards and there, sure enough, a little head was outlined against the dawn sky. Beaming, he waved a hand as the head disappeared. It was his smile that did it. For remembering her grandmother's words, Karina felt a caution, previously unknown to her. For hers had been a most secure life, wicked folk the stuff of tales, never of acquaintance.

Dummy tied a string around the rim of his bowl, clenched it between his teeth, and slowly went up the ladder. Setting the bowl on the parapet first, he drew himself up, and came eye to eye with a small girl.

"Mmm, Mmm," he pushed the bowl towards her, nodding in encouragement. Karina stared at him then flickered her gaze at the steaming cup. That, she thought, impressed that he had brought it safely up the ladder, was clever and kind. Yet when he mimed that she go down with him, suddenly afraid, she shook her head.

Watching him from her height seemed safer, so as he fried some mess over the fire, she just looked on. Again he came up, wobbling fearfully, a little brass plate in one hand which he offered to her. Again she smiled, nodded and took it. How good it was to have something hot and different from the dry left-overs of many days. Besides, she was growing afraid of being alone, with the sounds of dogs scavenging in the ruins below, their howls and fighting never ceasing. When she had finished, she put a small foot over the parapet and contemplated going down. Seeing the movement, dropping his work, he waved his arms at her frantically to wait and in moments was there, at the top of the ladder. Gently urging caution with sounds, he backed down again, close behind, guiding her feet while counting in strange noises, till at last they were on the ground.

Now he squatted and considered this strange little girl child before him. Dark curls framed a pretty elfin face and blue eyes surveyed him seriously. She was richly dressed in elaborate, gold embroidered pantaloons and blouse, with a large, plain leather jacket over the top. Beaming suddenly at her, he planted a kiss on her forehead. Surprised as she was, Karina felt her mouth turn into a smile, and carefully putting her arms about him, she kissed him roundly in return, on both cheeks.

Taking another helping of the food, he urged it on the child. The good smell had obviously attracted some dogs who prowled around, creeping ever nearer. With a stealthy movement, Dummy picked up a stone and with deadly aim, threw it. Tom woke suddenly, the yelping of the dog penetrating his sleep. Looking up, he saw the strangest sight. An exotic little girl, brightly dressed in rich, bizarre clothing, was sitting opposite to Dummy, in earnest conversation. Hands, fingers, mouths, heads and arms were used, with not a sound. As soon as he had turned his back to make water over by the tower, he came and sat with them. Dummy made the introductions.

"Ong," he said to the child, pointing to Tom. Karina looked at him, eyes wide. She had never before seen such blonde hair or such a huge man.

"Tom," he said, tapping his chest, "Tom," with Dummy nodding in agreement.

"Tom!" said the child, so they all smiled in satisfaction. Pointing to Dummy, she made her enquiry with a small frown, head tipped slightly to one side, a little hand stretched out with splayed fingers.

"Ummy," said Dummy, nodding happily and tapping his own chest.

"Dummy," said Tom, pointing, the child nodding and quietly repeating it. Then the child introduced herself most seriously.

"Karina," she said, very clearly, tapping herself. "Karina!"

Oh well, thought Tom, we almost have a proper name and at least this one can speak.

"Karina," he repeated, smiling broadly, inclining his head in a little bow.

"Ieya, Ieya," attempted Dummy uncertainly, and the child nodded, delicately touching his face with her fingers in approval.

The important thing was to be friends with these people, and to keep them there, until her family returned. So now, aping her mother and grandmother, she became the little hostess, and showed them around. Avoiding the ruined house, for with the stink coming from it, no one would wish to go in there, she led them up the hill, over the ridge to the farm. It was quite a sight in the morning light, spread in orderly fashion around a great yard. As they approached the gated paddock, she called, a high, wild cry, which brought instant activity. Clustering around her, vying for attention, the horses nickered as she stroked them, speaking softly while both men watched entranced. Then, selecting an especially pretty mare, she scrambled on its back and fingers entwined in its mane, she did a fast circuit, pursued by a handful of the beasts, while the men watched in admiration. Her little exhibition over, she showed them around the barns. It was easy to see that this was a wealthy place, for everything was neat and orderly, not the usual mess of a poor farm. Together, they explored, and holding her hand up at one stall, she indicated that this one must not be approached. Tom looked through the strong wooden fence. It was a fine stallion, hungry and cross. Even the confident child seemed wary of it.

"Harran," she said, meaning of course it was her father's horse. "Harran," again with a hand up. Which made Tom think that the stallion was called Harran, so that stuck. They fed the animals again, and cleaned out the water troughs and admired the order while always following and being guided by the girl.

Karina realized that none of the slaves were there anymore. Were they all dead? Had they been in the house at the feast when the earth shook and the whole place had burned down? If only they would come, Shimos, her mother and grandmother. They must surely come, but meanwhile, she would entertain these men.

Gradually Tom managed to explain to Karina that he wanted to buy the horses. Sitting on the bare earth, they scored their agreement with sticks in the dust. A small bag of gold was handed over with the indication there was more to follow. Tom knew it would probably never happen, for they had been ruthlessly robbed and home and more gold was far away. However, he had his orders. Lord Robert had told him to get horses and by the saints, he would. Pleased with the deal, Tom held out his hand enveloping hers in his in a rough handshake. It was obvious that she alone was alive in that place, and he felt a great pity for her.

He watched her secretly as every so often she gazed down over the dry, deserted plain, towards the well and the road, as if waiting for someone. Taking more gold coins from his belt he tried to explain his needs and what he was prepared to pay. Using a stick, he drew sacks of feed, rolls of hay or whatever, then placed a coin in her hand, and of course, being a clever child, she understood.

The first night they slept together was restless. The child decreed somehow that they move to the farm where the sickly smell of death did not offend them. A north wind blew down the hills toward the plain, and the views were far and clear. Laying their blankets on a bed of straw, they settled down for the night but the child cried out several times, till Dummy took her into his arms where she slept till dawn. Pointing to a small window in the tower, Karina mimed that they should get in there.

Although dubious at first, they soon discovered, with some hours of chipping, that it was possible to remove the iron bars of the store room window so they could go in. Once in, they found themselves in a comfortable, big but dim room. Taking up a small wick lamp, she held it for Dummy to light, then Karina showed them the cellars, which, to Tom's astonishment, were packed full of stores. What wasn't hanging up, was neatly stacked on shelves, an abundance. There seemed to be plenty of everything including dried food, bales of cloth, and barrels of wine. There were wooden drums of lentils and three kinds of beans. Sacks of two sorts of rice and something else he had not seen before, but obviously was good and filling. Cheeses, round and white like bleached skulls, hung in a slight draught before the meshed slits. Three kinds of nuts, still in their shells were hung in loose woven bags, beside fine bags of sesame and pumpkin seeds. Tubs of honey and clay pots of preserves were well sealed and stacked neatly on hanging planks, against the ants. Baskets full of fresh oranges and lemons smelt wondrous and Dummy went around touching and smelling, his eyes rolling in delight. The ceiling beams were well festooned with bunches of herbs, some in small cotton bags. After their months of often hungry, uncomfortable travel, it seemed like paradise. So their search for horses had also yielded supplies beyond their wildest dreams. Tom was dumfounded, all this would keep his party for weeks. There was a small, iron-studded door with a huge lock which the girl seemed to ignore. When Tom knocked on it, eyes wide with enquiry, she looked away, so he assumed they would not get in.

Taking down a bale of cloth, he offered the girl a coin which she accepted and going up to the light on the roof, he began making saddle bags taking his precious bone needles from a roll of cloth in his bag. Before long the three of them were seated cross legged on rugs, busy with needles and twine. They worked at it every spare moment, creating a good stack of large, roughly made, double bags, which when made, were tossed down.

Next, Tom asked her where they kept the leather. Frowning at first, she watched his hands caressing his bridle, then smiled. Climbing into the eaves of a barn at the farm, she showed them the stacked, tanned skins. So their next task was to soften, cut and stitch halters for all the beasts. Tedious, they did the slow task with more care, so it took time. Dummy excelled at this as with everything, and smiled shyly at the praise his work brought him. At times, Tom thought that he must be dreaming, the journey which had been a nightmare, now seemed so easy.

Every time he took or used something, he handed the child another coin which disappeared as if by magic. The days passed busy with preparation for their journey. Yet it was not all work, for Dummy and Karina were ever together, even playing hide-and-seek around the barns. The big man softened as he watched them. It was good to hear their laughter. Poor little creatures, what did their future hold in this dreadful land?

At last, it seemed as if everything was prepared for their departure. Every pony and horse save the stallion was to carry a load, and the stack of bundles grew while Tom estimated and cut more thongs to secure them. It grew cooler, and they watched the sky anxiously, for surely it would rain soon and then travelling would not be easy. Every beast had to have sufficient leather for a strong halter and belly straps. They had oiled all the neatly stored unusual saddles, and watched Karina knowingly make the horses ready. Then, to Tom's surprise, she emerged from a barn one day, a falcon on each wrist and grinning, invited him to join her in the hunt. It was a delight to be out, free, and doing something familiar in a different place. He was incredulous that his small companion seemed so knowledgeable in everything at her home. They did well too, with a good bag of hare and pheasant, and not only were the hawks glad of a change from vermin, Dummy rejoiced at something new to cook. Impressed with the little man's boundless knowledge, Tom watched him erect a crude smoker, so nothing was wasted. Having quickly spotted the gardens below the tower, he had regularly rummaged happily for fresh vegetables to add to their meals. With the smell of death everywhere, he avoided an upper area where he guessed lay some poor dead creature. So Adina's broken body was never found, and very gradually returned to dust.

All the colts, though frisky, were used to being lead, and every day, early and late, the strange trio of humans took a string of beasts each out for exercise, the stallion and ponies running free with them. Acknowledging that Harran needed exercise, was one thing, and coping with his temper was another. It was the girl's mare who seemed the magnet, for the stallion always followed her close. Of course she knew it was because before the earthquake, they had ridden almost daily together. Tom watched under his brows, fearful that the little girl might not be strong enough to cope. Yet it was obvious she had done it all before. What she did not have in size and strength, she had in knowledge and voice. Each one of the animals seemed to know her well, and she was a tough taskmaster, occasionally giving them a clip for bad behaviour. No, he could see this was a life she was used to, for there were few problems. Work which would have occupied ten men, was done by two and a child. Unbelievable! The days passed in busy preparation. Ready they might be, yet she kept finding some new reason to delay their departure, new tasks to do, new treasures to pack. Dummy was particularly pleased with the sacks of dried fruit which they bagged up, for he had a sweet tooth, and often took a handful to suck while he was working. Tom thought he understood and humoured them for awhile. Eventually, with words and mime, somehow he managed to suggest that he must leave, and that Karina must come with them.

Karina looked at him squarely. The pain in her tummy still sat there, the pain of loss and misunderstanding. They had gone. They would have been back by now if they could she knew. He was right. She could not stay here, even with all this money. Bad men might come. They would kill her and take her treasures and all the money. There was only one solution, for she had grown to like and trust these strangers who were now her friends. She would go with them.

The night before their departure, Karina produced a huge, iron key and nodding at the solid, locked door, stood back. She had hesitated in showing them this last treasure until, perhaps, she felt sure of their good intentions. Surprised by yet another new revelation, Tom grappled the lock open, and shoved at the door. Taking up a lamp he held it high and gasped. It would be years later, when Karina was easy with his language, that he would learn about the hoard laid there. For the cell-like room in the bowel of the tower, had its stone shelves filled with weapons. Swords, scimitars, shields, helmets and light armour, bows and arrows, pikes, daggers and axes, stacks of them. Beckoning Dummy to look too, there was immediate and frantic conversation with faces, hands and eyes. Yes, they would take them too, somehow they would put two or three pieces in each load. Karina stepped forward and carefully lifted out a particularly fine sword and held it close, her eyes watering. Drawing her to him with understanding, Tom realized it must have belonged to her father. Reassuring her with soft words and stroking hands, he tied the belt up short to make it small enough for her to wear. An old leather brass-bound box came to light when all the weapons were out, and the girl took that too, staggering with the weight, eyes down. It was late by the time they had sorted out the latest bounty, and exhausted, they went to sleep, to waken when the sun was well up.

As her last self-imposed task, Karina opened all pens and gates and fixed them wide with a rock. The sheep and goats, delighted to be free, bounded off, looking back to see if a human would as usual come with them. Eyes glazed, Karina visualised her grandmother working away hanging up the delicious fresh cheeses, or pounding the butter, in preparation of a feast. They would be alright, she thought, with the rains coming and new grass, they could manage alone although it came to pass that quite a few of the sheep followed them, as was their habit.

Loaded up, all her treasures in her father's small money chest wrapped in a sack behind her, Karina rode away from her home, clattering down the hill behind Tom, she did not look back. She was nine years old. They made an odd little caravan. Following Tom, with Dummy bringing up the rear, each lead a string of laden horses tied to their saddles. They kept a steady pace, following the road West, all the while followed by the ponies, sheep and a free running stallion.

It was easier moving slower rather than faster, easier than stopping and starting too often. Tying so many animals was a problem, so along the way they stopped to feed and water, only unloading and hobbling for a few hours at night. Even so, it was tiring, and, ever afraid of being set upon by bandits, Tom and Dummy tried to stay awake, night and night about. The falcons provided them with small game, and they cooked what they had, keeping some to eat cold along the road during the day. Dummy was well versed in camp life, baking small breads on hot stones, sometimes chopping dried fruit to work in the dough, for a change. All the time, they were alert, for with the dust raised from so many horses, they must be obvious from far off and tempting to the brigands who hid in the hills to the North. The watering places were the most dangerous, although with good pasture round about, the horses cropped hungrily. Yet they saw few signs of life along their chosen way, till at last almost with relief, they were born down upon by two men on fast ponies.

Urging his horse forward, Tom drew his sword, paused, then let out a bellow of laughter. The two scouts were well known to him, so after an enthusiastic welcome, one turned about and rushed ahead with the news while they followed.

Gradually, as the sound of an approaching storm, they heard the murmur of a great party of men and horses. As they pulled up on the brow of a hill, a huge, red and white fluttering flag waving camp lay far below.

Karina sat on her mare and stared in silence at the vast throng. As far as she could see there were tents, each topped by a pennant. Every inch of space seemed to be moving, like an ant's nest. It was incredible. Horsemen approached them and suddenly a ragged cheer rose as they were seen, followed by a great hearty roar.

"You are too modest Tom!" The dark haired lord slapped his friend the horse-master soundly on the back. "I told them," he glanced around at the admiring crowd which had gathered quickly. "I told them you'd be back, but oh my friend, you have done more than well."

Dummy and Karina sat on their mounts watching the welcome. Tom drew her forward and the tall, dark young man with startling blue eyes, laughingly took her hand to kiss it. Tired, Karina impulsively held out her other arm which was aching, on it sat their last falcon, the others having flown away. The bird turned its hooded head at the new voice.

"For you," she said simply on impulse, tripping over the words of the new language. Surprised, the dark man gently took the bird, his intense blue eyes glowing with pleasure, little knowing of Karina's relief. For she did not care for her father's hunting birds, however useful they might be.

"Come my friends," the happy man waved his free arm to include them both, "Come and eat, for now we have something to celebrate." But apart from Tom, they were too tired to do more, and were willingly led away to the horse lines by Lord Robert's proud grooms. A small crowd surrounded them, eyes glowing, fingers feeling. Lorimars and saddlers examined the exotic gear, feeling the beautiful fixtures and fine leather of the saddlery. Grooms ran their hands down quivering flanks and lifted hooves to inspect them. Dummy conveyed to them all, with extravagant gestures and wide grin, that the little girl was their owner and benefactor. Karina gazed at the sea of upturned faces, never having seen so many strange foreigners in her whole life before.

Somehow, pointing, and despite her fatigue, the little girl managed to explain to the grooms not to attempt to touch the stallion. Waving her hands at him skittering in the background, it was easy to understand her gestures of, "Leave him, leave him." With experienced eyes, the grooms looked over the great horse, liking what they saw with respect and with anticipation of fine foals. If she said so, they would obey. Happily taking over the fine new horses and the contrasting, rough little ponies, they had enough to do without getting kicked by that one. Somehow Dummy told Lord Robert's men to guard well the packs they unloaded from the weary beasts. You couldn't trust anyone, ever, and their booty was precious.

If it had not been for the reassurance of Dummy, Karina would have taken flight and run away. There were so many loud, big people, crowds of them, she was afraid. It was Dummy, understanding, who took her to a tent, brought water, washed her in a little wooden tub, then left her sleeping covered in his cloak. When she woke, he was there beside her with food and drink, and off she went to sleep again, a smile of thanks fading on her face.

Karina found the noise of the camp was hideous. Not only were there many huge men shouting all day, the beasts added their voices calling to each other. Then there was blowing of horns and the constant clang of smiths, repairing armour and equipment. The great horses, like the one Tom rode, carried big men, hither and thither. Karina watched, eyes wide as they rushed up and down, here and there, she considered needlessly, but apparently making preparations to leave. Her horses were smaller, she thought, more fine, and was gratified to see how they were greatly admired and squabbled over. It took several days to unpack their sacks and distribute their bounty, with Tom and his lord fiercely organizing their distribution.

Several, obviously important, lords gathered with Lord Robert and Tom, and a bargain was reached, for horses, ponies, stores and weapons, written down by a scribe, with signatures or marks. Then Tom showed it to Karina in front them, explaining to her, which she half understood, that all would be settled, in full, when they got home.

Just as the first drops of rain began falling from a leaden sky, the first wave departed, till soon, the camp was empty, leaving a ravaged, sodden and silent field.

They rode for more than a year, usually sleeping out, or if they were to rest for some days, in their tent. Once they crossed a great river of water, a terrifying experience for man and beast. Gradually they left behind the dry lands familiar to Karina, and the land they travelled through became ever greener. Some of the knights left the party along the way to go home, so they might rest at a castle for some days. Gradually the vast assembly of crusaders dwindled and became more manageable. Sometimes other travellers joined them, or they passed others going in the opposite direction, and so paused awhile to exchange news. Karina and Dummy always stayed close to Tom, who attended Lord Robert. It grew colder as they went North and Dummy sewed thick trousers and tunics for Karina, and cut her hair short on which he plonked a warm cap, so she looked like a boy. Having disappeared for two days, to hunt down a beekeeper they later understood, he waxed their cloaks, so the rain would sluice off. Always carrying their little fire-pot safely, wherever they stopped, he soon had a hot drink and a blaze for them to warm their hands over. Karina grew to love Dummy, ever by his side, trying to ease his labours and ever learning his wisdom. She also learnt Tom's language perfectly and the camp patois, forgetting her own, except in dreams.

Unasked, she attended what she still thought of as her horses who seemed always to know and obey her. They came the moment they heard her curious call, a yammering yell which caused much mirth along the horse lines. The grooms welcomed the bright little girl, feeling admiration and sorrow towards her, as of course, her story had spread. The stallion was slowly getting accustomed to his new life, and although still free, he came to Karina for titbits and a stroke. Feed was often a problem, so they spent much time hunting out grazing to avoid being robbed by the towns along the way. Even so, Karina mourned as her beasts became lean with travel, poor feed and the cold. The camp had soon got used to the odd little newcomer and her curious yell and generally viewed her with amused kindness, one of Tom's waifs. Good old Tom.

"So what will you do with her, Tom, when we get home?" they asked. Which troubled Tom as he rode along, for his Margaret might not care to take a strange child into her house. And yet as he well knew, Margaret was a kindly woman, who sadly having no children, might like a daughter after all. So he came to speak now and then about "home" and "mother" and Karina, a curious child, asked questions, always eager to know more.

In the middle of winter they rested at a great castle where Karina found the life confined and boring except that there were other children there, which was a novelty to her. Yet now she learned another language, for the grand ladies were intrigued by her, having heard a whisper of her adventures. In the dim, cold rooms, noses red and eyes straining, they spent their days making tapestries while the children played around them. When they danced, they taught her, which she much enjoyed and which certainly kept them all warm. She was naturally included when all the children were taught to sing and recite, how to spin and weave and more to her liking, how to play some new board games. Winter there was tedious and too cold she decided, never having experienced such before. At least the horses had good stables and could rest, and she was glad that the stallion was serving many mares, thus paying for his keep.

Her first meeting with snow so delighted her, her behaviour caused much hilarity. Warmly dressed, out she went with Dummy who showed her how to play ball with it, and later, to create a sleeping horse. So beautiful was it, so lifelike lying on the white earth, its head inclined in sleep, all the castle folk came out to admire it.

With spring, they rode on again, over mountains and plains, still cold but with a fresh wind blowing. It had come about so slowly, the greenery of the North, suddenly startling Karina into noticing it. The abundance of flowers! The colours of them! She was spellbound, often leaving the group to dismount and falling on her knees, to admire and gather them. It was all so new, so with childish enthusiasm she collected armfuls and made posies and wreaths for anyone who would accept them.

At last after many months more of tedious travelling, they rode down a hill and there, way before them, spread a grey mass of water which stretched for ever. Karina gawped, having never seen more than a lake or a river before. Shoving through the bustling town, Tom hastily took them to procure a room above the stables of a saddler which he had rented before. There the three of them moved in, all sleeping in one great bed together. Now, it was as if time stopped, for they had to wait for ships to take them and the horses across the sea. Whenever she could, Karina ran to the port or to the shore. Hugging her knees, she sat with her cloak drawn closely about her, and watched the comings and goings, fascinated by the ships, big and little. For although her grandmother had told her tales of her childhood on her father's ship, she had never seen the sea or ships before. What really astonished her was the enormous expanse of water. It was like the plain below her old home, always there, yet ever changing. When Dummy gave her some sea water to drink, she fell back with shock, laughing in amazement. It was all so new, and so good to be on the land again, on her own two feet, after travelling on horseback for so long.

They did however, take the horses out every afternoon, riding on the hills above the town, threading between the tenters working with the cloth, and ever, admiring the view. At last Dummy managed to tame the weary stallion into submission. One day he just seemed tired of fighting everyone, and more or less behaved himself. It was a time for man and beast to rest.

Karina became a woman there, and bewildered, showed her stained breeches to Dummy, who dragged her to the saddler's wife and fled. Mistress Saddler viewed the child with surprise, for she had thought it a boy. Rifling in her chest for soft rags, she instructed Karina what to do, then marched to Tom and demanded money. Obviously enjoying her new role and taking Karina by the hand, the good woman hurried through the narrow streets to a cloth merchant, where, to Karina's surprise, she was kindly made much of. Now this was a charming tale to tell, supplying cloth for gowns for a girl whom everybody had thought was a boy. Three lengths were chosen after long indecision and bargaining, and then the sewing began. Used only to stitching saddlery, Karina was sharply rapped for her clumsy efforts and firmly pushed aside. With her sharp eyes she soon took on the task of needle threader, thus gaining just a little praise.

Pleased with the project and change of routine, Mistress Saddler and her quiet daughter Louisa worked away every free hour of light, including Karina only in the simple tasks. Before long, they had created a new wardrobe and now set about making the lady to fit it. Even the dour saddler had to laugh at his wife trying to teach Karina to curtsey and to walk neatly and correctly, not as a boy. Holding her long skirts up, and trying to see where she was going, Karina made a poor job of it. Secretly, she was very displeased with her body for having let her down by changing her into a woman. But the two women regarded their handiwork with satisfaction. Not only content with it, they trimmed and washed her hair, and tied it up prettily in a cloth, hiding it until it grew. At least it passed the time for Karina, as Tom was often absent, and Dummy seemed to have a new awareness of the grown up Karina and avoided her, preferring it seemed, the company of the saddler's daughter.

For almost two hard years the odd little group had travelled and lived together as a family. It never occurred to Tom and Karina that Dummy would leave them. Yet, when at last a ship was found to take carry them across the water, he stood, eyes brimming with tears and shaking his head. He would not go, and that was that. What had been such an adventure to look forward to, now turned into a time of sorrow. Shocked, Karina felt bereft, suddenly and unlike her, indecisive, wondering if she shouldn't stay with him and not go with Tom, home and to Mother. To their surprise the matter was settled by the saddler's daughter, Louisa. It was she who quietly told them that she and Dummy were to wed, and that he would not only help her father in his business, he would open a livery stables. Somehow this revelation made the whole situation seem happier.

Mistress Sadler and Louisa helped Karina to pack, and pack again. They had grown so fond of the charming boy/girl child and now and again shed a tear that she would leave soon. Karina, grateful for the mothering when she had needed it, took two small jewelled buckles, ones she did not recognize, new perhaps, and pressed them on the two women in thanks. Touched, surprised and delighted, for they had little enough, being simple folk, their tears ran and if possible, they did more to send her off properly than before.

Pleased by her own generosity, and quite ignorant of worth or cost, Karina, now a young woman of eleven, took out her bag of gold coins, and pressed it into Dummy's hands. Waving aside his refusal and jabbering fiercely at the same time, she told him, tears in her eyes, that he could use it to get good horses and feed them well, while he got started. As it had been decided not to take Harran on the ship, she also gave him to Dummy who could use him for breeding, a very good way to attract business.

It was a still grey day when they left, and their mood was as low. The horses were tightly loaded on board so if the ship swayed, they would not fall over. At least their parting was so chaotic, there was little time for tears as they took their leave of the saddlers and Dummy. Forgetting her skirts, Karina climbed high as they set sail, tearfully waving, until the dot on the quay was no more. They were lucky, for although it was a slow crossing, it was not rough, with a light wind just filling the sails, nudging them along.

On land, astride again, her skirts happily changed for trousers once more, Karina rode on her own gentle mare beside Tom on his great horse. After so many miles and months together, the animals were fast friends now, and hated being apart.

Eyes bright, Karina took in everything new around her, the green little villages, the towns, the bright fields and the churches. The red and white pennants fluttering above them, they rode through the country, bringing folk out to wave, cheer and to give mugs of ale and flowers. Gradually the great party reduced in size as some left for their homes on a different road, here or there. Each parting was warm, for they had been through many and often bad experiences together and were truly brothers. Only when they approached home did Tom suggest that she put her skirts on again, over the trousers. A fast horseman had gone on ahead to give warning of their arrival and Tom and Karina were up front, riding just behind Lord Robert, banners high. They entered the town amidst bell ringing and the clamour of much rejoicing. More than four years had passed since they had left home, though some would never return, lying in a foreign grave.

"Home!" shouted Tom down to Karina, grinning happily.

Home, thought Karina, a strange, tight feeling in her heart. Letting her mare pick her way over the cobbles, she looked here and there, trying to take it all in, as they rode up to the town. She was intrigued. It was not unlike the little port across the water, yet it was different. Houses almost met over their heads, where women waved and smiled from open windows. Now and again when there was a gap, she saw a great tower at the top, and stared at it. So it wasn't so different from home. The road wound up and up, to a castle perched on a crag at its end.

A large gateway barred their way, and ignoring it, they veered left, ducking through a smaller arch in the stone wall, till they stood in a great square ringed by buildings. In the middle stood a well, surrounded by great stone troughs. Karina looked more closely at the surrounding houses and realized that they were stables. A feeling of satisfaction gently replaced her anxieties.

Their little party reined in with a clatter and Lord Robert turned to address them. Most of his thanks were for his Master of Horse, without whom, he might still be on the road, on foot. They laughed lightly, knowing that it would be them, not he, on their legs. Yet he didn't keep them long, promising that when they were clean and rested, he would invite them all to a feast to celebrate their safe return.

Unloading, sorting, rushing here and there, anxious to be off home, everyone hurried over their last tasks. Karina watched, as the horses were led off, and with a final wave, the lord disappeared through the great gateway. Tom smiled at her and indicated with his head that they must move on higher to his house. Clattering up a narrow road, they went single file, their bulging packs brushing the stone walls.

Margaret, the groom's wife, straightened her back from weeding her little garden. Unconsciously she touched her left breast where the bruise she had taken from a fall was at last, fading. Margaret was an able and much respected woman. Her house was the best, for not only had her father been Master of Horse, so too was her Tom. She had been the eldest of three daughters, and her father, sore at the lack of a son, had taken the orphan Tom under his wing. Youngest of three orphaned children, no one wanted the boy, while the girls were easily taken in for they were older and more biddable. So the horse-master had taken the little boy and trained him into a fine groom. A happy boy, always smiling, his blond good looks so easy to behold, Margaret had first loved him as a boy, then man. Although she was three years his senior, yet he topped her by many inches, a big fellow. When her father had died, she had taken up her skirts and her courage and walked up the cobbled road to the castle. There, looking more calm than she felt, she had asked the lady's permission to wed him, for as usual, the lord was away. So it was that few changes were made in her home as Tom stayed. A good bed was set up for them in the only room large enough for it, where stood the ingle nook and the hearth for cooking. Her mother and younger sisters were put under the eaves, and Tom took over as man of the house and his lordship's stables. After her sisters grew up and wed, life became quieter, as only her mother remained with them till she died. So since then, just she and Tom had rattled about the house. With a kind husband and fine house, her only sorrow was that they had not been blessed with children. When like now, he was away, she certainly felt a great loneliness. So she used her time in helping her neighbours and being a good housewife. Not many had such a good stone home, with three rooms, and a garden which she loved. She was an intensely house-proud woman, who kept everything spotless and shining. Very often, chores done, she joined the team of castle women to spin, stitch and weave for her ladyship, hence she kept busy from morning till night. It was coming down from one of their stitching sessions that she had slipped on a damp stone. Now she frowned, cocking her head, spoiling her lovely calm face. There seemed to be a commotion below. Wiping her hands on her apron, she went to the front door and enquired of a passing stable boy.

"His lordship is back," the boy called back, "and your man with him, with," the slightest smirk, "a girl alongside him," and hurried on.

A cold hand clutched at Margaret's heart. Had she heard right, a girl, with Tom? She began to tremble, looked this way and that, frantically trying to think what she must do. Then, running to the water pail she poured some to wash the earth off her hands, and smooth her hair, and going into the house, took out her best apron from the press. Then she blew up the fire in the hearth, hastily started a new batch of bread in the big wooden trough and covered it with a thick damp sheet. Running to the little store room, she unhooked the ham she had put by for just this day and lowered it in a kettle of cold water to soak. All the while listening, she ran out into the garden and plucked a basket of greens and what peas were ready. Then, having heard a hen announcing her news, ran to the coop and quickly lifted three new eggs, and laid them carefully on top of the vegetables.

By the time Tom and Karina clattered up from the stables, she was calm again, at least outwardly. There was no use denying it, she had feared he would do this for many years. For good and kind man though he was, she had not born him a child. Perhaps now he would put her aside and father children on the new girl he had brought. Others had done it, why not he?

A young stable boy, nephew to Tom, grinning at the horse-master in welcome, helped to unload their bags on the house steps before leading off the two horses.

"Wait just a moment, Karina girl, will you?" Tom asked softly as he went into the gloom of his house. And understanding, Karina turned her back to gaze down over the rooftops to a ribbon of silver, a wide river, of this, her new home.

Lifting up his wife in a great bear hug, Tom kissed her fiercely.

"Ah wife, but I have missed you," he said, nuzzling into the hair which escaped from her scarf, scenting lavender with wood smoke. Setting her breathlessly down, he surveyed her. "As lovely as ever I see, Mistress Groom my dearling," and kissed her again. Then, seeing the tears, "What's this then? Foolish bissum, tears to greet your husband? Woman!" and enfolded her tenderly again. Putting her away from him after a moment, he lifted her apron, noting it was her best and rarely used, and wiped her eyes. "I have so many fine presents for you, dear wife! Oh treasures indeed from far and foreign places. And not least my dearling," he tipped her face up so he could look closely into her eyes, "I have brought you a daughter, and she waits outside with longing to meet you, for she has no mother."

Standing straight, fighting her tears, Margaret heard him, uncertainty clear, all over her face. Very quietly, looking directly into her eyes again he went on. "A daughter, Margaret, hear what I say, a lonely child for you to rear, just as your good father did me. Yet it is a long, tragic story, of how I found her, which you will hear in time. She lost all, poor child, all and everyone in an earthquake. You shall learn it all, be sure," and kissed her again with a little grin. "I will tell you all of it," he spoke very slowly, word by word. "But not now, for she stands on the doorstep mistress, waiting to greet you, her new mother." Linking her arm in his he edged sideways out of the door, he said firmly, "Her name is Karina."

CHAPTER SEVEN

MARGARET

Margaret crept up the steep ladder to the little room under the eaves. Balanced on the top step, she strained in the gloom to see if the child was awake. Putting the posset cup down, she hauled herself up, wincing with the pain on her chest, then stood, stooped, for the attic room was low, and wondered what to do.

She felt calm and secure this morning, having had gentle and beautiful loving with Tom. How foolish she had been to fear, for she should have known that he was a good and faithful husband. The firelight flickering in the hearth, they had talked quietly, loved and talked again. After years away on that mad caper, there was so much to tell.

"She will be exhausted Margaret, my dear. I am, we all are, for it was a punishing journey, and more so for a child. Let her rest and sleep and eat and rest." He kissed her brow, thinking how lucky he was to have such a serene and capable wife. "But why do I tell you this, when I know well how kind you are with young things." Which earned him the warmest smile of gratitude.

So here she was with a posset of warm milk with honey and an egg beaten into it to give the child strength. Sitting on the edge of the bed she lifted the girl up, and carefully put the cup to her lips. Karina drank, smiled, and relaxed again, her eyes closing once more into sleep. It was like this for several days. A lassitude so great overcame her, that Karina could barely get up to relieve herself. Lightly kissing the worried Margaret, she would crawl back into bed again. When Tom came home he poked his head above the floor and patted her bum.

"Up, my lady! Mother has a fine pottage ready and hot for us. Up, put on your shawl and come down."

At last, one morning she was herself again, listening to the birds in the thatch and the comfortable sounds downstairs, she realized that she was home again. Another home but a home all the same, warm and safe.

Church bells ringing out suddenly caught her attention. For of course having travelled with a Christian host, she had learned about Sundays, and that it was a special day for their God.

Going backwards down the ladder she found Margaret and went laughing into her arms.

"Good day mother," words which were music to Margaret's ears. "I am me again. Sorry I slept so long. Now I will work. What shall I do? You tell me, I am ready."

Margaret almost laughed out loud at the funny little thing's quaint English. Kissing her roundly she indicated the water steaming on the crane.

"A good wash Karina? A bath?" Which met with instant approval.

As Margaret poured, so did the child scrub. Of course Margaret had bathed many children before, in this very tub, for she was a favourite aunt. Yet this one was different. While the others had been solid puddin' English with rosy cheeks and flaxen hair, this one was the opposite. Her skin had a golden glow to it, which of course might be from long travel and might even come off in time with scrubbing. Her hair was gorgeous, and Margaret soaped it with envy. For the colour was darkest red, or was it black? And the curls? But she was skinny, and Margaret pursed her lips. She would soon see to that.

"We must hurry to church my pet," Margaret combed carefully, trying not to hurt her. "Tom will soon be here. It is to be a great service, a thanksgiving you see, that you are returned safely from God's purpose."

Warmly dressed, eyes alight, Karina skipped between Tom and Margaret as they made their way down to the town square and into the fine great church.

"Meet Karina," Margaret said over and over again. "See what Tom has brought me from his travels, a daughter. But am I not lucky?" Tom's sisters came forward and leant to kiss the newcomer and were touched by the warmth of her response. As one, the people smiled and clasped hands and nodded in approval at the pretty, bright girl who dipped before them with such a style.

The service was eternally long. Karina gazed about, by now familiar with Christian temples, not unlike those in the city of her previous life, but different. They sat on low stools amidst the fresh-strewn herbs, crushing out the fragrance which added to the incense. Many of their fellow-travellers were there, smart compared with their dusty, travelling clothes on the road. Old friends, Karina grinned at them all with delight.

When it was over, the priests and officials slowly paraded out, dispensing blessings with the holy water. Karina caught sight of Lord Robert just behind them, and peeped around the throng, smiling at him in pleasure. He looked so grand and richly clothed, walking between a very fine old lady and elderly man.

"Ah," the lady on his arm stopped by them. "Ah, Margaret, is this your new daughter I have been hearing so much about?"

Margaret dipped low, her face flushing, for it was an honour to be singled out on such an occasion.

"She is, my lady," she replied, giving Karina a little push. "She is called Karina."

Taking her smile off Lord Robert, Karina looked at the lady, and quickly realized that she must be his mother and wondered who the old man was. Suddenly remembering to curtsey, she did so, very low, as she had learned at the castles along the way. Which caused a ripple of laughter.

"Karina!" the lady looked at her keenly. "What kind of a name is that child? Karina, never heard it before. Are you Christian? Have you been baptised?" Karina's eyes widened and she grew stiff in apprehension. Was she what? Her worried eyes fell again on Lord Robert, then she turned anxiously to look at Tom, frowning.

"Well child? Speak up. Well Thomas? Is she, has she?"

Now it was Tom's turn to look worried.

"I know not the answer to either my lady," and continued looking anxiously at Karina. "Yet somehow I doubt it, for I never saw church or chapel in her land."

"Father Michael, Father Michael!" her voice rang out. The procession halted untidily, the priest struggling back through the people to stand before the lady.

"A favour, Father Michael, a baptism. Now. We cannot let this charming child remain an infidel one moment longer." At the waving of her hand, the crowd parted and, intrigued, pressed behind as she led the way to the font.

Clutching Margaret's hand, Karina anxiously gazed at her. But Margaret smiled and held her close for a moment. "Fear not, my love, it is a ceremony usually done when we are babes, but a few drops of water on your clean head my dear, and then you will be baptised a Christian, the same as Tom, and me, and Lord Robert. If you are to live with us, it must be a good thing to do. Fear not."

The crowd pressed forward as water was hastily brought and blessed, the lady directing the priest, as if he did not know his work.

"Come child, now you shall be as one of us," and pushed her before the priest. Karina listened but understood not a word of the Latin. She lowered her eyes and tried not to smile as she realized she was the centre of attention and that this was an important ceremony.

"Who will stand as Godparents? And who names this child?" the priest asked. The lady stood forward.

"Margaret and I will be Godmothers, and my brother here, Sir Patrice, will be Godfather. She shall be baptised," she paused for effect, "Margaret Matilda." A rustle of approval moved through the crowd as Karina was thrice blessed with Holy water, more prayers were said, and once again, they all filed out into the sunshine.

"So Margaret, congratulations my dear, and you will bring our Goddaughter up to see me, so I may give her a proper and fitting gift. Margaret Matilda," she smiled, "go with God my child. This was a good day's work," and walked on.

Fairly astonished but delighted by the unexpected events, the little family walked home, Karina chattering all the way.

Margaret gradually introduced her new daughter to her way of life, her house and her garden. After the baptism, Karina still seemed tired, and chose not to go far afield. Days of quiet domesticity and talk, good food and plenty of sleep did its work. Soon after Karina had regained her strength, she asked to go to see her mare, so hand in hand, they went down to the great yard below the house.

Shocked by the unearthly yell which the child gave out as they approached the stables, Margaret soon laughed with the men there. For all her horses replied heartily, straining at their leads as she ran hither and thither, kissing their soft muzzles in delight. Ignoring the fact that she wore skirts and that her mare was not saddled, Karina scrambled up on her back and lay on the beasts' neck, crooning softly.

"Does she always call them like that?" asked Margaret still shocked. Tom nodded, grinning at her, eyebrows raised.

"She was the only one who could call them! Let it be my dear, early days yet."

Of course everyone knew that Tom had brought a young maid home, who was now Goddaughter to the Lady Matilda. At the start, while everyone was busy welcoming their tired men-folk, they stayed at home. Before too long, the callers began to knock on the door, curiosity getting the better of them.

Karina behaved perfectly. Mistress Saddler and Louisa had done a good job. Bobbing to the visitors, she demurely sat and spoke only when spoken to, jumping up to do her mother's bidding. Often afraid that she might laugh, Margaret gave knowing looks to her family and friends, later explaining that Tom kept on saying, "It is early days yet."

A message arrived from the castle asking for Margaret. Tidying up, donning a fresh head cloth with clean aprons for both of them, they slowly walked up through the great gate by the stable yard.

"The lady is very good and kindly, Karina. We are greatly honoured by her actions in becoming your Godmother and giving you her name. I want you to show great respect to her, as you know how, for we were bonded to the lord, her late husband and are also to Lord Robert." Her hand unconsciously to her side, Margaret rested, leaning against the wall, her breath laboured. "While Tom was away, I spent much time with her ladyship spinning, dyeing and stitching, for she is a great one for it, and has made some fine tapestries for the castle and the church."

It was a big castle, rambling and airy, not dark and damp as some they had been in on the journey. Karina followed her mother, carefully observing this new place which would, unbeknownst to her, eventually be her life. When they reached a great hall, it was filled with many people, speaking, coming and going. Gentle music was being played in a corner, and the mood was light.

They threaded their way between the throng to the great fireplace where a group of women sat sewing, supervised by the lady. Looking up with a smile, she greeted them warmly. Karina noted that she looked less severe without the elaborate head dress she had worn on Sunday. Margaret went forward to curtsey low, pulling Karina forward to do the same.

"Your ladyship, good day and God's blessing. Here is our new Goddaughter, my husband brought back from his travels," and shoved Karina forward.

Curtsying as low as had Margaret, she peeped up at the fine lady before her. It did not need telling that this was Lord Robert's mother, for he looked like her and now Karina found she was being examined by the same intense, blue eyes.

"Come child," she beckoned. "How are you these days? Rested? Well? Having heard much of you from Lord Robert, let me hear you speak some of your tale." So Karina stood before the lady, answering as best she could. A smile caused her to smile, her even white teeth shining and the silence was broken by a light titter from the surrounding company.

"Now!" the lady summoned her maid and whispered to her. "Ann will bring your gift, which is all ready for you."

Wrappings of fine linen opened to show a fine embroidered box with scenes from the Bible cleverly worked on all sides. The lady pointed here and there, telling the stories. The work was exquisite. Silver and gold thread was bedded with silk and real hair. She pointed to the black and the gold, which came from her family.

"As I have no daughter, Margaret Matilda, for alas, the good Lord took my little ones, leaving me with but just one child, this is for you to pass on to yours." Her eyes twinkled. "Open the lid child, see what treasure is inside." It was a cross, gold with seed-pearls closely set all over it and Karina, as ever impulsive, leant forward and kissed the lady. There was no need for words. Obviously pleased by the spontaneous gesture, the lady patted the soft cheek.

"Well, Margaret, I congratulate you, for she too is a treasure. Her eyes are blue like yours and in no time she will be you through and through."

They stayed a while with Margaret quite the centre of attention, which was for her a change. Picking up a corner of the work laid out on their laps, she began to sew, head bent over the work, with fine, neat stitches. Karina watched, feeling useless till she spied a spindle and took it up to spin.

"And she is diligent too, Margaret, so I must ask Tom to find me such a daughter next time he goes away." Then looking at Karina she said smiling. "For alas I only have one son, Lord Robert, and," she now spoke in French to herself, "he is tardy in taking a wife to give me grandchildren."

"Ah but lady, I hope he will not go away again and take Tom, for my mother did miss him," responded Karina, also in French. Which so astonished the lady, she burst out laughing.

"And you are right my child, I do agree with you. They have travelled in the name of God enough. We women must prevent them from going away for so long, for it is lonely here without them," and marked that the child spoke French, with a beautiful accent. Well at least one good thing had come out of that expensive failure.

It had begun to drizzle when they went home so they linked arms.

"I fell here last week, Karina mine," Margaret explained, pleased with the visit. "With so many men away, things have rather become slack, and the stones were dirty and wet. Now they will see to it, and many other things, but meanwhile my dear, it is comforting to have your arm."

The days now seemed to race past, and where before Margaret seemed to do things twice over to fill her hours, now, even with help, some tasks were neglected. It was such a joy to have the child around. They were easy together from the start, speaking lightly, no questions ever asked, but gradually, Margaret learned a lot about her child.

Tom came into meals when he was not working away. He and Karina were, as always, as of old, totally relaxed together, sometimes speaking French which Margaret didn't know, yet she guessed that he was merely asking if all was well.

Lying together in their big bed, Tom assured his wife that Karina was a wealthy young woman; not only was she a free woman, she had a fine dowry. All she had to do was teach her all she could, for they had no other worries for the future.

In time, the debts owed to her from the past came in, for a determined Lord Robert reminded his old companions how grateful they had been at a difficult, horse-less time. The little brass-bound box lay under Karina's bed, which to Margaret's astonishment was full to brimming with gold coins and jewels wrapped in silk scarves. Having not known such wealth even existed, she was fearful for it. When Karina tried to urge her to wear a pin, a necklace or a ring, Margaret held up her hands in horror. Having been a horse-master's daughter, and now the horse-master's wife, it was not her place to flaunt jewellery. Yet it was quite different when Karina urged her to buy cloth from the warehouses. Now that, with her love of fine fabrics, she did enjoy. With a lovely daughter to dress, cloth was an essential, not a luxury. They spent many an hour choosing till satisfied, they returned home, a boy carrying their purchases. Now began the planning and cutting and no hour was spent in idleness, for her hands were happily kept busy sewing fine new clothes for her growing daughter.

On good days, they occasionally went right down into the town to the riverside. Karina loved these jaunts and skipped along happily, which delighted the proud Margaret. The river boats were not big, like those at Calais. These had shallow draught. With sail, oars and current, they brought many goods up- or downstream, adding a touch of mystery to the old town. Some were simple flat boats, often piled high with fodder, or roots brought from the countryside, upriver.

Tom sometimes took Karina hunting, giving her more new experiences. Instead of parched brown earth and stunted trees, they rode through great dark forests and brought home game she had never seen before. Occasionally Lord Robert had guests and was always as friendly as when they were travelling, he always introduced her to them. For she was still something of a mystery and quite a talking point during the long winter evenings when they gossiped idly over a board game.

"Tom found her when he sought to buy horses to replace ours, for so many of ours were lost. Due to the great earthquake he supposed, no other human lived, just she. A little thing dressed in fine, rich clothing, all alone on top of a tower." Time and again they listened intrigued, while the story grew with the telling. "The place was huge and had burnt down, just the tower remained. And also to our benefit, the dungeons were full of weapons and food stores! In that desert place, they must have been important people, for not only did he return with many pack ponies, there were many beautiful horses, each was loaded high. A Godsend, indeed." He pondered, his mind flickering over past incidents. "It is my guess that her father was a local baron who had his own army. For it was obvious to Tom that it was a most organized place, with horses, flocks of sheep and goats and many falcons. The barns were full of feed, water came from a spring; everything was so organized, in that region, quite unusual." He pointed to the stand where Karina's last falcon brooded under its hood. "She gave me this one, her last bird. Not that I am entitled to own a falcon, but it was a gift and probably grows old now, so he can rest his days here." He shook his handsome head. "A mystery really, poor child. And now she is here, living with Tom, my horse-master, and my mother has taken her for Goddaughter!"

As the months passed, Karina's horses that remained, all regained condition, indeed they looked better than ever. Yet it was a surprise when Karina told Tom that she thought her mare was not only fat, but in foal. Yet again he was impressed by her instinctive knowledge. Gently, they examined the mare together, experienced hands creeping up her quivering belly, feeling the little bones of the foal within.

"You are right girl. Dear God but I think the sire could be our friend Harran!"

Then they waited, daily running to see the gentle mare until the foal was born. They saw, eyes shining, that it was Harran's offspring immediately.

"If only we could tell Dummy, another Harran," she cried, wringing her hands with joy. "Oh Tom, how can we send him word, for he would be so pleased." Then she sped home, for the news was so good, it must be told. Wiping her hands on her apron as usual, Margaret was dragged to see the new baby, and melted at the sight of the leggy little thing. Resting on her knees on the dried bracken beside her husband and child, she shared their joy. Oh but how sweet was her life now. Oh, dear Mary, mother of God, thank you for all you have done for me. Thank you for answering my prayers.

Inevitably, their lives levelled out into a regular routine. There was always so much to do. Apart from the house, cooking, washing, scouring the pots, the garden took up time. Karina struggled from the stables with buckets of old dung and Tom dug it in. Seeds were bought or exchanged, all with much thought and planning. For now Margaret filled every corner of her garden with vegetables, happy with a child to care for, she determined they must eat well.

"I have given a ship's master a message for Dummy, Karina," Tom told her, eyes bright with his success. "I heard him say he was to put in to Calais, and he was happy to do it, especially as Dummy has a stable and he can use a good horse anytime." So it was done, and perhaps one day, they might even have a reply.

Karina grew and filled out, and unbeknownst to herself, became a beauty. Not only the stable-hands glanced covertly at her when she wasn't looking, some of the gentry enquired, jokingly, if she was an heiress.

Tom and his lord were not only bondsman and master, they were good friends. Of an age, they had known each other all their lives and there was a deep trust between them. Both watched and heard what was said about Karina, and both were uneasy.

"Don't worry, Tom lad," Lord Robert rode beside him, reigns slack as they came home from the hunt. "Time will tell. A good fellow will turn up, you will see. Meanwhile keep her close. For with her rare beauty and all that you and I know she has in dowry, she can be fussy in her choice and not take the first comer."

Which brought him to remembering his own pressing need for a wife, and he frowned. His mother had been urging him with many fine maidens, yet none seemed right or agreeable. Still, it would make her happy. He must marry, that was for sure. An only son and no heir? Not good. Digging his heels in his great horse, he rode up through the town, determined to get on with it.

Karina wasn't sure quite when she first realized that her mother was ill. The hand to breast was familiar from the first days. Yet the breathlessness became worse as the years passed. Her memories of her grandmother Kareen'ala hobbling along with her hurting leg, crossed her mind. The drawn face was the same when she thought no one noticed her. As always, she tried to ease Margaret's workload, realizing that although she loved her home, it had now became all too much for her.

"Mother is ill," she announced flatly to Tom, whom she had tracked down in the stables. He looked at her stupidly and made to hurry. "Not now," she held out her hand to stop him, "for some time I think. She has a pain in her breast. She holds it and she is so breathless. We never go up to the castle nowadays. Or down to the river. I am afraid, Tom. I fear that she is really ill."

Perhaps it was her illness which caused her to catch every little sickness which came their way. Margaret was becoming an invalid. The smallest task seemed to exhaust her, so she increasingly left more to Karina, who sped through her chores in order to sit beside her mother and give her company. When the men went off to France, no day passed by without a sister or niece calling with some little fancy for the ailing woman. If they had found any fault in the girl, they would have banished her and taken over. Yet they saw, relieved, that she attended Margaret with such loving care.

"Margaret Matilda!" The lady stood on the doorstep. "I have come to see your mother, child, for I hear she is poorly," and swept in. Pleased with her visitor, Margaret sat up in her bed while Karina poked up the fire and set a kettle to boil to make a tisane for them all.

"Well Margaret, I have missed you and your fine hands. For have you heard? Robert has found a bride at last, the saints be praised. For I thought he would never do it." Agog with the news, the two women spoke of the impending nuptials and Margaret promised to embroider panels for the backs of gauntlets for Lord Robert. "For she is French you know," continued Lady Matilda, "and no doubt will think us very provincial I am sure. So we must show them that English wool-work is not world famous for nothing." She rose and kissed her hand in a farewell wave. "I have two visiting seamstresses from our cousin the duke who I will send down to speak with you. God be with you, Margaret," and lightly kissing Karina on her brow, "and you, Goddaughter."

The following day, two strange women called with cloth, scissors, fine coloured silk and wools and spoke for a while to Margaret of the work she was to do. At least one woman spoke all the while, for the other looked unwell and merely sat by the fire. Karina offered them ale or a herbal tisane, but they hurried away to hand out more work to the other needle-women for the wedding. To each home they gave wools, cloth and instructions, but they also gave a terrible illness, one which had been raging in their city. It was thought that the quiet seamstress must have brought it.

It began with a fever which seemed to burn the body into exhaustion. When it abated and it seemed that the illness was over, something stayed in the lungs, causing great congestion and difficulty in breathing. Karina heard that one castle woman had died, another and Lady Matilda were ill. Messages were sent to Lord Robert to return from France where they were finalizing the marriage contract.

The Lady Matilda died one week later, with Margaret the day after. Many others died after that, mostly women and children, the weak and old. All talk of a wedding was forgotten as the bell tolled and the dark, damp earth of the graveyard took the townsfolk till it seemed not one family was untouched.

A nephew told Tom of Margaret's death as he handed over his tired horse. Still, his weary face shocked, Tom crossed himself, his head bowed.

"Karina?" he asked the boy, who answered, eyes down.

"Ill."

Tom ran, three steps at a time, up to his house and pushed the door open. The fire was out, the bed stripped bare and the house was silent.

"Karina!" he shouted with all his strength. A sound above in the roof alerted him and he went up the ladder with all speed and listened in the gloom, for he could see nothing. A rasping sound, a rattling and a choking came from the bed.

"God's Truth!" he exclaimed as he reached out and drew the poor little body into his arms and carefully took it downstairs. Putting his cloak over her he quickly lit the fire, and looked around. Grief, what had happened? The bed unmade, he reached to the press for fresh linen. He hurried, trying not to fall over things in his haste. The whole house seemed in turmoil. Out in the store room he found just stinking, bad food and no water.

Bellowing from his front doorstep, Tom summoned his nephews who came running with all speed, for they were only used to a gentle Tom, who never a raised voice.

"Water!" he roared handing a pitcher to one, "wood!" thrusting a great basket to another. "Milk and bread," to the third. "And fast my lads, or I shall show you what a good beating feels like."

Back in the house, he threw a small stool on the fire for it was going out. Well it was the first he had made as a stripling, let it burn. When they came, he forbade them entry, but thanked them gently.

"Tell my sisters in their goodness, that is if they be well enough, to bring me what food they can spare, lads, for I think I must stay inside so as not to take the contagion elsewhere." Holding her up, Tom gently beat on the thin back so that Karina might spit.

"Out with it, girl, out!" he encouraged her to cough and spit. Every few hours he attended her, then wrapped her and put her back to bed again.

Gradually, as if he willed it, she got better. A fragile Karina, thin and so beautiful it took his breath away. Where was the little girl now? He bathed her tenderly, warming her feet by the fire, wrapping her in whatever he could find. Spoon by spoon, day after day, he fed her soups and teas, then lifted her like a baby over the piss pot, where obediently she let water. The nights were the worst. It was awful listening. Every breath so laboured, it seemed it was the last. Propped up in the day, she viewed him through half-closed eyes, so he knelt and smiled at her, willing her to heal.

"Spit, spit!" he demanded, and coughing and choking, she did her best. At last, just one month after Margaret died, Karina went out into the garden where she began to weep. For so much had over-grown, and so much needed doing, and she felt so helplessly weak. Strong hands led her tenderly to the log where Margaret used to sit and Tom worked away in the garden under instruction from Karina, resting in the sun.

It had not been an intentional move. While she was so grievously ill, Tom had slept as best he could, beside her on the edge of bed, to keep her warm, ever on call but where he would not disturb her. Now she stayed in the big bed which he had shared with Margaret and he was afraid to upset her by telling her to move back upstairs under the eaves. While she was still weak, she was often tearful and clung to him. Several times a day if they spoke of Margaret, or if she thought of her, the tears would fall. Having shed no tears for her own mother, grandmother, father or Shimos, now she wept. For this time there had been a body to weep over. White, oh sweet mother, so terribly white. Yet she knew this one really was dead. So Karina wept for all her lost loved ones and turned to Tom, the one person who remained to her.

No, he could not send her up, and anyway, hadn't they all shared a bed, many a time, on their long journey? Still Tom was troubled, for he somehow had begun to feel more for Karina than a friend, a brother or a father, and he knew it and he was ten years her senior. While his love for Margaret had been deep and loving, Karina put fire into his veins and a new longing tortured his body. Another winter passed and life went on as usual. All who had lost their loved ones prayed for their souls and tried to understand the will of God. Death was a familiar neighbour, coming to each and every home without reason.

Tom was usually out in the stables or with his lord hunting, and when he was home he seemed tired and despondent. Karina understood and was lovingly tender, making it more difficult for him. For she understood his sorrow as she too missed Margaret gravely and in the night lay close to Tom to give and take comfort.

In early summer Lord Robert went to marry and collect his bride with Tom at his side as usual. Kissing her roughly on the cheek, Tom slung his pack over his shoulder.

"Be well this time when I return, Karina girl eh?" making a great sigh. "Such a fright it was! To lose Margaret and maybe you at the same time! God forbid. Now!" He held her chin in his rough hand and gazed at her, "Go to the sisters, for they will care for you and keep you from being lonesome. It will be a merry time when we return you will see. With a young bride at the castle, there will be much fun and frivolity, and then you shall show them how you can dance!"

It was quiet without him. Ordinarily, at the most he might be away for two nights, but the time dragged and Karina took to visiting her adopted aunts who lived close by. If the day was fine, they sat in front of their little houses doing their sewing, for once more they had picked up the work which they had laid down on the onset of the sickness almost a year ago. Karina had begun on Margaret's work and diligently laboured at it.

"I wonder what she will be like," Karina said, biting a thread. To her own surprise she had become an able needlewoman, all thanks to Margaret.

"They say she is a very little thing," replied Margaret's first sister. "Dark hair and eyes, very French." They stitched on companionably.

"Perhaps this will give you the idea to find a husband Karina?" spoke up the younger, concentrating hard on her stitching. "For you will be sixteen soon won't you, and it is a good time to wed as I remember." The silence grew as they all looked overly hard at their work.

"I haven't thought much on it," Karina replied eventually. A tear glinted at the corner of her eye. "If mother were alive, she would advise me." Another silence.

"Well, Karina, we may not be true family, but we are here for you," the elder said, trying to catch her sister's eye. "If you ever feel a softness for any man, you just tell us and we will let you know if he is good enough to pursue. So think on that my girl, and for sure we will speak up honestly."

Karina, feeling that something was in the air, frowned and pricked her finger. There were too many taut silences; their talk was not as easy as usual. Yet she liked being with them, for they were so like Margaret, bonny and fair with soft blue eyes and kindly countenances. It was Tom she missed, indeed if she gave it a thought, it was Tom she felt softly for. Stopping and looking absently at a self-sown marigold by her feet, she suddenly said, "Would you think me very wicked if I told you that I feel sweetly for Tom? Not just as I did as a child, loving and trusting, but since mother died, and since the sickness I suppose, when we were so together all the time. More, far more than that."

As one they stopped their work and stared at her, mouths open.

"Is that wicked of me do you think? Is it a sin?"

How they laughed. Joyfully throwing their heads back, they laughed out loud.

"Are you the last one to see, you foolish girl? Have you no sense? Have you no eyes? Did you not realize? Tom loves you too. A great passionate love he has grown for you, just as if he were a lad. We saw it right away, probably before he did. A love very different from his with Margaret, for theirs was an easy marriage, having grown up together in the same house. Theirs was a union gone into as friends rather than lovers, by him at least." And they laughed again and in turn kissed her roundly but turned suddenly serious. "We were so worried about him Karina. At first we thought it was the sickness, for he was so dour." They spoke at once, butting in, jollying to have their say. "Then we could not believe what we suspected was happening to our brother. For he is always so ordinarily good is our Tom. So solid and proper. Yet we saw the fight in him because of his nature." They clasped their hands and laughed again. "Oh Karina, if you would love and wed with him, we will all be very pleased. For we know that Margaret would approve, loving him too, and wish him joy."

It seemed as if they were her older sisters. The years between them meant nothing as they plotted and planned and worked on the beautiful Karina to make her, if possible, more beautiful. While at the castle preparations were being made for the lord and his new lady, the horse-master's sisters were busy with their own plans.

"Master Dyer has a fine dress piece of deep blue linen, Karina, which will match your eyes. Can we afford it do you think? Dare we to dress you in such a fine, costly colour?"

As Margaret had forbidden her to tell a soul of her secret wealth, Karina went through her box and drew out the smallest gold coin she could find and gave it to her astonished elder sister.

"Oh Karina," she breathed. "You can have new shoes also, and we shall embroider them to match the dress so you shall be a beautiful bride."

Things never work out the way one plans, thought a trembling Karina, splendid at her doorstep waiting for Tom. From the clatter and racket below, she well knew that the bridal party was back, yet Tom did not appear. Sad, but not worried, she wearied of waiting and so sauntered down the cobbled steps to the stables to ask. Surely someone would know.

Lord Robert looked up, a hint of blue catching his eye. Most of his people wore browns and greens, such a blue being too costly. Ah, it was Karina! He turned smiling and bowed low.

"Karina, Margaret Mathilda!" and bowed again. "Madam but you look very fine! Yet why the sad face? What ails you?" All the while thinking how the girl had grown into a rare beauty. "Come, come," he caught her hand and dragged her away, as if she were a child still. Through the big gateway and chattering still, up, up to the castle. "You must meet my bride, and she must meet you, for you are of an age and she will be so happy, particularly as you speak French as she has no English yet."

So it was, when Tom came straggling in last, leading a lame horse, she was not there to meet him.

"My lady! Philippa!" Robert pushed through the muddle of stranger folk, trunks and packs which littered the hall. He bowed and pulled Karina forward. "Here she is then, my lady. Karina. The one I have told you so much of, remember? And see," he pointed to the pearl cross which lay on Karina's breast, "She wears the cross my mother gave her at her baptism. Her real name," he grinned at Karina, "her Christian names that is, are, Margaret Matilda."

Karina curtseyed low and then smiled at Lord Robert's new lady. She was little and dark and pretty in a soft way and she thought, probably sweet-natured, though nervous. Storing this unconsciously in her mind, she felt she must also observe the clothes and her waiting women to tell the sisters. But the clothes were dusty riding dress, and the women milling about her seemed grumpy in comparison to their mistress.

"Welcome lady," Karina said curtseying again. "But you must be tired and hot so I will go now, but I hope you will be happy here, for we have waited such a long time for you."

Pleased, Robert laughed in agreement. It had been a good impulse to bring Karina up; he could see that his new lady was pleased too.

They were all tired after the journey, for he had pushed them at the end, wanting to get home. It had been a thoroughly tiresome journey and he had been appalled with the number in her retinue who were not a stimulating party, forever complaining about everything. He must somehow send them home if they were not going to be happy. He hoped too that his bride would be content without them, for she seemed the sweetest thing and very different from all the poker-faced women she had brought with her.

In the stables, Tom had seen to the horse, over-fussing indeed so to give himself more time before going home. He ached, body and soul. Body from the journey which had been slow and tedious, due to the impossible ladies attending the bride. And soul. Oh his soul, how it pained him. He had heard minstrels sing of love, of the agony of it, and he had never understood. Now, so near and so far from his beloved, he hesitated, telling the boy yet again what to do, as if the horse were some prize beast. As if the boy didn't know full well what to do anyway.

His pack over his shoulder, he stomped slowly up to his house and walked into the dimness. The hearth burnt quietly and a good smell came from the pot hanging on the crane. He glanced around. Everything was just as Margaret liked it, clean and shining. Yet it was different, for Karina's hand had begun to show. Little things. A bright new cover on the bed, a fine linen curtain over the window instead of the shutter. Little pots of gay flowers were along the sill. His mind flashed to the little Karina, who riding into the green, North countries, delighted in the wild flowers. He dumped his pack on the floor and went through into the garden. Sniffing appreciatively, he saw she had another row of peas in flower and that not a weed was there for him to pull. Sitting on the log, leaning his back against the warm wall, he closed his eyes.

Karina saw him through the open door and her heart pounded. Standing in the shadow of the lintel, her mind whirled with what she must do, what his sisters had suggested. For perhaps they knew him better than she did, and she must be bold for he was not. Silently she stepped over the herb lawn till she stood before him.

Later, he thought that perhaps he did get the scent of her, yet still he kept his eyes shut. As a dream he felt her mouth touch his, tender and exploring. Her hands fluttering, holding his face, she crept over his mouth with butterfly kisses. Startled, his eyes opened. It was not a dream, it was real. It was she. Not daring to move, his eyes closed again, he let the tender mouth caress his, till despite himself, his heart hammering, his hands held her and drew her close. For many moments, there were no words. Their eyes spoke everything, their hands and their mouths. Somehow they went into the house, and somehow they lay together in the clean bed.

If heaven is like this, thought Tom, dear God, take me to heaven. Soon he forgot everything and gave in to his body, yet slowly, specially careful of her. It was at first a tender loving, exploring, seeking. He was kind, patient and very gentle. It was far more beautiful than he had imagined it would be in his dreams. He held back, afraid of hurting her, yet she drew him close with a gasp. After they had rested, entwined, whispering, joyful and incredulous, he took her with more force, greedy, needing, then contrite. Yet she laughed, loving it, not minding if it hurt just a little.

In the firelight she washed his hair and scrubbed his back as he contorted in the little wooden tub. Every other moment their hands reached for each other, their mouths touched softly, then hard. Perhaps they did sleep, perhaps they did not. By morning they were relaxed like cats who lie in the sun after a good meal.

"Margaret would be pleased you know," Karina was alerted.

"Do you really think so, for I do hope so, Tom." He nodded firmly.

"I will ask my lord today if I may wed you, Karina. And if he say nay, I shall go to the priest, put up the banns and wed you none the less," and kissed her roundly. "Now to the day, to work, and always trying not to grin like the happy fool I am." Taking her tenderly in his arms once more, he buried his face in her hair. "Thank you my sweeting. Thank you!"

CHAPTER EIGHT

PHILIPPA

Philippa gazed about the hall in awe, for it was so grand, and the feast so splendid. Lord Robert had insisted that they have a second marriage feast for his people, for so few had attended the feast at her home. Crowded boards, laden with thick brown trenchers, stretched right to the end of the hall, the noise of happy chattering was deafening. Now and again one could just hear the musicians playing as they edged their way between the rows of guests. It seemed as if the whole town were here, everyone wearing his finest.

At the great open fireplace, cooks toiled over ox, sheep, pig and fowl. Wisps of smoke filled the hall, and the good smell of roasting meats was tantalizing. Servants appeared from the far-off kitchens with other dishes held high. A feast indeed, way surpassing anything she had experienced before.

At the high table, the constable watched, eyes hooded, and was watched. For it was he, who with a raised hand, or indeed an eyebrow, directed the feast. The attentive steward, meanwhile rushed hither and thither, directing the castle staff in serving. Since the death of Lady Matilda, social life in the castle had been almost nil. Lord Robert had been a thoroughly lazy bachelor, albeit and thankfully, an easy one. Now all the officers revelled in their tasks, determined to show the party of foreigners how well things were done on their little island.

Handsome young squires carried bowls of fragrant water for hand washing, cloths draped over arm or shoulder for wiping. Platters loaded with cut meats, with little bowls of sauces alongside, were served first at the high table before going down the hall. Philippa watched as her silver plate was overloaded with the choicest titbits. Great herbal and parsnip pies, flavoured with bacon and topped with a rich crust came next. This dish, Mistress Chamberlain shyly told her, was a house speciality. Not really an old woman, Philippa had noticed that poor thing had very few teeth. No wonder she preferred pies, which were easier to eat than meat, all too often tough and stringy. Smiling her thanks, Philippa daintily took a piece in her fingers, and found it delicious. With a smile, nodding to the woman, she wiped her fingers. Gone, oh thanks be to God, were the lean days of fasting of her childhood. Dish after dish, sauce after sauce were served till she felt unable to even taste another morsel. For she was the slightest young thing, with birdlike bones and a waist, which her lord could easily surround with his great hands.

Without realising it, Philippa was becoming less afraid, daily more easy with her husband and new home. Her hand touched the magnificent chain from Robert's late mother, for he had given her Lady Matilda's beautiful embroidered box as her own. How lucky she was. It still all so surprised her, the proposal and, despite the delays, the marriage. She had thought to go into a nunnery, really she had, though in her heart she knew she had no vocation. For who would want her? Fourth child, and only daughter of a dead knight, who had left them with just the smallest, poorest manor?

"We will fast for Saint?" Her mother would pause to remember which saint day it was today, yesterday or tomorrow. All they did was fast. And why? In order to give the boys more. Philippa loved her brothers, tall and handsome and kind. Yet she was always hungry and cold, and longed to stuff herself with bowls of hot pottage and good succulent meats as they did. "They are our future Philippa, my dear, our only hope. We were so blessed, thanks to the Virgin, to have three such fine sons. So it is our duty and we must do without for their sakes, if we are short."

They were always short. By the time each son was equipped for his knightly duties, his men armed, mounted, clothed and fed, there was never enough for those left at home. Phillippa often thought that the peasants fared far better than she did. "You will see my child, it will be worth it in the end," said her mother yet again.

She gazed unseeing through a new wave of smoke which rose from the great fireplace. Something had spilled into the embers.

It was a lovely summer. Late sunshine shone through the great traced windows but inside, it was always chill. Her mind far away at home, she saw their meagre hearth and her pinched mother eking out their lives. She had loved her mother, yet now she was dead, she felt so far away and had little sorrow. No more scrimping and paring or being cold and hungry. No more unpicking and turning her mother's old dresses to sort the good pieces to make up into hers. She had been right then poor lady, it had been worth it, at least she hoped so.

The brothers, they who had always derided the rough great English knights, surprised them by bringing one home one day. A groom had ridden ahead to warn them, yet even so it had thrown her mother into a terrible fluster. It seemed that their guest was a keen horseman and admiring their mares, had suggested taking some of them to the port on the channel to service with an Arab stallion. Peeping out of a window into the yard, she thought the guest looked very fine on his great charger. At table, she had held the ewer and poured water for his hands. Then she had served him, for they had few servants and her mother thought it politic, a small smile on her worn face.

"Your second-best gown Philippa, hurry, hurry, and your best apron. Come now child, make sure to comb and silk your hair, for here is a fine young man who may look kindly upon you."

He had. Her mother had spent hours at her prie-dieu, thanking God, his Holy Mother and all the saints. For at last, a fine knight, even if an Englishman, had asked for her daughter's hand. She had recklessly used up their last wax candles in the chapel in her gratitude. Well the hives, would supply more soon enough.

Philippa had looked timorously up at him and felt her small hand firmly held by his. He smiled encouragingly at her as he kissed it. Now here was a gentle sweeting.

When her brothers had discussed the proposal, they told her gently of their arrangements. Trembling, Philippa had walked in the garden with the English knight, glad at least that he seemed more intent on her than the poor show of it.

"You will like my country, lady," his French was poor. "My castle is large and airy and we live in a pleasant part of the land with less rain and more sun than other areas. The hunting is good, if you care for it, and your brothers shall visit us often so you will not feel alone."

She realized he was trying to put her at her ease and smiled sweetly in thanks at him. Seeing her sweetness, surprised at his own actions yet pleased, he thought again that his mother would be happy. This was the maid for him.

When word came that the marriage was to be postponed due to a great sickness, the lord's mother had died, yet her mother had gone into a fury of fear. Her third brother was at home at that time and had great difficulty in consoling her that it was merely a postponement and surely all for the best. Indeed it was a touching consideration towards his sister.

By then her first brother had found a bride, a wealthy lady of rather low birth, yet whose father thought the match ideal for his purposes. Neither she nor her mother cared for Lillia the bride, a big raw woman who despite her wealth, looked odd, wearing impossibly tight and too bright clothes. Could he bear her, thought Philippa? So much scent to cover her stink. He who was so handsome could surely choose his spouse, from all the pretty girls of France? To be able to choose, lucky brothers, such luxury, unlike her. Yet she corrected the flicker of resentment being, as she well knew, secretly pleased with her betrothed. Yet why had he, her most fair brother, albeit poor, made such a proposal?

"For her money of course," had stamped her middle brother at the wedding feast. "If she had a sister with equal dowry, I'd have her too!" And Philippa quailed, for she had no dowry but for the few poor jewels her mother had not sold.

"It is a wife he needs, and, being an only son, he has no need for a dowry so he must have enough already. Yet I warm to him for it. So many are greedy and want it all. Yes, he just needs a wife," insisted her mother again rather smugly. "He has done well to offer for you. We are an old family, with excellent French blood lines and our breeding is successful. Look," she waved her arms nowhere, in pride. "Three fine sons and a daughter, all living and well. He is lucky to have you my dear," and savagely pinched her cheeks to try to put some colour into them.

It may well have been due to her strenuous activities, rushing about, preparing for her daughter's nuptials, the poor lady was found stone-cold dead one morning. Shocked, in a daze, Philippa sent for her brothers, wondering if this would mean another postponement to her marriage. But no. They decided their mother would want it to go ahead, although it would be a mercifully quieter affair as a result. Her brother's wife gathered some widowed ladies together for a retinue for her. Philippa was horrified. Surely this was not necessary? One or two maids would have been quite sufficient? Lillia introduced her to the ladies, having chosen them as suitable, and with much fanfare had made arrangements for her mousey little sister-in-law to be properly escorted. The quiet, country girl Philippa found not one to her liking. The agreement was they would stay with her for one year, and return, should they wish, when the weather was better again. No doubt they thought that if she, a mousey little thing, could find a husband, there might be other lords or knights for them. They were not, she decided again, very nice. No doubt word had got about that she was poor, and that she was lucky to have this offer. When the time came for them to sail, it would be a lonely journey without Robert. For Philippa had not found one lady to be friends with, indeed they generally ignored her, being so busy with their complaining.

The days before her wedding were therefore lonely, for she had no one to confide in. Feeling like a package, she was firmly told what to do and when, for the marriage. Then, after the ceremony she would leave for England. The day before her mother's funeral, her sister-in-law moved in and took over. The barest mourning and masses observed, she bent her considerable energies and wealth into organizing everything. There was no need for the words to be actually spoken; it was obvious they all thought that Philippa would never get another offer.

Every day for forty days was spent sewing and packing and planning and starting all over again, her new attendants ever squabbling between themselves. However, Philippa did appreciate being well-fed for a change, and the chateau certainly did look better with her sister-in-law's improvements. Despite her anxieties as to the future, Philippa softened her benefactor by freely saying so, and, for good measure, how pleased her mother would be. For it was true. The mellow old rooms blossomed with the fine tapestries and handsome furniture. Open shutters and fresh paint did wonders for dowdy rooms, polish and bright furnishings changed the mood. Well yes, perhaps she did now understand her brother's marriage if it brought all this comfort and plenty.

"You are dreaming my lady?" a voice cut into her reverie. Philippa looked into her husband's blue eyes. They were a rare, very deep blue, which fascinated her. Her own were a dull, mid-brown. It had not been so bad bedding with this kindly, gentle man. Indeed, to her secret surprise, it was even becoming pleasurable.

"I am thinking happy thoughts, my lord," she replied quietly blushing.

"Good, good!" Pleased, he stood up and clapped his hands. "Clear a space fellows, for it is surely time to dance?" Which brought a cheer and much activity and soon the centre of the hall was cleared, and the boards all stacked against a wall. Several youths took up brooms and shifted the herbs to the side, and the musicians struck up a tune.

Dancing was new to her, for at the chateau, life had been too frugal to ever have either occasion or enough people. It was the one thing, above all else, she really felt gratitude to her sister-in-law for. After her mother's death, they had dancing lessons every day. Surprisingly the great clumsy woman, Lillia, much enjoyed it and seemed to dance like an angel. So light on her feet was she, they had some meeting ground at last. Whenever a few guests arrived, instruments were brought out and up they got for a turn or two. At last Philippa forgot her fear of strangers and to her own surprise, danced well, almost looking pretty with bright eyes and flushed face. Now she took Robert's hand and went with confidence on to the floor to line up in front of all the dancers. Wearing her fine new clothes and jewels with style, no one could guess at the fluttering of her heart. In the half-light of evening, her hair pinned up with a lace cloth and a jewel at her brow, she looked almost beautiful. Despite standing tall, she was dwarfed by Robert, who stood on her right, with his cousin the duke on her left. There was much scuffling and laughter as others sought a place. It was hardly a formal affair and she quietly watched the duke to see if she could read his face. Forever the little mouse in the background, Philippa saw more of men's souls than most young women. He seemed amused with the entertainment, yet happy. Relieved, she gave him her best smile, having decided that he was pleased with their humdrum gathering.

Despite her foreboding, she had immediately taken to her husband's grand cousin. On their way from the coast, they had paused at the duke's castle for some days, where they had been royally entertained. Even her attendants had smiled. His was a great castle set on a strategic hill overlooking the sea. The town below was far bigger and more important than Robert's. They had shared the same great, great grandfather he told her, so were distant cousins, yet more important, good friends.

It was lovely to dance. A small smile of concentration on her delicate face, Philippa dipped, swept and turned to change partners with delight. Once she saw the strange girl in blue, except she was not in blue now, but deepest red. For a moment their eyes met and a chord of friendship rang quietly between them. If the crowd were not watching the Lady Philippa, they were watching Karina. For both were young and newly-wed and had such sweetness and grace in the dance, it was joyful to watch them. It was good to have young people in the castle again.

"Young Harran has served the mares well," Tom told Karina next day while he washed down in the sunlit garden, for the lord had insisted on bringing some of the French mares to mate with the son of the great stallion. "It will be a triumph if all the trouble to bring those mares across the sea is a success. His lordship will be pleased, for he told me his offer brought him to meet his lady." Rubbing his fair head vigorously he added, "What do you think of her then, the new lady?"

"I like her," answered Karina without hesitation. "I should like to know her better too, but not with all those sour-looking women with her. They are horrible, and I don't think she likes them either!"

Summer began to wane and Philippa's two brothers decided it was time to go home before the winter storms. Confident that the mares were in foal, they proposed to bide at the port till a good crossing was certain, before putting their precious cargoes at risk.

Having earnestly begged Robert to remove her escort, Philippa discretely suggested to the ladies that they might like to leave with her brothers. Despite their complaints, these irritating people hesitated. For yes, they had enjoyed the change, the good food and entertainment. But yes again, perhaps the winter would pall and finally, they all agreed to go home too. Once more the party gathered, loaded up with gifts, with the lords in the front and Tom behind in charge of the mares, and planning an easy ride, they set off one fine autumn morn. With a light heart Tom waved at Karina, till he no longer could see the blue gown anymore. He would not be away too long, as they wouldn't cross the sea with the party this time, just escort them to the port and wait till they sailed.

It took Karina three days to complete all her chores and find the courage to walk up to the castle to see the lady. Peeping round the door she found her sitting in the great hall with two of the castle women and they were mending Lord Robert's clothes. For, they told her, he was a great one for tearing them in the forests when hunting. As one they greeted her with smiles, for mending was a boring task.

"Lady," Karina dipped. "Having finished my chores, I hope that I may sit with you awhile, for with my husband away, I fear to get lonely." They smiled warmly at each other and Karina took up a hose from the basket to mend. "Tom does this too, my lady, but his hose are thicker than these, so they last longer." Chatting quietly, they worked their way through the pile and satisfied, the women bobbed and took them away.

"It is a fine day outside, my lady," Karina said, hoping she was not being too forward. Yet she need not have worried for Philippa was weary of being indoors and was only too glad to get up and go out.

"As I do not know the castle very well, Karina, will you show me around?"

There was a haze, as is usual on a fine day, and they stood high on the battlements and looked at the view spreading to the horizon. They were happy, just two young things, being girls together. There were no dullards left to drag their mood down, so they ran and leapt and crept into unknown places and explored as children do. There were few people at the castle at that time, most gone with Lord Robert, or out on their daily business. So they wandered about chattering lightly, feeling free to roam everywhere.

"Would you like to see my home, my lady?" Karina had suddenly thought she might. So almost furtively they sped down the stone steps and down to the horse-master's house where breathless, they flopped on the bed.

Philippa looked around the small room in fascination. It was white-washed throughout with dark, low ceiling beams. A great hearth took up one wall and a small fire was banked up in the centre, giving off sweet wood smoke. Over it hung a kettle which sang very gently. A press stood at one end, of dark, well-polished wood, covered with a white cloth. Copper, brass and pewter shone on shelves and in the corners. Philippa smiled happily at her new friend.

"It is lovely, Karina, so homely and comfortable. All one needs, I think."

Karina also looked about with fresh eyes. It was true. All they needed was here, every comfort and every tool.

"Come," she jumped up. "Come and see my garden." So out they went and Philippa was charmed again by the neat rows of vegetables and the little flowers which hid here and there. Karina unhooked a small basket and began picking some beans.

"I should like a garden, Karina," the admiring Philippa said wistfully. Surprised, Karina studied the gentle girl beside her.

"Then you shall have one, my lady! We shall ask Lord Robert, for I am sure he will refuse you nothing."

So they sat till it grew chilly, having shelled the beans, biting the grass stems, and discussing what they should grow and where.

"There is a walk," Karina saw it in her mind's eye, "right at the top of the old tower where we did not go today, it being locked. I will ask Master Watchman for the key. My Godmother, the Lady Matilda, had a small herbary there. It is facing south-west, and is quite sheltered. So it is warm, and the views are wonderful, as she often told me. Indeed I think she was more concerned with the views than her herbs," and giggled. "Water might be a problem," she went on, "but if we could catch some of the rain as it falls from the tower, in a butt?" Her mind was racing and watching her, Philippa saw immediately that she would get her garden. Still chattering, they went to the stables where Karina called with her strange cry, and so showed off her horses.

Then as night fell, they wandered, still chattering, up to the castle. There they were met by two almost hysterical women. Mistress Steward and Mistress Chamberlain, who having been left in charge, had feared her run away. Taking the lead from Karina, who was laughing at the idea, Philippa, at last the lady of her castle, ordered supper for two.

"Stay the night?" Philippa anxiously asked her friend. And Karina, who had slept on bare earth and rock and sand, often amidst the howls of wild beasts, agreed, understanding that she was afraid.

"Of course I will, for aren't we both alone, our husbands away? We shall still no doubt have plenty to talk about," giggling again. How lovely to be with someone as young as she. How good it was to chatter about all and everything without care.

"But while we are together Karina, we are friends understand. You will please to call me Philippa, or Pip, as my brothers call me privily. Please?" she added.

They began work on the herbary the next day. With her enthusiasm and charm, Karina goaded the stable boys to carry baskets of good, dry dung up, where the gardeners dug it in deep. A new air of youth and optimism filled the castle, and the officers' wives were glad that the poor new little lady seemed so content. Now if she could grow to be like the Lady Matilda, theirs would continue to be a well-ordered life.

The horsemen casually trotted along, man and beast looking forward to home and supper. Most days they went out to hunt, for in this time of peace, one must enjoy life and fill the larders. Lord Robert rode in front with the knights while Tom and a boy brought up the rear with the game. There were a few young squires and the odd page in the party, but this was not one of those castles which always had great numbers of people filling the rooms to overflowing, although visiting knights did come sometimes with their ladies and attendants. It was a useful arrangement to have good places to stop and rest while on a journey. It was the time to cement friendships, to converse, to learn and teach, compete and relax. With Lady Matilda gone, something, they quietly agreed between themselves, was missing, for she had been a good chatelaine, and this had always been a friendly place without too much formality.

Bowmen from round about came most days to compete on the butts and Lord Robert was generous in his praise and with his prizes. Who knew when the word would come for him to gather them up to go to serve the king?

When the gentry were not hunting, they practised sword-play and occasionally fell to jousting. They might all ride into the woods to picnic, the men to gather the elder and the yew so to have work on hand for the long winter. The days of autumn passed pleasantly, with Philippa happy now, with a friend of her own. When the weather was poor, man and hound grew bored, sitting about in the great hall, drinking and playing chess. Invariably, the tedium was broken by regular breaking up of dog fights and a whip was kept at hand as a warning.

"I see that our wives are the best of friends, Tom," said Lord Robert, watching the two bent heads across the room.

"Yes, my lord." Tom had nothing else to say for he was not quite sure about it.

"My lady could not have found a more pleasant and able companion. Though what they find to chatter about from morn till night I know not."

Both men smiled over to their wives, who feeling their gaze smiled back.

"It is mainly the garden, Sire," Tom said, feeling greatly relieved his lord was pleased with the relationship. "It is all I hear of at home while all the time I get orders of what I must seek out here and there. Last night it was honeysuckle. She wants at least two. Today it is roses, for they are planning a bower to sit in to escape the sun's heat." He laughed happily. "It is hard to remember that little girl riding in the day's heat. Days on end, indeed in all weathers, day after day, and month after month. And now she wants a bower to hide from the sun. So find the plants I must or there will be no peace."

Lord Robert smiled and rubbed a foot over his great hound. He had always been an easy-going, agreeable man, yet now he felt more content than ever before in his life. Marriage was good for him, and glancing at his Master of Horse, he noted that Tom also looked more contented.

"Well let us humour them Tom, for it is a gentle occupation which can only do them good. My lady asks for great barrels to catch the rainwater from the gutters. I am quite certain your little Karina thought up that one. It will certainly save much labour, carrying buckets in dry weather. Yes, I am happy that they have each other for friends, for a lonely wife might not be an easy one." So they spoke, idly, content with their regular cycle of life.

Karina begged plants throughout the town for the new garden quite shamelessly. She also dug up little plants from her own garden, wrapping the roots in damp moss and laying them in a shallow basket. When an idle stable hand could be found, he would carry it up to the highest walk of the castle. Her sisters-in-law also gave her seedlings, seeds and cuttings, so it did not take long for Philippa's garden to look as if it had promise. Often, if the day was fine, the two young women urged old Sir Patrice to sit with them. He came willingly enough, for they were merry company and made him forget his woes. For he was feeling his age, his joints all seizing up, and climbing the steps of the castle was becoming hard for him. Perhaps soon, he would ask for a chair?

When the days were poor, the two friends would closet themselves in Philippa's room to talk endlessly. Neither having had a friend before, both spoke freely of their lives, their anxieties and their dreams. Karina spoke of things she thought she had forgotten, about that past lost life, of her childhood. Philippa was entranced, her own life having been so dull, she took to urging her friend to tell more. Shutting her eyes, Karina would recall scenes and people, and once remembered, they would pour out as a flood. It never occurred to her that her stories might sound exotic and foreign; it had been her life, or rather, her previous life.

One day she was speaking about Shimos when Tom came and standing in the shadows, watched them, idly listening to their chatter.

"Of course," Karina was saying, "although he was a slave, he must have originally been a patrician. Or so my grandmother said, for she loved him very much, even though he was so old. He was very learned, and was our scribe. He spoke the two languages we spoke in our house, and Greek, French and Latin, as well as writing them. He was my father's tutor, but it was my mother who was better born and read and wrote the best." Philippa had stopped her work and gazed in admiration at her friend.

"Your mother could read and write?" she asked awed. Karina nodded.

"But what happened to him, Karina, your scribe, where is he now?" then quickly saw it was not a clever question and covered her mouth with a muddy hand.

"I suppose he is dead Philippa, for he left us and went to try to find help. I suppose that everyone else was dead too, and we were stuck on the tower, for the stairs had burnt too." Her eyes filled with tears. "Then my mother went, and she did not come back. Then my grandmother went." Pausing, she blinked back the tears and drew a deep breath. "Dear Shimos. How I loved him, poor old man. Something bad must have happened to him for he too never returned. Then Tom and Dummy came and saved me. So I will never know."

Tom held his breath. At last she was speaking about her early life. He recognized the old man, the tower, it all fit. So that was why the old scarecrow had been so determined to stop them. Knowing of the horses, he was glad to direct them to the farm, in order that they would find her. He had known that she was there, on the tower. He had probably been wandering on the plain for days, fruitlessly seeking help. Tom shut his eyes. He would have to tell her one day, but kindly, and make up some little story to ease her mind.

It came about very soon, that night in bed, yet in a strange way. For Karina seemed quiet, loving and rather mysterious. Then she told him, whispering shyly in his ear, that she thought that she was with child, and Tom's joy was boundless. After happy loving, he told her that he had overheard her speaking in the castle garden. Out came the story of how he had met Shimos, who was yes, old and weak, but who had certainly not forgotten her for he had directed them to the farm, in Latin. Just being the Master of Horse, not knowing much Latin if indeed any, he had not really understood what the old man was saying, but guessed that he was to rescue Karina. Thanks to the saints, it had happened all the same. It worked and he had given the old man figs to eat. Her happiness was doubled with his news. Perhaps she thought, somewhere, Shimos, her grandmother and mother were living together safely? Perhaps in the city, with her uncle? A great calm swept over her and she rejoiced in her life, her love, her friend, and in anticipation of her coming child.

When she told Philippa of her pregnancy, she was surprised to see her friend's face fill with colour.

"Oh Karina, my sweetest friend," she cried, "I think I am too!"

The months passed and in midwinter the men were called away, leaving their wives in the care of Sir Patrice and the castle staff.

"Now you take care my love" scolded Tom, stroking the ever growing belly where nestled his firstborn. "Lord Robert asks if you will move up to stay with his lady, and I agree, rather than having you running up and down all the time."

It was like a migration. The ponies and stable hands toiled up to the castle with everything she possessed, so she would not have to take the steps in bad weather and Karina was carried up in a chair.

In later years, Karina would remember each precious day as if it were just yesterday. How she and her only friend had laughed, and played and sang and so much enjoyed each other's company.

When Philippa saw into the treasure box, she was incredulous at Karina's jewels, and puzzled by her friend's apparent indifference to her fortune. It was no use. It would be impossible to even try to explain what she felt about them, so why try? Yet they played like children, donning all their jewels, this way and that. Sometimes, Karina, forgetting her thickening body, danced for Philippa, wild, foreign dancing, which delighted and scandalized her. When word came that the men were on their way home, Karina hugged her friend with wet eyes and went back down to her little house to make it warm and welcoming for her husband.

The men came home in early spring, Lord Robert with an arm in a sling; yet the wound, which was healing, was not too severe. They had lost a few men and some horses. Provision had to be made for the widows and children who trailed forlornly up to the castle for alms and comfort. Fighting at any time was grim, yet in the winter, it was doubly so. Those who returned were tired, even those without wounds had some infection, perhaps in the chest, or the gut, and even the feet. Glad to be home, they sat about resting, doing just the minimum. Even the horses were tired and glad to laze in their warm stables and eat good summer hay, dry from the lofts, instead of frozen grasses.

Despite his fatigue, Tom was thrilled with his rotund little wife and tenderly hugged her at every turn in the small house. At night, his hand on her belly, he chortled with delight to feel the activities of his unborn child. For days he slept long and ate greedily while Karina sat in the small window embrasure and sewed tiny vests as she remembered her mother had done. Of course she knew that it was much colder here than in that long-past life and here, babies were tightly swaddled. Still, she sewed them dreaming, missing Philippa, but happy to have Tom back. If she had a girl, she decided it would be called Margaret, if a boy? No name came, however hard she thought. With her stallion called Harran after her father, that was not an option. Anyway, the stable boys, finding the name strange, called him Harry, for Harran was a name not known to them.

Eventually the not unexpected message came from the castle, could she please come up. Refusing a chair, with Tom at her side she began the climb, resting at the top of each stair. At this stage of her pregnancy, going up was quite a trial, though she knew coming down would be easier. A tearful Philippa met her, having watched her slow progress up the hill.

"Karina, Karina!" she caught her friend's hands. "A letter is come from my brother that he and his wife will arrive soon, so to be here for my lying in." Tears poured down her pale cheeks and Karina was concerned, loving her. She also worried, as did the castle women, because the lady was such a little thing, with no spare flesh on her bones. Philippa's belly seemed enormous compared with Karina's. Her eyes were sunken in her little face and great black circles were etched beneath them. Karina glanced behind her, to see the anxious eyes of Lord Robert.

"What think you, my lord?" she asked as they went in, Tom still holding her arm. "Do you want them here? For we all know that however good the lady is, they have little real affection for each other." Robert looked wretched as he seated his wife close to the great fire, which burned warmly in the hearth.

"What can I do about it Karina? They just announced that they are coming. No question of whether or not we need them. Yet in some ways, it gives me relief as they are bringing two midwives with them, who will assist Philippa. Being from her own land, it might be a comfort." This was met with a cross "tsck" from Philippa.

"We," her hand indicated Karina, "have already engaged midwives here, one being Tom's sister. I know and trust them, and as I speak some English now, I am sure we can manage very well." She burst into fresh sobs.

While the women fluttered about, the men looked uncomfortable and were glad to be diverted when the butler brought ale and goblets.

"Try to be grateful," Karina urged gently. "For I am sure she means so well. And if, as you say, she has no child of her own, she must be so interested to assist you with your birthing." All the same, Karina was as upset as her friend, for they were so content with their own plans, and did not need company or interference from elsewhere, especially Philippa's sister-in-law.

They spent the rest of the day together, leaving the men to talk around the fire with their ale. Karina admired the huge cradle which had been brought out of store, and the heaps of sheets and swaddling clothes. Mostly they lay together on the great bed and talked quietly. Karina did her best to reassure Philippa about the expected visitors. It seemed she had lost her previous happy anticipation of the birth, and now dreaded it because of them.

"If only you could stay here with me Karina. With the good women, my maids and the midwives, we could both be confined here, support and help each other and I know we would manage very well."

"You know if they come it will simply not be possible, Philippa," Karina tried to speak calmly. "You are Lady Philippa, wife of our Lord Robert. I am Karina, the horse-master's wife. Your baby will be born in the castle, and mine will be born in the little house by the stables. That is how it is my dear friend. For friends we might be, yet our position in life is very different. Be careful with your family when you speak of our friendship, for they will not be pleased, feeling and rightly, that you should be moving in higher circles." After that, the friends sent daily messages, little gifts and posies to each other, but the climb was too hard for visits, even in a chair, the stones being slippery, and their time was near.

Karina watched from her garden as the retinue of visitors arrived, and felt anxious for Philippa having to entertain them. How she wished they could have had their babies together. Yet she felt so very well and so lucky. As her time neared, Karina was gently supported by Tom's family, who called every day and fussed over her, making her teas and tasty food, to give her strength.

When the pains began, Karina thought them mild enough for her to cope with easily. Standing on the wall outside the house, she called down to Tom's sister, who passed the word and soon came puffing up, all anxiety. The pains grew worse.

How could her mother have born seven little sons without crying out from the pain? Karina gasped and bit the roll of cloth which had been put into her hand and tried not to utter a sound. In between the waves of agony which consumed her whole body, she rested, and smiled at the dear women by her side. When the next wave came to engulf her, she shut her eyes and saw Adina's face and bit the cloth with all her might. Would it never end? On and on, hour after hour, her body was wracked with pain till she felt she couldn't bear it any longer.

At last, with the first rays of light, with just one great cry, she pushed her daughter into the world. Exhausted, Karina lay smiling to hear the indignant infant's cries mingled with sweet words of love and welcome. Tom came, unashamed tears coursing down his face.

"Her name is Margaret, Tom! Margaret Matilda," and was kissed for it.

She was a small, plump little baby with the fairest hair and milk-white skin.

"Well then!" announced the proud midwife holding her up grinning, "No prizes for guessing who fathered this one," and put the washed and swaddled baby into Tom's arms.

She was lovely. Karina gazed in awe at her daughter, examining the perfect ears, her tiny fingers, the pearl-shell minute nails. Her head was smudged with fine white down, so one could see she would be very fair when her real hair grew in. Without a doubt, she was the spitting image of her father.

Karina was asleep when Lord Robert came bearing a gift from his wife for the baby. Tom told her later how his lordship had peered most carefully at their daughter, "For he was instructed to take great note, so to make a full report on her to his lady."

Having seen how few jewels Philippa had of her own, Karina was touched with the pendant she had sent. A garnet, round and as bright as a cherry, it was set in gold, with tiny pearls all around it. Karina pinned it on the baby's bands, pleased with this first and fine gift. On the third day, the baby being strong and healthy, Tom carried her to the church in town to be baptized, with his sisters standing as Godmothers and Robert as Godfather.

When Karina heard that Tom had surely given her the names, Margaret Matilda, she wept little tears of happiness.

The baby was suckling well. Yet Karina's breasts ached, for they felt full and hard and she was always thirsty. Tom's sisters continued their loving care, each coming up once a day, telling her to be patient and assured her that everything would settle down in time.

On the morning of the fourth day, word came that her ladyship was in travail. Karina became fretful as the hours passed, worrying over her friend and wishing that she could be with her. Her sister-in-law cheerfully stopped by briefly telling her that Lord Robert had sent for her as he was unimpressed with the foreign midwives.

"Give her my love and tell her I am praying for her safe and speedy delivery."

Smiling kindly, her sister-in-law settled her precious new niece with a kiss and went to the door.

"I will, my dear, and be sure she will be glad of your love. But I must hurry, for between us, I am a little fearful that her ladyship is too small, her belly so big with probably a large child, it may be a difficult birth."

It was a long and anxious wait till at last, after two more days, the church bells rang out. The Lady Philippa had borne his lordship a fine son.

The following day, Karina dressed herself in her warmest clothes and fiercely brushing away Tom's objections, begged a chair to take her up to the castle. Knowing full well that he was bound to lose the argument, Tom trailed along behind, his daughter well swaddled and tucked warmly under his cloak.

In the stuffy, crowded room, Karina only had eyes for her friend. It was not only that the great belly was missing, Philippa seemed to have shrunk in every way. Yet her eyes lit up when she saw Karina, and weak tears began to fall.

"Oh wasn't it awful, Karina? I never knew that such pain existed." Kissing her tenderly, Karina noted how pale her friend was.

"But look, my dearling," Karina told her cheerfully. "After one week I am well again and so glad to see you. You will be the same, you will see. Just you must rest, eat and drink plenty, so you make milk for the little man," for they had decided that they would both nurse their babies, and Philippa would not entertain the thought of a wet nurse.

The baby Margaret was brought close and Philippa smiled at her.

"Tom!" she mouthed, smiling at the similarity.

Then the young lord was proudly brought forward by Philippa's sister-in-law. Karina gazed at her friend's child, amazed at what a big baby he was compared with her compact little miss. No wonder it had been a long and difficult birth. Later, she saw that the nursemaid was spooning camomile tea into his mouth with a silver spoon. He seemed hungry.

Karina's sister-in-law came in with soup for her ladyship and greeted her. By now, knowing her well, Karina could see from her closed face that all was not well. Generally having a smile, she was now serious as she drew back the sheets of the new mother and changed the blood-soaked cloths.

"It would be good if you could stay the night Karina," she whispered so that the strange women who wandered about would not hear. "She is happy with you near, and I am worried about her. For she is bleeding too much, she is too hot and the other midwives will not let me bring up cold water to press about her to stop it."

Karina did stay the night, lying on a pallet beside her friend, although sleep was impossible, for the little boy raged endlessly. In the night, when the exhausted women were snoring all about them, Tom's midwife-sister quietly brought the little lord to Karina to nurse.

"Forgive me for asking you my dear," Karina could see she was desperately tired. "They must seek a wet nurse, for this poor lady is too weak to nurse him. He gets hungry and angry with just the teas they give him, for he is a fine big lad and needs milk."

Karina put her friend's son to her breast and gasped in pain as he seized upon her nipple hungrily. After he had his fill from both breasts and was changed, he was laid beside Margaret in the huge, elaborate cradle. At last the room was quiet, and Tom's sister lay beside Karina and slept deeply.

In the morning, not one face had a smile, for it was obvious that Philippa was fading away. They held her up and tried to give her chicken soup, but it trickled from her lips as if she were too weak to bother. The only time she showed any life was when Karina spoke to her. Then her smile was so tender, it was heart-breaking. Trying not to weep, Karina sat beside her on the bed, ignoring the scolding of the foreign women. Lord Robert came, and on the other side, took his wife's ice cold hand, his fine blue eyes misted.

"Shall I give your boy to suckle, Philippa dearling?" she asked. "For he is such a big lad, and hark to him, he is so hungry." Philippa nodded silently, then watched as her son seized on Karina's red nipple, and contentedly nursed. Holding one of his little hands she whispered, "Will you have enough milk for little Margaret too?" and smiled, closing her eyes when she was reassured there would be.

"Is there nothing to be done?" hissed Karina in French to the frantic Lillia. "Must we just sit here and watch her die?"

The priest came and said the prayers for the dying and incense filled the overheated, stuffy, overcrowded great bedroom.

"Look after him won't you, dear Karina?" Philippa summoned the strength to whisper. "Make sure she looks after him please, Robert? Do not send him away? Promise? Promise?" Then, ever more faint, she whispered, "Look after both of them my dear friend." Kneeling beside her, pressing his lips on her cold hand, Robert promised.

Karina did not weep, although she wanted to. Everyone else in the room did, the wailing added to the prayers was dreadful. Instead she managed somehow to gather up the two babies in a shawl and left the room, to slowly climb up to the old tower and out into the sunshine. For a moment, her tears blinding her, she just stood. Then she carefully sat on the bench, the babies under her cloak on each arm.

Why? She saw the white face on the lace pillow, still warm. Why? Then the tears began to fall. Why did everyone she loved have to die? Rocking in sorrow, she held the children fast, her tears falling on their sleeping faces. Robert and Tom found her there later and wrapping their cloaks about her, sat close and silent beside her, gazing, unseeing at the glorious view far below them.

After the burial, Lord Robert took his son to the little chapel in the castle to be baptized. It was a muted affair, with old Sir Patrice and Philippa's brother and sister-in-law acting as Godparents. They named him Rupert, because for an unknown reason, the letter R was important in the family.

Surprisingly, there was no unpleasantness from Philippa's relations. They were too shocked at their loss, Lillia particularly so. It was unbelievable that after she had laboured so long and hard, the gentle Philippa had died, particularly after successfully giving birth to such a fine son.

"Be sure I will send him to stay with you when he is older," comforted Robert as after the masses, they rode away. "Meanwhile I will let you know his progress. I must be grateful that we have a good wet nurse in Karina. I am assured that providing she is very well nurtured, she will manage to feed both babies successfully."

Numb. Lonely. Her only friend gone, Karina ate and drank and did all that she was told to do in order to nurse the babies so that neither would go hungry. The sad, kindly castle women were constantly at her side, taking the babies to wash and change them, or holding them to bring up their wind. Once again, all her things were moved up to the castle. This time, Tom stayed with her, closing up their little house. Kind and loving, understanding her sorrow, he watched over her anxiously, for he alone knew just how much she had been through. He felt almost overwhelmed by a great sadness, remembering how many near and dear she had lost already.

When the babies began to smile, enchanted, Karina regained her good humour. Then, remembering the laughter she and Philippa had shared, she determined to put sorrow behind her. Whenever the day was fair, despite objections from the women, Karina took the babies into the garden, which had begun to look well. In a great basket, sheltered by a buttress, a cloth shading them from the sun, they lay gurgling contentedly or sleeping soundly. Sewing, or attending the garden, Karina, accompanied by the castle women, was content. For here she felt serene, somehow feeling her friend Philippa, all about her.

CHAPTER NINE

ROBERT

Robert smiled warmly at the messenger. What a relief that they were not being summoned once again to go to war. A visit, what a privilege! What was more, a visit from the princes would certainly raise his status. His mind sought as to when they had last had a visit from royalty. A long, long time ago, perhaps when he was tiny. He recalled his mother speaking of it. A pity it was not to be the king himself, but perhaps after all, the princes might be more interesting and less trouble. Besides, one or the other, was the king of the future.

Now if they could arrive in time for the Spring Fair? Ah, but that would be excellent, with plenty to do and see. He must send out word to all the knights in the district. They would make a great occasion of it, show their highnesses that even in the backwaters of the kingdom, enjoyable and civilized days were to be had. A month? Of course they could be prepared. His mind racing, he poured out more wine for the messenger and, trying to still his enthusiasm, he asked for news.

The burghers of the town were as delighted as he was. They gathered as requested in the great hall, intrigued by the urgent summons, relieved too that it was not for higher taxes, or more requirements for war, they threw themselves into preparations for the royal visit with enthusiasm. How happy their wives would be! How expensive their new clothes! Yet as one, they smugly agreed it would be worth it, for a smile from a prince would keep the ladies happy for a long while.

Messengers were sent to the outlying manors and the knights, sometimes with their ladies, rode in, all agog to hear of plans for the visit. Robert felt important and optimistic and set everyone on to what preparation suited them best. He would organize a tournament for the visitors and the local knights, which he must obtain permission for. There could also be competitions of every kind for the locals as well as on the butts. That very evening, it being fine, a host of men went out with their scythes and rakes to cut a fine lawn. They would have jousting for the knights and squires, archery for the bowmen, wrestling, for the lads who had more energy than sense. The castle grooms even spoke of a horse race on a circuit. And why not? The Arab horses were doing so well and were the envy of all who saw them. A display with them could only lead to more demands and higher prices. Yes, Lord Robert mused, they would put on a grand country show to gladden the coldest heart. The princes would not be disappointed in his place.

For a moment his face fell, for it was not yet five years since his good Tom, the horse-master had died. He groaned inwardly. For Tom had been a friend as well as a bondsman, he missed him even now. His first thought had been to summon Tom to talk over the plans with him. They had been through so much together in their lives, since boys. Then his face softened as he thought of Karina and the children.

"Robert!" Tom had never called him that before, always "sire," or "my lord". "Robert!" Struggling to speak, gasping for breath, his face contorted with pain. "Look after them?" a huge effort, pressing his hand, soft blue eyes staring into his, desperate.

"I will, my friend. As my own, good Tom, be sure I will. But courage, courage!" He pressed the urgent hands in his. "We shall get you home and get you well in no time, you'll see." But he was stopped short by a terrible gurgling from Tom's throat. Rich red blood flooded from his mouth in a torrent and the soft eyes glazed over in death.

"Oh God! Oh sweet Jesus!" Lord Robert had held his old friend fast in his arms, mindless of the blood which stained his fine jacket. "God take you and keep you always, Tom," and wept.

They drew him away from the body, washed him down as best they could, and murmured words of comfort. For they were all shocked. Tom! Not Tom, the best of men, as well as being the best horseman in the place, crushed by his own horse. How had it happened? A slip. Soft earth on a bank, and over they went, with Tom underneath. God take his soul. They carried him home on a rough-hewn stretcher covered with Lord Robert's cloak.

Karina had stood straight, her face cold and shut, as they laid him at her feet. This was the last one from her old life. Without a word, she indicated that they carry him down to their little house, there with his keening sisters to lay him out.

By the time the children were weaned, Karina and Tom had remained in the castle, together with Robert, as a family. The children had grown well, reared by countless nursemaids, one mother and two fathers. Both children ran and clung to Robert or Tom, whichever was closest, as their own. Yet both of them were Karina's children. Not only had she nursed them till they were over a year, she always had them by her, asking the maids for help only when necessary.

Karina was now full grown, a small slender woman, with an unusual and exotic beauty. Her eyes, like her grandmother Kareen'ala, contrasted so blue against the rosy glow of her skin. Her oval face was framed by red-black curls, which kept escaping from her head-cloth. She always wore fine, yet plain clothes, never putting on airs and graces because of her position as foster-mother to the little lord. Karina belonged now. Her origins were barely known, yet everyone, even knowing that she was a foreigner, liked and respected her. She was one of them. Yet her remarkable, un-English looks, made her stand out in a crowd.

Strangers noticed her, intrigued by her unusual beauty. They were perplexed too by the children at her side. The pretty little blonde maid had soft blue eyes and was tiny, while the dark-haired boy had hazel eyes and was tall and handsome. They were so different and appeared not to be related. Yet they both addressed the woman as "mama" while behaving as siblings, ever squabbling. If the strangers had bothered to ask a local, they would be fascinated by the story told. For it was obvious, that she was not a poor woman by her simple clothing, which was the best quality. The children too were, in contrast to most of the town's little ones, very well clothed. When it became known that the boy was young Lord Rupert, and that the lady was his foster-mother, they were impressed and gave her respect.

Karina loved her children with a great passion. Her little daughter was a delight. So like Tom, or perhaps, even his foster-sisters, she never tired of gazing at her, so fair and so different from herself. For Margaret really was a very pretty girl with yellow curls and flower-blue eyes like her father. Of the two, Margaret had been the clever baby. It was she who had crawled and walked first, she who had mouthed the first words. Rupert, a plump easy child, had sat, smiled, lifted his arms to be carried, and been totally idle. While his foster-sister had sped about, he had watched entranced, then yelled to go with her. The nursemaids had of course spoilt him totally, which had enraged Karina, who intervened whenever possible.

"How?" she had fiercely asked Lord Robert, "will your son ever walk or talk when he has these slaves running to do his every bidding?" Robert had smiled in his lazy way, amused at her fury.

"He will walk, Karina! He will talk! Then we shall have no peace, you will see." And he was right. A big lad, when Rupert finally got to his feet, he was as a charger, his one aim in life to torment his foster-sister till she screamed.

"Father, father!" the little Margaret rushed to him all too often, climbing onto his lap, plump arms twined about his neck. "Save me, save me!" Holding her close with a grin, Robert would fend off his robust son with his spare arm till someone could be found to distract him. It was a delight kissing the little wench too, his Goddaughter, his foster-daughter, daughter of his heart indeed. Great blowing kisses in her sweet neck brought forth such squeals and giggles, it was impossible not to laugh too. Even before Tom had died, the little girl had loved him, going to him as much as her own father. Then too Rupert had loved Tom. It had been a gentle and happy little family, the children growing up deeply loved and supremely secure.

"Shall I," Karina had stood before him, after Tom's funeral, her lovely eyes hooded, "return to my own house now he is weaned?"

Robert had been horrified. Go? Break up his lovely little family? Very firmly he had forbade it. It would be terrible for all of them. Having lost Tom, would she separate the children? Would she deprive them of their living parents? So life went on much as it had, they all missed Tom but with time, the humdrum days passed serenely as of old.

Karina had made the old tower into her home. With a door leading into Philippa's garden, she was happy with the rooms, which were private, being apart from the main castle buildings. The top floor became their everyday room as well as bedroom for the children and nursemaids. The room below Karina took for her own, an extravagance, a whole room to herself, but whenever extra guests came, she moved up to sleep with the children.

"May I cut up some of Philippa's clothes for the children, Robert?" she asked, a frown on her face. With the royal visit, she had so much to do, and feared that already the weavers and warehouses in town would be stripped of the best cloth. So she did, carefully choosing the finest of the good strong dresses, cutting them generously so that they would last if the seams were left big enough. The maids of the castle helped her, for they too were so excited. Everyone worked diligently and the castle looked bright and magnificent with all the hangings and the silverware gleaming on the sideboards.

Some of the manors sent staff to help, more cooks and servers for table. Wagon loads of produce had rolled into the town, the best carried up to the castle, there to be stored in the deep, cold buttery for the royal guests.

Robert had instructed the chamberlain that his room, the finest, must be given to the princes. It was, as with many castles, a muddle of additions, yet there were, if they could be cleared and cleaned, plenty of rooms for their guests and their attendants. Karina went in with the children so that Robert moved into her room in the old tower where, if he needed to, he could escape from the crowd. The tempo increased as the great day approached. Two little boys from a nearby manor were sent to learn about being pages and shadowed Lord Robert, always ready to run messages swiftly, here and there.

With a great fanfare and blowing of horns, the princes were welcomed to the town, then up, and into the castle. Karina and most of the women leaned over the battlements and light-heartedly sprinkled flowers as their highnesses entered. A beautiful afternoon with sun and blue skies, it promised a good omen.

Dressed in their new clothes, Karina led the children to the great hall as evening was falling. Sconces and brands lit the vast open space and it hummed with talk from many guests. Standing them on a bench by a pillar, Karina craned to see if all was well at the high table. She could just see Robert, who sat between the princes, looking very fine in his new clothes. The princes were handsome young men, not dark or fair, but in every way, middling. They were very finely dressed in silver and gold brocade and quite outshone the whole party.

"See," she whispered in their ears, "on either side of father?" The children stood on tiptoe on a bench. "They are the princes who have honoured us with their company."

After a moment, whether deliberate or not, Rupert slipped and made a grab at Margaret, who with a cry, fell to the ground. Cross, Karina reached over to retrieve her daughter who escaped her and raced away, intent on fleeing from her brother. Then they were off! Margaret in front, scurrying, peeping over her shoulder, speeding along, between the rows of tables, followed by the clumsy Rupert who had clambered down, pulling away from Karina's grasp.

Robert frowned as he was half-alerted to a disturbance at the end of the hall. Looking up, he unconsciously put his hand to the dagger at his belt.

The commotion was drawing nearer. Heads were turning, hands reached out, faces broke into smiles and all craned to see what was happening.

The princes were alerted too and looked enquiringly at their host. The guard crowded closer, for even in these peaceful times, you had to be careful. Suddenly a tiny maid scrambled out from under the board in front of the high table, and with surprising dexterity and despite her skirts, she was up on the dais.

"Father! Father!" and frantically made her way under the board between the fine tunics and hosed legs of the diners, up into the lap of Lord Robert.

"Save me, save me father, for Rupert is close behind."

A great laugh went up followed by light applause. Arms tight about Lord Robert's neck, the little lady gazed about, searching for her tormentor. Laughing, Lord Robert tried without success to prise away the little arms. Grinning at his guests, he shrugged his shoulders as his son emerged dishevelled, by the same route Margaret had taken. A castle soldier swept him up grinning, and placed him in front of the royal party.

"Well Sir?" Robert tried to look fiercely at his son, whose fine clothes were all covered with bits of the strewn herbs from the floor. "Do you even now torment your sister?"

The princes smiled at each other, liking the informal interruption. The handsome lad glowered, disappointed. As usual, she had been too fast for him. Another distraction alerted them. All eyes shifted to a beautiful young woman, who hurried up, face stern and firmly took the boy by the arm. Then seeing the princes' eyes on her, she hesitated and sank low.

"Karina," Robert called to her. "Come forward madam. Let me present you to their royal highnesses." Karina curtseyed low again, her hand still firmly holding Rupert's sleeve.

To the princes he said quietly, "This will need some explaining Sirs, for as you see, the rascal there is my son, yet my lady wife died at his birth. Margaret here," he naturally kissed the soft little cheek so near his, "is not mine. The Lady Karina was my wife's good friend. They were almost delivered together, so that when my lady died, Karina fostered my son." The princes smiled, liking the story and the unusual exotic beauty who stood before them. "More I will tell you later Sirs, for hers is a long and most interesting story."

Later that night when the children were asleep, Karina sat in the garden with three of the maids, discussing the evening, all too excited to go to bed. So it was that a message came to the tower for the Lady Karina to clothe herself finely, and to join his lordship and his royal guests in the solar. Eyes wide, hands fluttering over her mouth, Karina looked aghast at the maids who had suddenly stopped gossiping. She had been summoned! Oh and oh! Seeing their mistress's uncertainty, they quickly took control, eyes shining. Hurriedly going to a chest, sorting then pulling out a sumptuous gown which had belonged to Philippa, they dressed Karina in it.

Although she could never be as thin as her old friend, and albeit a little tight, the gown fitted well enough. Pulling her box from under her bed, Karina dipped her hands into the jewels which were never used. Clapping their hands, the maids pinned and hung them, pushing rings on her fingers, bracelets on her arms till she sparkled like a morning cobweb. She looked magnificent. The deep green dress set off her hair, which was adorned with jewels. Her breasts were pushed up, the soft apricot skin pulsing under the glowing pearls. The maids were entranced as they helped her down the steep spiral stair, holding up her skirts, and kissing her, they pushed her into the solar.

All talk stopped as she quietly entered. Twice she curtseyed to the princes, who had stood up and bowed low. Robert gazed in disbelief at the vision of loveliness before him and ordered a chair forward.

They spoke in French, pleased with her accent and with the change of conversation. For being late, they were weary, and men's talk had become tiresome. Robert told how he had met her, a little thing astride a fine Arab mare. How she had virtually saved them with her beautiful horses and fine stores, and how, at their first meeting, she had gifted him with a falcon. The princes listened fascinated, while the two reminisced of their journey. Occasionally asking questions, they went back to her childhood, and Karina tried to recall her life before the earthquake. With the good wine, and pleasant company, Karina found herself relaxed, speaking unusually freely to the two princes.

Tired, surprised and pleased with the unexpected course of events, Karina slowly climbed the narrow circular stairs and taking a shawl, sat under the bower in Philippa's garden. For she saw that the maids were asleep with the children and she wondered how she would manage to undress.

Having dismissed his man at the bottom of the stairs, Robert came into the garden quietly. He knew she would be here, for he had peeped into the room she shared with the children and seen the sleeping forms. A moon came out intermittently from behind scudding clouds giving some light. Some night flower gave scent, and a small owl called. It was damp, with a dew falling, so he pulled at his cloak and drew her close under it. Taking her hand, he kissed it.

Why, he thought had he never noticed her beauty before? But he had noticed her, every day, no one could not. The gentle, firm, capable Karina could never be overlooked. Wife and widow to Tom, mother to little Margaret and to his son, she was more than special. Very gently lifting her face, he bent his lips and pressed them softly on hers. His blood stirred. Tired as he was with the chaos of the past days of frantic preparation, he felt a great desire for this familiar little woman who was as a cygnet changed into a swan.

"Come, my lady. Let me help you disrobe, for the maids are all asleep and I do not think you can spend all night so tied up, or indeed sleep out here."

Down in her room, he stood her before the narrow window to get what moonlight there was. Somehow the gown came off, the petticoats, the stays and the jewels. Pushing her gently onto the bed, he stripped himself, dropping his fine clothes in a heap on the floor, and naked as she, slipped under the sheets beside her.

"You are so beautiful, Karina!" Hands and mouth explored the silky, sweet skin. Surprisingly, for he was a lord and could take what he wished, he whispered in her ear. "May I love you, lady? Will you have me, for I find that I desire you greatly."

Smiling in the dark, Karina moved closer to him and breathed in his man smell. Oh but how she had missed Tom and his gentle loving. How her body had ached to be loved. Strange that she had never looked at Robert in this way before. Always there, father and protector, she had never thought of him as a lover. Now, her breath suddenly short, she twined her arms and legs about him in welcome and gave herself to him willingly.

The visit was a great success and without exception everyone congratulated themselves. Robert was more than happy, his easy manners and winning smile infecting everyone. He again told Karina's story, ever more embellished, to the princes and their courtiers. They were charmed and enchanted by her and Robert felt his desire rise, coupled with pride when they exchanged smiles. So near, so far. They shared a few precious hours every night now, but the days were crowded with duties. Robert could not remember this strange and exciting feeling which coursed through his veins. His marriage with Philippa had been loving, but love, passion, desire? He could not recall any of those emotions for a moment. Whenever the party was in the castle, he summoned Karina and the children, for they were a delight and an entertainment. Having never been much of a ladies' man, Robert feasted his eyes on a newly beautiful Karina. His Karina, his own lady who each day seemed more lovely, and each night came to him with exquisite passion. He was so proud, for the princes and all his guests were not only charmed with her, they were truly amused with the children. They were, he realized, seeing them with fresh eyes, such a funny little pair, so different, so lively, if quarrelsome. Yet when Rupert tripped and fell, it was the little Margaret who sped to his aid, comforting him, just as her mother would.

Of course it was the greatest honour, yet his heart sank as the princes requested his company on their travels. That night he held Karina in his arms, spending himself in her as if there would be no tomorrow.

"Just when I have found you," he thumped his fist into the mattress, "I must leave you!"

His boxes packed with good travelling food and spare clothes, Lord Robert rode off with his men beside the princes with a bright face and a heavy heart. From Philippa's garden, Karina hung a great cloth over the battlements so he could see it for miles, and know that she was there, thinking of him. Little did they know that it would be a full year before he returned.

They returned at night, three men, out of the ten who had left on that bright day. It was not only skirmishes and battles which took two. One died probably naturally, for one morning he lay cold and stiff having been hale the previous day. Two more drowned when they forded a great river, being swept away by the current and the last two just disappeared.

The nightwatchman heard their approach and called down, asking who they were. Sending a boy scurrying to alert the chamberlain, he unbarred the gate and let them in. The hearth was blown up, water set to heat, and food was hastily served, for they had received no warning. Yet Lord Robert seemed quiet and grateful to be home and had no complaints, just wishing to get to his own bed again.

After he had left, Karina had became sad and lonely. Without a woman friend, there were only the little maids to speak with and their chatter was always inconsequential. One woman was different however, quiet and shy. Barely offering any opinion, Mistress Chamberlain was always there to help her. Karina soon realized that it was the two children who attracted her, for she was with them whenever possible. Slowly her story came out. Poor woman, her three little ones had been taken in an epidemic, and since then she had borne no more.

Glad of her kindness and her knowledge, Karina began to leave them with her, occasionally going to ride her old mare, just to get away from the castle. Sometimes she joined the huntsmen when they sought out fresh meat in the winter, loving the crisp hard ground, the hoar frost, her own and her mare's breath steaming in the cold air. It was a quiet friendship, centred around affection for the children. Mistress Chamberlain, whose name was Claire, would never be the delightful friend that Philippa had been, yet she was a companion.

Disturbed by the summons to her husband, Claire lay, wide awake waiting for the dawn. She must then go to Karina to tell her of the lord's return, prepare and dress her fittingly. For as most women, she loved romance, and it had been quite obvious that Karina sorely missed Lord Robert.

Creeping into Karina's room, she opened the shutters and turned beaming toward the bed.

"Stay here will you?" Karina pulled off her shift and struggled into her clothes, all clumsy with haste. "Have you seen him yet? Is he well? What time did he get in?" She was babbling in excitement, tightened her bodice firmly and took up her bone comb. "Oh Claire, what good news, thank you for coming to tell me."

Satisfied and pleased, Claire took the comb and tried to work quickly through the beautiful dark tresses without pulling.

He was still asleep, lying on his back, arms thrust out over his head. Karina looked at him in the half-light of morning and sighed. He had grown terribly thin. She did not know how long she sat, but eventually, feeling her gaze, he stirred and opened his eyes. A slow smile lit his face and reaching out he drew her to him.

"Ah, my Karina, is it really you? Or is it a dream?" Climbing onto the high bed, she lay beside him and touched his face with kisses.

"Welcome home, Robert," and snuggled close, holding him till he slept again.

It was well nigh midday by the time he rose, and finding himself alone, called down the stair for water and fresh clothes.

It was as if the castle had its soul back, for suddenly it was all life and bustle. Each member of the staff felt glad to be back in his proper work, instead of passing the days in semi-idleness. Word was sent out to the outlying manors to inform the knights that their lord was home and to summon squires and pages to attend him. The kitchens came to life, messages being given to the grooms to go forth to order fresh supplies for his lordship. Tasks which had been put off for lack of courage were now swiftly completed. The great place hummed with life, and everyone was happy again.

"We will wait up here until Lord Robert chooses to visit us," Karina insisted. "He is very tired, and it will take some days for him to settle in, patience children!" Of course they had not really forgotten him, and now were eager to see him again.

Karina had made many changes during her year alone and Philippa's garden was now an extension of their quarters. She had directed the masons to build a family room with broad glass windows onto the doorway to the long walk. Here she had made one end a kitchen with a fine hearth. With water from rain butts, and drains to take away the waste, it was comfortable and convenient. Here she, the maids and the children spent much of their time. For the climb up and down the steep stairs of the tower had been irksome, except if for a special occasion. The glass, which she bought with her own money in the town, caused the big room to be light and hearing of it, many folk came to see and visit. So if they did not go down to enjoy the life of the castle and town, it came up to them.

With a loom in the corner, and one of the new spinning wheels which a merchant had been gratified to sell her, they were busy all in the one place. Not that the children were without entertainment, for they were often taken down by Claire, the wife of the chamberlain, and the maids to ride their ponies or to wander in the town. It was Claire who controlled this activity, asking around if any illnesses were abroad. Only if she deemed it clear and healthy of ills did they venture down, even to the wharf, a special treat.

"Oh do take them down to the hall," directed an exasperated Karina. "Let them find him. If he is tired, he can always send them back." With no second bidding Claire, the maids and the two overexcited children were off, leaving Karina quiet for once, with her thoughts.

It wasn't till late that night that Robert found her. She was calm, yet tremulous, knowing that he would. He gazed at her propped up in her bed, the soft light of a candle being all the illumination there was. Her hair was loose, and a soft shawl lay about her shoulders. They smiled at each other, the quiet, sweet smile of lovers glad to be together again.

"I have something special to show you my lord," she patted the bed beside her. "Come. See!" and lifted the shawl to expose her breast where a baby suckled steadily. "This is Thomas. He is three months old."

Robert gazed in disbelief at the little thing and tentatively stroked the dark hair with a finger. Karina wanted to laugh, but restrained herself, just smiling broadly.

"You will see him better in the daylight, but there is little need, for if you see yourself in a mirror, he is there."

"Mine?" the word struggled out.

"Yours!" she whispered, then laughed, "of course!" as somehow, he managed to embrace her.

In the morning, his fatigue suddenly gone, Robert took his new little son to the window and gazed at him. Yes, she was right. Although Rupert was like him, his eyes were hazel from Philippa's brown and his blue. This one had the bluest eyes and look! He was smiling at his sire!

Karina showed him their new day room, solar and kitchen together. Walking ahead of him, she showed him the drains and privy and fine windows and he was impressed as she led him about proudly. It was a long, wide and handsome room, airy with good views and the garden, albeit smaller, joyful with colour all about.

"I found this pregnancy more hard than with Margaret," she explained. "He was born a big boy, perhaps larger even than Rupert. And I thought to make these improvements, to make life easier. It was also, I confess, a diversion, for I so missed you, and for what was the use of all that money sitting in the chest?" She stopped and faced him, looking up at him, she being much shorter than he. "You are not angry my lord, that I did all this without your consent?" Yet she need not have worried. Ever an easy tempered man, he was pleased with everything, not least their new child.

"I am determined not to go away again Karina." He sat by a window and looked out over the battlements to the town far below. "It was an arduous time, I am no longer a young man, I grow older. In the future, I will serve my king by providing men and arms, but I will no longer go with them. Now I will enjoy my home and my family. For which I will hold many masses to thank God."

Robert was especially pleased with his new son. This one was like him, he saw the good features and colouring which daily looked back at him from his silver mirror. Of course Thomas was a baby, of course he had no beard. But the eyes! And that winsome smile! He was glad that Karina had chosen not to have him baptized in his absence, so he wrote to his cousin the duke, begging him to do the honour of being Godfather.

It was arranged that they would all go to the duke's seat downriver, there to have the baptism, and spend some days being easy and discussing matters of the world. Robert was pleased by the invitation, and quickly arranged their journey.

"I wonder if there is a good jeweller in the city, Robert?" Karina asked absently. "My jewels seem outdated and strange compared with the duchesses. Perhaps I shall take them with me so that they may be broken up and re-made?"

The baby was baptised Thomas John, his second name being the duke's. He was a really good child, easy, smiling, and was a great success with the ladies in that court. Meanwhile Rupert and Margaret were barely seen for the excitement of the new place, the great city, the sea, not forgetting new friends.

Karina approached the duchess concerning a jeweller.

"I suppose the gems and gold are good," she said, "but the workmanship is a little crude. What do you think my lady," holding out some pieces for the duchess to look at. "Don't you think that having them re-made is a nice idea?" The duchess agreed. The pieces were interesting, perhaps a little too flamboyant. They would go to see her goldsmith on the morrow.

Karina was astonished to find that the court goldsmith was a woman, but when she saw her work, she was much impressed. Mistress Scrivener had her own workshop, which had been her father's, the goldsmith, who had died some years before. Two handsome young sons first brought out chairs for them to be seated, then trays of jewels for her to look over. The lady goldsmith's old mother offered them wine, and was pleased to speak in French with them.

"Well now you have something to look forward to Karina," said the duchess when the deciding was over. "Deborah is always an astonishment to me, for she is an artist in her craft. We are so lucky to have her."

They made to leave when the old mother approached Karina.

"Excuse me lady, I become rather deaf, but did I hear her Ladyship call you Karina?"

Taking the old hands in hers, Karina drew close and spoke clearly.

"Yes, mistress, Karina is my name, unusual, but then I came from far away, only to arrive in this land many years ago as a young girl."

The hands tightened and drew her closer.

"Karina? Little Karina, who mother and I made gowns for, when she became a woman, who, when she left, gave us two fine buckles?" Putting a foot out, she pointed to her shoe.

Karina trembled, yet the hands held her even more tightly. "Are you Karina, who was so generous to my dear husband when you left? Are you the little Karina who my Doume´ so loved?"

The words tumbled out then between tears and kisses.

"Louisa, oh Louisa, is it really you?" A reunion so moving and tender, the others in the room left, feeling that these two long-lost friends must be quiet together.

After that, during the days which followed, the Goldsmith family often sat with the ladies and once again reminisced and caught up on news about each other.

"You should marry your lady, cousin," said the duke watching them. "If ever I saw a good wife, she is one." And Robert heard and put it away in his memory.

When Thomas' godfather the duke died, they once again travelled downriver to attend the ceremonies. It was his first memory of being a grown-up boy, for he was sombrely dressed and walked with the duke's family behind the bier. His cousin, the new duke, was a tall, dark young man with deep, penetrating eyes. He, and his brothers, favoured their mother's side, while their one and much younger sister was fair and took after her father. At one point during the ceremony, he saw her weeping, so he put his small hand into hers and she squeezed it, giving him a watery smile.

Although he understood the sadness of the occasion, his own little world would be rocked by an event unrelated to death. Due to the funeral, many guests were staying in the great castle on the hill, and he rarely saw his brother Rupert as he was happy mixing with young fellows of his own age. One day his father sent him to find Rupert, for they were to get ready to leave for home.

They were playing some ball game in a court, as quietly as they could of course, in respect for the dead duke. Thomas stood and watched them, trying to catch Rupert's eye.

"Who is that handsome little lad, Rupert?" called out one of the boys, "he seems to want you."

Rupert looked across at his young brother in irritation, just when he was enjoying himself.

"Oh, he's just one of my father's bastards," he replied, his voice ugly, "don't mind him," and got on with the game.

One of father's bastards! Shocked, Thomas did not move. Well of course he knew what bastards were. Whenever one of the hunting dogs bred where it shouldn't, the puppies were put into a pail and drowned. Suddenly he felt a great roaring in his head and scampered away, the world going black, to slide down to the ground just around the corner and out of sight.

A bastard? Rupert said he was one of father's bastards. He wondered how many others like him there were, perhaps they had been drowned, only his mother wouldn't let anyone drown him.

"What is wrong with him?" asked Robert, as they lay in the barge going home. Feeling his little son's head and noting that it was cool, "Perhaps it was all too much, perhaps it was a mistake to bring him?"

For days he lay on his truckle bed in his mother's room. For days he could not speak, the sorrow and fear swirling about in his head with his brother's words. "Oh, he's just one of my father's bastards."

They took it in turns to sit with him, his mother, his sister, Mistress Chamberlain or one of the maids. They brought him all his favourite foods, urging him to eat, to tell them what ailed him. Yet he just lay there staring at the ceiling. His world had tumbled down.

"Now, Thomas my boy," his father hauled him up and, sitting on Karina's great bed, held him on his lap. "Will you tell me what ails you, my little son? For we are weary of worrying about you and wish to know the reason for your malaise in order to cure it." The child had been silent and not eating for four days. Something had to be wrong, for he was usually such a sunny little lad. He glanced at Karina who stood nearby, her face drawn with worry and lack of sleep. "Tell me, what worries you, my little son, tell me please?"

Thomas loved his father, and hearing his words, "my little son", leant into the safeness of his body. Surely, surely father wouldn't have drowned other little sons, even if they were bastards. With a great sigh, he asked.

"Why didn't you drown me too?"

Robert's eyes opened wide in surprise. What was the boy speaking about?

"Why should I want to drown you Thomas? Who else do you think I have drowned?"

There was a small silence while his parents looked at each other in alarm.

"Rupert said that I was one of your bastards. So I thought you had drowned the others, like the grooms do the bastard puppies."

Robert's first instinct was to bellow with laughter. Then it hit him, and a cold fury swept through his whole body. Carefully laying the child back on the bed, he turned to leave the room. Eyes blazing, he held up a hand to stop Karina from speaking.

"I will deal with this myself, madam," his voice was harsh. "Stay with our son while I go to deal with my son. Do not," he raised his voice, "interfere."

A great silence hung over the castle for several days, the maids whispering and scuttling about trying to be invisible. Robert spent many hours with his little son playing board games, or telling him stories about his travels, and of how he met his mother Karina when she was a little girl.

Slowly, normality returned, except that it was quieter, for Rupert had been sent to a great castle far away, to learn manners, so his father said.

The next big thing which happened, Thomas remembered joyfully all his life. His parents were wed, a great wedding ceremony with Margaret and he standing with them under a great cloth of gold in the church. It seemed it was an especially joyful occasion, for everyone seemed so happy, and they all received many wondrous gifts.

"Now you and Margaret are our children. You are no longer a bastard Thomas, for so says the church." He held his son in a great bear hug. "I have no other children, legal or otherwise but for you three, and you are my most precious one," he whispered, kissing him roundly, "funny one, as if I would ever drown you!"

CHAPTER TEN

DAVID

Perhaps a thousand miles away or maybe many hundreds, another root of the family must be told of.

At last the path levelled out, so the strain of hanging on to his big wooden saddle grew less. Then finally, after what had seemed eternity, they reached the top.

"Rest now, young master," said the rough voice of his guide beside him as he pulled at him to get him down. It was a remarkably big mule, and David tumbled down into the old man's arms, then found his feet. It was deep night, with no moon, and he had almost slept the past hour or so, whilst the powerful animal had toiled on, following the others.

"Trust him," his father had said, "as I do," and David had supposed, rightly, that his father had at some time helped this man. "It is essential that you reach home as quickly as possible, for you have much to do. It is a hard journey, but cuts off two days by going over the mountains."

It had been many years since David had travelled to the city to see his father. Times were bad, his father's people were always in trouble, so it had been directed that they had no relationship. He had watched his mother sorrowing silently, and as ever, wondered about the marriage of his parents. Now at least he knew, for the first, and as his father had hinted, maybe the last time, for they had spoken. Man to man. The pain lay heavily on his heart. Why did life seem so complicated? Why could they not just be?

It had been a day as ordinary as most. He had been down to the port far below the village and seen the copper-skinned captain, collected their goods together and sent them off as usual by pack mule. On his way back to the village he had stopped at their fields and spoken to the workers, gathered a few vegetables as was his habit, and taken his time in the noon heat, to get home.

His mother had been standing on the terrace waiting for him, and seeing her, he had hurried the last stretch. Always a quiet, serene woman, he wondered at the hands twisting in her apron and the unusual frown which now alerted him.

Only when he had left the vegetables with his mother-in-law and washed did he climb to the terrace to see her.

"Word came from your father." She was holding a tiny slip of paper in her hands, so he knew that it was urgent and that a pigeon had come. "You are to go to him immediately, come my son, get ready."

Generally, the mule trains came along the coast to the port and delivered any letters. Without fail, they exchanged small baskets, each containing three doves. He understood that his parents corresponded via the birds, but never knew more. Obviously this time he was involved, for it was the first time he was being sent for. She hovered as he washed down, squatting in a huge pottery saucer, Esther, his dearling wife, pouring jugs of water over his head, trying not to cry.

"I'll be back soon," he tried to reassure her. But she did not answer.

"Leave your horse at Carlos, the second inn, and take another. Pay him well to return it here, or he will lend it out and it will be ruined." She had packed a small bag of fresh clothes very tightly, and his mother-in-law, the cook of the family, had packed a basket of food.

The household consisted of women, except, he smiled, a touch of pride in his eyes, for his fine son Joseph. The second child was a girl, an adorable little daughter and now a third was expected. Truly he was blest, except that he had never understood his role in life, who he was, what and why?

His mother slipped a small packet into the secret pocket of his sleeve.

"Only remove it when you are with your father to give to him," she ordered quietly. "When you approach the city, there is a great inn on your left, perhaps you remember it?" He did and nodded. "Go round to the back where there is a small blue door surrounded by creepers, go in and wait."

It had all been a mystery, yet he had asked nothing. He had been sent for by his father, that in itself was quite out of the ordinary, and he knew he would get nothing out of his mother. If indeed she knew anything.

It had been a tedious journey, five days of riding on the poor roads in the dust and heat, for he had pushed himself as directed. The mule trains took seven, while most travellers took six, unless of course they were not in a hurry. He had enjoyed it in fact, an unexpected journey. It had been interesting seeing, observing, so many new sights and sounds. Almost all along the coast road, he had sensed and smelt Africa, far off, over the sea to the South. At twenty five, he thought he might have been fifteen years younger when last he travelled with his mother and they had stayed at the inn. He remembered his father most minutely, not unchanged from the father of his young childhood, who his mother even now wept for.

The tall, white bearded man had smiled kindly at him. (Oh my beautiful son, son born of love with my most precious wife.)

"Take care of this lady and her daughter," the voice had come softly. "Their husband and father has died. He was a close friend, I promised him we would care for them, and they will be safer out of the city, and will be companions for you."

So they had become a household of women, except for himself. It had been the easiest thing to woo and wed Esther, who was almost a sister, yet as his mother had explained, the same as he, of mixed birth, so it was clever to do so.

There had always been a mystery about his birth and his paternity. True, the women attended church as frequently as they should. True, he also went, but goaded by his mother, despite being utterly bored with it.

His life was regular and even. His work was to organize the goods which came over the water, to be directed to his father in the city. Mostly it was herbs for medicines, but there were other goods, and he never knew what it was for or why.

When he removed his hat, a welcome breeze ruffled his damp hair. It had been humid coming up, but now, nothing between this mountaintop and the sea, the air was cooler. He heard sounds of hay being munched and realized that his guide had tethered the animals and given them to eat. Now he was drawn by the wisp of a fire, and looked in the darkness for what he could do. But the man was used to his work and pushed him down onto some bundles.

"Rest," he ordered. "You still have a good way to travel tomorrow. Eat, drink, rest." A small wooden plate and horn cup were pressed into his hands. "I will keep guard."

As far as he knew, it was an uneventful night, although he knew that there were many wild beasts in the mountains. The tree under which he lay was small and scrubby, blown by the south wind into a grotesque shape leaning north, but like a roof, gave some shelter. His mind lively despite his aching body, he lay and tried to remember everything that had happened. After all, meeting your father and the rest of your paternal family, after so many years, was an event.

At first, he had not found the blue door. The inn was a chaotic and huge rambling place with much coming and going. Obviously the first, or last, inn, it was ever busy, and much used by long-distance travellers. A boy had taken his horse and another had taken his name. He had stood with his bundle and basket and gazed about at the turmoil. No one took any notice of him, so he prowled around the back until he saw a small flash of blue hidden in the vivid bougainvillea. Pushing the door open, he ducked under the low lintel. It was dim and cool inside. When his eyes had adjusted, he saw a table on which stood a jug of wine, some olives and figs in earthen bowls, covered with cloths. On one side of the small room there was a low couch, a brass ewer full of water and bowl beside it.

Pouring out water, he opened the basket and gave some to the birds who had not drunk since early morning. After washing as much of the dust off himself as he could, he sat on the couch, drank and ate. Despite intentions, tiredness with the habit of afternoon overcame him and he slept, only to be woken suddenly by a sound, aware that a figure stood over him.

In fright he tried to jump up but a firm hand pushed him down.

"Rest easy, brother," came a rich, low voice. "You made such good time, we did not expect you till this evening. I am sorry I was not here to meet you."

The figure before him was short and solid, a bearded young man, some years his senior, with dark eyes and a ready smile.

"You won't remember me," he extended his hand with a little bow. "I am our father's sixth son, Benjamin." He paused, scanning the upturned face before him. "I am so sorry we could not know each other before. Circumstances. For I always wished for a younger brother." He sat down on a stool. "If you are rested, we can go now, father might be home, and he is anxious to see you."

Silently they rode in file into the city, David casting his eyes left to right, drinking in all the strange sights. At last they wound their way through tiny back lanes till they came to a big door where Benjamin dismounted and knocked a tattoo. Silently it swung open and they entered a small courtyard massed with greenery. Dismounting his pony, Benjamin took the luggage in as David stiffly got down.

"I'll see to the birds now if you don't mind, they will need food and drink. I won't be long." He went away, carrying the basket, while a boy led away the horses.

David stood gazing about. He knew that he had never been here before. It was a strange, secret place, smelling of growing things and water. As he stood, he had the feeling that he was being watched from the darkness of a window. Evening was falling and a light hovered inside. Then a woman appeared holding a lamp, and quietly asked him to follow her.

Try as he might, he could not see her face, her head-cloth was so concealing. After she had shown him into a small room and lighted the lamps, she withdrew without a word.

"Who is she?" he had asked when Benjamin re-appeared. He found himself almost quivering to at last be meeting his mysterious paternal family. He gazed at his half-brother with barely concealed excitement. Benjamin smiled, his warm open face somehow familiar, even like his own.

"She is my," he corrected himself, "our, elder sister, Miriam. There is one more, just above me, Sara. Miriam is widowed now, so she and her children live with us, which is very nice because she is a good housewife and cares for my," again he cut short and smiled apologetically, "our father, very well." Then he frowned, his cheerful face worried. "Father is not back yet. We have difficult days, and we are always worried when he is late."

The door opened once again and Miriam came in bearing a tray. When she had left, Benjamin laid the table out, then turning to a small sideboard, took up a jug, offering to wash David's hands. Then he washed his own, and David heard prayers spoken, a sudden memory returning of his childhood, and the shadowy figure of his father. The food was delicious, and David ate heartily, suddenly aware of how hungry he was, and weary of packed or inn food.

They talked after that, Benjamin asking most of the questions, and during the conversation David learned that the goods he sent from the coast were for another brother's business.

"He is the only one in trade," explained Benjamin. "One is a teacher, and I and the rest work with father. We study and make up medicines, and gradually as father grows older, we are taking over his patients."

David liked this new brother. It was so good to talk, for he had few friends at the village, because somehow he was different with the habit of being kept close by the women at home, and busy while at the port with business.

"You probably know more about me than I of you," he remarked rather wistfully. Benjamin smiled again.

"I wish," David stopped, making sure he spoke the right words, "I wish to know you better." So Benjamin stopped smiling and stared into the flame of a lamp.

"We are in difficult times, brother. We seem always to be so, but now," he spread his hands extravagantly, "now they become well-nigh impossible." He shut his eyes tight, blinded by the lamp light. "I fear that very soon we may be obliged to leave this country, and find another, more easy on our people, to start again," then, very quietly, if to himself, "if such exists." Smiling once more he went on. "Father explained to me why you and your mother, and indeed why the woman of the late Rabbi Moses, are kept so far away from us. It is for your safety. You probably do not realize that here, our very lives are precarious. If it were not for our father's great skill as a surgeon, we would all either be dead or long gone from this place."

David frowned now, only half-understanding. He waited.

"At this moment, the duke is dying, his heir is childless and also not so well, and father is in attendance as usual. We are perhaps the last Jews left in the city, at least, the last unconverted."

They sat a moment in silence, and once again the door opened and Miriam came in, followed by a maid-servant who cleared the table. Looking at Benjamin, she spoke quietly, a strange tongue he did not understand.

"Miriam asks if there is anything else you want?" He shook his head and tried to catch her eye smiling, but she turned away.

"Please tell her that the food was truly wonderful, delicious." Which made his brother smile, as he passed it on.

"Perhaps then," Benjamin continued rising, "we had better go to bed, for it is late, and father has not come in yet." Now he crossed the floor and looked up at his tall, new, half-brother. "I too am glad to know you, David. I am sorry you were not here with me to grow up brothers, but our religion is so strict, I'm afraid," he coughed lightly. "When our father consorted with your mother, it was gravely disapproved of. Our people do not mix, it was not acceptable."

David watched the new brother/friend struggle to explain, sad but grateful that it had come out at last.

"Can you tell me any of their story, Benjamin? For my mother never speaks of it, though I know she deeply loves our father yet, and mourns her widow's life so far away from him."

This speech made Benjamin look up, a hint of surprise on his kind face.

"Well yes. I do not know much, for my sisters deeply disapproved and I just caught hints here and there." He leant forward and clipped the wicks of the lamps. "I understand that your grandfather, your mother's father that is, was a very fine herbalist who supplied my father for many years. Eventually some mistakes were made, so my father wrote complaining, most surprised. Then in time, it all came out when he visited your grandfather, and realizing his mind was going, so understood that your mother was trying to do all the work. Hence the mistakes, being young, and only home taught. Let us suppose that my father was lonely, my mother having died some years before, and as he guided her in their work, love grew between them. As much as he tried to keep it quiet, of course, in a place like this where there are eyes and ears everywhere, he could not keep it secret. I saw you once when you were a baby, for we went, father and I, to collect herbs from your mother, and I suppose he thought I was too young to understand. Yet I did. He was like a young man again. His eyes shone and he laughed as we rode along. It was outside the city and was a beautiful place, a house set within a high wall, full of herbs, flowers, bees and butterflies. And there was a lovely woman, who gazed lovingly at my father, always close to him. And you, who even looked like me and my siblings but with blue eyes. It was a precious memory, David, and young though I was, I understood. Hence over the years, I have supported my father as discreetly as I am able, for he deserved happiness, indeed now he does, for without him we would be long perished or gone, far away." He stopped, almost breathless and turned his smile warmly on his brother. "So there it is, David, brother. Now you understand why you were sent away, to be safe, not only from the prejudice of my own people, but from the authorities. I do know also that my father loves you and your mother most deeply." He paused, thinking, then went on in a rush. "Having seen what happiness a love match brings, for I watched two brothers and one sister suffer from their unsatisfactory arranged marriages, I insisted on choosing my own wife."

"And you are happy?"

"I am. She is as fair as you are, an artist and a musician, and as a plain little man," he grinned, "I have to say she has given me some very handsome, talented children." He rose, dusted his hands together and went across and kissed David.

"Sleep well. I will see you tomorrow. Leave one lamp, this one," he indicated a lamp with a good well, "God bless you brother," and was gone.

It had been a troubled night, a strange room, which because of his tiredness seemed to sway in time to the flickering lamp. Once he half woke, to find his sister Miriam leaning over him, a faint smell of cooking filled his nostrils while she looked at him intently while he lay stock still. Later another stooped figure, but by then he slept again, unaware that a shawl had been tenderly laid over him.

After he had bathed and changed all his clothing, they breakfasted together, he and Benjamin. The washing, praying ritual over, they set to with appetite. Fresh breads with honey and curd, preserved fruits, boiled eggs and watered wine.

"Come now, David, father is waiting for you." So with his heart pattering with anticipation, David followed through the dark low house till they came to an airy, sweet-smelling room. An old man rose and came to greet them, stepping forward, ducking to avoid the bunches of hanging herbs. Hands outstretched, for a moment, they gazed at each other, then suddenly, embraced close.

"Ah, David, my son, my son," the merest whisper. They stood thus for moments, and Benjamin, filled with understanding and love, quietly left.

They talked for a long time. Questions, answers; it seemed that at first all his father wanted to hear was about his wife, his love. The packet his mother had sent was accepted with reverence and tucked within a fold of his gown. Food was brought and after he had blessed it, the father watched as his handsome last-born enjoyed the good fare, happily complimenting it again, while he merely picked at it, in company.

"You will go back over the mountains, David, time is the important thing. If you can get home well before the messenger arrives, you can make preparations." The old man, who was his father, looked earnestly at the son. "It is a matter of days. The duke is dying. What happens after is in the hands of God. But we must be prepared, and do what we can for ourselves. If you do not hear anything, or if your mother ceases to have word from me, understand that the worst has happened. I have been prepared for it for a long time David, only I grieve for my family here, and wish I could send them to safety. I know I can depend upon you to help them if that day comes." He rose and ushered David out. "Rest awhile before you go," he ordered, and quietly shut the door and locked it.

Alone at last, the old man drew the little packet hastily from its hiding place. Carefully, the small piece of parchment was opened out with trembling fingers. Taking out an eyeglass he read:

"Slowly, how the years pass by.
When can I come? Together be
At last to hold thy hand and lie
Close, Safe, some hours with thee?"

The tears fell slowly down the old worn face while the thin shoulders jerked silently. He picked up the paper and pressed it to his lips, then, fearful that his tears might spoil it, dabbed at it with his sleeve. How empty he felt. How sad that he had sent her away, and this splendid son of theirs. Yet! Yet? He believed he had done right, which only time would tell.

But now, he cast around, he must reply to her beautiful letter, her poem of love. Finding a pen and paper, he saw her in his mind's eye and let the words flow.

That afternoon, when the day's heat was lessening, David set off again, a packet for his mother safe in his sleeve, a handsome basket bursting with food from Miriam. The leave taking was brief, not even intense. Somehow it had been enough to meet his father again, to share precious hours together; they both had a new peace, a peace which David wondered at.

Benjamin went with him as far as the single cork tree on a bend, where his guide had met him. Handing his horse to his brother, David had clasped his hand tightly, then mounted a huge mule. Without a word, the man had nodded to him to follow and turned off the road onto a track, up, ever up, a smaller mule following without a lead. Later, he had explained that the pony he rode was the mule's mother. It always followed her without question. His load seemed huge, but David later realized that it was merely rugs and sacks of hay with two wooden kegs of water to anchor it all down, hanging on either side. That night they walked till dawn, then unloading, slept, the animals tied up nearby with their hay. The day was hot, and they rode on with evening, silently up, ever up, till he no longer took notice of where they were going, his body aching with the strain. It seemed eternal, his journey through rock-strewn wilderness, parched earth and scrub trees. Quite different from the dusty, busy outward journey, where there was much to see along the way. That night it was cold, but he slept deeply.

"Wake!" he felt a shaking. "Wake, young master, for it will soon be dawn and you must go."

He had sleepily eaten the bread dipped in wine, dried figs and apricots from the basket, and drank his fill of water they had found in a clear spring.

"Attend please." The guide was kneeling on the earth, scratching a map in the dirt. The light still faint, David went on his knees too and tried to concentrate. The man explained, made David repeat everything three times, and grunting he rose. With just one more night to travel, he would soon come to familiar territory.

"Go with God, young master. Be careful, listen and if you hear any strange sound, hide and see what or who it is if you treasure your life. There are bad men in these hills. Put your hand over the mule's snout so he does not call out and wait till they are well gone before you ride on. Look out for smoke and dust and avoid both." Loading the bundles and the basket of doves securely onto the wooden saddle, he offered a stirrup with his hands, so David was hoisted up and rode away into the dawn.

The heat was crippling as the day progressed. David drew his hat down over his eyes, to try to avoid getting the sunshine right in them, for they were going due South. The mule however, ambled along at a good pace, with barely a nudge or pull at the reins to direct him. At one moment, David thought that he saw a dust trail ahead but to the West. As they were veering East, he kept on. Just once, having slithered down a steep slope, he found welcome shade, and so decided to stop and rest. First he saw to the birds, then, using his hat to dust out a hollow in a great rock in the dry stream bed, he half-emptied the keg of water out for the mule who gratefully drank it with all speed.

It was so tempting to stay there, laid out on a cool rock in the shade. He ate and drank sparingly, secretly rather afraid that if he lost his way, he would be very hungry before long. As far as the eye could see, there were dry, brown mountains.

As the day passed, they went ever downhill, and although the heat was greater, there was a breeze from the sea which he knew was there beyond the haze. With evening, he began to recognize landmarks along the coast which spread before him. He camped under a small cliff which gave him some small sense of security, and strangely, slept well. At dawn he watered the birds and mule, he hoped for the last time, he would soon find water, for the keg was empty, and after his own small repast, mounted and rode South. Now it became familiar, and heartened, knowing that the village lay far below perhaps just over the next brow, he encouraged the mule. Soon he saw the old palace on its great pinnacle of rock, but a deep gorge lay between him and it, which made reaching it directly impossible. Then at last, they came to the well, a fine row of stone basins built by a past lord where the flocks watered, but later, at nightfall.

Hearing voices, he was surprised to see some children, and when he dismounted, was shocked to recognize them as the children from the palace.

"Good evening young lord, little lady." He took off his hat and bowed to them. As courteously they replied, the boy bowing, the small girl dipping.

David looked at them in astonishment. They were not only in rags, they were filthy and barefoot. The only times he ever saw them was in church on big feast days, when they were dressed, as their mother, magnificently.

"Is your lady mother home young lord?" he asked.

Surprised, the boy paused, putting his water jar down.

"Yes!" he said abruptly. "Of course she is. But why do you ask?"

David observed the boy carefully. This was the middle one, the nicer one, according to his wife, who, as she occasionally sewed at the palace, as well as taking them herbs, knew them slightly. The elder son was reputed to be rather stern, undoubtedly conscious of his responsibilities as man of the family.

"I have just come from the city." He waved his arm to indicate he had crossed the mountains, "And I have a message for her."

"All the way across the mountains? Goodness," said the boy. "What, what message?" Which made David smile.

"For her my lord, not for you," and got a scowl for it, which he ignored.

First he washed his hands and face, then filled a bowl for the mule, but not too much.

"Shall you ride up to the palace? I think we can manage to put the water jars up also, if I unload. It will save your legs."

Now this was another story. Eyes alight, both children came and watched while he propped their full jars upright, unloaded his gear and set it behind a rock before hoisting them and their water up.

David patted the mule, asking forgiveness for this last lap and led him up the gorge towards the palace. He was shocked by the appearance of the children. Their clothes were in tatters, their skin burnt brown, their legs scratched and dirty.

"Is your well dry then?" he asked casually. The little girl nodded vigorously, her great dark eyes wide with the tragedy of it.

"Terrible, terrible," David said, "the worst thing ever, is to be short of water."

They plodded on slowly, careful not to spill the jars as they approached the faded pink walls of the palace.

It had been many years since he had been here. His mother had been frequently, most certainly, but he had somehow not been. He was shocked looking about, for it was all in ruins. Walls were badly cracked and had fallen, the lime-wash peeled. The roof tiles of the buildings had all slipped, and dust lay thick everywhere. As for the wonderful garden he remembered, there was none, just dried up weeds amongst the broken paving.

A great floppy-hatted figure came running to meet them and the children waved with excitement.

"Mother, mother, look, we have a ride." Quietening as the precious water slopped over them. As they came nearer, David realized it was the lady.

"Donna." He removed his hat and bowed low. It was simply not possible not to notice that she too had no shoes on, that her clothes were old, obviously made from sheeting, and that she wore a big, peasant apron. Her face however, when the hat was lifted, was as he remembered it, pale and beautiful. "Donna." He turned away to help the children down, carefully standing their water jars against a wall.

"He has a message for you," blurted the little girl, and smiled at David, with her beautiful eyes, feeling important having imparted the news first.

"He has come from the city," the boy cut in, "across the mountains. He has a message for you. Right across the mountains!" he ended high, incredulous.

David was shocked, but hoped he managed to hide it. Of course he knew that the lord of the old palace had been ill for years, since a fall from a horse. But that they were reduced to such poverty, he had not known. On the occasions they attended church, they seemed so richly dressed, so grand. Now he understood that their finery was left over from the city life, and probably only brought out for such occasions. He hurriedly tried to straighten his thoughts.

"Young lord, little lady," he caught their attention. "My poor mule has completed a long journey and just done you a favour and given you a ride. Please be kind enough to take him into the shade where he can rest, for he too must be very tired. In a little while, he and I must go down to the village to my home."

Off they went happily, dragging the even-tempered and tired mule, doing their bidding without fuss.

"A message from the city, Master David?"

So, she knew who he was. He looked around, and she understood he needed privacy.

"There is no one else here, sir, but come, let us sit, for I expect you will be tired." She led the way into the palace onto a great veranda overlooking the sea, which lay a vast and beautiful great panorama far below them.

To his surprise a couch stood against the balustrade and on it lay the lord, he who was ill, who his mother tended. Not knowing quite what to do, he bowed and muttered, "Good day to you my lord," and sat on the stone bench.

The lady had run swift-footed and was calling someone. Gazing out to the sea, David saw some tiny ships drawing near the harbour and realized that they were the fishermen coming home.

"The message, David?" The lady had returned and sat on the edge of her seat expectantly.

So in a firm voice, David told her everything his father had asked him to. That the old duke was dying. That the heir, their uncle, was himself ill, that they must be ready to return, she, her husband and their three fine, healthy children. This, he emphasised his words, to make sure that others did not intervene, jump in, try to take the duchy.

Without the hat, he saw that her hair was streaked with white, her lovely face was thin, and there were wrinkles in the corners of her beautiful eyes. Hand to mouth, she gazed at him in shock.

"What?" He noted how like her were the children. "What am I to do?" A tear glistened. "You see what we are sunk to. You see how desperately poor we are become. It is quite too much for me to bear to receive any visitors from the city. How can they?" she began to weep silently, holding her apron to stifle her cries. "They abandoned us here. Even the watering system has broken down!" and finally gave in to her sorrow.

"Elen, Elen," a soft voice came from the still figure on the bed. "My dear, what is it?" So she went across and sat and David was moved to see that the broken man so tenderly tried to comfort his wife.

An old woman approached with a tray and offered him water and a bowl of fresh figs. He guessed that the water was what he had just brought up now, for it was still cool. Then she went to the bed with a cup of fresh water and holding the patient, made sounds of encouragement, rocking as she did.

"When?" the lady asked, collecting herself. "When will they come, at the earliest?"

Again David told her what his father had said. At the earliest, six days from the moment of death, but he would have word by pigeon the same day, so had some time to prepare. Then, standing up, he announced the plans.

"You are our lord and lady, Donna," he began. "As we are your people, so are you ours. We are proud of you. If you become, as I believe you will, the new duke and duchess of our land, it will be a great privilege for us."

She was wiping her eyes on her apron, and the old woman and the lord were looking at him carefully.

"But just look at us," she blurted, "and this ruin," and began to weep again.

"Donna!" David raised his voice to get her attention. "By the Grace of God and your people, you will not be ashamed if anyone comes here in six days. That, I promise you. I and mine, and I trust every villager, will do our utmost to set all things right in that time. And," he smiled, "I think it might well be more than six days." He then leaned forward and gave her the plans from his father.

Elizabeth knew he was on his way for a pigeon had come safely to the dove house with a message from her husband. He had never been away so long from her, this one and only, precious son and she was gravely worried. She was standing on the highest terrace, hoping to see him.

The sound of hooves however, came up from the lane, then the gate was pushed and the familiar voice called.

"I am home!" So the women, his son and daughter ran to greet him, the servant smiling too, led away the mule while they clustered around the traveller.

Once again Esther stood over him weeping, silly girl pouring water over his head, rubbing his back with a cloth.

After they had eaten, all the while asking questions, interruptions so that David spoke more often than not with his mouth full, he went to the terrace with his mother. Esther and Grace took the children off to bed, so they sat in the gloom, waiting for the stars to shine.

"How was he?" she asked, almost fearful.

"So nice," replied her son. "So gentle, so kind, a wonderful man to have as a father." So that she smiled, and when he handed her the small packet, she in turn buried it close to her heart in the folds of her dress.

"But mother, I have urgent business from my father which cannot wait. Please go with the servant, go together. If the mayor sees you, he will know it is very important. Ask the mayor to come to speak with me, now. It is of utmost importance for all of us. The lord and his family, the village," he brushed a hand over his tired eyes and added softly, "and our family here and in the city."

While he waited, he rested, eyes shut, willing away the phantom sway of a mule, glad to be in his own home again.

"He is just finishing his meal, David," his mother returned very soon, for it was not a large village. "He understood the importance and will come immediately."

Then she sped away, taking a lamp to her room where she opened the packet with shaking hands and strained to read the letters there.

"Here take my hand
If even from afar,
Forget the trickling sand,
My love, my shining star.
My hope, our joy
Reminds me of blue eyes.
Our holy love, our boy.
Aye, how time flies.
Did I forsake you? Was I mad?
Can I forget with whom I lay?
Did we forsake us, for our lad?
Who I give thanks for every day.
Courage, hold fast my love,
And closely watch the sky
for thee and thine my dove,
Before the storm must fly."

Putting her head in her hands her shoulders shook. Why? A voice cried out silently. With a deep breath she pulled her shawl about her and silently went to place her latest treasure with the others in the secret drawer of her little chest. Tomorrow, and every day, she would read it. The final words had caught her attention. He told her she must watch for a dove with a message, and then they might have to flee. Well it was all prepared. She was packed, the essentials. Two captains had promised her safe passage for all of them. Now perhaps with a new duke, it might not be necessary. Composing herself, she walked back to her son, worrying, always worrying.

David briefly told the mayor, washed and changed into his best clothes, that it was almost sure that they would very soon be receiving very important visitors from the city. That they must clean and tidy up the village, and prepare for wealthy guests. More important was the palace up the hill.

"You see Don Mayor," David struggled to speak clearly despite his fatigue. "If we support and help, the lord and his family, they will never forget us. Don, have you been up there recently?" his voice anguished. The mayor shook his head, there was no need to toil up the hill. "Their poverty is terrible, Don Mayor. The children run bare foot," his loyalty to the lady prevented him from adding that so too did she. "They are in rags. The palace is falling apart." He leaned forward earnestly. "Let us call a meeting of the whole village first thing tomorrow morning and ask them to help. For it will be for all our benefit. If we fail them, we throw away a chance to improve our lives for all time, together with those in the palace."

The mayor surveyed the young man carefully. It must be true, all he was saying, for to ride over the mountains? What a dreadful journey, he had done it only once in his long life. At the same time he wondered if he should trust this young man who seemed always so distant and unlike the rest of them.

His mind veered back to the request. Well why not? The village could do with a good clean and paint, so he nodded.

Before the sun rose over the mountain the next morning, the mayor and David met in the square outside the tavern, if one could call it that. People began to assemble, intrigued. Something must be up, and as little ever happened in this place, they might as well at least listen.

Slowly, in a clear voice, David told them what he had heard. At no time did he mention his father or family, that would never do. He told them that all the talk in the city was of the impending death of the duke. That their lord up the hill was his second heir, and the first heir was poorly and had no children.

"We will receive a pigeon with the message when he is dead." The faces looked up at him, the morning sun lighting them. "Perhaps we shall then have six days at the most." A great sigh swept over the square. "You know I supply drugs to the city? Of course you do, some of you even supply me." A few heads nodded. "While delivering the last consignment, which was called for urgently, this news was whispered to me." He lifted his arms. "Friends!" They all rustled to attention. "We have the chance to improve our lives if we make a great effort for the messengers when they come. For there may be many, and they will be very grand and used to the very best of all things. We must entertain them as best we can. Give them shelter, feed them, and well," he shouted the last word. "If they are to escort our lord's family back to the city, after six arduous days on the road, they will need some days to rest before returning. Rooms my friends, surely we can sleep outside on the roofs for a few days. Clean and new-painted rooms with beds, clean and fresh hay in the mattresses, and your finest bed linen. Food my friends, the best we can manage. Not just bread and olives. We will send a message to the fishermen. Wine! Dig in your cellars my friends and charge those city slickers properly for they can surely afford it. Music?" He looked around. "Miguel?" There was a muttering and a thin girl was pushed forward. "Ah Maria, you are here. Where is your father?" The whispered reply was taken up and hurled at him. "Well someone find him." He snapped, searching in his mind, then his brow cleared. "Maria, you will sing, as you do so beautifully, while your father plays. I will here and now before our brethren, guarantee your father one jug of wine for every day of the year for ever more." He stopped and raised his finger. "If, he stays sober for the necessary days, and plays for us in the evenings, lunch time too if needs be, while we have the guests here. For no one," he raised his voice to hush the sniggers, "in the city, no, in the south of Spain, plays the guitar as does Miguel." There was light applause. David laughed. "I do hope my friends, that you will help me to supply him with wine for every day of his remaining life." There was then, a burst of laughter.

The priest came with a slate and sat at a table brought out from the tavern. They stood in an almost peaceful line, each to offer what he could, while the priest wrote it all down.

"To work my friends," David held up his hand for attention. "When the news arrives, my mother will hit her big dye pot from our terrace." A ripple of laughter tripped about the square. "Start work now, so it won't be too hard later. And don't forget, every last one of us will be rewarded, one way or the other, for our efforts. Good luck," he ended, making his way, shaking the odd hand, hoping that he was right and that he had got it into their thick heads.

David faced his women. He well understood that pregnant women were sometimes tearful, yet he felt impatience with his wife.

"We will have it all back my love," he entreated. "It will be just a loan. They have nothing, nothing," he sighed. "We have so much. Just keep what we will need, barest necessities."

So every chest and cupboard was emptied. Cloth for sewing was put to one side so that the Donna could choose, which the mothers would make into clothes for the lord's family.

Clothes which he had outgrown, put safely away by his careful mother for his son, were now brought out for the lord's sons. Hung out in the sunshine, brushed and sponged, with some added frippery, they would have to do.

"The cloth is not as fine as what they have in the city, but it will be understood as being practical and cool for country folk."

With the mule well laden, David and his mother made several journeys up the hill to the palace, small pieces of furniture strapped on. There were not enough hours in the day. Eyes were strained and fingers were sore, yet the women toiled on, somehow creating passably fine clothes for their lord and his family. It was quickly agreed that the palace children might be better staying in the village at David's house, for they were excitable and underfoot up there, where work had begun.

They were charming children, thrilled with everything new and the two little girls played for hours together, locked in another world of make-believe. David's old clothes were quickly enriched from those outgrown from the palace, which were stripped of every reusable decoration.

Twice the young lords accompanied David down to the port, there to take in the exotic smells and sights with barely concealed excitement. Sitting in the shade of a great grapevine, he treated them to a fine fish meal, with strange vegetable dishes, brought over the sea from the South. The three children were delighted with their new clothes, even if they were not indeed new, at least they were fresh and clean, which was more than were the visitors when they arrived.

At first, it seemed as if nothing was achieved, for throughout the village and in the palace, there was chaos. Many wished to work at the same thing and squabbled while David, the mayor, and in the village, the priest acted as intermediary. Slowly it happened with each passing day, until early one morning, the sound of a bronze dye pot being beaten alerted the village and galvanised them into more speed.

Six more days.

"Donna?" David stood at the doorway waiting for the lady to come out. She rose from where she was working and smiling, came swiftly, feeling as they all did, urgency in the very air.

"David! Thank you for coming. Yes it is working again, thanks to the sweet Virgin, God and your men, so we at least have plenty of water and work goes faster." She stood before him, a lighter, brighter woman than of a few days past. The little girl Magdalena, as her mother, rushed up to him. She had enjoyed being at his house he knew, and the new clothes were almost ready.

"Master David," she held out her hand to show him a shell. "Your Maria gave it to me. Can I keep it?" He smiled, glad that his little daughter was enjoying a new friend.

"If she gave it to you, Donna Magdalena, it is yours."

They watched, as with a radiant smile, she rushed away again.

"I am deeply indebted to you, David," the lady said very quietly. "Your mother has lent me all her wonderful linen and charming furniture. You have organized new clothes for all my family. The water is running again. The palace is clean and freshly painted," she stopped and looked out over the gardens. "Even the gardens are almost tidy," and sighed. "I will miss this place, David. However hard it has been, however bitter I have felt against the family for their neglect of us, I realize now that we will be leaving, that I have had much happiness here and I fear that my life in the city will never be so free and peaceful again." She turned to look at him again. "How can we ever thank you?" David dropped his eyes and did not reply. Yet she persisted. "When you have need David, whatever it is, remember this moment, this time, and ask. Whatever is in my power to do for you and yours, I promise, by the Cross, I will do it."

At last the lookout called from the hilltop. A great column of dust approached; they were coming. Renewed frenzy hit the village as a storm. They rushed, colliding, laughing and finished those last little jobs. Everyone hastily washed face, hands and feet and changed into their best Sunday clothes. Fires were lit and delicacies were made ready to lay on the hot coals. No spindle lay idle, as the women sat outside their freshly-painted little houses eager not to miss a thing. At last hushed, they waited as one, for the approaching host of visitors.

"I thought you said that this place was a dump," the dandy concentrated on paring his fingernails which had become filthy on the journey. Oh the relief being off that uncomfortable mule, sitting in the shade on a bench outside a pretty little village house, enjoying the sea breeze. He took an appreciative sip from the wine goblet beside him. His companion glowered at him. The vine trellis above them was laden with grapes, and the insects were humming in happiness as they leeched the sweet juice.

"It was I tell you. Of course it was years ago, when we escorted the young lord and his bride here. They must have worked hard to get it so pleasant, for yes, that is how it was I tell you, a slovenly place fit only for pigs." He scowled again, leaning heavily against a sturdy support of the vine arbour which shook it free of some ripe grapes. An immediate flurry of hens caught their attention, so in silence they watched as sharp beaks picked up the tasty morsels. Which they absently thought, might explain the delicious eggs. After that terrible journey, anything would be paradise. The roads! The inns! The food! Yet he had felt it might be clever to come with the escort, after all he had known the young lord in childhood. Even he did not seem so ill and hopeless as story told. Somehow it was all rather surprising. The peace and contentment of this far place, where they had been obliged to come, to claim and escort the heir from.

It had been as a dream to arrive in the late afternoon to find a freshly-painted, clean village where the people were kind and welcoming. Totally unlike every village they had stopped at during their journey here, for there had been no time to arrange any better. In comparison, this place was really almost paradise. Six days along a dusty road, where they had slept three to a bug-bound bed, eaten fresh-killed, stringy he-goat if they were lucky, and barely slept for the heat.

This, he thought, is how their country should be, beautiful, clean, vibrant, with good food, wine, and the music? Divine. How an old scarecrow like that could coax such wondrous sounds from his battered instrument, he did not know. An antique instrument, looking like a cross between a pumpkin and a great onion. Yes, it had been heaven, and his skinny daughter sang as a lark. Each little house had been offered for simple hospitality. True, they were sparse but clean, the wood and string beds freshly made with good country hand woven sheets, rough and delicious. The scent of jasmine swept over the tired group with the evening sea breeze. Exhausted, they had accepted the advice of the mayor to rest here for the night, while word would be sent to the palace of their arrival. He was very persuasive, the mayor, the lord must be warned of their arrival. Yes, they understood it would be better for everyone to go up there in the morning. They were even offered baths! Tasty and plentiful food was served, almost as if they had been expected. Which was of course impossible, for hadn't they come as fast as they could, and no one had overtaken them.

So they relaxed, enjoying the first evening, which was a delight after the nightmares preceding it. Again, politely urged by the mayor, they arranged for just the important few to stay at the palace, while for the following days the rest partook of the village hospitality. Even the horses rejoiced at being put out in little fields, to run free there, instead of being hobbled or shut in a filthy stable.

Then in the morning, they had trooped up to the palace, impressive and gleaming white on the hillside, and had been graciously received by the lady. True, the noble children had seemed rather wild, and their clothing was distinctly rustic. But no doubt it was practical being lighter-clothed in the summer, better than the elaborate dress of the city palace. Fortunately someone had thought to bring some chests of clothes with them, in which the lord and his family could be hastily fitted before returning to civilization.

They stayed for five days, charmed, rested, enjoying their little holiday in a far village, ever gazing at, and never tiring of, the magnificent view out to sea. When the time came for them to leave, it was almost with reluctance.

And it had been so cheap! The board and meals, the fish, so fresh, dripping in oil and garlic, so tasty. Not forgetting the wine and music, so nice to find such a natural place still. Such a shame it was so far away. Goodwill oozed.

"I hope we shall meet again, David," she said quietly, a twinkle in her eyes. "Do you know, I had forgotten how foolish they are," she tipped her head slightly towards the chattering throng. Leaning down from her fine horse, hiding her face under her wide new straw hat, she held out a handkerchief to him. "At this moment, as well you know, I have nothing else to give you. Yet mind this well, for if you are in need, send it to me and I will buy it back." His fingers about the cloth, David realized there was something hard within.

"No Donna," his hand still high, refusing the gift. "I cannot." But she brushed it away.

"It is all I have to give, all else was sold. I had it for my baptism, from the king I believe. It has my name on." She smiled down at him. "My daughter has a small copy of it, so I will never forget it. What you have done for us is worth far more, good David. So! Remember what I said won't you? I and my family will never forget you, yours and your service to us. Perhaps one day," she paused and made to gather up the reins, extending a hand, "never forget?" He kissed it and bowed.

Behind her the children crowded to say their farewells. The little girl was weeping, sat up in front of her elder brother, stretching her hands out to them. David's little daughter did the same, bawling loudly in return, causing smiles with her racket.

Joseph lifted up his sister as high as he could, and for a second, the little girls touched fingertips. Oh what tragedy to have found so sweet a friend, and to lose her so soon.

Both the young lords, proudly astride their new ponies, bent to take their hands in farewell. Lifting their hats seriously, they turned to leave without a word. Yet words were not important and David took off his hat and bowed with his son, his womenfolk dipping low, and surprisingly, all eyes glittered, blurring vision.

"Come and see us sometime, your graces," he called after them. But he knew they never would. He stood as they disappeared down the road, a sudden anticlimax filling him. Still, he had done his duty. And, somewhere along their conversations, he had given the lady the name of his father, without telling of the relationship, just that he was the court physician who sent pigeons when he needed medicines. She had looked hard at him, and he had held her gaze. Maybe she knew then. Well, perhaps it was a good thing. "Write us a letter if you need anything from here Donna," and laughed lightly. What was there here worth sending?

As they had arrived, like a flock of bright birds, so they went away. The dust and heat was fierce by the time the last had left, and as one, the village shut its doors and went to bed.

Handing the kerchief to his mother, he repeated the words. In the cloth, lightly stitched, Elizabeth found an exquisite gold and jewelled cross. David watched as his mother lifted it to her lips and kissed it.

"Ah poor, good lady, such a gift!" she shook her head in disbelief. "This was the one piece of jewellery she had, from her baptism she told me. David my son, we are greatly honoured." Swiftly, as if it might disappear, she took it to her secret box, and reverently laid it there, another treasure.

For days the village spoke of nothing else, and all but essential work was forgotten while they regained strength as from an invasion. They laughed, exchanged stories, they drank themselves senseless most nights just because there was so much coin about, no one was careful of their cellars. Miguel continued to play for them, incredulous at his sudden fame and good fortune. His fingers ran over the mellow strings as he basked in the warmth of praise, for his golden music had surely been the honey on the cake.

Oh but what silly people they were, they all agreed laughing, those city dwellers, those fancy fops, with money pouring from their purses as if they minted it.

After a few days, David went up to the palace with some borrowed beasts to reclaim their property. After several journeys, for they had stripped their house of all their furniture and treasures, he just stood and looked about. Once a magnificent palace, now held together with whitewash, the empty rooms echoed and he was sad. Then realizing that his task was done, he shut the doors and left. Although he wondered if it would stand for many more years, he hoped that the old woman who had not returned with her lady to the city, would care for it.

CHAPTER ELEVEN

JOSEPH

"We have to leave, my son," his grandmother had her back to him, busy with a wooden box, but he knew she had been weeping for he had heard her. "You have to leave also." Joseph had collected his few treasures together, his shells, his knife, his perfectly round, smooth stone. That had all been a long time ago, and now, all he had left was the jewelled cross which his grandmother had sewn into his vest, which ever lay hard upon his breast.

"Never lose it, my dear child," she had whispered in his ear, as if she were just kissing him. "Go with this man, who is kin, learn from him, and live with him, Joseph. Understand, my dearest child, our lives are fraught with danger, and we must part, if just for a while. Remember, that cross was given to our Donna by the king for her baptism. It is of great worth. One day it might help you. Go with God, Joseph," and then she backed away, the tears falling quietly. He never saw her or any of his family ever again.

Now he touched it and prayed. But it was no use. The pain in his armpits was cruel, and he could not breathe. All about him lay the sweet, foul stink of death. It seemed as if no one lived. The plague had once more swept through the little seaport, and just the gulls screamed, all human voice it seemed, was stilled forever.

He reached for the last of the water in the pitcher which he had fetched for his master, when he was dying. Carefully he poured it on his face, trying not to cause himself more pain by his movements. Then he slept, and in the morning, found that the buboes had burst, the filthy muck draining down his sides, stinking into the hay mattress.

He knew that he must somehow get up, he must get out of this ghastly house full of death. Rolling off his mattress he crawled to the window and somehow managed to push open the shutter. The bright light of day pierced into his eyes, so he closed them quickly and dropped the shutter. Later, after he had rested, he opened the shutter again and peered out, using his last strength to prop it open. He could smell vinegar. Well that wasn't anything new, for Madame Doume´ was forever making pickles, which she sold to the sailors down at the port. Exhausted, he lay half out of the window gulping in the un-fetid air when a thought struck into his mind. If Madame Doume´ was making pickles, she must yet be alive. Perhaps he could call to her and ask for help?

He listened as evening approached, yet there were few sounds in what had been a busy quarter of the town. Usually, he could hear much coming and going, the stamping of the horses feet next door in the Doume´s' livery stables. They snorted through their noses, nickering and whinnying a welcome when they heard their stable-mates return from a journey. Yet for some time, all had been quiet, just the smell of vinegar came pungent from the next door kitchen.

At last he dragged himself to the door and, pushing it open, peered out.

In the house next door, Louisa laid her head on the table and wept. Whatever was she doing, pickling gherkins by the barrel, when there was no one to buy them? Yet the garden was full, and being her pride and joy, how could she let the vegetables rot on the vine? And where was Doume´? He was never gone for more than a few days, a week at the most. And the horses? The groom boys? Where were they? Now it must be a month since she had heard Doume´ whistling through his teeth, his bright eyes twinkling as he swept her up in an embrace. She wept afresh knowing full well that he, like most of the world, was dead or dying, somewhere.

It had been a strange marriage, yet happy. Plain, quiet, she had been glad to take him as husband, with the stables as her dowry. And Doume´ had made it grow and prosper with his fine horses and his great love and knowledge of them. That there had been no children had been a disappointment to her, yet it was God's will. Like this terrible sickness.

A sound alerted her and she frowned. Was it the evening wind rattling a shutter? Or was there another being nearby knocking? Taking up the big wooden spoon which she stirred the pickle, she struck the cauldron hard, three times. Joseph heard it, his breath coming fast, he gathered his last strength and knocked back hard, three times.

Three days later, he began to feel his energy returning. Where she found the food to feed him, he knew not. All he knew was that she poured spoons of good chicken broth down his throat,

"Thank you," he had whispered, over and over again. "Thank you Madame Doume´."

She had stripped him of all his puss-sodden clothes, carefully unpicking the jewelled cross from its bag, and dropping it into the lye bath which she used to bathe him. The fire under the cauldron burnt bright with the clothes, and the smell was foul. He felt awful. Weak and ashamed and very humble. Here was a woman he barely knew, who he had perhaps greeted a few times, "good day", and she was saving his life.

"Madame," Joseph said when he was almost well. "We must leave this place, for it reeks of sickness and death. Will you come with me to see if we can take a ship, and cross the water?"

Louisa looked at him under her coif. It had been good for her to have him to care for, as it made her forget her fears for her husband who she guessed was dead. And what about her future? What was there for a barren woman to do with her life? There were no horses in the stable now to bring in the money to live. Everyone had either left or was dead. This man with his gentleness might be kind to her in gratitude for helping him in his need.

"Please call me Louisa," she said, dropping her eyes. "I know you are Joseph." Wiping her hands in her apron she pondered for awhile. "Yes, you are right. It might be best to leave this place, for there is little left here for me anyway."

They dressed as best they could and walked carefully through the filth-strewn streets to the centre of the town where miraculously there seemed some life. Louisa approached the mayor's office and holding the deeds for her house, stables and garden, asked if they would sell them for her, eventually.

Joseph then explained about his employer's death, and that bodies still lay in his house, waiting for decent burial. It took days before anything happened and finally the corpses were trundled out of town to be tossed without ceremony into the communal pits.

"Do you know where he kept his gold?" Louisa asked. Joseph stared at the cobbles, which from lack of traffic now grew weeds between them.

"I think so," he replied. He did.

"He will not need it any more Joseph, or the precious stones," she said calmly. "Bring them, and I will sew them into your clothes with your cross. If you are to start again with your work, you must have materials to work on. Why not we take it, instead of leaving it for some stranger?" Then she added as an afterthought. "We will have masses said for his soul. For he was kin, was he not?"

There were few ships on the quay, yet Louisa went each day with a small jar of her pickles to bargain for passage for them. At last, after several weeks, the skipper of a small ship, liking her gherkins, agreed to take them. With surprising strength, Louisa insisted that the mayor pay her for her property and squeezed a pitiful sum from him, glad of that. Only when they were installed on deck with their few possessions, under an old sail, did Louisa get a cart and bring the little barrels of pickles. It was a wretched crossing, the small ship wallowing like a tub, so that Joseph felt once more that death would take him.

Leaving him lying on top of their things on the port cobbles, she set her jaw and with the mime she had learned from Doume´, she found them a tiny attic room for some days. Joseph listened to the new language and wondered if he would ever learn it. His birth tongue having been Spanish, he had learnt French, which was not so difficult. But this, this English! So he left it all to Louisa who with amazing skill, seemed to not only manage well, she amused the folk in their new country by her determined efforts.

They moved on now and again according to circumstances. Just when he thought they were settled, something would happen, and off they went. He realized that Louisa must have money secreted about her person, and quite a lot of it at that, for his little efforts to work with the odd goldsmith barely fed them. Yet it pleased him to work, and he listened and learned.

At last they came to a large village by a river where they rented a house which seemed to lean right over the water. It had three rooms, one above the other, and Louisa swept and cleaned till it was to her satisfaction. Still barely speaking the new language, they managed quietly, until one day she came home all smiles, carrying a small cheese with the news that she had found someone who spoke French.

So it was that Joseph set up his little workshop at the back overlooking the river, his fire set on a wide stone. Ever afraid that his raw gold and stones would be stolen, he devised a way to lift the stone, where a cavity underneath held them safely.

Each day Louisa went to the well in the square and carried two pails of water back, only using the river water for washing. A tiny garden blossomed under her care, where she somehow managed to grow abundant vegetables and life became routine once more for both of them.

On special market days, eyes alight, Louisa went to the square, for she had found a friend at last. Joseph listened as she told him of the fair good looks of Mistress Woodman, her handsome husband and beautiful little twin daughters who came downriver to sell her wonderful cheeses and who spoke French.

Once, when Louisa complained about the rats which came in from the river, Mistress Woodman brought her a kitten. She was enchanted, for it was the prettiest little thing, and without a child, she lavished all her affection on it. Joseph smiled, pleased to see the quiet woman which life had unexpectedly given him, laughing as she played with it. Almost into middle age, Louisa had never been a beauty, yet now, with her delight in the little animal, her features softened and she became almost pretty.

As there was no goldsmith in the area, Joseph found himself getting a little work now and then. Not that it was a rich village. It was not, yet it was growing and the burghers were pleased to call and draw on a slate, and consult with the gentle foreigner. Even more, they were pleased by the work he created, so that they vied to deck out their wives with his jewellery. When it came time for him to need more gold or pearls or stones, they went with him for safety to the city, where he somehow found just the right thing. Life went on quietly for them and they made a place for themselves in the small community.

When Louisa became ill, Joseph suddenly realized that he had grown to love his quiet woman and he worried deeply. While she lay abed, he struggled to do the marketing and to cook up some broth for her. For hadn't she done the same for him in the past?

"Go to the church steps on market day," said a neighbour. "Find yourself a little maid to do the chores for you."

Ill at ease, Joseph went and cast his inexperienced eye about the poor souls who stood about seeking employment. Where to start? Who to choose? With his poor English, he felt so afraid, having eyed them all, he turned and slowly walked home. A step behind him alerted him that he was being followed. Slowing, he listened to be quite sure. There, some paces behind him limped a small woman, grossly all bent over to one side. She smiled at him shyly.

"Is it help in the house you need, master?" she asked. He saw that most of her teeth were missing and she was poorly dressed in virtual rags. He nodded. "Then shall I come along with you, for I am eldest of a big family and know all about keeping house." Joseph trembled, for she was not a comforting sight, so gave no answer. Nevertheless, she walked into the house behind him and within moments she had found the broom and had begun putting the place to rights.

Louisa was aware that someone was busy about her, sweeping, changing the bed, opening the window shutters and cooking-fine smelling food.

"She'll be alright master," said the self-appointed new maid as she served up an excellent pottage. "She'll be alright when the babe is born."

Joseph lowered his horn spoon into the bowl and felt the colour drain from his face. A babe? Louisa with a babe? Was it true? Did Louisa know? A child! They were to have a child! Oh Praise the Lord.

So Bibby became part of their family, nursing and loving the sick Louisa through her first, last and late pregnancy. They paid her a pittance, which she gave to her mother on Sunday afternoons when she went home, yet she also took food and contentment. Bibby, Louisa and Joseph were all vastly satisfied with the arrangement.

"A beautiful little maid," she exclaimed as she delivered the infant after a wearisome labour, "and perfect." She who was born so crooked. They had her baptised Deborah, for it was a lovely name which the priest had spoken in church where Bibby stood Godmother, while the mayor stood Godfather.

They were incredulous with their child. For they considered themselves old, and Louisa had thought that she was barren. Here then was this gift from God, a beautiful girl child.

In the spring, Louisa went to the first market after the winter to show her baby to her friend Mistress Woodman and to see if all was well with her. Back she came smiling some time later, to introduce her friend with her beautiful daughters to Joseph. It was the beginning of a long friendship, a friendship started between the mothers, which would go on with the daughters.

Although Bibby had helped to bring up her many siblings, another one was never too much trouble. For she adored her little charge, taking her about in her arms, then by the hand, ever telling stories or singing. Once, when Deborah was ill with some childish ailment, she persuaded Joseph to allow her to take the little girl to visit with the Woodmans upriver. Having hired a flat bottomed boat, they found their way to the marsh tower where she soon got well again with the good country food and plenty of childish company.

Deborah learnt from her country friends too. Not only did she speak French from her parents, she insisted that she learn with her friends upriver. The one thing she was dissatisfied with her mother over was the lack of a baby brother or sister. For the Woodmans had a new baby every other year, and Deborah loved them.

Watching her father working, she began to help him as she got older, as she drew flowers and all things from nature on her slate, so Joseph made jewels, using her designs. Gradually, as his sight dimmed, his daughter began to tap the precious, golden metal into shape. Her hand was light and sure, and she became ever more fascinated in the creation of jewels. Bending over the fire, pressing the little bellows to heat the charcoal, sweat beaded on her upper lip. It seemed she was naturally gifted, for she took to coaxing wondrous shapes from the precious metals, into jewels for ladies, and sometimes men.

Louisa and Bibby watched their mutual child grow into a lovely young woman, whose interest in her father's work astonished yet impressed them. It was no surprise to them when one day the mayor arrived accompanying a splendid courtier, sent, he whispered, by the city dignitaries, to see the work which came out of their humble workshop.

For Joseph's work was lighter, more fragile in appearance than the other goldsmiths. His jewellery had a taste of faraway places, a slightly exotic air, and he seemed to use less gold than most, therefore his pieces were less heavy and less expensive.

"Perhaps I can arrange an audience for you," the courtier said, cousin to the mayor. "Our duchess is from across the seas, and I believe that she has jewels not dissimilar to your work Master Goldsmith."

It took some years before this advantageous interview came about though. Joseph was not perturbed, for he was more interested in a quiet life, with gentle and regular work rather than pressure. As long as the box, where lay Deborah's dowry, lay safe beneath the floor boards and they had enough to eat and pay their rent and taxes, he cared for nothing else. At times he watched his daughter in amazement and wondered from where she took her height, her deep red hair and amber eyes. From the day that Bibby had entered their house, she had been a surprise, a joy, a gift from God.

His coming together with Louisa Doume´ had been casual, more friendly than passionate. Although she was the elder, they had both been past their first youth when they had arrived in this cool, green land. Sometimes he dreamed of his childhood in Southern Spain, where the hot wind blew red dust from across the water, smothering the very herbs of the parched earth. It did not do to think on his family. His father and mother, the two little sisters or his grandmothers. Then, at the end, before they walked down the rocky hill to the port, his strange old grandfather had arrived, with an entirely new family straggling behind him. It was an intense meeting, with many tears of joy and sorrow. He had waited for them to come for him for years, remembering his grandmother's last words. Yet they never came. So now he had his own family. The wife of the dumb owner of the livery stable from next door, and now his own child. Not forgetting Bibby, poor crooked, dear little Bibby, who ran their lives diligently and with love.

"We need pearls, father," said Deborah, while she idly sketched on her slate. "I'd like to come with you this time, for last time they were not really quite right."

She was a kind girl, so she did not say that the pearls which he had bought were too yellow, too misshapen. Besides, she felt a stirring of dissatisfaction with her life, here in this dull little backwater town. No word was spoken of a marriage for her, though she knew that her father had accumulated a fine dowry which he kept under the floor. Why should she grow old, without any bridegroom in sight, while her friend Clary already had children.

She knew that they were different. Her thoughts roamed casually about her parents. They still spoke in a foreign way, after years of being here, in this town. Her father was prematurely old, a stooped man, probably from bending over his bench. His once dark hair was streaked with white and his blue eyes were rheumy. When urged, her parents told her the story of their meeting across the water, far away and how her mother had tended her father out of the great sickness.

"Yes, I'd like to come with you, father," she repeated, "and I'd like to see what else is available for our work."

It was impressive, the huge town which lay sprawling below a great castle topped hill. The sheer volume of noise hit her, as if the world were all babbling at once. Their own important market days were very poor affairs in comparison. They put up in a tiny inn run by two foreign sisters. Deborah understood that they were privileged, and that it was no common hostelry. A boy unloaded their bags, and led their hired ponies away. Deborah tried to keep close to her father, as if she was concerned for him, and not afraid.

That night, strange people came to talk with her father while she pretended to sleep. Through slitted eyes she watched as he opened the cloth bags and showed them the jewels inside. With her heart beating, she watched their faces in the dim light. They liked the work.

"Debbie mine," her father rarely called her that childhood name nowadays, "we will go to the other, larger castle towards the sea, tomorrow. A friend has arranged a meeting with the duchess, who recently gave birth and the duke wishes to present her with new jewels. This is a chance to show your work." He seemed excited.

Putting on her best red brown dress, which matched perfectly with her hair, Deborah dipped her comb in the wash water and smoothed it down.

"Put your cross out on your breast my child." he said, gazing at her in proud disbelief as usual. "This is no time to hide it away. You are Christian, so be proud of it. And that cross is all I have left from my family."

Damping a cloth, Deborah sponged down her father's jacket and wished he had a newer one. Gazing at him with love, she sadly realized that he looked far older than his years, yet knowing his story, she understood why.

As they rode up the steep streets to the castle, Deborah gazed about in fascination. Everything here was bigger and better than at home. Houses hung over the street almost touching at their upper windows, and throngs of people jostled this way and that. Mind you, she wrinkled her nose, the muck and stench were terrible.

They were seated with dozens of others in a great audience chamber. Courtiers wandered about settling people to wait, writing down names, being important.

Joseph let his mind wander back, back, to his childhood, to the only other such place he had been in. There in his mind's eye he saw a great airy white palace set on a red hillside, blinding in the sun. This one was dim, smoky candles giving off a poor light, so the scene was hazy.

Eventually they were called and following a little man, they were led, men at arms before and behind, through long passages till at last they stood before a great carved door.

"Leave your arms here," instructed their guide, pointing to a table by the door. Joseph looked surprised at the courtier, who, a hint of impatience in his voice repeated himself.

"We do not carry arms, Sire," he said mildly, "we are goldsmiths, come to show the lady jewels. We have no arms."

It was a big and airy room full of women whose chattering paused as they entered. Joseph bowed and was pushed forward. Deborah dipped low, her eyes darting about, intrigued and impressed with all before her. It was a beautiful room, hung with fine tapestries and it seemed that every pair of hands there was working on something, none lay idle.

A round, copper-topped table was brought forward and Deborah opened out their little bags on it, placing each jewel on top. Then the table was lifted and carried to the duchess, who sat in a fine chair, surrounded by her women. Soon little sounds of appreciation floated over the scented air towards them. Each piece was closely examined, whispered over, and handed on. Joseph and his daughter stood silent and still, waiting.

A white, bejewelled hand beckoned them forward.

"Can you make me a necklace, something like this," a piece was held up. "But with white pearls?"

Joseph cleared his throat and turning to his daughter asked quietly, "Can we?"

Deborah took a step forward to see which piece it was. Then, realizing it was her own, she nodded and replied, "With certainty."

"Is this your work, or is it Master Goldsmith's?"

Deborah dipped slightly and nodded.

"It is my work, lady."

A buzz followed, while the piece was re-examined and curious eyes surveyed her.

"Come forward please," a stool was set beside the lady. "Let us discuss what I want, come!" the voice was kind.

Taking her slate from the bag which hung from her girdle, Deborah settled herself beside the lady and looked up enquiringly. The beautiful face peered down at her, but not quite at her, for the dark eyes were concentrating on her breast, or perhaps on her cross which lay, magnificent, there. The white hand fluttered towards it, then to a smaller cross which lay amongst other jewels on her breast. The voice, small, uncertain began, then stopped.

"Your cross, miss? Where did you get your cross?"

Deborah touched her jewel, as she had often before. Feeling the fine filigree gold work, the smooth water-worn rubies, the glowing pearls, she watched the pale face before her grow even paler. Suddenly the women attendants clustered around their duchess, fanning her, holding scent before her nose while the two watched horrified, and men at arms ran forward from their places to add to the panic.

Calm returned gradually, as the colour returned to the aristocratic face. Quietly now, the duchess leant forward and addressed Deborah, who still alarmed, nervously clutched her cross.

"Can you tell me miss, how you came by that cross?"

Now Joseph took a step forward and bowed slightly, never taking his eyes of the lady.

"It came to me from my father, lady, many years ago. It was given to him by our duchess, in a far-off land. It was a gift to him, in thanks for a favour."

The silence stretched, all eyes were on the bent man, who with his streaked head and beard seemed to be desperately trying to see clearly, the lady before him.

"What is your name sir?" her voice seemed to fade away.

Joseph cleared his throat and took a deep breath.

"I am now known as Joseph Goldsmith lady, but my birth name was Joseph, Davidsson."

The lady stared, and stared, then leaning forward snapped an order in another tongue, so a page ran off, and the silence stretched, seemingly forever. Deborah slowly raised her eyes from her clenched hands to watch her father. Rising slowly, so as not to cause alarm, she took up her stool and setting it behind him, gently pushed him down. Consternation broke out in the silent throng and another stool was quickly found and given to her. This time Deborah drew it near to her father, and sat close to him, almost touching, holding his hands.

A distant commotion alerted them that something was happening so they looked up. Joseph was bewildered by the recent events, and wished he was home, quietly working at his bench and watching the river roll by.

The lady rose and swiftly went to the door where a group of courtiers surrounded a figure. Joseph couldn't see what was going on, but his daughter whispered in his ear. It seemed as if a great wind rustled through the room for every person there rose, and dipped low, their gowns sweeping the floor.

Deborah looked down on a small, wrinkled woman, richly jewelled, coifed and dressed all in black. Yet again dark eyes scrutinised her face, then dropped to her jewel.

"Who are you?" a clear thin, accented voice demanded.

Bowing, they introduced themselves.

"Joseph?" The new arrival peered even closer so to see properly. "Are you indeed Joseph, David's son?"

Deborah saw that her father was trembling and put her hand on his arm.

"My father was from far across the seas, lady," she dipped again. "He does not see so well anymore, for there are curtains across his eyes, but he hears well."

Then the old lady began to speak quickly, in a foreign tongue, while the younger lady held her arm, just as Deborah held her fathers. The trembling grew even greater and Deborah was alarmed and tried to hold him tighter, but he pushed her away.

"Donna, Donna!" his voice came tremulous. "Ah Donna, my lady, and Donna Magdalena, is it really you?" and fell to his knees and took their hands to kiss, tears pouring down his face. Again the whole company rustled and strained to see and hear.

When she told her mother and Bibby about it later, Deborah had to sort out her impressions, for what happened next was all a jumble. Turning to her blindly, Joseph, his voice choking with emotion, begged her to give her jewelled cross to the lady. For it was hers by right, for it had been a gift from the king at her baptism. It was an emotional scene, for the old Donna took it, kissed it, hands trembling and put the chain over her head to lie on her breast as of old.

They then all rose and were escorted together to an exquisite small room, there to sit and talk for hours. Joseph told, tripping over his words, searching for the old language, laughing and returning to his poor French or English, all his adventures. Of the day when a pigeon had arrived with her message and together with all the family who came soon after, they had left, to sail south, to Africa. He told of their being taken by pirates, of fear, thirst and death, of paying ransom. Of how his grandfather, the old physician, had died in his grandmother's arms, a smile on his face. Of how, eventually he had been sent off alone with a strange man, never to see or hear of them again.

With cries of sorrow, the Donna exclaimed on every adventure, wiping her eyes on a fine linen cloth, or holding his hand, wiping his eyes.

Then it was her turn for she told him how they had eventually settled into the great city palace where her poor husband had eventually died, and how her son had become the duke, and despite wars and sorrow, they had at last succeeded and prospered. Nodding to Joseph she added, all thanks to David, his father.

Then, smiling at the young duchess, she told of the strange love match which had formed between her only daughter and an English duke, who had come with an embassy and how, she had come to settle in this cold land, to be with her.

With her cross in her hands, the Donna seemed no longer old. Her eyes lit up when they spoke of the white palace on the hill above the village, which had been pink. Forgotten were the privations of that long past life, the heat, the flies and the poverty. Just the beautiful memories remained. The sun, the little fishing boats on the distant shimmering sea, the sweetness of the figs and apricots.

"And the music," interrupted Joseph, "I miss it and that old man, playing, his daughter singing, like a bird." He mused on it. "Before we left, my father gave Miguel a very good small vineyard, for his own, a debt he said. Those days when the people came from the city to fetch you, are deep in my memories, Donna, for before that, and indeed after, little of import ever happened in our lives in that little village." Then very seriously he added. "Although I do not know what happened to my family Donna, I give you thanks now, for sending us word that we must leave. No doubt my sisters are somewhere in the world, wives and mothers now, all due to you and your concern for us. My next sister, who for those days was your friend," he addressed the younger lady, "never ceased to speak of you and mourn your departure."

Fragrant food was brought, and Joseph savoured it, rolling his eyes as childhood memories flooded his mind as did the saliva in his mouth. Yellow rice with succulent pieces of lamb, rich with spices and grilled fish laid on foreign vegetables was piled on a silver platter. Soft, savoury breads, warm, covered with a linen cloth were passed around. Golden wine was served in fragile glasses. It was an informal meal, as amongst kin, and Deborah had never experienced the like before, or seen her father so animated.

Back in their room that night, he could not sleep, and spoke as never before, telling his child about his childhood, long past, far, far away. Of the day when the donna had ridden away with her children, giving the cross to his father in gratitude. How the young duchess was just a little girl, friend of his sister, and how they had cried at parting. It was as if a floodgate had been opened, and Deborah listened, entranced, at last learning her father's history.

Next day they returned to the castle, and this time were shown straight to the duke's rooms by a courteous page. People milled about speaking quietly, all waiting their turn for audience. A door opened, and two men came out smiling broadly with their farewells. Deborah started, for surely they were so like Master Woodman, they must be kin. But her thoughts were interrupted for they were called and ushered into an office where the duke sat behind a fine, carved table. Rising, a smile on his face, he bowed lightly to them as he waved them to two seats.

"What a pleasure to see you Master Davidsson!" he settled on his chair again. "My wife and mother-in-law were in such great spirits, I felt I must meet you, for, of course, I have heard about your family, from days long past." He nodded to Deborah, "and I understand that you too are a master goldsmith young mistress, and that you will do drawings for my wife and create my gift to her, for the birth of our new child."

A diffident courtier sidled up and discretely placed a leather purse on the table. The duke nodded briefly with a half smile and took it up.

Deborah noted that he was an affable man, as fair as his lady was dark, with golden hair and whiskers, and deep blue eyes.

"No expense is to be spared my friends," he pushed the purse towards Joseph. "Go now to make decisions and entertain my ladies again, and come to see us often, for as I have said, rarely have I seen them both so happy before."

Sitting with the duke's ladies, Deborah drew on her slate, rubbed out and drew again until they were satisfied. Quietly, the Donna of his childhood handed Joseph another purse of gold, in payment for the jewelled cross, which had lain on his breast for so many years, over so many miles. Despite his reluctance, she insisted he take it.

It seemed that everything changed from then onwards. During their search for good gems, instead of being kept waiting with bare courtesy, they were royally treated. Instead of being fobbed off with second-grade pearls and gems, the best were laid out before them, and at competitive prices. For word spread as a tide throughout the town, that the duchess and her mother had found old friends from their own country. Joseph and Deborah Goldsmith were to make the fine set of jewels which the duke would give to his wife.

Back at home, they worked as never before. Together they sat, side by side at the bench, the little crucible often in use, the sound of gentle tapping, ever in the air, Joseph assisting his sure handed daughter.

The ladies were pleased with their work. Passing each piece from hand to hand with smiles, they glowed with pride. For this was a constant reminder of the work done at home, in that far off country.

It was not so difficult to persuade Joseph to move with his little family to live in a small annexe of the castle. There, safe and never short of work, they settled with the faithful Bibby.

"And what about our finding a husband for you, Deborah?" asked the duchess. For she was happy with their resident goldsmiths, and wished to keep them close in order to have their wonderful skills always to hand. Joseph glanced at his daughter. It was true, he had been tardy in finding a husband for her. The truth was he needed her by his side, for it was she who now did the delicate work, while he, his sight ever dimmer, merely did little jobs which she gave him. He nodded and cleared his throat.

"Donna," for he was remembering his childhood language and delighted in conversing with the many Spanish ladies of the court in practise. "Donna, I would deem it a great favour if you would assist me in this. For surely I have been a lazy father, although I have accumulated a good dowry for her, you are right, my daughter surely needs a husband."

Had he but known it, they had already found him. With little else to do but sit, sew and gossip, it had been a task they had happily set themselves. And not just with her welfare in mind. For they wanted the goldsmith family to stay in the castle, and so a groom must be found who would be happy to stay there also.

He was a scribe, a young man highly gifted in languages, with a beautiful hand, who wrote letters for them in many tongues, as well as official letters for the duke. His family had, like the Davidssons, once been Spanish. It was understood that unlike the Davidssons, whose womenfolk had been Christian, they had converted, at least officially. Jonathan was a tall, dark man with sallow skin and deep set dark eyes. If accommodation could be provided for them, then everyone would be content.

"I have a letter going off to Arabia soon, Joseph, I understand theirs are the finest pearls," said the duchess, carefully unpicking some faulty stitches. "I suggest that you speak to Jonathan the Scribe so he may write your requirements." She picked up a little bell from the ornate table beside her and gave a sharp little ring with it. A page appeared, eyes eager. "Ah, good Simon, run and fetch the scrivener for me."

Which is how Deborah met her husband.

Life in the castle was pleasant. If they cared to join the throng in the hall, they could. If not, they stayed in their rooms, and Bibby either marketed in the town for their small needs, or scrounged from the kitchens. Deborah did not let her marriage or motherhood interfere with her work with her father. She loved it, forming beauty from a lump of gold. It fascinated her deeply, and after each piece was made, she looked at it with a critical eye and vowed to do better next time. Meanwhile her mother and Bibby cared for her children, fine boys, Joseph and David, who had her good looks and their father's excellent brains.

The years passed swiftly and they were all content. Joseph could barely see now, the curtains over his eyes a silver shutter. Yet as his eyes failed, it seemed that his hands became more sensitive for he sanded, polished and drilled, with Deborah's guidance.

CHAPTER TWELVE

CASTLE POMEROY, THE HEALER, ANOTHER ROOT

Ducking under the heavy curtain, he paused on the small landing for a moment, the darkness all about him, heavy as a shroud.

Everything was ready. Of course, and as usual, he had too much. He thought of the pile of bundles all neatly tied up, sighed, moved a foot carefully toward the top step and began the decent.

"One, two, three, four." He liked travelling light, but it rarely happened. "Five, six, seven, eight." Nice though it was being given gifts of gratitude, his needs were really few. Tools of his trade, a change of clothing, that was all he needed. Long tapering fingers lightly touched the rough stone on either side as he went down, circling, circling, sure. "Nine, ten, eleven, twelve, thirteen."

He paused at an arrow slit, pushed his face into the cavity as far as it would go, drinking in the moist air and peered out. Still dark, just a gentle drizzle. The thin and distant call of a village rooster barely registered.

"Fourteen, fifteen, sixteen, seventeen, eighteen, nineteen." Now he paused, holding the walls with outstretched arms and flat palms, nudging his toe over the broken step. He had got to know this circular stair over the six months he had been there. It needed attention, but as he was leaving, and no one else ever used the old gatehouse anyway, he had not mentioned it. Over the hurdle of cracked and broken stone he ran lightly down the last three steps and stopped. Reaching up automatically for his cloak draped on a stout wooden peg, he felt it still heavy with rain from the day before. Oh well, April. One never knew from one hour to the next what it would do. Fortunately the cloak was of good thick felt. He wrinkled his nose fastidiously, funny how the stink of wet sheep lingered forever. Without looking down he nudged his feet into the pattens which stood on the bottom step and moved out of the doorway into the great courtyard. A faint sign of dawn broke the dimness as he clacked his way across the cobbles of the bailey to the hall.

The fire was lit, indeed he noted that there seemed to be some activity which was unusual so early. One brand and the fire caused the huge hollow darkness to flicker and move with shadows and light. Lee pulled up a stool and sat by the fire, observing the pots and pans which stood about on trivets nestled into the hot ashes or hung from the chains. He wondered if Mistress Joan was preparing a good send-off for him. His face softened. He would miss her, that severe-looking and excellent woman. A light sound caused him to look up and she, about whom he had just been thinking, came in. Without pausing to greet him, she went to a small pot on the embers, lifted the lid and ladled out a spoon of some herb tea.

Lee breathed in deeply, puzzled. Perhaps she was making it for the last of the young men for their journey, although he really did not feel it necessary, their wounds were well healed. After six months, they no longer suffered pain.

"Good day, Mistress Joan," he broke the silence.

With a slight nod she acknowledged him with a murmur, turning to leave as quietly as she had come.

Now Lee was intrigued. Something was happening and he wondered what. Leaning forward he investigated the several pots in the embers. Something yes, but able woman that she was, she had not asked for his help, so he would not enquire who was ill. Finding a pot with mint tea in it, he helped himself. Realizing he would just have to wait and see, he hung his cloak up on two of the big wooden hooks to dry and settled himself more comfortably.

He would be sorry to leave this great barn of a castle. It had turned out far better than he could have imagined that first wild and wet evening in autumn when they had arrived, the ford impassable.

Dumbly they had stood gazing at the raging torrent, unaware that it must have rained very heavily in the hills.

"Now what?" he had thought aloud. There he was, entrusted by the abbot and Brother Edward with this pitiful group of wounded men. Their injuries had been deemed not so severe, so they should at least try to return to their own homes before winter. So they had set off, full of hope in the bright, early morning. Now, with night approaching, the rain increasing, and no way to cross the river, they were not in an enviable position. They clustered closer together, silent, while the horses fidgeted.

They had just passed through a pitiful huddle of a village with no inn that he had noticed and not one hovel showed light or smoke. All the inhabitants were no doubt wrapped in their ragged blankets inside trying to keep warm. He knew the story only too well, poor brutes. Then almost smiled at his foolishness, poor brutes were they, and what about us?

"Now what?" he said again.

A small movement at his left alerted him. One of the less injured men had detached himself from his task of stretcher bearer and approached. A cough. Lee looked up. It would be pneumonia in no time. He sighed. They should never have left the warmth and safety of the monastery.

"Yes?" he asked.

The man reached out and plucked at his sleeve, the other hand clamped to his mouth in an effort to stop the coughing. Lee followed him to the fair boy. So young, so fine, and although he believed him too ill to journey, Edward would have none of it.

"Yes?" he bent down.

"I have kin here," the boy said weakly. He raised an arm, apparently pointing to the sky. "I was page here, to Baron Pomeroy." The effort had drained him, but the eyes gleamed. "They will take us in," the last a whisper.

"Right!" said Lee, greatly encouraged and gazed skywards. Sure enough, towering above them in the gloom was a great crag which he had not noticed through the dripping trees in his hurry to reach the ford. He guessed that they must have passed a track somewhere to the castle on the top. Quickly he turned them about, hoping against hope that they would be taken in; the alternative was grim.

Sheltered under the great gatehouse, breathless from their climb, they had knocked until they almost gave up. A voice had called down at last, from somewhere way above them, which is how Lee had known there was a good window up there and had eventually explored, and taken over the gatehouse as his quarters.

They had been made warmly welcome although the baron was away. A handsome, severe-looking woman seemed to be the chatelaine, or housekeeper. She was addressed as "Mistress" or "Mistress Joan", and in a very short time, Lee had realized that she ran the place, and that very well.

The first days and nights were a blur of fatigue, for the journey had surely been too much for most of his patients. In the dimness of the hall, the castle folk scurried about obeying orders from the woman. Cauldrons of water were set onto the built up hearth, warmth and light welcome so he could almost see what he was doing. It seemed to Lee, as he asked for something, it was there, at hand. Tactful, in the shadows, Mistress Joan had watched as the skilled hands changed sodden dressings, and heard the kind voice giving orders and courage.

Despite the constant care, they lost two the second night, an old priest appearing like a spectre, to mourn his prayers over them.

As usual, Lee was angry. Angry with God for allowing them to die, so young, so fine, and all for what? Silly skirmishes. Politics! Angry with the King and the dukes for their quarrels. Just angry.

After the hasty burials outside in the dripping garden, he had followed the priest, and discovered the tiny and ancient church where he railed against God helplessly. Later, he found it so peaceful a haven in the busy castle, he often just went to sit, his thick cloak tight about him, and contemplate in that tiny, holy place, replacing sorrow with good memories.

"It is God's will," the abbot had a habit of saying.

"Rubbish!" hissed Lee, only to be scolded by the gentle Edward, his only friend, the herbalist at the monastery.

"Join us do?" asked Edward pleading, again and again. "With your healing skill and my knowledge of herbs, we can help so many people with the Grace of God." The truth was that he enjoyed his friend Lee, his unusual mind, his casualness. He also was aware that Lee was different, more clever perhaps than anyone else he had ever met, and above all, a gifted healer.

But Lee did not want to join the brethren, much as he liked the quiet life of the monasteries, the singing, the security. His was a different way. To go where he was needed, to go without plan, like a leaf blown in the wind.

No sooner was one task done, another presented itself. Most thought him a lay brother, well he almost was, for much of his time was spent in monasteries, for they all knew and indeed seemed to welcome him. His way was to seek the sick, and to try to help them. And all the time, in small ways and large, he learned. His hunger for knowledge was boundless, and when he felt he had a jewel worth keeping, he wrote it down in his book, sent it to Edward, and gave it to whatever monastery he was next at, to use or not, as they willed.

His own tiny book he kept, with miniscule writing, all he learned, maybe he would need it as reference, one day.

Now ready to embark on his travels again, he sat staring into the idle flames of the fire, warm and calm, unaware that this day would probably be one of the most important in his life, with being born, and dying. So deeply was he into his memories, nodding off, he did not hear the woman step lightly beside him, her hand on his shoulder awoke him.

"I need your help, Master Lee," her voice low, weary. "You know I would not ask you if I could manage alone. But I have toiled all night, and now I despair." A tremor in her voice alerted him to her tiredness and need.

"Ask?" he said simply.

Taking a cup she ladled a spoon of the mint tea for herself, then him. Despite being the first sweet leaves of the year, it was well stewed and getting bitter. None-the-less she drank deep before answering him.

"I hoped it would be safely over, and you away on your travels, but I fear I must ask your assistance, even knowing that you do not like to be involved with women in childbirth."

Lee stared at her intently.

"Someone is having trouble birthing?"

She nodded.

"Then why didn't you call me, mistress? Liking is one thing, duty and care is another." He stood up and stared down at her bowed head. "Tell me."

Putting the cup down the woman smoothed her hair into its cloth and straightened her shoulders.

"None of us even knew that she was with child, no one!" She pondered. "She was always such a quiet little thing. Fine-boned, not really frail, but then we gave her light tasks, to suit her build. Sewing," she spread her hands, "spinning of course, dyeing, all which she did so well, it seemed her rightful work. She was never idle, she was always quiet and went about her work with diligence. I never even noticed she had a man!" She sighed and lifted her arms, to drop them in despair. "It is always so busy when the baron comes with his guests. How should I notice all what is going on in every corner of the castle, for not only am I too busy, I do try to keep a low countenance." A look of exasperation, then resignation. "Being winter, all bundled up with heavy clothes, I just had not seen her condition and now," she drew in her breath sharply, "she cannot push the child out, she has no strength. I am very afraid that they will both die."

"Shall we see her together now, Mistress Joan." He offered a hand to lift her up. "Perhaps we can manage a birth together," and followed her through the endless dim corridors and stairs of the castle, her lantern flickering in the draughts.

It was true, he did hate childbirth. Not that he hadn't helped many a babe into the world, but it was normal that he was usually called only when there was trouble. Then, he usually despaired of the filth, the conditions, so late, watching the exhausted woman fade from life, all too often taking her unborn child with her.

The girl lay, a slip of a thing, light hair wet and dark against the sheet, eyes wide with pain and fear. He took her hand and felt the light flutter of the pulse.

"We shall be alright now, Fleur," said Mistress Joan with regained authority. "I have brought Master Lee, thankfully he had not left yet, we are lucky." Pinching the lamps to make them flare, drawing off the covers, she busied herself as usual. Lee knelt beside the low pallet and put his hands on the swollen belly while the girl kept her face averted. She was thin, perhaps, he guessed, in her fourteenth or fifteenth year. A tightening under his hands told him of the wave of pain and deftly he turned the slight body on its side and pressed his palm deeply into her back.

When it had passed, the girl looked at him, eyes grateful.

"Tell me when the next pain comes," he said kindly, "I'll try to ease it from now on with a good back rub, it always helps." Then he turned away and spoke rapidly to the woman. "It is her small size, maybe a poor position. I need salve, mine is all packed, can I use yours?"

Together they collected what they needed from her basket of simples. Lee then considered first his hands, then Joan's. Without a word, he took hers, drawing out his tiny nail-scissors from his belt pouch, and carefully, very short, he trimmed the nail of her index finger.

"Now wash," he ordered, "very well," and turned for the moment to rub the girl's back again. In the next lull, staring intently into the older woman's eyes, he explained what he wanted her to do. Slowly, carefully, his hands raised in example.

"There is a passage through which the child comes, with a tight ring at the end. Now, I want you, your finger is smaller than mine, to put your well-salved finger inside and stretch that ring. You will feel the hard head of the child. By helping with the stretching, the body usually starts to work again, so we will have the child in no time." He gazed into her shocked face, "You MUST," he hissed, "now." Turning to back-rub once more, he spoke softly to the girl when the pain was over.

"Now this will hurt, Fleur, but you are brave, and you are tired, and you want to see your babe don't you?" He went on without waiting for an answer. "Mistress Joan will try to stretch the ring which is stopping your baby from being born. Be brave, try to help us, there's a good girl." So sitting on the bed he held the slight body in his arms while a trembling Joan knelt between the thin, white legs, and did her work.

"Good, good," said Lee.

"I feel the head," said Joan, a new look on her face, incredulous, hopeful. It seemed as if the pains grew more frequent and severe.

"Be brave, Fleur," said Lee, pulling the girl's knees up, "push now."

It was a girl. In a rush of bloody fluid it came, a tiny, thin, fair child, face first, which mewled like a kitten when Mistress Joan, face alight with wonder, lifted her up for them to see.

Without realizing it, Lee bent down and pressed a kiss on the brow of the exhausted mother.

"Oh well done, Fleur, you have done well, a fine, live daughter, who will, I am sure, be as fair and lovely as you." Which brought about a sweet, weak smile.

When she had washed the tiny girl, Mistress Joan handed her to Lee. For the first time, in all ignorance, Lee gazed tenderly at what would be his whole future life, before laying her beside the young mother.

With the dawn, came the sun, a glorious spring day, and with it came all the well-wishers. Joan brought her three handsome, tow-headed sons who stared round-eyed at the tiny thing in the crook of Fleur's arm.

Next came all the astonished and chattering womenfolk of the castle to admire the unexpected new baby. Everyone brought some small gift, and Fleur weakly smiled her thanks, accepting them.

A perfect day indeed to begin his journey, thought Lee, yet he hesitated. Exhilarated, knowing in his heart that he had been the cause of the successful birth, he was reluctant to leave so soon. He knew that Joan would not have known how or dared to probe without his instruction. It was quite likely the girl and child would have slipped away by now. Curiously happy, he visited the young mother and child several times during the day, brushing aside all talk of his departure. Instead he waved-off his party, wishing them Godspeed and good health, and for sure they would meet again. They had a bond together, the last few. Their shared injuries, the dark months close together, sorrow and joy. Nothing would ever break that.

Later, an afternoon visit to his new patient caused a flicker of fear in his heart. The blood loss was too severe and caused him to order cloths soaked in ice cold water from the deepest well, to be wrapped about the poor girl. He would wait till she was strong again before making his way.

"What is a day?" The adrenaline causing him to feel good, so it was easy pushing away the fears.

That evening, a frown between her eyes, Joan sought him out and they walked together down into the village, for it had become obvious that the young mother was not yet able to feed her child.

"My Goddaughter Joany, is I fear, also with child and due soon. If Fleur cannot nurse hers, and if we can keep it alive with the pap pot, surely Joany will be able to nurse the two babes, for she is a fine big girl. There is no other nursing woman in the village," she added surely, for she knew everything. As they came to the open mouth of the blacksmith's shed, smoke and a great clamour came from within.

"John Smith." Her voice was loud and hard. Lee understood immediately that she had no love for the dirty brute who emerged. "I've come to see my Goddaughter." She pushed past him, through a leather-curtained door into a dim room behind. "Joany!" she called, her voice kinder.

A girl, well-wrapped in a shawl rose from a poor bed.

"Aunt," she sobbed, "oh aunt, I asked da if I could go to you, for I have such terrible pains, but he would not let me."

Immediately understanding the trouble and with her usual authority, Joan stepped into the village street, raised her voice, causing the neighbours to scurry around and a pony was soon brought up.

"Shame on you, John Smith," eyes blazing, she faced him. "Your girl is labouring with a child, and you do not let her come to me, her Godmother, your own wife's best friend. Oh but if she was alive today?" A catch in her voice made Lee realize that Joan was near to breaking with exhaustion, having not slept all night, having done her tasks and cared for Fleur all day. Quickly he bundled them out, hauled the girl Joany onto the pony, and supporting her as well as he could, set off at a smart pace.

"Who is her man?" asked Lee. But Joan did not answer, her face severe and he dared not guess. "Go on ahead Mistress Joan," he ordered, in charge now, sensing she really no longer was able to make decisions. "Put on some more herbs to brew," he mentioned the strong ones, ending with a shout at the hurrying figure, "and get plenty of water heating, this girl is filthy!"

It was as different a birth from Fleurs' as night is to day. Firstly they drew out the big wooden bath, once again everyone running to obey orders. It was chaotic. Set behind a clothes maiden before the fire, the unwilling girl was stripped and manhandled into the steaming bath. Very soon, more water was on the floor than in the tub for Joany was a big, raw-boned girl, filthy, verminous and furious. Lee found he was smiling to himself at the mutual abuse of Goddaughter and Godmother. Mistress Joan, exasperated beyond words, landed some good slaps on whatever area of bright pink flesh she could reach. When a pain swept over her, Joany raged like a mad creature, cursing, like a smith at both of them, so surely all the castle could hear.

"Out!" screamed Mistress Joan, when anyone dared to enter the hall, even though it was evening and everyone wanted their food. "And keep out till I tell you."

Gradually the herbs did their work and the girl quietened so they got her clean somehow. Lee skilfully cut off as much of her hair as he could in the melee and tossed it into the fire. Finally, the three of them, wet from top to toe, the girl draped in a great thick sheet between them, left the hall and made for the room where Fleur lay.

Rested, clean, secure with her Godmother, Joany quietened for the moment but as the pains quickened, once again began yammering like a hog being killed. No amount of slaps caused her to quieten, even being told that she was upsetting Fleur. With each pain, she gathered breath and hollered till she croaked.

"If you will stop that noise," Lee tried, shouting above the racket, "I can rub your back as I did Fleur's, which really takes away the pain." He looked across at Fleur. "Isn't that right Fleur?" As Joany just happened to hear what was being said, and seeing Fleur nod, she turned her back to Lee who gratefully set to.

"Now take great breaths, good girl."

Peace. Joan and Lee almost smiled at each other despite their fatigue. At last the birth was near and Joany, unable to control herself, once more set up her din. With one last yell, with astonishing speed, she shoved a great strapping bright-pink boy into the world, who carried on with gusto the noise his mother had left off.

Father Jerome came with the night, the maids lighting his way, carrying the great silver ewer and bowl, for Mistress Joan had sent word that she was fearful for Fleur and her daughter. By the Grace of God, they must have rites, and be baptised.

Somehow, despite the muddle and her weariness, she had found the necessary cloths and Holy head-bands for both babies. A baptism must be done properly, even, and especially if, the infant died.

Swaying with fatigue, Mistress Joan stood beside Lee while the old priest droned his liturgy, the women responding, hands fluttering over breasts.

"Shall we call her Fleur after you?" Lee had asked, holding the ice cold hand, now furiously admitting to himself that he had failed. The fingers pressed his as she murmured her agreement. Drawing the healer down she whispered, "Promise me you will care for her?" Lee looked down at the white face, the candlelight flickering over the gold hair, deeply sad.

"I promise." First kissed her hand, then her brow. "I promise."

The old priest baptized them, first Fleur, the lightest bundle on his skinny arm, who did not even murmur. Then Jerome, twice her size, who squealed like a half-grown piglet. For Joany, once more her old self, announced she wanted a fine name, and what better than Jerome from the priest? The old priest blinked at the compliment. Mistress Joan and Lee stood as Godparents for both babies.

There was no celebration. Joan was led straight away after the little ceremony by her irritated husband to her bed, while Lee, having closed up his room, decided to sleep on an extra pallet with the new mothers. Twenty four hours after he had put his foot onto the cobbles of the courtyard, exhausted, he fell asleep, so he did not know the exact hour when Fleur, mother of his new Godchild, quietly broke her ties with the earth.

Of course he did not leave, for the moment anyway. Joan was so tired, he stayed to help, to guide the rumbustious young Joany in her duty as mother and wet-nurse. Clean, her cropped head healing of its sores, and tied with a pretty head cloth, Lee saw a good-looking young woman emerge, as a butterfly. Thankfully she had enough milk for the two babies and more and revelled gratefully in the good and plentiful food and ale supplied to her.

"You shall stay here with us now, Joany," announced Mistress Joan. "I promised your mother I would care for you, and I have been tardy in that duty."

It was Lee, not because he had to but because he felt it wise, who marched into the smithy, plonked down a purse of coins, and informed the smith that his daughter was now living at the castle.

"Find yourself a wife to cook for you and pay your dues with this."

Days went on to weeks, and still he did not leave. Then months, then years. Till eventually, in the fullness of time, he too was laid to rest near the gentle Fleur. But that was not for many long years, long after he had reared her daughter as his own.

CHAPTER THIRTEEN

JOAN

Holding each one firmly, Anders scrubbed his sons meticulously, till clean and pink, they were done. He gazed at them, as he often did, in disbelief, for they were a light to his eyes, the bonniest trio ever. Now he tidied up, put the milk in the ashes of the fire, threw the bowl of water down the sluice and told the eldest to get down three bowls.

"Bread and milk, with," he turned and grinned at them, "a dribble of honey on top."

The elder clapped his hands to be instantly mimicked first by the second, then by the third. Anders laughed out loud. Who could imagine he could be so happy, even if this was woman's work. Tearing up the bread, he distributed it into their bowls, poured on the warmed milk, then the honey and then, taking the smallest horn spoon, he pressed the bread to soften it for the little one.

Even bringing the warm milk from the fire was a new experience, he'd always had thin ale. And she always laid a clean cloth on top, insisting he did likewise, so smuts didn't fall in from the fire. He had learned a lot, even if at first he had riled about what he thought was nonsense. Of course he had never argued from the start about anything, or complained about her fussiness. But then no one argued with Joan, for she was special. Hers was a curious role, not only in the castle, but about the whole district. It didn't take long to understand that she was much respected, and had an unusual air of authority. Handsome to look on, she was also wise and fine, and was ever being asked for advice and help. Generally she sorted out the problem, and if she could not, she stated firmly that it could wait for the baron. There was no bailiff at the castle, which seemed unusual at first, because his Joan saw to everything. At the same time, she was an excellent wife and mother, although he did often find himself a rather more active father than most. Deftly he popped the spoon into the open mouth and watched the baby munch away with his bare gums in obvious enjoyment. Now he was weaned, he wondered if another baby would be coming along. Joan said not, but secretly he thought that even she could not dictate that sort of thing. Taking the little one on his lap, he nursed him to sleep while the older two played. He frowned. Now why hadn't he thought of cutting up slices of logs for the boys to play with? He watched them intent on their building, chattering quietly together, deep in their child's world of make-believe. Very carefully, he laid the sleeping baby in his cradle and covered him with a shawl.

Taking the bunch of goose wings from outside the window embrasure, he sorted them out. Even the feathers were banished outside, against bringing flies in. He smiled at his wife's nonsense, his hands busy, gently tugging the feathers out. However careful they were to recover their arrows, many were lost, and with hunting days ahead, he bent his head to work. Simon the fletcher had taught him while his foot was bad, and he felt now that his arrows were almost as good as his teacher's. Edging his stool close to the hearth, he tried to get the shavings in and not on the floor, another of her little fussy ways.

Whatever Joan said about that healer, Lee, he could never like him. Too smooth, too silent, an odd creature that he was, creeping about the place on his felt shoes. And now, with the two newborn children, it looked as if he was going to delay his departure further. Anders would not have even guessed that he was jealous of the newcomer, but he was, mostly because of his wife's friendship with him. Not that there would have been any grounds for jealousy, for Joan was a faithful and loving, if stern wife, while the healer usually kept much to himself. Until the babies arrived that was. That big raw girl Joany, nursing two squalling mites, he compared her in his mind's eye with Joan. There was no comparison. One was a rough village girl, coarse and slovenly, while his Joan was a lady. His thoughts went back to the friendship of the healer with his wife; it sorely irritated him.

First he had arrived in the night with a group of injured young knights with their men. It seemed as if they had taken over the castle, so soon after the baron had gone, just when they were enjoying the peace. Although she never complained, he knew that Joan had been sore-pressed to provide for them, the baron's party having emptied the store rooms. Now the man was totally engrossed in two little babies, and he had to admit, they took much of Joan's time too.

"It won't be for long my dear," she consoled him. "Joany is my Goddaughter. She must learn and I have great faith in her. Her mother, my childhood friend, was an excellent woman, who made one big mistake by taking up with that ruffian, John Smith. I never understood her, even though, true, he was most handsome when young. Be patient Anders, for my sake, who was so lucky to have made a good marriage. Little Fleur is so tiny. Imagine if she were ours. When they are well-established, things will get easier again, you'll see." Pausing, she smiled warmly at him. "Besides, husband, it is grand to have more children in the castle, they will be friends for our three, no place is right without little ones about with their laughter and noise."

Soothed by her words, even so, Anders did not like the healer, something was funny with him, sly. He tried to force his thoughts away from that tedious subject.

Soon, the baron would be back for the summer with his wife and her sons and their squires and grooms and hangers-on. A hunting party took some organization and he would be so busy, there would be no time for such silly thoughts. And Joan, she too would be run off her feet coping with those spoilt and demanding people. He pulled himself up shamed. What a cur he was to be grumbling away to himself when life had never been so sweet.

It had been about six years ago when she had waylaid him. A tall slim young woman, nice to look on, but reputed to have a sharp tongue. Well how should he know, he had barely exchanged two words with her.

The castle was strangely quiet after the annual hunting parties had left and this time it had been especially busy. The baron had recently married an older lady, and it was with the baroness' household that he and his father had come as grooms. Being a widow with sons already, lads barely younger than the baron himself, it was put about that it must have been she who organized the match. A haughty woman, she had chosen the baron no doubt for his lands, for he was hardly a handsome man. The day before they were to leave, as luck would have it as it turned out, a horse had stood on Anders foot, breaking the bones. The pain being terrible, it was obvious that Anders could not leave, so with a curse and cuff, his father had told him to stay till he was healed.

It was she, Mistress Joan who had tended him. Ignoring him, she had concentrated on his foot, bound it in splints, smeared comfrey poultices on, and wrapped it up like a great onion. During her ministrations, she barely spoke, just giving orders, and yes, a kind of comfort.

When it was healed he rarely saw her, for autumn had come with the usual harvest work to be done and stores to be brought in. All the daylight hours were filled with preparations for the winter.

One day, he was hobbling across the cobbled bailey with his crutch, when Mistress Joan had barred his way.

"How are you, Anders?" she had asked, peering at his foot, then him.

"Good, good," he had stammered his reply.

Then not looking at him directly, "may I have a private word with you?" she had asked, not waiting for a reply. Ignoring his surprise, she had led him into a small garden he did not know existed. Holding the door open for him so he could scuttle through, she closed it firmly and went to a seat. The smell of chamomile rose as their feet crushed the lawn.

"No doubt you are wondering why I wish to speak to you?"

He had nodded, dumbfounded. She patted a seat on which lay a cloth. "Be seated," she said in her strange polite way, and taking up a piece of stitching lying there, she sat opposite him.

He was uncomfortable. Say if any of the other lads saw him? They would tease him forever. He waited. The little garden was filled with bees, exploring the late roses, getting their last stores in for the winter. A small damson tree stood in a corner with ripe, deep-purple fruit hanging low, and the wasps were already seeking out the falls. He realized that it was very peaceful here, that the girl opposite him had just bitten her thread, and was surveying her work. Still he did not speak.

"The baroness," she paused as she re-threaded her needle. "The baroness," it seemed she was struggling for words, "informed me before she left, that she would be seeking out a husband for me," she paused and brushed away an enquiring wasp. "That the next time they come, she would arrange my nuptials." Silence. He watched a bumble bee struggling to take off, so well-loaded with pollen, its leg-baskets so heavy it could barely fly. He imagined the baroness, wondering if her choice of husband would be as haughty and unpleasant as were she and her sons.

"I do not wish this," she continued in a rush, voice squeaky for a moment. "The baron is unable to support me against his wife, so I would be obliged to marry whoever she chooses." Pausing, she held out her stitching to look at. "The lady does not, alas, care for me, so I am sure that her choice would not be agreeable to me." Another pause while she searched for the colour thread she needed with exaggerated care. "Therefore, Anders, you will please excuse my forwardness," another pause and deep breath, "I am asking you, if you will wed with me?" Silence.

He had heard and been dumbfounded. He switched his gaze from the bee to her, eyes wide in shock. He noted that her face was very pink, and her eyes were cast down on her handwork.

Silence.

"Is it distasteful to you then?" she asked quickly. "Am I so plain? Have I no appeal to you?" Her voice seemed funny. "I hoped that you liked it here, and that you would care to make your home here, after your foot is well. I do have a small dowry," she hurried on. "I am well-versed in all womanly tasks, which perhaps you know, having been here for some months. I would endeavour to be a good and loving wife to you."

Silence, then.

"Why me, mistress?" he asked, struggling for words.

Another silence. She tussled with her work, and when she glanced up at him for a moment, he saw her eyes were brimming with tears.

Quickly he moved as best he could to her side, took away the sewing and put it deliberately down on the seat beside her.

"Certainly I would like to take you to wife," he felt suddenly very manly, holding her hand, gazing on the top of her head which hung down. "You have been so very good to me, and clever to heal my foot. I see that you are such a fine maid, who would not? But." She drew her hand away, lifted her apron and blew her nose.

"You have a reason for not wanting to wed with me?"

Anders hopped around and carefully sat beside her, his bad foot stuck out in front as usual. Again he took her hand, feeling very daring, for he had little previous experience with women; his father always saw to that, ever intent to be there first.

"I think it sounds a very agreeable thing to do, Joan," he added, greatly daring. "More than anything I would like to stay here with you. If you do not care that I am a simple bonded man, without even the money to pay my lord the due to wed? Can you see I am no great catch, though I believe I am a good groom and I enjoy my work." Watching her face for her reaction, he saw only a pursed mouth and lowered lids. "Then I thank you for the honour you pay me. So yes, you must choose the day, and meanwhile I will try to make my foot completely better so that I may work again and so be a good husband."

They spoke more, quietly, kindly, trying to learn something of each other. She told him that she found his looks pleasing, which surprised and delighted him. She said that she saw how brave he had been in pain, and that his ways were kindly to the beasts, which was why she had taken special notice of him. He told her that never in one hundred years would he have dreamt that such a lovely lady would take him for her husband, which caused her to smile.

Christmastide was her chosen time, time enough for his foot to mend, and for her to make arrangements. They kept their plans quiet, yet it didn't take long for it to be observed that they were spending time together. Hers was a strange position, for already she was in charge of so many things in the castle. True, there was Father Jerome the priest, Agnes the woman in charge of the girls who did the cleaning, laundry and dairy work and Peter, her old husband who seemed to be steward in all but name. For it was, for most of the year, a small household, a very old castle, mainly used for hunting in the fine forests around about, not really a home fit for gentry.

To his great joy, she had given him the most precious gift for their marriage, the best surprise in the world. A filly foal, barely off its dam. She was a beauty who with love and care grew into an angel horse. Small and fast, she moved beautifully, the light rippling on her flanks, a light chestnut. Man and horse became as one as they hunted in the service of the castle. Yet she was his own mare, his very own, a marriage gift from his wife.

All he had to give her was a polished great piece of light gold amber which hung on a plaited-hair cord. Eyes glowing, she had taken it up and held it first against her breast, then to the light.

"Oh Anders! It is so beautiful," which, because it had been his mother's, gladdened his heart. So he was able to tell her, the only person in the world, that Michael the groom had not been his true father. His natural father had been, according to his dying mother, another Anders, a tall, fair man from across the seas. It was he who had given her the amber before he sailed away, and Michael who had taken her to wife soon after.

"She would be pleased to know you have it, my wife," Anders felt his throat close with emotion, remembering the day his mother died. Would he ever forget the pain of her dying, how she suffered, the great thing growing in her belly like a child, but growing to kill her.

"Take it, hide it and give it to your wife one day," had said the old hag who had laid her out. "Make sure that he," she glanced to the curtain from where came the sounds of drunken snores, "doesn't get it, for he will drink it up in no time." Grateful, the young Anders had slipped it into his shirt, surprised at the gesture. Any other would have kept it for themselves, but this was a kindly woman. Quietly he went to the flour pot and felt about at the bottom. He handed the two small, flour-covered coins to the old one, which she took with a slight smile, then as he slipped it into her clothing. Yes indeed, that is what he would do. Simple though it was, just a lump of pure sunlight, he would give it to his wife as a wedding present, if ever the day came.

The first foal out of his mare, another fine filly, he had given to her, to mark the birth of their firstborn son.

Due to the obvious disapproval of the baroness, they retreated to their room whenever possible. At least, in private anyway, the baron had given them his blessing. For he and Joan were kin. Generally, life was sweet, safe and comfortable. At first, he had been just a groom, Mistress Joan's husband. Now he, becoming respected almost as she, was head groom and huntsman; it was official.

Carefully he rose to look at the sleeping baby in its cradle. Next he passed the piss-pot to his older boys who did their best, then clambered into the truckle bed he had drawn out for them from under the tester bed he and Joan slept in. It never ceased to amaze him that he, Anders the groom, who all his life had slept on straw, more often than not in the stables too, should now sleep on a fine big bed in the castle.

"Come," he drew her close as she came in, pressing his mouth to her head, smelling the cleanness, the baking bread, the pottage, the fragrance of her. "Make yourself easy Joan, for you look tired." As was their custom, he poured her a glass of good red wine, while he took ale. This was another strange thing about her, she with her expensive tastes.

Yes, he had much to be thankful for, so he must dismiss his irritation with Lee the healer, the uninvited guest who never left.

Still, beside her, Anders made his plans for the hunt tomorrow. Joan had yet again told him what was needed, though being the sixth year, he knew well enough. By the week's end, the store room would be well hung with venison, boar and game; there had to be plenty when the baron was in residence.

The baroness always brought her own cooks with her, fussy nuisances that they were. They would arrive shortly before their mistress, and with as much reluctance. At least it meant that Joan would have a more quiet time and be able to be with the children instead of rushing about running the place. From the first, he had noticed how she kept to herself when the baron's party were in residence. Gladly it seemed, she relinquished the reins of the castle to the visiting staff. Gladly too she took back the reins when they left, and quickly set about getting the place to rights again.

The village, indeed the whole area, had been informed and would be arriving with their dues and wares. The animal pens were fixed and ready for the livestock. Larder, buttery and pantries swept and lime-washed, were already laden full of produce which Joan had gathered in. So for two or three months, as long indeed as there was good hunting and good weather, their home would be a mad place. The extra horses had to be stabled and fed. Hounds, every size from almost ponies to lap dogs would abound, ever on the lookout for a fight or something to steal. The falcons, irritable messy things always on their perches, and in the way. Worse than the creatures, were the humans who came with them, ever jostling and squabbling because they felt they should have better accommodation. Grumbling endlessly, over the discomforts of the old castle, and yearly trying to oust his family from their one room. Anders frowned to himself. It was just one of those things which had to be tolerated, a time to be lived through. The lords he could cope with, but their servants, he did not. With their stuck-up ideas of their own importance and ridiculous demands, acting gentry themselves, it was sickening. Then the food! How he craved the daily pottage and good brown bread which Joan made. Filled with good things, the pottage was always tasty, never mushy as of his childhood where everything was stewed to a pulp. The fuss of those cooks astonished him. The daft things they did with wild colours, feathers, even castles with marchpane. He was unimpressed, taking bread, cheese and cold cuts to their room, there, whenever he could slip away, to eat in privacy. Sometimes Joan would make a small pottage just for them if she could collect together the ingredients. They had brought her small loom up to their quarters after the first boy was born, so during this time, she managed to weave enough cloth for all their needs for the coming winter.

"I cannot be worrying over him, and running all the time to see if he is well." Now she leaned over the growing cloth, drawing up a thread, never able to be still, always busy, ever seeking work. It seemed that the boys needed new shirts. Anders smiled to himself, he till now who had only owned the one shirt on his back. He never ceased to wonder at his wife's knowledge, patience and efficiency. How he came to be so blessed he could not imagine, yet blessed he was, thanks be to God.

Deftly, she worked the pattern into the weft.

"I was born here," she laughed at him, happy to have the time to talk, the new Joan, the lighter, brighter Joan that she was since their marriage. He swelled with pride. "Since as long as I can remember, the hunting parties came, with all the fuss and to-do they make for us who live and labour here." Obviously she enjoyed it too, doing it well, and thus, he knew, irritating the baroness, who did not like her; silly, idle woman.

"I'm used to that too," had smiled Joan when he questioned her. "The baron's mother, the Lady Jessica, always made my life a misery, for it was well known that I was her husband's natural daughter, though born before he knew her. She could never forgive my very existence. After sending us away, my mother, who was seamstress for the previous baroness died, so I returned. The baron was ever kind to me, and when the son was born, I was pressed into immediate nursemaid. What she did not realize was that I adored my half-brother. A loveless child needs to focus its affections somewhere, so Roland was my all. He was my baby brother, my precious little frog. He was the one human who truly loved me, and thankfully still does, albeit now he is married, with discretion. And just as well too, as the old baroness was a silly woman and poor mother. Then," gazing unseeing she remembered. "Nature has a strange way of giving justice you know, husband, for she gradually lost her wits, so it was I, the despised base-born child, who cared for her." She laughed quietly. "In the end, she always referred to me as "daughter". I suspect she indeed thought I was too. Roland and I do have some features in common, although I favoured my mother, thank goodness; for father was a very plain man." She smoothed her hair, tucking a stray wisp under her coif. "I do admit however, how grievously I am disappointed that the baron has no heir. Especially while we have been blessed with three fine sons. It is said that his lady is a lot older than she admits, certainly she is many years his senior. How many times I have asked myself why he married her, silly boy." A great sigh as she smoothed the fabric on her loom. "Anyway, she is happily more involved with her own sons, so apart from the initial spite, she grows used to me and leaves me alone." Leaning across to surprisingly kiss him lightly on the cheek she ended. "Thank you for marrying me Anders. It would have been unbearable being wed to a stranger of her choice, someone who would despise me for my birth. While you dear husband?" As she left the room, he felt a warm glow, yet wondering at the question at the end of her sentence.

CHAPTER FOURTEEN

PETERKIN

Much as he hated leaving the children, Lee was loyal to his old friend Edward at the monastery. Several times each year, he rode on a borrowed pony, most of a day at that, then stayed some days, before hurrying home.

He was not sure that bloodletting was always a good thing. It must be for healthy older people, but for the young, weak or seriously ill? No he wasn't sure. Why drain them? If they were sick, it was far better to give them nourishing food, light soups, good air and gentle entertainment. The face of his teacher flashed into his mind. "Use your common sense," was his motto. "Don't kill them by bleeding them to death." He smiled fondly with the memory. Gratitude filled his heart, for he had learned all he knew from that strange yet fine person. Most of the monks seemed to benefit from the letting, and he felt he owed it to them, for many reasons, not least because of their friendship and the good herbs which came from the monastery. He found that he enjoyed the routine and the order compared with the often hectic, secular life of the village and the castle.

It was also quite a good thing to have a change from the castle, especially while the baron and party were in residence. He increasingly appreciated the contrast of life, the monks, their orderly lives, the plainsong and the beautiful buildings. It seemed as if every year he went there, more buildings rose. Of course the church was very wealthy. What with their lands, the wool and their wealthy patrons, they could certainly be extravagant. Besides, building gave occupation to the many artisans who came from far and wide. Which in turn gave occupation, and a better life to the locals. Like a pebble thrown into a pond, it touched everyone eventually. Deep in thought, he let the reins loose on the pony's withers. The pony, guessing it was going home, made a healthy trot along the soft forest floor.

Lee never feared these solitary rides despite advice from everyone. Who after all would want to harm him? He carried nothing that a robber might want. So he was unprepared, when hardly into the shade of the deep woods, his way was barred by three big rough fellows who stood right in the middle of the path. The pony slithered to a stop, its nostrils flaring. Lee flicked an experienced eye over them. Big men with even taller long bows, they must be brothers with their red hair. Each was clad in rough homespun and skins and was uniformly filthy.

"Well brothers," Lee raised his hand in greeting. "What can I do for you?" yet trying to quieten his beating heart. The leader came forward and held the bridle.

"Are you Lee? The healer?" he asked roughly, peering up through his wild hair at the monkish figure astride the pony.

"I am he," replied Lee and waited for the blow which didn't come. Still holding the bridle, the ruffian turned and led the pony off the main track down a narrow path, the others close behind in single file. Feeling his feet catch against the saplings at his sides, Lee tucked them in and hung on. Before long, they came to a clearing where a simple shelter stood, a small fire burning before its open door.

The leader cupped his hand under Lee's foot and helped him down.

"For the love of God, healer, see to our young brother who lies sorely sick, inside."

Surprised at the apparent sincerity of the man, Lee stepped inside the shelter and sniffed. Oh dear God, he thought, gangrene!

"Get the fire up, man," he ordered going to his pack on the pony. "How long ago did this happen? Why didn't you bring him to the monastery before? The wound is bad, bad, can't you smell it?" Anger rose in him, anger at the ignorance of these people, and at his own helplessness. Silently, the three men brought wood, then water from a small stream, setting a pot on the fire to boil. Together the three of them carried the patient out into a patch of light, and Lee could see that he was a mere stripling and in poor shape. With his tools laid out on a cloth beside the fire, Lee knelt over him. The stink was terrible. Muck was oozing through rough rags swathed about a foot, which he swiftly cut away and threw into the fire, which hissed and sent up foul smoke. Searching through his meagre supplies, he brought out herbs and soft wool and washed the filthy wound so at last he could see it clearly. Then he drew out his pot of leeches and put them to the side.

Where there had been toes, there was putrid meat, with bone showing through. He would have liked to ask how it had happened, but thought the better of it. The lad was weak, there was no time to waste. Could he stand an amputation? He would die anyway, his body succumbing to the rot which now surely coursed through him.

The three men watched him silently. It crossed his mind that whatever he did, he might not live to see the morrow, or the children again. Sitting back on his heels he turned to look at them.

"You have left it very late, perhaps too late. If I do not remove the toes, he will die. If I do remove the toes, he is so weak, the shock may cause him to die. You are his folk. You must decide. I will do my very best, and by the Grace of God, and good care, he may survive. Now. Go and decide while I give him something for the pain."

Testing the bitter brew which was simmering on the edge of the fire, he took up a cup and spoon, and holding the filthy head on his lap, eased the spoon into the mouth. To his surprise, the reaction was strong. Well now, perhaps he is not so weak after all, for he was a lad and robust.

"Don't fight me, son," he said very firmly. "The medicine is bitter, yet it will ease your pain. Come on now, man, your brothers have brought me here to help you; now you must take the medicine." As with a little child, the mouth opened and Lee spooned it all in.

"Do it," a rough voice spoke at his elbow.

Awed, they did as he asked, sharpening their best knife, cleaning it in the hot ashes, washing it in boiling water. Their coarse faces fearful, they held the sick boy down and while he screamed, Lee cut away three toes, much flesh, and again, threw it all on the fire. Praying silently to himself, he willed his stomach not to rise and spew up its bile. Feeling for the fluttering pulse, Lee hastened to sew, anoint and placing the leeches there, covered the whole mess lightly with a bandage. Settling his patient, he laid the leg up high on a rolled up skin.

Then, sitting on his heels, he thought of the tiny box secreted in his clothes, the most precious drug of them all which Edward had generously given him. Well, if the boy was to die, let him die in peace. Taking it out, he carefully opened the box and fudged about inside. Taking a tiny portion, as a pea, he rolled it in his fingers, then, opening the boy's mouth, pressed it high into his cheek.

"This is a very special herb, brothers, given to me by Brother Edward at the monastery, for serious cases. Now we wait my friends. If he is strong and the poison has not taken over his whole body, he will live. The wound is clean now. He needs rest, good food, and let us pray he will live to be a grandfather." On impulse he moved up onto his knees and hands together, quietly began praying, and the three fellows seeing it, meekly followed.

It was a bad night. Lee lay beside the boy, to hold and comfort him, who tossed and moaned endlessly. Rising now and again, Lee added more wood to the fire even though, being midsummer, it was not cold. As the leeches bloated and fell off, he put them back in a jar and replaced them with others to do their wondrous cleansing work. The three ruffians snored in ragged heaps nearby, obviously unable to keep awake. Lee realized wryly, that with him there, they had shed their responsibilities. It often happened, for no doubt, they were exhausted. Bathing the fevered brow, spooning more chamomile or willow bark tea into the resisting mouth, the night passed and with the dawn, Lee slept too.

When he woke, he found surprising order in the camp, the fire still burned and a fresh new pile of wood lay nearby. The patient slept, though on touch, Lee saw he had a high fever. Still, as he pressed his fingers into a pulse, he thought that he might live. He was obviously a strong boy, and the shock had not killed him. Considering for a moment, he thought again of his own teacher. What would he do? Then suddenly decided that he should bleed him. The poison in the blood must seep away and let the body make new. Finding a vein under the ankle of the bad foot, he let it bleed, hoping that the poison was going too.

Glad of the chamomile and borrige he had brought from the monastery, he brewed a tea, gave some to the boy and drank the rest. To his surprise, one of the brothers brought him a jug of ale and some barley cakes which he soaked in it and ate gratefully. He was hungry and while he ate, he watched them from under his hood. Despite their rough appearance, it was obvious that they were a united brood, deeply caring of their youngest brother.

Two more days passed and the boy seemed better. While he slept, Lee wandered nearby, gathering wild mushrooms and some unusual herbs. These he dropped into a pot bubbling gently over the fire, set on a strong wooden crane. The brothers quietly went off in twos, returning with rabbits, wild garlic leaves and cooking herbs, and the smell of good soup filled the little clearing. The mood in the camp changed subtly, optimism and humour filling every face.

"I would like to go on my way now, my friends," Lee spoke with more courage than he felt. "Let us put the boy on my pony, he can travel now and he must come with me, for if I do not continue to tend him, the wound may go bad again, and he may die yet."

Doubtful looks were exchanged.

"Do you think I will let him come to any harm, brothers, after working so hard to save his life? No!" he forged on. "He needs good care, good food, and I promise you, that if he lives, I will bring him back here in one month."

It was a slow and difficult journey, with Lee leading the pony, two holding the boy on the saddle while the third held up the injured leg.

As the road widened just before the village, and they came into the light, Lee left them to slip down to the river. Dipping his tunic in the water, he gently cleaned the boy's face, and saw that under the mire and with time, this could be a good looking lad.

"Mistress Joan will set about me if I take such a dirty lad into her kitchen," he said cheerfully to reassure them. "Yet she must be pleased, for not only has she a heart of gold, she is a fine cook." He looked over his companions and even felt a fondness for them. "Now do not worry. All being well, and with the Grace of God, he will heal, even if he limps all his life. I promise you we will come to your place in thirty days, by then, God willing, he should be well on the way to good health." He turned and walked on a few steps and leant against a tree so that they had some time to speak together privily.

Their faces showing astonishment, yet quickly, one by one, they swept off their hats and took the proffered hand and shook it. Men of few words, used to the silence of the forests, their rough faces showed every emotion.

Lee looked up at the sky. At least it was fine, but dusk was falling despite it being summer. It had been a slow, tedious ride. He looked at the boy anxiously, touched his brow and smiled. Turning to the three men he lifted a hand.

"Godspeed, my friends, and we to a decent meal, and good health-giving broth for our lad here." He clicked at the pony and they started very slowly up the cobbled slope to the castle. Setting the boy down on a mounting block, Lee called for the pony to be taken away. Gingerly, he lifted the boy, despite his ills no light weight, and carefully edged through the door into the great hall. Every eye watching him, Lee sought out Mistress Joan, studiously avoiding her husband, who he knew would be scowling.

Barely raising an eyebrow, Mistress Joan came forward with quiet greeting and tended the boy as she would any other needing child.

"More work for you," said Anders later, anger in his voice. "Must he always bring in these waifs for your attention?" But Joan smiled serenely into her loom, then turned and giving him an unusually tender smile replied.

"Well, Anders my love, as well you know, I have a speciality in caring for lads with injured feet!" Which melted him so, he forgot himself, and shamed, went to her, and cupping her breasts from behind, pressed his mouth to her hair, drinking in her scent of lavender and good pottage.

"Ah dear wife, you are right as usual. Forgive a old silly bear." And harmony quickly returned to their lives once more.

The foot healed slowly. Eventually, when he had lost his fear and gained confidence, the boy told them that he was called Peterkin. Joan once again took up her shears to clip his head so that she could wash it, and eventually he -changed colour with her attentions. Anders was away purchasing necessities for the winter, which made things easier, for even now, despite himself, he could not help resenting the extra work which the healer seemed to lay on his wife.

Lee went unerring to the little place where he kept his medical stores and found a goodly crutch. There had been a woman in the village years past, sitting by the ford with a girl-child, selling baskets and pegs, they were poor, maimed creatures, with their head cloths almost completely covering their faces. Curious, he had squatted down before them and gently moved their cloths so that he could see their disfigurement. The elder had one side of her face grievously burnt, causing her to be lopsided. The other merely had a severe hare lip. They looked up at him, without fear he noted, and he in turn noted the wonderful blue eyes of the child. Overpaying them for the crutch, he took some calendula salve from his basket and gave it to the woman.

"Rub it on your face at night, it will ease the tightening," he told her, stroking the child's head, "such lovely blue eyes, lass, God be with you." So he had, thankfully, a crutch ready and waiting for the boy.

With the crutch, and a new felt shoe with soft wool stuffed in the toe, he gently urged the boy to get up to go to the privy. Before long, Peterkin was being led about by the children, who were delighted to have another playmate. For the newcomer seemed to have endless patience with them, and taught them many new songs and games of dice and knucklebones and disappearing a coin, pulling it out of their ears.

Unaware that he might receive disapproval from Anders, the boy began hobbling to the stables, and ever careful with his foot, tried to help with the horses. It seemed he had an affinity with beasts as well as children, for they softened to his touch and seemed to realize that he was lame.

After thirty days, Lee got him mounted and with a bag well-stocked with medicines and food, they retraced their way through the forest, yet at a slightly faster rate. At the clearing, they met with silence. The shelter looked abandoned and not used of late. Lee swept aside the embers of the fire and laid his palm there, but it was cold. He looked at the boy, puzzled.

"We will stay here for the night, in case they got their counting wrong." While they set up camp, as they opened up their packs, a slight sound alerted them. Hand raised, Lee listened intently. Suddenly a poor little wretch of a cur crawled toward them on its belly, ears down and whimpering. Peterkin fell to his knees and stretched out his hands. Lee watched as boy and dog embraced with sobs and frantic licking.

"I see you have an old friend here Peter?" Lee said kindly. "So we will be glad of his company as guard while we wait for your brothers. Methinks a good meal might be welcome to him too."

They stayed for three more nights, and were very glad of the food they had brought. Lee was pleased to see how the boy kept busy and automatically took over as host. He was off into the trees, shadowed by the little dog and struggled to collect wood, sweeping the hearth with a root broom, yet all the time his face worried.

The weather changed, a great wind blowing, thrashing the branches, foretelling rain. Lee saddled up the pony and faced the boy.

"Now, Peterkin, I wish to return home. If you want to stay, I cannot stop you, yet I do think you should come with me, for your foot is better, but not completely healed. When they come, they will see from your work that you have been here, and they will come to the castle."

They never did. At first the boy watched anxiously every time there was the commotion of arrivals at the gate, but gradually, he gave up. Eventually, Peterkin became one of the castle folk, his anxiety and search for his brothers dying with time. Lee noted with surprise that on his return from business in the town, Anders was kindly and seemed to take a liking to the boy, often finding uses for him, with unusual praise. Lee puzzled lightly about the change of heart and supposed that the good Joan had brought it about. When Anders was away, buying or selling, doing jobs for the baron, he always left Peterkin in charge of the stables. Puzzled yet glad, it would be some time before Lee would understand why. Perhaps even Joan did not fully understand her complicated husband. It was enough that his kindness and help were giving the boy confidence, dampening his irritation towards the healer.

By the time Fleur and Jerome were three, Joany had long since finished nursing them. Having been a good mother and foster-mother, she was now nursemaid and friend. Scarcely past being a child herself, she understood and loved them both deeply. Very often, she took Mistress Joan's three sons along with the two little ones and their laughter rang out across the valley. There was no need to call, for you just had to stop and listen to learn of their whereabouts. Lee smiled fondly. How fortunate they were to have such happy children, how lucky to have such a good girl to mind them. Joany had grown into a fine, pretty young woman, her rich golden hair gleaming with good health, her skin rosy and fresh. Her agile mind had soon picked up much herb lore, so Lee was always confident if he was short of something, Joany would search and find it.

On fine days, the women of the castle always gathered in the walled lady's garden, there to gossip while they spun, sewed or sorted seeds and pulses. The most tedious task seemed easy in that sheltered cocoon. Roses and honeysuckle sprawled over the wall, and cheeky little birds pecked about without fear. While the children played on the camomile lawn, Mistress Joan taught her Goddaughter all she knew, and Joany, having been bereft of a mother's care for so long, learned with a fierce enthusiasm. Biting off a thread, the older woman looked at the girl with affection.

"You are so like your good mother, Joany," said Mistress Joan. "It is like old times when we were girls, when we sat here with old Baroness Jessica, and learned, just as you do now." Then she brought out stories of past days and people, which Joany would never forget, with the peace and joy of her life at the castle.

The years passed with only the chaos of the annual invasion of guests, when Lee did not notice that Joany had a beau. One of the visiting groom's eyes lighted on her golden hair and happy face, so he took to hanging about. A handsome young man, it soon became obvious that whenever he had time free, he sought out the little family to play with the children and flirt with their nurse.

Lee had by now given up denying paternity of the children. Explanations were tedious, so Godfather soon became Father, and that was that. He was Father to Fleur, to Jerome, and somehow, even to Joany. At least that is how she addressed him, naturally, without guile, and about a hundred times a day.

"Father, can I take the children to the river to play? Father, Jerome has hurt his knee. Father, Fleur needs new shoes. Father, please may I make myself a new robe?" So yes, he was their father, all of them. For he not only loved them, he directed their lives and provided for their every need and zealously watched over their health.

Most of the year, they slept with Joany in the room off the halfway landing, which had probably been the gate-guard's dormer. Soon after their birth, they had opened it up and swept the chimney clear of bird's nests, and had made it into a comfortable nursery. Mistress Joan saw that the many repairs required by Lee had been made to the gatehouse, particularly in the winding stair, so they were safe and comfortable. So much so unfortunately, that they were obliged to vacate it when the annual guests took it over. Then the trio moved up the winding stair, delighted with such an adventure, into Lee's small eyrie. Joany's low bed was struggled up the stair, and piled with fresh-filled hay mattresses, the little ones snuggled up close to her in sleep. On the high shelf which was his bed, Lee watched them in the dimness of the night, loving their beauty and abandon, feeling strangely so proud and so happy. At least, when he went away to escape the visiting crowds for the regular blood-letting at the monastery, with them there, he felt his room and possessions were safe. For despite all intentions, Lee had settled into the castle as his home. His precious books were high on a shelf, covered with a length of fine linen. His medical equipment and medicines were safely stored in a chest which even had a great key to lock it. In the draught before the narrow window, bunches of herbs swayed gently drying while the dried ones, having been powdered in the mortar, were bagged up neatly and hung between the rafters.

It had not taken long before news of his gift of healing spread far and wide, and not many a day passed by without some sick soul coming to Lee for treatment. Aware of the jealousy of the trouble-making town physicians, he never charged a fee for his services. Dressed simply as a lay brother, the blessing of the monastery protected him. Even so, grateful patients often brought gifts. The wealthy always slipped a coin and there was a full purse hidden behind the wainscot. The poor brought what they could, according to their means. None came completely empty-handed, honey, wax, herbs, eggs and sometimes charcoal. Lee especially appreciated the fine woven, long strips of linen which he used for bandages. Simply made by a few clever women with basic waist and comb looms, he washed them carefully in lye, to use again, and again. These and carved wooden utensils, were received with such gratitude, so that the patients parted with them happily due to the lavish words of praise given by the healer. If he was asked, Lee always requested some simple thing, for it was best he found, not to refuse gratitude. If a woman came with her children suffering some childish ailment, he would give them tisane and lozenges, salves and powders. If the good wife offered him a basket of twelve eggs, he would take four, "one for each of my little family. Keep the rest for your little ones, mistress, for you must feed them well to help them to get better."

He blessed his luck in having the tower room over the gatehouse. Well enough away from the busy castle, it still was central enough to know what was happening and who was coming or going. Without fail, every time he climbed the stair, he carried a small basket of charcoal for the brazier, so in time, the dank walls dried out and it was cosy. In his early days, Lee had set up a rope along the stair to hold onto. He found that by suspending a small bronze sheep bell at the top, he was well warned of impending arrivals.

Perched on a great outcrop of rock, the castle had no moat, a feature Lee disapproved of, stinking, putrid mess they usually were. In an alcove on the half landing was the blessing of a garderobe over which Lee hung a strong cloth for privacy. The slope below seemed to flourish with the human waste and the ashes from his brazier, making a green carpet, well washed by the rains.

Not only did he heal humans, often some hurt creature was brought to him, and even if the poor beast was destined eventually for the pot, he tried to heal it.

Fleur had grown into a long-limbed, fair-haired, and beautiful, delicate-featured childing. Lee loved her with a great passion, and zealously watched over her, ever fearful that some harm might come to her. She was unusually quick to learn and spoke perfectly, constantly chattering gaily on this or that. Already she knew the herbs he gathered, and at his elbow sought to help him. She loved him, Jerome her brother and Joany. Indeed she seemed to love everyone in the castle, her dazzling smile winning all hearts.

Jerome had grown into a very big, sturdy boy, yet, to Lee's concern, unlike Fleur, Jerome did not speak. It was assumed that Fleur did his talking for him, for his bright eyes missed not a thing. So despite his silence, his quick intelligence made him a useful little person to send scurrying for things. He understood everything said to him, yet he remained mute. As time went on, worried, Lee tried to teach him. He sat with the boy every spare moment, urging him to say "Fleur, Father, Joany". Holding up objects, a cup, flowers, an apple, urged him to speak. Yet though he mouthed the words, no sound came. Nonetheless, and didn't everybody know it, he could bawl, and did so with vigour, if he fell, or if someone displeased him.

"Perhaps one day?" mused Lee to Mistress Joan while they were stripping dried beans for storing. "He is not stupid. It interests me to watch him and Fleur speaking together." Eventually, after careful examination of Jerome's mouth, Lee believed that he had a severe malformation, which prevented him from speaking.

Lee looked up as a shadow fell over the sun. Joany stood before him, another figure behind her in the doorway.

"Father," she came forward, almost a timid smile on her usually cheerful face. "Father, this is Dickin and we want to speak with you." Lee closed his book, cleared the table of pens and sat back surveying her with surprise.

"Of course, Joany my child, come in, come in young man."

They stood awkwardly, the boy tall enough to have to bend a fraction to avoid the roof beams.

"So what ails you on this fine autumn day?"

They exchanged glances, and the boy took Joany's hand and they both looked down at the floor. Lee watched and waited, surprised and mildly irritated that he had not noticed the two before. This was one of the baroness's entourage. Thank God the whole tiresome bunch would be leaving soon and peace would return.

"I've come sir," the boy spoke quietly, drew courage and began again more firmly. "I come to ask your permission to marry your Joany. I shall be leaving shortly with his lordship, I am an under-groom, my father is head groom at his lordship's other castle. Joany and I would like to wed before we go." He stopped, cast a quick look at Lee and continued. "I know that since your lady died, Joany has cared for the little ones, but sir, I would like to wed with her with your blessing and take her home with me."

Lee glanced at the girl. So that was the story. Well why not? She was a good girl, and yes, she had cared for the children, even if they were more hers than his.

"Joany," he addressed her, his face mild, "be a good girl and run for a jug of wine and three cups. We cannot speak of such important matters with dry throats."

While she was gone, he questioned the young man. A few years older than Joany, he was well-built and amiable looking. His family had been bondsmen to the baroness's late husband for many years.

"I will take good care of her sir," he stated, now feeling encouraged. "Not only do I love her well, I see she is a fine girl, with much learning from you, sir. My mother will be right glad to have her with us, for my sister died many years since and my mother is lonesome."

"And she has much sound knowledge of medicine, young man, mark you," cut in Lee suddenly realizing that he would miss her sorely. "Any place will be lucky to have her with her knowledge of herbs and healing. Indeed," he sucked in his breath for effect. "How I shall manage without her, I do not know?" He looked severely at the optimistic young face before him. "And mind, Master Groom, if I do permit the marriage, and if I ever hear that you beat my Joan, I shall come after you with a brace of ruffians and give you your share. Be sure I shall then bring her home with me, after having some strong words with his lordship. Mark my words young man, for I will not tolerate my girl being ill treated, for we are a gentle people here, and do things a different way from most." He stopped at the tinkle of the bell.

A breathless Joany arrived hotfoot with the wine, which put an end to the scolding, much to the relief of the young man. Sipping from their cups, conversation slowed, then stopped and Lee fell into thought.

"We must discuss this with your Godmother, Joany. And we must hear if the baron gives his blessing. It might be better if you wait a while, if you are promised for one year before you are wed and leave us. I will have to find a nursemaid to take your place to look after the children. This is all very sudden." He ended abruptly and shook his head mournfully.

The truth was, he was panicking. How would be manage? Obviously the plan was to leave her own child, Jerome, and how would he manage with the two children, by himself? Of course, his mind raced, two were better than one, and certainly, it would be awful to separate the children. Knowing that the women of the castle were always ready to mind them, even so, he saw his orderly, contented life falling apart. Poor girl. He remembered the day she had arrived. The blacksmith's child, filthy, bruised, rough and noisily labouring in childbirth. Smiling he drew her close in a light hug. And here she was, so fine and so wishing to be his, Lee, the healer's daughter. If it was what she so needed, she lied, and certainly, he would not let her down.

It was Mistress Joan who persuaded him and, if he did but know it, far less easily than getting permission from the baron. But not to wait a year, Joany was grown and ready for marriage. Lee was going to let it happen anyway, but he felt it his due to make just a little parental fuss. Once agreed, there was no holding back. The busy women gladly abandoned their regular chores and worked overtime with their needles to send one of theirs off with a decent dowry. The lady's garden seemed overfull and busy as a hive, with chattering and laughter, till they were done. Incredulous and proud, Joany packed a small new chest with three robes, two skirts, a cloak, shawls, hose and many fine things, almost like a young lady. Then, on her wedding-day, Lee took her to one side and handed her the leather purse.

"Go with God, my child. Take this for your dowry and mind it well. But I think your Dickin is a good man and that you will be content together. Make sure to try to come to see us each year when your man comes with the baron. And why not, something for us all to look forward to!" He held her close, surprised at the emotion which welled in his throat.

Despite their imminent departure, guests joined the castle folk with flowers and good wishes and witnessed the marriage being blessed by the priest in the church doorway. The children ran wild with excitement, clutching their wildflower posies, their hair decorated with simple wreaths, even the boys. With the celebration, the usual chaos of the departing hunting party seemed minimal. The most awkward of the high ladies, and pompous men, forgot their little grievances for the moment. It was a relief to find tempers were less short than usual, which added ease to the celebration for the handsome young couple. Everyone liked Dickin, a cheery lad and a good groom. Undoubtedly, many of them owed a debt to the bride's father, that odd healer-fellow, Lee. So led by the baron, Joany received rather generous gifts, considering she was not of the gentry. Music was played in the hall and a noon-day feast was laid, which cleaned out the larders completely.

The little family stood on the grass mound of the keep while the party straggled out of the courtyard and through the tall gatehouse. It was a fine sight on a bright autumn day. All the grand palfreys were milling about with dogs underfoot, and ill-humoured falcons balancing on mounted wrists. At last, after much kissing and hugging, Lee's family waved to Joany, whose eyes were perilously bright with tears. Their little rosy faces were filled with excitement as they were childishly ignorant that she was going for good. People did go away, they well knew. Lee their father, Anders, the other father, the baron and family. They went. And they always returned. Joany would come home soon.

When the last pack-horse had clattered out over the cobbles, an unusual silence fell upon the castle. It was always like this. Every year, the excitement when the hunting party arrived, and when they left.

As evening fell, Lee took the children back into the hall, poured them buttermilk and set them onto teasing wool with the other children. Sitting in a corner on piles of fleece, they laughed and chattered, their little fingers seeking out herb and burr. It was a game, a useful game too while Peterkin sat with them, a new self-appointed guardian. Lee watched them with love, but also with a tinge of fear. Could he cope? He must of course. And well he knew he was not alone, for the excellent Mistress Joan, Godmother to them both, she would help him.

"Be of good cheer, Lee," seeing his face so down, she smiled as she handed him a cup of wine. "Our Joany did well. As her mother's friend and her Godmother, I am pleased with the match, and that we could aid her in a sound marriage. And mark, my friend, even the baroness gave them her blessing!" Pulling up a stool she sat near him, closing her eyes against the brightness of the fire. "It was good chance that she came here when she did, or her life would have been hopeless in the hands of that brutal oaf, the smith." It seemed that she dozed off, but presently she spoke again. "I was thinking what a good thing it was she went to another place. For you must know Lee, that every castle has much inbreeding. Often indeed, the blood lines are confused or are unknown." She absently untied and retied her head cloth. "I could only guess at who was my friend's father, a visiting nobleman I heard, not at all unusual. Yes indeed, she was a fine girl. Pity was that she chose John Smith. Anyway, and mainly thanks to you, we can be proud of our girl, Master Lee. Certainly we will sorely miss her, and I will pray for her tonight, and indeed every day. Let us hope we have not really lost her, and that we shall see her now and again."

Joany did not come the first year, yet her man came, glowing with pride that she had born him a fine son, who was yet too little to travel. The following year she did come with her little son and although Fleur and Jerome had forgotten who she had been in their lives, yet watching their father, they greeted her joyfully.

So it was, when she was in-between bearing children, Joany came bringing them, swelling the hunting party. It was coming home, she told Lee and Joan, and while she was away she dreamed to return to the old castle, and slipping happily back into the tempo of life, as if she had never left.

Despite his good attentions to the boy Peterkin who Lee had brought, Anders still could not bring himself to accept the healer. He did not understand his feelings himself. He just did not care for the man. It took a personal tragedy at last to change his mind, which overnight made them as blood brothers.

One winter day when he and the men were hunting in the forest for fresh meat, his beloved pony was attacked by a wounded boar.

Peterkin had ridden back to the castle, calling frantically for Mistress Joan and Lee, and sobbing, had explained the trouble. Lee pursed his mouth, a gashed belly, the guts all hanging out? Bad, oh bad. Quietly, he told Joan what to collect together, then ran up the tower for his medicine bag, breathless. Gathering a few more men with axes and ropes, they hastily mounted their horses and followed Peter into the forest, till they came to Anders in the gloom, nursing the injured pony surrounded by anxious men.

CHAPTER FIFTEEN

ANDERS

The pain in his legs had gone now, for with the weight of the mare's head on his lap, they were quite numb. Hearing the approach of horses, Anders raised himself a little and was relieved to see the castle party returning. His wife and the healer dismounted and hurried towards him.

"Anders," she was on her knees beside him, eyes anxious, voice tender. He acknowledged her despite his discomfort, mightily relieved that she had come. The horse quivered at the familiar voice, as a kind hand caressed it. Lee too was on his knees, but looking intently at the horrific wound on the horses' side, where the guts had tumbled out onto the turf, stained red with blood and pulsing.

Leaving Anders and his wife, he went over to the group of silent men and spoke fast. Heartened with the chance to take action, they first unloaded the horses, then went off in groups. Some to fetch, "the cleanest water", others to hew saplings to make a shelter, the remainder to gather fallen wood to keep a fire going. Very soon the distant sound of wood cutting filled the air. Others undid the bundles, bringing out all that Lee had asked for. With great tenderness he laid a great woollen cloak over the injured beast, then knelt at its head. Lifting a lid, he saw the animal gaze at him and gently laid a thick cloth over its eyes so that it could not see. Feeling for his precious little jar, he scooped out a nut and gently stroking the soft head, he opened the corner of its mouth and pressed something unseen into its lips. It chomped lightly, but the healer held the lips closed and nodded to Peterkin to take over.

Soon a good blaze was burning, with pots hung on crude cut branch cranes, hissing as drops of water fell on the flames. Men reappeared, dragging wood as quietly as they could, for the healer had told them fiercely to be quiet, as they would for an injured man.

Swiftly looking at the land about the fallen horse, Lee dug his heel into the soft earth at four corners, mouthing "here" each time. Next he indicated by the rump of the beast, where to dig a small ditch for waste to run off. While the pots heated, a good, rough shelter rose with surprising speed above the horse and master. When the structure was done and lashed securely to nearby branches, the men drew up earth all around, salvaging anything to hand to thicken the walls and sloping roof. It was a poor stable, but, if it rained or snowed, would give a modicum of shelter to those within.

His mind whirling, Lee worked out the procedure. It had been many years since he had seen such a wound, and that time it had been a man. Those were the days of his apprenticeship, so now he pictured how his master had worked, step by step. Only this operation was on a larger scale. Turning to the woman he signalled her to his side.

"Could you change places with your husband, Joan?" he asked quietly. "We can make you more comfortable perhaps, and I will need his help."

Gently, carefully, they lifted the heavy head from Ander's lap to release him. While Joan lowered herself to his place but onto a sheepskin, two men lifted Anders and held him fast for some moments, so to let the blood back into his legs. A bowl and soft soap were brought for the stiff man, to wash his hands, and steadying himself on braced legs, he did as he was told.

A clean linen cloth was laid out before the fire, for it was dim in the forest despite winter and few leaves, and night would come soon. Here the healer laid out his tools, then covered them with another cloth, all eyes watching his every move. Sprinkling some herb into the water, he eased the pot over the fire. When the water was warm, Lee took up a full bowl and began to splash cupfuls over the exposed guts to clean them of leaves and dirt. At his side, Anders anticipated his every move, gently shifting the warm mass here and there, till satisfied, a clean cloth could be placed under it all. Confident that the wound was clean, Lee carefully looked the mass all over, glad to see that at least the guts were not punctured. Now he poured warm wine over everything, small cups here and there, and together, he and Anders lifted and pressed the slithering mess back into the hole. Taking up a needle, he threaded it with hair from the horses' tail which had soaked in boiling chamomile water. Fascinated, holding brands aloft to make light, the men clustered around to watch.

Taking a deep breath, his eyes closed, Lee once more ran his mind over the past and his instruction for such wounds.

Anders watched intently at the still figure crouched beside him. Was he praying? He was praying! Anders felt his heart flip. Praying for a horse, his beloved horse! So he too closed his eyes and prayed also.

Stitch, knot and cut, stitch, knot and cut. The belly quivered with each jab, but it was drowsy from the drug, poor beast, and probably this was no worse than the horse flies of summer. Bit by bit, the wound closed, and each time, warm wine was poured and Anders carefully tucked the gut in, till at last, the inner wound was closed.

Cramped, Lee sat back on his haunches, flexed and rinsed his hands and reached for the soaking hank of linen thread to complete the job. At last when it was finished, sewn up like a passable tear, the healer gave instructions to Peterkin, who aching to help, had, wide-eyed, watched every step. First he disappeared to return with an elder branch which he hollowed out with a fine dagger. Lee again washed it in the boiling water and tucking one end into the lowest end of the wound explained, "This is to leak off the badness."

Next, Peterkin flung himself down behind the pony and using hands, knife and a long spike, struggled to tunnel underneath the mare. When it was done, for there were many eager hands to help, a tight-rolled linen sheet was pressed right through the hole. Muddy, satisfied and uncaring at their condition, they stood about and watched as the sheet was drawn up, opened revealing the clean side and a great bandage was tied around the swollen belly.

"Now we wait," Lee said to Anders. "If we can bring her home tomorrow or the day after, so much the better, but now, she will be shocked and must rest." Turning to the men about, his authority unquestioned, he sent them home, just keeping six all told, with a couple of dogs at the camp. "And you must go too, Mistress Joan, but hasten back tomorrow I beg you, for there is yet work to do." Once more, slowly, with infinite care they changed places, and Joan gave her seat back to Anders. With a list of things to bring in her head, Joan touched her husband's arm, nodded to Lee, and mounted her pony for home.

Night and the cold fell swiftly. Drawing up the fire closer to the shelter, the men put more wood on and talked quietly for awhile. Eventually a silence fell over them, so they rolled up in their cloaks, settled as close to the fire as they dared, and went to sleep. Leaning against a corner pole of the shelter, Lee closed his eyes, now and again placing his hand under the cloak on the horse, to satisfy himself it was still warm.

Next day, barely with the dawn, an anxious Peterkin arrived ahead of the others. On his knees beside the horse he stroked and kissed it, murmuring endearments. Lee and Anders exchanged glances, barely nodding.

Mistress Joan had sent oats which had been ground fine in a quern and Lee now messed it with warm water, like a gruel to feed the mare, who surprisingly took it, a few sips at a time. With urging, she also began to drink, her head held up, over a shallow bowl.

Lee watched the dressing and saw the slow spread of matter seeping through the elder shunt, but it was not red, the wound was holding.

The second night was the worst, and Lee was alert to the fever which consumed the poor beast. Pouring herbal teas into its mouth, using every trick he knew, he managed well enough. Determined, he held her head up, even if she wanted to lie down, for if she did lie down, she might die.

There was, each day, constant and unusual traffic from the castle. Everyone was concerned, for it was well known that Anders treasured his mare greatly, and that she was a jewel. Each brought, as if to a child, little gifts, sweet hay and ground oats, honey-comb and barley cakes, all to tempt her appetite. Tasty pottage was brought for the men and all manner of little treats to keep their spirits up. The men took it in turns to stay over-night, but Anders and Lee stayed always, usually with Peterkin and his little dog.

Somehow, the silence and the shared anxiety over the injured beast brought together the two men. Lee covertly watched Anders, who frowned, seemed to want to speak, yet hesitated. Then suddenly, on the third night out he came with what was troubling him.

"What was that you put in her mouth," he touched his own breast, the place where Lee kept his most precious drug, "and what did you place in the bindings, Master Lee, right at the end, in a fold of the cloth?" Lee stared into the fire, silent for a while. So, he had seen. "Joan told me you did the same with the boy's foot, a stone she said. And I think that I remember you did the same for me. Is it magic? Witchcraft?" Again Lee was silent, searching for the right words. It was so important.

"Magic?" he asked, "Well maybe, yet I know not how. Witchcraft, certainly not, for how can a simple stone make witchcraft? But I will tell you what I can of it." He stretched to try to make himself more comfortable, playing for time. This questioning had happened before, yet always with simple folk who took his answers easily. This one, the clever Anders might not take it as others before, and it would not do to have witchcraft coupled with his name. Never. "It was given me by my teacher when he died, together with all the tools of his trade. And yes, he seemed to value it, for he had received it from his teacher, and perhaps it had a longer history. Whenever he had serious injuries, he used to press it onto the wound. As his apprentice, I observed, like you, not understanding. In my early days, he told me that the pressure of it stopped the blood flow. As time went on, he confessed that he thought it did more than that, and actually helped the healing, though he did not know how. One day, not long before he died, he showed me that it did have a magical property, for it could lift up metal. On its own. I will show you when we change the dressings on your mare. He told me that it was called a lodestone and that it did aid healing to a remarkable degree, but to keep it safe and quiet. For there are foolish people who might accuse us of witchcraft, and, it has been done, perhaps burn us. The stone is just that, a stone. Round and flat and smooth. But it has some special property and I for one believe in it, for I have seen desperate injuries heal miraculously, probably because of it." He stopped, still staring at the fire. "The drug I placed in her mouth was a precious gift from Brother Edward at the monastery. You saw and you asked, Anders. Now I ask you, for the love of God and all sick men and beasts, to keep this privily to yourself. Let this be just between us, for there are other folks, without your intelligence, who might not understand. How else can I carry on the work which was taught to me by my teacher, and his teacher, and back, goodness knows how long?"

Anders nodded, not understanding but believing the healer and satisfied, they resumed their silence

"Why?" Lee dared to ask Anders, later, during the small hours, "Did you suddenly change your mind and take to the boy, Peterkin, Anders? Forgive my impertinence in asking you, yet it seemed to me a miracle, when I knew you disapproved of me and the waifs I take under my wing, inflicting them on your good wife and the castle." There was a long silence, and just when Lee thought that he had spoken to a sleeping man, Anders spoke out softly.

"I am glad you ask, Lee." He replied low. "To say that I saw myself in him might be almost true," he began. "For hadn't I stayed at the castle just because I had injured my foot years ago? Never as sorely as that boy's, yet it was Joan who cared for me, and afterwards, you had done your work for Peterkin too." The silence stretched. "Does he sleep, Lee? For I would not wish him to hear what I am about to tell you."

Lee quietly got to his feet and on the pretext of laying more wood on the fire, looked to see if the boy was sleeping. Nodding to Anders, he lowered himself down again and drew his cloak up well about himself.

"I vowed that I would keep this story in my heart, and never put the burden of it on any other soul. But it has been a heavy load to carry alone, Lee, and I will be glad if you will share it with me." The fire flared up with the fresh wood, and the mare stirred, to be comforted by her master with soft hands and loving voice.

"She saw it all too, this one, Lee. She carried me that day when Joan sent me to the town to buy special stores, just after you brought the boy home." With the crackling of the fire, Lee strained to listen, then rose, and moved close to Anders, so that none other would hear. Nodding with appreciation, Anders coughed a little, spat and went on.

"After I had made my purchases and left my orders, I began to set off home. My way took me though the square, and there seemed some commotion so I asked a man what was going on. A hanging, he told me, three in fact. They were making ready the gallows right then, with three nooses. Well you know, I am not a man for such things, so I kept going, glad to be off." Staring into the fire, Anders recalled the scene in his mind. Clear and terrible, and closed his eyes as if to shut it out. "Unfortunately I found myself in the thick of the crowd and saw the condemned men who rode, well tied up, in a cart. It was their hair, Lee, their red hair, which caught my attention. Then when they were close, I saw that they must be Peterkin's brothers, for I had seen you coming to the castle with them, three big red-haired men."

Lee nodded to himself, for yes, they had even taken off their caps when he shook their hands in farewell.

"'What crime have they done?' I shouted to anyone who might know. 'They killed Will the roper,' they shouted. 'Why?' I called out again. Till finally one man yelled some story that they had hung him up by his toes, and that he had died."

"Imagine my shock Lee. It fitted, something was familiar. The boy's toes which Joan told me were injuries from just such a wicked deed." He put his head in his hands and groaned. "Oh dear God."

Lee waited, his mind alert, his thoughts racing.

"Then I looked at the men, who seemed aware of our words for they stared at me. Meanwhile I was being jostled by the crowd, and Angelina here was getting fretted. But somehow, I had to know so I urged her nearer to the cart, and called to them, 'Are you Peterkin's brothers,' I called again, more loudly above the noise. And, eyes-wide they yelled 'Yes' as one, straining their bonds to see me clearly. By now the throng was dense and almost stopped in a narrow of the road. But still I kept at it. 'Why, I shouted, did you do that to the roper?' And they started together, then, he who must have been the eldest yelled to me that the roper had strung up their little brother Peterkin by his foot, so they did it to him in return, using his best twine. Meanwhile the bailiff's men were getting rough with the crowd, swinging their staves and trying to get the cart moving again, but the crowd wouldn't budge, intent with me and my questions. Then I asked, as you can imagine in a loud voice, for it was a noisy crowd, 'Why did the roper do that to Peter?' And you know what he replied, Lee?" A sob escaped him, and the tears began to fall. "Oh dear God, Oh sweet Jesus, if you knew how heavy this ugly tale has lain on my heart, Lee, so even I daren't tell my good Joan for to distress her." Quietly he wept, his shoulders shaking. "What will you be thinking of me, Lee, a grown man bawling like a babe, but the tragedy of it, oh the sadness." And wept on, till at last he quietened and could speak again.

"It seemed that Will Roper had caught Peter's little dog foraging about, as they do. Catching it, he was belting it, so the boy fell upon him and bit his leg till it bled. So angry was the roper, he caught the boy and tied his foot and hauled him upside down from a branch, went off to bathe his leg, and probably forgot him. By the time the brothers found the lad, the foot was bad, well you know it. And the lad was exhausted from calling. So you can guess what happened. The brothers set upon Will Roper, and did the same for him, using his best hemp rope, except his heart must have failed, for he was a big man."

"Now the crowd heard all this, and began to scream at the bailiff that the brothers should be set free for they were just protecting their own. God had punished the roper, and so on. It was an angry crowd with much jostling and pushing and I was in the thick of it. But the bailiff yelled that they were outlaws, guilty of many other crimes as well, and hang they must. By then we were back in the square, and the bailiff's men were wielding their truncheons and staves with vigour. Yet the brothers couldn't take their eyes off me. So what could I do, Lee? I shouted to them that that Peterkin's foot was healing, and not to fear, for we would take care of him, as our own. That he was helping me with the beasts and that he had a gift of kindness in him which they seemed to understand. And, Lee," he began to sob again. "They were pleased, Lee. Going to their death, they grinned at me, Lee, thanking me. Nodding and looking at each other, smiling, glad. Yes indeed, glad they were, Lee, right glad to know that the boy was with us, that we would care for him." Once more Anders lost his courage and wept silently, his shoulders heaving. "Even when they were on the board with the noose around their necks, even then, they grinned and nodded and they kept thanking me, Lee. Me, who was angry when you brought the boy. Right to the end, how they could, as they could, strangling, they looked at me with their eyes full of gratefulness and at last I yelled with all my strength. 'We will mind him well by the Grace of God, and, we will pray for you!' And then I turned her head, for I was choking too, and dug my heels and bless her, she pushed her way out of the throng and how we did it I know not, but we came home somehow." Blowing his nose with his fingers, Anders gave a great sigh. "So now you know, Lee, and I thank you for hearing me. And my friend, while there is kindness between us, I tell you I am right sorry that I have shown you coldness. I ask your forgiveness. Knowing that my Joan is clever in all things, I should have known that if she trusted you, then so should I."

Taking a soft cloth from his bag, Lee dipped it into the pail of fresh water and leaning over, he gently wiped Anders face, as a babe, then patted it dry. Drawing the exhausted man close to him, he put his arm about the hunched shoulders, rocking, very, very gently.

"We will pray for them together Anders. We will quietly ask Father Jerome to say a mass for them. And I will pray for you, and thank the Almighty that I have a friend who is near to a saint. For Anders, what you did was valiant. Such a kindness only comes from a great and noble heart. Another man would have turned his back and ridden away. How can I tell you how fine I think your deed was to stay there, to comfort dying men. To keep on, to forget your own danger, to help them in their sorrow. Oh well done my friend, oh well done!" The soft, steady voice of the healer droned on. "God and his saints know of your goodness Anders and now it is very clear to me why the excellent Joan loves you so well." On and on, with soft words, like silk. Smooth and gentle, strong and precious, on and on he spoke, until level breathing told him that Anders slept.

Lee sat awake till dawn, when he carefully shifted the weight of his new friend so that he could get up to begin the day. Kicking up the fire, he hung the water pot up once more.

It was clear now, the whole story. And Lee felt a new hope fill him, an unusual belief in the goodness of man, a great gratitude for life.

They took the mare home that day. With two great plough oxen, lengths of good cloth, flexible saplings and many men, they got her home. Somehow they lifted her, and slung between two oxen, she had tottered along, weak but courageous, even nickering to her companions, despite no doubt being in pain, glad to be on her feet once more.

Back at the castle, the mare settled in her stable, Lee gave Anders into Joan's loving hands. Sternly he bade her to brew the special herbs to make him sleep while to Peter, he gave the responsibility of the mare.

"You will help me with her wounds, Peter. You will see to her every hour of day and night for Anders is ill with tiredness and sorrow. Three times each day, you will go to him and tell him of his beast. What she ate, when she ate, how many times she passed dung or water. And Peter," sharp fingers plucked and held the boy's ear. "I do believe you might make a fine animal doctor, that is if you will have me teach you what I know. And," Lee released the ear but held his finger up to get full attention, "when we take out her stitches, you shall help me." The expression of disbelief and joy on Peter's face were answer enough.

For three days Anders lay in a state of exhaustion and aided by Lee's concoctions, his body and mind rested, so that when he rose, he was well. At the mare's side once more, Anders caressed her and silently gave thanks for the healer. Without a doubt, as he now well knew, his dear beast would surely be dead. Frowning with inner thought, he turned to Lee who was putting salve on the wound.

"One last thing I remember Lee, though it makes no sense. One of them," he paused, looked about to make sure they were not overheard, "you know." Lee nodded. "Right to the end he kept on calling to me; 'The tree, tell Peter, the tree.' He looked enquiringly at his friend. Lee frowned too. A tree? He thought for some moments. Then his face cleared.

"They must have kept their treasure in a tree somewhere. That must be it, a hollow tree, perhaps in the clearing where I found him. I tell you what Anders. Next time I go that way I'll take the boy. Then I'll tell him that I dreamt of his brothers, who told me to remind him of the tree. That should do it don't you think?" Pleased, they settled the horse for the night and went together, close, as brothers, to their meal.

CHAPTER SIXTEEN

FLEUR

Fleur lay silently watching the narrow window, willing the day to dawn. She and Jerome were in father's turret room in the gatehouse, which was because the baron was in residence with his party. An adventure, she still felt a flicker of excitement over it. It was a small, low room, full of father's books and herbs, where he worked and more, had all his lovely things. Sometimes, he let them touch them, if they were careful, and told them stories about where they had come from in their beginning, and who and why of the giver.

One thing she loved greatly was a lamp, made of brass and likened to a star. It had little windows all around, in different coloured glass, and when they put a candle stub inside, oh but it was beautiful.

Stealthily, she put her hand on Jerome, to see if he were also awake. Yet he was not, for as well she knew, Jerome loved to sleep. But she sensed that her father was, because she felt his silence and his listening.

"Why don't you get up, my dearling?" came his quiet voice across the room. "Put the water on for tea, my lamb, there's a dear." Fleur smiled, jumped up and crossing to his bed, felt for him in the gloom. Putting her face close to his she kissed him and whispered.

"I knew you were awake!" So he grabbed her, hauled her into bed and roughed and tickled her till she squealed.

"And how did you know that, my little baggage eh?" he hugged her, breathing in deeply the child smell of her. Patting her little behind, he gave her a shove towards the door, "Go now, use the pot."

With her little felt slippers properly on her feet, and her night shawl tied over her night shift, Fleur went out onto the landing, then, relieved, seriously did her housewifely work. Deftly she blew up the small brazier on which Lee made up his concoctions, placing new charcoal on the embers. Reaching up for the mint jar, she spooned it into the kettle. How she loved being useful, pleasing father and doing little tasks specially for him.

It started out a day, as any other. That is, a day when the baron was there which was different from when he was not, sometimes exciting, other times tedious. For a start, there were so many people, it was hard to find a peaceful corner, except of course when most were out hunting. Even then, the grand ladies, who did not go, had little patience for the castle children, theirs all grown. So the five of them, Anders' sons, Jerome and she, if they were not helping somewhere, went down to the river, into the woods or even to the village for their sport. Fleur thought that the pages who came with the gentry, and even some of the squires, were a mean lot. Instead of playing, they loved teasing, when of course, there was no one about to see. Pretending to trip and make them fall, they seemed to enjoy spoiling their games and toys, and generally working off their own frustrations on the younger children. Fleur hated them, for they turned her orderly and happy little life upside down, and were cruel and taunting to her brother Jerome, who did not speak.

"He can speak!" she raged, pink and breathless and all too often shaking with rage. "Just he doesn't care to speak with you," and taking Jerome's hand, she would drag him away, pleading with him not to listen. Alas, they were beginning to find that the pleasant Jerome of quiet days was not the same as when the baron was there. All too often Lee had intervened in a fight, where despite being hopelessly outnumbered, Jerome seemed to be doing the most damage.

"I will not have my boy turn into a ruffian, hear me Jerome!" Exasperated Lee would then speak to the foolish pages and implore them to stop their baiting, "for he is a good lad and this is his home. Be quite sure that he is really, far more clever than the lot of you put together if you could but learn it."

This was the one day in the week when Lee went down to the village to the new Moot Hall which he had persuaded the baron to build. There, a little market had grown up, and Lee went with his salves and bandages to doctor the simple people, who would not otherwise have treatment, being too poor and shy to approach the castle, especially at busy times. The lords and ladies had mostly gone off hunting as usual, so the castle was comparatively quiet.

"Can we help you, Aunt Joan?" the two stood before her, an incongruous little couple, like a sweet garden pea and a big, coarse field bean. Mistress Joan smiled lovingly at her Godchildren. Fleur was so fair and dainty. Intelligent and willing, she was always thinking of little things to help and please. Beside her Jerome seemed a child three years older, for he was a robust tall lad. Blond, snub-nosed and strong, he did just what his sister told him.

"Well now," she made a few suggestions, and the one concerning their father immediately appealed. Should they clean out his room and strew fresh herbs? Taking two new brooms from her storeroom, she handed them over so they went proudly to the gatehouse and began to sweep.

"I'll do father's room," stated Fleur, always the one to make decisions. And you see if you can sweep our room, so that when they leave, it won't be too bad for us." For the overflow of attendants had taken over their room as usual. She considered for a moment. "Then I'll sweep the stairs and meet you on the landing, and we can do the rest together." Ever willing, Jerome nodded, pleased to have a task, for he was bored these days, always trying to keep out of the way. With his usual noisy enthusiasm, he set to work.

If he had not been sweeping, Jerome would have heard the three pages creep up, past his room, to the turret. When he paused, he cocked his head sideways at the noise that Fleur was making. A great deal of activity sounded on the boards above his head, and surprised, he put his broom down and slowly went up to see what she was doing.

Because it was the turret of the gatehouse facing toward the village with a good window, the screams drifted down, till one by one, everyone below stopped their work and chat to listen.

By the time Lee had raced back up to the castle, it was over. Mistress Joan, having been alerted by one of her sons had sped to the source of the noise. A bloody scene met her eyes. Jerome was sitting astride one boy, holding the necks of the other two and crashing their heads together. Fleur was lying on the floor, her clothes almost ripped off her, screaming hysterically. The moment Jerome saw his Godmother, he stopped, got off the fallen body on the floor, pushed the bleeding and dazed pages towards her and turned to embrace the sobbing Fleur. There was so much blood everywhere, it was difficult to know who was hurt.

They never learnt the truth of it. Yet Lee was white with anger, refusing to tend the sobbing boys, for it was more bleeding noses than true damage.

Picking up Fleur and taking Jerome by the hand, he sped down the stair and stalked away from the castle. Ignoring all he passed, he stared ahead, thin lipped and more furious than he had ever been in his whole life.

Had they deflowered his Fleur? Had they abused her? Was that what they were doing when Jerome found them and put an end to it? Trying to still his rage, he took them to a favourite place downriver where they always swam and laughed and had been happy.

Struggling to stop shaking, he struck and lighted the tinder and soon a good fire was burning. Jerome, helpful as ever, was already gathering wood without being asked. He knew what to do, and not bearing to look at his father or sister for he was so afraid, he waded into the shallows, gathered up their regular stones, so big and round and smooth, and rolled them into the fire.

While Lee nursed his daughter, carefully removing her torn clothing, kissing her all the while, Jerome scooped out the sand and pebbles from their hollowed out rock, cleaning it, ready for their bath. When it was done and they were waiting for the stones to heat, Lee drew his blood-spattered son close, kissing the top of his tow head, praising him, thanking him, assuring him that what he had done was fine and valiant. Jerome pressed close, relieved, safe, the occasional tremble still going through his little body.

"I thank you, my son, for my dear boy, with me gone, it was your loving duty to defend your sister. You will be a most valiant knight one day I know, for you have true valour."

After they were clean and warm and almost calm again, Fleur wearing Lee's tunic top over her torn clothes, Lee walked them right around the castle far away up the hill to the sheepfold, and put Jerome into the safe hands of Josh, the shepherd.

"For, my friend, there has been trouble with the gentry, and I fear for the lad. He protected his sister from some wicked pages, and gave a very good account of himself. Keep him here, I beg you, and you will find him a most useful boy, kindly to all beasts."

Bending to speak to Jerome. "It is wise to stay here with Josh my son, better to stay away from the castle, the gentry and trouble. Help Josh well, and we will come to see how you do very soon." Then whispering in the boy's ear, "I fear that Fleur is not at all well, so I must put her to bed for some days. God bless you, Jerome, my brave little knight."

The hall was still in uproar when later, Lee returned to the castle carrying his daughter. Everyone noted that there was no sign of Jerome.

The three pages were still fussing over their wounds, with Joan offering soothing teas which they refused.

"No, I will not attend your page, Sir," Lee's eyes were slits of hate. "I am staying close to my daughter, whom your pages have abused. Her need is greater than theirs. See to him yourself, for if I get my hands on him, he may end up worse."

Even to Joan, he refused, knowing that she, close to the family, would be suffering gravely, and, quite without reason, he hit the wall, grazing his knuckles. So much trouble, because of three stupid and badly-behaved boys.

The next day, Joan arrived at his turret followed by a breathless baron. Seeing the still, white form of the child on the bed, the healer beside her holding her hand, they laid their offerings on the table and waited, mute.

Realizing that he must speak, Lee looked up at his guests and drew out some stools. Poor Joan, he could see that she had slept badly because of the fuss. And Roland the baron, he too looked bleary eyed. Shaking his head he began gruffly, "I'm sorry, Lee. Just a prank you know. Silly lads, bored, my fault, I should have taken them hunting, even if they are always a damned nuisance."

Lee flickered his eyes over the pair, seeing the strong family likeness, as usual liking Joan, even feeling sorry for the man.

The silence stretched, then Joan, coughing a little asked, "How is she?"

"Shocked, Joan, deeply shocked in soul and body."

The woman walked quietly to the bed, sat beside the child and kissed her.

"Here is your Godmother, my dearling," she murmured, "your Aunt Joan. I have brought you some supper my love, which I made specially for you. See, a little venison pie with damsons, just how you like it." Still the child did not move, staring at the ceiling, silent.

Desperate, Lee sought what way he could entertain the child enough to forget her ills. Suddenly remembering seeing a Book of Hours, he determined that Fleur should have her very own prayer book, like a fine lady. He, Lee, healer and scribe would make it for her. He would write and paint with more attention to detail than ever before. She would have the most beautiful book he could make. Sorting through his sheets of vellum, he took down his precious tiny pots of paint powder. The next day, having begged an egg and some feathers from the kitchen, he began by painting the lady garden from memory, and finally Fleur took her eyes off the beam above her, and onto the delicate little painting.

After the shouting had died down, the castle fell into an embarrassed silence. People talked in whispers, the castle folk furious, doing their work for the guests with an ill grace, while the visitors pretended everything was alright. The injured children were swiftly taken away and returned to their homes, there to explain to their distraught parents, how they came by their broken noses.

"Sir," Lee addressed the baron who sat in the solar with his lady and Joan, "I think perhaps it is politic if I leave, taking my children, who as you know, are not my children, with me. It is no more your fault than mine that this sorrow has befallen us. Yet alas what has been done, cannot be undone. My anger at those silly pages, their uncaring knights, the proud attitude of their ladies for my daughter's plight, so fills me with rage, I must go. Hear this, I never, ever, wish to see any of them, again."

The shocked silence hung heavy, no one moving even, stunned at Lee's words. For there was no question about it, they were more than fortunate to have Lee with them. How should they fare without him and his gifted hands.

Now the baroness spoke up. A haughty, foolish woman on most matters he knew, who nevertheless Lee guessed was more than clever in matters of husbands, lands and money.

"There is no need, Master Lee, for you to leave this castle, for we have decided to make our other castle our main residence. It is much more suitable for our large parties of guests than here. We will not hunt here in future, but develop our other forests for our hunting parties." A small movement and wide-eyes showed Lee that this was news to both the baron and his sister.

"We know how valuable your medical knowledge has been to all our people, even to healing a horse," she bent a small smile on Joan, who stood still and stony-faced. "I have arranged a considerable gift from the knights of the three pages, to be given to you for the girl. As we are not certain as to the extent of her," she hesitated, "what really happened," she stumbled on, "I think you will agree it is most generous, most kind and thoughtful, a dowry for the girl." She placed a small leather bag on the table beside her with a goodly thump.

Lee gazed out of the opened windows at a tree which was turning yellow. Autumn would be here soon, berries galore and mushrooms to be gathered, he thought on aimlessly. He had grown to know and love this place. He sighed and turning into the room he addressed the baroness directly.

"Lady. My daughter Fleur, mark you her name is Fleur! My daughter needs no dowry from anyone, especially from careless knights or badly-reared pages. If one of their daughters was deflowered at her age, how great would her dowry have to be I ask you?" He jutted his chin at her, eyes angry, "What fine lord or knight would accept her, impure?" Every eye in the room watched in disbelief as Lee approached, very close to the baroness. "I will pay my own daughter's dowry, explaining why and what, and be sure who. They shall have the slur, not she. And I will let it be known far and wide, to high and low, how we decent, quiet folk suffer these insults and indignities." He raised his voice to a shout. "Yes, suffer!" then dropped it to a whisper, turning again to the window to look unseeing through tears. "From arrogant, proud, useless, people like you, who never do a day's work in your life, as leeches, sucking the life-blood out of our bodies." Turning again, shocking them by the tears which coursed down his face he raged on, his words loud and harsh. "Have you seen her, lady? Have you looked into her eyes? And you, foolish woman, talk of generosity. Bah! Nothing, I say nothing, can undo what is done."

Now Joan sped forward on quiet feet, tucked the purse into her gown and put her arm about Lee, drawing him away.

"Enough, my dear," she held him tightly, willing him to stop. "At least," she spoke quietly, just for him, "some good will come of it, if they do not bother us again, and stay away."

Fleur lay still and quiet on the bed, barely acknowledging her father. Obediently, she accepted her milk and ate her bread and pottage. Silently she used the piss-pot or went down to the landing to the garderobe. It seemed as if she had suddenly grown very old, her little face was so still and serious. Her replies were mute, nods and turning away. Lee felt more anxious each day and wondered how long it would last. The only time she showed life was when Lee showed her his progress on her Book of Hours. Only when he was called did he leave his room, and so spent many hours meticulously working on her book. Slowly, as she watched its progress, she relaxed and began to smile at him.

One Sunday morning, Lee pottered about and with his warm clothes on announced he was going to see Jerome. It worked. In moments she was up, dragging her warm shift on and washing her face and hands at speed till she was ready. Lee watched her with relief. She would mend.

They found that all was well with Jerome, who had quickly learnt the arts of being a shepherd boy. He loved the lambs and being out of doors all the time. The hut that he and Josh lived in was some way from the castle, above the water meadows and the big river. Each day he and the shepherd walked the flock to a different pasture, returning in a great loop at dusk.

Their days were regular and ordered. Milking early and late, the dairymaids came with a pony mid-morning to fetch the milk to take back to make butter and cheese. The life suited Jerome well. It was quiet and beautiful, without cruel people to taunt and tease him. Josh was glad of the help and company, for he was getting old and a lad had many uses. Cutting a strong reed, he made the boy a pipe and taught him how to play it. If he never spoke, now Jerome delighted to try all the songs he knew to play for Fleur every Sunday.

A routine was agreed on by the two shepherds. Old Josh would go with the dairymaids to the village on Saturday to pass the day with his daughter. Then he returned with the maids on the Sunday morning for his turn to take the sheep out. This meant that Jerome was in charge alone for a whole day, which made him very proud. It also meant that Sunday was his to be with his family, either at the fold if the weather was fine, or to go back to the castle. While the gentry were there, the three of them went instead starting before dawn to an old hunting lodge further up the marshes. A single tower, almost a ruin, yet quiet, a long, long ride. Yet on fine days it was a delight to explore and enjoy the tranquillity of nature. Every bit the little mother, Fleur insisted that Jerome should have a weekly bathe, which was also fun, and a change of clothes, which she organized, so their day was always busy. The stores they brought for him each week, had to be carefully hung up in the rafters of the hut, out of the way of the huge dogs which protected the sheep.

"Try not to eat it all at once," admonished Lee, knowing his son's prodigious appetite. But he knew that they would not go hungry, for when they ran low, the dairymaids took bread and cheese, ale and occasional cuts of meat with them.

Fleur remained quiet, except when she was with Jerome. As he did not speak, she chattered as she always had with him, answering her questions herself by reading his expression. Lee was perplexed. At home she was once again normal, but silent. She nodded and obeyed requests, just as Jerome did. Yet she never opened a conversation, spoke or replied unless pressed. Shock? He pondered. Or was she missing her brother, for Sundays had become the highlight of their lives, when they visited the sheepfold. Fleur would chatter as of old, while her father and brother sat and happily watched her, round-eyed with pride and delight, for she was a beautiful child. Soft blue eyes were set off by palest fair hair which framed her sweet face. Tiny freckles laced her nose and when she smiled, her teeth showed small, white and even. Heart full, Lee realized his daughter would be a beauty one day.

Conscious that his son had a good mind, Lee sought what he could give him to do to keep it active. Playing the pipe entertained him happily, yet Lee felt there must be something else to occupy the boy. Always short of vellum, it suddenly came to him. Jerome was there on the spot when lambs were still-born or died young. He would teach him how to make vellum and if he did well, he would pay him as good vellum was hard to come by, his the result of bartering at the monastery. He never had enough for the baron's accounts or letters, or for his little healing book and now for Fleur's Book of Hours.

Jerome learnt swiftly. After burning his hands with the caustic lime once or twice at first, he soon took more care. Lee showed him how to peg the skins out on a board, how to scrape off the tissue and fat till they reached the soft white layer. The endless scraping, stretching and scraping again were easy for Jerome, his big hands surprisingly careful not to rip or tear. Turning the skins in a barrel with a stout stick, he soon learned to gauge when the hairs would slough off before lifting them out. Recalling a fine chalk bank, Lee took Fleur to collect some good, clean white lumps of it. When they were completely dry, he rasped them, then shook the white powder through a fine hair sieve to sprinkle onto the new vellum. Within the year, they had a production which was enviable. When he had enough good sheets to show the monks at the monastery, he was pleased that they were much impressed and happy to pay. After showing his son his earnings, all Jerome's money was hidden away for when he was a man and would need it. Lee was delighted that all their careful work had not been in vain. It was a relief to genuinely praise the boy, first to show him the coins, then take them to save for him.

Almost every week in spring and early summer, Lee took the completed skins home to do the finishing. It was a fine thing to be busy.

It seemed natural that not only did Lee doctor human beings, he readily accepted any creature which was sick or injured and did his best to cure it. Many was the time when a wounded bird or beast was brought to him, mostly by children, who were more tender-hearted than their elders. Just one of these little patients was to be the cause of Fleur finding her voice again and would be the cause of much merriment for years thereafter.

A small owl, no doubt dropped by a hawk, was brought by a gentle child from the village. Having given the child a barley cake, Lee examined the feathered patient, set its wing and anointed its wounds. It was a plucky little bird, who having recovered from the shock of its assault, soon perked up and settled into his new home, Lee's room. He was beautiful in every way with round, bright eyes, soft grey feathers, and a kindly disposition, for he never bit, when Fleur used to stroke him under his neck, crooning softly.

When at last Lee deemed it well enough to join its brethren in the woods, he sat it in the window and poked its head out into the world. So it sat for two days, flapping its wings in between watching for mice in its adopted home. Then, with a deal of rustling, away it flew, and Lee clapped his hands, while Fleur wept.

"What, tears my dearling?" He took her on his lap and held her close. "But no, you must rejoice, for he is well again, and gone home to his family. No tears my love, just pride that we mended his wounds and that he can fly again to catch the mice in the barns." Yet she would not be consoled.

The following morning Lee was summoned to the hall to speak with a messenger, so he left Fleur up in bed on her own.

Then the screaming began. Piercing, frantic screams came from the battlement landing outside their room, and whoever heard it, first ran to see who it was, then rushed, wide-eyed into the hall, to call the healer. It was fearful. On and on it went, the little figure at the top of the gatehouse, waving its arms, mouth wide open, screaming, imploring. A fair crowd gathered in the bailey, while Lee rushed breathless up the stairs and clasped Fleur in his arms. Moments later, he reappeared, the child still in his arms, laughing till he was speechless.

"The owl!" he gasped when at last he was down amongst them again, holding the child, holding his side, trying not to laugh. "The owl has returned!" The laughter, the petting and kindness, the praise for healing the owl, all must have been the right balm for Fleur. For she not only laughed too, she began to speak again, and the owl lived with them thereafter, coming and going at will.

Thankfully, the baroness kept to her word and they were no more outraged by the annual invasion of the hunting parties. Word came that extensive works on the other castle had greatly succeeded in pleasing the lady and her friends. The baron however, did visit his old home very often, always warmly welcomed and fitting in naturally as ever. It was quite obvious he was more happy in his own home, than in the grand new place of his wife. Always taking a few neighbouring knights with Anders and Peter and a few of the grooms hunting to stock the larders, it was obvious how they enjoyed their sport, without the grand gentry. When the days were fine, the baron rounded up all the local men and shouted himself hoarse on the butts. For there were again worrying whispers of war and fears that they would soon be summoned. It was Baron Pomeroy's obligation to the Crown to supply a party of skilled bowmen. Even when it was wet, Roland sat contentedly by the fire in the solar, working on arrows with his bowmen, laying them in the embers to straighten and harden. Otherwise he was joined by his sister or Lee, playing chess and reminiscing over past times. Yet they were lucky, for the years passed peacefully, the routine of the castle and the seasons as a pendulum.

CHAPTER SEVENTEEN

ROLAND

It would not have occurred to the baron that all the agreeable changes which came about in his life had actually stemmed from that child and that awful day. In his head, he thought of it as The Catastrophe, little did he know then, that it heralded wondrous changes for him. Neither did Lee, the child's father, her foster brother, (that idiot Jerome, cause of all the trouble), and last but never least, his own, dearly loved sister Joan.

What was the world coming to, he thought a hundred times, when well-born young pages should rape a ten-year-old girl, and, in his castle? Somehow it was that which riled him most, though he didn't realize it.

He, an innocent man, had found himself in the thick of it, he who was happily hunting with his guests, miles away at the time. How he came to be blamed he simply could not fathom, for not only was his lady outraged with him, the castle folk avoided him as best they could, leaving him feeling very poorly done by.

Somehow, his life had not turned out as he felt it should. He had always dreamt of living here, in his childhood home, where throughout the vagaries and changes of history, he and his family had managed to survive. Their other castle, lower down the river, was, true, more modern, larger and lighter, more, according to his bride, a gracious seat. But this had been home, and always would be.

His earliest memory was of sitting in the lady garden with Joan. Who had made him a daisy chain for his head.

"There my sweeting," she had said, kissing his hand so as not to disturb his crown. "You are Baron Roland and you even have your golden circlet on to prove it."

He remembered the sun always shining, and riding beside his father on a barrel-bellied pony, his adored and caring sister, close behind. They had been the magical days of childhood, when he was lord of all and everyone.

Even, when at eight, he had been sent to their cousin the duke, far down the river by the sea, the days of agony had been few. For his tears, rages and refusal to eat, had soon brought his sister Joan to his side. It was she, in his mind his real mother, who had cuddled him in bed, and calmed his fears with sweet words and old songs.

"I am here now, Roland my dearling," she said a hundred times, soothing the hiccups resulting from his tears, which shook his square body. "You and I shall be pages together, and Father will be so pleased with us."

True to her word Joan had defied all authority and stayed by his side for the months it took for him to gain confidence. Slowly, he later realized, so cleverly, she had left him now and again to do tasks for the ladies, till at the end, they met only at meal times and in chapel. It wasn't till years later he understood that perhaps she had benefited far more from their years with the duke than had he. For few knew that they were not full kin, that Joan was base-born, and sent as nursemaid to mind him as she had always done since he was a baby. From things she said when they were adults, it had been a precious time of learning for her. While he had bumbled his time away playing with the other high-born pages, she had absorbed everything offered to her. Here she avidly soaked up everything the ladies taught, be it embroidery, music or French.

"Your son is a happy lad, cousin, but he will never have the mind of your daughter," said the duke every time when their father came to take them home for holidays. "My lady tells me that Joan is a jewel, who she will sorely miss. Indeed she claims that Joan is the best maiden she has ever had in her household. She has gifted hands, the keenest mind for learning, together with the kindest disposition. It would be well not to forget her in your will, cousin, a decent dowry, for I doubt if your lady wife has care enough to look to her future."

With the seeds sown, their father had deeded a house and good farm to Joan, the least a man could do for his child, even if she was base-born.

While he lived at the castle, Roland never noticed that his mother's mind was roaming. Yet Joan did, and slowly, quietly, it was she who sent away the uncaring waiting maids and took over their duties, for they were lazy in their lightest tasks, and laughed behind their hands at the witless woman. It was Joan, who gently directed her father's wife in every way, and every day, and Joan who took the reins of the castle into her able hands.

At that time, as was expected of him, Roland often went to court, as squire, then knight, to idle his days in occasional tourneys, games and songs, none of which he excelled in. Having always believed that he was the most handsome and clever boy, it smote his heart sorely when he found that indeed he was neither. Still, he was a good horseman and wielded his sword with strength and loyalty, so he stayed on the fringes of the court, always hoping to be noticed.

Although he would never know of it, he had indeed been noticed and the court scribe wrote in a great ledger by his name, "Trustworthy," a rare compliment.

Of course there were others like him, who were not of the highest echelon, the Lady Sybil being one of them. Somehow he did not have a great interest, as did his peers, in courting the young ladies with songs, flowers and trinkets. All his life he had been shielded from competition, for at home, he was the best, the young baron. It would not occur to him that a widow, with, as he soon learned, sons already, might find his solid character more interesting than other young men who were in pursuit of prettier prey. For Sybil was an astute woman, who at thirty-five, was tired of hardship and struggling to rear her sons alone and this boy baron might just be her last chance. Flattered by her attentions, and delighted that his romance was noticed by the king and court, so that they even attended his marriage, Roland never even considered whether this was a sensible action or not. It was only when they got home and he introduced his new wife to his beloved sister, that he had pangs of doubt. For, in his slow way, he had expected Sybil to love his sister as he did. And he expected Joan to love his wife, even if he had doubts that he himself did. Yet it was too late and life went on and the women skirted around each other, so at least there was little unpleasantness.

"Why?" said Sybil, fanning herself extravagantly with one of the new-fashioned, imported fans, "doesn't your half-sister live at her little farm, at least while we are in residence?" Roland considered her slowly. His immediate thought, ever conscious of his own comfort, was and who will run this place? Yet he hesitated, the germs of diplomacy beginning to sprout in his thick head.

"Well my lady," he replied, "and why not? I fear that I have been careless of your rights. Forgive me that I did not see that you are fretting that you do not hold the castle keys. Of course you wish to run our home, to make all the orders and arrangements. So I will speak to my sister this night to correct it. Forgive me Sybil, I simply had not thought."

To which the shocked Sybil, eyes down, hastily sorted her own thoughts and replied hastily.

"Ah but no, my lord. That you must not do, for I do see that she runs your castle to your liking, while it may take me time to learn so well. Better to leave arrangements here as you wish. So let us leave it my lord, and I will strive to be a good chatelaine to your other seat, which," she paused to fan herself again, "I freely admit to preferring to this dark, damp place."

True, unknowingly, she had spoken in French to her husband, careless, derogatory words about his sister. Seeing the young woman turn swiftly to leave the solar, she had raised her fine-arched brows at him in query.

"My sister," said Roland very deliberately, feeling an unusual quiver of anger course through him, "speaks excellent French."

So with one thing and another, that is how they rarely came here, for Sybil was happy holding court downriver. It had especially irritated her when the bastard woman had gone behind their backs and taken herself a husband, no doubt even slyly getting the baron's approval to do so. For, disliking Joan and wishing her away, Sybil had planned to wed her to her late husband's widowed cousin. She had feared greatly, that she might have been forced into that role herself. For her high-born relatives managed everything. Being widowed was an unenviable position, particularly having again married a younger son. What ill fortune she had endured, that both young and healthy husbands had died leaving her with sons and little else. If the relatives had the mind, they could send her to her kinsman, if not as wife then as housekeeper. The thought made her shiver. For he was a cold, cruel man with many children, who lived in the far North-country. A woman like Joan, true, base-born but with blood from one of the old Norman families in her veins, might be of use. Now she reasoned that with no child of the baron, her new husband, there was little reason why her sons could not be his heirs. Sybil was happy with the way things were working out, and chose to ignore her husband's sister and childhood home. After the scandalous occurrence when the three sons of her friends had been well nigh murdered by the brute child of the healer, who would want to go there anyway? A cluttered, crowded place with few comforts, even if the hunting was good.

From the start, Roland was clearly aware of his sister's silent disapproval of his wife, for even if they were just half-siblings, they were deeply close in character and thought. He knew too how she grieved when time and again his party came to hunt, and the spare body of the Lady Sybil showed that she was not fulfilling expectations to produce an heir.

So it was inadvertently, that the uproar following the catastrophe with Lee's daughter turned out for the best. It caused the lady to remain at her chosen home, so when Roland came to the old castle, he came with a light heart. Now it was just like the old times. He took his place at the great board, drank, ate, sang and regularly as usual, gave judgment on local matters as they arose. He jollied all the youths from round about, and set them to practise on the butts, rejoicing in their success. Now and again he did his knight's service and rode at the fore of his little army of bowmen and joined the king, whichever one it was. Inevitably, England continued to have troubled times. Roland, Baron Pomeroy, prided himself as he led his well-liveried and armed men, his boar's head pennant aloft, yet always with the real hope to return them home safely to their own hearths. If some were lost in battle, he left it to Joan with her wisdom and kindness to aid the family how she thought best. He usually took Lee with him, so with their good stores and their clever healer, they coped better than many.

Increasingly, he remained at his favourite castle, only to return to the later, more elegant one, when summoned by the Lady Sybil for some special occasion.

He and Joan resumed their close bond, and he enjoyed her husband and sons, as he did Lee and his fair daughter. The castle was a happy place with the sound of young voices echoing through the dark corridors. He felt at ease again, enjoying the sound of the children playing, which his lady wife had not, ever shooing them away. Through Joan he knew everything that was happening about him, be it in castle or villages. Without her, he would know little. It was she of course who lightly broached the idea that Lee had suggested that they should build a Moot Hall so to encourage a local market. When it was done, she next suggested they replace the old wooden structure and build a fine stone church in the village. For it was growing, a quiet prosperity was causing more folk to settle there, with their strong new houses rising on narrow lanes, less like cattle shelters. Roland liked the idea and his eyes sparkled, so with Lee he went to see the bishop, and exciting plans were made. A new pride filled Roland, for this was Godly work. The arrival of workmen swelled the village further, which meant more houses. The pentices along the side of the castle walls were cleaned and repaired for the men. Gradually they filled up, with hewers, sawyers, masons and carpenters. Small merchants set up their shops in the street while the country people worked harder to supply the newcomers with vitals. In the first years, a rough wooden bridge was strung over the ford, but later, to transport the materials better, it was crowned by a proper stone bridge.

Ignoring his wife's complaints, he found himself ever in demand, busy with the architect, the head builder and the monk, whom the bishop had sent. It was all fascinating, and it absorbed him as had nothing else in his life. One day he had found the little Fleur, Lee's daughter, in the hall, drawing leaves and flowers on a slate. Leading her to the stone masons on the hill, he showed them her art, and soon she was drawing faces, animals and much else, for them to copy. Theirs would be a fine church. Even if God did not give him heirs, he would give God a church.

His flocks were growing too and Lee was proud to tell him that without a doubt, it was because his boy Jerome was now in charge. He had grown into a huge young man, very blonde and strong, with kind, soft blue eyes. Yet apart from his piercing whistles and occasional raucous laughter, he never spoke. The baron had been impressed and approved that Lee had deemed it sensible to leave him with the shepherd to learn a goodly trade. Although there was little need to read or write, Roland was relieved that the healer had taken on the task of scribe. He and the boy Jerome even produced, according to the monks, very fine vellum and parchment. So it had worked out well for the boy, keeping him in a worthwhile occupation and away from any more silly visitors. One uproar had been more than enough for all of them.

The church grew, and with it, Roland's confidence, for they received many important and interesting visitors, who came to watch its progress. Not only their praise delighted him, but they made donations for the fabric, which was always a help. Yet, and of course as baron, he had to dig deep into his pockets, which caused the Lady Sybil to be none too pleased, but in God's name, it would be the finest church upriver for many miles. Amongst the many travellers and visitors who arrived and sat at the board in the hall, came one day a tall, silent man. He did not mix, or state his business openly, and Anders remarked quietly to his wife that he was not to be trusted. After greeting the baron, he spent many hours closeted with him in the solar, papers spread all about. It cannot have occurred to him that the woman who brought lights and wine might be able to read what was written on them. That night Joan went to Roland quietly.

"Be careful what you sign brother," she stated bluntly. "Lady Sybil will try to take all you have. Let her sons wait at least till you are dead." He stared stupidly at her in the gloom of candlelight. She was right! He had not thought of it, the man had such a smooth tongue, he had almost thought to give them everything now.

So he retracted the rough drafts, insisting that Lee assisted in the new. Next, he deeded the other castle to his wife in trust for her eldest son, right there and then with Lee and Joan as witnesses. The smaller castle, he willed to her sons on his death, and let them squabble over it as they wished. It was a perplexed lawyer who rode away, wondering what he had done wrong.

After a skirmish by Roland's little band with another lord's men, Lee made himself a little hospital in the room on the landing where the children had slept. Fleur had long left this room, a quiet, sweet natured girl, who only spoke when spoken to. Instead of joining the other maids as one might expect, to giggle and gossip, she now slept alone in a tiny room in the main building, near to her Godmother Joan.

The old dormer made a good sickroom, for even if the stairs were tricky to ascend, once there, it was all comfort. With the warmth of a wooden floor, a good chimney and a garderobe on hand, it seemed more practical than having sick bodies lying about underfoot in the hall. With the work on the church introducing new materials, Lee had begged the architect to get extra glass. Now his little hospital was light and warm, so he could see to do his work better. As it was often occupied, accidents being frequent on the building site, his extravagance was justified.

Word had no sooner come that the plague was about again when a messenger arrived late one evening. Lady Sybil and many others had been taken, leaving two sons alive, he told them breathlessly.

"Away!" cried Joan, pushing him out of the door. "Away! While you bring news, do you bring us the contagion also?" and sent Anders and her sons to drive him away, even from stopping in the village, their whips belabouring the rump of the poor exhausted horse till they were well gone.

Shocked and almost in tears, Joan took up a broom and swept the very ground where he had stood. Then, calling the women, they scoured the midden and set about burning old bones in braziers and in every chimney place, to drive away the feared disease with the stink. Next day, she sent the baron with Lee to tell all who lived in the nearby villages, locals and workmen, not to leave or allow a living soul in from outside, at their peril. In narrow places along the road, strong hurdles were set up to keep all comers out. Fear caught their hearts and silently they prayed wherever they were, doing whatever task. But this time, they were lucky.

"Perhaps now the baron will choose a younger bride for himself?" queried Lee. "A fruitful wife would be good, for I do not like the look of those stepsons one bit."

Joan laughed lightly, now her anxieties over the sickness coming to them had diminished.

"Ah, Lee, if only? But I fear that my brother is lazy, as was our father. Either a wench will choose him and get him as did Sybil, or we must arrange a bride for him. He will never stir himself sufficiently to find and woo one for himself."

As usual, Lee went to the monastery to help with the blood-letting, Peter as always, groom and companion. A well-loved and trusted young man now, Peter had not only collected the treasure from the hollow tree, he had accepted that his brothers were dead. With part of a foot missing, he still found walking a difficulty, yet rode better than most.

Although he did not realize it, the baron terribly missed Lee while he was away. He was a good and clever friend, one with whom conversation was never dull, for he had travelled, been in great castles and met extraordinary folk. What was more, he played a fine game of chess. Roland intended to beat his adversary one day. One day.

Joan understood her brother was bored and missed Lee during his regular short absences. Despite her efforts to entertain him as well as run the castle, she felt unwell, a summer fever perhaps. Taking to her bed, she hoped it was not the plague and appealed to God, his holy Mother and the saints, to heal her of whatever it was. Hearing of it, always a child in these things, Roland also took to his bed. So Fleur found herself nursing them both, forbidding entry to the other women, for fear if it were a contagion, that they would be ill too.

Anders listened to Fleur and gave his wife herb teas to lower her fever and calm the cramps which tore at her belly. Satisfied that Joan was comfortable, Fleur then attended the baron. Feeding him light soups and teas for the fever, which she observed he did not have, she also played chess with him, always winning, to his astonishment. Of course, being Lee's daughter, she had learned from him and not only was she clever, she had grown into a beauty.

When Lee returned, he found that the baron had lost weight, which suited him greatly and seemed to give him more energy. Mistress Joan too was thinner, but with laughter in her eyes, as she told Lee privily, that she was with child again. After all these years and at her age! Soon the news had spread all about the castle and into the village and without fail, everyone rejoiced.

"It is time," Roland announced loudly, pleased with his new figure and his sister's news equally, "there were more children around here. This old castle is as a morgue, no noise, no laughter, no children!"

It was a difficult winter. The weather was so mild, rain, mud and impossible roads together with endless colds and coughs made life tiresome. Joan could not believe that this pregnancy could be so difficult compared with those when she was younger. Sick for months, she could not bear to be near the great hearth in the hall, the smell of food turning her stomach. Fleur and the women managed as they could, yet everything seemed to go wrong. Without Joan's discipline, the men brought in mud, great clods of it and the place was always filthy. The dogs and falcons, bored by inactivity, fought each other whenever they could, causing injury to themselves as well as to the humans who sought to separate them. In tears, Fleur sat by the baron, who was making the most of a bad cold, unseeing of the chess men so at last, jubilant, he won.

Lee was pressed too, for there was much illness about, and fresh food was short because no one could hunt in this weather. The barrels of salt beef and herring were empty. The dovecote was getting low on squabs, and they dare not kill the parent birds or they would be short next year. At least the clever Jerome kept them supplied with mutton through the dark days of winter. Work on the almost completed church had stopped. For how could they bring the great oak roof beams through all this mire? Lee was worried about Joan too, whom he missed sorely, realizing that without her, the castle was going to pieces. And what about his dearling Fleur? Bundled up against the damp, white-faced and miserable, she tried to help him to help everyone.

Joan's daughter was born in early summer. It was as hard and long a birth as Lee had ever seen, but a healthy little girl brought smiles to her face and free of her burden, Joan was ecstatic.

They called her Moya, after Anders' mother and both the baron and Lee stood Godfathers, while Fleur stood Godmother.

Anders and his sons were incredulous at their new little woman. While their Joan regained her strength, they toiled to make her life easier. For the architect was back, as always full of ideas. It was he who organised changes in the old castle, a heavy job as it had been solidly built long years ago. With roof gutters directed to butts, carrying water was greatly reduced most of the time. With leaden drains taking the waste away to pits in the garden, life seemed sweeter and far easier. During the work, while the place was upside down, Joan removed herself to her own house at her little farm. A mere mile from the castle, her menfolk commuted daily. It was a good half-timbered house on a stone base, and for the first time, Joan found herself mistress of her own home instead of the rambling old castle. Here she enjoyed the garden, her swaddled baby in a basket by her side, only missing Fleur, who was still unwell and trying to cope with everything, and so did not visit often.

Fleur dragged herself up the narrow staircase, resting on the garderobe, then painfully and slowly went on up to Lee's room. Here she lay down, wishing that he would come, wondering if she too had the plague and was dying.

Lee rode back from his regular visit to the monastery, wondering why he felt unease. Having let Peter take his pony, he left his bundle of newly acquired herbs on the step of the gatehouse and went in search of Fleur. She was nowhere to be seen. Puzzled, he knew she was not with Joan for they had briefly stopped there on the way. Taking up his bundle, he slowly ascended the circular stair to his room. It was a sound which alerted him, for there she was on his bed, and his heart lifted.

"Ah there you are my dearling, I have been seeking you and was worried." He went over and touched her brow. It was wet.

"Fleur!" Fleur?" he fumbled as he struck the light and finally got a flame on a candle, so to light the brazier. "Are you ill my child?" Fear clutched his heart. For there was the plague about again, he had heard at the monastery. Which was why, in his anxiety, he and Peter had paused to swim in the cold river, to cleanse themselves in case they had brought it with them. Gentle hands drew back the covers, and he lifted the lamp so he could see better. Feeling under her armpits, he frowned, nothing. And perhaps she had no fever, then why? A moan escaped her and she drew her knees up in agony.

"I must have eaten something bad, father," she gasped, "oh the pain. But I am glad you are come at last," and began to weep.

A terrible thought filled Lee. Not again? Could she be with child? Her mother had done just this. Carefully he crept his hands over her.

"God have mercy!" he whispered, feeling the hardness of her small, yet rounded belly. That was it. She was labouring with child but it must be early, for her belly was small. His hands shook as he drew the clothes over her once more, then ran out of the door and leaned over the battlements.

"Peter! Peterkin!" and yelled till the scurrying of figures in the bailey way below showed him that he was heard. Limping across the cobbles Peter stared up at the frantic waving figure of his friend the healer.

"Go with all haste to fetch Mistress Joan, Peter. Fast, oh go quickly," and turned back into the room where he tried to stem his shaking hands to make preparations to deliver her.

Just once more he spoke to her in between pains, his kind, strong hand relieving them as he always did for women in childbed, indeed as he had done for her mother so many years previously.

"Who was it, Fleur?" voice tight, trying to control his anger. "What man did you lie with?" Then waited till the pain passed and she took his hand and through her tears murmured one word.

"Roland."

Joan arrived just in time to receive the tiny boy, and watched Lee mark his head with water and baptize him "Roland", before he quietly died. The only one who did not weep was Fleur, who lay silent.

"Help me, Joan, for we will not lose her as we did her mother." Working together they took away the afterbirth and cleansed the thin body and made her comfortable.

After he washed the still white form of the tiny child, he wrapped it in the softest scarf from his chest of treasures and laid it into Fleur's arms. Though small, he had seen that in all things it would have favoured her. For it was fair of skin and fine of bone and no doubt at all would have had the palest hair.

"He is dead, my dearling. Born early I must guess. He was too little to breathe properly so he is gone to the Lord, my sweeting, for at least he was baptized." Fleur looked down at the still face and a tear rolled down her cheek.

"I did not know, father. Believe me I did not, for I bled monthly as always, though little. Father, do not be angry with me," she began to weep weakly. "You were away, and he was sad and lonely as was I, and after we played chess, he took me to his bed, because I was cold. He was always kind to me, father, especially when I missed you, while you were away." Quiet sobs shook her body and in the gloom, and Joan gave Lee the fiercest look.

"I am not angry, my dearling," his sorrow overcoming his rage. "The shame is that we did not know, for Roland would have taken you to wife, and here was an heir at last!" He bent his head to rest it on the bed to hide his tears. "But now be sure he will wed with you when you are fit enough. And you will carry him a good strong heir while we care for you. It was a hard time trying to run the castle without Joan. If only we had known, we would have helped you more. Do not worry, my angel," yet the words failed him as he tried to stem his distress. Rising from his knees he addressed Joan.

"I will send up broth for her, Joan, I beg you to stay till I return. For now she must sleep and rest to get strong again." Reaching for the tiny, lifeless bundle, Lee kissed his daughter on the brow and taking it in his arms, straightened his back resolutely. "Now I will go to Roland, my dear. Rest well and do not fret. You are young and you will bear more children and next time," his voice hardened, "we will mind you better."

He found Roland in the solar idly playing chess with Tim Bowman. Nodding to the man, Lee jerked his head at the door, asking him without words to leave, so that he could speak privately to the baron. When the door was shut, his face unusually severe, Lee knelt before the baron, opened his cloak and held out the shawl-wrapped child his hands.

"Your son, my lord."

The baron peered at the offering, gawped, then back at Lee.

"What? What?" he mumbled stupidly.

"Your son, my lord," insisted Lee, his voice hard yet close to breaking. "Your son, sire, born of my daughter Fleur. See he is dead. Take your dead son, sire. Note what a beautiful child he might have grown into."

Still Roland stared, his eyes popping from his head, his throat working.

"What?" his mouth gaped, "what do you say?"

"We baptized him Roland the moment before he died, so at least he died a Christian." Pushing the bundle toward the astonished baron he repeated himself, this time louder and more harshly. "Your dead son, my lord, take him! Take him, he who would have been your heir!"

The baron reached out with trembling hands and took the little thing, peered at it, his face incredulous, breaking and unconsciously he began to rock. Despite his own rage and sorrow, Lee felt pity for the bowed figure, as with the little body in his arms, his face crumpled and he wept as a child. Great drawn breaths of sorrow racked his body. In between them came sobs and wet kisses on the tiny head punctuated by "No! Oh sweet Jesus, no. My little son, my little Roland, dead!" So began his wailing all over again.

His anger still with him, Lee hardened his heart to practicalities.

"Shall I order a beautiful little casket to be made for him, my lord? We will bury him in the crypt of your fine new church, don't you think, first of your line." Unable to reply, the distressed man merely nodded his head, still intent on the tiny lifeless child in his arms. "Mind him now, while I go to Fleur," went on Lee relentlessly. "Mind him and I will send Joan to you when she has finished with her care of Fleur." Turning on his heel, pain and anger thick in his throat he went out.

When Joan came to her brother, the baron wept afresh against her breast as he had countless times as a boy. Unbelieving, distraught, he rocked as he clutched at her familiar, kindly body, the tiny boy, son and nephew, pressed between them.

His little son! His own little heir!

"So beautiful too," said Joan gazing at the waxen doll, "so beautiful."

It was Anders who stayed up half the night working on the little box, deeply sad, realizing the truth of the matter. That in her care of his Joan, Fleur had birthed her child too early. In sorrow he strove to make the little casket as fine as he could, thinking of his bonny, living daughter. Joan nodded in approval when he gave it to her, and recklessly taking a fine robe which had belonged to the old baroness from the great press, she cut off part of the skirt and carefully lined it.

Word flew from the castle to the village to the outlying farmsteads and by mid-morning, a great crowd had assembled in the courtyard. Jerome had been told by the dairymaids and he came, eyes frightened, to be held and fiercely comforted by his father. Led by the priest, intoning prayers for the dead with the baron carrying the little box, they all walked silently down to the incomplete church. Here the stone over the vault had been removed, and after the prayers, Roland descended and laid his child on a stone shelf. His sorrow was moving, and few had a dry eye in sympathy.

"Help him out!" ordered Lee to Jerome, who obediently went down the stone steps and all but lifted the grieving baron out.

Then the women went down, partly from curiosity, partly from kindness. Touching the box with a prayer, they laid simple flowers, just recently gathered and still dew-fresh, on the little box and all about it. For all too many of them knew the grief of losing a newborn. One after the other they came, curtseyed their reverence to the baron and at last, stood back to let the family pass and go home.

So, they whispered, the baroness had just been too old to bear him children? They chattered quietly between themselves as they returned to their chores. Imagine Fleur bearing him a son? Oh but the pity of it dying, poor little soul.

Gathered in the solar, with only Jerome missing who had rushed to his sister, they drank a glass of the best wine and spoke quietly. Lee again reassured the priest, well backed by Joan, that they had baptized the child while it breathed. But as this brought forth more tears from the baron, they were silenced.

"Well, baron," Lee spoke out in a firm voice. "Now you have had one child, I see no reason why you should not have more." He was interrupted as Roland wiped his eyes and blew his nose noisily. "I propose to you that if he calls the banns now, in six weeks time, when Fleur is churched and well again, you ask Father Benedict here to marry you."

Joan, Anders, the priest and the baron looked at him. Surprise, uncertainty, pleasure and approval flashed across their faces. Roland was the first to take Lee's hand.

"Will you allow it, Lee? Yes indeed, I should like that. For it is a grand idea. She is a lovely little lady, so good, so kind and gentle. Yes indeed, Lee, with your permission and blessing, I would be so glad to take your daughter to wife."

Lee narrowed his eyes at his old friend, soon to be his son-in-law. It was as well he had agreed, for if the fool had refused to wed his Fleur, he would have found a way to kill him, painfully at that.

"It is the honourable thing to do, sir," Lee went on, his mind running ahead with plans. "God willing, as she is young, you will have more children, and nothing here will change in your life, which is quiet and agreeable to you, but my lord." He had it now, and he would insist he had his way. "I expect you to sign a nuptial agreement with my daughter. In the event of your death, that she and her children will be well provided for. For I am sure we do not want a repetition of your late lady's situation to happen here. And with two of your stepsons still living, there might be problems with the inheritance. For, as we well know, it is not uncommon amongst kin."

Taking out two of the best sheets of vellum, he began that night, writing out two documents. Heavy-eyed yet satisfied, in the morning, took them to the baron for his approval.

"This castle my lord, one thousand acres and the old hunting lodge by the marsh." Lee had worked it out, a clean, tidy, block of land, according to an old map he had borrowed from the baron's chest. "Your elder stepson has the other castle and the lands beyond it. They will not want the marshes with the river winding through it as it does. Your younger stepson will have a good sum of money and will just have to marry an heiress. For I believe you have done your duty and twice over for your late lady's family. Now," he spoke very clearly, "you must forget her and make correct provision for your own future family."

The baron smiled for the first time since his little son had died. His own family!

Six weeks later, Baron Roland Pomeroy, descended from Geoffrey Pomeroy who landed in England with the great King William, married Fleur, daughter of Lee. He grinned cheerfully as he put his clumsy mark on both documents with a flourish, witnessed by Joan and the priest and gallantly kissed his bride's hand.

"Lady Fleur, a flower indeed."

A great banquet was held in the castle and mostly local folk attended, a few knights from not too far away, but no stepsons. Roland did not care, for he felt bright and young again, and happy as of old. Life was now as he had always hoped it would be, as it was when he was a boy. Unaware that again he had been manoeuvred into a marriage, he behaved like a successful wooer, jolly and optimistic.

Fleur, dressed in fine clothes at her father's insistence, looked lovely, quite the lady. No longer did she toil all day about the castle as of old, for Lee had employed women to do the work. Fleur's task now, he insisted, was to thrive and breed. Instead she began the great labour of embroidering magnificent tapestries with her maids, as did all the other ladies of the land. Joan sometimes joined her, although she generally remained at her farm which her sons were running. Anders kept his post as the head groom, with Peter taking over ever more of his responsibilities. Much changed yet little changed. They were getting older every one and youngsters were taking over their task of running the great old castle.

One year after her marriage, Fleur gave birth to a full-term, bonny daughter. It was a very different birth from the last. In the great bedchamber, the bed with fine new drapes and hangings, Joan looked down at the squawling baby and laughed.

"Oh my word," she gently wiped the face and held it out for Roland to see. "She is your mother, the Lady Jessica all over again!" and laughed merrily. "So long as she is not as awkward as her grandmother, we shall manage."

They named her Jessica, and very soon they learned that she was indeed awkward. Yet Roland was spellbound by his progeny and spent hours gazing into the great cradle in which she lay.

"Flesh of my flesh," he thought proudly, "bone of my bone and blood of my blood." Life had new meaning; the empty old days of Sybil and artificiality were forgotten, for this was all so real, so very satisfying.

Jessica was a solid and demanding child, and they soon had to find a wet-nurse as Fleur could not feed her herself. Fleur was relieved, for somehow this child did not warm her heart as did Joan's daughter. At two, Moya was a delight, all smiles and charm. Grateful that the wet-nurse, whose own child had died, seemed to take to her daughter, Fleur gratefully resumed her place in the solar at her embroidery frame.

Roland on the other hand delighted in his daughter, who so resembled his mother, and indeed himself. He was forever visiting her, holding her fingers and kissing her roundly. As she grew, it was he whom she loved and was obedient to. Apart from her grandfather Lee of course. No one dared to disobey him, though, being of a very stubborn nature, she obeyed even him with a poor grace.

So it came about that Jessica spent as much time as she could with her father, be it inside, or out. This meant the castle was restful and Fleur encouraged her to go with her father rather than have her complaining underfoot. In no time, a small pony was found and she became an exceptional and fearless horsewoman, always going hunting with him and his friends. As she grew, taller and wilder horses were found for her, yet with her streak of determination, she managed them all and well.

When her father had guests, she was there close beside him, laughing like a man at the men's jokes.

"She has to be curbed, Fleur," insisted Lee who found her behaviour unladylike and embarrassing. "I see the guests' shocked faces at her bawdiness, interrupting, speaking out of turn. Something must be done, and always wearing brais and hose, like a boy."

A painful subject, for no more children arrived, no heir, and if the baron was satisfied with his daughter, Lee was not. "She must be sent away to learn manners, yet how can we send her to a great family with her dreadful behaviour?" He had been pondering over the problem for some time. He was feeling old, he must organize something for her or it would be too late and she would end up unmarriageable. "I have heard of a lady not too far from here, who takes children from good families and teaches them. Perhaps she would do better than we do."

So it was arranged and when in the spring, the roads were passable, a furious Jessica was taken to the Lady Felicia de Alencourt who had a small manor two day's ride away. The baron rode with her, all the way trying to convince her that he and Joan had done the same, and how he had come to enjoy it, even if he had hated it at first.

Roland was to do that ride again two weeks later, for a letter had come from the Lady Felicia demanding that he send Jessica's cousin Moya or take her away. For it seemed that Jessica would not settle; all she did since arriving was to weep and wail and refuse her food. Joan packed up her daughter's clothes, a small smile on her face, funny how history repeated itself. Anders hovered, unhappy yet knowing in this as with most things, his wife would have her way. Yet he was glad for his daughter, even if minding Jessica was hardly a happy task. The main thing was that their only daughter would not only receive a good education, she would mix with the gentry, and perhaps find herself a good husband.

Peace descended on the castle, quiet as of old, without the indignant cries from the baron's daughter, which usually rent the air all too often. And yes, when she came home for holidays, they quietly agreed amongst themselves, Jessica was more tractable.

CHAPTER EIGHTEEN

MOYA

Moya gazed at her mother with shining eyes. So she also was to go to Lady Felicia's manor to learn, not that she didn't already know to read and write, for Master Lee had taught her. Of course she had learned much else from her mother and father. All household tasks and to sew, spin and weave, though the latter not really so well because mother always did it. But, oh joy, another place, different, new, exciting? She glowed, her heart beating rapidly as she folded her third dress and laid it neatly in the small chest. Then, startled, she saw a single tear slowly course down her mother's cheek. Swiftly, arms outstretched, she gathered Joan into her arms and held her close.

"Mother, mother!" she rocked the ample body of the beloved woman. "Do you shed a tear because your baby is leaving home?" Holding the chin in one hand she tenderly smiled into the soft blue eyes. Joan fumbled for her apron and blew her nose into it mightily, smiling tearfully.

"Indeed I am, my dearling," she wiped her eyes and smiled properly. "Yet I am glad you are going, for it is a great chance to better yourself and meet other young people. Well I remember how much my time away did for me."

Together they tucked oddments into corners of the chest which Anders had made for his daughter. Stockings and kerchiefs, aprons and gloves, they disappeared in its lavender scented depths. "Strange how things repeat themselves," mused Joan. "For I was sent for to mind Roland all those years ago, and now, you, my love, will be doing the same for Jessica." She straightened her back and surveyed their work satisfied.

"I want you to have my amber, dearling," Joan said, voice firm. "Your father gave it to me for a marriage gift, and as it was his mother's, your name-sake, I think it fitting that you have it now. Only," she held the golden glob of ancient sap against the light, "keep it safe, my love, for I do think it not only a lovely and precious thing, I believe it brings luck. It did to me anyway." Recovered, she smiled warmly at her only daughter and last child. "I have been so blessed Moya, so very blessed."

The girl took the amber in her hand and felt its warmth. Turning it this way and that, she gazed at it, absently wondering about her dead grandmother, and of how she came by the gem. Impulsively she leant forward and planted a gusty kiss on her mother's rosy cheek.

"Thank you, mother, I will wear it always and hope to be blessed too."

At the manor, her cousin Jessica had seemed extraordinarily pleased to see her. Thinner, which suited her, Jessica grasped her hand and proudly showed her around.

"It is not so fine as our place Moya," she explained, "but the light!" A hand waved to indicate the many glassed windows about them. "This is what we need. Windows! Then the castle won't seem so dark and gloomy."

Moya surveyed her cousin quietly. There were times when she almost wondered if Jessica was right in the head. Our castle indeed! Well she knew that her Aunt Joan had her own farmhouse beyond the village which did in fact, have windows. Yet Moya had grown wise being the elder, knowing all too well if she pointed that out, there would only be an argument.

"Why don't we carefully remark on it to the baron," she murmured, "certainly, apart from the solar, the castle is very dark."

Moya loved the manor. Indeed she almost loved the Lady Felicia, who was not nearly as daunting as her appearance implied. A tall spare woman, the lady seemed most kindly disposed to her, and Moya smiled to herself, imagining the hideous tantrums Jessica had subjected them to which had brought her here. All now was sweetness, and light, she smiled remembering. Soon Jessica almost grew to like the other children, indeed they all seemed as a happy big family. Sir Gervaise, who was ancient, was the father-figure, even though he did little all day. The Lady Blanche was old too, but it was she who ran the household, with the helpful orphan, Maria, by her side. Order was their theme. All work was to be done well and speedily according to the task and the time of year. Moya rejoiced with learning new things, and as usual, diligently put her mind to her work, thus gaining praise from the elders. Just once at the beginning of her three years at the manor, Moya had found herself alone with Lady Felicia.

"Lady," she said glancing about to make certain she was not overheard. "Please do not give me too much appreciation or my cousin will mind, and she is often quite difficult to cope with, if I get more praise than she."

Lady Felicia looked at the girl, squinting around her coif. Charming girl, she thought, clever, lovely and good, quite unlike the silly cousin of hers. Smiling, a bony hand resting for a second on the young cheek, she murmured,

"Thank you, child. You are of course, quite right."

So it worked. They learned and they worked at many tasks which would eventually be of use in their adult lives. Every morning they had lessons. Thanks to the bishop, they had books to read from, so lessons were pleasant and passed quickly. Their letters home were their writing test, and it was Sir Gervaise who gently rapped knuckles if he considered their slate practice not good enough. On dull days, they sat by the windows and stitched tapestries for the churches to be collected by the bishop who visited quite often. Moya gazed at the woollen yarns which the bishop brought from their own dyers and admired the vibrant colours. This she must learn to do, but it seemed no one at the manor had much skill in dyeing, so she only managed simple, ordinary colours, which they already did at home. Still, it was a busy yet contented life at the manor. On fine days they picked flowers and herbs to hang and dry for winter. Maria taught them to make reed and straw mats, so every holiday, little gifts were taken home to be proudly admired and much appreciated.

Not only did they learn their book lessons and good housewifery, they learnt manners, table service, archery and games. Jessica was always bored with indoor work. Yet, being a good rider already, she surpassed at outdoor activities. Indeed, as was often remarked, she was more like a boy in her behaviour, than a young baroness.

Apart from Jessica and Moya, there were three more smaller girls and four boys. Maria was almost grown up, and she, with the other children, did not go away as they were orphans, so lived at the manor, all the year round.

Of the boys, Stephen was the oldest and most handsome. Moya watched him when she thought no one could see her. His was almost a saintly beauty. Tall and fair, his skin was smooth and his demeanour gentle.

If only, thought Moya, I could find a husband as appealing as Stephen. For not only was he wondrously handsome, he was a delight in all ways, with the makings of a fine knight. Yet he was younger than she by several years, though he stood taller already.

After the three years had sped by too quickly for Moya, they returned home for good, their education finished and adult life stretching before them. Instead of living at her parent's farm, Moya usually stayed at the castle. The baron was growing old and her aunt Fleur needed help with him. Help, they all knew, which should have come from Jessica but did not, as Jessica had resumed her old life, of riding and hunting and avoiding any task which irked her, such as woman's work. Without a doubt, she was an exceptional huntswoman, using her bow with a rare expertise. The baron was enchanted, blind to her often loud and rough ways and proudly exhibited the meat on the spit which his daughter had felled.

Occasionally visitors came to stay for some weeks, either to hunt or view the new church which was nearing completion, the baron's other pride and quite the talk of the county. It was good to hear visiting knights with their ladies lavish praise on the church, and its main benefactor, Baron Roland Pomeroy.

Several young men came to court Moya, yet she turned her face away, a face much like her mother's, but fairer and without the stubborn mouth of the baron's family.

"Why?" laughed Anders, "won't you smile on the young men who come to woo you? Be kind my girl, for having heard your praises, they come from afar to see you."

Moya pulled a face, then smiled at him, knowing full well her mother's story.

"Because father dear, when the right man comes a-wooing, not only will I smile at him, I shall ask him, to wed with me." So they laughed.

Although old Roland did not go to the court or to do his knight service with the king anymore, he still did his duty and sent a good party of fine bowmen when the need arose. Once again there were whispers of war. Disputes with the king and his heirs and endless intrigue and treachery were the gossip, and Roland was glad to be far away from it.

"Thanks be to God and his holy Mother," Roland allowed his wife to knead his stiff shoulders which was lovely even if it did hurt. "I could not bear the silliness of court now. When I was young I thought it great sport, but now," he took a slender hand and kissed it, "home and wife are all I want. And," he raised his voice, "I thank God I am not obliged to go to war anymore. For even war is changing. Such stories of explosives, cannon fire, new fangled weapons which debase the chivalry of knights. That I live to hear such tales is bad enough."

When Moya brought in a tray with pewter goblets and wine she was pleased to see the affection between her aunt and uncle.

"Uncle, a message has come from Sir Godfrey, your younger stepson," she said offering him his wine. "He is in the hall and would see you tonight." Roland frowned. He did not like either of his stepsons, they were prissy, unreliable, proud and greedy men. A visit meant trouble, and he wondered why he was being honoured with a visit. Lee came in and set up the chessboard, but Roland was uneasy and his indigestion was troubling him, so he played a poor game.

"You eat far too much for your age, Sire," said the healer mildly, taking a knight. "How you can sleep with your belly struggling so, I do not know." Then turning to Fleur he asked. "Have you any anise left, my child, for the baron might need a tisane before he retires."

Uncomfortable in more ways than one, the baron refused to see the visitor that night, adding sourly that the morning would be too soon. So it was Moya who went down and politely passed on a milder message, and led the young man and his squire to a room.

"So you are Joan's daughter," Sir Godfrey said, casting a skilful eye over the comely figure of the young woman. "So we must be somehow related." Moya straightened from attending the fire. All her senses told her that this was not a good man, so she lifted her head and said as politely as she could.

"Hardly related, Sir Godfrey, perhaps connected might be more correct."

For a moment she thought he was going to put his hand out to her and she stiffened. "Good night to you, Sire," dipping slightly, "the day will be fair tomorrow so perhaps you may care to spend some time with your stepsister, for I know a hunt is planned." So she avoided more talk as she gracefully slid out of the room and hurried down the stairs, feeling somehow unclean from the bold eyes of the visitor.

He was not pleased. His stepfather had fenced all his requirements most cleverly, which had surprised him. The old boy surely hadn't the wit on his own, which is why the curious healer always sat in the background. Talk seemed light, yet it was not. Godfrey wanted the promise from his stepfather of the castle and lands, which he politely reminded him, was what he had been promised upon his death. That was all. His so called stepsister, base-born no doubt, whatever was said, could marry well, live elsewhere, so that he could take over the castle. Mind you, it needed much work doing to it, so therefore he must find a rich heiress. Pity, he mused as the fine figure of Moya passed swiftly by. Now there was a lovely young woman, modest too, unlike her awful cousin in every way. He thought hard on the subject. Who could he get to marry the Lady Jessica and so get her out of his way?

"Now," said the baron lazily, "the best solution would be for you to marry my daughter. Then my lands shall remain in the family, and be yours jointly."

Sir Godfrey felt the blood drain from his face. He was so shocked that he had no words for some moments. The healer was watching him keenly.

"I,er," the young man felt for words. "I,er was not thinking of marrying quite yet," he stumbled over his words. "I,er hope to fight for the king soon, and must gain my spurs properly before I offer myself to a bride."

"Well perhaps," the thin voice of the healer cut the silence, "you might become betrothed to my granddaughter before you go. A sensible move I consider."

Godfrey gazed at first one man then the other. He had not remembered that the baron's shadow of a wife was the healer's daughter. He coughed and searched for words frantically in his thudding head, his face now turned a hot pink.

"When I return from the war, Sires, yes," gaining confidence, "that might be a good plan." But in his heart he thought only of escape. For marry Jessica he never would, castle or no. Now if her cousin were the baron's heir?

He rode away before lunch after kissing hands and doffing his hat valiantly. He even managed to smile at Jessica, pug-faced, ill-humoured girl that she was.

Lee sat with his hands under his chin, deep in thought. He asked Moya to give a message to her mother to come on the morrow if possible for they needed to talk.

"You must write a watertight will Roland," he insisted. "That young man has the king's ear, the good Lord knows how, and as you well know, kings often do silly things to please their favoured subjects. We must thrash this out together, so in the event he does succeed in bending the royal ear, we shall have the law on our side. For, Roland," the old baron sat up at the surprisingly severe voice, "we will not live forever and we must protect our ladies. It must be done."

Lee sat up all night with his worries. Fleur's daughter must inherit a good portion, for how else would she find a husband? Lee loved his granddaughter with misgivings. She really was not an attractive girl, in face, word or deed. The only person she revered was her father. All else was as dirt under her feet. Joan had told him that she strongly resembled Roland's mother, in every way. She too had been a difficult, wilful and spoilt woman. Wearily Lee went to his couch, hoping that a wise solution would enter his brain, for till now, there was none.

They conferred, Roland, Joan and Lee. This way and that they turned the problem around, till at last, hoping to cover every loophole in the law, Lee wrote the will out in triplicate, no mean task, and Roland signed them with the other two as witness.

All lands, castle and buildings would be shared between groom and bride on their marriage. If they did not marry, then, adhering to his previous will before Jessica was born, he left the marsh tower and one hundred acres to Godfrey his stepson. In the event of his death without issue, it would revert to Jessica. If Jessica did not marry Sir Godfrey but another, the tower hunting lodge and all the rest of his lands, something near one thousand acres, he left to his daughter. In the event of her death without issue, it would go to Godfrey.

It was not ideal, yet it was the best they could do. That night Lee slept for the first time in days. He watched Roland carefully. A big man, florid and loud, Lee saw all the signs of his irregular heart, ever under strain, and wondered how long he would live. At times when they had guests and Roland became more noisy and red-faced than usual, Lee made up a hawthorn bark tea for him. Just to steady his labouring heart, a small gesture. He liked his baron, son-in-law and friend, and feared the day of his demise, which would rock their precious family as well as the contented castle.

Yet it was Lee who went to his maker first. A simple cold it was, probably caught when treating the villagers who came regularly to him for their ailments. Then, because he did not heed it, his chest began to bubble and he felt too weak to cough up the muck which was drowning him. At last he took to his bed and Fleur moved back into the childhood haven, leaving Moya to run the household.

For three days Fleur sat beside her beloved adopted-father. Unwrapping her precious Book of Hours from its silk scarf, she quietly read to him, page by page. Lee, hearing her voice, was calm, for he saw in his mind's eye, the vivid painting and letters he had written so carefully. He remembered each page, the coloured scenes, the gold leaf and the little illustrations of meadow and castle. It had been a labour of love, using fine vellum made by Jerome which they had so lovingly worked for her, oh years ago, just after the catastrophe.

Everything he had taught her, she used in her fight for his life. On the fourth day, she suddenly understood that he was going to die. No! Her mind screamed silently. I cannot do without you.

"Father, father, I beg you, sit up, cough, spit, get well again. Oh father, do not leave me I beg you."

Lee heard the sweet anguished voice from afar. Of course he was aware that she was always near, yet her cry seemed to give him new energy and he sat up, coughed and spat, drank the foul tea she gave him, and determined to talk with her.

"I have a confession to make to you my dearling, one which has lain heavily on my soul for many years. A sin I committed against you my love, oh if you will hear it and forgive me?" He coughed and spat again.

"He came, a fair and handsome man, a wondrous minstrel, when you were just a little thing. I saw at once a likeness, and fearful, I whisked you away to visit Jerome at the sheepfold. I feared that when he saw what an angel you were, he would want you and take you away. And then my heart would break, for by now I really felt that you were truly mine." Resting back on the pillows he let Fleur wipe his face with a damp cloth. "I am certain he was your natural father Fleur, and I never told you."

Smiling warmly at him Fleur took his hands and kissed them.

"Ah but father, Aunt Joan did tell me. And that he was looking for my mother who he had abandoned, probably to take his pleasure with her again, not even knowing about my very existence. So Joan in her wisdom, told him the truth, that my mother had died, and omitted to mention me." Very gently she held him and kissed him. "You were my father and mother from the day I was born, Joan told me all about that too. That but for you I would not have lived, how deeply loving and caring of me you were, from the very first."

Smiling with her words, he slept for a while, then woke coughing, and exhausted, lay back, anxious again.

"There is another thing which lies heavy with me. Something which no living soul knows of me. Will you promise me one thing, my Fleur?" She nodded and pressed his hand. "You," he made his words clearly, "you alone must lay me out, my dearling, you hear?" Fleur bent her head to hide her tears and kissed his hand. "I never have told you, but now I must, for you are as my own flesh and blood, my sweet child." He rested, trying to still the burblings which rose in his throat. "I was about seven years old when my mother took me to my teacher, the physician I have so often told you about. I remember it well, because it was so strange and new." Again he rested, his mind roving into the past. "My mother was weeping as she put my hands into hers. Yes, for my teacher was a woman, a normal healthy, perfect woman." He coughed and spat out the muck into a bowl which Fleur held out for him. Exhausted he lay for a time before starting again.

"It seemed that her great driving force was to be a physician, and women were not allowed. So she became a man. Not until she died did I know it. And as I ask you now, so too did she ask me to lay her out, no one else."

Fleur reached into the bucket of charcoal and carefully placed some pieces on the brazier for she was anxious to keep him warm.

"She, who I thought was a he, put me on a table, lifted up my tunic and examined me. Then she nodded to my mother, probably gave a coin, which was her way. I never saw my mother again. So I stayed with the physician and at first ran errands, all the while learning. He was kind to me, gentle and good and for the first time in my life, I had enough to eat. I came to understand eventually through my work, that I am neither man, or woman, but have something of each. It was he, no she, who told me to be a man, for then I could learn all from her, and be a physician too. It was, she said many a time, easier in life to be a man. Only when she died did I really understand her words, seeing her in death, that she was wholly a female, so that is how she knew."

They were silent then, holding hands lit only by the soft glow of the brazier. Fleur felt nothing, just sorrow that he should want to unburden his heart to her because he felt his time was near.

At one moment Moya came with her parents, who together with the priest, prayed softly at their old friend's bedside.

Later, struggling for strength, "all my fortune is in the flower tubs on the battlements outside, my dearling. Just take out the shrubs and you will find jars of gold, it is yours and Jerome's for whatever you need." Again, a silence. "I remember when you were born. I was to leave that very day and Joan asked for help with your birthing." His voice was so low, Fleur bent forward to catch his words. "So now I will go, and leave you at last." The savage cough ripped through his thin body once more. "Don't go Fleur. Stay with me." So with tears falling quietly, she took the cold hands and held them and began to pray too.

Three times a day, Moya climbed the steep spiral stair with a tray for Fleur.

"Will I sit with him for a while, for uncle is asking for you, and I tell him he must not attempt to come up here." Fleur shook her head, absently sipping the chamomile tea.

"It won't be long now Moya dear. I ask you to call your mother to look after the baron for me until it is over. And you are right of course, he must not come up, besides, my father would not be able to speak with him." Taking Moya's hand she kissed her. "One more favour dear child, please go and bring Jerome. Take the baron's great horse, for Jerome is too big for the others. Bring him speedily, for I fear it won't be long now."

Lee heard the soft women voices and smiled. How fortunate he had been to come to this place so long ago with those wounded boys. How lucky he had been to find himself a father to two beautiful children. How good his life had been in this place where he was of use as well as being surrounded with fine and gentle people. He struggled to breathe, his face contorted with pain every time, which wrenched Fleur's heart. Suddenly she remembered the stone, the precious healing stone, which her father used only in great emergency.

"The stone, father! Where is the stone?" Blankly he looked at her, trying to understand her words. Then his face cleared and he glanced up at the small carved wood box on the topmost shelf. Fleur climbed up quickly for it, and sure enough, there with his most special knives, was the fine linen bag, heavy with the stone. Taking it, she tucked it into the folds of his robe, right on his heart, and hoped it would make a miracle and help him. Grasping her hand, he tried to speak, then coughed again, exhausted. At last she heard his words.

"You must keep the stone, Fleur, keep it safe. But be very careful who knows of it," he struggled to speak. "Folk do not understand. Witchcraft, Fleur, it is not. It is a precious gift from God, for the gravely injured. Mind it. Use it, but be cautious and use it very carefully." Perhaps she imagined it, but his breathing did seem easier.

Moya rode with speed first to her mother, then, with Joan up behind her, passed by and left her at the castle before going to the sheep fold.

Jerome had very quietly taken himself a wife some time back to their surprise and joy. A small woman, she appeared to be afraid of her own shadow, so must at last feel safe with the big, handsome shepherd. Several fair children ran out of the simple wood dwelling to meet Moya, for she was a favourite aunt. As she ducked under the thatch into the house, Moya smelt delicious baking from the hearth stone and was glad that she had smoked venison in her basket. Having brought her own blanket, for she intended staying until Jerome returned, she set to teaching the children their letters. Being busy would help to pass the time and ease the sorrow.

A scrubbed-clean Jerome came before night to the castle and sped up the familiar stair to silently embrace his sister and wipe a tear from her cheek. All night he sat beside his father, his big rough hands holding the cold slender hand in his.

"Look after your sister." Lee whispered at one moment and Jerome nodded, blinking back the tears. "Give your children learning my son," he gasped, "for even though being a shepherd is good, perhaps they might have another calling." There were other unexpected sentences in the night, so they knew that between naps he was still thinking. Each time they caressed the dying man, Fleur with loving soft words, Jerome just nodding. Hadn't they learnt about loving from him after all?

A bubbling and coughing rose painfully and Lee seemed to fight for every breath. Fleur now climbed onto the familiar couch and took her father's light body onto her lap, raising and supporting his chest up to ease his breathing. Jerome sat close, holding the cold hands while Fleur pressed kisses on the cold brow.

So Lee died peacefully, in the embrace of his two beloved children, who were not his children at all. With the first streaks of dawn, and the thin cry of a rooster, Lee thought himself to be floating. He felt safe, loved, even warm, held gently yet close to their healthy bodies.

"My children, my children," his lips smiling he murmured as he slipped away. Lee was buried in the baron's crypt.

"He is family after all," sobbed Roland, still unbelieving that his old friend had left him. Many came to offer sympathy and to lay little bunches of wild flowers on the tomb. For this had been a friend to all, with his clever healing and his quiet generosity. Fleur and Jerome stood with the baron, heads bowed as the prayers for the dead were spoken. He had lived a long and useful life they knew, yet with him gone, something of their life had gone too.

They were lost, all of them. It was always as if they expected the quiet footfall, the gentle voice, the kindly words. They felt him everywhere, yet he was not there. The women occupied themselves by going three times a day to say mass for his soul and consoled themselves that such a good man would surely already be in heaven.

Roland was not able to go with them. His weight and his bad legs prevented him from moving very far from the solar. Occasionally and with help, he might just go to the hall. On fine days, Fleur persuaded him to sit with her in the lady garden and enjoy the air and they used to reminisce of their lost loved one. The big, brash Roland grieved as they did, for perhaps Lee had been his one true friend, as Joan was the truest sister and Fleur the loving, caring wife. His solace was to drink. Without the moderation of his friend, without the chessboard and without the easy conversation, Roland was desperate. He became childish and belligerent when the women chided him. When they resorted to watering his wine, he soon found out because three of them inadvertently doctored the same flask at one time and he was furious.

One month after Lee died, Roland became ill and within a few days was in the crypt beside his old friend.

Now the women were truly bereft and more, they were afraid, for women alone were always cause for violence from greedy men. The gate was kept locked, and the doors too and Jerome was installed in the castle, great man that he was, while Peter was helped by his young sons to do his work. They now depended on the gentle, silent Jerome to protect them, even if they knew not from what.

Moya slept with her cousin Jessica in the baron's great bed because Fleur had oddly chosen to leave it and go back to the gatehouse. Winter came, and with it some security, for not many people chose to travel through the forests with snowdrifts and wild animals, let alone starving robbers.

Secretly, they rolled up Fleur's fine tapestries, the good silver inside and put them in Moya's house. He would come for sure, and he would not be taking their treasures.

With the first sign of spring, a messenger came saying that the new baron would shortly be taking up residence and asking for the ladies to remove themselves to their own land. The new baron? They were aghast. Who could that be? Guessing of course. Yet it was commonly known that Baron Roland only had one daughter, his firstborn son having died early. Moya went to see her mother and the two clever women conversed well into the night.

When the grand party arrived they were ready for them. Jessica had insisted that she be dressed in her finest, her grandmother's jewels heavy on her breast. As she was Baroness Pomeroy and lady of all her father's lands, she would show them. They had told her that she must be charming to the young man, for, if they were to wed, life would not change at all.

Sir Godfrey looked over his stepsister with disdain. She not only had not improved, she had grown fatter and more pug-like than ever. Hideous, despite the rich dress and jewels, he found it hard to look into the small eyes which tried to beguile him. It was, he assured them, tightly holding the leash of his huge, ill-tempered alaunt, just a short visit to look over the castle to see what improvements needed doing. Little men ran about prying, poking, measuring everywhere and the women hid from them in the solar in fear for the future.

"The Baron Roland suggested a marriage between you and his daughter, sire," said Fleur, in her clear quiet voice. "This would mean you would share the castle, not just have it with one hundred acres and the tower, but share the Lady Jessica's one thousand acres with this castle."

Sir Godfrey looked haughtily down his long, cold nose at the baron's widow. If that she indeed truly was. Yes indeed, a good-looking woman, but base-born.

"Mistress," the whole gathering sucked in their breaths audibly. "Mistress," he repeated more loudly, to make his point of doubt as to the legality of her position. "I fear that you are mistaken in your numbers, for see here, my father's will." As one they noted the lack of "stepfather". "He left me one thousand acres and this castle. To his daughter, he left the one hundred acres round and about the old tower by the marshes." He held an open vellum in his hand, then rolled it up quickly and handed it to his secretary.

Joan, Fleur and Moya stood stock-still, faces white. The liar! The thief! Only Jessica opened her father's chest and drew out one of the three copies of his last will.

"You are mistaken, sire," she opened the roll and went to the window. "It is as clear as day. If you wed with me, you shall share my castle and one thousand acres. If you do not, you have the marsh tower and one hundred acres, no doubt improving your lot by marrying another heiress as my father suggested."

Swiftly, like a snake, the knight strode forward and snatched the scroll and made to read it.

"A fake, I do not doubt, recently written since the old baron's death." He stepped close to his secretary and shoved it under his nose, "A fake methinks, and only fit for the fire," and almost before the words were from his mouth, he pushed the vellum into the heart of the fire behind him.

There was no sound in the room but the crackling of the burning will. Moya put out a warning hand to her mother and aunt who she knew had the second and third signed and witnessed copies. Frowning at them, she barely shook her head, knowing too, that Fleur held her marriage agreement from Roland also. This was not the moment to reveal them. They understood and were silent.

When Sir Godfrey and party had left, they sat in the solar, four women, related by blood and love and they trembled.

"He will win," said Joan, bowed now with sorrow and loss. "We are helpless; women have no say in such matters. We are but dust under his feet and he will walk all over us. He is as his mother, greedy and dishonest. They are all the same and Roland's will is for naught. We are all lost."

Fleur sat silently, hands folded in her lap. Thoughts roared through her head in disbelief, yet she said nothing. It was Jessica, shocked by the recent events of their lives, who began very noisily to weep.

"Father," she cried miserably, "oh father, come back we need you."

"It might," ventured Moya after a while, "be quite a pleasant change you know, Jessica, to move to the old tower, and do it up. We are not short of money or men. Do not be downcast, dear cousin, for it might be better to be far from that evil man with two legal wills in our hands and our lives, than frightened here, with his wicked ways."

The next fine day she and Fleur rode out to the tower with Peterkin and a groom. Joan had returned miserable to her own farm while Jessica stayed abed and refused to move. No sooner it seemed had they left, a party of horsemen arrived and shoving aside the elderly groom, they marched into the bailey, led by Sir Godfrey.

"Where is Mistress Fleur?" He demanded roughly. Impatient, he strode into the hall, where two maids were setting the linen into the press. "Your mistress?" he threw his cloak on a chair, then irritated by the lack of response, shouted at them again. "Do you hear me? I ask where is Mistress Fleur?"

Old Agnes was true, hard of hearing as well as being short sighted. Yet her breath came fast at the roughness of the man she knew full well was Sir Godfrey. Not bothering to curtsey, she spoke out clearly.

"Her ladyship is out for the day, master," and lifted her chin in defiance. With a bound, the knight strode forward and landed a resounding blow on the side of the old one's head. There was a sharp crack. For a moment, Agnes felt pain, then nothing as she gently crumpled senseless to the floor. Unseeing his error, Sir Godfrey sped out and up the stairs, two at a time, up to the solar. A whisper had reached him, that his accursed fool stepfather had made three copies of his will. Or rather, that sly healer had, the father of Fleur. Bursting in, he was surprised to find Jessica sitting by the window, a young maid idly combing her hair. She was barely decent in her shift, and he smirked at her. Terrified, the little maid fled from the room.

"Jessica!" He was suddenly delighted with his find. "I understood that you were all out for the day, but how nice," he tried to catch his breath. "We shall have some time alone together." Jessica gazed at him stupidly, picking up the comb. "Here," he went to stand by her, "let me, fair sister. Let me comb your hair," forcing it out of her grasp.

Never in her life had Jessica experienced such fear. For with a strange twisted smile on his face, Sir Godfrey dragged her head back savagely and began pulling the comb through her hair. "Tell me now, sister?" he jerked her head back to stare into her wide eyes. "What are these whispers I have heard that your father left three wills?" Another jerk. "Tell me, fair Jessica, are they true?" With his hand turning ever tighter, her hair was pulling painfully from her scalp. Trembling, she raised her hands to try to push him away and got a vicious swipe across the face for her pains. "Tell me!" he shouted, twisting if possible, ever more cruelly, yanking her head this way and that. But had he known it, this was not the way to extract information from Jessica, who began to whimper with pain and fear. Furious, the knight threw her to the floor, and for good measure kicked her violently as she lay there, before storming out.

Now he raged through the castle, opening chests and cupboards, throwing the contents to the floor, searching fruitlessly for the other wills. Somehow he did not bother to climb up to the rooms above the gatehouse, and of course, Joan held her document at her own farm.

It wasn't till the party returned the following evening that they found the castle in chaos, dark and silent with Jessica traumatised, still lying on the floor. After rushing through the whole place, they at last found the cold and weeping castle staff all locked in the buttery, Agnes' stiffening body with them. It took time to find a good axe, and finally the thick old door was opened. Fury, indignation and fear filled their hearts as they comforted Jessica and their people. Word would spread, slowly but surely like poison. Sir Godfrey would eventually, of that they were quite sure, get his deserts.

Unaware of the sorry happenings at home, the little party had ridden swiftly through the dimness of the forest, their horses hooves but making scarce sound on the soft track, and none of them spoke. The great oaks towered over them as a deep green tunnel, and the sounds of the woods filtered through as did the sunshine. At the sheepfold, Jerome joined his sister and niece and they quickly rode on, even racing their steeds into the lighter, more open land, as it fell down to the marsh. There, like a single tooth stood the tower as a sentinel. Carefully crossing the broken-down causeway, they toured the tower, which left them silent with their disappointment. Although the structure was good and strong, the roof leaked badly, indeed a young tree grew from it, and the surrounding pentices were all collapsed. Moya had noted wild raspberries along the way and left the siblings together, to gather a few in her horn cup, to give them courage. They camped in the middle floor of the tower, Jerome bringing wood for the great fireplace, which even the most busy jackdaws had not been able to fill. It was a troubled night but after bread, wine and wild raspberries, they decided they must leave. After firmly embracing his sister, Jerome stayed behind when they left. He would use his great strength to make a start, so next time they came, they would not look so crestfallen. Gathering his sons to help, he began clearing and tidying whenever he had some free days, so he could see what building work needed doing.

Early one evening, tired and dusty, Jerome sent his sons home and went to check his snares, took the conies to clean then washed at the stream edge, gazing over the rising mists of the marshes. Later, when he was curled up in front of the fire in the first floor room of the tower, he thought that he heard voices. The mist by now was swirling and thick, and the voices sounded one moment near, then far. Putting his fingers to his mouth, Jerome whistled loudly. An anxious cry answered him, so he strode out across the causeway, towards the voice. A pony train straggled along with three wet men, who were more than glad to see another human being. Jerome waved them to follow him back to the tower where he put the beasts in the ruined byre and helped with unloading them.

When he told Fleur the story some days later, using hands, eyes, his usual mime, she laughed with him yet with angry eyes. For it seemed that the brute, Sir Godfrey, had ordered glass panes for the castle to use for windows in his improvements. The head drover had been all too willing to accept hospitality out of the damp night. Not only did the great lout help with unloading the baskets, he gave them roast rabbit and barley cakes with ale. This would be a tale to tell. Taken in at a ruined castle, by a great dumb man, they were more than glad to keep warm by a good fire. At least their host seemed not deaf. For surely, he nodded most vehemently when asked if this was the baron's castle and strangely, he played a pipe like an angel. In the morning the drover and his men followed Jerome with their ponies, relieved of their burdens and to be shown the way home, on higher ground, their task done.

With wry laughter and new courage, the women made their plans, delighted with the unexpected, God-given gift of real window glass. Now they would make a new home for themselves, and the devil take Sir Godfrey.

Word went out to engage builders, masons and carpenters and to move the timbers left over from the church roof, which lay weathering by the river.

No one knew much about the solitary tower which stood overlooking the marshes. For years it had been used as a hunting lodge during the water-fowl season. It was old, that was all they knew, and that once the main river had flowed past it, but now with the ever-shifting meander, it was gone, just leaving marsh, and seasonal streamlets. As the weeks passed, the roof was renewed, the floors repaired and narrow windows glazed, so at last there were two great rooms above the entrance and a tiny chapel set in the thickness of the wall. All about the outside, the tumble-down buildings were temporarily propped up for shelter for the animals. More work could be done in time.

Word came again that Sir Godfrey would be arriving for Martin Mass and that he and his retinue would be moving into the castle. A week before Martin Mass, his staff arrived with their loud voices and rudeness, all of which was shocking to the regular castle folk. Men-at-arms seemed everywhere, to rudely jostle the women, cleaning their swords in silly places, a coarse and constant, unspoken threat. Jessica began to tremble violently, her jowls shaking as she clung white faced, close to her mother or cousin. They kept to the solar, barring the door, and the castle servants could barely carry up a tray of food, without being roughly molested on their way. None had ever known such unspoken terror.

The women left two days later. Moya took her aunt and cousin to her mother's house so that they could rest safely for awhile, before leaving.

"You are to leave all chattels, furniture and beasts which belonged to Baron Roland, Mistress Moya," the new bailiff spelt out his words slowly as if she were daft and could not understand. "My master has instructed that all tapestries and plate, all utensils and tools belonging to the castle, must remain."

Moya curtly nodded her head and silently gave thanks that they were long gone and were already making the tower look just a little like home.

"Are these?" the man went on, glancing about, his voice sour, "the old baron's only hangings, mistress?" Moya looked at them trying to hide the tremor of her mouth.

"Yes indeed Master Bailiff," striving to keep her voice calm. "I do believe I remember them from my early childhood. They were I think, part of the dower of the old Lady Jessica," knowing full well what she said was true, and that the glorious tapestries worked by the Lady Fleur were safely away. "I do not think that Sir Godfrey's mother, Lady Sybil, ever embroidered or provided any new hangings to grace the walls here. Perhaps her handiwork is at the other seat?"

In fact, grimly determined to keep some of their rights, they had stripped the whole castle, leaving behind only bare necessities or that which was too heavy or old. Moya herself had counted and packed the silver and left the battered pewter and wood utensils proudly polished and set on the board in their stead. If Sir Godfrey could cheat Jessica of one thousand acres, she could certainly take her godmother's fine tapestries and a few pieces of family silver with her.

The best horses, hawks and hunting dogs had been slipped away to the tower at night. In their two's and threes, their hooves muffled, the horses had been quietly led away, leaving but the few remaining poor old beasts, which hopefully to stranger eyes, made the run-down old castle appear as normal.

Not only did they leave their old home empty and forlorn, they left a shattered pantry door, for Peter had hacked it down with his axe to free the poor things locked inside. It would be many a year before the great old key was pulled from the depths of the castle well where Sir Godfrey had thrown it.

Moya wrote to the Lady Felicia, telling her as mildly as she could of their change of fortune. Well she knew that the astute lady would read between the lines, and together with what she heard, fully understand their predicament. To their great surprise a reply came announcing the lady's arrival. Another small upheaval ensued while they arranged place for her, and her party. With the lady came Stephen and two manor children, the priest and two grooms, so it was quite a great task finding beds for them all. The days of autumn were beautiful and the water-fowl from the cold north came to land on the marshes, filling the air with their many and strange calls. A surprisingly recovered Jessica took Stephen and the other two guests hunting, proudly using her small bow with precision, so they always had good game to eat. This was Jessica's best gift and the dogs followed her about, just as in the old home. Indeed it seemed all that she excelled at, riding and hunting, and at such times she was unusually gay and bright for a change. Thrilled with the chase and to practise her arts before Stephen, whom she had always favoured, she almost looked pretty.

How it happened no one knew, but suddenly at supper one night, flushed with the day's riding and the good wine, Jessica announced loudly that she and Stephen were to wed. There was a shocked silence while every eye first gazed at Jessica, then at Stephen.

"What a fine plan," the Lady Felicia announced in her clear voice, obviously not at all surprised, "two of my children to wed each other, so to make me a grandmother." A light applause broke out, and tentative smiles replaced astonishment. "We all know that there is no impediment, so we can dispense with the banns." She gazed around brightly, "we can use the little chapel here for the ceremony, I have my priest and so there need not be any delay."

Moya felt the blood return slowly to her face though her heart continued to thunder. Oh Stephen, dear, gentle Stephen, what are you doing?

It was a strange marriage, swiftly executed, almost indecently so. A few more guests came, Jerome and family, Joan and Anders and their sons, for this was a family affair. Try as they might, the women felt their hearts heavy as they re-hung the drapes on the great bed, cooked and cleaned once more. The only person who seemed happy was Jessica, who had of course, yet again, had her own way.

Meanwhile, Lady Felicia held the reins of law in her bony hands and told the priest what to write in the marriage agreement. Should Jessica die before Stephen, the land would go to their issue, and if none, to Stephen. The sound of scratching of the quill filled the great room and knowing the old lady, Joan saw what was in the shrewd old aristocrat's mind. At all cost, Godfrey must not get this land too, and poor Stephen had done what he was told.

After the ceremony, Moya returned home with her parents. Fleur had looked desperate when she voiced her intentions, but when Moya had reminded her that her parents were getting old and needed her, she accepted it. What she did not realize was Moya's deep pain that her cousin should wed the gentle Stephen. She bitterly blamed herself for the latest events to shatter her life, for in writing to the Lady Felicia about their new situation, she had directly been the cause of it.

Not unsurprisingly, Stephen quietly took to his new life with energy and was a boon to the workings of the small estate. As winter closed about them, he and Jerome together with his sons, toiled hard to complete the works on the buildings. At dawn, Stephen left his wife's side, only to return exhausted, at dusk.

Fleur soon realized that her daughter was with child and rejoiced at it. Here was something to look forward to, a babe, which she fervently hoped would favour its father. Jessica apparently thought little of the coming child, just resented the nausea which gripped her for months, and deeply resented her mother restricting her food. Most of the time she lay in bed, for the winter was hard and she was not allowed to go hunting in case she slipped on the ice. In despair with the constant complaints, Fleur drew a coat of arms on a canvas, begged wools from the manor, and set Jessica to work.

"You must have something of me in you," she said crossly, "can you imagine how dreadful this barn of a tower would look without my hangings? Sew daughter, sew," and angrily thrust the basket with threads and needle into Jessica's hand.

Surprisingly it worked. It seemed that indeed the one thing that Jessica had from her mother was her gift to embroider. One by one, the wonderful tapestries came from her hands as the winter passed. Mechanically, each one the same, with slight variations in colour according to the yarns, Jessica churned out surprisingly fine work. Fleur had taken the Lady Felicia's arms and drawn them together with those of the Pomeroys. Remembering Lee's laughter when he had drawn a small fleur de lis, joking that she was indeed, Fleur de Lee, she tucked that motif in a spare corner. It made a handsome crest, and watching the gifted work emerge from her difficult daughter's hands, a surprised and greatly relieved Fleur lavished unusual praise on her. Meanwhile, as the winter passed, it kept Jessica busy and quiet.

As her pregnancy progressed, Jessica simply kept to her bed in the upper chamber. They had moved it near to a window, newly glazed, so she had some light. The only time she left it was at night when her husband came in, then she went down to eat her fill at the board, now that the nausea had passed. Then she became gay and bright and stopped complaining for an hour or two. However, Fleur was increasingly exasperated with her daughter and wondered how Stephen remained patient with her. At the old castle, there had been others to share her and Jessica's vagaries, but now, apart from the few servants, Fleur was in charge. She longed for the birth of the child, knowing that it would in part free her of Jessica, who would no doubt resume her old ways and be more out than in. As the two women had never had a close relationship, Fleur didn't even know when the child was due. Did indeed Jessica know? She watched her closely, knowing in her bones that Jessica would cause the greatest trouble during her lying in, and as spring progressed, she wrote, urging the Lady Felicia, Moya and Joan to come to assist her.

For once, Fleur was wrong. Knowing that her guests would arrive any day, Fleur was extra busy. She was surely becoming happy in their new home. The men were doing well with the building of a proper house about the tower, a house designed by Stephen, like the manor and, thanks to Jerome, with many windows. Already she did most of the cooking in the great hearth of the new house. No more did she have to toil up two steep stairs of the tower carrying wood and food to cook in semi-darkness. Now she lifted the two coddled eggs from the water with a wicker spoon and laid them in a basket alongside some fresh little buns and a soft new cheese. With her time so near, Fleur tried to feed Jessica with light yet nourishing food.

It was her habit to go up to greet her daughter every morning, rather than send a maid and, breathless, she paused at the top of the stair and balancing the tray in one hand, pushed the door open. Going to the small high window she took up the rod and drew back the curtain. Sunlight fell blinding on the scrubbed wooden floor and golden rush mats.

"So let us hope that they arrive today Jessie," Fleur opened the bed-curtains and looked over at her daughter. "It is a fair day to travel, so let us hope." Then she stopped short, the tray halfway onto the bed, for Jessica was smiling at her.

"Look mother," she held out her hands. "Look, I have a little baby."

CHAPTER NINETEEN

THE VAGRANTS, BEE

The rain was coming down so hard, the flimsy roof of their shelter seemed to vibrate. There were countless drips, and Annie had tired of trying to catch them in whatever poor receptacle she could find. Now the earthen floor was awash and the only place it was more or less dry was the bed-ledge in the corner where Bee lay.

In a way she was glad that it was raining so hard, for otherwise the hideous sound of laboured breathing would have driven her to distraction. She edged more into the bed and tucked her icy cold feet under her. Reaching out she checked that Bee was covered, for all she could do was to try and keep the poor sick woman warm. Some hope to do that, she thought sourly. Warm? They were never warm in winter, how to keep warm? She had even been chased away from the churchyard where she was gathering twigs to try to make a hot drink. Night came, and with it more cold because the rain stopped. The laboured breath beside her seemed interminable. Annie sighed in despair at her uselessness, surely there was something she could do? She took out her little pouch where she kept her sliver of flint and one of the last pieces of fire lighters.

"See!" would cry Bee joyfully, "just when we are running short too." And swooped down with her sharp knife to cut the strange horseshoe fungus, which they sliced up carefully, and kept in their fire lighting pouches. Either they had none or there was an abundance, it depended on where they roamed. Bee had taught her so much, now she tried, despite the damp, to light a fire for warmth.

Everyone in the village was tired of her and her begging. So old Bee was dying? People did die, and may God rest her soul. Yet it was she, Annie, who had to sit and helplessly listen and wanting to ease her pain, could not. True the young wife of the squire had given her a bowl of pottage which was warming, which she at least had enjoyed. Bee was past eating or even drinking, but the weaver's wife had given her a good piece of woollen cloth which she had used to cover the sick woman. Now she edged under it, feeling its softness. Mistress Weaver seemed such a stern woman, yet, she had always been kind to them.

"'Tis because we are good spinners, Annie my dearling," Bee often said. "She knows well that she gets good value from us. So it suits her if we stay here, for our work feeds her loom and saves her the trouble of spinning much herself."

The other thing about Mistress Weaver was that she alone in the village seemed not to notice their ugliness. Not once did she flinch or look away.

Although she had given up asking God why he had inflicted her so, now Annie did so again. In fury, raging silently, she asked the Almighty why Bee and she should be any different from his other children.

Mind you, she mused, at least Bee had been born perfect, or so she said. Daughter of a miller, hers had been a good life without hunger. She had been taught many things with her sister and brother, her mother having been a learned woman who had married beneath her. Bee was pretty too. And that she could believe, for the good side of her face showed that. Then when she was fourteen, their house had burned down, and Bee, whose real name was Beatrice, had run in to try to save her granny. The flaming house had fallen, a burning beam had struck her on the side of her face. So, when it became certain she would live from her wounds, first she was hidden away, then she became an outcast, scarred, ugly, unwanted and unmarriageable.

"We have our uses," she used to say, "we are not useless just because we are not good to look upon. We are both good spinners, so can earn our bread, and," she paused, remembering, "all the unwanted, maimed, ugly children are given to us to take away from the sight of normal folk, those that is, who do not get killed, suffocated or starved to death. Yet it is surprising how many survive for one reason or the other. I was one, you another. So we are banished, barely fed, clothed after a fashion, and thus their guilty consciences are appeased."

Annie used to listen, for Bee certainly was clever. She could not remember life before Bee, her own parents, her home or village. She had become Bee's child, and Bee had become her all.

"At the mill!" Bee began many a sentence while Annie listened fascinated to hear tales of a normal, busy, happy family life.

"When I die," she sometimes said, "you will continue my work. There will always be poor little unwanted children for you to care for. Even with the children I used to spin every day. I have had four, sadly only you lived long enough as proof of my loving care. But the others," she thought of them, gazing into the fire, "however much I loved and cared for them, they were poor sickly little things, nothing I could do would change that. The good Lord wanted them so he took them. And listen well, Annie my dearling, in order to survive, you must work hard to keep them well. No children, no life, no freedom and no food!"

But Annie knew that Bee was not right in that, at least, for they had always roamed free in the woods and forests, and fed well off the fat of the land. They knew the secret places where they picked the bounty of nature, and yes, sometimes stole from man. Even so, Bee had her code of honour.

"As you take, so must you give, my Annie," she would state firmly, which meant the quiet repair of a broken fence or wall, the swept barn or yard in the early hours when no one was about. "We would not like it if someone stole from us now would we?" Meanwhile tucking four warm eggs into her pocket, for their breakfast.

They were careful in their wanderings, watchful and listening, and knew when to sink into the brush silently, to hide when necessary. Otherwise, they laughed and played when alone, far away from habitation and mankind. Theirs was an easier life than that of the village people, who toiled away endlessly in order to live their utterly dreary lives, to pay their taxes and to serve their lord.

Just because they were hideous to look upon did not mean they could not work. For work they did, gathering fruit and nuts, making baskets and pegs, walking sticks, crutches, little cradles. When a fair was due, they worked with fever, knowing that all they made sold well at markets far and wide. Their wares were willingly bought too, for despite their hideous appearance, it was known that their workmanship was good. They had a great circuit which they did about three times a year and people along the way got to know them, so strangely, albeit shunned, they felt appreciated.

"Come," Bee would take out their good head cloths. "Let us cover our faces, so as not to drive them away." So, well-shrouded, just their eyes free, they sat on the steps of the church, or if it was raining, under the moot hall, by the bridge, or anywhere where people passed by to see their wares spread on the ground.

"Our lives are more free, Annie my love, than those poor fools who toil for a crust from dawn till dusk." Bee tossed her head as she strode along, her long legs outdistancing any man. "See how well you have grown compared with many village children? And so you will, with the good food we get. Ugly we may be, but we have good strong bodies."

Until now. Annie understood a little about illness, but not about this terrible cold in Bee's chest which seemed to be choking her, all night it went on, the laboured breath, the fevered brow. Annie tried to cool it with a damp rag, but Bee shook her head and just reached for her hand to hold.

"Have I taught her everything?" Bee asked herself in the mists of departing. "Does she know enough to survive this cruel life?" Panic took a hold of her as she tried to breathe, coughed, then exhausted, drifted off, floating, flying, secure with the warm little hand in hers. Dying was not so hard, especially when she knew she was not alone.

Before dawn she seemed quieter, so at last, lying close, utterly exhausted, Annie slept too. When she finally woke, it was morning, quiet, and Bee had died.

Bleary, still tired, Annie gazed at the still white face of her only friend in the world. She looked so calm, so lovely, her burnt side underneath. Annie smoothed the fine hair, kissed the cold cheek and fear cramped her heart. How would she manage without Bee, she was herself just a girl? Yet she remembered, for Bee had told her just what to do, so she lay thinking in the dawn, listening to the birdsong and the occasional drip still coming through the leaky roof.

"First," Bee had said with her bossy voice yet again, quite absently stripping the bark off a willow, "lay me out properly, you know how, just as we did dear Tommy." Annie had nodded. It had been a blow losing Tommy, for although he was not right in the head, he had been a sweet boy, someone to play with, and his parents had given them what they could more frequently than her own parents had, according to Bee. "Then go to the priest to have me buried." Satisfied with the willow, she put it down with the stack already done and took up another. "He has the money already mark you, but he is a good man and will see to it and have some masses sung for my soul."

Annie remembered it all word for word, for how many times had Bee told her?

"No mourning or weeping mind, my dearling. You have a stout heart and a good head and you must remember all I have taught you." And had placed a resounding kiss on Annie's cheek which made her laugh as usual.

"If we have another child in our care when I die, you just carry on as always, look after it and teach it all you can, everything that I have taught you. Are you listening, Annie?" She had nodded, yet fearful at the thought that this warm and clever woman might one day just not be there.

"If we do not have another child, then you must seek some out. You know what to do. Go to the squire, priest, monastery and tell them you are willing to look after a poor little soul whom no one else wants. Tell them that you will continue as I have, keeping away from mankind, not causing any witchcraft or trouble, you only need some oats every month, some milk, a goat, perhaps specially, if it is a little child, and some cloth." Twining the bark about her bundle, she hoisted it on her shoulder. "You spin well for a young girl, so you never need be hungry. Just listen out for anyone who needs work done, a dowry, a shroud, or go to the weaver. That will keep you fed and safe, even if it is boring."

Bee took the hideous little face in her hands and gazed into the fine eyes intently. "Keep away from men, Annie. Marriage and families need men, and they are not for the likes of us. For they will use your body, then desert you. Hide your face, roll yourself up tightly in the blanket and keep to yourself." She gently shook the thin shoulders. "Hark well, Annie my dear." And Annie nodded and took heed.

At least the rain had stopped, the sun was out, so now she could go to find the priest. As she walked along, her tattered skirt hoicked up, she was careless of the puddles, merely walking through them in her bare feet. The sorrow which she felt for her lost Bee almost overwhelmed her. Steam rose from every damp flower and leaf along the lane. It was so beautiful, and again reminded her of her lost Bee who had told her all about it. Bee had been so clever, she had known everything. So the steam would rise into the sky for the next rain shower, like in the lid of a kettle.

Ahead lay the old, moss-covered wooden church. They had rarely gone in, for people did not like to see them and recoiled. Instead, faces covered, they had stood outside to beg, and to show their neighbours how Christian they were, many worshippers put a coin or two into their bowl.

Annie lifted her ragged skirt and wiped her eyes. Then seeing a cleanish puddle, scooped up some water and washed her face and hands. Bee had always said that it was clever to be clean, and stupid to be dirty for water was free. Squaring her shoulders, she approached the door of the priest's house and knocked firmly.

In single file they walked to the hall where the squire was just breaking his fast. The priest spoke to him quietly while Annie gazed about, her scarf well over her mouth. It was a huge, dim and smoky hall, sunlight slicing in from the high un-shuttered windows. A wide board was standing on trestles near the great open fireplace, and there were stools set all about it where they settled themselves. A servant came in, and seeing the visitors, hurried away.

Then the squire's wife came running, and Annie smiled, for she knew that this was a good person. In moments, bowls of porridge and horn spoons were put first before the priest, then into her hands. Gratefully, for she had not had anything yet that day, Annie drew down her scarf so as not to mess it and began eating.

Silently, they watched her, fascinated. Her face was split from the mouth right up into the nose and it amazed them how she managed, true with much noise, to eat. Her ugliness was amazing and they could not stop staring at her. Fortunately Annie was intent on her bowl, which she scraped clean, so she did not notice.

"More?" enquired the squire's wife kindly. So the servant took the bowl and plonked in another ladle of thick oat porridge, then poured some milk on. Anne smiled at her, although having had a good meal the day before, she was in fact no longer hungry, yet she well knew that no offer should be refused. Who knew when the next meal would be?

"Any time you are by, Annie," the squires wife went on when she had finished, "do not hesitate to come in, for we can always find a bite for a hungry girl."

Annie smiled again, then immediately saw the shocked eyes before her and pulled up her scarf. For her teeth were not neat and tidy like other children's, they were all over the place like thrown dice. Safely hidden under the scarf she smiled again and mumbled, "Thank you mistress."

Taking the bowl away, the squire's gentle wife felt a pang of guilt at her reaction to the child's ugliness.

"You have lovely eyes, Annie," she said sincerely, "like cornflowers."

Annie gazed at her in disbelief, then seeing the sincerity there, smiled again. She never forgot those words. Cornflowers! Lovely eyes! She hugged the sweet words to her heart and thereafter, always sought out in high summer, the beautiful and elusive flashes of pure blue. Making little bunches to gaze on, she might leave one in a church or, when she was in this village, on Bee's grave and to the squire's lady.

Several good folk came for Bee's funeral, out of curiosity of course, but also from sympathy. For who knows which of them would be struck down, or have an afflicted child. They all prayed most earnestly to God to forgive them their sins, so that he would spare them such a terrible burden.

Someone, probably the weaver's wife, had provided a shroud for Bee, yet as the earth fell on her still body, Annie felt like screaming, for they might be hurting her. Gently the priest led her away in understanding, while the men finished their task with the clods.

As they walked away, the squire and priest urged her to stay and take up work, perhaps weeding the fields or spinning, but she shook her head.

"Thank you kindly," she said in her strange nasal voice, Bee said always to be polite. "I will go and grieve for awhile and start to seek out a little child to look after to keep me company." They listened intently, yet understood but half of what she said, a tear escaped from her eye, and seeing it, the squire reached into his pocket for a coin and others followed with their tiny bit.

Back in their pitiful little home, Annie went through their few possessions. She would keep Bee's cloak, which was lined with pockets and was so useful. At this time, the pockets were mostly empty, for with Bee's illness, she had used up all their meagre stores, but at least it might not be too heavy for her to wear. It was much heavier than her own, but it was good thick felt and kept out the rain. Often, when they had little shelter, they had both crouched under it and kept warm together. Next she surveyed the kitchen. The stones of the hearth had a good stick for suspending the pot on, yet as she could easily cut another stick, she put it right at the back under the roof. Of course she would take the bronze pot, their most precious possession. It was not big, but heavy and a little awkward with its three feet. Yet it meant life-preserving hot pottage and heavy though it was, she could not do without it. Carefully, wrapped in a rag, she put into it, their two wooden bowls, their horn cups, horn spoons and the big wooden stirring spoon. Bee's horn cup, given to her at her baptism, had a small silver band on it and impulsively, Annie kissed it, swearing to keep it safe always. Into the inner pockets of the cloak she tucked their spindles and whorls, and Bee's knife, with hers at her belt as usual. The rest of their pitiful possessions she wrapped up in a bundle in her own cloak and walked again to the hall to leave it till she returned.

All was tidy by midday, so without a backward glace, Annie walked out of the village wearing Bee's good cloak with her bundle on her back. At thirteen years old, she was again unwanted and alone. She set her jaw, sucked in her breath so not to cry, lifted her head and smiled. Cornflowers. Her eyes were like cornflowers.

Manage she would, somehow. But go to live with people? Never.

CHAPTER TWENTY

ANNIE

The first year after Bee died was strange and lonely. Annie wandered without purpose, travelling by familiar paths to known villages in an ever-widening circle. Her search for a child to nurture was not successful.

"No," they all said, "the mother of God has been kind to us, all our little ones are whole." Then, seeing the sadness in the blue eyes, they realized their harsh words and drew out a coin, or went into their house for bread and cheese.

It was becoming a burden, the purse of money hanging under her shift. Bee had always cared for it, she had just occasionally bought a trifle at a fair, but now, it weighed heavy. Whatever she bought, it was always the poorest, with familiar bargaining. For it was expected and she always paid with the smallest coin, for people had eyes and it would not do to have them think she was worth robbing. As the weather grew cold with autumn, she began sleeping in the wayside inns as she and Bee had done. Laying her cloak down on the rough floor, then untying her blanket, she rolled herself up in it tightly. Whenever possible she chose a corner far from the hearth and where the other travellers gathered. Watching the shadows on the low rafters, she listened to their bawdy talk and drunken laughter, till they finally slumped into sleep. Never forgetting her prayer for Bee, she then slept despite the snores and coughing which racked the smoky room.

Generally she was ignored by most people, though many of the inn folk knew her and were roughly sympathetic at her loss. Usually they welcomed her willing hands as she helped serve at night and cleaned up in the morning. It was the unspoken agreement that if she helped the inn-wife in some task, she paid nothing for her bowl of pottage, her night and ale. It came to her very quickly how much of the work Bee had done, and how hard it was working alone. Weeping, she struggled with a willow cradle, yet found it too hard, and so turned it into a rough basket. So for the first months, she made pegs and walking sticks, carefully noting good shapes in the hedgerows and woods, marking them for later if they were not yet big enough. Gradually, she began to get proficient in her tasks and if she came across a good willow stand, stayed close by to work at her wares till it was cleared of usable wands. Fortunately baskets were not heavy and she stacked them inside each other till she had enough to sell.

A year passed, and twice she had returned to where Bee lay, carefully cleaning her grave and planting little wild flowers upon it.

Back again in the little rough lean-to shelter on the edge of the village, Annie decided to clean it up and repair the poor roof so that it would be there for another time. Strangely, she felt almost happy working there, feeling Bee all about. As she toiled away at pulling off the poor thatch, repairing the roof boughs, and started again, she sang in the strange nasal drone which was her way.

Despite days of toil, it was a poor job. The layer of ling was not really thick enough, and the turves barely met, so for sure the rain would come in for a while anyway. With time, the turves would grow together and it might be almost rain-proof. Yet to her, it looked so fine, she felt a huge pride. Next she went to the river and hoicking up her shapeless clothes, she grubbed around for flat stones. Laid on the floor, she spread sand from the river's edge in between the cracks, and basked in pride at her work. Lastly, she surveyed the poor hearth on the floor and decided to start again there too. Having taken up two roundish flat stones, she was just about to relay them, when she found the pot. Eyes wide, she carefully cleaned about it till it came loose and lifted it out. The pot she recognized. It was from the family of tow-headed potters way over by the big river. A cloth was tied strongly on the opening over a wooden bung. Everything about it was familiar, Bee's hand.

So this is where Bee had hidden their money. Annie sat on her hunkers, the dusty pot on her lap and thought yet again, "Clever Bee!" What a wise place to put it, and no doubt in the deep of night or early dawn when no one was about. Carefully she drew out her purse and keeping just a few coins, added her little fortune to the pot, re-stoppered, tied it, and gently placed it back in the hole. Then with all haste, as if someone were watching her, she replaced the stones, filled it in as it had been and lit the fire.

That evening she made a good meal of a roasted fish which a boy had given her in exchange for a small fish basket. As there was no one to see her, she left her head cloth down and smiled and smiled, amused and impressed with her find and filled with warm memories of her much loved Bee.

Mistress Weaver seemed glad to see her and kept her busy for some weeks spinning, which at least meant she did not have to think of feeding herself.

Twice, she went to the church where the priest said a mass for Bee. Feeling well and rested she eventually set off again, somehow lighter in spirit as she was in her purse. It was a grand feeling, blessings on Bee, being secure, knowing of the treasure under the hearth.

At each special little place where they had stayed, a cave, a half cave, a rough lean-to, she decided to tidy up. When she was quite sure she was alone, she remade the hearth, and each time found the same little cache of treasure, clever, clever Bee. Yet strange that she had never told her.

The second winter alone, she found herself at a monastery where she helped make a willow hedge in the physic garden. With her scarf high over her nose and held tightly in her teeth, she followed the silent brother who poked holes in the earth for her to plant the cuttings. Deftly she wove the wands into intricate patterns, pleased to learn and happy with the wordless praise from the monk. This was new and exciting and she had all sorts of plans to make good her little resting places, to screen them from people or beasts. They had good food there too, so she forgot about being hungry and lonely. Indeed, for the first time since Bee had died, she found herself deeply contented, realizing how pleasant it was working again with another person.

When the work was done, she was paid and although not asked to leave, she did, feeling it was what was wanted. Pulling her cloak tight about her, her few possessions tied in her bundle on her back, unusually low in spirits, she moved on.

That winter was very hard. Snow fell early and the cold held it as rock, so travel was difficult, and there was little work. The nights were terrible and no matter what she did to keep warm, by the early hours, she was frozen. Each evening she heated stones by her hearth, always careful to have wood at hand to feed the fire through the night. Without fail she kept a little pottage in the bronze pot as a last hot meal so her stomach would be full. Almost warm, she would fall asleep, only to waken to the sound of the forest wolves, the fire low, the stones cold, and her feet as ice. Begging an onion from a farmer, she smashed it up and put it on her sorry chilblains and wrapped her feet up with rags. It did help.

Finally she decided to seek shelter in the small town nearby and work her way. Although Bee had always assured her that if she stayed within sight and sound of man, the wolves would not hurt her, she dreaded their mournful howling. With no Bee to clutch close for comfort, she had become fearful, and so decided to try her luck with some people who had always been kind to them. The inn was a big old place of many rooms, ramshackle, the thatch dark with mould and moss, yet it was busy and warm enough inside.

By lucky chance she arrived at the inn at the same time as a chapman with his string of ponies. Heads hanging low, the poor creatures heaved white breath from the effort of coming up the river road. As they were being unloaded, Annie ran to help, observed by the inn-wife who was glad of the speedy girl who understood what was wanted and worked quickly.

So again she did not pay for her pottage, bread and ale, and Annie continued to seek out tasks, thus befriending the inn-wife who was glad of her help. It was agreed that she should stay at least till Twelfth Night was over. Carefully tying her bundle high on a corner beam of the main hall where she could always see it, Annie stole some bracken from the barn and made her bed with it. Several times a day while serving ale, or fetching new wood for the fire, she checked that her corner was unmolested. So she gratefully established herself in the inn where she was busy, fed and almost warm.

As Christ Mass approached, the inn-wife was especially busy, for, as she explained, the mummers were coming. Her excitement was infectious, and Annie worked hard, for the inn would be crowded. Her tasks were numerous and endless. She went to the rooms under the roof where the guests stayed, tossing and replacing the herbage, turning the straw mattresses on the low pallets, folding the worn blankets before she swept. When they finally rose mid-morning, those travellers in proper chambers who had stayed up most of the night drinking and merry-making, she shook their mattresses, emptied their piss-pots and tidied up. Whatever the weather, she cleaned the roots in the yard in icy water before chopping them for the huge cauldron of pottage which ever hung in the great fireplace. While she plucked fowl or skinned hare or rabbit by the great ingle-nook, she was glad to sit in the warmth and watch the busy life of the inn all about her.

Those beasts which had not been slaughtered at Martin Mass were now close penned in the yard. Barrels of good ale, flagons of mead and even fine wine were set up in the cellar. Every day the country folk came in to offer goods for sale, fowl of every sort, piglets, smoked fish and the promise of fresh meat. The peelings from the roots she gave to the poor, cold beasts waiting to be butchered.

"'Tis a task, Annie my girl, to know just how much to buy in now, whether to wait, whether to buy in case others buy before us. It would never do to be short, yet I do not care to overbuy, for after Twelfth Night, the mummers go their way and we are back to normal, which at this time of year is empty and quiet."

She was a jolly, buxom woman and kindly. Her raised voice could be heard throughout the dim, low rooms and well into the yard. Despite her girth, which together with her layers of clothes made her look double, she ran hither and thither and breathless, was grateful for the poor ugly girl whom chance had sent.

"Well but I am glad of your help, Annie girl," she would exclaim when she had a moment. "Fetch us a mug of ale, good lass, and one for yourself, so that we can have a sip and a sit, and a natter," her laughter following Annie to the cellar where she filled the mugs.

The mummers arrived, a troupe of a dozen, with three old nags carrying their bundles and a mad dog which did tricks and seemed to understand everything.

Many was the time when Annie had stood at the back of a crowd to watch the performance, be it one performer or a troupe. They fascinated her, these lively, exotic people with their crazy antics. Sometimes they had a bear, which she did not like, for the poor beast always seemed so sad. Other times they had a monkey, a furry, odd, tiny man with a tail and sharp teeth. But this lot were real mummers, mostly men, but she knew there were two women for she saw them at the privy. These, the inn-wife told her solemnly, were special performers, for they were engaged by the lord at the castle up the hill for the full twelve days of Christ Mass.

Using any excuse, Annie watched them at rehearsal. They seemed so noisy and sometimes bad tempered as they worked out their acts. They drank deeply and slept long, only coming to life for meals and practice. Just before their first performance, they donned their colourful, fanciful costumes and at last Annie enjoyed watching them openly. A dress rehearsal, they bowed and doffed their caps at the riff-raff in the inn, drank in the applause, and larked and fooled with great vigour.

It was the masks which really caught her eye. With just the top half of their faces showing, their masks covered their beards, or, with the women, their lack of beards. The eyes glittered and smiled through the eye slits, and it was nigh impossible to know who was inside the guise. A little flicker of thought ignited in her mind. Perhaps if she wore a mask, she could join them. Quietly slipping away while they were at the board, she took up a simple mask from a pile they had left and held it to her face. A polished sheet of copper served for their mirror and she gazed at herself in the gloom. Why, she looked just like them.

Greatly daring, she approached the kinder of the two who were obviously the leaders. Taking the mask from behind her back she put it on and faced him.

"Master," he looked up from his ale. "Can you use a drummer? For I like to beat the drum and would be so happy to play with you."

He had frowned at her, trying to understand the nasal voice and to remember who she was. He raised his voice and fired questions at her just when the inn-wife came in. Then, something happened which Annie never forgot. With rare understanding, she sided with Annie, her arm about the girl's shoulders. So it was all arranged. No pay, just to join in. Annie was ecstatic, her blue eyes flashing with excitement. They found some colourful hose and doublet and as if by magic she was a handsome boy. They let her use the mask she had chosen, for it was nothing special, and a small drum was unearthed from the depths of a great bundle, faded coloured ribbons flowing from it prettily.

"In time, in time!" the leader shouted. So Annie beat time and lightly hopped about the room, making them laugh at her enthusiasm. Pity filled them, and a strange joy, unusual in those hardened travellers. When she could be spared from her work, they found some parts for her and Annie threw herself into the world of make-believe and found herself in heaven.

For the first time she was one of many. For the first time, no one stared at her. When she leapt and danced, indeed they laughed and clapped which excited her to do even better. If only she could wear the mask forever.

Soon the inn was full to brimming. Musicians arrived, rubbing their poor cold hands together, begging hogs fat from the inn-wife, so that they could play their instruments. Immediate rapport formed between them and the mummers and the noise and gaiety increased. Glad of the chance to earn before the cold, empty months before spring, they practised hard, for if they did well, they knew that the lord would reward them nobly.

At last the feast days were upon them. Firstly, they all went to the church as usual and afterwards walked up the hill to carol at the castle. Annie stood and stared. It was quite different from any place she had seen and she gawped through the sweet apple smoke at the fine room, high ceilings and beautiful tapestries. A great fire was blazing and there were many pitch torches and candles which added to the warmth. The floor was strewn with special sweet herbs, obviously dried in early summer and kept for the feast days. The only great building she had ever been in before had been the monastery. This hall being not dissimilar, was not only grand, it was beautiful. It was like being in a forest, she thought, gazing spellbound all about her. For every rafter was strung with greenery, a great bush hanging as the centrepiece under which people kissed and laughed and might try to kiss again. All the decoration and the fineness of their clothes and the headdresses of the ladies! Oh and oh, thought Annie, if only Bee were here to see them.

With her mask firmly on, Annie clutched her drum abandoning her staring and joined the musicians where she could see better. Set on a dais, they worked hard at their instruments, their feet tapping and playing merry country jigs. It was so simple to slide behind them, pick up the tempo, and beat time all the while gazing spellbound at the gay throng of people.

In a space in the centre of the hall, shining-faced revellers grouped, joking and laughing, egging each other on, till at last there was dancing. A great lad came by with a tray of mugs and Annie accepted a horn cup and turned to look at a hanging in order to raise her mask to drink. This was some hot sweet drink, elderberry wine perhaps. It was as a dream. The music and laughter were infectious and she tapped her foot in time. Edging closer to the musicians, she gazed in admiration at them and wished that she could learn to play a stringed instrument. Yet sadly, she accepted that with her poorly formed mouth, she could never play a pipe.

The usual homemade small ale she was used to was very poor stuff compared with what they now served for the feast. Exhilarated, she thumped the little drum in time with the musicians, and whenever her mug was filled, she swilled it down as fast as they did, eager to play again.

Now and then the musicians were silenced for an announcement from the steward. These moments gave them the chance to eat and drink and regain energy, for it was hard work. Meanwhile great dishes were borne in to much applause and taken to be served to the lords and ladies first. Then with a wave of his hand, the steward told the musicians to start up again, which they did with renewed life. Annie was enjoying herself so much, she did not want to stop to eat. Yet the food smells were so good, she did help herself to what was offered, reluctant to turn her back on the crowd in case she missed anything. Surreptitiously, a habit of old, she tucked what she could into the string pocket under her tunic.

Strange, sweet pies were handed round, all quite new to Annie and as she savoured her piece, she begged for more. Good warm bread came round, each with a slice of venison laid upon it. Once she even had a piece of sweet white bread, and remembered Bee telling her what hard work it had been at the mill, sifting the flour through fine linen for some high feast.

Amused by her enthusiasm, the musicians made sure she was fed and her mug well filled. Eyes glowing above her mask, Annie had never had such a happy time in her short life.

Then with a fanfare, the mummers ran in to perform. After some short plays they whistled for her and light as a fairy, she leapt and bounded about the hall, beating her drum all the time. Gradually she learned when she would be wanted, and ran into the centre to dance and spring between scenes. They were pleased with her, patted her back, smiled at her, admiring her bright blue eyes and treating her as if she were one of them.

Late every night of those twelve days, warm, fed and completely happy, she tagged along with the crowd when they returned to the village. Back at the inn, laughing and silly from too much good food and drink, she hung up her mummers' clothes and slumped into her blanket to fall instantly to sleep.

The twelve days of Christ Mass passed as by magic. From early till late, she toiled for the inn-wife, anxious to please her. Yet when the mummers set off to the hall at the castle, she joined them, excitement making her forget her tiredness.

The great feast for Twelfth Night was, she was told, the most important. They must do their very best performance for the lord and his guests.

By now she had become known to everyone as the Sprite, a fairy, for she was so small, nimble and graceful a dancer. Of course with her mask on, no one knew who she was, or indeed, that she was a girl in boy's clothing.

This she was told, would be the great gift-giving feast. If they had pleased the gentry, they would be well paid as well as being given some gift.

"Nothing is free in life," she remembered Bee's words and sought in her mind what to give and to whom. Of all the grand folk at the feasts, she had noted a girl, perhaps her own age, beautiful and calm, sitting at the high table. Obviously of some importance, she was seated between a stern lady and old gentleman who must have been her chaperones. In the hours after they had cleared away the midday meal, just before the sun set, Annie ran to the river and swiftly cut some fine rushes. Sitting close to the fire to keep her hands warm, she deftly wove two tiny cradles, one for the gentle girl, and the other for the inn-wife. Then with her small sharp knife she whittled two simple babies from soft wood, cut a scrap of vellum from the skin off the side of her drum for haloes, and wrapped each babe in a strip of fresh linen as the Christ Child. Hastily made, they were utterly simple, therefore, if she had known it, all the more delightful, an infant Jesus.

Shyly, she offered one little gift to the inn-wife, who touched, was careless of the hideous face and roundly kissed it. That night in the hall, when the opportunity arose, she danced up to the high table and made a theatrical bow which she had learnt from her troupe. Carefully, without a word, she put the tiny cradle on the table in front of the young lady.

Ah, but what joy to be so happy! And what joy to see the sweet smile on the pretty face. Together with the two elders, she peered and praised and they waved their hands at Annie, as she ran away. Now with real interest, her simple gift was passed up and down the high table to be admired, the Christ Child, a jewel indeed.

When it was all over and the guests had left the hall, they were each given a purse of money, and to her surprise, even to Annie, who after all, was not really a mummer. As they moved in a crowd out of the hall, one of the pages pushed through the crush and stopped Annie to press a small cloth napkin into her hand.

"It is from my young mistress, who thanks you with this small token," and was gone in the press.

Standing under a torch, Annie gazed enthralled at the tiny brooch in her hand. Silver, it was a knot of twisted wire, fragile-looking, yet strong and very pretty. She was astonished to be given such a precious gift. Never had she been so happy. The twelve days of activity, laughter, theatre, plus plenty to eat and drink and now this. Stuffing it into her pocket for safety, with a pirouette and leap, she joined her companions as they left the hall.

The rest of the evening went by in a blur of singing, dancing and firelight. It was bitterly cold outside and the great jug of drink which was passed around seemed so warm and strong and Annie did not realize that she was drinking far too much. Laughing, they followed their leader, clutching at each other, fearful not to slip on the icy path. Clapping and playing their instruments if they could, they streamed out of the yard and into the orchard nearby. With steaming breath and spluttering brands they held hands in a great circle and danced about the oldest tree. Calling to it as if it were an old man, they gave it drink and music, and breathless they sang,

"Wassail, Wassail."

At last, with a few torches alight to see them along the road, they all went home, huddling together for warmth. In the thick of it, her mask still in place, Annie held hands with her neighbours and danced and sang, the little drum silent at last, bumping on her back. In the inn, she veered away from the crowd who noisily demanded more ale and crept to the sleeping room. For the last time removing her mummer's clothes and mask, she draped them on the rack by the hearth to dry. Back in her own dry clothes, she dizzily went to her corner to sleep. Yet sleep evaded her and the firelight seemed to make grotesque figures move about the ceiling timbers of the empty room. Uncertainly she mulled over her thoughts. Could she join the troupe? With the mask, might she be able to live as a mummer? They knew she worked hard and they seemed to like her. Certainly she appeared to have done well, having received much praise as well as money. She patted her inner purse unconsciously. As her thoughts rolled about her mind, so too seemed the sleeping room. Just once, many years back, she and Bee had crossed a great river in a boat, a funny, round, cap shaped thing which bobbed and swung to and fro. Everything swung now, just the same and she tried to cling on to the sides of a boat which wasn't there, or Bee or anything. But there was nothing and she felt a wave of nausea engulf her. In the mists of her consciousness, she reached out. "Bee, Bee!" as she had years ago. Now as then, she felt strong arms holding her. Gratefully, she clutched at them, and felt herself held close to rough homespun weave, smelling of wet wool and wood smoke. Yet after a moment she was shocked to be roughly pushed away. Her blanket was being dragged off her, the stink of sweat and drink was close. A sudden terrible fear hit her. Something was wrong. Feeling the cold as her clothes were hauled up, she tried to roll on her belly, but it was no good. As her skirts were thrown over her head, she was pinned down and could barely breathe.

It went on and on, seemingly many brutes took their delight in her little body.

Afterwards, all she remembered was great strength, roughness, huge weight, a deep and terrible pain, and her screams being stifled by her clothes and strong hands. On and on it went, like the swine on the village green, humping and grunting. It seemed that she was torn asunder. A cry, then silence.

Early next morning Annie crept up and quietly packed her few possessions into her blanket. Taking her bundle, hurting, she carefully stepped over the sleeping forms and went to the kitchen. Relieved that no one else was stirring, she gently drew open the great bar on the front door and left, careless of the snow and her bare feet. Sore and frightened, she went on and on in a daze, determined to get far away from the inn which had been a happy place, but which now only held fear for her. Far she would go, away from her violators, whoever they were. Sobbing as she stumbled along, calling Bee, calling God, at last and near to death, she was taken in at the monastery. They asked no questions even if they guessed much. There she stayed all winter, always useful, always quiet and tactful. Brother Matthew made her wooden clogs which he lined with fleece, and rubbed herb and lard on her chilblains. All happiness gone, Annie did her chores silently in deepest shock. Ever tactful, Brother Mathew had her helping with the many small garden chores of winter, till her willow hedge showed sweet green leaves, and thanking the good brothers, she set off on the road once again.

During the early spring, Annie felt a great sickness overwhelm her and feared that she was ill. Whatever she ate, she brought up again. Creeping, as a wounded animal to its lair, she went from one little sanctuary to the next, grateful for the pot under the hearth stone, blessing Bee who had been so thoughtful, for as she was too wretched to work, at least she could buy bread.

With summer, she felt better and constantly hungry. Now she walked for miles and worked at her trade, creating fine baskets which sold well for the harvest ahead. All and more that she had taken from her secret caches, she now diligently replaced. Now sixteen years old, Annie had grown in height, her clothes were too short, too small, tight, as well as being filthy and ragged. Imagining what Bee would do, she bought some cloth and using her precious bone needle, stitched two shapeless shifts, under and over, for herself. It was a moment of pride when she stepped, washed and clean, out of the river and donned her new clothes.

As summer waned, forgetful of the bitter cold and the wolves, she decided to try to stay at one of her favourite places over winter.

Above a slow-running river, a great beech forest stretched southwards forever. On the Northern bank, a sizable village straggled, where she could buy bread, providing the wooden bridge was not swept away by the winter floods. The thought of sleeping at inns with many others now made her afraid. Memories of the last night of Christ Mass haunted her. Impatiently, she pushed them away, accepting how foolish she had been taking so much strong drink when she wasn't accustomed to it. All the while, she felt Bee's disapproval.

"After all I told you!" she heard the dear voice in her head.

High above the river was a half-cave which went deep into the bank, great beech roots holding the earth and rocks together safely. Over the years she and Bee had worked at it, digging it out to make a comfortable shelter. On the hills above the village in stream hollows, grew willows which she cut to make her own little fence. Secretly, she worked early and late when smoke rose from the poor hovels and the village folk were inside. Nimble fingers plaited and twisted with great care, so a thick wall would one day grow a screen in front of her home.

Carefully, she wandered far and wide and bought in stocks, just a little here or there, so as not to draw suspicion or interest. Each village or market she went to, she bought stores for the winter. Often she merely traded her wares rather than part with a coin. Having washed the remnants of her old clothes in the river, she used the cloth and stitched some little bags. One by one she hung her winter provisions up high on the roots which threaded her ceiling. There were several small pieces of salt bacon, a flavour which lifted the poorest pottage. Stockfish, again for the salt, although she did not much like it, always preferring her own fresh caught bream or chard, trout or salmon. Still, the thinnest sliver of the hard dried fish had enough salt in it to add flavour to anything. Three good bags of wheat from the farmer, loose barley and oats to thicken her stews. Her small supply of salt she hung directly where the warmth of the hearth would keep it dry. In the woods above her home she searched for mushrooms which she dried and hung up where the smoke would preserve them. Wherever she went, she picked and ate berries, staining her mouth, relishing the sweetness. As the nuts ripened, so she gathered them too, returning again and again so as not to miss any. It amused her how the roof of her little home was festooned with bulging little bags and bunches which bumped her head. Lying on the shelf which was her bed, she gazed in admiration at her stores and felt very safe.

One day, wading through the river, she spotted a stone which would do as a grinding stone. Slipping and struggling, she got it to the bank where after scrubbing it with an old root, she left it to dry before dragging it up the slope. Pleased with her find, she pushed a flat stone to and fro on grains of barley till she had enough flour to make some little flat breads. It made her so happy and they were delicious. Some days if she was lucky, one of her fish traps provided her with a meal. Having cleaned the fish right there by the river, she baked it on another stone beside her fire, turning it gently till done. The late summer days were calm and lovely, and she was quietly content except for her craving for meat. The little bronze pot which had been Bee's, which was the only part of her dowry she had kept and her pride and joy, provided her with good thick pottage, but she was bored with it. It would be a long time yet till Martin Mass when perhaps she could get some fresh meat from the culling.

Every day she went down to the river to check the fish traps, wash herself and her pots and fill her water jar. As her money grew, she mulled over the idea of keeping a water jar at every shelter. If she hid them well, they might be safe. Somehow now, the jar seemed daily more heavy as she struggled up the bank, so she began to just half-fill it. Her solitude did not worry her, in fact she avoided mankind. Very often, sitting silently, she watched the wild creatures of the woods, who barely moved, so familiar had she become. Fearful of her little home being found out by people, she tried to take different ways to and from it, so as not to tread a regular path to tell them of her existence. On one such sortie, she was alerted by an unusual rustling in the undergrowth and on investigating, found a rabbit jerking in a snare. Quickly she held it by the back legs and chopped at its neck with the edge of her hand. Surprised, pleased, she stood looking at it, her mouth watering with the thought of the meaty meal she would have. For moments she stood and watched and waited for any sign of life. There was no sound but the soughing of the beech trees and the twitter of little birds thinking about preparing for the night. However, Annie felt she was being watched, her senses alert, she waited, but nothing stirred.

Darkest brown eyes surveyed her from mere yards away. The boy was just coming to get the coney to make himself a meal when he saw the woman approach. Still and silent as an animal, he ducked down instinctively and observed every detail.

Suddenly breathless, Annie sat down, her interest caught by the snare. It was a fine buck rabbit and she planned to skewer the legs on green twigs and roast them over a low fire for supper. If only she knew how to set up such a snare. Carefully she looked at it. Simple, made with twigs and twisted grass which was everywhere, it might mean many good meals in the future. As she got up, she again remembered the old rule Bee used to often say, "Nothing is free in life", so smiling with her warm memories of Bee, she took out her pocket and felt in it for a coin. Considering for the moment, she chose a good one, just in case the snare layer might leave another rabbit for her. Plucking a big red leaf from a tree nearby, she first put a flat stone on top, then the coin, and another stone to cover it.

The boy watching, saw suddenly the hideous split face as the scarf fell aside, and just stopped a gasp. As she set off, he noted that she was not so old, and that she was large with child. Pity flooded through him, for he too was one of the unwanted, an untouchable.

After she had gone, he ran to the stone and took the coin, bit it and grinned. Rabbits were his everyday fare, but now he could buy bread, which he craved.

The rabbit was delicious and lasted her three days with a soup at the end.

Whenever over the next days she went along the path, there was another rabbit, and another, and each time she left a coin, disturbed yet grateful.

During the night, the boy crept silent-footed to peer over the willow fence into the little cave-room where the woman lay. He was skilled in tracking, man and game, as skilled as he was in disappearing. So she was an outcast too. He had, in his eleven years seen others so afflicted, but none as bad as this one. Poorest of the poor, even so, pity flooded him as he unconsciously touched his dark brown yet perfect face. It must be hard to be so ugly and to be alone without man or kin and be great with child.

Days passed. Then one morning, the routine altered. Knowing that she went to the river early in the mornings, he crept to see if the coin was there instead of the rabbit so that he could go to the village to buy bread. Shocked, he stood and stared. Already the flies were surrounding the carcase and of course, there was no coin. Frowning, he took the dead rabbit and silently walked down to her place.

Even before he got there he understood what was happening, for the moans were regular and heart rending. Uncertain, he stood nearby, wondering what he should do. Memories of his own mother labouring in birth came back to him and he closed his eyes tight shut. It did not do to think of her, for without a doubt, he would never see her again.

Stealthily, slowly, he approached. Yet she heard nothing, too far into her own agony to care for outside sounds, only trying to stifle her own. As another pain engulfed her, she bit onto a rolled rag to stop herself from screaming. Peering in, seeing her water jar, he leaned forward and quietly lifted it up. It was the least he could do.

That evening he returned, the rabbit laid on a broad piece of bark, roasted and delicious in garlic and marjoram. The boy squatted outside, holding his ears against the continuing sounds of agony which came unceasing from within. Absently, he began to eat the rabbit, pulling at it with his fingers, still, quiet, afraid. Once again he silently lifted the water jar, observing that some had been used, filled and returned it.

With a tearing scream, Annie pushed mightily as her body dictated. An explosion so great burst from her, she felt as if she was torn apart. Exhausted with the effort, she fell into a faint, while her body once again pushed, emptying itself. The pain gone, the weary body relaxed into sleep as night fell. Just once in the predawn, she reached for the water jar and drank deeply. Aware that she was bleeding, her exhaustion was so great, she ignored it, pulled up her cloak over herself and slept again.

As the sun rose and sliced through the willow wall, Annie rose and weakly went down to the river to bathe. Realizing that she was bleeding heavily, she recalled that she had not bled for some time.

"Stay near water during the days when you are bleeding," had instructed Bee. "Keep quiet, away from folk and wash often."

A terrible thirst overcame her as she washed in the icy water, so she drank and drank, then washed her face, and slowly returned trembling with weakness to her home under the beech tree. It had rained in the night and the bank was slippery as she struggled up. Suddenly the sun rose over the woods on the other bank of the river and the willow wall, flooding the small space, lighting it clearly. As she dragged her cloak up to cover herself once more, she suddenly saw something lying there. Shocked, she stared in disbelief. The still, white and silent body of an infant, lay sprawled on her rough couch. Blue white, as butter-milk, the life-giving blue cord was twisted tightly around its neck in a stranglehold.

How she got to the monastery they did not know. Brother Matt working as usual in the physic garden on, hearing her noisy weeping, had lifted his habit and ran outside to help her in.

"I didn't know, I didn't know!" she sobbed over and over again, leaning into his rough habit. Kindly the brother patted her, himself aghast, speechless, sadly looking at the poor dead child, listening to the strange voice, which from long practise, he now understood.

"It is God's will, daughter!" he said forgetting his vow of silence as he unwound the cord and laid the stiff, lifeless thing on the camomile lawn. "She is in the arms of the Blessed Mother of God now, Annie. Cry not child. Heaven is a better place than here, and a blameless babe such as this, surely will be there." On and on he spoke the gentle words of comfort, while Annie sobbed weakly in sorrow and anger at herself for her ignorance, till at last she slept, right there, in the garden.

Washed and swaddled in a soft white shroud, the dead baby looked beautiful and perfect. Annie stared at it, amazed that she, ugly, wretched Annie, had given birth to such a perfect child. Numb, she knelt beside the tiny grave, head bowed, uncaring that her face was showing, she heard them, the men of God, give her words of comfort, listened to them chant their prayers and saw her child gently placed in the earth in the corner of the garden.

"Bee!" she cried inside her head. "Bee! Take my child. Look after her for me." And wept again. Exhausted in every way, aware that she must get to the river to wash herself, she thanked them. Taking the last coins from her pocket, she pressed them into the hand of the monk, then without another word turned and fled.

Cleansed again by the cold river water, she climbed the bank slowly and sank onto her couch to sleep once more and deeply for many hours.

The boy observed her yet again, realizing that she must be as hungry as he was. Greatly daring, he took up her bronze pot, peeped into each little bag hanging up, and going some distance away, made a little fire and began to prepare a good stew. Squatting by the river bank, he deftly skinned and jointed a rabbit. Next, he fried some cut fat bacon then added dried wild garlic leaves and the rabbit. Then he poured a cup of water in so that it could simmer into tenderness for the meat was too fresh. Scouring the woods, he found several good mushrooms and a small bullace tree. Helping himself to a taste, he nodded and planned to buy himself just such a pot. Well probably not so fine, an iron one would do well. Lastly, he tossed a handful of dried peas and barley in and put a flat lid stone on top, to keep in the steam.

Back at her den, he noted the mess of the after-birth and using a stick, lifted it out and carried it away to hurl into the river. Something would find and eat it no doubt. Frowning, wondering at the silence, he wondered if she had the babe cradled to her. Carefully, silent on bare feet, he laid the embers of his fire on to her hearth and gently blew up the flames. Packing the fire with slow-burning green wood, he hung the pot high above on the root crane and silently as was his way, left.

With the dawn, Annie woke dreaming that she was about to eat one of Bee's special pottage. The smell was so good. She sniffed. Eyes wide open, she sat bolt upright and looked around. A shaft of sunrise struck through the willow fence onto the lazy smoke curling up into the roof.

It was wonderful! Ravenous, she stirred up the barley from the bottom and poured out a little at a time into her wooden bowl so that it would cool. Never mind who had made it, never mind that she hadn't heard a sound. This was just what she needed, for she was weak and very hungry.

Utterly calm now, she thought dispassionately about the dead baby. It was gone, as if it had never been. After washing herself carefully in the river again and drinking, she returned to lie down and rest and to think. Perhaps she must move on?

When the pot of food was finished she raised herself up and after washing again, walked to where the snares usually were. There was no rabbit this time, but there was a snare set, and several others laid on the grass, as if in stages. Annie knelt and studied them. It was a lesson. Astonished, she undid one and tied it again. Then another several times, till at last she felt sure she had it right. Listening, looking all round, still there was no sign of life. On her way back to her place, she set two of the snares where she knew rabbits burrowed. Next day, they had caught two. Jubilant, she ran back to her place, stopping for a moment at the remains of a small hearth near her home. So this is where the kind stranger had cooked. Foolishly, for a moment she thought it might be the ghost of Bee come back to help her. But this she quickly dismissed knowing how Bee would scold her as a superstitious fool. Gathering wood and dried grasses, she struck her tinder stone and set it alight. Her hearth must go out for a while.

Creeping down the slope that evening, the boy was startled when he saw her cooking pot hanging up above his little hearth, a wisp of smoke still keeping it warm. Smiling, he took out his own wooden spoon, squatted down stirring it, and ate his fill. It never ceased to amaze him how even with the same ingredients, some one else's cooking was so much nicer.

For the next two days, Annie went to swim in the river. First she cleansed herself, then she pressed her aching breasts to release the milk which gathered there. The worst thing was that she was always so thirsty and being young and ignorant, she drank copiously, unaware that by drinking so much, her breasts would engorge.

During these days Annie ate, bathed and made food for herself and her invisible helper, waiting till she felt strong enough to leave. Digging up her now cold hearth, she took out all the coins, bar three. Up the hill by the first snare, she made a small hole and poured them in. Three red leaves and a stone on top for safety, Annie looked about, almost willing whoever her benefactor was, to show themselves. Nothing stirred. Her house in order, Annie loaded up her stores in her blanket, pulled on her cloak and securely drawing the little hurdle across the entrance of her home, she went down to the river path.

The boy stared in disbelief at the wealth in the hole. He realized that she had gone, for the entrance to her home was firmly shuttered. In a way he was sad, for it had been a good feeling helping someone as poor as himself. Carefully secreting the coins all about his clothing, in the little secret pockets, in his cap, his bundle, he turned excited, yet with a tinge of regret, to go uphill and away. He had never possessed so much money. The very first thing he would do was to buy bread, the next, a good cooking pot.

Annie walked beside the river, only stopping to drink, wash and press the milk from her hard and aching breasts. It was seven days since the birth, and now she felt ill, a fever making her dizzy and weak. On she went, scratching her legs on brambles, sobbing with pain and fear. For she felt so unwell, burning, burning. Eventually, a clearing along the river showed her a beautiful round pool, shallow and clean. Leaving her cloak and bundle on the bank, she slowly got undressed and stepped in. The cold water would help her fever. Gradually she felt it lessen a little, as she floated in it, gazing through fevered eyes at the golden leaves which drifted down to cover her.

CHAPTER TWENTY ONE

MARTIN

It was very quiet in the village and the dye shed was empty save the dyer, Martin, who was, as was his way, worrying over the vats. Even the click clack of the looms were silent for once. He wiped a wet hand over his eyes. He was tired, well who wasn't? His messy, dye-splattered face seemed severe as he lifted the cloth up from the vat with a stout stick, and surveyed the colour.

Martin was a tall and handsome man, and had, in the past, been the despair of all the mothers of daughters far and wide. For not only was he handsome, his great haunting dark blue eyes captivating them all, he was a freeman. And there were not too many of them about as eligible husbands. Yet his shyness held all away. Never rude, always with a small smile, he yet managed to avoid or escape their attentions. His father had been brother to old Mistress Dyer. He too had been a distant man, only seemingly concerned with the dye house, which in the long run benefited them all. They were even reserved with their dyer relatives, preferring not to live in the fine stone two-roomed house but in a narrow pentice off the dye house. As a family they had kept very much to themselves, not unfriendly, but perhaps shy. It was commonly known that it was their knowledge and diligence which paid great dividends, for Rekeshill was famous in the district, indeed far and wide. No one else could boast such varied and wondrous colours and the abbots who were in charge made sure that nothing would disturb the tranquillity of the smelly little hill village.

Martin sighed deeply. The past days had been dreadful. The screams! Why did God make women suffer so? Why after all that had the poor girl died? He knew that he should clean up and go to the church to her funeral with all the villagers, for she was kin, but they were very behind with all the fuss, and the cloth should at least be soaking in the river as soon as possible. Cousin Blaise Dyer might be distraught at his wife's death, yet they had a living to make, the monastery to supply and people to pay. For this small village in the hills lived off woollen cloth, and far better than most round about. The monastery shepherds tended huge flocks of sheep on the granges, which provided much good quality soft wool. Most was sent abroad, loaded high on pack ponies, which trudged off to the far coast to send across the water. The finest, softest and whitest wool was kept, by order of the abbot, for the local women to spin.

There were three looms in the village which the women shared and all the daylight hours were taken in turn. No moment otherwise was allowed to flee without a spindle in the hand, a basket by the side, ever filling with skeins of woollen yarn. When the day was fine, the younger women would venture out in the woods and downs, the children glad of the change, running alongside. Knives and baskets in hand, eyes darting hither and thither, they scoured the land for dye plants, broom, walnut, alkanet or lichen, according to the season. Returning home well-loaded down, the dyers would do a tally before sorting, cleaning and hanging up bundles to dry for future use. This small extra payment would mean smiling faces and everyone was happy, for even if life was poor, here at least it was secure. Every family was obliged to daily carry their piss-pot to the dye house, which was at least down the hill. No urine, no dye house, no living. Downstream, the dyers grew woad on their small water-meadow and sometimes, as now, though the stink was loathsome, they used it to get the fine blues and greens requested by the abbot for the gentry. Life in the village was ordered by the dye house. Living there, none was overly conscious of the stench from the urine filled dye pits and vats, unless they went away, and returned. It did not occur to anyone that the main reason their village remained safe and peaceful was from the stink, for it was far worse, even than the towns, with their poor drainage. Anyway, few folk came to Rekeshill. One or two chapmen or pedlars might make the detour and stay a day or two, not so much in hope of making money, but to winkle the odd hank of fine-coloured wool out of Mistress Dyer on the quiet. After the shearing, the packmen came, as rough and short tempered as their ponies. Once or twice a year someone from the monastery came with orders, so life was measured and calm by all standards.

Martin liked his work, though he was unaware of it. It was and always had been his sole occupation, learnt automatically beside his parents and dyer relatives. It fascinated him, the thrill that herbs and roots and barks could make such fine and various colours. The expectation, the delight in success, the frustration when it did not go well was his life. He was always splattered with many colours and despite scolding from his aunt, the older Mistress Dyer, he ignored it. There was no point, he told her gently, waving his hands as was his way, for Martin rarely spoke and then so quietly it was hard to hear him. Why to clean up, change his clothes or wash his face? For what? For who? Over the years he was despaired of, yet warmly accepted, quiet, diligent, colours and all.

Martin waited till the dye water had mostly drained away back into the vat before he lifted the baskets onto the donkey's back. The beast grunted with the sudden weight, yet it steadied itself for it was a willing animal and trusted the man with whom it worked. Quietly they ambled down towards the river, glad to get away out of the squalor of the rough village, to the solitude and beauty of the woods.

He could still hear the screams through his head. There had been no getting away from it. The women of the entire village, frantic, seemingly ever rushing up and down, wringing their hands in despair, and ever waiting for the next scream. Days it had been, till ever weaker, quieter, then worse, no more. Now it was deathly quiet, the lifeless form of the poor girl laid out on a bier in the wooden church, to be buried later that day. He had been glad when his cousin had wed, for who would take over the dye house if there were no children?

Hanging on to the saddle, Martin tried to help the donkey from slithering too fast down the path to the river. After unloading the baskets, he led the donkey, all the while encouraging it, for they must not take too long. Truly, he must go to the church for his cousin's sake. The donkey needing feed, hurried to a grassy knoll where it gladly put its head down to eat the sweet grass. Thick yellow water still trickled out of the baskets as broken egg. Due to the past desperate days and its over-long lie in the dye pot, the cloth would be a fine, rich colour. Dragging it towards the river, he folded it over and over, so it was not too heavy. With his hose hoicked up, wading in the cold water, he hardly felt the wool cloth rasp his bare legs as he anchored it down with rocks. Having done that, he rinsed out the baskets and left them in the shallows before getting out.

There were three small stone shelves at this point of the river, and this was the pool where he did the first rinse. Right now it ran gently, more like a stream. Yet with the winter rains it roared as a torrent and work in it was well nigh impossible. There were two more pools above, so the cloth had to be hauled out to drain, before going up to the next stage. Martin loved this place with its peace and memories. Few came here; then just the women to wash their clothes before feast days, or in summer after the shearing to wash the wool.

Still reluctant to go back to the mourning village and the church, he wandered up, noted the teazles nearly ready for cutting and planned to gather them to dry, so to strap them onto paddles for the weavers to brush up the cloth. Passing the contented grazing donkey, he finally stood breathless above the first pool. It was a favourite place of his and very beautiful. A small waterfall splashed into the round pool, now gently. Yet he well knew that the basin had been formed over time, when it fell with great force, churning the stones in it, like a pestle and mortar. For as long as he could remember, he and his mother had come here with the dye stuffs to wash. While the cloth was soaking, they had amused themselves and had by happy chance discovered a small space behind the top fall, a secret place where he used to hide. It was surprisingly dry, deep under the shelf, just the air being damp. One day the shelf would fall for sure, but not yet. There had been plenty of headroom for a child, yet now he had to go on all fours, where he went to rest in the heat of summer. It was only during the hottest days that the villagers came to lark about, wash and cool off. Martin had always been a loner, a shy young man who kept to himself. So on hearing their rowdy approach, he had always ducked under the sheet of water and waited in his secret cave, till they left, before emerging, cold and damp.

Just then the sun shone through dark scudding clouds and a gust of wind caused the first autumn leaves to filter through the branches onto the water. The brilliant blue, summertime, maiden flies had gone, but the golden, falling leaves were beautiful in their turn.

Suddenly, Martin realized that although he was looking at the fallen leaves, there, just under them, lying in the water, was a human body.

His breath stabbed painfully in his chest and he gasped. Was it a person? Was it dead? Skirting the scrub trees on the bank, he came to the little beach where he usually spread the cloths to drain before putting them on the tenterhooks on the hill above. From this angle he could see nothing however hard he looked. Wading in, careless of his clothes, his hand touched the cold body and grasping it, he struggled to the bank. Exhausted with effort he sat for a moment, then gathered his wits and stared. He had never seen a naked woman before. Even when his mother had died, he had laid her on the bier in all her clothes, before covering her with a sheet. This body was as white and still as death, yet the firm, taut-nippled breasts rose and fell, shining with the sunlight on droplets of water. Long dark hair concealed the face and there was no sign of life.

Looking about frantically, he saw a bundle on the far bank and again mindless of himself, waded across the river to fetch it. Finding as expected, that it was her clothes, he spread the mantle and blanket about the girl, then tucked her clothes under her head which fell sideways away from his gaze.

His head in a turmoil, he thought for an instant, then fled, dragging the surprised donkey with force up the path and mounting it, kicked it hard.

Where to go? Who to call? If she was dead, the priest would have to come. But they were all at the funeral. His face lightened as he kicked the donkey onwards. Jennet! She alone was not at the church, he knew, for she was at the Dyer's house with the new infant, which had not died with its mother. At last at the house, falling off the trembling donkey, forgetful of the pain in his legs, he beat on the door.

Exhausted, Jennet left her work and sourly peeped through a crack in the door. Seeing it was Martin, she opened it a slit, for she was in charge and Mistress Dyer was a hard woman. Not only had she been left behind to care for the tiny, hungry babe, she had been ordered to bake breads on the hearth, and set up a huge cauldron of pottage to serve out after the funeral. Seeing Martin gesticulating desperately, her eyes softened. He was about the only person she could tolerate right now, for of course, she was being blamed by everyone for the death of the young mother. Drawing back the door she nodded him in, then watched aghast as a pool of water formed about his feet. Mistress Dyer would not be pleased.

"Jennet, Mistress Jennet," he gasped, unaware of her disapproval. "There is a dead woman, well I think that she is dead, dying anyway, in the top pool." Grabbing her skirt he pulled her towards the door. "Come, I beg you, I have taken her out of the water, and covered her, but," he pulled again, "I beg you to come."

The woman stared at him in surprise, for in all the years she had known him, these were the most words she had ever heard from his mouth.

Widow Jennet was the village herbalist and midwife. Her man, Eric the sawyer, had died under a falling tree years ago. Having no children and presumed barren, she had not found a new man, so her life had become one of poverty. Sadly, fearful to marry again, she had become the general do-everything in the village, till now, she was a valued member of the small community. She was as simple as she was good, with a simplicity so clever, she read people's minds. Now she saw the desperate need and truth in Martin's face, and taking up the newborn infant and wrapping it in her breast warmly under her shawl, she sent Martin back to the river while she fetched the priest.

If there had been excitement in the little community before, now it was doubled. So little of note ever happened in Rekeshill, two emergencies in two days, was extraordinary. Mouths fell open when Jennet came bursting into the church, running up to the altar, calling on the priest and young men to assist, till eventually, all but the Dyer family, followed her down to the river.

Martin knelt beside the still form and tenderly moved the wet hair from the face to see blue eyes staring up at him. A hand rose to cover the mouth. So she wasn't dead. Sitting back he surveyed her silently, taking in the blueness of the eyes and the thick wet lashes which framed them. With surprising noise for a subdued people, he heard them coming long before a breathless Jennet arrived with the whole village. Thankfully, the old grave-digger had a second bier made ready, so this was passed down the bank and the body lifted on it.

They laid her in the dye house and fussed about while Martin quickly lit the fire under a cauldron. Eventually, thoroughly exasperated, Jennet firmly chased everyone away. This was woman's work, they should go to the funeral. Disappointed, they trailed back to the church behind the priest.

With her skilled eye, Jennet noted everything about the girl who lay silent on the bench. First she noted the very bad hare lip. Next, that she had recently given birth and that her breasts were hard and cold as stored lard. Using warm cloths and kind words she gently pressed the milk out into a pap pot, barely able to hide the excitement and huge relief flooding through her. The Mother of God had sent a wet-nurse for the Dyer's child. She shut her eyes and gave thanks, for well she knew just how hard it was to rear an orphaned babe without a wet-nurse.

"Go quickly to the house," she ordered Martin suddenly, "This young woman must be very hungry. Stir up the pot well and bring a good bowl of pottage quickly, and a spoon," she added, knowing how silly men could be. Having got the girl, it was important that the shock of the cold river didn't stop her milk.

Warmed by the food and the fire, safe and cared for, Annie slept deeply while the voices of the returned villagers raged round and about her.

"She is a witch I tell you," screamed old Mistress Dyer. "You only have to look at that face and floating naked in the river. A suicide without a doubt and you want her for my grandson's wet-nurse. No I say, take her to the courts for I will have none of her. A witch she must be, who put a spell on our daughter, wanting her child because her own had died. A witch she is and only fit for burning, I say."

Martin stood in the shadows and listened, appalled by the violence. His old aunt had always been a strong woman, and yes, she was grieving for her daughter-in-law, sure her grandson would not survive either. But a witch? No, surely not.

"Let me speak with her quietly," said the priest, silencing the outburst and hushing the fascinated onlookers. Jennet gently shook the girl's shoulder.

"Listen to me, girling," she said kindly. "The priest here wants you to answer some questions. Do you feel well enough now to sit a little and speak with him?"

Annie nodded.

"Why were you in the river, my child?" asked the old man. The blue eyes steadily gazed at him. He repeated himself, more clearly.

"I was hot," the strange nasal voice replied, not easy to understand. "I had a fever, so I went in to get cool."

Jennet translated, jubilant, recognising the truth in her words. It was the fever caused by the built up milk in the hard breasts, she explained professionally.

"Did you recently give birth, my child?" the priest persisted.

Now the blue eyes slowly filled with tears and the head dropped to one side as a small sob escaped the ugly mouth. Jennet quickly comforted her, wiping her eyes with her cloth, smoothing the brow with a kind hand. After a few moments, Annie spoke quietly only to the woman, who in turn told the few around what was said.

"Her baby had the cord tightly about its neck and was dead. Brother Matthew at the monastery buried it." Hugely satisfied with the answer, Jennet propped the girl up and urged her to drink some good ale. For it was important, to get her strong again as quickly as possible and ale made milk.

Now everyone was all attention and quiet, for if the monastery was involved, all surely was well. For the village, indeed land for miles around, was owned by the church. It was the monks who dealt with the wool, grading and selling it. Everyone knew that they took away the fine dyed cloth which provided for every living soul. Theirs might be a poor hill village, yet they knew their worth, for no one produced such fine-coloured wool cloth as they did. No, there could be no fault here if the monastery was involved. A still silence hung in the dim dye shed.

"Who will go to the monastery to find out what we should do?" The priest surveyed his flock, yet no one moved. None wished to leave the village at this time. The morning meal had been poor in every home and they were optimistic that Mistress Dyer would put on a fine meal later. In that poor place, any extra food was more than welcome.

"I," said Martin simply. He waved to indicate some sacks hanging on a beam, knowing they were destined for the monastery "And."

They understood him, for this was how he spoke. The bundles were the last consignment of cloth ready and waiting to go to the monastery. This was the solution.

"How?" asked the priest, turning to Jennet, "Will they understand what he is saying?"

Jennet viewed Martin with new eyes.

"He can speak perfectly clearly if there is need, Father, for didn't he come to tell me of the girl in the river? Of course they will understand him. If it is important, he will explain very well."

Every eye gazed from Jennet to Martin, then back to the priest who nodded.

"Go," said Jennet, her position of authority restored once more. "Wash yourself and change your wet clothes. Then come back here before you leave and someone will help you load up the donkey." Yet when he returned, at least dry if not cleaned of the colours which were all over him, he was grateful that she had a good bowl of food and some fresh baked breads ready for him. Hungry, he ate them quickly before loading up the donkey himself.

Casting his experienced eye about the dye shed, he took up a stout stick and gave the woad vat one last good stir, slopping it over with his vigour and splashing his brais and feet as he did so. With a strange reluctance, he looked once more at the sleeping figure of the girl. Silently he stoked up the fire with another big log so that she would keep warm and led the laden donkey out of the village once more. Nodding to him, Jennet closed the doors to keep the cold air out.

There were two ways in and out of the village. The most used was downstream, where it joined the main river and the road, which marched alongside it. The other, which Martin took now, was upstream, a path which though narrow and sometimes difficult, was much shorter. Only the village people used it and then only to go to the monastery, so it was rarely used. Swinging his little axe, Martin walked ahead cutting brambles which would trip the donkey, or lopped boughs which hung heavy with autumn berries. Martin had only once gone the other, longer way, and then it was with his father and uncle. He did not care for the thought of going alone with the precious cloth on the main road, for one heard of terrible things. Now he tried not to think of the pain in his legs and forced his way up the overgrown path.

As it had been a fine day, it stayed light quite late and Martin arrived at the monastery to the tolling of the bell as dusk was falling. He had hurried and now went to the stables where he unloaded the donkey before leading it to a stall where he gave it water and a good handful of hay stolen from a neighbouring and fine palfrey.

He knew and liked this place of old. The order and neatness appealed to his sense of beauty. Hurrying across the deserted courtyard towards the lighted church, he spat on his hands to smooth his hair down as his mother had taught him. For a second, he paused to admire the silhouette of fine carved stonework, exquisite against the deepening blue night sky. Straightening his mantle, carefully brushing his hose, he pushed the small door open and crept inside. Kneeling at the back of the church, he muttered some prayers before standing to look over the heads of the monks at the altar, beautiful, all lighted with, he thought, a hundred candles. It was so very different, this fine new stone house of God, compared with the poor little wood and sod church in the village.

"Kyrie, eleison." The abbot's fine voice floated over them.

"Kyrie, eleison," came the response, and Martin forgot that he normally did not bother to speak, and fell into the rhythm of the mass.

"Kyrie, eleison."

"Christe, eleison."

On it went, the beautiful old familiar words, lapping against the walls and into the ears of the faithful.

A brother in front of him turned fleetingly to look at him, then away again.

"Christe, eleison."

"Kyrie, eleison."

There was a slight shuffle of movement while several other brothers turned, saw him, then hurriedly resumed their responses.

"Kyrie, eleison. Kyrie, eleison."

The monk with the censor blew into it quietly and began to swing it gently. The abbot, noticing the movement, gave one of his most severe looks at the young monk for the unwanted extravagance, who stopped immediately.

"Gloria in excelsis Deo." Frowning, the abbot had raised his voice, aware of the stir within the church. "Et in terra pax hominibus bonae voluntatis."

Puzzled by the lack of attention, the abbot paused for longer than usual and silently drew his breath in through his nose. What?

"Laudamus te. Benedictus te. Adoramus te. Glorificamus te."

With the barest movement, the abbot held forth his hand, so the monk with the censor should see it. With deft movements from long practise, a curious glitter of understanding in his eye, the young monk swung the censor into life once more, so in moments the smell of incense filled the church.

("Oh God!" the abbot struggled to keep calm, "What is this terrible stink?")

"Gratias ãgimus tibi propter magnam gloriam tuam."

The restlessness seemed like a wind heralding a storm. Nostrils flared. Eyes grew round. The monks tried not to look at each other. Instead they cast their eyes at the roof, the floor, the altar, anywhere but at their fellow sufferers. The younger ones bit their lips to stop the mirth. The older ones tried not to breathe at all.

Martin alone was not one bit disturbed and did not notice the hasty glances in his direction, for he was deep in prayer.

Martin did not pray often, yet this beautiful church inspired him and he shut his eyes tightly to pray for the soul of the young woman who had just died and for his mother, and for the young woman who he had hauled out of the pool this day. For a moment he saw the white body, naked, beautiful, and he shut his eyes tighter. These thoughts were wrong, especially before God.

"Dominus vobiscum."

"Et cum spirit tuo."

"Oremus."

The abbot wiped his brow, suddenly feeling the heat from the candles. How was he to get though this mass?

("Oh God!" he appealed. "Help us, miserable sinners.") trying not to breathe. (Could it be perhaps, because the mid-morning meal had been overly full of onions?) He drew his breath in deeply, then choked on the combined stink and incense smoke which filled the church, recovered and continued.

It was by the moment worse, the heat, the incense, the appalling stink.

"Sanctus, Sanctus, Sanctus, Dominus Deus Sabaoth."

("Almost there, forgive me Lord, but this is terrible.")

"Pleni sunt caeli et terra gloria tua. Hosanna in excelsis."

As a flash from heaven it came to him. Woad! The stink was woad! He covered his mouth, suddenly feeling an almighty laugh rearing up through his corpulent belly.

"Benedictus," he crossed himself with a great sincerity, "qui venit in nomine Domini."

("Forgive me, Oh Father in Heaven for my weakness, yet I am so grateful I can soon be OUT," he realized he had spoken the word aloud but cared not, "of here, your blessed house.")

"Hosanna in excelsis."

Only Brother Mathew, who understood the problem, had been silently edging towards the door. With a quick movement, he took Martin's arm and silently pushed him through the small door. He had realized immediately what the smell was, for having been brought up in Rekeshill, he was familiar with woad and its stink. Still holding on to Martin's arm, he herded him surely through the gloom to the wash house where with a smile, he gently explained to the ignorant dyer, that not everyone could cope with the stink of woad.

"Wait while I fetch light," he hurried away leaving Martin looking down at his hose, which yes, had been splashed with woad water so recently.

"Off!" demanded Brother Matthew, tugging at the offending garment, while Martin hung on to them. "Off I say, Martin, don't be a prude, man, give them to me to wash, while you cleanse yourself. For we must hurry to the refectory or we shall miss supper and I for one am hungry." At last he had the smelly hose down and off, with the flickering lamp light, Mathew saw the splattered and blotched legs. Jumping up he tossed the hose into a tub and turned away in shock.

"Wash yourself free from the stink as best you can, while I fetch you some soap and fresh hose for you to wear, Martin," and whirled away.

Outside, Brother Mathew leant for a moment against the door. He hadn't known. Had anyone known? Did Martin know? Gathering his habit up he fled, his thoughts racing too, to fetch fresh hose from the poor store and then to the kitchens for a pail of hot water, and a small pot of soft soap.

"Oh dear Lord, help me," he prayed as he walked as fast as the pail would allow him. "You dear Lord, who put your hands upon ten lepers, help me to put my hands on just one."

Martin was standing stock still in the half butt of cold water. His eyes were dark with fear as the monk came in. Had he seen?

"Here you are my friend," he carefully poured the hot water into the butt. "Now take some soap and wash well, for, Martin, you cannot imagine how woad offends the noses of those who were not, like us, brought up with it! Wash well now while I see to your hose so they will be dry for tomorrow." Turning his back, he lifted his habit, kicked off his clogs, stepped into the water tub and started stamping the offending clothes.

"If," he prayed silently, "it is your will oh Lord, I submit to it."

When the Mass ended, the abbot turned and willed himself to be dignified, so they trooped slowly out as usual, following the Cross.

"Ten, eleven, twelve," the abbot counted his steps carefully, knowing the length and breadth of the church. "Nearly there, Oh God, then I can breathe again."

As they neared the door, it seemed as if the stink were double in strength. With a grateful swoop, he was out, sucking in the fresh air in gulps, the brothers close behind him, all doing the same.

Then the laugh which had threatened in the church began to rise in him, like a pot of boiling broth, it bubbled and rose, till at last, he held his stomach and bent over double. The monks watched their abbot in horror. Was he ill? Why was he doubled like that, quivering, shaking? Not one of them liked him one jot, yet they were good men, and seeing a fellow human in obvious pain, they rushed forward, hands outstretched, supporting him in concern.

It was no good. He could not hold it for one more second. Standing up straight, gasping for breath, he let it go. A huge bellow of laughter pumped out of him, a roar, a grossly uncouth yell, a belly laugh of great proportions, flowed unchecked from within him, into the sweet night air.

For seconds they stood transfixed, shocked, amazed. Then, understanding dawning slowly, as one they too let their breaths out and lifted their voices, tentatively at first, then with relieved gratitude, to join his in laughter.

How long they stood there, they never knew. They howled, they wept great tears, they rocked and bent over, holding their bellies in an agony of mirth. As a pause came, they looked at each other, then as children with some silly joke, off they set again, revelling in the sheer joy of freedom to let themselves go in laughter.

Weakly, they trailed to the refectory as the brothers in charge, tripping as they wiped their eyes on their habits, sped to the kitchen to bring the meal.

By the time Brother Mathew and Martin arrived, all was quiet, yet there was a strange new feeling of fellowship and love, barely discernible, yet never to be lost.

"Come," called the abbot, "Brother Mathew, bring our guest to sit near me, for I would hear news from him." They all shifted to make space, surprised yet pleased. So he was a good man after all and they had been wrong. A man with humour and kindness, which had only needed something like the stink of woad to release it. Little did he know, poor abbot, just how much he had been disliked. Yet now, and in the future, life would be so much easier and kind. All because of a simple dyer covered with spilt woad, a little miracle. It was a new thing to relax themselves into such brotherhood and laughter. As for the abbot, could he ever put a day to the change of heart and manner of his house?

He would look back on this night as a gift from God. Laughter! Oh but such a glorious and wonderful feeling it was to let go, to enjoy the pure animal force of joy, and to share it too. When they made him bishop, he remembered this night, and whenever he gave the beautiful dyed cloths or yarns to the ladies in great houses and convents, he delighted in the tale.

"Tell us?" they begged, all the charming, pretty gentlewomen who thought how fortunate they were to have such a worldly, kindly bishop. "Oh my Lord Bishop, please! Tell us of the night of the woad?" And pretending not to want to recount it, he would eventually, with more and more embellishment, which everyone enjoyed.

When they finished their meal and it was cleared away, somehow not wanting to end this eventful night just yet, the abbot asked to view the cloth. Sack by sack they were brought from the stables, opened and admired. Yet now and again, a glance, a smile, and backs would be turned while more laughter shook helpless bodies.

"Martin Dyeson," the abbot smiled warmly at his dyer. "Tonight in my prayers I will give thanks to the Almighty for you and your craft, for surely your efforts bring forth great beauty." Martin stood, head bowed, amazed at being so kindly addressed.

"And brothers," the abbot raised his rich voice to attract everyone's attention. "We are surely blessed, are we not, for this good man who toils so hard, often in difficult conditions, to produce such beauty?"

Understanding perfectly, as one, smiling they nodded.

In the light of many fine candles, Martin told, hands waving with a few words, about Annie, the death of young Mistress Dyer, the accusation of witchcraft, and was heard with coldness.

"Foolish people," announced the abbot sternly. "We know the girl Annie, who poor soul, carries a heavy burden already. She has helped Brother Matthew for many months, living quietly, soberly, never once giving any trouble of any kind. Yes," he looked at Martin with kind eyes, "you did well, my son, to save her from death, and I lay it on you to look after her most diligently. For she is an innocent girl, and if Mistress Jennet says she had milk fever, surely that is why she went into the water, to be cool." While he spoke his mind was racing. For that poor village of Rekeshill was an important small part of their lands. Their wool was not really so very special, but their dye workings were exceptionally good. He himself had never before seen such fine colours, and no fuss or trouble must interfere with that.

"Brother Matthew," he actually smiled at him. "Go with our friend here, sort out any troubles for me. You well know what a good girl Annie is, that the poor innocent soul was used by some lout, so gave her the child, which by the will of God did not live, poor mite. Go with Martin and quieten things down at Rekeshill, for is it not your home village?"

Matthew nodded, surprised that his abbot knew anything about him.

"It will be good for Annie to be wet-nurse to the motherless babe. The Dyer must attend to his work, and having a good nurse for the child will be a great comfort for him, having lost his wife." He thought for a moment. "See in the poor store and find some more clothes, Brother Matthew. Some for Annie, and if you please, for Martin," now he really grinned. "When you come again, which I hope you will, please my friend, wear fresh clothes so we may breathe the sweet air that God has given us."

Early next morning, orders were given for a pony to be brought for Brother Matthew. The empty sacks were once again loaded on the donkey, some mysteriously full, which they would be happy to explore and find good things in when they got home.

"And Martin," it was as if the abbot was loathe to have him leave. "I recall that our Brother Matthew has been requesting a rooster and some hens for a little while now. By chance you could find some in Rekeshill?" He drew out a small string purse from the folds of his robe and handed a handsome coin to the astonished brother. "Choose the worth of this, Matthew," he ended, "but keep them in the kitchen garden if you please, away from the clean courtyards." He turned and left, still smiling.

The fear was slowly leaving him as they prepared to leave. Martin watched his companion for any signs, but no, there were none. He cannot have seen. Indeed the monk seemed as natural as ever. On their way out of the monastery Mathew pointed out the fine willow hedge which Annie had planted, then the tiny grave set by it.

With the donkey pleased with the company of the pony and less laden, they made good speed and were back at Rekeshill by nightfall. Martin led the animals into the open end of the dye shed, unloaded them, gave them water and turned them out into the little field. Only then did he take his new friend inside. Hearing them from the kitchen of the house, Jennet appeared and later brought out a pallet for the monk and two good bowls of broth with bread. In the morning they would call together the village with the priest, and Brother Matthew would tell them the orders sent by the Lord Abbot. Now they would sleep, for strangely, both men were tired.

They soon grew used to her, the stranger who had arrived miraculously to be wet-nurse to the dyer's infant. In a village where they were usually all well covered up, often over their faces too, she soon blended in. Besides, with Mistress Jennet in charge, it was the wisest thing to do to accept her. For Jennet was extremely happy with her new life and would take no nonsense. She was now once more in a position of authority, blessed by the abbot no less. Living in the Dyer house, she was totally in charge, sleeping with the girl and the babe in the kitchen by the fire. It was a fine change from her own pitiful, dank cottage where one wall of the only room was all falling in. Added to being in charge of the girl and child, she had regained her name in midwifery. All now agreed freely that Blaise had been unwise to wed such a fragile little thing, (may God rest her soul). Annie might be ugly, but she had plenty of milk, besides being a thoroughly biddable girl and excellent spinner.

They got along so well too, the daughter she had never had, and Jennet taught Annie all she knew with a great pride. Together they adored the little boy, the centre of all life in the Dyer's house. Even Mistress Dyer began to soften when she saw her precious grandson thrive, smile and even put his arms out to her.

On the fringe, always in the shadows, Martin watched with a half-smile, glad, oh so glad that things had turned out so well. Although he never went into the kitchen, the women always took him a bowl of pottage or a dish of meat on feast days beautifully cooked in herbs and wild garlic.

Even if she would not admit it publicly, Jennet found that she was learning from Annie too. Some surprising things, she was secretly impressed as well as being astonished. They had never eaten so well either, so they felt unusually fit. For almost every day Annie went out into the woods, the baby strapped close to her for warmth, never returning empty-handed. If it wasn't a brace of conies, it was a basket of mushrooms, or damsons, nuts and in the spring, mallard's eggs. Smelling the rich cooking smells from her cold room, Mistress Dyer would join them occasionally at first, increasingly so with winter. It was very agreeable to sit on a stool by the fire, dandling the child and be part of a family again, so long as she didn't look too closely at the ugly girl.

Annie understood that at last she was truly happy. Jennet was totally different from Bee in all ways. Yet she was just like Bee. Theirs was a warm companionship albeit a new one, a give and take relationship which benefited them all.

The three women were unusually well balanced and it was a peaceful home. Blaise Dyer was relieved with the peace in his household for he was often away and it was good to return to a happy house. The loss of his wife hardly mattered now that his home and work were well run and fruitful.

For Annie, the foster-child which had so unexpectedly taken over her body, was a constant joy. Lying on the pallet beside Jennet, she would quietly pull the baby from his cradle and snuggle him close. He was a golden child with fair hair and blue eyes, his skin rosy and healthy and there for her to tickle. He loved everyone, giving his smiles freely. Yet in her heart she knew that he loved her best, almost her own little boy.

The dye house was a constant fascination to Annie, who wondered at how the magical colours could change and set. And Martin? He taught her too, beckoning her to come and see, proud of his art, delighted to have her company and interest. They rarely spoke. All communication was done with few words, mime and eyes. It happened so slowly, so quietly, both she and he did not see it coming, until one day, there it was, they were in love. There was no union, no touch, few words, but a love so tangible, that even Mistress Dyer remarked on it to Jennet.

"Leave them be, mistress," advised Jennet feeling unusually sentimental. "A great love like theirs must move slowly, with the seasons, not rush and tumble like ordinary folk." So nothing was said, no snide remarks, no jokes and the love grew.

In late summer of the second year, Annie was out as usual, this time cutting willow to make some strong baskets for the dye house. As little Blaise was almost weaned, he was left behind with Jennet. Without him she went further a-field than usual, seeking a variation of colour to make the baskets different. Loving Martin as she did, she had to show him in her little ways, with her hands. Never had she made such fine baskets, let alone with such variations of colour. She smiled at her foolishness, but happily. With her skirts hitched up, Annie waded in the shallows of the quiet river. It was so peaceful, in the heat she lay for a moment on the bank gazing at the brilliant maiden flies flickering on the water till gradually she fell asleep. Here Martin found her and sitting quietly beside her, he gazed at her with love. He did not see the ugly mouth and scattered teeth or indeed ever hear the nasal voice so different from other girls. He saw her hair glinting in the sun, her rosy skin, a tiny pulse beating at her neck and hidden under the closed lids, he knew lay beautiful, cornflower blue eyes. Breathing in deeply, he blessed the day he had found her. His was a deep contentment. He had never loved before and this seemed to him the reason of his life. More than that he did not think, each day was a joy, to see her, to be near her. It was enough. It had to be enough.

A sound caught his attention. It was far off, but alarming. Holding his breath he turned his head to hear better, then on bare feet ran silently up the bank where he would hear more clearly. In the distance he heard the baying of hounds, a horn, the crash and clamour of many hooves. Swiftly he swept the girl up and putting her on her feet dragged her by the hand, fearfully looking over his shoulder. On, quickly, oh run, downriver, faster, towards the village.

Alarmed, Annie saw his face, and trusting him, ran too, even before she heard the sound which seemed to be approaching so fast.

He knew that the horsemen were gaining on them and never sure who or what they were, he just wanted to get to and warn the village. But it was no use and suddenly Martin veered down into the river again, to put the hounds off their scent and reaching the top pool, still holding her hand he ducked under the waterfall, and held Annie close.

Astonished, Annie tried to catch her breath and ease the pain in her side which had come on from running. Her heart was pounding and she could feel Martin's against her back as he held her so tightly. The evening sunlight shone through the curtain of water, and Annie wondered at this beautiful secret place she had not known about. They stayed there for some time, gradually regaining their breath and held fast to keep each other warm.

"Stay!" he mouthed, then for a moment held her terribly close, loving her. "Stay till I return," and then was gone.

It was dusk when he returned, slipping as a shadow under the curtain of water, a coarse blanket under his arm. Annie tried to see his face, but could not in the gloom. He said nothing, just wrapped the blanket about them, held her close and strangely, fell asleep. Without realizing it, she too must have slept, for a shaft of light woke her, shining off the river, straight into their hiding place.

Stiffly, quietly, they emerged with the dawn. Martin's face was so severe, Annie dare not ask him what had happened. As one they washed and drank in the river, Martin watchful and silent as usual. In single file, they approached the village cautiously but there was no sound, just smoke.

There was little left of Rekeshill. The band, angry at the lack of food, drink and valuables to be bought off with, had wrecked the place. In half a day they had pillaged, slashed, raped and burnt. Even now the thatched roofs smouldered, and there was a different, terrible smell.

One by one, the survivors emerged. Terrified, some burned or slashed, they wept as they tried to help each other. The shepherds had returned to find desolation. Just they, and Annie and Martin were unscathed.

His anger a goad, Martin dug a wide grave and one by one they laid the bodies in as neatly as they could. The priest was dead too, so there was no one to tell the litany for the dead. Mistress Dyer and Jennet were dead, and gone were their salves and simples in the conflagration. Martin had found them in the burnt out dyer's house, huddled in a corner, their bodies trying to shield the baby. But he guessed the smoke took them anyway, for at least there was no mark of violence on their bodies. Despite her efforts rooting about in the smoking embers, Annie could not find a single good sheet to wrap any of them in. Surprisingly she found her cooking pot and absently, bitterly, put it to one side with the few other things worth saving.

Martin laid them together, the baby in the dead arms of the two women who had so loved him while Annie knelt and wept silent and bitter tears. Of a village of fifty souls, twenty survived and some of them would die of their wounds. The earth fell into the shallow pit, a dull sound, covering her precious child for ever.

"Annie?" she looked up at him, her eyes red from weeping and smoke. "Will you go to tell the abbot? We need help. Brother Matthew, food, clothing." She thought for a moment then nodded. He and the other able bodies must stay to look after the survivors, she must go.

"Annie?" again she looked at him, "come, I will walk a little way with you." So they retraced their steps till they reached the river. Stopping and turning to face her he stated very clearly.

"I love you Annie, with my heart and soul, and with my body too."

Surprised, she heard the beautiful words, yet knew that somehow they were not a promise. "If I could, I would take you to my wife. But dearling, I cannot."

Strangely, he bent down and rolled up his fire-blackened, dye-splattered hose. Then he straightened. "I am a leper, Annie, see?" he pointed to his legs. "I took it from my mother, who caught it from my father, who got it from who knows where."

Eyes wide, she looked at his legs, then into his face. Never before had he addressed so many words to her.

"It will spread, Annie love, eventually all over my body. It is, so my mother told me, contagious, so I hide behind the dye as my parents did. That is why I live a solitary life. I dare not touch anyone, which is why I never held you or the baby, much as I longed to. From the moment my mother saw that I too was afflicted, she told me I must never wed or take a woman to my bed, for she, as my good mother, would also succumb. For you surely may have caught it. I could not. I cannot. Loving you, I cannot wed with you and inflict this illness upon you. I watched my parents suffer long and die, always afraid of being discovered, in such pain, always afraid of being driven out. So to avoid taking up the leper's rattle, I let the dyes cover my body, as they did."

They stood, lost in time, a huge emptiness, lost, lost. He pushed a small bundle into her hands and from the weight she understood it must be her bronze pot. "Go now, my Annie, my dear love. Help us please, bring help to the people of Rekeshill. Be careful, for maybe that band has also attacked the monastery, go with caution." Forgetting his intentions he reached out and held her close, a sob shuddering through his spare body.

Fumbling in her pocket Annie brought out her one treasure, the little silver brooch she had been given at Christ Mass.

"It is a love knot, Martin, please take it and remember me by it." They stood close, eyes wet, the little brooch held unbearably tight in his hand. Martin said, "Thank you, my dearling, I shall keep it with me always, all my life. Now go my love, and never come back. But also never forget how much I love you." He bent to see her eyes. "You hear me now?" and turned her with a little push. "Go, never return, never forget. I love you."

As if in sleep, she walked away from him, numb, unbelieving, his words echoing in her mind. How could happiness flee so suddenly, so unexpectedly and leave oh so much sorrow, such emptiness. She turned to see if he was still there.

A smile so tender, so bittersweet, crossed his face as he gazed at her. His heart was full. He had loved. He did still love and would till his dying day. As she came to the bend, she turned once more and raised her hand. For a moment he did nothing, willing her to come back, to stay. Then, putting his hand to his mouth he raised it high. He had loved, he loved, and no one, not even she, could ever take that away.

As with all who truly, selflessly love, Annie and Martin remained with each other in their thoughts, every day of their lives. The sight of anything sweet or beautiful which crossed their paths, made them stop and stare unseeing, and love filled their souls, love which surely flew across the miles.

Gradually, slowly, Rekeshill recovered and once again the dye house supplied fine, coloured yarns. Blaise Dyer married again, a buxom, wide-hipped girl who bore him many children, so the dyer's art survived. Yet the time would come when, without Martin, it would gradually lose its fame. For the colours which Blaise got were not exceptional, as of old. They lost their depths and brilliance without Martin's infinite care, they faded and washed out, because it was he alone, who knew the many and strange dyer's secrets.

The next tragedy to befall Rekeshill was when Brother Matthew came one day, stumbling, ragged and ill, down the path alongside the river, to the edge of the village.

"Martin! Martin!" he called loudly from the river bank, and when Martin appeared, puzzled, at the dye house door, shouted at him, "keep back, keep away, do not come close to me, for I am ill." He leaned against a tree to get his breath. "Bar the lane, Martin," he gasped, "set a hurdle across and keep guard day and night for the plague is rampant and let no man into the village or you will all perish."

Martin ran forward to help his friend, then backed away seeing the wild, feverish eyes.

"Keep away from me, you simpleton, did you not hear what I said? Let no man in, do you hear. Do it now, Martin, for the love of God and your people, keep all strangers out, which includes me."

Martin hesitated, then seeing Mathew stagger back the way he came, he ran into the village, told the new priest and together with the young men, they set up strong hurdles and barred the lane.

When it was done, Martin took up a flagon of ale, bread and cheese and his cloak and went in search of Matthew. He soon found him groaning with pain, lying on the narrow path beside the stream.

"Fool! Fool!" said Matthew through frothing lips, but gratefully drank deeply of the ale, then fell back in Martin's arms, his eyes wide and frightened. "Do you want to die also?"

But Martin wrapped him in his cloak and held him gently, and sought through his mind for the Latin words which he had, all too often, heard the priest speak for the dead and the dying. Matthew heard his words, right or not, they seemed to help him, for suddenly a peace overtook him. The smallest smile on his lips, he looked at his old friend, and understood.

Martin went to the dye shed and quickly took up a spade, the little earthenware pot which held his treasures, his other cloak and returned to bury his friend. Having done it, a poor shallow grave but with some good rocks on top to keep the wild beasts off, he drove a stake in at the head and tied Matthew's cross on it, so that all would know that here lay a man of God.

Then, exhausted, he went down to the water, washed and drank, and in his mind's eye, saw a still, white, body floating there, covered by a carpet of golden leaves.

Wrapped in his cloak, he lay under the waterfall as night fell and thought of Annie. With the little pot securely wedged on a shelf above him, he willed her to come and fetch it one day. He remembered her lovely eyes and her sweetness and told her that he loved her, and that he would surely find her in paradise. The sickness came upon him swiftly with a fearful agony, and by morning he was dead.

So many times Annie had passed near enough to go to Rekeshill, yet her courage had failed her each time. By now Odi was a big boy, and her life was even and almost orderly. Yet she never ceased to yearn for Martin, to see him once more, to know how he fared.

At last she came, settling Odi with their last barley cake in a hollow outside the village by the little madder field. Telling him to stay with their things, she said that she was going to find bread in the village.

Much had changed. Many new cottages stood where last she had seen smoking ruins. Knocking on the rebuilt stone house of the dyers, she pulled up her cloth to hide her mouth. A strange young woman came to the door, obviously great with child, with several children about her. Looking at them she started, for surely they must be Blaise's young, so like they were, to her dear lost boy.

"Martin?" The young woman looked at her curiously, "they don't know where he went. He just came running one day to tell that Brother Matthew had come, very ill, to the edge of the village, crying that they must bar the lane, for the plague was all about." Annie stared at her in shock. "We heard later," the woman continued, "that more than half the brothers at the monastery died from it, and Matthew came to warn us, then went away again. They searched for Martin, but only found a grave, so guessed that he had buried Brother Matthew, whose cross hung at the head."

Annie thanked her quietly, and trembling left, knowing surely where he had gone to die. The familiar little path by the stream was so overgrown that she had to fight her way through the briars to get to the three pools.

Unafraid, she crept under the waterfall which fell softly, the days being dry, and there in a tumble of rotten cloth and mud lay a form, white bones showing here and there.

"I'm here, Martin my love, I am here!" she said and wept bitterly. A shaft of sunlight filtered through the water as the sun set in the west and

Annie saw the earthenware pot on the shelf above him. Taking it down, she carefully emptied out the water, and some coins fell out into her lap. Then, a tarnished twist of silver. Her brooch! Her love knot. The tears fell again. Oh Martin, oh Martin my love! Gathering up the coins, she put the pot outside on the bank and began to work. Collecting rocks as large as she could manage, she made a little wall around Martin's bones, then, filled it in with as many smaller stones that she could find. At nightfall, cold and exhausted, she picked up the little pot and made her way back to the sleeping Odi. Covering them both with her cloak, she lay for half the night remembering, till she finally slept with the dawn.

That day, they went into Rekeshill where she met her few old neighbours and was given a good welcome, with pottage and ale, cheese and barley bread. Then she went to the new little church and kneeling, prayed for all her lost, loved ones. Lastly, she left Martin's coins with the priest, to say masses for his soul and then she left the village forever.

Later, finding a little windfall damson, she rubbed the silver brooch with it until it shone. She always wore it after that, proudly pinned onto her shift, touching it, smiling with her memories; it gave her courage.

CHAPTER TWENTY TWO

ODI

What made her walk on after alerting the abbot she did not know. Her tears had simply dried up, there were no more left to shed. She felt empty. Her eyes were so swollen and red, she could hardly see. A quiet moaning came from somewhere deep inside her, but she did not care about anything, anymore. Somehow she felt her loss was so acute, it told of her whole life, everything of the past. Her brief, happy life at Rekeshill was over, gone, all gone. Lost too was her dearling child, lost forever. And what of her love for Martin? Had he loved her? In her ignorance the word she used was not love, for never had she experienced girlish whispers of romance. At least that had been a beloved, healthy, beautiful child, before God chose to take him too.

The monks were kind and comforted her before they went to Rekeshill. A good party of them left the next dawn, loaded with tools, clothes and food, so she slipped away, unable to face returning herself.

Once more she felt ill with the milk pressing against her bodice and again in ignorance, drinking at every little stream she passed, made her pain worse. Instinctively, she wandered to the home she had last shared with Bee, sweet friend and loving companion, never to be forgotten. Her little shelter where Bee had died was all in ruins. Perhaps it was neglect of two winters. Or maybe the village children had played there. Through feverish eyes she gazed at it with sorrow. Turning, she walked slowly to the village and to the weaver's house. For Mistress Weaver had always been kind to her and might aid her now. As she approached, she saw a light in the byre so crept up.

Standing in the open doorway she watched the weaver's wife struggle with a creature who made such a noise, half human, half beast. Silently, Annie stood there, noting albeit the shadows, how worn the woman looked, and how her face was wet with tears.

Approaching, she laid a hand on the woman's shoulder which made her start and cry out. In the gloom of evening, the small horn light hanging on a beam, Mistress Weaver saw Annie, the poor ugly waif girl and strangely, her spirits rose, for she was feeling very lonely, as she did so often these days.

"Oh Annie, dear child, I have been praying for you to come for alas, I have a child for you to mind. We were afraid you were dead as you have not been by for so long." Then her face crumpled and fresh tears fell. Unable to speak she pushed the creature in her arms towards the girl. Annie took the bundle and lifted the shawl and saw it was a child, an angry child, for it opened its mouth and screamed with rage as a wild animal.

"He is always hungry, Annie," she blew her nose hard, using her apron. "I thought I was barren. Master Weaver and all the village thought I was too, but just when I was forgetting to be a woman, he came along." She sighed hugely. "So, the good Lord gave me a child, but see," she paused, shook her head and wiped her eyes. Pulling the shawl away to reveal the head, Annie gasped.

"Oh my," she whispered, "oh my!"

There on the other side of a normal baby face was a huge eye. An eye like a cow or horse, far greater than the other eye. So big was it, that the lid could not close. Fumbling her right hand free, Annie crossed herself. Never in her life had she seen such. It was an abomination! The noise it made, wailing, deep and angry. Mistress Weaver took up a horn spoon and a cup of thin gruel, stirring it.

"He seems determined to live," she said, struggling to push the spoon into the raging mouth. "So feed him I do, with milk, I have none, but from the goat, and now gruel, to silence him." The child spluttered and fought, gasping in Annie's arms, arching its back. "Truly, my man must be right, he surely has the devil in him."

Despite her horror, Annie suddenly felt a great pity overwhelm her. Poor mite! Another ugly thing such as herself! Deftly she undid her bodice and pressed the taut breast to the child who seized upon it so she almost fainted with pain.

Thus it was that Annie got another child to care for. And so soon after her beloved perfect foster-baby, although she wondered how long it would last, she did still have a little milk.

Mistress Weaver heard her story clicking her tongue in sympathy. Pushing the girl in the hay and drawing the good thick covers over her, she told Annie she would bring her food, and then she must sleep, mind the child and she would be by her first thing in the morning.

For a while, Annie lay, cradling the child, letting it ease one breast, then the other. Of course, having gorged itself, it belched loudly and threw half the milk up again. Wiping herself down with hay in disgust, Annie felt her heart harden. In the early morning she fed it again, wiped it down and returned it to the nest of hay in the byre. Then she went to her old home before folks were about and carefully dug out the hearth, for although the abbot had given her a coin, it would not last her long. By the time sun rose, she had made a good start in tidying up, a small fire burning on the hearth drying it all out.

"Oh my dear," Mistress Weaver arrived breathless, the child in her arms. "I was afeared you had gone." She began to weep, seating herself on the ledge which was the bed. "I beg you, Annie, to take this poor child. My man is so angry with me, saying it is my fault, he will not allow it in the house. I am no longer welcome by his fire or in his bed. He barely speaks to me. For getting a child at last he was so filled with hope. Now, Annie, his anger and disappointment are cruel." She sobbed afresh. "What would I do for a perfect child to love and for comfort in my old age."

Annie took the child and nursed it, careful to cover its great bulging eye with the shawl. It looked quite normal with the eye covered. Yet she felt nothing for it. Her pain of loss of her baby, Martin, Jennet and her contented life at Rekeshill had left her numb.

"I'll stay awhile, mistress never fear, and I'll nurse your baby till my milk goes." Which was all Mistress Weaver wanted to hear, so she hurried off to collect food and blankets, a small milking pail and returned sometime later laden, leading a small nanny-goat. Annie strapped the boy about her as she had her first foster-son. Each day she wandered off, leading the goat to fresh pasture, avoiding the villagers. The goat's milk was good and she drank it all, twice a day. For the new boy was happy with her milk and perhaps the goat's milk helped hers flow.

Her old home looked better than before, for Mistress Weaver came often, bringing what she could to make it comfortable and to make it look nice. When she was not busy, she sat with Annie and they span together, and Annie told her about her wanderings of the past years.

That winter she stayed there, tending Bee's grave, spinning for the hall or the weavers. Somehow she kept busy, but if she could, stayed further away from the villagers than before. For the child she was suckling really was a monster, its huge eye staring at her, even while it slept.

Perhaps because she kept to herself, Annie got through the winter without being ill and the boy thrived. He grew heavy and when she turned his big eye into the shawl, she saw the small eye surveying her, and it smiled. Very gradually her emotions thawed and she began to enjoy her new charge. Mistress Weaver continued to support her in every way, loving her monster child despite herself and glad that it survived. Just the two women took the boy to the church to baptize him, and Annie stood Godmother. He was named James, but already the name given him by his father had stuck.

"It is Odin come again!" the surly weaver had shouted. "Look at that one eye. What kind of child is that?" So somehow the poor babe took the name Odi, short for Odin but with the two women's love and care, he grew into a fine boy.

Annie began her wanderings when the weather grew warmer. With the boy on her hip and her pack on her back, she set out, with the little goat following. There was no need to tether or lead her for she came when called although she had no name. Every winter she returned to her own village where Mistress Weaver welcomed her and helped her through the bitter weather. The slips she had planted about her shelter grew a fine wall onto which she added twigs and daubed with mud so to keep her little shelter warm.

Odi was a fine boy, strong and, apart from his eye, handsome with deep red-brown hair, his little head round and shiny as a horse chestnut. Annie learned to slick his hair over the eye so no one could see it. With a bonnet perched on his head to keep the curtain of hair in place, he looked very bonny. Yet there were times when Annie was afraid when ruffians taunted her while she went through towns or villages. Then she would draw aside the hair to expose the hideous eye, drop her headcloth so they could see her face, and laugh hysterically as they ran, frightened away. With time, few bothered her, and she resumed her basket-making although with her savings under each secret hearth, they were never hungry.

Standing outside the churches always brought enough alms to buy food for many days. The pious would cross themselves and shudder at the two ugly humans and thank God in his mercy for their own normality.

There was scant order in their wanderings. According to weather and whim, they went where they willed. Sometimes they walked along barren beaches and rejoiced over shells, gathering driftwood for their night-time fire, marvelling over the wondrous iridescent colours which rose from the salt laden fire. Other times they wandered over hills and downs, occasionally dropping down into the valleys to buy food and sell baskets. There were great forests to cross, but by now Annie knew the way and stopped by the friendly charcoal burners who were always glad of a chat in their lonely work. Despite her strange voice, Annie managed to tell some fine tales and news of the world. In exchange they allowed her to gather up the fallen charcoal, so when the strange pair left, they had another bundle to carry. Although big it was light and a source of warmth and fire for cooking for many a day.

When Odi was about five years old, they were, as usual, on the move and found themselves on a high moor. Annie had promised a dyer that she would gather a bag of crottle for him. Whenever they passed boulders on the moor, she would examine them, and if they were right, would patiently scrape off the fine yellow moss which grew there. It was a slow job, yet it paid well, for red dye was expensive and few had the time or patience to gather it. As they struggled through the heather and ling which was wet and scratched their legs, Annie saw a great eagle soaring above them.

"See my dearling," pointing skywards. "There he is, hunting for food for his little ones while his mate keeps them warm." Odi was proving an inquisitive child who wanted to know everything. She supposed, forgetting that she had been the same, forever pestering Bee with questions, that it was because he had no children to play with, so in her own way, she tried to be substitute for them. When they were walking through the great forests they would play catch, hide and seek or blind man's buff. Whenever the opportunity arose to teach him something new, she remembered Bee's words.

"Tis a wondrous world we live in dearling," said Bee, "so much to see and hear and learn." And, she would draw the girl close, "aren't we so lucky to be free to do so, and not toiling away in some smelly village as other folks."

They watched the great bird soar high above them for some time, lying in the shelter of the heather while the goat browsed around them. It could be that they slept for awhile, for they woke with a start at a terrible scream and sitting up, saw the eagle had dropped something which fell with a soft thud near them.

Up leapt Annie waving her arms to ward off the bird as it swooped low, huge and menacing so close to them, seeking its lost prey.

"It must be near, my boy, come quickly, let us seek out what it has dropped." So they searched and there lying in a heather clump they found a small kitten who for the moment was stunned and silent. Eyes filled with pity, Annie swept it up and tucked it into the darkness of her shift where it would be warm.

"You find something else you bird," she called up to the sky. And so they wandered on, the kitten still in Annie's shift close to her beating heart where it felt safe again and lay still. At last, with evening in a little camp out of the wind under an overhang of heather roots, Annie made a little fire and they toasted some old bread and drank the goat's milk. When the kitten began piteously mewling, Annie drew it out and holding it by the loose skin of its neck, surveyed it. Limp and un-protesting, it had some spots of dried blood from the eagle's talons on it, yet it seemed otherwise quite well. Putting a drop of milk on a horn spoon, Annie offered it to the kitten, who when it had stopped spitting, fell into it messily. Squatting on his hunkers, Odi was excited by the new arrival and curious to see it.

"Can we keep him, Annie?" he asked, trembling with excitement.

"Well my boy, I think we shall have to, for heaven knows where his dam is. Let us try to feed him, and yes, then we will keep him, if he survives that is. For maybe he is sorely injured by that eagle. But we shall see," and tucked him back into her warm shift where he slept again.

Now they were four, two humans, a goat and a tiny wildcat kitten. Fortunately the goat had kidded again that spring, so had plenty of milk and the kitten throve. Eventually he stopped spitting at his new family, and instead purred mightily while they stroked him.

They called him Eagle. A fine name with meaning, announced Annie, pleased that it was a boy cat, so at least there would not be lots of kits to cope with. With the good goat's milk, and with the half-chewed rabbit meat Annie spat out for him, he would became a fine sleek cat who deeply loved his family, even the goat on whose back he sometimes rode.

If they had been a spectacle before, they were more so now, yet with kindness. People smiled as the little goat followed her people, a kitten firmly attached to her back. So, often they would be given a couple of eggs, barley cakes or even some scraps of meat. Yet the best thing of all was the friendship in people's eyes.

"It must be a real wildcat," said a wandering friar, who gently examined the kitten and had a good bite for his kindness, "as you found it on the moors, far from dwellings. Yes I do believe it is." He patted Odi's head. "You are very privileged, young man. For wildcats do not normally become tame. And though he bit me, I see he loves you dearly."

Every other year their little goat was mated and stank of billy goat for weeks after. However, this they had to tolerate for they loved her and when she gave birth, took just a little of her milk so that the kid would thrive.

Here was another sweet little creature to play with and laugh at except that when they returned to the village for winter, Master Weaver always took it.

By the time he was seven, Odi was as tall as Annie, and more sturdy, for she treated him as does a mother bird, stuffing his mouth whenever he opened it. The fruits of the earth were abundant and varied for those who knew where to look.

One shelter they especially liked was on the edge of the forest. Except that the stream was some way off, it had everything. It was a cave, set in a pile of great boulders. If they climbed up and sat on top, they could see for miles all the way from East to West. It was usually warm there, being shielded from the North by the forest, and if the sun was shining, the stones stayed hot all day. It was not too far from a small lane either, so if anyone came by, they saw them and made the decision to speak, or stay hidden. Occasionally they realized that someone else had discovered their site, for the hearth had been used and there was a certain untidiness all around. At least Annie thought gratefully, they were not so tidy as to re-make the hearth. For when Odi slept, she hastened to dig up the hearth to add or take of the hidden treasure and found that it was always intact and her money safe.

"Rom," said Annie knowingly. "Because they never live in a house, they are never tidy," forgetting, that they also did not live in a house.

On one occasion, when they were settled in, Annie set off in the early evening with the child, leaving the goat to graze and the cat to forage for itself. By now, she knew the best places everywhere to set her snares and absence meant that plenty of new life abounded where she had culled it. Deftly, for by now she was an expert, she set them and on the way home they dallied and collected firewood in the slanting evening sunlight.

Odi stopped suddenly, his face turned so he could see with his good, the smaller, eye. Something was hanging on a branch, a pitiful little noise coming from it. Tugging at Annie's skirts he pointed. A long piece of cloth hung from the tree with a bulge at the bottom.

"Oh!" said Annie, dropping the wood and putting her hand to her mouth. "A babby!" They approached it cautiously and looked about. Annie opened the cloth and beheld a pretty little dark brown baby. Lifting it up, she began cooing to it with Odi hanging close by, thrilled with yet another creature to join their family.

"Can we keep it?" he breathed, his face a picture of delight.

Annie hoisted him up to unhook the cloth sling, then sat down with the baby in her lap. It had stopped crying and looked up at them, glad to see faces, it smiled.

"It must belong to the Rom," said Annie surely, "for they are always brown like this and have so many children they must have forgotten this one." She held it close. "Little dearling," and rocked it as it began to mewl again. "Are you hungry?"

It was a problem indeed. Much as she would like to keep it, feeding it would be difficult for she had no milk or a pap pot, even if the goat was still milking well.

"They can't have gone far, Odi my dear. Perhaps we should try to find them?" She cast about the clearing, examined several small paths leading off it and eventually chose one which was well beaten down. Odi ran on ahead, stopping to listen now and again. Annie hurried after, firmly patting the baby to try to stop it from crying.

After some way, Odi almost fell into a big clearing where the Rom were making camp amidst a clamour. There were many women and children, a few men and some fierce-looking dogs.

"A babby!" yelled Odi, to gain their attention, his cap askew, his great eye exposed from his flight. "A babby!"

By the time Annie arrived the screaming had reached fever pitch and with the dogs baying, it was a terrible din. As she stopped, behind the shocked Odi, they had all disappeared into the surrounding undergrowth, just leaving the threatening dogs.

Catching Odi to her fast, she comforted him, for he had been terrified by the noise and trembled violently. Many dark eyes watched her from the dimness of the forest. Then a young man stepped out with his hand raised, palm out, towards them. No word was spoken. The forest was suddenly deathly silent.

"The babby," said Annie, holding out the cloth-bound bundle towards him. "Be it your babby?"

The young man swiftly stepped forward and took the child, his face breaking into a grin, fine white teeth bright against his dark face. He laughed and said something, in his own tongue twice over, throwing his words over his shoulder into the dimness.

"Don't be afraid, little man," he said kindly, patting Odi on the shoulder. "They meant no harm, just you gave them a fright coming out of the trees so suddenly." He smiled gently to Annie in sympathy.

Annie carefully straightened Odi's cap, the hair in place a curtain again and the man nodded in understanding. Then he clapped and whistled and one by one, all the tribe came out from their hiding places, the dogs silencing at last. The mother who had forgotten her baby roundly slapped her eldest daughter who was meant to mind it. Yet before long, laughter and gratitude replaced the fear and tears. Annie and Odi had found new friends.

That night and the next, they stayed with the Rom. A huge fire was built, big stones all around so it would not creep and set the whole forest alight. Odi was shy at first, for he was not used to company and the children stared at him. But the young man was speaking in their own tongue very firmly to them, so eventually they began playing with him. The little brown baby safely at her mother's breast again, they laughed and rejoiced and a splendid meal was made of roasted coney, while a fine iron pot soon bubbled with a herb and barley pottage. The young man was especially friendly and later, when most were sleeping huddled together under piles of ragged rugs and skins, he sat by Annie and talked quietly. He told her his name was Han and asked her the age of the boy, and if he was hers. Annie felt easy with him and told him of her own dead baby, her lovely foster-son who had been killed and how she came to rear this one.

"He is a fine, bright boy," said Han. Which warmed Annie's heart for of course, she had come to love Odi most deeply, as her own. Her distaste for him of early days long gone, he was her family now. They sat in the darkness of the night, the fire flickering and making shadows on the surrounding trees. Han passed an earthenware flask of mead which warmed them and loosened tongues. Now and again he threw scraps to the dogs who crept about the fringes looking for food and eventually, they all slept around the dying fire.

In the morning, Odi and some of his new friends went back to the cave to fetch the goat who badly needed milking. The cat had disappeared, no doubt distrustful of the strangers, but it would surely reappear. Annie was happy to share the milk with the children while the mothers baked little breads on the hot stones.

"I must go look at my snares, Han," Annie said. He listened carefully, for she was not very easy to understand, speaking through her nose because of her deformity.

"I will come too," and rose to go with her. Then, while they collected the rabbits, he laid the snares again. Annie watched him frowning, feeling something familiar. Seeing her expression, he began laying a snare on the bare earth of the forest floor. In stages, very slowly, he laid out the sticks and twisted grasses without a word. When he had done he looked up, smiling broadly at the silent woman again.

"It was you," she barely murmured, "you who helped me. You who taught me how to catch conies," and surprisingly began to weep.

"And who was it who left good money for a hungry lad to buy bread with?" Han held her fast, rocking her, soothing her with gentle words while he stroked her hair. "I am glad we meet again Annie, for be sure, we are good old friends."

Annie had not been so happy for a long time and now she laughed and cried and all the tribe were told the story and the fine iron pot was shown to her and so it was that fate had played a hand which would be with them for very many years.

When the elders of the tribe were not foraging, they sat about the fire and sang or talked. Odi tried to speak like the other children, for he understood now that he need not talk through his nose as Annie did. Easily, being an intelligent child, he soon picked up their Rom words and enjoyed their games. Han cut a branch from an elder tree and whittled away at it, at last making a tune. Handing it to the boy, he nodded encouragingly. Odi was enchanted with his little flute and began to play. An older man gave him a tiny, sharp knife, "for finding the babby", so he learned how to make his own little pipes and soon was quite proficient at making them as well as getting sweet sounds out of them.

They always looked out for the Rom after that. Annie never gave them money, for she felt it wise not to do so. But she always gave them something, if not food then clothes. For compared with her, they were desperately poor. While she had just one child to mind, they had far too many and she noticed how the little brown children barely wore clothes, often shivering with cold. As every year Mistress Weaver made far too many clothes for Odi, she always managed to carry some extra, just to give away or leave where she knew they would be found. Word spread to other tribes of Rom. The woman and boy were good. So it was that the grateful Rom mothers looked out for her and in return for her bounty, they had occasional company and Odi had children to play with.

"If you see Han," Annie would say, "give him my best." Which they would, for messages and news were precious with people who no one wanted and who neither wrote or read.

Odi would remember their meetings with the Rom, and their warm communion with them. How they were welcomed, unlike other folk, and warmly accepted into their camps. He remembered how Annie delighted to speak with the women, all day and often till late at night, usually while making pegs or baskets on the edge of the green-wood. Whenever possible he sat close and listened to their gossip, learning of women's ways; of coupling and childbirth, neither things which he and Annie knew aught of.

Pointing to an elder daughter one day, an ancient, toothless Rom woman, told them of how, when she was a girl, and far too young to breed, she too had been taken and gotten with child.

"She began birthing right there in a village, so we carried her out and laid her on the sward by the road. How long we stayed by her I don't know, it seemed like days; it was terrible. I was sure she would die, for the babe was stuck fast, and she no longer even screamed, for her weariness." The old one lifted her ragged skirt to wipe her rheumy eyes which not only watered as was usual, but now shed tears in memory of that dreadful occasion. "Then a monk stopped by us, where all others had run past, careful not to look. It seemed he was a healer, for immediately all was calm, with him on his knees by my girl. In no time he had us running to make a fire. He boiled up the yellow flowers and washed his hands and her down with the water, speaking quietly all the while. Then," she covered her eyes with a dirty hand, "he put salve on his hand and first went into her to discover what was wrong. Then," she paused for effect, "he took out fine scissors and cut!" Even Odi gasped, but no one noticed him for they were all intent on the story. "He cut her down there, to the side, not the centre, for he told me it was the best place to heal. There was blood everywhere and a little foot came first, but the next moment the babe was free, and came quickly into the world, bawling loudly."

"Oh my, oh my!" said Annie, as she always did when she was amazed.

"He told us that the babe had been lying around the wrong way, and together with such a young girl, was unable to come out," she wiped her eyes again. "Anyway, for sure he saved her life, eh?" she called across to her daughter. "And now she is a grandmam too."

For a long time Annie shook her head repeating, "Oh my, oh my!" at the tale while Odi mulled over it and kept it stored in his excellent brain.

Once, Annie and Odi, having missed their road in a fog, took a longer route than usual. They followed the river which grew larger every day as new streams joined it on its way to the sea. The days were fine and autumn was merely threatening. Yes, it was lovely having one more journey before they must return to the village for winter. One day they went with a little boat, crossing to the other side just to explore a ruined castle. The fisherman even gave them two fine trout for their supper, happy with the day perhaps, or the tiny coin which Annie handed him. They climbed to the top of a knoll where tumbling stones littered the steep banks. At last at the top, they looked across the river, while the sunset lit a magnificent and colourful sky. They sat for a long time gazing from their vantage point, enjoying the beautiful view. Annie hugged her boy to her. This was a time of contentment, when she really appreciated her freedom. The little nanny-goat was gone now, but the cat still came with them, as a dog. Except when strangers were near when he melted away, to reappear maybe hours later. Perhaps he followed their smell, or their voices. But he always reappeared just when they had become fearful, so happily endured an extravagant and loving welcome. By now he was a huge cat who fed himself off the land, and sometimes even fed his humans.

They had found a half ruined hall and laid out their cloaks and made a fire to cook the fish on, all the while scolding the anxious and hungry cat. Luckily the place gave them some shelter for in the night it rained and a cold wind blew. Annie looked where the view had been now covered with driving rain and regretted her dallying. They packed up their few things and set off down the hill again, hoping to find a boat once more for they were on the wrong shore. The river now roared with the night's rain, and crossing would not be easy. Still on the wrong side, they slowly made their way up-river till at last they came to a small town with a wooden bridge so they crossed safely. Now Annie hurried for they were still out of their usual familiar country and they were wet and cold and anxious to reach one of their secret shelters. Greatly daring, Annie stayed on the road for it was so dark and blowing, she knew few folk would be abroad and she was afraid that she would get lost if she tried to take a quicker route across country.

So it was that they met Han again. A different Han, black from head to foot he was, a great sack weighing him down and leading a heavily loaded pony. Annie stared at the white eyes and shining teeth of her old friend only recognizing the voice.

"Han my friend," she went forward and stood before him. "Are you now a charcoal burner then?" Ruefully Han shook his head.

"Tis coal, Annie. Not quite the same as charcoal and much more heavy." They walked along, all feeling more cheerful with the company and bent into the rain as it blew horizontally. Han told them he had a wife now and that he had gone to dig up coal so that she and her old mother would be warm in the winter especially as his wife had just born a little one. Annie was intrigued with his story and before night fell they came to a poor village where Han kicked open the door of a mean cottage and led the pony in, his friends following.

"Who you got with you?" a querulous voice called from the dark interior. Han murmured to Annie and Odi to wait a moment.

"Tis friends of mine mother," he unloaded the coal in a corner with a thump onto the earthen floor. "They will stay the night for it is right bad outside. And see," Annie heard his messing with the poor fire, "I have brought coal to warm us."

A rush light was lit and Annie saw Han's wife through the smoke, a pretty, very fair girl lying by the fire with a swaddled babe in her arms. So he married out of his tribe, she thought. Pretty girl too, as she hunted about in her many pockets for some candle stubs she had cadged from a monastery some time back.

With daylight, they saw they were in a very poor one-roomed cottage. The thatch was all black and rotting, many of the roof beams broken and rain fell in hissing on the fire. The pony stood with a sheep on one side, hanging its head, obviously relieved to be rid of its burden. Han fussed about fetching water for it and an armful of greenery. Then he unhooked a brace of coneys from a hook in the roof, skinned them and drew up the embers of the fire with a stick. Soon the coney were roasting, giving off a good smell and Annie and Odi crowded near the fine heat and admired the tiny baby which seemed to please the young mother.

"Her name is Hannah, after her da," the girl said shyly.

"Poor black little thing it is too," grumbled the mother not moving from her pile of bracken. "A boy was what we needed, a fine handsome boy, fair like my daughter, and look," she spat deftly into the fire, "what we got, a black little gypsy girl."

"And her da is black too from digging coal for a grumpy old mother," Han strove to keep the irritation out of his voice. "So I shall be off to wash at the burn, you come along with me Odi, so to help me carry more water back."

Despite the ill-humoured old woman, they had a pleasant enough evening. The girl, who was called Gilly, seemed to come to life in the warmth of the fire and company and she sang sweetly. Odi and Han played their pipes while Annie tapped on her bronze pot, so the evening passed well even with the old woman's continued grumblings and the rough surroundings.

In the morning with the light, after milking it, the old woman went out with the sheep and Annie took Han to one side.

"Here is a gift for your babby, Han friend," she said, and pressed her one real treasure into his hand. A small gold coin, it was none-the-less shining and beautiful and Han felt first surprise, then a surge of gratitude. "I found it," she said, "long time back and I want your little maid to have it for luck."

"It is too much, Annie, too much." But Annie stubbornly shook her head and nodding at Gilly said, "It will be useful one day no doubt. If you pierce it, you can put a cord through it so the babby can wear it round her neck."

Gilly was entranced, turning the coin this way and that, biting it, rubbing it till it shone ever more brightly. All the while a bewildered Odi watched the present giving and receiving with surprise, for he knew how much Annie loved her golden coin, that and her precious brooch of twisted silver. He well remembered when they found it, for as Annie said, it was truly a gift from the earth. They had slept under a curtain wall of a ruined castle, well sheltered from weather and folk when in the early morning, Annie had nudged him awake.

"See, Odi my love, see there, straight before us, Master Mole is digging up little hills while he searches for his breakfast." They watched idly as the sun rose, fascinated by the ever growing row of mounds of fine earth. Then, something shone amongst the spoil and Annie crawled from the warmth of their bed and went to see what it was. "Oh my, oh my," he heard her mutter as she spat and polished and then showed him the little gold coin. Now, held in Gilly's hand in similar awe Han said, "We shall do that, Annie girl. Next time you see us, she shall be wearing it be sure. Thank you, Annie, thank you," and kissed his daughter with, "lucky wee Hannah."

They left before the old woman returned. Annie pressed her covered mouth to the baby's brow and Odi did likewise, kissing the tiny thing extravagantly. He loved babies, any sort of babies, be they of man or beast.

The plan was to retrace their steps to where Han had dug the coal, for Annie was intrigued and determined to carry just a little with her for their evening's fire. They plodded along skirting the wide puddles along the dirt road. As directed by Han, they turned up a track in order to go over a hill which had outcrops of coal on the other side. Other folk were already there when they arrived, black as had been Han, with a few head-hanging beasts waiting to be loaded. They ignored the new-comers and went on with their hacking and digging. Annie went forward, looking in surprise at the black face of the hillside, for she had never seen the like before. Picking up a piece she weighed it in her hand. It was heavy and big, very black and shiny, not at all like charcoal. She hesitated considering that they already had good bundles which were heavy enough by the end of the day. Still just a little might be interesting so she bent and picked up another piece, remembering the comfort of the night's fire. Suddenly something struck her on the face. Shocked, she looked up to see a bear of a filthy man bearing down on her.

"Taking my coal, is yer?" he yelled and threw more at her. "Get off, thief. Dig your own. Get away from my coal." Seeing she did not move, he picked up a huge black lump of slag and hurled it with all his might at the silent, shocked woman. Odi began to scream. He was big for his age, strong and well-covered from a good life and his scream was fearful. Picking up what he found at his feet he tried to defend Annie by hurling them at the man. With his youth and rage combined he did well but it only brought forth more abuse. The others hurried closer, each with their hands full of rock and slag and they showered down on poor Annie who by now had fallen to the ground. Pulling off his hat, Odi screamed even louder, showing his great eye which as always terrified the foolish and so they fled, leaving the two crouched in each other's arms on the black earth.

But something was wrong, for Annie moaned and held her face with both hands and could not speak. How they got back to Han's poor house Odi did not know, for he was weeping all the way, while Annie moaned quietly as she leant on his shoulder. The jaw was broken and Han looked sorrowfully at his friends, realizing that he should have gone with them. There were other wounds too, on the side of the head which he tried to bathe but it was all congealed with blood and coal dust.

Han bound up the broken jaw and laid Annie on a rough bed of bracken close to the fire. They poured a trickle of milk into the corner of her mouth but it all came back messily. The girl Gilly seemed frightened while her old mother kept up a running complaint at the return of the newcomers. Ignoring her, he curtly told his wife to mind Annie and with the boy beside him, Han strode back to the hill where the coal cutters were.

"I'll have her things now. Now!" Waving a stout stick at them. After much shouting, he got their bundles back and had a lump of slag thrown at him for his pains as they left. Then they hurried home to find Annie no better.

Han realized that Annie was dying, for her breath became ever more ragged and she seemed unable to do or say anything. She died in the night, fortunately while the boy was sleeping. Well aware that she must have her treasures secured all about her person, Han went carefully through her clothing and put the coins in a cloth which he tied up tightly for the boy. Taking a little silver knot brooch from her shift, he pinned it onto Odi's and held him close for a moment. When he was done, hoping that the old woman had not been watching, he covered her carefully and went out into the cold dawn to dig a grave behind the house.

Distraught, the boy sobbed himself into exhaustion while they buried her. As soon as it was done, Han loaded up the pony and led Odi away, feeling it was better to be on the move than let the boy mope in that dreary place.

"Will you show me the way lad? I know that you spend every winter at Annie's old village, where your parents are the weavers?" Dumbly Odi nodded and they silently set off, each with their own thoughts and fears. It took them three days.

At the little shelter on the outskirts of the village, they stopped.

"I won't come any closer, Odi my boy," said Han patting him lovingly on the head. "Tomorrow when I am gone you must go to see the priest about masses for Annie and find the weavers. Many folk do not like Rom, thinking that we bring bad luck and if they see you with me, it might go badly for you." Gently he lifted Odi off the pony and sat him on the couch at the back of their winter shelter. As usual, it was messy as they had not been there for some time but despite new tears, Odi began tidying up from habit. "I will light the fire while you go and bring water."

Once more Han held the boy tightly in his arms. "Odi. You are a good boy. Now my lad, hear me. You must not be afraid for we shall meet again be sure but meanwhile, I am going to teach you how to get help if you need it." He bent down, looking carefully into the good eye. "If you are in a crowded place and are in trouble, could be one of our people will be there too. Now to show that you are one of us, you must learn this." He lifted his handsome head, opened his mouth and a strange sound came from his throat. Odi was first surprised, then a flicker of a smile crossed his face. Han made the sound again and urged Odi to try to do it too. Side by side, they repeated the sound until Han was satisfied.

"It is like a coughing owl," said Odi and Han beamed.

"Exactly, clever lad. Now you remember if you are lonely or in trouble, try it, chances are that someone who knows will hear and come to you. And Odi my boy, now you know it, if in turn you hear the coughing owl, you must seek who it is who is calling. Look after yourself and the cat and be sure to eat well so you grow into a fine, strong man. Do no wrong to any soul and you will be rewarded somehow, some day." Turning him around he gave him a little shove. "Go my boy, go find the priest and the weavers while I tend the fire, be sure we shall meet again."

Odi was surprised by the kindness of the welcome he received from the village people. The squire drew him into the hall and sent his wife running for a bowl of bread and milk while a maid ran to give the news to the weavers. Arriving still wiping her hands on her apron, Mistress Weaver even kissed him, then shed a tear at the news that Annie was dead. Yet Mistress Weaver was desperately anxious, for with Annie gone, who would look after the boy? The weaver ignored the crisis and got on with his work, banging the loom bar harder than usual so all the village could hear it, just to show his disapproval.

Having explained as best he could of Annie's death and her burial, Odi spoke with the priest and offered to pay with the money they found on her for masses to be said for her soul. That done, the problem of the boy remained and after he had tidied Bee's grave as they had always done,

Mistress Weaver led him from the church weeping, her hands twisting in her apron. Taking him to the stable where he had laid when a baby when Annie had come, she told him to sleep there and she would see him in the morning.

As soon as it was dusk, Odi left the stable and returned to the security of the shelter outside the village which was home to him. Odi was in shock. He had no more tears. She had gone. His Annie. His mother, sister and best friend had gone and had left him alone. He knew about the money under the hearth stones for Annie had grown careless when she hid it away so he was sure he would never be hungry. It was being alone which he found so frightening. Later that night, the cat crept in which was a comfort and snuggled down beside him, keeping him warm. The soft soughing of the wind in the trees eventually lulled him to sleep.

When he was a man, Odi would look back on his wandering the land with his gentle foster-mother as the happiest childhood, his first life. Now as the child slept, mentally exhausted by the recent events, little did he know that a new life was about to begin, a life of terror and sorrow. A life alone, a life without Annie.

CHAPTER TWENTY THREE

THE ARISTOCRATS, FELICIA

Oh that nasty, fat, pasty little man! She pursed her mouth and drew her breath in sharply through her thin nostrils. How dare he keep me waiting so long. Insufferable, uncouth, pig of a man, an abbot indeed. The Lady Felicia wriggled on the hard chair she had been offered, and raged inwardly at her misfortune in having to be there.

"You must, my dearest child. We need him," her aunt had coaxed in her gentle way. "How can we manage to survive without the Church's help? You know as I do, they are so powerful, so wealthy, and know everyone."

Felicia had picked at her food. It was all too true. They could not manage. Life had gradually become too hard, every problem insurmountable, their dream, their lovely little dream was on the verge of being extinguished.

"I will try, aunt," she had said, really meaning it. But her opinion of most of the holy men she had met had been very low. Just once had she seen this abbot, at Easter, two years previously. A small, round man with chins, little eyes, and clammy, pudgy fingers. Having to kiss his hand! Ghastly. Those beady eyes watching you, those sideways whispers to his monks. What was he saying? What unpleasant things did he find about them to pass on to his fawning acolytes?

She gazed around the little room, admiring the panelling, so fresh and new, unlike theirs at the manor, which was dark with smoke and wax. For the thousandth time she asked God why he had taken her parents and sister from them. Not forgetting Etienne of course. She had been unwell, with, what her aunt had supposed was some childish ailment so they had gone to court, taking Nicola with them. Despite her disappointment, she had enjoyed staying behind with her aunt and her old husband Sir Gervaise. Having no child of their own, they loved her, whereas it was common knowledge that her parents loved the beautiful Nicola. She had, in so many ways, become their child. Just things seemed so hard without her father, who always coped with the financial storms of the small estate, the taxes and the bills, which so frequently beset them.

It must be close on one hour now, she fumed. He must be trying to break my courage. What was the man doing? What did abbots do anyway? Apart from going to church, and eating, which reminded her that she was hungry, breakfast was far behind, and supper a long way off.

A knock on the door caused her to sit up straighter, and a wizened old monk put his head around it and beckoned her.

What, does this woman want of me? Adam, whose real name was Adun, the abbot frowned and bit his lip. He feared and mistrusted these high-born ladies, with their bony noses and flat chests. He doubted it would be money, for although his informant had told him that they were always very careful, they were not paupers. With a charming demesne such as theirs, good land too, and interesting connections, with old Sir Gervaise in charge, now that Sir Nicholas and lady were dead, he wondered what it could be.

She entered and made a curtsy, just right, not too low, yet not an insulting bob. To avoid kissing his hand again, she moved swiftly to the one chair in front of the table where he sat.

"Good day, Lord Abbot," her voice moderate, polite but not gushing. "I am grateful that you will spare me a little time, but as my ride home is a long one, forgive me if I come straight to the point of my visit."

So, he thought, she is reprimanding me for keeping her waiting is she? At least she didn't try to kiss my hand. He inclined his head for her to continue.

"Since my parents died, we have been somewhat at a loss as what to do with our lives. My family, you understand." He nodded.

"Our sorrow was so great at their loss, for almost a year, we were unable to take part in life of any kind, just staying within our bounds, mourning."

He nodded. So what was all this leading to? Haughty, ugly girl.

"My parents sadly lost all their sons, just we two girls surviving till adulthood, and alas my sister, also now departed." She paused while her mind's eye dwelt for a moment on her sister, Nicola who always got her own way, the pretty one. Dismissing the thought she went on. "Our manor is a small one, albeit beautiful and fruitful. We all feel that in thanks to our forefathers and to our Lord, we must do something worthwhile, something which will make our lovely place alive once again." How am I doing? Does he appear to be listening, understanding me? Am I going fast enough, or too slowly? She coughed delicately.

"Last year," she raised her eyes to make sure he was attending, "we found a baby boy left literally upon our doorstep. Of course we took him in, and by the Grace of our Lady and with our inexperienced but loving care, he thrived, and is well. I named him for my late fiancé, Stephen. We suppose that word had got around that we had taken in one foundling, for then on Saint Anne's day came a baby girl, an enchanting little thing, Anna, a sister for our Stephen. My uncle and aunt now find themselves grandparents, while I, a single lady, find myself a very busy mother." She smiled, as she had practised in the one mirror they possessed. Which, he observed made her almost look pretty. Perhaps he could recommend her to smile more often?

"As you may know," she continued, "there is no charity house or orphanage in this area. I do not wish us to become such either, for we could not cope. But we would like to offer a home to children from good families. Perhaps orphans with some means so to be able to contribute towards their own keep. Or, and you will have to excuse my bluntness," she paused, "we would welcome any base-born children, for it is not their fault that they were born out of wedlock. We would be their family and our name and home will be theirs."

She stared at him fascinated, for it seemed his eyes would pop out.

"Of course, some financial help would be most useful, and they would be safe, educated, introduced to good families, perhaps later, advantageous marriages made for them." She took a deep breath, thought swiftly of more intelligent things to say. Heaven knew she had practised enough.

"Whatever the background of the children, we will teach them, according to their gifts and abilities, and every child, boys and girls, to read and write. My aunt and I will teach the girls how to be the best housewives, with all the womanly arts and crafts. My aunt and I are passably good embroiderers, which of course they must learn to be too. My uncle, will teach the boys estate management, hawking, hunting. Last but not least, they will learn manners, and how to conduct themselves in high society, should their way so take them. My uncle," she raced on, half aware of his shock, "requests you to find us a gentle priest to live with us, so that the children might learn the ways of God in their daily life. We have a simple chapel. However base-born they might be, we could legally adopt them if their natural parents so wish. He is a loving and caring man, my uncle, and likes the idea of being a patriarch."

Oh God, my Heavenly Father, she knows, they know! Help me, a sinner. Oh blessed Mary, Mother of God, you know how I have tried to make up for my sin. Oh woe. Someone has found out about my lovely Maria. All my care, my efforts to protect her have failed. Lord, in your mercy, help me to protect them.

"My Lord?" Felicia watched horrified as the man before her changed colour, first red, then white. Despite her tender years, she was used to making decisions and giving orders, so seeing a small hand bell on his table, she rang it fiercely. In remarkably short time, a young monk appeared, breathless.

"Wine if you please, my lord abbot is feeling the confines of this room."

Still very much in charge, she held the glass steady for the trembling man to drink.

"If you have a cloister," knowing full well they had, "shall we walk and talk there in the fresh air. This room is a little stuffy."

They walked, somehow Felicia had placed his arm upon hers and she made a brave show of supporting him. They walked in silence for some moments, Felicia peeping under her headdress at the charming cloister.

"Forgive me if I shocked you with my words, my lord. I do understand that you lead very secluded lives here. Away from the evil world of wayward men who abandon foolish women to the shame of bringing a child into the world without God's blessing of marriage. But," she found she was babbling, "oh if you could but see our children! They are angels. No one can blame them for their base-birth. Whoever they are, of whatever place in society, high or low, they are the children of God. It is we who are blessed with their innocence, which is why we so badly need help with their schooling, their books, their everyday needs. If we could find just a few more children with reliable sponsors, they could all share together, and we could give them all, a good life."

He had recovered himself a little, perhaps after all, she did not know his secret. He even offered a slight smile as he moved to a seat and offered her to sit.

"What if you should marry, Lady Felicia?" he asked sensibly.

She did not answer immediately, considering his question seriously, a good sign. Her request was not being dismissed without consideration.

"I was betrothed for a short time, my lord. My affianced was a gentle knight who alas died in the same plague epidemic which took my parents and sister. At first, I thought my life would end. I considered going into the church myself. Then the little boy Stephen came to us, then Anna, so I understood that God had a life for me, apart from marriage, a life with love and children. Yes," she took a deep breath, "I cannot say now that I will not meet a fine knight who appeals to me, but my uncle and aunt have sworn that they would not oblige me to marry against my will. I loved Etienne most deeply, yet it was a young love. Perhaps when I am older, I am yet sixteen years." She hesitated. "But then as you see, I am not a beauty, my sister had it all, alas my plainness and small dowry would not attract many men," and laughed lightly.

"But you do have a charming smile, lady." There, I have said it. Which caused her to smile and yes, she could, as he had observed before, be almost pretty.

The cool air and time had made him feel himself again so to practical matters. The abbot looked at the sundial, almost time for church. He rose and led the way slowly back through the beautiful cloisters, to his rooms.

"You must take some refreshment before you leave, lady." He beckoned a hovering monk and gave an order. "Come and sit in this little guest room and refresh yourself before you set off".

The room was light and airy, simply furnished with table, chair and couch. Felicia stopped short, gazing at a woven mat laid on the floor. Apparently without thought she sank on her knees to see it better, her stiff habit billowing out around her. Feeling the texture with her fingers, looking on the underside, she was filled with admiration for the work.

"I see you like our mat, lady, a gift you know, from the hands of a good widow woman." Liar, liar that you are. Elspeth is your wife, your life, your all, but the world knows her as a widow. And so she is, my poor dearling, a widow of the church.

"It is so fine my lord, so much better than the eternal messy herbs which we strew. And look," she lifted a corner, "the dust goes right through, so can be swept, beaten and turned, so clever. Now if only," she paused, "My lord, a favour." She sat back on her knees, eyes bright with enthusiasm looking up at him, greatly pleased with herself. "Will you ask the maker of this fine mat to come to visit us so we can learn from them. We can even pay, just a little, for we have many fine rushes in our moat, and this could be something we could teach our children. We could make mats for our own use, even for others, another small income perhaps." There, aunt dear, it is done, as you instructed me.

The tray brought was lightly laid but with delicious scones and fresh cheese, a small smoked fish, a pair of eggs and some salad. Felicia ate thankfully for otherwise she would surely be feeling quite weak by the time she got home. She thought about Robert and Giles the grooms who rode with her, but consoled herself that they could look after themselves very well and no doubt had.

All the way home she mused on the visit to the abbot which she thought had been a success. Perhaps she had been too harsh in her judgment of him, after all, he could not help his looks, any more than she could.

"Was it worth it?" pressed her aunt. "Will he send any more children, paying children too, for we will not manage otherwise."

"I think so, aunt, I hope so." Felicia bit her lip, trying to remember.

"Do you think he guessed that we know of his woman, the mat-maker and of his daughter?"

"No, aunt, I truly do not think so, I was very careful."

A mere seven days passed when a letter came to reassure them.

Most gracious Lady Felicia,

I am trusting this letter finds you and your good aunt and uncle and all your household, in good health which by the Grace of God I found you last week.

It has been my pleasure to think about your requests, and feeling that your ideas are gracious and kindly, I do believe that I may be able to help you, as well as some needful children.

Meanwhile, the good lady who plaits the straw and reed mats tells me that she will be honoured to attend you at your manor. Sadly she is not in robust health, but can certainly teach you enough for you to learn to go on yourselves. As she has a young daughter, a good, gentle child, she asks if they may both visit you, the first week of next month, and stay as long as you have patience for them, or need to learn from her.

I await a reply by the messenger who carries this letter, and end by assuring you that my prayers to the good Lord will be to send blessings upon you, your aunt and uncle, and the little children in your house.

I am your most obedient servant in God, Adam, Abbot of Phillby.

"Aunt, aunt, quick, pen and ink, he will help us, and the mat-maker will come to teach us." Eyes shining she whirled about, lifting the fair boy child at her feet and swung him round too. "It will be alright after all, my little Stephen, we shall survive."

Mistress Elspeth was quite the most charming, gentle and humble guest they could wish for. Her daughter Maria, a serious little girl of ten years, was just the same. Felicia and her aunt worried over the fragile health of the lady, feeding her good country soups, and healthful tisane. On fine days they went to the moat and full of laughter and a lot of mud, cut their reeds.

Maria became the elder, greatly loving sister of the two toddlers, soon losing her serious demeanour with their childish games.

"However did we manage without you?" was constantly heard, for Maria was truly, a blessing. No one at that time ever thought that she would remain at the manor for ever, assisting Felicia with their growing family of children.

The abbot was true to his word in all ways, not only sending children, but provisions. He visited regularly twice a year, seemingly unable to stay away from the relaxed, happy atmosphere of the small manor. A new peace came over him as he watched his loved ones become part of a family, safe, cared for and really appreciated. God is good, oh but I thank you Lord, forgive me for doubting Your greatness.

He had of course, discretely delved deeper into the family affairs of Sir Nicholas de Elancourt and found that his connections with France were responsible for the original wealth which caused the manor to be built, and what a manor? With so much glass in the windows, the house shone from far off like a jewel. His had been a new blood-line born of trade, while his lady had been of the oldest, most elevated status of the land. It had been a love match he understood, something which gave him a small flash of pleasure. It was all too rare for the gentry to be able to choose their spouses, the families ever jostling for more advantageous matches for their young. Which is why he, a poor scribe, had been firmly dismissed from courting his Elspeth. How could they, the thought milled in his head for ever, marry her to a man older than her father? Yet, in the end, poor old man, he was the loser, and after her husband had died, Elspeth had welcomed him, borne his child, and now was more or less safe, by the Grace of God, under his protection.

No fine knight ever did come to woo the Lady Felicia in marriage. True, she was no beauty. True also, her lands were small and hardly worth the sacrifice when there were plenty of heiresses with greater estates to pursue. The manor was, perhaps and thankfully, off the beaten track, a good thing in those troubled times, so they were unmolested. The years passed joyfully, their family grew, the women the hub of the house, while old Sir Gervaise grew to a great age, the nominal head of the family.

He, Mistress Elspeth and one little child succumbed to a great sickness which swept the land. How it came to the manor they did not know, for hearing of it, they kept much to themselves.

"My Lord Abbot," Felicia wrote with her neat small hand, "it is with anxiety I write to you in all haste to request your presence here for we have the Sickness, and our Mistress Elspeth is gravely ill. By your goodness I urge you to ride with all haste, for in her delirium, she asks for you."

By the time he arrived, Sir Gervaise was laid out in the little chapel, and Mistress Elspeth lay fading fast. Holding her cold hand, Adun the scribe, prayed for her soul, imploring his God to take her into his hands, forgive her her sins, and keep her safe. So that when the Day of Judgment came, he implored, they could stand together and proclaim their love as never before.

Felicia watched him silently, seeing his anguish and sincerity. Only she came into the sick room now, for fear of the rest of the family taking ill. The shutters were closed so it was dim, and fragrant smoke filled the air from the small brazier. She was tired, tired to death really, having stayed close to her uncle, and now to Elspeth, dear friend. The children had been driven out to the loom shed, a new building just built last year, fresh and light and hopefully healthy. Meanwhile it was all a new game to them, except Maria who understood.

While he prayed, Felicia wandered about the room, tidying where it was not untidy, straightening, where it was already straight. Children's voices rose from the garden, and going to the window, Felicia opened it, letting a shaft of sunshine fall on the bald head of the abbot.

"Adun?" a frail voice came from the bed. Felicia watched quietly as the hands were kissed fervently, and saw the smile on the dying woman's face.

Felicia turned her back so she could not see their agony. Elspeth, her only true friend was fading and soon, would be gone. Strange how that ugly little man had such a gentle woman so devoted to him. Love was such an odd emotion, as an illness, catching here and there without reason. She rested her head on her arms and closed her eyes.

When she woke, she heard him praying for the dead and knew that her friend had gone. Swiftly she moved to the bedside, seeing the tears streaming down the ugly face while the lips murmured the prayers. Carefully she crossed the hands of the dead woman, and wound her rosary in between the still warm fingers.

"What great solace, my lord, that you were here to help her passing so gently and with such love." It was as if he did not hear, for he continued until he had finished and then, turning, through swollen eyes he looked at her.

"I was so wrong about you, Lady Felicia, forgive me," he spoke softly but clearly. "I thought you were just a foolish, proud, aristocratic woman who despised me, knowing me for what I am, a simple man." He took the napkin she offered and carefully blew his nose and wiped his eyes. "She told me many times that I was wrong, that you are special, kind, great-hearted. Now I understand that she, in her wisdom, saw clearly, without the foolish false fears I had."

Felicia stood silently beside the bed and listened.

"I had such ambition lady, to become a bishop, if you please. I tried to deny my love, my precious wife in God, my beloved child. But love is God-given, so she told me, a precious gift not to be used lightly, or ever denied. So till this moment, from the day you came to me first, I owe a great debt to you, and your family. For Elspeth knew such contentment here with you, my child too, and learned so much. All I pray now, good lady, is that you keep Maria, as your other children, for she will miss her mother, even if she has known in her heart that her death would come soon. For myself, lady," he stood up, "I will go into the forest and find a cave and leave the rich trappings of the monastic life. I will worship and give thanks to God in another way, innocently, with purity, living simply instead of in comfort."

Felicia's heart and mind raced, juggling his words, trying to see the future. If only she were not so weary. To pass time she took up a small ewer and brought a basin, poured out scented water and offered it to the abbot to wash.

"You are in pain, my lord," she began, feeling for the right words. "Time will heal, but now, do not do anything too hastily, for this is when you might make mistakes. Be kindly to yourself, as you would to another who has suffered a mortal blow. Think carefully on your future, and for those, as Maria, myself, our little family, and how we depend upon you and the bounty from the church. Will the next abbot be as thoughtful and generous to us as you have been? Shall I be able to care for the children as I have with your help these past few years? For feeding and educating a growing family needs worldly wealth, which, as you must know by now, we have but very little. So I ask you to think again, not to abandon your ambitions or to abandon us in this small manor. I ask you, my lord, to make no hasty decisions, mourn now and decide later, when you are calm and rested."

The silence dragged in the quiet room. The sun slanted down to the West and the evening sounds of cattle being brought in rose to their window. She knew that she should go down to help prepare the evening meal. Yet knew too that the women of the house were doing it right now, realizing that she was needed upstairs. These moments were so important. They must not be lost, for if he did become a hermit, abandoning his present life, it would be very bad for them.

"Elspeth told me your story," she spoke quietly, steadily. "How when you were a scribe to her father, she loved you. How her father's mismanagement in trade caused him to fall into such debt, that she was married to his creditor, an old man, kindly, but not you. She told me that the moment he died she found you, a monk by then, tempted you and drew your child into herself. Poor Elspeth, she never forgave herself for her sin, which is why she endowed the most part of her late husband's wealth to the church. Yet she told me more than once, she had no regrets of her actions. For she so loved you, and was ever grateful that your love bore fruit." Surprisingly, she took his hand and held it strongly. "Never fear that your secret will be broken. Be easy that Maria will be our child, yet welcome you as our abbot, a special uncle, when you visit us, as you have, when possible. Fear nothing, my lord. Mourn your loss privily and we shall all pray for her soul publicly."

So Elspeth had told her all. Well, it was a relief. No more pretence, no more lies. Someone knew all about it, and that Maria was his daughter. A calmness began to fill him, a gratitude so warm for the dead women on the bed, the tears began to fall again.

"Ssh, ssh, my lord. Guard your sorrow now. Do not forget her for Maria's sake, for that is what you will do. Especially with your assistant monk who even now must be wondering why we take so long here." Going to the door, she held it open. "We must tell Maria and the family now, my lord. You must lead our prayers and prepare for her burial tomorrow together with Sir Gervaise." She straightened her back and looked at him kindly. "You will do," as she scrutinised his face, dabbing it with a cool, wet cloth. "Enough with the tears, take courage, for now you must give comfort."

Even after he became bishop, Adun visited the manor, and for some few days forgot his burdens and rejoiced in life. Those who had thought him a pompous, jumped up-fool, very gradually, almost changed their minds. For surprisingly, he did become a true man of God, ignoring the wealth and fripperies which were to hand, and used his time and good mind to help the poor and needy.

The Lady Felicia was surprised when she became famous for her family and school and more children were sent to her than she could cope with. Other houses were set up about the country, often by widows not wishing to remarry, or childless couples. Bishop Adam took a deep interest in them, and visited them all. Well they might smile at the little man who seemed more like a pedlar the way he passed on gossip, poems, stories, patterns or wondrous coloured wools for embroidery. Yet they were pleased, even touched and often more than grateful to him for his care.

Maria became Felicia's quiet and efficient assistant, firmly refusing all offers of marriage. She had grown into a serious young woman, lacking the bright smile of her mother, yet with such a great tenderness for the children, so they loved her. Little Anna, the second waif whom Felicia took in, made a fine marriage to a wealthy widower. Small and young though she was, she ran his house efficiently, took over his children and soon had a brood of her own. Word went about in the big houses that the Lady Felicia nurtured good girls. So if little dowry was required, there were pliable, well-trained potential wives in her care, who were surely worth a fortune. Felicia grew old gracefully, for the dream had succeeded.

CHAPTER TWENTY FOUR

STEPHEN

Stephen regarded his work with satisfaction. He was learning, he smiled at Jerome who grinned back. Altogether, his new life was far more satisfying than the old. For much as he loved the manor and the people there, this was his place and the new house was progressing well and going to be beautiful. Carefully he honed his adze and chisel, wiped them and wrapped them in a cloth soaked in pig grease against the damp.

He had learned so much in the past year, it was marvellous. Jerome had scoured the forest for a suitable outcrop of rock, then got in quarryers and stone hewers to cut the stone. At first Stephen had helplessly watched the men drag the stones on sleds through the forest rides, then across the causeway. He watched in awe as confidently they first set up the hurdles for scaffolding, then the stone foundations of the house, abutting the tower. For the plan was that the house would envelope the base of it. As it went up, timbers and stone together, he began to help, till by now, he was almost a craftsman himself, who tried his hand at everything. He stood back and surveyed the door which he and Jerome had just put up. He had wanted a fine door, being the main door of the house. It faced south, with the tower shielding it from the north wind. The front door was oak, strong and thick graced with fine ironwork made by one of Jerome's sons and yes, it was strong but also beautiful. Jerome had been perplexed at first, but now he too was proud. Stephen wondered when they could start building a new house for Jerome and his family, for theirs was a very poor affair. He understood that it was not because of a shortage of money, for Lee, the healer, had left his children well provided for. He had watched, impressed as the Lady Fleur had handed out silver and gold coins to the builders, very different to Lady Felicia at the manor who guarded every penny. Indeed so fair had Fleur been, paying up without delay and well, there was never difficulty in finding good workmen. The hewers, sawyers, masons and thatchers passed the word far and wide, so not only were they never short, their workers were good. He pitied the fool Sir Godfrey who thought by his title and castle, he could order the men to come to work at his place at his will and for a pittance. But those days were gone, and the artisans of England were free to come and go and work when and for whom they chose.

The Lady Felicia would be arriving any time now and he felt excited by the thought of all the things he had to tell and show her. It had dawned very slowly in his uncomplicated mind, that the Lady was his natural mother. Little things which had slipped out over the years, showed him that he had not been an adorable baby boy left on the doorstep, but that he had been born in the manor. The Lady Blanche and Sir Gervais, had, when they were old, also let slip little things which had puzzled him. Then, last year, when they had ridden here, the Lady had almost confided in him, urging him to marry the Lady Jessica. Not only were the Pomeroy women in serious need of a man to protect them, it was necessary to get Jessica married. As they knew her, it seemed that it might be a sensible match for him. Stephen had been shocked, for Jessica had never appealed to him, whereas her cousin Moya had. Not only was Jessica rather plain, sadly not favouring her mother but the old baron, she was rough and frankly unladylike. He did not speak for some miles, riding along with his thoughts going this way and that. He well knew that if The Lady had a plan for any of "her" children, no one could change it. It would never have occurred to him then that she might also plant the seed of the idea into Jessica's mind too. Undoubtedly, as he realized later, that was why Jessica had announced they were to wed, not even waiting for adult intervention or for him to ask her.

It was a tiresome marriage. She was, as always, not an easy young woman and if it had not been that Stephen was the mildest, kindest of men, no doubt it would have been tumultuous. He had soon learned never to argue with his wife, but to just let her have her way and go his. Hence he had immersed himself in the building of the house, which was proving so successful, even to his gaining of confidence in himself. Having been raised by a powerful woman, it was really not so difficult to cope with the new one. At least she was with child. That had been the greatest good fortune, for it had eased his duties towards her, and she seemed happy to laze about, day after day, getting ever fatter. Seeing how Jerome loved his children was also an inspiration to him. He now looked forward to having a little son to teach everything which he had learned, to share his life.

A sound alerted him, causing him to pause and frown. It was a thin, piercing cry, not a marsh bird, not familiar at all. He cocked his head to listen and it came again. Was it his name being called? He walked out into the open and looked about. A cloth being waved from one of the small slit windows of the tower alerted him. Then he realized it was Fleur calling, and putting his tools down, he ran.

"Water," the call floated down, "fetch water." So he changed tack and filling two oak buckets, ran carefully up the stairs, two at a time, into the great upper chamber. It sounded as if the birth had begun. Lady Fleur greeted him gratefully as he put the buckets down by the hearth, glancing towards the bed.

"The child is born," she said rather abruptly, "a most exquisite little girl child. Call the women," and returned to her work. "Come back in a short while, after I have made them tidy."

It seemed that everything happened at once. No sooner had the women stripped the stained bed and re-made it, a shout came that the guests were on their way. Running hither and thither they worked, and in between their labours, they all praised Jessica who sat up in bed, her face a picture of surprise and pleasure to be suddenly so popular. With the babe washed, bound and tucked into the old Pomeroy cradle, they were just ready when the sound of voices and many steps on the stair announced their visitors' arrival.

It was, they all sincerely agreed, a most beautiful child. Even the Lady Felicia, forgetting her disappointment that it was not a boy, almost shed a tear of emotion when she saw the tiny girl. Fair, it had a look of both her father Stephen and her grandmother Fleur. Privately Fleur saw for a brief sad moment, a likeness to her long past, tiny dead son.

Stephen never forgot the day when his daughter was born. The fairest day, warm and bright, and how he and the guests were all enchanted by the new arrival. The general mood was light and joyful, even Jessica was happy. That it had all been incredibly easy, was an added bonus.

She was baptized Felicia, of course. The Lady Felicia and Moya stood God-mothers while, and from old habit, there was Jerome, who stood as Godfather. The Lady had thought to bring many fine gifts, silver spoon and cup and spurs, thinking it would be a son. Moya, pleased with her new role, had nothing, so gave her one treasure, the lump of amber.

During the happy days which followed, Stephen showed The Lady his handiwork and she was generous with her praise. She thought that she was still a young woman, strong and determined, yet she seemed softer now with the passing of years and her love of and pride in Stephen were quite obvious.

The little Felicia throve, with Jessica mostly always happy, pleased with the diversion and company. Joan was especially kind to her niece, brushing her hair, dressing her, all the while telling her tales of her father the baron, when he was a baby, making them all laugh.

Before the party left, Joan took Fleur to sit on the log seat by the stream. In her heart she knew she would not come here again. She was old, and her home was the one place she wanted to be. There, together with Anders, she hoped to pass their last days peacefully, especially now as their sons had good wives to run the place.

"Fleur my dearling," she took her hand and pondered at it absently. "What I must say, I must, though in truth I may well be wrong. Yet say it I really must, or I would be tardy in my duty. For I am getting old and fear that I will not be visiting you here again."

Fleur looked at her bewildered. What was all this about?

"You remember my telling you of when I was a girl, when my own mother died and the old baron my father, took me back to live in the castle with his new wife?" Fleur nodded. "It came to me very slowly, because I saw her every day. Something was wrong, the forgetfulness. Not," she added hastily," like me, getting old, more than that. Vague. Silly. It seemed that the older Lady Jessica gradually lost her hold on life, which was more noticeable to me, when Roland and I went away. Each holiday she seemed worse, till at last I realized, young though I was, that she was losing her wits. I did not think there was anything which I or anyone could do for her, except give her kindness and understanding." Joan stopped and stared at a flock of water birds, startled from their feeding, who took off with loud cries of alarm. "It is some time since I saw your girl, Jessie, over a year at least. And Fleur, dear God-daughter, it is so familiar, her demeanour, her giggle, everything." She covered her face with her hands for a moment. "Roland escaped it, even though he favoured his mother in looks, his humour was all from our father's side. I am fearful my dear, fearful that your Jessie is the same as her grandmother." They sat silently for a moment. Fleur sighed.

"Well as you know," Fleur replied quietly, "Jessica has ever been a trial to me, and if there is nothing to be done about it aunt, at least I am forewarned, and I thank you for telling me your fears."

Stephen had also noticed his wife's vagueness and alert to the many perils which might befall his precious daughter, he did many things to protect her where her mother did not. He built light wicket gates for the top and bottom of the stairs. Other ones, great reed arcs, for each of the hearths. He blocked all paths to the stream so that when the little thing began toddling, she might be stopped, before falling in. Not that Jessica was any trouble. She had indeed grown milder and more biddable with time. Her one occupation was to stitch their family arms onto canvas, over and over again. It was surprisingly fine work. Even when the little Felicia was weaned and toddling about with her father, grandmother or the maids, Jessica showed little interest in her, even eventually indeed in anything, in her hounds, falcons or her past delight of hunting. The tower, then the house, was slowly filled with cushions, table runners and cloths and hangings, all depicting the arms which Fleur had drawn up for her. As Fleur's tapestries graced the walls, it did not matter if Jessica failed to create anything new or of note. So long as her hands kept busy she was quiet.

By now they were mainly living in the new house. Bright and light, it was big, yet nowhere as huge and tiring as the tower. No longer was it a desolate neglected place, for they had soon created gardens, a summer-house and all the new buildings round about were strong and handsome. Even Jerome had, urged on by Fleur, at last built a fine new timbered and thatched house for his large family, which he could stand up straight in, unlike the previous low one.

If visitors came, they were put up in the tower. They were usually family, but occasionally strangers came, tax collectors from the king, and very interested in everything. Unpopular men generally, they ate and drank their hosts out of house and home, and then demanded grumbling, to know what was left to give the king.

"As you see," Stephen quietly waved his arm to encompass their surroundings. "We have little. One hundred acres of marsh land with water fowl, fish and eels, and little else. The best we can send to our liege lord are reeds for roofing for his houses. Of that we have plenty." And so it was agreed, for it was obvious even to those hard men, that there was little else.

When Felicia was three, she was a very personable little maid. Pretty with her fair curls framing the sweetest face, she strove to help her grandmother and father all she could. Her mother, ever sitting and sewing, she barely noticed, except to pick up the fallen yarns to give back to her. Jerome's sons now had children and so she had cousins to play with, except that they were set to working very young, while she was a young lady, only fit for light tasks. Kneeling beside her grandmother, planting seeds or picking fruit, her little fingers worked deftly while Fleur's grew knotted and painful from work and the damp earth of the marsh. It was a peaceful life, with few interruptions to routine, for they were well off the beaten track.

Few travellers chanced upon them, for they were on the edge of the forest, by the marsh, and not on the way to anywhere.

By the time Felicia was four, her mother had retreated into a world of her own. Fleur and the maids washed and dressed her, put her sewing into her hands, and setting her food in front of her, at least she still managed to eat alone. Stephen had long since abandoned all thought of more children, ever fearful for the one treasure he had already. Yet he was kind to Jessica in a practical way, building seats about the garden, with little creeper-covered shelters so that she could sit out on fine days.

"Come Jessie," Fleur drew her along a path, little Felicia taking her other hand. "Come and sit in the sunshine and watch out for the dragonflies, the kingfisher, or watch the fish rise." Fleur carried a thick felt cloak which had belonged to Roland and wrapped it about her, for there was a capricious little wind. Whenever possible she took her daughter out, far away from the house and where she worked, for Jessica never stopped talking. True it was quiet speech, a mumbling to herself, occasionally cut by foolish laughter, but it irritated Fleur and her patience ran thin. "Wait for a moment, Jessie, for we have forgotten your work basket. Wait while Felicia brings your sewing." Taking her granddaughter's hand, she turned to go back to the house brightly telling her, "father will be home soon my love, he has gone to see to the eel traps."

Jessica sat on the bench and obediently looked over the water at the fish rising suddenly feeling pleased, for Mother had said that Father would be home soon. She smiled. She hadn't seen him for a long time, he must have been away. Whenever father came home, he brought her a gift. She smiled in anticipation, wondering what it would be this time. Holding the cloak tightly about her she watched for fish and thought again, father will be home soon. A fish jumped, silver and gold, beautifully reflected in the shimmering water of morning sun light. She leant forward to see where it had gone to, watching the ripples disperse, ever widening. Then a shadowy movement caught her attention and she leaned out further to see better. There, smiling up at her in the stilling water, was her father, wearing his thick felt cloak. Her smile ever wider, Jessica held out her arms. Joyful, she called out, reaching for him, "Father!"

Puzzled, Felicia gazed about wondering where her mother had gone. In her hands she held the basket of sewing which she put down and wandered back down the path calling for her. An hour later, the frantic searching at a standstill, Stephen noticed something green in the dusky, marsh water, just under the surface. It was Roland's cloak, which had covered Jessica, trapping her under its thick folds. Careless of his thick brais, Stephen jumped in and dragged his wife's body from the dark water, calling out loudly, that she was found.

They took her next day on a bier to Castle Pomeroy to bury her in the crypt of the fine new church beside her father, brother and grandfather. Riding through the forest, Jessica's bier on a dray, they stopped at small settlements to tell the people, all well known to them, all knowing too well the Pomeroy family and their story. Messengers had ridden out speedily with the news, so soon Lady Felicia came with a small party, as did a few other gentry from round about.

The new self-styled baron, Sir Godfrey being away, the bailiff reluctantly did what was correct and opened the doors of the castle to the mourners. Fleur looked straight ahead, her heart and face cold. She was certainly not mourning the death of her daughter, who she considered had been lost to them for a long time.

The air was thick with dust so she knew immediately that the hall had just been swept and re-strewn. The walls were also newly hung with painted cloths as a ladder still stood in place. She eyed them critically. The colours were too bright and crude, the painting rough and hardly artistic. So they had not replaced her hangings which now adorned the marsh tower, using cheap wall coverings instead. Yet, quietly taking in the condition of the castle, she mourned her old home, where she had been born and grown up. Here she had known security and happiness. Here her father, Lee, had taught her everything he knew, and here in the end she had been baroness.

"As soon as we decently can, Lady Fleur," said the Lady Felicia in her penetrating voice, "we must leave this filthy place." Her words carried out of the hall to the anteroom where the bailiff and his slovenly staff lingered in apprehension. "Never have I seen this castle so neglected, my lady. Your husband the baron would be utterly shocked by the condition."

Joan and Fleur exchanged glances and Fleur smiled to herself. Never before had the Lady ever addressed her as anything other than Fleur either. Lady indeed! And as for Roland being shocked? Roland who only thought of food and drink in ample quantities, he who had noticed nothing? Ever!

No sooner was Jessica buried, than they returned to their new home in relief, the Lady Felicia with them for a few days. Little changed, except there was less work to do without Jessica to tend and mind for.

Now Fleur delighted to work in her stillroom, urging the willing Stephen into making racks on which to hang her herbs, shelves on which to set her jars. If her knowledge was not as great as Lee's, her enthusiasm made up for it. Besides, with the marshes, there were many and new herbs to work with, so she searched in his book, poring over his detailed drawings and descriptions. As her eyes faded, Fleur used the bright eyes and clever fingers of her granddaughter. Felicia seemed to know instinctively what she was searching for as they wandered along, baskets on their arms.

Many of Lee's old patients still came for help for their ailments. Many new ones, on hearing of Fleur's art, found their way through the forest rides and along the marsh paths for theirs. Wounds and broken bones were laid before her to mend, and Fleur thought back to her life with her father, and felt happy. As of old, one never knew what each day would bring, but it was very good being useful, her father would approve. Bluntly she told herself that her life was as she wanted it, quiet. For with Jessica with her endless chattering gone, the silence was quite like old times at home with her quiet father and silent brother.

They had become a very small household. One old dairy maid had returned to the village to be with her family, leaving just a young girl to help Fleur. Not for long however, for one of the Jeromes took her to wife. A poor little girl, she was lucky to find such a fine husband, while he was glad, for there were few girls about who were free to marry.

Stephen worked as two men, not only hunting and fishing, he tended the garden, growing fine vegetables and fruit in the rich marsh soil. Once or twice he left to do his knight service and then, Jerome's family came daily, bringing logs for the fire, or rods for the peas and beans, withies for eel traps and baskets for produce. The two families helped each other, dependent yet independent. While Jerome provided milk, cheese, butter and meat, Stephen's small family supplied fish and eels, fruit and vegetables. They bought flour together from the miller, often trading their produce for it. Jerome fretted because he wanted to grow his own barley and oats for his beasts, but had no field or space. Life was however, satisfactory for both families, becoming rather commonplace, yet contented for all of them.

The first winter after Jessica died, was a hard one. First it rained eternally, so the water rose and Stephen had to block up the new front door, taking a ladder up to a window to get inside where somehow they were always wet and cold. The new house seemed to have gained new cracks with its drying out and the wind came in. The icy wind swept off the marshes, froze the milk in the dairy and made the fires smoke. At last, in despair, they moved back into the tower, lighting huge fires and burning charcoal braziers as well. Huge it might be, but the middle room was protected from above and below, the thick walls and glazed windows keeping the winter fury out. Here, Fleur slept with Felicia in Jessica's great bed, while Stephen, drew out a truckle bed from underneath for himself at night.

When at last the rain ceased, it became still and bitterly cold. They stayed in the tower, but at least they could go out in the winter sunshine to visit Jerome and keep warm by gathering kindling. It was a time Felicia would remember all her life for the marsh was frozen and she enjoyed new games with Jerome's grandchildren. Voices shrill with excitement, they went sledding and skating on smooth slices of ox bone made for them over the years, on the miller's great stone wheel.

It was during this time that one of Anders' sons came to plead with Fleur to go with him for his parents were both gravely ill. Packing up her big basket with herbs, Lee's precious stone close to her breast, Fleur kissed her granddaughter Felicia goodbye and left within the hour. For the days were so short in mid-winter, they must hurry to be there by dark.

Felicia always remembered her grandmother although she was by then just five years old. Little things. Being in the still room hanging up bunches of herbs or putting a horn spoon of honey in her mouth, because her teeth hurt. A song she remembered, a spinning song, soft and repetitive. But her little world was empty, with her grandmother away, and every day she asked Stephen, when she would return.

Stephen learned what happened late one night when Moya appeared, half dead with cold and sorrow. Pushing her into a chair close to the fire he went down to the stable to welcome Moya's brother and to attend to his horse and the poor pony, which being Fleur's, at least had found her way home and led them through the snow safely.

It was as if Moya could not speak with her sorrow. The fire burned low, a heap of hot ash still warming the room, yet the ice was in her heart. Moya gazed into the dying embers remembering the horrors of the past weeks. Illness everywhere deep, agonizing coughing which racked the body and left it broken, so it could no longer fight for life. Fleur had arrived when Anders was already slipping away, the frantic Joan worn out with her own illness, desperately trying to reach him to draw him back. Nothing could help him but Fleur worked on her God-mother, trying to give her nourishing soups and potions to ease her cough, thus to keep her strength. Yet it seemed that after Anders died, Joan just gave up, refusing to take anything.

All about them people were ill and dying. Fleur treated others in Ander's family, yet one daughter-in-law and two little grandchildren went with Joan and Anders. Others in the village came and begged for help, which Fleur gave unstintingly, until she too, by now utterly weary, became ill.

"Go to the tower, Moya," she begged, gasping for breath. "Go now, before this epidemic gets you. Ask your older brother to go with you. Take my pony, she knows the way even in the snow, and," reaching into her breast she drew out the stone, "take the stone and book and mind them well." Telling her quietly what her father, Lee had said.

Moya could not believe that both her parents were dead. Yet it was not yet finished, now this precious one, God-mother, aunt, kin, friend, healer, now perhaps she was going too.

"Do as she says," ordered her eldest brother, who since the death of his parents had become as a rock to them all. "Sit at the board, Moya, and eat a good bowl of pottage before you go. Wrap up very warm and I will tie sacks on the pony's feet so that she doesn't slip. Come, my dear, for you are needed to care for Fleur's granddaughter. Only then will she rest easy. The family will see to her, only go." No sooner had he arrived at the tower had he left, anxious for those left at home.

Stephen held a horn cup to Moya's cracked lips and urged her to drink. Hot milk and honey. After the first sip, she took it, feeling the comfort of it course down her throat. Gently, Stephen eased the cold clothes off Moya, wrapping her in a great soft woollen sheet and carrying her to the bed where he and Felicia slept. With rag-wrapped hot stones at her feet and back, Moya began to feel warm for the first time in days. Then she slept, Stephen laid on one side, the child on the other, a long, safe and healing sleep. It was well into the next day by the time she woke, wondering where she was in the still dimness of the tower.

Two days later, another brother came with Jerome, to tell them that Fleur had died, but quietly, in her sleep. So perhaps her heart had just stopped, exhausted. They had already laid her to rest beside her baron, son, daughter and father in the crypt. In turn, they silently embraced the desolate Jerome, who gazed out over the marshes, his eyes empty, gone, the last one, his precious sister. Stephen raised a finger to his lips and turned his eyes at his daughter. Need she be told yet? She was so delighted in having Moya there, and copying her grandmother, was tending her. Better leave it for the moment. Yet it seemed as if the child knew, for she no longer asked for Fleur, even speaking about her often and so naturally.

"I think it is wonderful," said Moya when the day was done, Felicia was in bed and she and Stephen were sitting by the fire. "Like a miracle. As if she knows, still loves and always will love her." They sat staring into the fire. "She sacrificed herself for me, Stephen. She wanted me to come here, to get away from all that illness. And see," she looked directly at him, her hair escaped from its coif, glinting gold in the fire-light. "I am not ill. But had I stayed, I surely would be now."

Stephen put more wood on the fire wondering. The Lady Fleur had been the strangest woman he knew, so quiet, so wise, so able. Nothing like his lady mother Felicia, with her imperious manners, yet she had also organized her family in the same way. Had she guessed that he loved Moya? He pondered on it. He thought that perhaps she had and was biding her time, for she had often spoken of Moya, singing her praises and worrying that she did not wed.

"She loved you dearly, Moya, for she often told us so. Indeed she had plans for you to come to stay in the spring. So dear lady, be easy in your heart, for she was very wise, very kind. I believe that she would have far rather had you for her daughter, than poor Jessica."

Spring came at last, and to their surprise they found many changes on the marshes. Once again the river had gone its own way, cutting corners and by chance in doing so, causing their land to raise up considerably. They first laboured long and hard on the house, living upstairs while it dried out. It took time in finding a mason to cut square stones to lay on the floors as the water had ruined the beaten ox-blood and earthen floor. Moya taught Jerome's family to make strong rush mats, and struggled to make salve for her own poor cut fingers. For most of the herbal salves which Fleur had gathered, had been used up during the terrible winter, and Moya merely knew the common simples which everyone knew, not Lee's secrets. There had been no need to learn, with first Lee, then his daughter always there to care for and heal them. Perhaps she might seek knowledge in Lee's old book which together with Fleur's Book of Hours lay wrapped in silk in the dry salt niche in the great fireplace. So it came about that she and the little Felicia sat and went through Lee's herb book, and when they were out, would try to recognize them and gather them.

"We must try, dearling," said Moya deep into the book, "and you can learn your letters from it, for it would be a grave sin to let all this precious knowledge be lost."

To those, who not knowing of Fleur's death came for help, Moya did her best, but asked them to pray for her God-mother's soul, and for guidance for her. Even when she studied Lee's book, she was afraid that she had no gift for healing, there was so much to learn and she often wished she had done more, when Fleur was alive.

Stephen, Felicia and Moya became a family. At first it was a calm and caring relationship between them all. Yet gradually Stephen felt a new yearning for Moya, a strong, all enveloping need which he could barely conceal. Moya felt it too, a powerful lusty desire which set her body on fire, and made her ache unbearably. Yet having never had a man, she held back, a grown woman, not a maid, yet a maiden.

They came together by accident, which was the best way, with their tender souls. Felicia and the children had gone with Jerome to fetch flour from the miller, always a popular outing, and Moya was warping the loom, a job she did not care for. With a grunt of disgust, she forced herself to go on when she was interrupted by Stephen who came in, his finger cut from gathering reeds. Taking a dab of pork dripping and a wisp of clean wool from a basket, she wrapped it tightly around the cut and held it firmly to stop the bleeding.

"Why are you looking so sour, Moya?" he asked, happy to be held so close to her. She was surprised, then smiled.

"I do not like setting up the loom," she replied, "and I am no longer feeling sour, because you interrupted my work."

They were so close. He looked down at her and marvelled at her fair good looks, her strong bones and her soft mouth, so close to his. Moya felt a curious faintness at having him so close and noted his fair beard and strong teeth stretched in a smile above her. Then, leaning forward a fraction he pressed his mouth on hers very softly, then, quite forgetting the finger, he took her in his arms. As if in a dream he pushed her towards the great bed where they all three slept every night, and lifting her onto it, he took her face in his hands.

"I love you, Moya. I have loved you since I was a little lad, and now my body yearns for yours and I will take it."

So astonished was Moya, so impressed with Stephen's manliness, she gazed speechless at him while he lifted her skirts and ran his hands over her flanks. It was a glorious loving. At first tender and exploring, then frantic with need, they embraced and joined and with a cry were one.

Afterwards they lay spent, on top of the bed holding hands.

"What now?" asked Moya quietly.

"Now," Stephen replied smiling, "I make a little truckle bed for Felicia," Which caused them both to laugh merrily. Moya had never thought that she could be so happy. Remembering the little Stephen when she had first gone to the manor, even then, by children's standards much older than he, now she felt him older, her love and so manly. True, he was far taller than she, and in many ways wiser. It was a good thing she realized, that they were just three in the home. For their need to love, touch, smile, and when Felicia was out of sight, to caress, were all powerful.

Having lost both mother and grandmother so young, so close together, seemed not to effect Felicia at all. For her home was happy, she was secure. Moya watched the years pass, with only one regret, for no child was born of her union with Stephen, despite their love and passion. Even so she had a child, a wonderful daughter who gave her pride and joy every day of her life. In order not to send Felicia to the manor, Moya taught her all she knew at home. What a foolish thought, as if anyone could keep the precious child away from her paternal grandmother? So Felicia went away, as had her mothers Jessica and Moya. Even her grandfather Roland and her aunt, had gone away to learn. As Moya had taught her so much and so well, she already spoke French and Latin, even if there was room for improvement in household tasks.

An unexpected letter came from the Lady Felicia imploring help from Moya. She read it several times, consulting Stephen on what the truth was behind it.

"My dear young kin, Moya,

I trust that you all keep good health at the marsh house, as do we at the old manor. It is with sorrow that I give you the news that our good friend the bishop has died. Maria, whose benefactor he was, is especially sad, and I ask you to receive her when Felicia returns home next time. We are also very short of fine coloured yarns for our tapestries, which Maria is now trying to learn about. It could be that round and about your home there is fine material for her to work on. A gentle occupation which might fill her mind as it seems to make her happy. So my dear child, in the name of the Blessed Mary, I ask you to help her where you can at this sad time. For it will also benefit us all, as lately, our source of fine colours has gone, and our supplies are all used up.

My constant prayers are for you, Felicia and Stephen, Your devoted friend always,

Felicia."

Stephen read it again and handed it back.

"It is quite clear to me, for I believe that the bishop was Maria's natural father. Looking back to my childhood, and you know how children observe things, I remember how he loved her, especially after her mother died. Hence she is mourning so deeply for him." He thought silently for a moment then brightened. "Yes it is a good plan, for if the dyers made so many wondrous colours, why in time, shouldn't you and Maria. It will be a happy occupation for you to work on together." In saying so, he lifted her up and kissed her deeply.

By the time they arrived, Maria was already more cheerful according to Felicia, who had proudly escorted her along the way. The grooms too enjoyed the change, although they returned after a few days, their pack ponies laden down with good things from the marsh. For Moya was learning how to smoke the eels of which they had plenty, and the Jerome men had become expert in making little wooden casks in which to transport them. The Lady Felicia had sent many gifts as was the custom, so they gladly sent by return, what they could.

Maria really did brighten, it was true. For years she had lived at the manor, always a willing helper to the lady yet her happiness came from the bishop, whom, she told them, she had known all her life. It was he who provided them with the wondrous coloured wools for their needlework, he who had been so kind towards her widowed mother. Stephen looked at his food in rapt attention at these words and Moya busied herself over the fire.

After that, Maria came every year, sometimes twice. They planted a dye garden on the rich marsh loam and soon there grew a small patch of madder, English marigold, another of alkanet and some distance from the house, a small field of woad. They happily scoured the woods and marshes for other plants to get interesting colours from, and Moya was thrilled with the new interest and furiously busied herself with it. Having been the last-born to a highly capable woman, she had rather lagged behind in housewifery duties. There had been no need for her to toil hard, for with her mother's efficiency, and her brother's wives learning from her, the young Moya had never had to work. Now she span every spare hour of the day in order to try out new colour experiments sometimes to their joy, others to their disappointment. One of the Jerome wives even taught her to make woollen stockings, which she surprised herself by excelling and every evening she had her basket by her knitting away. There were always folk so happy to be gifted with them, which gave Moya an unexpected thrill. Jerome's sheep were studied for the softest, whitest fleeces, and bought before they were shorn, to be cleaned before shearing.

It was a huge flock by now, indeed, just as did Jerome's family seem huge, with sons, grandsons and even great grandsons. They all seemed to look the same which Maria remarked on in confusion, tall, blonde, with snub noses, pale blue eyes, and rosy cheeks. Apparently always cheerful, their outdoor lives seemed to suit them for they were rarely ill. If they did not tend the flocks, they cut reeds, wood, or made charcoal. Very gradually, so as they barely noticed it, the woods gave way to open land and bordering what had been the old forest marsh road, there were now little fields of oats and barley about Jerome's large toft.

Every year Stephen organized the cutting and delivery of reeds as agreed with the tax collectors and because of their obligation, the Jeromes had built several flat boats to use when cutting in the bitter winter. Then they poled them down-stream, there to hand them over to the authorities at the first town. Little did they know, but their reeds were considered the best and much sought after. For not only did they cut them long, the marshes about the tower were distant, the reeds undisturbed and of good quality. Each year Stephen expected the return of the tax men, yet, unusually satisfied with the honest and prompt delivery of the reeds, they stayed away.

When Jerome died, quietly as was his way and an old man, his family buried him in the forest by a little spring, and forewent the services of a priest. The people from the tower, the miller and his family, and a few others attended. It was a strange yet beautiful funeral with Stephen reading from Fleur's book of hours, and every one who came, brought a rock according to his ability, to lay upon the grave. When it was done there was a fine cairn there, a fitting memorial to a good man. As they rode home, Stephen pondered sadly on how Fleur had left just one child of her body, Jessica, then his Felicia, while Jerome had left a veritable tribe.

The years passed with a gentle rhythm. Felicia grew tall and beautiful and was a joy to her parents. For although Stephen and Moya never wed before a priest, they were the most loving parents any child could wish for.

Once more their lives were ravaged by a terrible winter of storms when it rained constantly and the water rose again flooding their precious gardens and ruining the causeway. Great trees came crashing down, taking others with them. At least it saved the Jerome family from cutting them down, and they provided great stacks of logs to re-build the causeway, and for burning to dry out the house.

Now in desperation, Stephen decided he must put in willow hurdles all about where the garden had been, so that they would grow, a protection against future catastrophes. Instead of cutting reeds, he and some of the Jeromes took the boats and cut great bundles of withies and planted them to make a safe island for the future, should they be beset by more storms.

When the water went down, they saw that yet again the river had changed its course for the miller came, wringing his hands. His mill race had dried up and he could no longer mill the grain.

All the neighbouring men came to the old mill to consider this new catastrophe, for they depended on bread for life. An old mill, no one knew quite how old, it was obvious from the ragged foundations all about that it had been part of an ancient and large settlement. Coins, old and of no use and bits of bronze, bright glass and pottery were ever being turned up, apparently from a once wealthy village. It would be very tedious to have to get out the old querns to grind their grain again. There seemed no solution but to find a new site downstream, build a new mill and move the great stone wheels, an enormous task.

No sooner had they begun dismantling the wheels than the miller and his son mysteriously left for the town, "to borrow money" so said his wife, who was left behind. They were all rather bewildered by his sudden departure, yet went on with shifting the stones when other work was slack. Meanwhile, with many complaints, the women got out the querns and bread was subsequently scarce, whereas before it was a staple.

Moya felt sorry for the miller's wife, for now no one called by and she seemed so alone and miserable.

"Won't you come and live with us for the time being?" Moya asked her kindly. "Just until your men folk come home and the new mill is running? Yet Mistress Miller shook her head, twisting her apron in her hands and looked away.

"Whatever is the matter with Mistress Miller?" Moya asked her family, a frown between her eyes. "She seems afraid of me, me, who was always a friend to her."

As the following winter drew nigh and more trees came down, Stephen went alone to the poor, lonely, cold house where the miller's wife lived and ordered her to pack her things, for he would not allow her to spend another winter there alone. Still fretting, she eventually agreed and got her things together in her fine big bride's chest. Hoisting it on his horse, some bundles of chattels on the other, they walked back to the tower together.

At first the poor woman just sat beside the fire wiping her eyes, for surely her man and son should be back by now. Gradually, as the months passed, not only did she amply contribute to the spun wool for the loom, she joined in with the running of the home, always gently treated by the family who remained bewildered by her timidity. Stephen had put her in a wide bed with Felicia so she had company at all times. It was a small, upper room which looked out west on the road so she could watch out for her men folk. Her bride's chest was set beneath the window and they laid on it two fine cushions from Jessica's hands. Yet as far as they knew, the miller's wife never opened the chest, and they made no enquiry as to what she kept in it.

A year passed and the forest and marsh families were becoming desperate without the mill, the women tired of turning the querns and the men of never having enough bread to eat. Eventually, after much discussion, and permission from Mistress Miller, all the men went downstream, found a good site and began the huge task of shifting the mill stones and great timbers in order to make a new mill on the river's edge.

In the end, by trial and error, the Jeromes got the new mill working, yet still the miller did not return. So one of the big blond men and his family became millers and at last there was flour and plenty of good bread.

Despite their entreaties, Mistress Miller refused to go to the new mill or to accept money for the mill stones. With the passing of time she had become secure and happy at the marsh and tearfully asked if she might live her life out at the tower. A quiet woman, she had grown fond of her new family and enjoyed the company of women which she had not had at the mill. To Felicia she became a grandmother and to Moya, a constant help in all things domestic. They never heard of or saw the miller and his son again, so it was a satisfactory situation for all the family.

Having taken a cold from the February winds, Mistress Miller died quietly with Moya at her side. Right to the end, clasping the strong hands in hers, the poor woman gave thanks that she had been taken in so kindly and told Moya that her bride's chest and all in it, were hers.

Being ever busy, it was some time before Moya opened the chest and drew out many beautifully woven sheets and covers, a few clothes and some fine pottery. But there, right at the bottom, well wrapped in cloth, lay several objects, beautiful worked wine cups, bowls and a great oval platter which to Moya's inexperienced eye, all appeared to be of gold. Showing Stephen, eyes wide with enquiry, they spoke long into the night about this secret treasure. It was all guessing of course, but they thought that perhaps the miller family had stumbled upon it, for it was well known others had found precious things thereabouts. Perhaps the miller and his son had taken some pieces to sell in the city in order to pay to have their mill re-built in a better place? Perhaps they had been robbed and killed, or even having sold it, had taken the money and gone off to a new life.

"They would never do that," said Moya, "for they were happy, part of a good community and would never have left Mistress Miller. No, I fear the worst. Valuables invite trouble, so we shall shut this chest and forget it."

It would be years after Mistress Miller's death before Stephen would hear from some distant woodmen, that they had discovered two bodies wearing men's clothing in a shallow grave just inside the forest. There was nothing of interest or value found with them.

CHAPTER TWENTY FIVE

THE WOODMEN, ROBIN

It was mid-morning by the time the three horsemen rounded the river road and passed by the new little hamlet which had grown up near the Marsh Tower. The miller had told them about it, yet they paused, held by its beauty. The mist was still rising, so the top of the tower was not visible, yet the house, its windows gleaming, and the surrounding gardens, were as fairyland. They reined in their great horses, for a moment, and gazed spellbound.

It seemed as a castle surrounded by a moat yet there was a broad causeway to it, a solid wooden gatehouse barring the way in. The house seemed to surround the base of the tower as a kirtle. It had upper stories with wide overhanging eaves roofed with oak shingles. A wisp of smoke rose from the chimney, and the smell of bread wafted to them through the stink of the marsh.

Grinning at each other, the woodmen, James, John and Robin, urged their horses forward over the damp earth track till the leader raised his hand to halt them, and stood up in his stirrups so to see better. There was a fine, spring-green hedge all about the garden. Young willows were set in the water, as a wall, grown all over with briars and honeysuckle. As they paused, they heard the sound of singing which drifted towards them, as the bread-scented wood smoke. Now cautious, eyes alight with curiosity and humour, they silently urged their horses forward, intent on catching the words and if possible, to see the singer. A sweet young voice rose and fell, pausing, no doubt in some chore, before starting again.

"So, Oh, dig and delve and muck and rake for Mary and the Apostles' sake.

Come help me do good honey bee,

and sup the nectar from the briar,

or taste of the sweet strawberry

and rest upon the water lily.

So, Oh, dig and delve and muck and rake for Mary and the Apostles' sake.

Iris, pinks and gillyflower,

faces bright with sunny smile,

growing around the lady's bower,

carpeted with camomile.

So, Oh, dig and delve and muck and rake for Mary and the Apostles' sake.

Come work for me you humble worm,

pile up your casts upon the lees.

The day so fair, toil on the lawn

for man and beast and hearts ease.

So, Oh, dig and delve and muck and rake for Mary and the Apostles' sake.

Periwinkle, fair lavender,

oxeye daisy, germander,

beauteous, scented, growing free

flower for Felicity.

So, Oh, dig and delve and muck and rake for Mary and the Apostles' sake."

For a moment they waited for the next verse and realizing none was coming, grinned at each other, eyes bright and raised their voices in hearty unison.

"So, Oh, Dig and delve and muck and rake for Mary and the Apostles' sake!"

Which echoed cheerfully across the water, yet brought no acknowledgement from within the garden, just a rustle of wind in the trees. They stood stock-still waiting, hopeful, but the only sound came from the bridles of their beasts shaking their heads. Then the leader spied a movement behind the willow canes and doffed his cap with a laugh.

"Good morning. I call to the little lark who serenades us all so beautifully in the fair light of day." The canes rustled again and were still. Eventually, realizing that the singer had disappeared, they exchanged glances of amusement and digging their heels into their mounts, made for the gated causeway.

A good-looking blond man stood on the far side of the gate, an axe in his hand. They looked at him in astonishment thinking it was the miller, then realized that this must be a relative, brother or son, and hailed him courteously. Andrew Jerome looked the visitors over briefly, far more interested in their fine horses. War horses they were, huge and well fed. Yet the men up did not look like warriors, indeed they looked very ordinary indeed.

"Right," said Andrew, swinging his axe casually, "and what can I do for you, sirs?"

"Could be," one of the three rode forward, "you are kin to the miller who sent us this way to meet with Sir Stephen?"

Andrew nodded and opened the gate. If his uncle miller had sent them, they'd be alright. A boy came running in answer to his whistle and was told to call Sir Stephen and then Andrew led the way to the stables, his mind full of the fine horses.

They were shown into a hall, light and airy, hung with fine tapestries and graced by a board well set with silver. Long benches stood along each side with two fine, carved upright chairs at each end. Everything shone from care and the smell of wood smoke was subtly interspersed with that of lavender. A woman was at the hearth, stirring a great pot, and as they entered, she straightened up and tucked her wayward hair under her coif.

"Sir Stephen will be with you shortly, sirs, if you will sit awhile and take some ale?"

They looked about them impressed, for it was a new house with great windows, rush-matted floors and was especially clean and neat.

"Ale?" asked the lady again, wiping her hands on her apron, setting horn cups and a big shiny pewter pitcher on the board before them. Footsteps sounded outside along the paved way and the door thrust open. A handsome fair man came in, his brais and shoes trailing muddy water.

"Got him my love!" he exclaimed, holding up an arrow on which a dripping dead rat was impaled. "Got the devil with my second arrow, fair and square I did, except he dove into the water with my arrow still pierced right through him." Then he noticed the visitors and gave a short bow. "Sirs, forgive me, for I had man's work to do. My daughter has for some time been complaining of a bold great rat who digs up her flowers. Well," he grinned and held his bow up again, "I watched for him up in the tower, so he won't any more!"

It was a good beginning to a long friendship. The visitors could not help but laugh, so they all sat down and drank the good house ale with a dish of chewits and talked about archery and the art of killing rats.

"Are you all born together, Sirs," asked Moya, intrigued by the three dark and handsome men who were so alike. Again they laughed, for it seemed that laughter came easily to them. They pointed at each other, speaking all at once, till at last one spoke alone and told them that "Yes", indicating his twin and himself, "we two were born together, but", he made to tweak the ear of the third who ducked, still laughing, "this one came along to break our peace, just two years later."

When the introductions and laughter were over, they got down to business and explained that they were shipbuilders and they had come looking for great oaks. They had a contract with the king; for every ship they built for themselves they would build one for him. It seemed the king felt the need to form a navy to protect their shores, and the finest oaks of England were in these forests.

Stephen was intrigued. Shipbuilders? A navy? Talk went on to the current wars, the men of power, the sickness which came and went. Man talk, it switched to prices and shortages and Stephen was happy to hear the news.

Moya had returned to the hearth, and putting a rod into a cauldron, carefully lifted out strands of wool, a beautiful rich green. Unhooking the pot from the crane, she lifted it to one side of the hearth, there to cool.

Just then the door opened and a young girl came in, her skirts dripping. Ignoring the company she addressed her father, handing him an arrow.

"I got your arrow back, father," she said and tiptoed with her bare feet across to the hearth, as her father, trailing marsh water.

The men watched her, eyes glowing with pleasure for here surely was the lark who had been singing in the garden, a lark who was now receiving a good scolding from her mother at the wet skirts.

Robin was enchanted. Such a beauty! Such a clever lass too, to fearlessly find the arrow, a fine one at that. And those pretty feet? Despite the ale being mild, Robin felt himself intoxicated and burst into song.

"So, Oh, dig and delve and muck and rake for Mary and the Apostles' sake."

Stephen laughed with the rest of them while the maiden scowled.

"And my little lady," Robin persisted, "are you the Felicity of the song?" Felicia looked directly at him, unconsciously noting his dark good looks, his fresh complexion and his mud green-eyes. Barely dipping, she introduced herself.

"Felicia."

"I could not find the right word to rhyme with it," interrupted Moya. "But it is the same name indeed."

The men, obviously reluctantly, went out with Sir Stephen and clattered over the causeway to find the wood-cutting Jeromes who lived deep in the forest. They would know every great oak that there was, Stephen assured them, pleased that here was good work for everyone in the future.

Sir Stephen made them very welcome each time they came, housing them in the tower, and always giving them good, country hospitality. Sometimes they hunted with him when meat was short, and gradually many great trees held their mark, for the Jerome men to do the felling in the autumn.

The following year they came with great bullocks and drovers to shift the trees, a slow and arduous task which at least gave many men a livelihood. Not all the three brothers came every time, and it soon became obvious that Robin came most often, and just to see Felicia. For he never failed to bring a gift for her, and usually also for her mother. It might be a damp basket with some new plant. Or a small carving which he had done himself. The best gift he brought was a puppy, a small, whiskery little thing which he assured them would keep the garden free of rats and so he did. Felicia loved him as passionately as he loved her. They were inseparable, and because he arrived in July, she named him Julius.

"I fear that young Robin thinks too kindly of Felicia, Stephen," said Moya, carefully intent on her needlework. "I think it time you warned him gently that she is not available for a woodsman to woo."

Stephen paused for a moment. They had killed some geese lately and he was cleaning the feathers for fletching and putting some aside for letter writing.

"I like him," he said simply.

Moya rustled impatiently.

"And what has that got to do with it, sir? What will the Lady have to say if your one child goes her own way or makes such a poor marriage? No." She bit a thread and crossly surveyed her work. "You must tell him, and soon, before any pain is felt by any side." A silence hung between them. "And well you know that the Lady will choose a husband for her willy-nilly, whatever we or she has to say about it."

Stephen was unhappy with the conversation, for he still thought of Felicia as his little girl. Oh the pity of it that he and Moya had no children. Having just the one child was a truly heavy burden to bear.

It came sooner than they expected, for Felicia had a gift for her birthday, sent by the Lady, her God-mother, who alone remembered it. An exquisite chatelaine, worked silver, practical as well as being beautiful. Scissors and purse, needle case and key ring, each was a delight to behold, and of course Felicia proudly wore it always.

"So," said Robin, face serious for once. "Will your little maid be open to receive suitors now Sir Stephen?"

Giving a silent thanks to the saints for the opportunity Stephen replied as lightly as he could.

"No my lad, I think not. For her God-mother, the Lady Felicia is arranging a fine marriage for her. We shall have no say in it, I am sure. But then you will understand that being my only child, and though I say it myself, sweetly comely, we want the very best for her too."

The next time Robin came, Moya noted that he was better dressed than usual, keeping his old clothes for the forest, yet changing into his best for company. The gifts too, became more precious, so that Moya again felt that Stephen must speak out firmly.

"I cannot my dearling," Stephen held her loosely from behind, cradling her breasts and breathing in her hair. "How well I remember loving you so helplessly, always so near and so far. I feel his pain Moya," and held her very tightly. "I remember it. Poor boy. For I like him so well, and would not object if he made Felicia happy, and that I say most plainly."

In the garden, Robin stealthily approached Felicia and covered her eyes with his hands. She did not move away but lightly touched the hands which blinded her and sighed.

"Robin," very softly, "I know it is you, for I spied you coming along the ride."

They faced each other, eyes filled with hungry longing. They both knew that it was hopeless, yet because they were young and their love was so sweet and so tender, they still had hope.

"But he is not even a wealthy man, Stephen, let alone a knight." Moya paced their room, anguished by what she saw in the eyes of her beloved daughter. "She is so young. It is puppy love and will soon be over. It is our fault. Mine. I have kept her so close, when she should have gone to some great castle and met many other young people. No," whirling about to face him, "to give her heart to the first handsome man she meets."

They pretended not to notice, yet Moya clung to her daughter's side be it in house, garden or on the chase. Now she wished the woodsmen had never come, however much she liked them and welcomed their company and the good they did for the people.

"Both of us are from fine if unusual families," Stephen pleaded with her. "Do you know how miserable I was when I was sent to be squire. 'Base-born', they whispered behind their hands, 'Poor', things which had never bothered me before, in the happy home of the manor. So I did the worst tasks, things the others turned away from and always dealt with the least-liked lords, cruel, arrogant men who everyone shunned. I knew that the Lady made many enquiries for a fine bride for me. Titles, from a great house, rich, beautiful. Poor lady, she wanted the impossible for me, and was always refused. For every parent wants the best for their child, except for me. I want my Felicia to be happy, to be loved. The Lady was never married, although I believe that she must have loved my father, or else I would not be here now." He sighed deeply. "It must have been very hard for her. So in despair I suppose, there being in her eyes no other option, she gave me Jessica. When I would much rather have wed with you."

They sent her away then, their much-loved child, this time first to the manor, then to Stephen's foster-sister Anna's great house. Little Anna, Lady Felicia's second foundling, was now a grand lady, who considering Felicia to be her niece, warmly welcomed her.

It might have been fate, or gentle interference from the Jeromes, that on her homeward ride, Felicia met with Robin. Sitting together on the river bank, they spoke for the first time in many months, their Jerome escort suddenly busy in the woods searching for mushrooms to take home for supper.

They gazed at each other, hungry, fearful. She saw that he had grown leaner, more bronzed with the summer and if possible, more handsome. He felt himself quivering for love of her, noting that she had grown just a little and filled out into a lovely young woman. For Felicia had inherited all the fine good looks from all her family. Her nose had the slightest of aristocratic bumps from the Lady Felicia, but was not and never would become the bony beak. Her hair was straight and corn-coloured and her skin was fair, smattered now with a few tiny freckles, despite her coif.

"You have been in my heart ever since you have been away," said he.

"I have," she answered simply, "and you in mine."

"What can I do to persuade your father to give me your hand?"

She looked straight at him with a directness which must have come from Jessica her mother.

"It is not my father you need to see, but the Lady Felicia. She is the one who directs our lives. Go to see her."

Which he did, abandoning his work for a few days, weary of the forest, the labour and his heartache.

"But who were your parents? Your family?" the Lady looked down her long nose at the young man before her. The truth was, she was shocked. For this was the first time she knew anything of an attachment, if indeed such existed.

"Nothing Lady," Robin chose his words carefully. "Nobodies. They were just ordinary folk who worked hard and honestly, and now we have ships, and are ever building more for the king and for ourselves."

"But you are working in the forests cutting trees, hauling timber. I expect a man of far greater standing and ability than that for my grand-daughter."

Robin stilled. Had it been a slip, or had she meant to say God-daughter?

"Lady," he pressed on with his plea. "I am the youngest brother. So it is my task to oversee the selection of the great oaks which we use to build our ships. We are more than fortunate in having the Jerome family to do the work, for they are fine craftsmen, with a gift to do things the right way. However," he paused, secretly glad to see her interest. "It is not just the cutting down which matters. It is the storage and the transport and normally we would have a rough sort of fellow, who only cares that his belly is filled and that he can take home his pay. My father and brothers entrust me to organize the choosing, felling and transport of the timber. These two years have been easier for me for I enjoy the work and being out in the open, not being cooped up in a port with its stink, noise and blather. It has been fine living half the time in the forests, having Sir Stephen's company and hospitality sometimes. And one last thing, Lady, hear well," he raised his voice a fraction. "My great respect for Sir Stephen and his family have been complete, and I have never taken advantage of any of them from respect and true love."

Yet she would have none of it and wrote a withering letter to Stephen, informing him of his appalling slackness in allowing a common woodcutter free entry into his house.

"I am decided grand-mother," deliberately using the word, Felicia sat with hands folded and eyes cast down, "I shall enter a convent for I believe only then will I find the peace I crave."

Now the Lady really was shocked. Now this she would not have on any condition. The last of her line, Stephen's only child. Her heiress! She worried her nose with a lace kerchief to cover her alarm.

All winter the Lady Felicia sat at her desk and scratched letters inviting suitors to come for the hand of her God-daughter and heiress. Her hands grew stiff from holding the quill and her nose seemed sharper, it was so cold and red. Yet with every opportunity, the letters went out, so when spring came, so too did the many suitors.

At first Moya was amused with the visitors, for any new company was pleasant after the long dark days of winter. After the third had arrived, and there was some quiet discord amongst them, she realized what had happened. Approaching the mildest of the three suitors, a stocky little man by name of Sir Giles Derefield, she learned about the letters sent out by the Lady.

It was not a comfortable time. Felicia did not make herself agreeable, either hiding from them or not speaking at all. Some days she disappeared altogether, visiting, as she told them later, the latest Jerome baby. Gone was the cheery girl who sang in the garden and played with her dog and who was never disagreeable to anyone. Stephen was so upset by the changes in his household, he rode one bright day to the manor to object and tell the Lady of what was going on.

"She will have to choose, Stephen. I have only written to decent, kindly gentlemen, knights all of them. And if she persists in being difficult, then yes, she can do what she wants and enter into a convent."

Stephen was appalled. Now this he could not bear, his lovely girl shutting herself away in one of those frozen, semi-prisons. Never! As the spring progressed and the days grew fair, more suitors came, until there was barely room to house them all and Moya curtly described herself to her husband as an "inn-keeper's wife".

While the little hamlet toiled as usual with their various tasks, the tower seemed an idle place of music, feasting and competition. For the guests had created butts for archery competition on the lawns. When they were not vying in poetry or singing, they were letting loose and losing their arrows in the marsh.

Felicia gradually came to look more like her grandmother, the Lady Felicia, for she lost weight in her misery, and her nose grew bonier, her eyes cold. Not that her parents could fault her behaviour really, for although she was polite to the young men, she was overly, correctly aloof. One by one they despaired of gaining her attentions and reluctantly rode away.

It was Felicia who announced that she wished to go to stay awhile at the manor. Although their supplies were unusually low because of the guests, Stephen and Moya hastened to gather up what gifts they could.

They were both physically tired and emotionally drained by the weeks of artificial revelry and delighted in the peace which once more descended on the tower. The Jeromes, who had watched aghast from a distance now returned, their homely faces once more wreathed with smiles.

Although there had never been the grinding poverty of most villages in the forest hamlets, the woodsmen had brought a new prosperity to the area. For bullocks and drovers had to be fed, so the oldest to the youngest of the huge Jerome family had been pressed into service to profitably provide for them.

A wandering friar, an unusually young and good one too, had set himself up in a tiny shelter on the fringe of the village. What little ministering the locals needed, he provided in exchange for some meals, and company. Occasionally, he went to the tower where Moya greeted him kindly, wondering about the quiet man. While she gave him ale, cheese and barley cakes, they talked of this and that, until, inevitably, he asked to see Fleur's book of hours. Eyes alight, he reverently unwrapped it from its silken shroud and read the sweet prayers out loud while Moya quietly toiled at her duties. He was then, they understood, a learned man, yet had no book, and she wondered if somehow they could get one for him. Perhaps the lady might have some to give, for she knew that the bishop had been more than generous over the years.

Meanwhile, Felicia settled in to the manor again, observing that it was Maria and the priest who did all the work with the children. The Lady mostly sat in the solar, writing endless letters, yet as her eyes became increasingly dim, barely reading.

"Shall I read for you, Lady?" Felicia asked almost daily. Which she did, taking the books down from their shelf and sitting by the window for the light. The Lady Felicia observed her grand-daughter carefully from under her coif. Yes, she could be proud of this one descendant of their family. The sun caused the corn-coloured hair to glow, and the clear, melodious voice made the words from the book beautiful. So why was she here? Stubborn girl!

She was not sleeping well, and had begun to think of her immortality. Trying to still her tossings so as not to disturb her bed fellows, Maria and Felicia, the Lady spent hours thinking over her life, her successes and her mistakes. Foolishly she knew, she would go back to her girlhood and imagine if that almost-forgotten young love had lived. Would they have had more children? All handsome and gentle like Stephen? Sons, and daughters like this Felicia, who had so much of her sister Nicola and even just a little of herself? At last, unable to stop her nightly searchings, she waited till she and Felicia were alone together.

"Now my girl," she sat up very straight as was her custom, and peered down her long nose at her. "When are you going to tell me the reason for your visit?"

Felicia closed the book and carefully re-wrapped it. Then she looked at her grand-mother, calm, eyes slightly hooded. Lying really was not in her nature.

"I am so glad you ask, Lady, for I was wondering how to tell you." The expectant silence stretched between them. "I have heard, in a discreet sort of way, that some of the children here are base-born, and that you, in your mercy, harboured their mothers prior to their births, then kept the children."

The Lady gripped the carved arms of her chair and breathed in deeply. Very slightly, she inclined her head.

"As I am with child to Robin the woodsman, I came here for succour, so as not to disgrace my parents. So, Lady, that is why I came, to throw myself into your merciful hands."

The Lady Felicia closed her eyes as the room swayed. The muted sounds of day suddenly became overly loud, and it seemed that a great wind swept through the room. An arm was about her shoulders, and a cup of wine was held to her lips.

Her pale face blanched white, and she tried to breathe in deeply so as not to fall.

"I have you, grand-mother," a quiet voice said by her ear. "Try to drink a little wine, it will steady you."

They did not speak for some time, until the Lady turned to look directly at her namesake.

"So you know or guess everything, you minx? So you think just because many years ago I made a grievous yet highly fortunate mistake, you can. Was this done deliberately? Tell me miss, for if it was, then I shall not be pleased with you."

They stayed talking quietly for some time until the bell rang for prayers. Felicia, heart pounding, tried to behave normally and assisted the Lady to the chapel.

"You do understand don't you," she said the next day, "that you, being last of two lines, will, by marrying a common woodsman, lower yourself and all our family? I had great hopes for a good marriage for you. After all, you have good blood on both sides, especially good from my mother, a grand-daughter of the royal house, something to be proud of." She held out her left hand. "See, I still have the royal ring which was hers. But the woodsman, what are his roots then? Where does his line come from? What is his fortune apart from a few ships?"

Felicia sat still, her hands folded neatly on her lap and gazed at the floor, appreciating the elaborate pattern on the rush mat. She had never managed to do such a style, this surely had been a labour of love from Maria's clever hands.

"Over these past two years, Lady, I have gained not only love for Robin Woodman, but a great affection and respect for him and his brothers. They are honest men, and when I saw how agreeable they were in company with my father, I understood they were men similar to his good character. Of all the suitors who came wooing me, not one had as much good sense and natural manners as they. If I married one of those knights, I know I would soon despise their empty lives and foolish interests. The woodsmen are true, lowly men. Yet, father told us they are men of the future. For with the aftermath of the great pestilence, such men are highly valuable to re-build our land. They are widely travelled, Lady, and have diverse interests because of their work. I have seen how particular Robin is in his choice of trees, and their subsequent treatment. He wants and gets only the finest quality, never taking second best. For he says it is a waste of time and money, which might even end with loss of life."

The Lady Felicia listened, and to her surprise she liked what she heard.

"Does your man know that you are with child?"

For a moment Felicia hesitated, then shook her head.

"Very well my child," the Lady said with a sigh of resignation. "If as you say they are clever, they will rise up in the world, and not pull you or our family down. I shall send for him immediately and arrange your marriage with all haste."

Now Felicia began to eat again, so the gaunt look which threatened her beauty quickly disappeared, her face filling out with youthful speed. Once again she was the happy, helpful girl, who sang in her work and had love and kindness for everyone.

Just twice it seemed as if her happiness would be shattered, for although Robin had been sent for, he was not to be found. Apparently in his misery, he had agreed to take a vessel to a far port for delivery and was biding his time.

Then Maria, who was privy to the Lady's plans, almost spoilt them for one day she found Felicia furtively washing the cloths which she used during her monthly bleeding. Shocked, Maria stared at the telltale evidence being scrubbed in cold, lye water, by a silent Felicia.

"You will not tell, Maria, I beg you? For it was the only way you know. Otherwise they would have made me marry one of those dreadful foppish knights and how could I when I love Robin so." Wiping her cold chapped hands on her apron she clasped Maria's. "I beg you sweet Maria, do not let me down. By Our Lady and Saint Margaret, I tell you that I am indeed not with child. In fact, Robin is such a good man, he knows nothing of me, or of my little lies and I promise you, that I am not with child for I am yet surely a maiden."

Shocked at first, later Maria had to smile to herself. How clever were these Felicias, who willy-nilly always got their own way.

"And one more thing I beg of you, Maria. For the love of your good father and mother, help me to warn Robin of my wickedness. Help me send a small letter, to be got to him with all speed, for he might and rightly deny responsibility of something which is not. Oh please Maria, help us?"

So, the gentle Maria, who had known no suitor or love, aided Felicia, feeling some joy and girlish excitement in their secret.

Worn out with the rough return voyage, Robin was greeted by his brothers with several letters. He sat down in their small town house above the harbour and read them, his eyes gradually lighting up, his mouth softening into a happy smile.

"She does love me, brothers!" he exclaimed, holding her letter close. "She even lies that she carries my child, which is not possible I do assure you, in order to wed with me. Hasten brothers, for we have a marriage to attend, and be sure I will do my best to make her with child as soon as I can, so to save her pretty face, the wanton!"

The marriage was held at the manor, which, with a host of Jeromes, was bursting.

"They are kin," announced Felicia happily, as she embraced them.

"They are not!" said Moya under her breath to the brothers. "But one day I will show you what is written in the book of hours. For Lee, who made it, the physician who became part of our family, wrote it all down most carefully, in the back pages."

"So, Master Robert Woodman," the Lady still tried to show her disapproval. "You have married a lady, from a long line of knights, indeed kings and she is an heiress too, of this manor and the marsh property. As you seem to be ready breeders, I hope that you will do better than our recent generations. For it is not good to have but one child, and I hope that the Lord will bless you with a great family."

Which in time he did. But no sooner had Felicia and her bridegroom returned to the tower, than a letter was sent to the Lady, that obviously the ride had been too long, too strenuous, and that she had lost the child.

Hardly had the lady recovered from her bitter disappointment, when another letter came, announcing that Felicia was again with child. And this time, every reassurance was given, they would ensure that she took no risks in order to produce a fine heir.

"I love you more than life," said Robin, holding his wife's head as she puked into the piss-pot, "even if you are a scheming wench, who caught me by false means. Oh how I love you." He wiped her mouth tenderly, and leant her exhausted body against his arm. "It will soon pass my love. Come now, drink this camomile, sip by sip. For many a time I have thought to puke my heart out on the seas, and this is the best remedy."

As the months passed Felicia's belly grew and grew, until it seemed that she was all stomach and eyes, for she became very tired.

"Could it be," one of the kindly brothers asked, "that she is hatching a brace, such as us?" They all gazed at Felicia who squirmed, ever trying to ease her discomfort. Even the numerous Jerome women had no experience with twins, and Moya, who had never borne a child, grew fearful.

"I am told," she wrote to the Lady, "that it is unusual for a firstborn to be so large. And dear lady, I become ever fearful, as our girl is truly huge, and suffers many and diverse discomforts, all the time."

It was Robin, who in the deepest of winter suggested that they build a small church. For at that time, the bulk of the little population lacked work, and heaven knew, they had enough wood. So here was a diversion which occupied everyone, delighted their young priest and took their minds off Felicia, her belly and the bitter cold.

Both she and Moya span all the hours of the day, delighting in making their colours in the dye pot from dried herbage. The Jerome women also brought hempen thread for Moya, who sat thereafter at the loom while Felicia span, for it was well known that women with child must never weave. While Felicia sat twisting her drop spindle near by, Moya wove lengths of strong cloth for them to work on. Taking a tiny drawing from the book of hours, they began stitching a fine tapestry to hang behind the altar, while the village laboured on the church itself. By spring, it was done, a sturdy structure with stone foundations and stout wooden walls, in-filled with mud and topped with a thick turf roof. It was dim inside, but sorting out some precious panes of glass left over from the house, Stephen had a window made, which set to the east, gave sunlight on the fair early mornings.

An unusual, strange new pain, deep in her body, alerted Felicia that perhaps her time had come. Needing somehow, just some more hours of peace alone, she went out into the garden, her feet in strong wooden clogs against the damp, a thick shawl over her shoulders. Ever alert to her child's moods, Moya watched her from the window. Even the little dog seemed to sense that something was different, for he stayed close by her, anxiously looking up at his mistress as she tried to suppress her moans. Carefully walking as far as she could, she reached the seat from where, so they told her, her true mother Jessica had fallen to her death. Pressing her hands to her sides she drew her breath in and tried to remember her, but could not.

"If it is a girl," she whispered in a lull, "I will name her for you, mother Jessica, and for your grandmother Jessica. For it is a pretty name."

Unable to bear it any longer Moya took up her shawl and strode out into the garden.

"Come my dearling," she put a hand under Felicia's elbow. "It is time to come in now."

The village midwives were called and Robin and his brothers joined Stephen in the tower where they drank and played chess and dice, to pass the hours. Which dragged on, and on, while they tried to be casual, listening for a step with the news.

With the first streaks of dawn, Moya came, tired but jubilant.

"A perfect daughter Robin. Fair and bonny, and looking so much like Jessica, Felicia has named her thus already."

As one they rose and embraced and clattered down the stair at speed and into the house, there to see a tired Felicia lying, smiling in the great bed.

It was as Moya said, a bonny child, fair and perfect, from what they could see of it left un-swaddled. It was also heartily healthy too from the noise it made.

"Out, out!" said Moya, shooing them out of the door. "She must sleep now, for it was a hard long labour and she needs rest."

"I will take the midwives home and go to tell the Jeromes," Stephen said, far too excited to take to his bed by his wife's urging. So they all went down to the stables to saddle up the horses and Robin went a little way with him to give the news to his men as he had promised.

Moya sat beside Felicia and gazed at her in admiration. For surely it had been a great travail and unlike some other women she had overheard in child bed, she had barely uttered a sound. The room was once more tidy and empty of the women who had been pleased to go home to spread the news.

"Mother!" a sudden and anguished cry came from the bed. "Mother!"

Panicked by the unknown, Moya drew down the sheets shocked and just in time to receive into her hands another child. Wrapping it in a cloth she quickly gave it to Felicia to hold while she ran downstairs. Wildly she told the news to the astonished brothers who sat beside the hearth, while she found her scissors and twine and ordered them to bring up water.

Having set down the pails, the men stood by the bed, grinning broadly down at their sister-in-law.

"How clever you are dearling sister!" exclaimed one joyfully.

"Twins, like us," said the other.

Somehow between the three of them, ignorant and unabashed, they helped Felicia, washing her down again, swaddling the little thing somehow, who mewled softly as they lay her down in the great, carved oak Pomeroy cradle, beside her sister.

"Clara!" announced one of the brothers, Clara being the name of his lady of the moment.

"No, Isabelle," said the other, it being the name of his current lady.

They squabbled quietly for days, like dogs with a bone, until the child's father lost patience with them.

"Clarissa she shall be, something of both. Now enough I beg you, for we are all weary of your bickering."

Jessica and Clarissa grew and throve with the constant attentions of their mother, grandmother, and the maids who, for lack of other work, had left the Jerome households in the forest to help at the tower. They were very pretty, fair-haired little things, as peas from the same pod; Jessica was just a little plumper than her twin, while Clarissa was a little longer. They were good children, feeding, sleeping and growing well, soon to smile and laugh at the many adoring folk who surrounded them.

Over the next ten years, four more little girls were born. Joan, Fleur, Leah and Maria, all as fair and beautiful as the twins. The Lady had her descendants, but no son as yet.

During this time, Robin and his brothers had quietly become wealthy ship-builders and owners. They were always active, ever thinking of new things to do, once bringing strange men from over the seas to drain the marsh, so once more there was work for everyone who needed it. Gradually the forest retreated and hamlets sprang up along the old river road. The drovers intermarried with the Jeromes, and in that little corner of the land, there was peace and security.

The gardens of the tower no longer edged onto the marshes, for the water had drained away leaving fine, fertile land. Now instead of the silver glint of marsh, great fields of wheat, barley and oats stretched golden there, with sometimes the blue of flax. When the drovers were done with their work, they took their slow oxen to turn the thick, black soil and there was plenty for everyone in that little backwater, all year round.

Stephen and Moya were summoned by the Lady, who growing old, announced that she needed them with her for her last years. Gradually the manor had ceased to take in young people, for it seemed too much for them to cope with. And after all, wasn't Robin supplying them with money and more? All their needs he attended to, whether doing repairs to the roof, draining the moat or paying their taxes; he saw to it all.

With six beautiful daughters, Robin thought seriously about their dowries. True, neither he or his brothers were knights, but they had by marriage and hard work, become highly respectable citizens. His brothers did not marry, seemingly to be too close to each other, they had wooed and left many lovely women, apparently content with sharing their younger brother's family.

If ever land came up for sale round about, Robin bought it, extending their holding way along the river and into the edges of the forest which of course still belonged to the crown. Times were changing and with the not-so-long-past pestilence, there seemed to be more land available than men to work it.

The flocks of sheep grew, and a few cows were bought in. Felicia organized the Jerome family into making hard cheese and butter, smoked eels, salt beef and hams and anything else which would keep, and thus advantageously for everyone, supplied the family ships.

The village downriver had gradually grown into a sizable town and occasionally the family went to market there by boat, returning with one of the great horses towing them home along the river path. For the little girls, trips to Marsh Newton were the greatest treat, for on saint days there were stalls, mummers and jokers, and best of all, they had found a new, interesting friend.

Deborah was the only child of the goldsmith, and an only child, was to them, a rarity. Her parents were older people, foreigners too, who delighted in speaking French. Deborah even came to stay sometimes, usually with her nurse Bibby when she had been ill and needed a change of air. How they vied for the attentions of their exotic friend, so different from the local children. Father even ordered some pretty crosses to be made for each of them in gold from the hand of Master Goldsmith, and Mistress Goldsmith loved their cheeses and chattering to mother.

Felicia too enjoyed the relationship with their new friends. So she made great efforts to visit as often as time allowed for it was a change, her daughters so enjoyed it and the little excursion did them all good. So they made little cheeses and smoked eels to sell, packing them into thin, wooden boxes as they did for the ships. Their fair hair tucked under bonnets, the little girls chattered as birds as they cruised downriver. Only the younger two had pig's bladders tied to their waists, for the uncles had insisted on all of them learning to swim, living as they did, so close to water.

Just once the Goldsmith family came to celebrate the day of the Virgin, bedding down in the tower, fearfully impressed with the beautiful place. The friar was now well established as priest in the new little church, even with the blessing of the new abbot, for priests were in short supply after the great pestilence.

Many of the neighbours and forest people came, all bearing what they could towards the feast which was held afterwards at the marsh tower. The excitement was tangible with children rushing about over the lawns, the day magical, warm and bright after the early mist had risen.

Inevitably the Jeromes had brought their flutes and drums, so when everyone was fed and well filled with strong ale and wine, there began country dancing, the children leading the way, eyes bright. When they tired and lay in heaps, still so excited they chattered, Sir Stephen got up, took Moya's hand and did a graceful court dance, which some tried to follow. In the lull that followed, Master Goldsmith had stood up, and clapping his hands for tempo, had begun a curious dance, all the while singing in a very strange tongue. Slowly, the crowd joined his clapping and watched transfixed as the strange, usually quiet man strutted and stamped, gyrating in a dance none had ever seen before. When the lightest titter came from one corner, with a severe look sent in their direction, Sir Stephen got up and joined their guest, and did his best to copy the strange but fascinating dance. Then Robin joined them, then the uncles till the clapping rose wildly in delight to see the five most respected men, seriously and elegantly dancing together.

"Why do you weep Louisa dear?" Felicia put her arms about her guest.

"Because," whispered Louisa, "he looks so young, his years of toil and sorrow gone, dancing the dance of his childhood." and sobbed happily afresh.

It was the most perfect day which none would forget and the Goldsmiths went home that night amazed by the event and wondrously content, escorted by the uncles.

They were the most special uncles, disappearing for months, then returning, laden down with wondrous gifts for them all. Robin had, at her birth, made each of his daughters a bride's chest, with her name and year date carved on it, and here they kept their many and increasing treasures.

"Look now," said the uncles, proudly gazing at their beautiful nieces sitting on the lawn all about them. "Look carefully at the sky and tell us, how fares the weather for tomorrow?" So the little girls learned about the sky from those experienced seamen and delighted in their unusual knowledge.

Strangely, Felicia noted that her two firstborn were not like their uncles, for although certainly twins, their characters were completely different. John and James Woodmen were so close, calm and happy, they could not be told apart. Whereas her girls although identical too, were easily identified, for one was as cranky, as the other was peaceful.

"If you could but remember Jessica your mother," remarked Moya, "You would see how alike she is. Indeed I recall my own mother telling me how difficult the first Lady Jessica was. So you named her well." She looked over to her favourite, the other twin, who had slipped into the world, into her hands. "Now Clary? Well who knows where she comes from, Fleur your grand-mother I think. She was a quiet and gentle soul too."

It was in the town during one of the big annual markets that farmer Lucas, from by the ford, saw the beautiful little girls clustered around a small table piled high with fresh cheeses. Eyeing them and their busy mother, his heart felt heavy.

He was not a happy man. Life was hard, and even harder since his wife and two little daughters had died, leaving him to bring up the two boys alone. Buying a single cheese, he cut it into three with his knife, handed a piece each to his sons and ate it quickly. It was excellent. So he went back, and to the astonishment of the pretty cheese wife, bought up the rest, intending to smoke them when he got home. Now if only his boys could wed such clever farm wives, all their lives would be sweeter.

CHAPTER TWENTY SIX

TOBIAS INNMAN

Sensing that they were nearing home, the ponies quickened their pace, first to a brisk trot, then breaking into a canter. The girls too, were excited, forgot that they were tired and encouraged their mounts to make haste, so they ended their journey by racing each other amidst much happy noise. The two grooms glanced at each other ruefully, then grinned as they spurred their horses to catch up. Well! It would be a relief to hand over these lively, young ladies, that was for sure, particularly the eldest. Now they would have a few days rest before setting off home again to Sir Stephen's manor, escorting the next three grand-daughters. They both hoped that they would be more biddable.

The whole household came out to welcome home the travellers. After much embracing and chatter, they all gathered about the great board in the kitchen to exchange news and drink ale.

"Grand-mother sent back the Book of Hours, mother, with a letter," Jessie carefully took the wrapped treasure from a pocket hanging at her waist feeling important. "Grand-father has filled in all the latest family additions in the back, so we are to keep it here." The letter and the precious book was passed along the table and taking them, Felicia put the book back in its proper place in the niche in the fireplace beside Lee's Herbal. The letter she would read later when she had some quiet.

It had been a pleasant month with three of her daughters away at the manor. At least, it had been very peaceful without Jessie, for the next two girls were always easy enough. Now Clary and the younger two were off, and she hoped that Jessie might be the helpful older sister in her place.

They raced about the garden, showing new happenings, telling the little things which had occurred during their absence. Then they saw the new looms which father had built, a fine big one and a braid loom for the young ones to learn at.

"I suppose," said Jessie, eyeing the big loom, "we shall be put on your old loom while you work the new one?"

"No," said Felicia, pulling her breath in with irritation, and drawing off the cover, "you will start tomorrow if you like, for see," her hand smoothed the cloth already there, "Clary has already started, see what good work she has done. You girls must now weave your own dowries, for I cannot, as I am with child again, but I will spin for you."

Jessie heard her mother's words with shock. With child? Her mother who was so old? A feeling of revulsion filled her. Really, that such old people should be still mating, how could they?

None-the-less she did sit at the loom the next day with Clary beside her, who, being aware of her twin's sudden ill-humour was determined to ignore it with her happy directions.

"It is a marvellous loom, Jess," she said. "Look, a flying shuttle! So quick and easy, isn't father clever? It won't take us long to fill our dower chests," and giggled. She for one was thrilled that mother was with child again, she couldn't wait to tell her grandparents. Perhaps it would be a boy this time, after the gap in years since little Maria. After six girls, she really hoped so, for everyone would be so pleased.

They left three days later for their month at the manor. They went every year and looked forward to it and spoke about it for the rest of the year. First of all the journey was exciting, riding on their ponies through the great forest, past little hamlets and greeting the many Jerome cousins. They always stopped for a night at Castle Pomeroy. Not that they stayed at the castle, although it was always empty, because it belonged to an unpleasant kinsman who never visited. They stayed instead just outside the village with their other cousins the Anderssons at their farm. Then they rode on to the manor where they were spoiled and made much of and had the happiest time pretending to learn but really just enjoying themselves.

"Why the sour face, Jessie?" Robin was aware of the undercurrent of unease in his house. "If you come back from the manor with your mouth so turned down, I shall not allow you to go there again." Jessie banged the loom bar with more force than was necessary and wished she could go to live at the manor always. Except it would mean she could not go to Marsh Newton on market days and see Luke Byford.

"You stay at home, my love," Robin caressed the gentle swelling under his wife's apron. "I'll take the girls and the goods, and I will see old Lucas from by the ford. You are right. If Jessie wishes to be betrothed to his boy Lucas, I think we should encourage it, for they have known each other for many enough years, and he seems a good steady lad. Jessie needs her own home, man and children to occupy her mind and hands. We shall have no peace until she is wed."

Not only had Marsh Newton grown into a fine little market town, there was a splendid stone church almost completed. The Jerome mill now stood on the very outskirts and supplied flour to a great area and it was there they stopped to leave the horse, for he would be towing them home. Now Robin greeted his wife's kinsman and asked for all the news. Who better than the miller to get it from, for he was worried about his elder daughter. True, she was only older than Clary by a couple of hours, but older in other ways. He must find out all he could about the Byford men, and what the miller thought about their betrothing Jessie to the older boy.

It was luck that they came then, and that Robin put his questions to the miller, for he had just heard that two hundred acres were up for sale on the south side of the river by the ford.

"It is good land, Master Woodman, or with good husbandry, could be" the miller's son told him. "Good river land, dark and rich, if a bit boggy in places, indeed I should say marshy. But that can be seen to in time."

Deep in thought, Robin hustled his daughters back into the flat boat and paddled it into town, there to tie up just behind their friends, the Goldsmith's house.

While Robin went to attend to business, the girls clustered around Deborah Goldsmith all chattering at once. Eventually they too wandered around the town, old Biddy with them, enjoying their lively company so much that she forgot her ailments for the moment. All heads turned to admire the gaggle of girls who were so pretty.

As a host of butterflies, they drifted along to the church, then quietened as they went into the beautiful new, cool interior. They gazed about in awe; it really was a very fine church, even if it was not yet completed.

Luke Byford stood behind a pillar at the back, and brightened when he saw them coming in. Knowing that his father was meeting with Master Woodman, he had come here for quiet, to pray and to sort his thoughts. It was difficult making out the girls, who came in different sizes but otherwise they seemed all the same, fair and lovely. Then one looked around and caught his eye. His breath quickened. Surely this was she? Startled, the girl quickly looked away. His heart seemed to turn over. What a lovely lass! So he kept his eye on her firmly, till the mass was over and kept as close as he dared as they drifted outside.

Was he imagining it, or was there a tiny mole, or was it a mote, just under her jaw-line? Then, because of the crush, he lost sight of her momentarily and frowned.

They were gathered outside in a bunch about the Goldsmith's old maid when he approached and bowed lightly. After all he had been acquainted with the family for many years now.

"God's blessing this day, young mistresses, are you all well?"

As one they dipped, and smiling, he hastily cast his eye over the taller two. They were exactly the same. Then, one spoke up.

"And to you, Luke, will you walk a little way with us?" Then said Jessie, aside to her sisters, "You may run on while Luke and I accompany Biddy slowly."

Marsh Newton had become a prosperous little town due alone to the rich alluvial earth of the water-meadows. There they produced plentiful and good hay, therefore good stock and plenty of milk and cheese. To one side lay the forest and on the lower, where the land had settled down from the vagaries of the meandering river, lay fine fields of wheat, barley and rye, with flashes of soft blue flax tucked here and there for linen. Robin was interested to learn that there was even talk of a corn exchange to be built. The innkeeper who had just taken the cheeses from Marsh Tower, liked to speak with Robin Woodman, whom he considered a worthy successor to Sir Stephen, even if he were an ordinary man. There were no put-on graces about him. Master Woodman was, he considered, the best kind of "new man" in England.

They talked of this and that until Robin asked about the rumour that some acres were up for sale by the ford. The innkeeper sharpened his ears. Interesting. Now why would he be wanting more land, and at such distance from his home?

"It is water-meadow, Master Woodman. Often subjected to flooding, they tried to work the land but it was too heavy. Now the widow talks of moving away to be with her daughter by the coast, and that is why it is up for sale." He paused, refilling the mug of ale which he pushed over to his customer. "By chance you are thinking of buying it?"

Robin sipped his ale; it was very good, medium strong and with a good nutty flavour.

"You know that old Lucas Byford has been asking for my eldest daughter for his first son?" He went on without waiting for an answer, "well it occurs to me that some acres around his holding might make a fine dowry." He looked directly at the man before him. "I'd take it as a favour if you would make enquiries for me of the price, Master Innman, discretely of course."

"Of course!" repeated the innkeeper, pleased. It was a good thing to be in with folk like the Woodmans, with their connections, land and, he understood, sea-going vessels. More than anything he would like to import good wines direct from France and Portugal, develop a business in it, and this might well be a way to do it.

"We shall hear from Tobias at the inn before long," Robin told his wife that night. "He is a decent man, as I see from his ale. I think he will have our information in no time."

Robin was right, for word came that the innkeeper would like to see him.

"Are you certain, Felicia mine, that this Byford boy would be able to handle Jessie?"

Felicia eased her discomfort by getting up and stretching. This was either going to be a large child, or a brace again. "Come now, Robin, what a foolish question to put to me. I, who cannot handle my own daughter? Of course he will not be able to handle her, only Clary can do that. The poor lad will have his hands full, but if he wants her as much as old Lucas wants her for him, they must cope."

It was a problem.

The next time Robin went to town he met Lucas Byford in a small private room in the inn, where they discussed their children's nuptials. Lucas was a tall, spare man with a stern countenance. Robin understood that since the loss of his wife and daughters, he had become morose, having been a jolly fellow in his youth. Having a beautiful and loving wife himself, Robin felt sympathy for the man. Now it seemed he wanted his son to take a wife to replace his womenfolk, and Robin seriously worried that Jessie, not being the busy, capable lass the man imagined she was, might well turn out a disappointment. However, Lucas did not seem to understand the indecision, and certainly he obviously liked the idea of one hundred acres of water-meadows as dowry.

That evening when the little ones were abed, Robin kept his older daughters in the big kitchen.

"You understand that I met with Master Lucas from by the ford, Jessie? And that he still asks for you for his older son?"

Jessie smiled, eyes bright, and sat up straighter.

"Now he seems a good man, if a little morose since his wife and daughters died, but the boy looks a nice enough lad and I ask you what you have to say to the idea of the match."

"I like it, father." Jessie replied, looking very pretty with her enthusiasm.

Turning to his second twin, Robin asked, "And what about you, missy? Do you think that it sounds a good match for your sister?" Unaware that he was frowning, he looked at her. They were so different, these two, born together from, he understood, the same egg. To look at superficially they were the same apart from a tiny mole; even some of the family had difficulty in telling them apart. A small pain stirred in his gut. He was not at all sure about anything.

"I do, father, although he is a little quiet, I think he is a good man. We saw him at church today and he was very attentive."

"Then the next time my brothers come, we shall visit the Byfords and see what kind of home they have, and if it is suitable for our girl."

So it was left for awhile, and Jessie was unusually biddable while Clary was away, and worked hard at the new loom making fine linen for her dowry.

One month later, when Clary and her little sisters returned from their month at the manor, they found her rather silent. When pressed, she told them that she feared that her grandfather was not well. As one, they looked at her intently. Somehow Sir Stephen had always seemed so young, so handsome with his fair hair which had discretely turned white so that it was not really noticeable. Puzzled, they continued to press her, what was his trouble? Did grand-mother Moya notice or say anything? Miserably Clary shook her head, sorry that she had spoken of her anxieties.

"He kept telling me about his youth, tales which I had never heard before. About our ancestry, which he even made me promise to write down in the back of Lee's book. As he had filled it up so recently, I wondered at his insistence. He was, as always, so loving and tender, but," she faltered looking up at them, her eyes shadowed, "I worry for him. Forgive me for telling you my fears?"

Yet she was right, for by summer's end Sir Stephen was failing, and because of her advanced pregnancy, Felicia could not go, so letters were sent frequently, and a cloud descended over the family.

Robin did buy the land in an almost distracted way not bothering to bargain too much as was the norm. Tobias, the innman, assisted in the purchase, and when it was settled, refused to take payment, stating that friendship was a far better gift.

"They grieve for Sir Stephen, although he is not dead yet, for I suppose they must be a very close, loving family," he sighed, holding his wife to him, his thoughts racing, "not as we had eh, my love?"

Barely out of childhood, Tobias had been stable-hand to Mol's grandfather, a cantankerous old keeper of a very poor inn. He had quickly noticed the pinched little girl and her frequent tears of fatigue, so with his kind nature, had tried to ease her lot. She was probably the reason why he stayed there, for the pay was as poor as was the food and conditions. Having lost his family in the plague, he warmed to the lonely little girl, and gradually became the man of her life. Tobias had looked about at the filth and decay of the inn and taken off to the moor to cut armfuls of broom so to make a start with sweeping up.

It was during his obsessive cleaning that he found it, literally a pot of gold. There was an old barrel by the stable filled with water from a streamlet which sometimes ran in bad weather. Full of holes, much of the water drained away all too quickly, so Tobias had waited till it was empty before taking it down to mend. There, in the bottom, immersed in sludge, lay a pot, and inside the pot was a rotten, linen bag filled with gold coins. Tobias was shocked. He knew not what to do. Should he take it and run? It would certainly take him far and give him a fine new start in life. Then he heard Molly singing, little Mol who never sang during his first year there but who was now happy, and probably beginning to love him. Carefully he cleaned and caulked the barrel and set it up again with the gold back in, still in its pot, minus just one coin. She had never asked him where he got the good things he bought for them. Every time he went to town, he bought good fare, some cloth for a new dress for her, a trinket or new clogs for himself when it grew icy in winter. He was always very careful, it would not do to draw attention to extravagance. When that coin was finished, he took another one, so their lives improved in that awful place, and the old innkeeper, bad-tempered old man that he was, half blind, half deaf, noticed nothing.

After he died, in a fit of rage, Tobias sat with Mol and discussed her fate. They both knew what a miser her grandfather had been, but now here was a chance to either stay and make good the inn, or leave it to go elsewhere. They decided to sell, for there were few good memories in that place to keep them there.

Once again Tobias cut great armfuls of broom and set about cleaning the place up in order to sell. They collected red clay from a river bank nearby and worked it into dung and lime wash, stirring the barrel till they got a fair, soft, ochre-red colour. When it was painted, the outside of the inn looked fresh, warm and inviting. They worked well together, eating well too, so they had strength as well as hope.

"We shall be out of here by winter, Mol," said Tobias confidently, "and if you will wed with me, we can find another inn to run as we like, and well."

Eyes glowing, Mol had nodded. Life without Toby was not imaginable.

With his instincts alert, Tobias ripped out the inside and made good the old inn, and sure enough, he came across three more little caches of gold which the old man had hidden away and obviously forgotten. This was a fortune indeed, which he kept in his saddlebag under his head at night. He none-the-less savagely fought to get a good price for the inn, waging war with the buyer to have sympathy for the orphaned girl.

They travelled for six months after that, with ponies and a pack-horse, almost respectable folk, staying at inns in villages, towns and cities, all the while observing how they were run. At last they came to a growing village on the edge of the marsh and lodged with a widow, for there was no inn there.

"I should like to stop here, Toby," said Mol certainly. "I see that there is no inn but much building going on, and we can make our own place how we like it. Besides," she smiled at him sideways, "it is time we were wed, Toby mine, for next year we shall be three."

Widow Tims was as small and neat as her home. Situated on the edge of the village, it was a two-roomed wood-framed house, filled in with lath and plaster, it had a neat reed roof which was exceptionally weather-proof. One end wall was stone, and had a chimney stack set in it. Tobias was impressed. For it was rare for simple folk to have such, usually living in one smoky room with a hole in the roof. They settled in to the small room while Widow Tims slept in the room with the chimney piece and as it appeared that her guests were to stay for some time, she was quietly happy. Usually people stayed for a night or two on their way elsewhere, yet it seemed that the young couple intended not only staying, but building an inn.

They did their sums. Neither really knew how much their inn would cost, but they guessed that if they made great plans and worked slowly towards completing them, they would manage. Tobias asked around for land for sale, land in the centre or edge of the village, where they could spread if needs be. None seemed available or ideal. They began to despair when Mistress Tims found Molly retching into the privy at the back, and delighted to hear of the coming babe, immediately offered to sell them the little meadow alongside her house.

It was ideal and Tobias was jubilant. Now he engaged a head builder and together they endlessly drew on a slate in front of Mistress Tims' fire till a plan was agreed on. A long low building would be built first, with allowance for a second floor and, later, as the money began coming in, they would expand and build stables and barns at the back about a courtyard.

The people of Marsh Newton were pleased. An inn! A decent place, to accommodate travellers, hopefully with fine ale and good food. Now their village really was on the way to becoming a town, and then they might get a charter and who knew what else?

When Molly gave birth to their first son, Mistress Tims was as mother and grand-mother and stood for God-mother, begging that the boy be named Michael after one of her lost sons.

Over the months, her story had come out slowly, her sorrow finally causing her to speak. One day a fine fellow had ridden into the village and spoken to the men, urging them to leave their poor lives and their hard work on the land and come with him to seek their fortunes and fight for his lord. Foolish men, they had picked up their scythes and pikes and on a fine summer's morn had marched cheerfully out of the village, never to be seen or heard of again. Timothy the hurdler, with his three strapping lads were amongst them. What was the point of keeping the field when it was quite obvious they would not be coming home?

"There, there," said Molly, kindly, rocking the grieving woman close, "we are your family now, dearling, and be sure we shall mind you well."

That had been ten years past and everything which they had dreamed of came about, mostly due, they well knew, not only to chance but to hard work. Mol had borne five children, three boys and two girls, but in the last bitter winter, two little boys died of the cold and they were devastated.

"I'll not have any more," sobbed Mol, "just to lose them." To be roughly comforted by Widow Tims who was like a mother to her. "And you will so, my love, if the Good Lord designs it."

It was a good inn, clean and airy and well run. Tobias bought good wheat flour so theirs was the best bread in town. He walked around the market and chose the best beef, mutton or fowl, which, either roasted, on the spit or cut up in pies, were succulent and tasty. And the cheese, brought downriver from the great Jerome flocks of sheep, was delicious. Even the pease pottage, thick with mint and onion, with tiny bits of crisp bacon in it, was special. They had built on stables with reed roofs at the back, and remembering his past, Tobias made good space under the eaves for the stable-hands to live, dry and warm. Gradually the inn grew to envelop Widow Tims' house, but she lived with the family now, above the kitchen, dry, warm and loved.

Tobias seemed very thoughtful for days, and the women walked around him quietly. At last he spoke, having mulled over his problem long enough. He cleared his throat and spat into the fire.

"If Lucas Byford, a yeoman farmer, can get one of the Woodman girls as daughter-in-law, why then can't we do likewise?"

Molly looked up at him from her great crock of lardy-crust. Her hair had escaped from its cloth and a smudge of flour sat thick on her cheek. She all but gawped at him. Was the man going soft in the head? "Never," she crossly brushed the hair aside, "have I heard you talk such nonsense, Tobias. Them's gentry, lad, while we are simple village folk. Daughter-in-law indeed," and bashed her fist into the dough.

"You did not hear me well enough, wife," Tobias responded calmly, "I said yeoman. Yeoman. For that is what Lucas is, just a humble peasant farmer with an itsy-bitsy bit of land by the ford."

Mistress Tims listened, intrigued, but said not a word as she brought the great pans from the larder to have their pastry lids laid on.

"I heard you well enough Toby," repeated Mol, "but you forget yourself with your fancy ideas. They'd never look at the likes of us."

Tobias looked fondly at his wife, noted her floury face and hair and felt a great surge of love flow out of him. "You are a silly besom, woman. You do not see beyond your kitchen and your children, you do not see how life is changing all about us, going up, and down." He stopped and cleared a space on the board before him. "Think of the river Mol," he set a knife down. "For years it runs straight and clean. Then," he reached for another three knives and set them down too but in a fan, "a catastrophe happens, it rains too much and the river breaks its banks, causing floods and calamity. Things change, sometimes for the better, often for the worse."

Now Mol stood up, having deftly completed her task, brushed off her hands and glared at him, hands on hips. "One moment, Tobias Innman, you speak of one of our children marrying above his station. The next, you speak in riddles of the river."

He caught her as she flounced past. "Affairs in families go the same way, wife. Think on it. Sir Stephen de Elancourt! Baron Roland of Castle Pomeroy! Oh yes," he banged the board so that the knives jumped, "don't think that I haven't done some listening as well as quiet asking. They were lords of our land for generations. Now what are their descendants? Woodmen, good woodmen mind, honest and decent and probably a lot better than their forefathers. So they are down now, and we, simple folk as you rightly say, are on our way up. Is there," he kissed her firmly on the un-floured cheek, "any reason why our Michael should not, in a year or two, take one of the Woodman girls to wife?"

With this in mind, he nurtured the friendship with the Woodman family, encouraging the little girls to play together, and always arranging that the great, ten-year-old Michael, was free of his tasks, to watch over them.

Robin's brothers came in autumn as was their habit, and the tower house was filled with love and laughter. After each girl had received her gift, she sang, recited or danced for her uncles in thanks. Felicia saw her children's dower chests fill up with ever more beautiful and precious things. Due to their travels, or by giving orders to their captains, the uncles had access to much that was fine and rare. Something from every precious cargo was put aside to bring to their nieces. Trade was good, and who but family came first?

Gradually over the years, many of the folk round and about the tower became involved in supplying victuals for the ships. It was something which had happened slowly, so trade with the area grew, bringing about a greater prosperity. The ever larger Jerome family provided the bulk of the goods sent by flat, reed boats downriver to the port, there to be squabbled over by the captains, for food on board was too often poor. Vegetables in pickle, waxed cheeses, pots of butter, double sacks of good flour, tubs of honey as well as smoked meats, were highly prized. Peas, beans, dried mushrooms in season, and smoked eels in barrels, intestines filled with fine, clarified lard and dried herbs all helped to cheer long voyages. Fresh and cleanly packed, they lasted much longer than the usual shoddy port stores.

Felicia began to dry, cooking and medicinal herbs to send to sea with her brothers-in-law, who encouraged her to do more for all their ships. So Robin had built the little braid loom for their younger daughters to weave little bags in which to pack them. They used different colour borders, colours which indicated what was what. This was a way, Felicia said, to help folk who were not well versed in herb lore, or could not read.

After the brothers had toured the forest and marked what trees needed felling, they went downriver to see the farm by the ford.

"Don't expect too much," Robin said as they floated along, the horse walking along on the bank beside them. "Tobias Innman told me that since Lucas' wife died, his farm is a sorry place, all run-down. But he did say something about a good spring with pure water, which in this day is certainly something. Firstly, being downstream from Marsh Newton, the river will be none too clean. Secondly, if it is a spring, the girl won't have to pull up water from a well or the river to carry to her kitchen."

It was much worse than they expected. A great ramshackle barn-like hall stood alone on a rock bluff above the river by the ford to the town. The brothers glanced at each other as the flat grated on the gravel and Lucas greeted them. They were so close, the three of them, a mere look, lift of a finger or eyebrow told aeons.

They walked, the last one leading the horse, in single file behind Lucas up to the farm, there to be met by the two sons, clean, their fair hair newly-cut and well-washed. They bowed and shook hands in welcome. It was the same inside. Quite obviously a great deal of cleaning up had been done for their arrival. Yet it was plainly one of the old hall farms, where man and beast lived inside at night, summer and winter. The brothers deliberately did not look at each other.

"Tobias Innman told me that you have a fine spring, Lucas," Robin spoke jovially, trying to hide his dismay. "Shall we see it, for I have a great thirst on me for pure, cold water."

Again they walked West, a short distance from the hall, one behind the other silently, till just below a small rocky overhang there stood a fine spring falling into a great stone basin. In turn they drank and washed their faces praising the coldness and purity of the water. Then they looked about and saw lettering on the rock face, still clear despite being weather-worn.

"It's Latin," said a brother, bending to see better. "It is a dedication to an ancient god I think, built by one Lucius, son of Lucius Scholasticus." He stood up, suddenly intrigued. "Have your family been here long Master Lucas?" he asked.

"For ever," came the reply, "as far as I know." They looked at him then in the early evening light, a stern, craggy face and wondered.

That night they sat about the hearth and watched the moths circle in the smoke as it rose to escape out of the roof hole. They spread their cloaks on the piles of hay which had apparently been fresh cut for them, for it smelt good. They did not know where to begin, for they were, for once, lost for words.

The sons, Luke and Piers, served them at the board which was at least good simple fare. Robin recognized the Jerome cheese in gratitude and tore at the bread no doubt from the Jerome mill. A salmon had been roasted on a stone by the fire and they picked at it with their knives and fingers, finding that Master Byford had an unusual way with herbs, if little else, for it was delicious. So somehow, they found some things to praise and the evening went well enough.

In the morning, Robin was taken by Luke to look about the farm. It really was a poor place though the views across the river to the water-meadows were beautiful. Robin stood gazing out, and asked quietly. "If you take my daughter, will you let us make many changes to your hall and round about? We will of course pay for everything, as part of her dowry."

Luke nodded.

Robin then turned to the elder boy and asked him if he agreed to everything.

"Well lad, speak up, or don't you want Jessie after all?" Robin looked at the boy and saw a flush rise up his neck and into his face. Luke would have liked to say there and then, that he did not want to wed Jessie, it was Clary, the quieter one whom he liked.

"What about the other?" he asked, stumbling over the words.

Suddenly, Robin thought he understood. Of course. The lad must be close to his brother Piers and want him to marry too. And if Piers were to wed with Clary, it would be pleasant for all of them. That then, was the answer. It would be the best plan for them all, for really Jessie could not cope here alone with three men, however many improvements they made on the place.

Back at the hall, Robin looked over the younger son with new eyes. Smaller, lighter and perhaps finer-looking than his brother, it seemed he might suit his gentle Clary very well. Knowing her, his favourite child, he knew that she would be in agreement. This then would answer many problems. They would make the place habitable and fit for his daughters, within the twelve month. Greatly relieved, a weight suddenly lifted, he announced his plan.

Both sisters would marry the two brothers, and for their dowries, they would each bring one hundred acres, furniture, linen and chattels, plus the entire renovation of the hall.

After a stunned silence, they all smiled broadly, pleased with the plan. All but Luke, who bit his lip, wondering quite how it had come about. Still, there was time, and Piers was an easy boy who wouldn't mind which bride he had, as anyway, they looked the same. As the brothers left, they thanked their host and promised that they would organise the starting of work as soon as possible. Old Lucas actually looked happy for once.

Back in the inn, they agreed that Tobias would organise the papers to be drawn up, and when they were ready, he would accompany them to the Byfords as witness.

"Tell me, Master Woodman," Tobias speared a good piece of meat from the platter and offered it to Robin. "Is there an inn at your place, for my wife asks to go to visit the cheese-makers, for she is mightily impressed with their produce. Since we lost two little sons last winter, she could do with a little change."

Robin laughed lightly, "No inn, Tobias, but your mistress is welcome to stay with us any time. Bring the girls, for ours do love them so. It would be good if she could come soon though, for my wife is waiting to deliver, and company would be a great diversion for her."

With Mistress Tims and young Michael in charge of the inn, the brothers went with Tobias to settle the agreement with Lucas Byford and his sons. As they went downriver, so did Mol go up, her little daughters wild with excitement, their mother not for a moment letting go of their clothes in her clutch.

Never had Mol seen such a beautiful place. Never had she slept in a great tower in a huge bed, her daughters on either side of her, under a down quilt. Eyes wide, she gazed at the fine carved furniture, "made by our grandfather Sir Stephen when he was young," said one little girl. "And by our father," interrupted another with indignation.

The walls were hung with beautiful tapestries, their colours vibrant, their scenes unworldly. Embroidered coats of arms were everywhere, on everything, and she supposed it was theirs. Walking in the gardens, she begged cuttings and seeds from Felicia, for the inn would certainly benefit from some joyful colour in the spring. Mol found herself looking at the little Woodman girls with new interest, perhaps Tobias was right, perhaps one of them would do very nicely for their Michael.

Felicia was glad of new company. She was so tired of her pregnancy, so huge, so clumsy. The innman's wife seemed a lovely bright young woman, so helpful too and her daughters sweet and well behaved. Although she could not accompany Mol to the Jerome farms where the cheese was made, the girls went too, also happy with the visitors.

All packed and ready to leave when the flat boat returned in the morning, Mol sat with her new friend in their grand, light kitchen till late, chatting quietly, exchanging stories of their lives. As Mol made to leave for the tower, she heard a small cry, and turning, saw Felicia standing up, gazing at her feet where a pool of water grew larger by the moment.

"My waters have broken, Mol! It is a little early, I am not yet due. Oh my dear, thank heaven you are here. Please first help me upstairs, I'll call Clary, but I beg you to be silent, for it is better Jessie does not know and stays abed."

Having heard the quiet call, Clary appeared, her shawl loosely about her shoulders, "Yes, mother," then stopped seeing Felicia's face. "Rest easy, mother, I'll go to fetch the midwife," and on silent feet ran lightly down the stairs. Slipping on strong shoes, she went out to find the stable boy, helped him saddle up the best pony and away, and then began making ready the kitchen, poking up the fire. Drawing water from the well, she filled the cauldron and pushed the crane over for it to heat. Putting the maiden in front of the fire, she laid out towels, together with the sheets and bindings for the babe. They had been through all this, for Felicia was determined that her daughters should know all there was about birthing. Satisfied that she had completed her tasks, Clary trimmed the candles, put more logs on the fire and ran up to her mother's room again.

The two little boys arrived in quick succession before the midwife arrived. Mol took the babies as they were born, and handed them to Clary, who incredulous, quickly wrapped her brothers up in warm sheets.

"Tie a piece of wool on the firstborn's wrist," said Felicia smiling happily, "For they are as peas from a pod, as you were, and we will want to know later."

When the midwife bustled in, she delivered the afterbirth, telling them that these were, as had been the first brace, identical. Then she washed and made tidy both Felicia and the babies, and made them comfortable and sat herself down in a chair to wait till dawn.

Robin and his brothers arrived back from town the next day to be met by eight wildly excited girls who all spoke at once, noisy, unintelligible and joyful.

"Let father go in first on his own," Clary barred the door as the others crowded round. Then, after a while, a beaming Robin opened the door and they all streamed in, the uncles, almost weeping with joy, for here they were again, dark-haired twins, just as they had been.

A messenger was sent to tell Sir Stephen and Moya the good news. Clary had written a hasty letter in her fine hand, telling them all about it, and her thrill of attending the birth. What fine, big and beautiful boys they were. How wonderful Felicia had been, uttering not a sound, now resting after her travail, glad to be free of her burden, wondrously happy.

Of course, Molly and her girls did not leave the next day but stayed a full week more to help. The change had done her so much good! She had enjoyed every hour of every day, culminating in the joy in the delivery of her new friend of two fine sons. The honey on the cake came when she was invited to be God-mother to the boys, so she stood proudly beside the uncles whose names, James and John, they took.

Gazing about the lovely little wooden church, at all the happy faces of kin and friend, she suddenly realized that her Tobias was really a very wise, far seeing man.

As there was no inn around about, it might be clever to start thinking about it, and their Michael might indeed woo and marry one of the Woodman's daughters, who could help him to run it. Tobias was right, things did change, and now she felt a flicker of confidence that it might be possible.

Trailing her hand in the water, she idly watched the young groom trotting on the tow path beside the river, and thought of all the wonderful things she had to tell Toby and Mother Tims. Then she thought of the two new born-babes, her Godsons, smiled softly and again realized that perhaps Tobias was right there too. Maybe they should also have some more children.

CHAPTER TWENTY SEVEN

PIERS

How the winter did drag! How boring life was, being cooped up inside all the time with babies and children, washing and shutters closed and misted windows. Jessie unpicked her sewing, angry that her mother had scolded, saying it was not good enough.

"Who will look at the stitching on my shift mother?" To which Felicia had simply narrowed her eyes at her daughter and said nothing.

No one came to visit, that is, no one of worth. There was no news from the outside world, just the small happenings and gossip of the village. Jessie scowled into her sewing. Their two dowry chests were filled to brimming, yet her mother goaded them on to do more.

"You will be grateful one day," said Felicia, utterly weary of the winter too but mostly because of her elder daughter. "When you have a home and family to care for, mark me, there will not be so much time to spin and weave, and a full dower chest will go a long way to ease your lives, and last a long time."

Felicia was tired. Her baby boys were the light of her eyes, bonny, good little things, but now, she frowned, she feared her milk was failing, and then how would they fare?

"Why the frown, sweet wife?" Robin was about to go out, so lightly touched his wife's head cloth with his lips. She sat silent for the moment, a babe on each breast.

"I fear that my milk is not sufficient for them any more. They drag at me, making me sore, yet they are too young to take other food. I'm afraid that we must find a wet-nurse." A tear glistened at the corner of her eye.

Robin felt a surge of fear in his chest. This was woman's work, something which he had never even thought of. He gazed anxiously at his sons. To him they were perfect, plump, smiling and good babies. He was terribly alarmed.

"I have been putting off going to town for many days now, Felicia my love," trying to sound normal, his heart hammering. "Now this is important, so I will go and while on my way and in town, I will pass the word that we need a wet-nurse to help you at least with nursing the boys."

Head bowed, Felicia realized that this was the wisest action, however much she hated the idea of her babes at another woman's breast. She smiled weakly at her husband. They were so blessed she knew. Eight fine children and unlike most people, they hadn't lost one, so unusual. Fear gripped her heart and she held the boys tighter.

Clary came in and took a baby up, her face aglow with love. Deftly laying him on her shoulder, she patted his back until a fine burp erupted to their mutual satisfaction. She loved her baby brothers passionately, and was constantly at her mother's side helping with them.

"Your father is going to ask around for a wet-nurse, Clary," Felicia said rather tearfully. "I don't want one, but I get sore as they are hungry. I fear that I do not have enough milk for both of them any more."

Clary's face grew serious and her eyes widened. After giving her mother a hasty kiss, she ran out to the stillroom and returned with a brimming jug of ale.

"Drink mother. You know it helps to make milk." Then she went to the physic cupboard and returned with a small pot of comfrey ointment. The best hog's fat well cleansed and gently melted with comfrey finely chopped in it, then strained, made an excellent healing salve.

Felicia gratefully did as her daughter asked before tightening her bodice up again. "Thank you my dearling," she said, still tearful, "how ever will I manage without you when you are gone?"

Robin went to town as usual in a flat boat with two Jerome men, a boy riding the horse along the river bank. He should have gone last week and the week before but with the weather so bad, had put it off. Now the boat was loaded up with goods to take to the town, and he had work to do with Tobias about the Byford farm. Seeing the fine inn which Tobias had built, he had asked him to supervise the extensions to the Byford hall. For the plan was that the girls would wed in early summer, and there was much to do.

A thin sun shone on the river as they glided down stream, the only sound, the dull thudding of the horse's hooves on the towpath. A small but bitter wind hit them, face on, and they drew up their cloaks and pulled down their hats. Robin told his companions of his anxiety and quest to find a wet-nurse for his twins and they promised to pass the word.

Tobias was glad to see Robin, and Mol brought out hot mutton pies with ale for them to eat in front of a blazing fire. Winter was always quiet, with travellers sensibly staying at home except for emergencies. So the innman had taken on the project of the Byford work with enthusiasm, for after all, it was quite a compliment.

He told Robin of their progress, drawing on a slate to back his descriptions.

"I do believe it will be a fine place for your girls, Robin," for they were now good enough friends to be on Christian names. "This cold weather has been a boon as far as bringing in the timber, and soon the reeds will be cut and ready to go on the roofs." He paused thinking for a moment. "I must admit my friend," he grinned, "I thought that your idea was grossly extravagant at first; two, separate houses more or less, tacked on each side of the hall! But now I see the sense of it. For being so different, it will be good if your twins each have their own quarters, with the hall centrally there for all to use." They mused for awhile. "Old Byford is giving me a little trouble mind, grumbling all the time. But why he should, I do not know, for he doesn't even have to feed the builders. They cook for themselves with the provisions you provide."

Robin raised his eyebrows.

"Why should he complain then? As there is little work in the winter, he can sit by the fire and watch his place grow bigger and better by the day! He is a lucky man."

Mol was concerned and sympathetic to hear of the need of a wet nurse. She was again with child, so felt anxious for her friend Felicia and her godsons, so promised to enquire about most diligently.

Robin then walked through the cold and silent lanes to the Goldsmiths' house with their regular cheeses where again he received a good welcome, and again passed on his request for a wet-nurse.

The days being very short, Robin decided to get home as soon as possible. He looked at the sky, frowning. Snow? Back at the inn he was surprised to find Lucas Byford waiting for him with his younger son. They were all ease and smiles and a slight wink from Tobias caused Robin to grin wryly to himself. Once more they sat by the great ingle-nook and Robin heard all over again of the great works going on at the Byford farm.

"How are the girls?" asked Piers, which caused Robin to look closely at him. A handsome, soft boy he felt, glad once again that his lovely Clary would be well suited.

"Well, lad, well, but bored with the winter and being indoors." Then on impulse and addressing the father too he said. "Why, my boy, don't you come home with me to stay for some days? I know work is slack at this time of year, and it will do us all a lot of good having your company." He raised his eyebrows at first the father, then the son. "Well what do you say then? For my wife and daughters would be right glad to have you."

So Piers returned in the flat with Robin, his eyes aglow with excitement, for he had hardly been further than town, and certainly never before this far from home. As they trudged over the hard ground towards the lights of the marsh tower house, Piers gazed raptly all about him. He had never seen such a fairy-like castle before. Dimly rising up, soft lights picked out from windows, he took in the beautiful, rambling building dominated by a single tower.

As they entered, at his call, Robin was surrounded by a host of golden-haired girls, all vying to be kissed, so Piers stood unnoticed in the shadows for the moment. Then Clary saw him; their eyes locked, and running forward she dipped, took his hand and drew him forward, flushing prettily.

"Look who is here!" she cried, "Piers has come with father." Then turning to Robin asked in a rush, "Did you not also bring Luke?"

Laughing, Robin took off his cloak and Piers did likewise helped by many slender hands and smiling upturned faces who told him all together, where to put his things.

"I chanced upon Master Byford and Piers just as I was about to leave. After we had some talk about the building work, I suddenly thought, work being slack at this time, that Piers might be spared to come and give us his company, so drive away our boredom."

It was all excitement and fuss as girls ran hither and thither to set another place, fetch ale, more food, a napkin. The guttering candles were pinched and burned brighter while the fire was encouraged with more logs. It was such a happy evening and they all stayed up later than usual. A pallet was laid in a corner of the kitchen, for it was too late to prepare a room in the tower, and Piers fell asleep with a smile on his face, dreaming of golden girls.

Next day, Robin having insisted that Piers borrow some of his warm, working clothes, they all went out to explore. The girls showed him all around, up in the tower, the stables, the frozen gardens. Then they ran through the village greeting their neighbours, introduced Piers, gathered kindling and picked some branches of red-berried holly to take home to cheer mother.

It grew dark very early that afternoon for the sky hung leaden, laden, so everyone told him, with snow. They were right, for the following morning the earth was white and great, lazy fat flakes were still falling.

Felicia watched all her daughters' delight in their guest. Carefully, she observed Clary, then Jessie. It was as usual. In between helping her mother with the babies, Clary did most of the work preparing the meals with old Mary, their last maid. Of course the younger ones helped with many small tasks like cutting vegetables, setting the board and replacing the tallow candles. But it was Clary who organised them in their tasks, while Jessie idled around, pretending to be busy. Piers observed all this too. He quickly found he could identify his bride, from her twin, merely by her activity. As she sped past him on her errands about the place she would flash him the warmest smile, before rushing on. He was glad that he had been given the second twin, for the first, though quite as pretty, seemed not nearly as pleasant.

Then one morning, the sun shone and the sky was blue so out they raced again, sledging, playing snowballs and creating a snowman till they were pink and breathless.

Another diversion unexpectedly came to entertain them. A pony-drawn sled arrived with some Jeromes aboard, well bundled up against the cold, a plaintive goat stood up behind them. It was Beth, one of Jerome's granddaughters, a childhood friend of Felicia, with her man, two little daughters of about six months and little over one year and five older children, all boys. There was happy reunion between the women, and suddenly the house, which had always seemed so big and airy, seemed small, crowded with people of all sizes.

"Come!" said Robin, picking up a great log basket. "Let us make the chamber in the tower comfortable for all you young people, so give the mothers some quiet."

Excited, all eager to help, Jessie picked up their best tallow candles, and everyone carried something and rushed around while the men lit the fire. Mats and stools were shifted to the side, clogs were taken off and lined up neatly by the door. Then Beth's man pulled out a little pipe and began playing, so Robin ran hither and thither placing them in two rows, boys one side, girls the other. Eyes alight, they lined up and began to dance, the older ones guiding the younger. Clapping their hands, weaving and crossing, dipping and skipping, they were in no time, very warm.

In the kitchen Beth and Felicia talked babies. Beth had heard about her old friend's fears and had decided to come to advise her and also take her squabbling brood out of the house while the sun shone.

"It was the same with me dearling," said Beth. "We were that pleased to have girls after all those boys, but when the elder was about half a year, and I was so quickly with child again, I suddenly became fearful that my milk would fail and I would lose her."

Felicia observed the little girls who, hopelessly impaired by their clothing yet none the less determined, crawled about the floor, exploring. They were bonny and obviously very healthy. "So how did you manage, Beth?" she asked, greatly interested.

Beth drew up a large sack and began to take things out of it, talking all the while. "We bought a goat, then I ground oatmeal," she showed Felicia the little quern at the bottom of the sack, then opening a little bag, took out a pinch of powder, "very fine. Once a day I boil the milk and mix in the meal to make a soft paste, sweetening it with a little honey. She took to it immediately, so I gave her the breast to start, then some pap, then breast again." She crowed to her little ones who beamed back at her. "Now I feed both the same way. As they got older and grew teeth, I slowly added other things, and if it agreed with them, kept on. If not, I stopped. Everything is best done gradually. Now we mush up what we eat and add some goat's milk to make it sloppy and they take what ever is offered to them."

Felicia shook her head in wonder. She had never before heard of half yearlings being given food other than milk.

"Of course," Beth added with a wry smile, "they still love mother best, so while I have milk, we shall just go on, even if it is just for comfort."

Felicia was impressed, and while she handed a son to Beth, Clary slipped in, pink faced from her exertions.

"Sorry mother. I forgot to help you, for we have just been so enjoying some jolly dancing!"

Felicia clicked her tongue in mock scolding. Then she told her daughter all that Beth had said, so there and then they took turns to grind up oatmeal very fine, took some milk off the goat, and made a small pan of pap to offer the babies.

When a happy and tired party of dancers re-emerged from the tower, they found the two boy babies intent on opening their mouths wide for the next spoon. The general enthusiasm and laughter even brought smiles from the little boys, who for the moment were diverted, from their new and interesting sustenance.

Felicia thought rapidly as to how she would feed so many mouths, for it was a low time of the year, with little of interest to put into the pottage. Taking down their largest cooking pot, she scoured the larder shelves for little treasures which she had put by for just such an occasion.

All about the long board, the family and guests sat, peeling and chopping, faces glowing in the fire-light. First a good lump of goose fat went into the pot sizzling merrily, to be followed by a bowl of chopped onions and dried garlic leaves. The smell was wonderful. Next, tiny pieces of ham and bacon to fry, followed with water, because they needed longer cooking than the vegetables. Happily assisted by Piers, Clary climbed up to the highest shelf of the larder where the dried stores stood. She unhooked a ring of shrivelled mushrooms, took a measure of peas and a little bag of damsons, all of which she sat in boiling water, to soften them. While the pot heated, parsnips, neeps, and cabbage, were peeled and all neatly chopped, to go last into the pot. All the while this work was being done, they sang, cheerful young voices vying to sing the loudest, sweetest, or the next song. When the water was boiling up again, Felicia tipped the mushrooms in, then added a good measure of barley and stirred it well.

Every type and size of bowl and horn or wooden spoon was set on the board, some having to share a bowl, for there were not enough. No one seemed to mind for the mood was gay and they were all hungry from the cold and the dancing.

"What a good pottage, Felicia," said Beth, savouring it, and Piers agreed fervently, determined to do the same when he got home. Blowing to cool it, for her little girls were anxious to have a taste, Beth thought of her dull winter pottage and planned on gathering next autumn's mushrooms, damsons and bullace to dry for such occasions. "You give me ideas."

A silence fell on the great kitchen, as every eye and spoon concentrated on their meal. When the pot emptied, good brown wheat bread was shoved around to sop up the last of the gravy, and every soul smiled as each stomach settled comfortably. Felicia and Robin smiled at each other over the young heads which crowded the benches about the board. Life was sweet.

That night, Beth and all her family slept in the tower, and left in the morning loaded down with little gifts. It had been a joyful little interlude during the dull days, one none would forget.

A goat was bought the very next day and Beth's advice carefully taken. Felicia watched in awe as her sons grew before her eyes, particularly as they also enjoyed their new food. Clary sat beside her mother at meal times and in turn, took a boy in her lap, spooning the creamy pap into a wide mouth, while the other nursed. They liked their new menu, with eyes as round as their mouths, were always alert for more. Meanwhile, all the family enjoyed the novelty and laughed to see Felicia's rueful face at the mess the twins made of her breasts.

Piers left for home the next time Robin went to town. Despite the many souls who filled the house, he and Clary had managed some precious moments alone together. Once he came across her walking a baby to sleep in the garden. She looked so lovely, and he could not help but put his arm about her, to walk with her quietly, close. Jessie particularly seemed to make a point to be by them all the time till once, when Felicia had suggested that Clary show him her bride chest, they had some more moments together. Quickly, he had taken her into his arms and kissed her. It was wonderful, this being in love, especially with such an angel.

"I shall miss you gravely, Clary, my bride."

Clary smiled, a slow sweet smile of pleasure. "It won't be long now, Piers."

"It will feel forever," he replied, fervently, holding her tight.

"We can write?" She looked up at him to see a shadow cross his face.

"I cannot write, my love, or read," He buried his face in her hair. "And you must understand, my sweet girl, that our home is a very poor place beside yours. I fear you will be deeply disappointed," his voice filled with anguish.

Now Clary reached up and put her arms about his neck, and on tiptoe kissed his mouth, for she knew something about his place as her father had hinted such. "You are lovely, Piers. It is you who I love and will wed. As for your home, we can make it beautiful together," and they kissed again, this time deeply. Voices outside heralded the arrival of some little sisters so they quickly drew apart, yet glowing. For they were true lovers now, having kissed and held each other close.

All the way home, well bundled up against the cold, Piers thought of his love. He was so lucky! She was an angel! Yet he also saw the marsh tower in comparison to his old hall home. His was a barn, that was all.

"Well, tell us, Piers?" Luke eagerly requested of his brother. He was deeply disappointed, yet resigned now to wedding Jessie, for it was obvious that his brother and Clary were well matched. It had been a great shame that it had not been he who had gone to market that day with his father, for then, he as the older, could have staked his claim. "Tell us all about it."

Yet somehow Piers could only drop hints of his days away. Almost reluctantly he spoke of little incidents, the dancing in the tower, the lovely little sisters and twin boys. He could not bring himself to tell of the fine furniture, the beautiful hangings, the decorative candlesticks or the obvious superiority of the marsh tower, compared with their place.

True, the builders were making great progress. Wooden skeletons graced either side of the hall, east and west. Luke had already decided he wanted the east house, "so to wake with the sun." Imagining his bride, Piers began helping with the west side. Every free moment he had, he was there beside the carpenters and the masons, imagining how she would like it, and guiding them. The Masters Woodman had sent window-glass too, so when the glaziers came, it seemed that the house was ready. Gradually both sides of the hall took shape. Here the two couples would sleep and rear their families independently, while using the hall, where old Lucas still slept in a cupboard bed, as kitchen and living quarters. Both east and west houses had a great chimney opening on both sides, giving warmth and cooking place in the hall and the house. The Byford men were quietly aghast at the extravagance. Two fireplaces! But when the uncles Woodman glowed with pride at their innovative idea, they had to agree.

Piers imagined the sun setting, and he and Clary sitting in the evening after work, shelling beans and peas for drying. He thought that he would make a vegetable garden on the side of their house, so began collecting river stones and discarded masonry from the builders, to make a wall to keep the beasts out.

When with spring, Piers was out with the flock, he noted all the little clumps of bright flowers along the hedges and water's edge; violets, snowdrops, primroses and grape hyacinths, and dug them up to replant along the bluff above the river.

At the tower, preparations grew frenzied, everyone trying to outdo each other to make gifts for the brides. With their nimble little fingers, the younger girls peeled the skin off reeds and dipping them into melted lard, made rush lights, providing each bride with a fine boxful for the winter. Of course they already had a good stock of tallow candles lying in the cool of the stillroom, but as Master Byford had bees, they were not being sent with any wax candles.

At last their wedding drew near. It was to be a grand affair, the nuptials held in the fine new church at Marsh Newton, with the feasting laid on at the Toby Jug inn. For it had been decided it was the best place, between the two properties, and Tobias and Mol, being good friends, turned over their accommodation entirely to the wedding party.

Despite all advice, the extremely old Lady Felicia, insisted on being present. Sir Stephen and Moya brought her in easy stages, staying a few days at each place. Ruefully they told of how while they were exhausted with their travels, she seemed to thrive on it. Sir Stephen looked so thin, frail, his hair a beautiful, snow-white. Yet he remained as ever, charming and gay, with love and time for everyone, so all his grand-children doted on him.

It seemed that not only the whole town turned out for the wedding, crowds of kin, or not kin, as said Moya, came in by boat and cart, emptying the forests and hamlets about the marsh tower. Every one brought generous contributions for the feast, and the meadows above the town before the woods, were dotted with carts and tents, or merely strong cloths stretched from cart to ground. For although the townsfolk had opened their doors to the visitors, accommodation in Marsh Newton was limited.

The day before the wedding, Felicia went with two flat boats loaded down with things for the Byford hall. The two bride's chests, woven mats, utensils for the kitchen and a few small boxes and barrels. Moya and Louisa went with her, glad to get away from the mounting excitement, leaving Bibby and Deborah with the little girls, and the brides with their hands full, looking after the twins.

Felicia was so relieved that the festivities were not taking place at the tower. The work involved would have been overwhelming and not a day went past without she blessed Mol Innman for offering to organize the feasting at their place.

As the boats drew near to the ford, the three woman gazed at the hall perched above it. The two fine new wings virtually covered the sides, broad brick and stone chimneys jutting from both of them. Felicia had been aware of her husband's misgivings about the hall, but she thought, now looking at it, that it was indeed, not so bad.

The Byford men came down to the river to meet them, then loaded a pony with the goods and went carefully over the ford which was low. After everything was unloaded, the three women were shown around the hall itself first, then the new wings. Piers covertly watched his love's mother, and noted that she averted her eyes. He wasn't surprised in the least. Despite the many improvements, their place had no comparison in grace or comfort with the marsh tower.

Felicia took charge, directing the chests here and there in a flurry of activity. Incredibly, by the time the three women had unpacked and arranged everything, a new life seemed to come into the gaunt old hall, and the new wings looked quite cheerful and homey. With the beds made up, covered with colourful quilts, and beautiful hangings on the walls, it was a veritable transformation.

Back in the hall again, the women almost ignored the men as they removed the few poor things arranged on the rough board at the side. Here they first scrubbed the old wood clean then proudly set up shining and handsome pots and pans, horn and pewter cups, colourful earthenware pitchers and pewter and wooden platters.

"Well!" Mistress Felicia said firmly, "that's a start anyway. The girls will want their things their own way, I dare say, so they can see to it in time." Turning to the Byford men, who stood silently gazing in admiration at the transformation of their home, "we would just like to see the spring which my husband told me of before we go." Following the men up the rise they gazed in admiration in turn, at the great over-flowing stone bowl, washed their hands and faces and drank the cold, pure water.

"Now that is a splendid spring Master Byford," giving him a dazzling smile. "It pleases me greatly that my girls will not have to carry water up from the river or have to draw it from a well. So we shall be off now, and thank you for your help. May you all sleep safe and well and we shall see you at the church tomorrow."

Once back over the ford, the three women at last dared to look at each other. Nothing could have prepared them for that barn of a place, yet they knew in time, with energy and imagination, the girls would surely make it a fine and beautiful home. Then, not realizing how voices carry over the water-meadows, they began to laugh, holding their sides, wiping their eyes on their aprons. As one or the other remembered some other horror of the place, they began all over again. Alarmed by the sounds of mirth up behind him, the pony widened his step so they returned to Marsh Newton in record time.

Clary and Deborah sat on the little jetty behind the Goldsmiths' house with their feet dangling in the river. Each had a sleepy twin lying in their arms and looking over the water-meadows on the other side, they spoke softly.

"Aren't you at all nervous, Clary?" asked Deborah.

Clary considered for a moment, trying to sort out her thoughts.

"Well yes, I suppose I am, just a little. It being unknown," she smiled shyly at her friend. "But Piers is such a nice, soft boy, I am sure he will be gentle and careful of me."

"Have you never then?" Deborah's voice trailed off.

"Goodness no!" Clary spoke louder than intended and disturbed the babies, so giggled quietly. "It was so difficult when he stayed you know, so many people all the time, and Jessie hanging close by me as chaperone." She giggled again. "We did kiss though and he held me in his arms. It was lovely, I felt quite dizzy! It even makes me dizzy when I think about it."

Michael Innman had set a fine new cart, decorated with flowers and greenery by his sisters, right in the centre of the inn courtyard. Here everyone laid their gifts, to be looked over and admired by all-comers. The provisions brought were handed over to Mol for the feasting, and for safe keeping, food gifts for the bride's store cupboards, to take to their new home. Not for the opportunist cats which roamed about the inn, keeping down the rats and mice, but who also were always on the lookout for something to steal.

The three elders from the manor were given the best bedchamber, where they all shared the huge tester bed. The rest of the rooms were taken over by the Woodman and Jerome families. It seemed that the Byford's had no family, for on the wedding morn, just the three of them arrived, looking unexpectedly splendid. Lucas had taken his sons to be fitted up for fine new clothes at a tailor in town, downriver. They were handsome as peacocks in their new hats, doublets and hose. With hooded mantles as well, the grey and dark green, yellow and chestnut, were colourful compared with their usual rustic, work-a-day clothes. Later, in the privacy of their room, Piers proudly showed Clary his new brais and shift of good linen.

Moya had given the brides, yards of lace, which she had bought from a pedlar boy and they had sewn it carefully onto the necks and wrists of their gowns. Jessie had insisted on red. So dipping into the madder stores, they had dyed a length, such a long and complicated task, and made up a beautiful gown for her. Clary had chosen blue, thinking to use woad, of which they had plenty. But this time, her father had sent to his brothers for indigo, which was an exquisite colour, rarely seen out of the city. A dyer came too, and it was a thrill for them all to watch and learn from him, how to use the precious dye. So they looked quite a pair with Clary in a deep blue gown, while Jessie's was a good red.

The morning of the wedding dawned dull, a fine misty rain just causing the cobblestones to glisten. Yet by noon, the sun had broken through, and by the time the wedding party had arrived at the church porch, it was quite pleasant.

They were met by the new priest, Father Benjamin, a tall, thin young monk, with palest grey eyes which seemed to see into the soul. Now he carefully appraised the twin brides who stood before him, and in seconds had their characters clear.

Piers was enchanted with Clarissa, as the priest had correctly addressed her. But then, so was Luke, for she was truly lovely that day. Clary's eyes seemed more blue, enhanced by her deep indigo gown, while Jessie seemed too red and loud, her gown doing little for her. Without realizing that he did it, Luke gazed at his brother's bride at every opportunity. His disappointment that he had the wrong twin was keen, yet here he was making promises for the sister he did not even like. Later that day, after the feasting, minstrels came, joined by the many musical Jeromes with their various pipes, and it was a splendid evening. They danced every dance they knew; some for the elders, gentle and sedate, and lively ones for the young. Some were line or ring dances and no sooner were they finished, with a change in partners, they began all over again.

With her twins, sleeping on her lap, Felicia carefully watched her daughters and their new husbands. Was she, or was she not, imagining that Luke, Jessie's man, was watching Clary with lovelorn eyes? Very carefully she put the question to Robin, who despite the noise, understood and in turn watched surreptitiously. He frowned. Why did women always see what was not meant for them? But unfortunately, he too did notice that Luke watched Clary far more than he did his own bride. Which was as well, for Jessie was behaving like a loose woman, laughing and flirting, dancing with all comers. No doubt, thought Robin irritated that he had not curbed her somehow, having taken a glass too many of the good wine.

Mol was carefully watching too, but not the bridal pairs. Smiling into her mug of ale, she saw her Michael courting Joan, the next Woodman daughter, with sweetest attention; which the young lady seemed to enjoy. Tobias was right, they did make a handsome pair. She leaned down and spoke into Mistress Tims' ear, so the old one nodded smiling. How good it was to be part of a family again.

A fine new flat boat was brought up to the jetty closest to the inn, a gift, it transpired, from the uncles who had organised the town's children into decorating it with wild flowers and greenery. Stripping off their fine jackets, Luke and Piers handed their brides into the boat, then taking up paddles amidst cheers, guided it out into the midstream, so on, downriver.

It was still light, it being early summer, so when they arrived at the hall by the ford, both girls could clearly see their new home as they approached it. The soft sunset framed the hall against the rise of the hill, and it looked a most lovely and tranquil place.

It was dim inside, and the moment they entered they were greeted by the beasts who were in pens at the far end. They could not help but laugh, and having looked at them, the girls then sped around exploring, exclaiming and admiring everything.

"Let us have a last glass of wine before we go to our chambers," said Jessie too loudly, as she continued to look about. Clary reached for the fine glasses, a past gift from the uncles of course, while Piers brought the flagon of wine.

Both men seemed to disappear to do tasks, fetch water for the animals, see to the fire in the hearth and so forth, so Clary kissed her sister with, "Good night, Jessie. May God and the Virgin watch over and keep you this night and always," and left for her side of the house.

Having made sure that all the beasts were safe and watered, their domestic tasks done, the brothers returned to where Jessie sat alone at the board with a glass of wine in her hand.

"I'll say good night now, brother, sister," Piers gave Jessie a small bow. "Sleep well," and strode off to his house, on the west side of the hall. Taking Clary into his arms he kissed her roughly, tossing her up in his arms, laughing at her, loving her.

"Mine!" he held her face in his hands, "well almost mine anyway," then he sought in a purse at his side and drew out something small and shining. Taking her hand, he tried the ring on till he found a finger to fit it snugly. "Deborah made it for me," he said proudly. "It is three different coloured golds plaited together," ardently kissing her hand, laughing and hugging her all the while. Then, suddenly becoming serious, he whispered, "I will love and serve you till my dying day, mistress mine, and I will thank God and the saints for you, every day of my life."

CHAPTER TWENTY EIGHT

JESSIE

Picking up his boots and cloak, Lucas quietly rose from the pallet in the main room of the inn, and carefully made his way over the other sleeping bodies there. A chink of light through a shutter showed him that day was dawning, and the roosters of Marsh Newton were just beginning to try out their voices in reply to the Byford ones. He wasn't quite sure what to do, for no one else seemed to be awake, and he wanted to go home. Other forms lay on heaps of straw around the sides of the courtyard, their cloaks tight about them.

An old dog, sensing rather than seeing him, gave a gruff bark. Moments later a figure emerged and Lucas was glad to see it was the innman.

"Good day, Master Byford," he said quietly, then led the way to the well where he hauled up a bucket of cold water and offered it to his guest to wash, doing the same himself. Then, he led the way to the privy, and the two men stood wordlessly side by side, relieving themselves. Having done, Tobias led the way to a small parlour which must have been made ready the night before, where he lit a candle. Pouring out two mugs of ale, he plucked a basket off a hook on a beam, removed the cloth and offered his guest a fine white roll, before taking one himself. After he had broken and dipped his bread in his ale, he ate quietly, carefully not looking at the stern old farmer before him.

"Can't say that I've ever seen a more happy coupling as we had yesterday, Master Byford. Such handsome youngsters, you must be complimented. My, but they will breed fine families I can guess."

Lucas nodded, his mouth full.

"And I was happy to see that my boy Michael took a fancy to Joan, the next lass down, and she seemed to enjoy herself too. So maybe, Master Byford, in a year or two, God willing, we shall have another such wedding. Though," he hastily added, "nothing could better yesterdays."

Again Lucas nodded, carefully wiping his beard of the delicious crumbs. It was the first time he had tasted white bread, and he had enjoyed it. "Thank you kindly, Master Innman, for your words and for the great feast which you put on for our families. As you say, it was a grand do," he drained his mug and covered it with a hand in refusal of the offer of more. "Please give my best greetings to the Woodman family and tell them we expect them at midday, you too if you have the mind. I'll be getting back to the farm now, for there will be work to be done, beasts to see to," a slight smile, "and no doubt the young people will not be abroad yet."

But they were, at least three of them, for Jessie had stayed in bed.

"It is so beautiful," said Clary, eyes glowing as she took in the slow moving silver river and the early morning mist on the water-meadows below them. "I don't believe I shall ever be tired of looking at this view."

Piers only had eyes for his bride, whom he considered far more beautiful. "Come, my dearling," he caught her hand, "let me show you the rest of the farm," and drew her behind a hayrick to kiss her once more.

Seeing them, Luke picked up the milking pails and with a heavy heart went to milk the sheep. He loved his brother, that was for sure, but now he realized that he also loved his brother's wife, and nothing could free him of the burning passion he felt for her.

By the time old Byford had walked home, all the tasks were done, the hall swept and strewn with fresh herbs, just cut from the river's edge. The beasts were out, tethered in the meadow and Luke was getting a fire ready, for they were to roast a young bullock for their guests, and it needed many hours burning, till the embers were low, grey, very hot and just right.

Back in their new quarters, Piers playfully manhandled his bride onto the bed, but was surprised to see point-blank refusal in her eyes. "What! No?" he chided her in turn. "Will you refuse your lord and master so soon?"

Clary caressed his face and smiled sweetly up at him. "Never, my lord, but!" she tried to tickle him, "only at the wrong time!" and wriggled out of his grasp to run to her dower chest. "Come help me do, sweet Piers, for we have a great host of guests coming, and we must prepare for them." Then, she stood up and faced him squarely, "And you wouldn't want to make me sore so soon, now would you?" Surprised for the moment, then contrite and understanding, he kissed her neck tenderly, smelling the lavender and fresh, dewy sweat of her labours mixed. Together they carried her things to the hall to make ready.

Their visitors began to arrive as the sun was directly overhead and the day was hot. To their surprise and pleasure, despite their age and apparent poor health, Lady Felicia, Sir Stephen and Moya came too, intending to stay the night with them, before travelling on the next day. All the girls came from the marsh tower, running to help, laughing, admiring, carrying the little boys for their mother and filling mugs of ale for the guests. Of the inn folk, Mol came with Mistress Tims and her brood. The Goldsmiths came, including Bibby, as well as some town notables. So it was a merry party, the more so because of the uncles, who dashed into the river in their underclothes to cool off, urging all the others to do likewise. It was a happy, noisy scene with the brave diving off the flats moored along the riverside.

The smell of roasting beef wafted out of the hall. New little breads, just made by the girls, were handed round to quieten rumbling stomachs. A huge bowl of pease pudding was setting in the coolest corner by the spring, a cloth tied tightly over the top. Mol had brought all the left-overs from the wedding feast, so until the bullock was done, there was plenty to keep the hungry busy.

"You three will sleep in our chamber great-grandmother," insisted Jessie. "Luke has already put a mattress in the loft above for us, so do not worry, we shall be very comfortable."

Surprised, Felicia looked again to make sure that she was hearing the right twin. Yet she was. So what had come over Jessie? Had one night of marriage suddenly made her sweet and generous? Felicia felt unease, something was wrong.

The good holiday humour of all their guests did much to hide that first, definitely shambolic, entertainment. No one minded under-cooked buns or over-cooked beef. Why, with the river to swim or paddle in, the view to gaze at, the new wings onto the hall to admire, everyone had the happiest day.

At dusk the tower people left in their flat boats while the townsfolk went home on foot, or pony and cart. The two girls assisted Moya in putting Lady Felicia and Sir Stephen to bed, each with a cup of milk, laced with honey.

"It was a lovely day, Piers," said Clary as she snuggled in his arms, "that the elders should come too, such a compliment to us!" Yet she also was aware that something was wrong with her twin, for her behaviour, all day, had been unusual. There had been a certain brittle charm in all her dealings with the visitors. She had been too attentive, too kind. It just was not her. Clary bit her lip frowning. It was no use discussing it with Piers, for no doubt, he would just not understand.

The following day the party of elders set off at a sedate pace with their grooms. As the day was still fine, the girls went running along beside them for a while, loath to see them go. For who knew when they would meet again.

Byford Hall soon became a tidy and beautiful place. Before long, a barn was put up on the north side, so that water could run from the spring to the beasts along hollowed out logs so they would not make a mire about the well. The hall immediately became clean, with fewer flies now that the animals were out. With some difficulty they re-erected and repaired an old loom which had been put away after the death of Mistress Byford. The next one to go to town would seek out the warper, for warping up a strange loom was a specialised job, one which the girls could not do. Old Lucas seemed pleased by their efforts to get the old loom working again, and took it upon himself to repair the combs where some of the teeth had snapped.

Clary had asked her father-in-law for a place to grow vegetables, herbs and flowers, so they chose a spot where the cattle had once been penned, where the earth was good and rich. Piers built a wall, using the stones he had collected, it would make a fine vegetable garden. Seeds brought, bought and begged for, were soon sprouting, and any spare hour would find Clary out there planting with her dibber and weeding with her hoe.

Clary watched her sister quietly, when she thought she wasn't observed. Jessie was angry about something, her mouth down at the corners, her voice sharp. Yet when they sat at the board at night and drank the good wine sent by their uncles, she was unfailingly merry and foolishly flirtatious with her husband.

"What is wrong with them do you think?" Piers asked. "Luke is a misery, while I am more happy than I have ever been." So Clary wound herself about him pleased, for now she was quite sure she was with child, having missed two months of bleeding, now she could tell him and make him even more happy.

Eyes shining, they told old Lucas the next day, who actually smiled his pleasure and leant out to kiss both of them, for the first time ever. Yet they hesitated in telling Luke and Jessie, for they seemed to keep to themselves and did not invite any confidence.

Felicia and Robin were delighted and sent letters to the manor with the news. All seemed well with their families, except, Felicia noted when they met at Tobias' inn, that her twin daughters seemed to have little to say to or about each other.

Of course Jessie found out soon enough. Joan, their next sister down, who delighted at the prospect of being an aunt, had inadvertently let it out.

"So why did you not tell me, Clary? Why did I have to hear it from Joan?" her face flushed and angry.

Clary sighed, sorry that it had come to this, and wondering quite why it had. She was beginning to feel unwell in the mornings, and already her breasts pressed hard and painful against her bodice, and her stomach had a new and gentle swell to it. "I'm sorry, Jessie," her voice quiet and miserable, "it was just that somehow you weren't friendly with me, always keeping to your side of the house, never talking, confiding, as we used."

Jessie flounced out and went to her room where Clary heard her sobbing, which made her feel even worse.

Mol Innman had another son, to their delight, and named him Robin, who stood for Godfather. Every time the Woodmans came to town, Joan made quite sure that she came too, radiant in her love for Michael, who obviously felt the same as she.

Clary quickly grew large and heavy and found every task irksome. So Piers worked twice as hard to ease her toil. When Felicia and Robin came in the late autumn to bring them nuts and dried fruits, they considered their daughter.

"A brace again methinks, Clary my love," said her mother. "It does run in the family, and I see that you are too large, too early for a singleton."

"Well maybe it is an on-time singleton," cut in Jessie, in a hard voice, "conceived out of wedlock." There was a gasp, followed by a shocked silence.

Then Robin got to his feet and stood over his elder daughter, his hand raised, his voice tight.

"Never, ever, have I raised a hand to any one of my children. Never, ever, have I so much wanted to beat one till now. Get up this minute, Jessica Byford, and beg your sister's pardon, for you have gravely insulted both her and Piers, in a wicked, public and disgraceful way."

Jessie saw her father's fury, and frightened, burst into tears.

"Tears will not do, Jessica!" he shouted, still standing before her, resolute, "must I finally beat you, you who have earned beatings all your life, while your sister never did?" Felicia tried to catch his sleeve but was brushed aside. "Yes, wife, and don't you know how often she deserved a beating? And how we refrained, because we thought that we were gentlefolk, and gentry do not beat their own." He paused and looked at Luke. "As her husband, I urge you to beat her, daily, or every time she deserves it, for she obviously needs it, and I have been amiss not to deal more harshly, as she deserves, with her myself." All the while, Jessie wailed and wept, so Robin had to raise his voice to be heard. "Well Luke, do I have your permission to beat your wife or will you do it?"

Then Luke, who had been as shocked by the events as everyone else, rose and putting his arm about Jessie's shoulders, led her away to their room.

Clary sat white-faced, Piers and her mother at her side with a cup of ale, Robin, seemingly exhausted, sat down, head in his hands. Then old Lucas spoke up.

"That was just what was needed, Master Robin," he said in his quiet voice. "I have been watching these young couples, and saw that these two," he waved towards Piers and Clary, "had from the start, a real affection for each other, which the others did not have." He paused, as if searching for words. "I think it very possible that Luke wishes his wife were as sweet and gentle as is Piers'. Jessie has been uneasy in all her ways, causing Luke to be discomforted." He paused again, glancing towards the sound of the subsiding sobs which still came from the east room. "I have the feeling that those two have not even coupled yet, which is why Clary's happy news brought about that jealous outburst."

They sat in silence after that, while the old man poured more wine into their glasses. Gradually as they became calm, the sobbing stopped.

It must have been as old Lucas said, for after that day, things seemed happier in the hall. Jessie smiled naturally now, was kind because she was finally content, which made the dull days of winter almost agreeable. While Clary stitched cloth from her dower chest, Jessie sat at the loom and wove while they sang or chattered as of old.

Noting the unity between his daughters-in-law, Lucas, who barely stepped outside, letting his sons do the bulk of the farm work, spent much time with them. He had in his youth been good with his hands, so now began again, starting with simple things as spoons and stirring paddles. Finally, he began to make a cradle, carving it beautifully. A large one it was, of oak timbers, which had been left high on the hall rafters to mature. It was hard too, and he was ever sharpening his knife on the hearthstone.

Clary was frightened. Despite her total contentment and love for her husband, she felt increasingly uneasy about the birth which drew close. Finally finding the courage, she spoke with Piers, begging him to allow her to go home to the marsh tower for her confinement.

At last a day came when winter was ebbing and a weak sun shone, and the sky was clear. Hugging Jessie with tears, she was carefully lowered into the flat, a hot wrapped stone at her feet and well-covered with shawls and sheepskins against the cold. Piers rode the horse along the river bank, drawing the flat against the current, always looking back at the muffled figure, calling out and singing to her.

It was wonderful to be home again. Her parents and sisters surrounded her with love and attention, and her little brothers, walking now, gave her constant amusement. Beth and two other midwives agreed to come for her delivery, and they cheerfully made everything ready in the tower bedchamber, where they had all had been born.

Three weeks later, in the dark still hours just before dawn, Clary gave birth to her two sons. It had begun, the merest niggle of pain, the mid-morning before. A pain so deep, so new, she realized immediately what it was. Unusually for her, she had begged Piers not to go out with her father to the forest where they were sawing great trees, ready for the teams of bullocks to haul to the coast. Knowing and loving his wife deeply, Piers agreed immediately, for she had been so quiet and easy in her pregnancy, making few demands despite, he realized, often being uncomfortable.

So they walked close together in the garden, wearing pattens through the dew-wet grass. Then as the sun came up and steam rose from every glistening surface, they sat in an arbour, where they spent private, loving moments together, not speaking aloud, but with their minds. At last they went into the great kitchen where the children ate their morning meal, to play chess, which Clary won.

"Time to go up, my dearling," said Felicia tenderly, having already sent word to the midwives and remembering the birth of her first twins.

One came, head first, blue-white and silent. As they bent over him, they did not see the other come, feet first, the cord about his neck tight. Listening outside, Piers understood immediately that a birth had happened and aware of the silence, rushed in. The women were working on the first child, rubbing it, tying the cord, while Clary lay faint, exhausted. Seeing his second son lying, white, still on the bed, the good husbandman that he was, he took up the limp little body, unwound the cord from his neck, and blew, as he had done countless times with lambs, into his mouth.

They were trembling, all of them, working on the lifeless little bodies. Beth with her helpers, Felicia and Piers, frantic, desperate, till as one, the infants began to mewl, then with lavender-scented air new in their lungs, they bawled mightily.

Cutting, tying, washing down and all the while weeping, they forgot to tie the wool on the firstborn's wrist, so they never really knew, ever. At the time, it was getting them to breathe which mattered, not who was to be heir, to what?

Then they saw to Clary, cleaning her up and making her comfortable, still weeping with relief and joy. Unlike Felicia's twin sons, these were fair, yet again, identical. One, the larger, they had to guess was the firstborn, they named Lucius, from the carved stone above the spring. The other, Clary begged and was readily agreed to, was Stephen. Word was sent to the manor, where despite a difficult winter with many ailments, the old ones had clung to life, no doubt looking forward to hearing the good news. In a land where so many died young, it was a rarity to be a grandmother, let alone a great-grandmother.

Little had she thought, the frightened, lonely thirteen-year-old, Lady Felicia de Elancourt, that the tiny life which grew unwanted in her womb, would eventually create a large family and cause her to be a much respected matriarch.

Robin rode with his third daughter, Joan, to the hall by the ford, there to congratulate old Lucas, who unashamedly shed a tear. Insisting that the old man return with him to the tower to see his first grandsons, he suggested to Jessie that Joan should stay as company and that they go to Marsh Newton to give the good news to their friends. With this outing as compensation, the girls were happy, and Joan was especially joyful as she had not seen Michael Innman for many months.

Deborah Goldsmith hired a flat boat and arrived carrying two fine gold crosses of her own making, in time to stand as Godmother to her friend Clary's two sons. It was a small but happy ceremony in the small, wooden church, with the old friar, whom they now called Brother Francis, officiating. Gifts came from the manor, too many and too precious to Felicia's eye, who sensitive to the ways of her parents, worried.

Piers returned to the hall, satisfied that all was well with his new family and ready to make up for the time he had neglected his share of the work. Old Lucas remained at the tower for forty days after Clary's deliverance, bemused by the delightful children, the comfort and splendour, understanding at last what his in-laws must have thought of his barn of a home.

No sooner had calm returned to the marsh tower, and Clary was back at home with old Lucas and the twins, when tragedy fell.

Late one night, the dogs barking woke Robin who went down, lit the candles and went to the gate-house where the saddest site met his eyes. A raggle-taggle caravan of three wagons piled with furniture was accompanied by two carters and several shrouded old people. Moya had arrived, and apart from a few of her aged staff, alone. A much changed and gaunt Moya, riding on the first of three wagons, she looked down on Robin, tears falling, shaking her head. Hastily calling Felicia and the older girls to help, they lifted her down and put her and her tired old companions to bed.

Much later next day, seated in front of the fire, rested and warm, Moya's story came out. "It was a contagion brought by the priest," she said, "we all got it, but my dearlings died while I was so ill, I didn't even say goodbye." They watched sadly, holding her icy thin hands, pressing a linen cloth to her face to dry the tears. "Those who were not too ill, or were over it, put them in the crypt of our little church. I had no way to send for you. My dears, forgive me?" and wept again. They just sat, nodding, murmuring kind words to comfort her and let her speak how and when she wanted to. Now and then the three other old ones, long-time servants, indeed friends, from the manor, put in a word here and there.

"They decided it all, together, before they died," she told Felicia. "They arranged to sell everything to the family who have been renting our fish-ponds for years and who had been offering to buy the manor and lands for some time. They thought it best to do it while they lived, and not leave all the troubles to you."

Felicia was aghast. The manor sold? No more a part of their lives? It was Robin who calmed her, explaining that Sir Stephen had hinted as much. It was too far away, too much of a liability. Who would take care of it? Their circumstances had changed as had the area where they were now settled. It was the wisest decision, and while Moya lived, she always had a loving home with them.

"They wanted the children to share everything," said Moya, "the furniture and hangings, the plate and their books. Everything of worth, and even of little worth but sentimental, is packed in the drays. The deeds are signed, the money which I have is yours. For although," she almost smiled at them, "you never knew that Stephen and I have been wed for many years, I do not want for anything. All my own possessions are in the great chest given to me years ago, by Mistress Miller."

Felicia and Robin talked into the early hours, trying to come to terms with the loss of beloved, albeit elderly relations, and to prepare themselves for the new order of things.

"Funny that they never told you," said Robin, comforting his wife against his shoulder. "Like us, they shared a great love. Like us, they were so lucky." Felicia pressed against him, grateful for his sound sense and comfort. "I am sure it was she who refused marriage, because she never had children. I am equally sure that father insisted that they did wed. I am glad. She was a wonderful wife to him and mother to me, not to mention grandmother to our brood."

They decided to allocate the furniture themselves, to avoid any squabbling. Jessie would have Sir Stephen's great bed, while Clary would have Lady Felicia's. Telling a gentle lie, Moya told the other girls which pieces their grandfather had wanted them to have. There was enough and more to go round twice over. Sir Stephen's clothes and personal things would be put by for the little boys. When Jessie heard the news, inevitably it was she who made trouble.

"How could they sell the manor without consulting all of us? How could they? And why should Moya keep the money from the sale, when she is not our real grandmother nor even wed to grandfather?"

Once again Robin cut her short and, without raising his voice, told her, steel in his eyes, the true facts. "You may think what you wish, Jessica, but, as ever, I am gravely ashamed of you. It is long overdue that you learned to still your tongue. Work on it, for sadly, not only in this, you are sorely lacking."

The only extravagance Moya indulged in, was to have a magnificent tomb built for her husband and his mother. Masons were called, skilled men who had known Lady Felicia and Sir Stephen, and they carved two fine effigies who lay side by side in the little church near the manor. In soft, golden sandstone, it was the pride of the little parish, hidden away in the woods and remarkably, it survived the roughest periods of history and brutal desecration. In time, it was inevitable it would be forgotten that there lay mother and son, so they were simply Sir Stephen and Lady Felicia de Elancourt.

Well settled into her new home with her baby sons, Clary understood that her sister's marriage had at last been consummated, but still there was no sign that she was with child. As each month passed, Jessie would become excited in anticipation, then, deeply disappointed and subsequently impossibly difficult for some days.

At night, Piers and Clary clung together and wished that they could not hear the high, angry voice of Jessie, through the thin lath walls, berating poor Luke about some nonsense. The old man lay in his cupboard bed and heard it too, for although his eyes were going, his hearing yet remained sharp, and he fervently wished that it was the other way around.

Old Lucas Byford was content with his life in every other way. His sons were fine strong young men, diligent and content in their work. Piers, who favoured his dear dead mother, was the lucky one, for his wife was quite the sweetest and a very hard working young thing. Whenever he could, he helped her in her garden, for he soon realized that she had much knowledge in herbs which she used most successfully when some accident befell man or beast, and when his joints ached.

When he thought of his grandsons, Lucas smiled in the gloom, such fine, robust little lads, so cheery too. It was his constant delight to sit with them while their mother was busy, hold their hands when they walked unsteadily, and kiss them when they tumbled. It was a pity that Jessie was not breeding, but with her poor disposition, it was not so surprising.

Tobias Innman had his way when his son Michael asked for the hand of Joan Woodman, and two years after her sisters' wedding, there was another celebration at the Toby Jug.

They decided to hold the ceremony the day before the Midsummer Fair, a new and highly successful innovation in the town. This meant that kin and friends from far and wide would come to town anyway, so killing two birds with one stone in busy lives. Despite earlier plans to open another inn at the marsh tower hamlet, trade was so brisk at the Toby Jug, that the young couple were still needed to help out there.

Once again the builders arrived and a new wing rose, attached to the inn, with extra rooms to support their ever-growing families. Tobias had built up a fine livery stable and kept good stable-hands which meant gentry would stop by and change their horses if needs be.

Marsh Newton was ever growing into a successful and attractive small town. Apart from the handsome stone church, there was a good Moot Hall in the centre which encouraged traders to visit. The town elders had also put aside money for the upkeep of the road to encourage travellers to come their way, instead of going to the south, the other, longer, route to the city. Warehouses stood by a strong jetty to accommodate the farmers who lived up river. Grain and reeds came down on flat boats in their season, and a small corn exchange had been built to serve a wide area.

Sadly for the town, their one and excellent goldsmith had left, taken by the duke at the city to fashion his beautiful foreign-looking pieces. But, they admitted, trade in such luxuries in their little town must have been poor, for the local people were not accustomed to extravagances. Even so, as well as the miller downstream there was now a baker in town, a butcher, a weaver and a potter up-river, where the floods had left a good layer of red clay for him to work. Yes, Marsh Newton was a thriving little town of which they were very proud.

At last, Jessie announced that she was breeding. A sigh of relief swept quietly through the family; now perhaps, they thought, she would be calm and happy. Where she had often been impatient with her little nephews, she gave them every attention, studying them, wondering if she was carrying a brace too, and if they would be like her sister's.

Very early on the wedding morning, all but Lucas, who insisted he stay behind to guard the hall till the last moment, left for the town. Bright, in their red and blue wedding gowns, the girls were carried laughing, over the ford so as not to wet their hems. With Jessie, the twins and their gifts and contributions for the feast loaded in the cart, they set off while the larks sang. Clary walked alongside, helping the men push when they came to particularly deep ruts, laughing as they did so. As well as lettuces, eggs, cheese and a great ham leg for the feast, Piers had brought six beautiful, cured lambskins to sell in the market. For Clary had announced that the boys would be sleeping on their own truckle bed this winter, the cot too small now, and they needed a good goose-down quilt to cover them. She would like to buy some geese.

The marriage ceremony was splendid, with more folk attending than previously. Once again Father Benjamin noted the bride with his cold eye, not unlike her sisters, but light and gay in a yellow gown, which matched her flower-adorned golden hair perfectly.

Clary kissed her mother and grandmother Moya, all her sisters and handsome little brothers most extravagantly. The relief on hearing of Jessie's breeding was very evident. No more were there looks or words avoiding that delicate subject and Jessie looked radiant in her happiness, while even Luke looked relieved and less stern. Now, Clary told her mother, if, as she hoped, she got with child again soon, she would not be afraid of Jessie's wrath. For the boys would be near to three years old by the time a new one came, a goodly gap.

That evening, the stalls for the fair went up on the meadow above the town, colourful stalls of every shape and size, simple and grand. The weather being fine, most slept outside under makeshift tents alongside their carts with their goods, so to make an early start in the morning.

The four Byfords wandered about looking at everything for sale; admiring, feeling, discussing and enjoying the happy atmosphere. Each brother had a twin high on his shoulders and all heads turned to admire the bonny sight. There were tumblers and acrobats in ragged, colourful clothes, standing on each others' shoulders, leaping from one to the other, never falling. There were sheep penned which they passed by, thinking that their own were far better. On the fringes of the market stood lowing calves and bullocks, yearning for home and dam, frightened by the noise and strange smells all about them. Gypsy children darted here and there, hands outstretched, begging, while their mothers stood selling their pegs, rolling pins and brooms with noisy abandon, their beautiful dark-eyed babies tied on their backs.

A wrestler challenged the young men to compete with him, but smiling, the Byfords moved on. A tinker mended precious metal tools over a tiny, charcoal forge pumped with a blown up skin. Then they saw a pedlar boy, selling lace, a huge black hat pulled down over his eyes, a shaggy pony and fierce great dog at his side. Jessie bought some yards, pleased, for it was so like the lace on her wedding gown, and Luke, relieved to have a happy wife at last, indulged her.

On the edge of the wood stood the horse dealers, their poor beasts tied all day to branches, seeking shade from the sun. Yet they didn't linger there, for they were not thinking of buying anything other than a goose for Clary.

With his skins over his shoulders, Piers gained courage and soon called out the merits of his wares as heartily as the rest. In no time, he had sold them all four, to the wife of a town notable, who wanted them for making shoes for her little children. Joyfully catching Clary's hand, Piers went to the poultry line, where farm-wives hovered over baskets, beckoning and tempting, holding up their fowl by the legs, pinching their plump breasts. But Clary had spotted a goose girl, who turned out to be a Jerome, so after fond embracing, an honest deal was struck, and holding a cord attached to the mother goose's leg, Clary walked happily on, the six goslings busily piping, close behind.

Piers suddenly disappeared mysteriously, then returned, swooping upon her joyfully, love in his eyes with a gift of a little leather chatelaine. Thrilled, for didn't her mother also have one, Clary took out and admired the scissors and thimble, the knife and the tiny leather coin purse. Tying it securely to her apron strings, she told Piers to take the boys back to the inn for their supper, while she followed with the geese more slowly, allowing them to have their evening meal. Glad to see her so happy with her new creatures, Piers gave Clary a great hug and smile as he strode off down the hill, a boy under each arm.

Tobias was tired. It had been a very busy few days, yet he was greatly satisfied for he believed his Michael had made a grand match. Hoisting a new barrel up from the cellar, he un-stoppered it and banged in the spigot. He would be back making ale the moment things quietened down, for there was some heavy drinking going on. Pouring a fresh mug, he carefully observed a newcomer from under his bushy eyebrows. Tall, dark and strong, he considered with his experience of men, not one to be messed with. It was none of his business of course, but he didn't think it wise to put away so much strong ale if you were travelling on horseback. This much he had learned from the stranger. He bred horses and had some for sale at the fair.

A small commotion alerted him, and he waited as his elder daughter hastily picked her way across to him. He frowned as she whispered urgently, then nodded. It was a shame that Michael had to work right after his wedding, but as soon as it was quiet, he would see that the young couple went to the marsh tower for a few days. Striding across the courtyard he stepped into the furthest stable where a crowd of gypsies were clustered about an old one who lay on the straw.

"What is it Cilla?" he asked of the tall woman in charge. She looked drawn and worried from her place on her knees beside her mother.

"She had one of her turns today. Rambling terrible she is, worried, frightened, yet we can't make it out at all."

Tobias knelt beside the old woman and took her hand. Memories flooded swiftly through his head. It had been she who had held his hand when he was a stripling, no more than five or six years old he had been, when the drunken brute innkeeper he toiled for at that time had beaten him senseless. They had gathered him up and carried him away, but first he had heard the scream. It was terrible, long, drawn out and ended with a gurgling. For they had held the drunken brute down, and had cut his lower lip; right down the centre to the chin, so it flapped. Here was one who would not find drinking easy ever again.

When he was well after days, weeks, he knew not, they had dropped him off at the back door of another inn as if nothing had happened.

"We'll see you again laddie," had said the old one, and made a sign over him, before melting into the night. Later when he thought about her, he presumed her sign was for good luck. And that he certainly had had, meeting his Mol. Apart from a sense of right, he could well afford to pay his debts.

He still had the scars of that beating, which only his Mol had seen, weeping, she poor lass who had had her share.

"Mother! Mother!" he lent forward close, "it's Toby here. Tell me what it is, my dear, so that I might be of help."

The old eyes gazed blankly at him, then sharpened. Suddenly she gripped his hand tightly and tried to speak, but instead she just dribbled. Turning to Cilla he asked again. "Try to remember what she said."

Cilla sat back on her heels and closed her eyes. "It was when she saw them girls, red and blue. She began to have a fit, like she used to have, but not for a long time now. She kept on saying, "be ware blue, be ware". But with the racking about and frothing, it was hard to understand."

Tobias thought, wondered if it was something to do with the older Woodman girls who were wearing red and blue. He had always known that the old one, a pure Romany, was strange, special, saw things. Now he kissed the cold old hand and rose, nodded absently to her anxious people about her and returned to the inn. There he told one of his daughters to run quickly to the stable with a thick shawl and a jug of ale. He might have words said at his back at his tolerance of the gypsies, but never forgetting, he always remained loyal to them. Tobias looked about the crowd of folk in the inn and noted that the stranger had gone.

Then a flicker of red caught his eye and he saw the Byfords coming in, the sleeping babes in their arms. Expecting blue to follow the red, he frowned, passed his work on to Mol and threaded his way to the door.

"Where is Clary?" he asked. They smiled a greeting, happy, tired.

"Oh she is coming along behind slowly, with her new goose and goslings," said Piers happily. "She'll be along presently."

CHAPTER TWENTY NINE

JASPER

He looked around the inn, appreciating the size, order and service. Not that for a moment he could understand his own appreciation, for his life had not trained him to. Yet he felt unusually easy there, in the hustle and bustle, without any of the usual fear, which he had grown accustomed to. Of course this was a new area, one they had chanced upon because the river had flooded after a wet winter, and had changed its course. No one knew them here.

He caught Sam's eye and gave the merest recognition. The rule was they stayed apart. Just in case there was trouble. And there usually was. But he hoped that they might come here again, for he was actually enjoying himself.

A young girl passed him and he caught her, handing her his mug for a refill. The ale was good too. Wonderful smells were coming from the fireplace where an old woman was cutting and serving meat, helped by another young girl. A sister no doubt he guessed, she who now stood in front of him with his ale. Searching in his pocket, he gave her a coin, winked at her and was rewarded by a cheeky smile.

He'd like to bring his mother here, he thought, then changed his mind. For of course, his mother had probably never been in a common inn in all her life. The scene of home and her, sitting in that great chair all day long, cast a cold hand on his heart. How could she have got into such straights? If she had had a normal life, then he might have been better born, in a house, or castle, which she had often hinted of. He went over to the fireplace and waited in line for his portion. The old woman smiled at him with rheumy eyes, and wished him good appetite as she handed him a wooden dish on which sat a great slice of bread, topped with meat and sauce. He sighed, remembering that this night they had to start back to the hills, or his mother would be worrying. He continued to observe while he ate, trying not to mess up his clothes which he had recently acquired. Being taller than most, Jasper didn't fit into many men's cast offs. But some days before, they had met a tall lad and after sharing an evening's drink with him, had followed him into the night. There had been a moon, so they had waited till they reached the shelter of some trees before getting him to the ground.

"Don't mess them up," Jasper had hissed, anxious that the clothes would not be bloodstained. So he had strangled the lad, while his men held his arms behind his back. For a moment, Jas had felt unusual regret, for as he died, the lad tried to speak, entreaty in his eyes. The clothes fitted well, so they had tossed his old ones and the body into the river and ridden on, making good distance that night. The added bonus was that he had found coins stitched into the jacket, coins which he now spent most happily. For any money they made horse-dealing, had to go straight to his father, well accounted for. They were always expected to steal their daily needs.

Again he caught the eye of the young girl, again he gave her a wink. But this time she did not respond and looking about he realized that something was amiss, for the innman and his wife wore anxious frowns, as did the girl.

He considered staying another night, for he really felt good in this place. It had been jolly watching the marriage which took place midday. There were so many lovely, fair and smiling girls about. Unlike the miserable, pinched wenches they had at home. And it was a nice change being warm, well fed and enjoying unusually good ale. Some time later, he felt that the innman was observing him rather too carefully, and his instincts warned that it was time to move on. Catching Sam's ever attentive eye, he jerked his head a fraction towards the door. Moments later six men were silently moving out of town toward the horse lines.

It was a lovely evening. Jas found his horse in the stables, and was pleasantly surprised to see that he had been groomed and fed. He tossed a coin to the boy who brought his saddle. This was the life, he thought again, all decent and open and above-board. Where you paid for services, and didn't cheat and kill for them. If only he could get away, take his mother and find her a home, where she could be comfortable in winter, with the warmth of a house and fire, to ease her pain. Yet he knew, sighing unconsciously, that his father would find them. That brute of a man, who they both loved and feared. Setting his horse to an easy canter, he rode through the town up the hill towards the woods.

The sunlight lay like a glow on the sward, and there, against the greenwood was pictured a pretty sight. A girl in a deep blue dress walked, idly holding a long wand, guiding a goose with a gaggle of goslings. He watched his men pass and greet her, and saw her smile kindly at them, sharing some joke. Now why couldn't he have such a woman? Fair and clean, rounded and bonny?

As he came up to her he lifted his hat. "A fair evening to you, Mistress Goose-girl," he called down to her.

"And to you, sir," she replied smiling.

Just then the goslings set up a frantic piping being alarmed by the great horse which stamped its hooves so close by. They scattered and the girl began to run hither and thither, trying to round them up once more.

It happened so suddenly, she was caught unawares, busy with the geese. One moment the horseman was helping her round them up, the next, he had seized her and hauled her up and over his pommel and they were streaking into the wood and through the trees. She heard a shouted order, as they joined the group of men who had just gone by, and struggle as she did, Clary could do nothing but sob into the shoulder of the sweating horse. How long they travelled she did not know, but it was deep night before they dismounted and her abductor lifted her to the ground.

Shivering with fright and cold, she hugged her knees and watched as the men tied up their horses, fetched water from a streamlet and lit a fire. She was very afraid so didn't move or speak. When all was orderly, they all rolled up in their cloaks and lay about the fire. Then, the dark man, her captor, put a hand against her mouth, pushed her down and hauled up her gown and shift.

Clary fought furiously, kicking and biting, yet it was no use. Amused at first by her resistance, he laughed, enjoying the challenge. But Jas soon became angry and hit her hard against the side of her head, causing her senses to flee for a moment.

She was aware of his mounting her and savagely taking his pleasure and in her mind she screamed, "Piers, Piers," and just lay sobbing helplessly. Smothered by her clothes and his hands, she tried to get away, for she could not breathe, but he caught her and hit her again, then drew her gown out on the forest floor and lay on it, so she was anchored and could not move.

It was a terrible night of fear and cold, and despite herself she was glad of the warmth of the body so close to hers. She must have fallen asleep finally, for she was woken, light barely filtering through the trees high above, by a nudge to her shoulder. One of the men, who she had greeted the evening before, a small bent man, squatted beside her, a steaming cup in his hand. Nodding, she sat up and accepted it, yet avoided his eyes. It was mint tea, nothing more and she drank it gratefully, aware that she was hungry. Seeing that she was alone with him, she considered trying to escape, but then thought the better of it. Her head hurt, her face was swollen and if she did but know it, her eye was discolouring from the blows he had given her. Then she felt a seepage between her legs; she must wash. But it went on, a trickle, more than just man-seed and her eyes widened for she knew it was her monthly bleeding. She closed her eyes again, realizing that despite their joyful efforts, she was not with Piers' child as she had hoped. Having at last stopped nursing the boys, she had been sure it would happen quickly. So carefully, with an involuntary groan, she got up and looked around.

"I thank you for the tea," she spoke directly to her guardian. "I need to wash."

Without a word, he led her a little way to a streamlet which meandered through the forest, then sat down whittling on a stick, his back against a tree, not watching her, but obviously keeping guard. Investigating the stream, she found a small pool and lifting her skirts, squatted down and washed herself. It was dreadful! She had no cloths, and her beautiful blue gown would be stained. Suddenly she decided to use the bottom of her shift, so, thankful for Piers' dear present of the chatelaine, she took out the scissors and cut off a wide strip. If the man noticed what she was doing, he made no sign of it. By the time she had arranged some sort of protection for herself, sounds indicated that the men had returned, so understanding his wave, she followed him.

An old nag was brought up for her, and despite only having a cloth over its bony back, she found it more comfortable than lying face down over her captor's pummel. It occurred to her that she should observe the way they were going, for one day soon, she would be escaping, that was for sure. Yet the forest seemed endless, always the same, so easy for someone who didn't know the paths, to get lost.

It seemed that they were climbing, and eventually the trees thinned out and the country changed, becoming ever more rugged. On the third, or was it the fourth day, they reached their destination. Looking about her with distaste, she realized that it was some sort of permanent camp for, the men started shouting their arrival, and women and children emerged. Ragged and filthy, they clustered around her, gazing in awe at her rich, blue gown, no doubt also noticing her swollen, bruised face.

A dark little girl threw herself at the man she now knew was called Jas. Surprised, she saw him lift up the child and roundly kiss her. Barely more than a boy himself, she wondered how old he had been when he sired her. These really were a very poor, uncivilized people.

Their home, it transpired, was a huge cave, a fast flowing-stream at its mouth. The child, who said her name was Emma, led her to the centre fireplace which the women and children returned to, sitting close. It was damp and cold, and Clary noticed that they were all thin and pinched. Never in her life had she seen such poverty and filth. The damp, earthen floor was littered with bones which some pups were gnawing on. The fire was sulky and smoky so her eyes began to smart so she lifted the hem of her dress to wipe them. Her every move was observed though no one spoke and she felt totally lost and helpless.

"What is your name?" asked the child, Emma. Clary cleared her throat and tried to speak but her face was so swollen, her voice came out as a croak.

"Mary!" said the child, turning to tell the gathering. "She says that her name is Mary," beaming, satisfied.

So Mary she became, and despite herself, felt a warmth for little Emma who was the eldest of several scruffy children in their cave, and the most friendly. After a while, she came to understand that Emma had no mother, and the three other poor wretches around the hearth had five little ones between them. At first they viewed her with suspicion, for they were pathetic looking girls, probably from poor homes and of big families. Perhaps they had come willingly with the handsome Jas, unlike her. Gradually, when they saw her fix a broom from twigs and set about tidying their home, they brightened and began to take more of an interest in her and indeed everything about them. There seemed to be little food. The men brought meat, but no bread, and there was no pan to heat water for a tea or to wash or to make pottage.

Having realized that she was bleeding, Jas left her alone at first, for she furiously refused him and she supposed that was something. But then he had three other women available in which to relieve his heat. Of course, before long, he approached her one night and forced her again. Clary fought him savagely, but it was no use, for he had his way and again beat her roundly for her opposition. The next day Clary lay where she was and did not move or speak, just letting silent tears stream from her eyes. How had this happened? Why had she been so foolish as not to return to the inn with Piers and the boys? When could she escape and return home to him? Fear clutched her as she realized Jas might well get her with child before she could escape.

Early the next morning she rose silently and made her way out, down along the banks of the stream and into the woods of the hillside. She did not know where she was going, but it was good to be out of that cold, damp place, and she walked on steadily, the sun warm on her back.

They caught up with her, led by their great dogs, at about midday and with his eyes narrow with anger, Jas roughly pulled her by the arm and once more laid her on his pummel, now and again hitting her backside with a fearsome blow. Dazed, hungry and exhausted, she was once again dumped on the damp floor. Emma came to sit beside her, eyes anxious, kind. A little while later she disappeared and when Clary woke, she found herself being observed by a stranger.

A pair of violet-blue eyes, sunken in a lined white face, was framed by wispy snow-white hair which escaped from a ragged head cloth. A fine-boned hand seemed to support one side of the horribly crooked face and the stranger observed her keenly.

"Mary?" Even the voice was distorted and strange. The hand seemed to rearrange the jaw and she spoke again, more clearly. "I must warn you my child, it is pointless trying to leave. They will always find you and bring you back." Clary closed her eyes and tears leaked from them. "Believe me my child. Do not go again, for Jas will damage you, to forcibly prevent you from ever trying again. See what his father did to me." Clary heard and thought over the words. She opened her eyes and looked properly at the woman beside her. It was plain in the firelight, that here had been a great beauty. So what had happened?

"Did he do that to you?" she indicated the jaw. The woman nodded.

"Not only to my face either, my child," she tried to stretch out her legs, "he also broke my leg so that it set crooked. Firstly, I could never go far, and secondly, who would want such an ugly, maimed creature ever again?"

Clary was horrified and reached out a hand, held the thin, cold one in hers.

"I am so very sorry, lady," she said, unaware that she had used the word and was rewarded with some sort of a smile.

"And call me mother if you will," adding, "there are no ladies here," almost with a laugh. Then Jas came to stand near them, and his mother looked up, her hand supporting her poor face all the time.

"Do not hurt her grievously as your father did me, Jasper. This is a lovely maid, quite different from the other poor things you brought before."

Clary listened amazed. If she closed her eyes she would surely believe that she was at the manor, and that Lady Felicia was speaking in her beautiful French.

So, she was a lady, one who spoke French. It took moments for Clary to absorb it. Then strangely, she decided not to confess that she understood and spoke it too.

There was no help for it after that. Clary decided to make the best of her unfortunate circumstances but would never cease waiting for the chance to escape. Always accompanied by the little girl Emma, occasionally by the other little children, she roamed the hillsides in an ever wider circles. Collecting herbs and berries, she tried to improve their diet, always doing her asking through the child, never prepared to ask Jas for anything directly. Soon a handsome pot bubbled daily on a wooden crane over the fire. Whenever they ran short of barley, onions or beans, Emma would ask, and eventually it would arrive, no doubt stolen as was everything else, from some unfortunate. When a little boy tripped and fell into the embers, Clary whisked him up and held his foot in the icy water of the stream. Then, leaving the mother in her place, she ran out into the hills till she found the herb she needed to treat him and from that time on, she gained reluctant appreciation.

Realizing, resigned, that she was with child, she cared little for her own needs or the demands of her body. At night she could visualise the child, black-haired, fierce-browed, just like its father. A plan formed slowly in her mind. Jas might plant a child in her, but she did not want it and she would kill it the moment it was born.

Gradually she got to know all the members of the group and their women. The leader, Jas' father, was as his son, a big man, broader and blacker but much more rough in his ways. There seemed little system to their lives. Now and again a group of men would head off, their huge hunting dogs at their sides, either with horses to sell, or with the intention to steal them. Sometimes they cooked up great pots of walnut haulms and dyed any greys they had stolen to a motley brown. Other times they arrived with a flock of sheep which they slaughtered, feasting on the meat for days until they were all gone. Observing a young sheep large with lamb, Clary caught it by the back leg as it ran past and, finger to lips, pulled it into their cave while the others went on. Then she and Emma took the sweet creature out every day, so that when it lambed there was just a little milk for the small children. Meanwhile, the lamb was a constant joy and toy to all of them and they laughed and clapped their hands, watching its antics.

When she found a fine walnut tree not far from a stream, Clary enrolled help from anyone she could so that a channel ran in a great ring about the tree, watering it. When autumn came, they had a great crop of walnuts, some of which Clary planted, urging the children to help so that there would be more walnuts for the future. By then, Clary had found herself a tiny, private place where she slept. Virtually a cleft in the cave wall, she thought that someone had slept there before, for above the sleeping shelf, there were markings on the wall, none of which she could understand. Here she hid her chatelaine, only telling Emma where she had put it, and now and then took out the scissors to cut the hair, finger and toe-nails of the children.

There were times when she almost felt contented, then something would happen which threw her down into despair again. With her growing belly, Jas was pleased, and tried to be kind to her although she always rejected him.

Then the night came, in autumn, when Jas's great hunting bitch whelped, and in her private rocky cleft, Clary did not realize what was happening for a while. Puzzled, she listened to the unusual and ribald laughter which regularly rent the air. Finally she got up and went over to the fireplace to investigate, just in time to see a pup birthed, its dam lovingly clean it, and Jas, slamming a rock on the tiny head before throwing it into the fire. Appalled, Clary sat down beside Emma, who worried, looked anxiously at her.

"How many is that?"

"Eight, replied the child.

"You won't kill them all, will you, Jas?" probably addressing him directly for the first time."

Surprised, he looked up at her. "And why not? Winter is a hard time, and there will be little enough food for us all without extra mouths?"

"But surely," Clary persevered, "you will leave her with one, just for the milk?"

"No!" he replied shortly, ready with his rock.

They all watched as with his other hand he held the leash on the bitch's neck, ready to pull her away from her licking. Quickly, Clary leant forward and scooping up the pup, placed it in her bodice and without a word, turned to go back into her little place. It was suddenly very quiet, and everyone stared into the fire, not at each other.

Later, when the bitch came snuffling into the cleft, Clary stroked her, murmuring endearments and offered her the pup to suckle.

It was a lovely, soft-grey pup, quite unlike its dam, smaller, smooth-coated and fine, like a racing dog, and Clary wondered at its blood-lines.

Fearful of Jas's wrath, she carried it about in her bodice and only took it out when the mother came, grovelling, tail wagging, to clean and nurse it.

"Shall we call her Dove?" suggested Clary to the children who clustered around. So Clary now had a dog to love and Dove was her name.

The winter was hard, cold, wet, windy and often there was snow. Fearful of the frozen path by the stream, they scattered ashes there; and to her surprise, Clary realized that there was a caring air around her and her unborn child. The man, Sam made several spindles and whorls for Clary who taught the women and girls how to spin, so at least the children now wore little knitted woollen shifts and were not quite as cold as before. Still firm in her intention to kill her child at birth, none-the-less Clary made a shawl and gathered moss, setting it to dry in fissures of the cave walls. She had persuaded Jas, as usual through Emma, to build up a wall on the front of the cave, so that the cold wind and spray did not sweep away what little warmth the fire created. Gradually, despite being very dark, the cave slowly dried out and now and again Jas's mother was carried down to sit with them. Without realizing it, Clary had begun to tell stories of her life to amuse the children, their mothers quite as avid listeners as they were. She told of the farm, mixing it up with the tower and the manor, spoke of the family, all as siblings, never ever indicating for a moment that she had been married or had two little sons.

The child moving in her womb constantly reminded her of the coming birth. She reckoned that it was due mid-spring, when hopefully the days would be brighter and not so cold. Half of her realized that it didn't matter where she birthed the child, presumably there were the odd accomplished women amongst the raggedy few who lived in the caves round about them to help her. Her other half cried for privacy, a little hole to creep in, away from eyes and ears where she could cope with her agony, give birth, then snuff out the new life, so no one would know. As if they'd care, these hard people who treated life as naught. Unconsciously she kept alert for the ideal place, going further a-field, her little Dove by her side, in her search for herbs and roots, which in winter were much more difficult to find.

Then she saw it. A great ivy-grown boulder with a shelf on the top, and did she see the darkness of a small cave above and behind it? Making sure the children were far away, she struggled up, setting her bare, cold toes painfully in the ivy branches, forcing her accursed growing belly up, over the top till at last, she lay breathless on a wide ledge. When she was rested she found it to be the ideal place, safe, private and known only to her. Automatically she began to clear away the debris of ages, till the cave seemed to grow, going deeper into the hill. Carefully she piled the sticks in a corner, and satisfied, struggled down, determined to put supplies there for when she needed them.

She had found half a broken pottery urn in the stream bed, and somehow tied it in the shawl and pulled it up, slowly, inch by inch, terrified it would snag, drop and break. Set into a hollow of the shelf, it would catch rain water and make a fine basin. Next she cut bracken and moss and made a good, soft couch for herself, right at the back. During her cleaning, she discovered some flint slithers, like knives, sharp, with serrated edges, and wondering at them, put them in her chatelaine for future use. One day she made a tiny fire on the ledge, then put it out quickly, fearing to use too much of her precious wood or be observed. It was the height of her refuge which worried her. It would be a matter of getting up quickly, between pains, for it was high for any person to climb, let alone a woman large with child and labouring.

Winter was slow to leave the hills, but at last the catkins and pussy-willow blossomed and aconites poked their flowers through the leaf-mould.

A new fear possessed Clary. Say if she was bearing twins again? She felt her belly, feeling the sharp little heels levering up her ribs, and a bony butt shoving at her stomach, preventing her from eating. Comforting herself, she felt that she was not as large as she had been with the boys. It must have been due to his mother, for Jas was most attentive in his supplies for her welfare. Even so, she thought with relief, that this time it would be a singleton. Killing one baby would be hard enough, two, filled her with dread.

The pains began in the evening. They had eaten, a rather dull pottage as usual and her hands were itching because of the young nettles she had plucked to throw in. Carefully she made her plans, humping up the bracken on her bed, making sure that her knife and scissors were in her chatelaine. Twice she went out and came in on some pretext. Throwing rubbish into the stream, bringing in more wood, suggesting quietly to no one in particular, that she felt like visiting the mother. Satisfied that all was calm, she barred her little cleft in the rock so that her dog would not follow her, and stepped out into the night. Using a stout stick for support, she hurried, only stopping when a pain engulfed her, eyes closed, breathing deep. Getting up to her ledge was more difficult than she had imagined, but there, she lay and rested, gulping air as she had been told Lee had written in his herbal. After she lit the fire, she put green wood on, for perhaps her labouring might go on for a long time.

It was terrible alone, with no kind hands rubbing her back, no soft voices giving courage and no gentle faces to look on. In the early hours, exhausted from the efforts of expelling the child from her womb, she lay sleeping for a moment, to waken to the mewling of a newborn. Too tired to do anything else, she took it up, wrapped it in the shawl and instinctively held it close before again falling into a deep sleep.

The sunrise woke her, and for a moment she was confused till she heard the snuffing of the child on her arm. Looking down at it, the evil black-headed boy she had dreamed of, just wasn't there. Instead lay a beautiful, very fair girl child, and Clary's heart melted.

It was Dove who had led him to her of course. Suddenly Clary heard the barking of her little dog, and eyes wide, knew that she was discovered. The next moment Jas's head showed above the ledge, and then he was beside her, holding her in his arms.

"Oh the little angel," he said, "it must be a she, for she is the spitting image of my mother."

Clary looked, and hearing his words, nodded.

"Why did you run away?" he said, but kindly, "why did you come here?" he gazed about realizing that she had planned her confinement well in advance.

"I was afraid and needed to be alone," she said weakly, "I just could not be there, in the cave, with so many people. Say if I cried out? What would the children think?"

Somehow they got her down, and seating her on a pony, walked slowly back to the caves, where the women and children ran out to greet her and see the new baby.

"Oh, my dear," Jas's mother peered at the little sleeping thing through the gloom, "I do believe she looks as I was, and that she will also have white hair." Clary stared at her surprised, having thought that her hair was white from age. "Perhaps it is too early to tell yet, but I do believe that she also has my eyes." They looked, and perhaps yes, they were the same unusual, violet-blue. They smiled at each other. "Will you name her for me, my dears?" and Jas, so kindly and handsome, now he was happy and smiling, looked at Clary for her agreement.

"Ursuline? Yes, it is a fine name, mother, we thank you for it."

"No doubt she will be called Lina as I was, except for special occasions of course, betrothals and so forth." There was a sudden, strange silence, as if she had been speaking in another tongue and nobody understood her.

Lina proved to be a lovely baby, sweet to look on and sweet in nature. The white down on her head did not change, and her eyes were surely an exquisite blue, just as her grandmother. There was no other such fair child in the caves, all having dark hair and eyes. Anyone with spare time, came to see her, and when she began to smile, to compete for them. Jas was strangely proud of his new child, even showing her to his sullen father, who like the rest, soon fell for her charms.

With summer, the men went away more often, sometimes for many days. Clary moved up to be with the mother for company, who was more comfortable in her own place. Summer suited her, for her aches and pains seemed less. There was an open patch of land with sunlight right on the top of the outlaws' settlement, where she managed to struggle to on her bent, broken leg, which caused her to walk crabwise. Here Clary attended the sad, older woman by cutting, washing and braiding her hair, and trimming her finger nails. Here too, Clary confessed to speaking French, to the amazed delight of the mother. Somehow it all came out then, broke down barriers and they spoke freely thereafter. Clary told of her marriage, Piers, her twin sons and how desperately she wanted to return to them.

Then, as if in a rush, Ursuline told of how she came to be there. How as the younger sister of the duke, two betrothals, to much older men, had ended because of their death. Of how as a headstrong, foolish fourteen year-old she had escaped, when out riding one day, hiding from her grooms, until she was lost in the forest. There, eventually the outlaws had found her, and thinking it all great sport, in her innocence she had gone along with them. Believing that they would escort her home, she had been charming, especially to the tall, dark and handsome leader. But he had other ideas and giving her strong drink, had taken her. Sure that her brother's men would find her, she played a waiting game until she realized that she was with child, so urgently needed to return home to visit the wise woman. For she knew, that another marriage was being arranged for her, and a child was not in her plans. Her attempt to escape had soon ended in capture and violence. He had been furious, taken in with her guiles, and had beaten her so savagely, she was near to death.

"He broke my jaw, and my leg, and there was no physician to help me. His remorse was great, never would you believe the tenderness which that ruffian showed me. When I told him I was carrying his child, he cared even more carefully for me. So I stayed, a broken, ugly woman, for I could never go back to my brother as I was, so great a disgrace. I tried to keep my dignity, tried to rear my only child with some sort of decency. Despite my infirmities, I keep on living, he makes sure of that because, strange man, he loves me."

They both wept. Clary for those she had lost and the tragic woman before her, and Ursuline because of what she had done as a foolish child. She knew that she would now lose Clary and the enchanting baby Lina; that her brief months of company and comfort would end, and that she would do everything in her power to get them away.

"Of course you must go, my child," she tried to dry her eyes as well as hold up her jaw. "I shall miss you both most dreadfully, but I know it is the right thing to do. It was a terrible thing to tear you away from your legal husband and little sons. Besides," she held Lina's little fist and crooned to her. "Besides, what kind of life will this angel have here? No life. Yes my dear, I will tell you when, you must surely go."

Carefully, so that the children would not notice, Clary baked little barley breads at the hearth till they were very hard, so they would keep, and tied them into a bag with some walnuts. Her dress was in tatters, stained and wretched, so she steeped it in a hollowed-out stone on the streamside with hot stones, the walnut haulm juice turning it a good, deep brown.

The days were long, the nights short, and the men being away, Ursuline helped Clary to leave. Giving her namesake her horn and silver spoon and pressing a small purse of coins into Clary's hands, she wept, for by sending them away, she knew her loneliness would again fold in on her.

"Go north," she said, "for they will expect you to go south. Try to travel early and late so as not to pass anyone. Hide the moment you see any sign of life or hear any sound. And," she stroked the silky grey head of Dove, "for the love of God, keep your dog close by you or she will lead them to you."

Then Clary did a strange thing, before she left she turned, and as Lady Felicia had taught her for high society, she sank into a curtsey so graceful and low, Ursuline gasped, and began to weep again. It was very many years since anyone had paid obeisance to her.

"I will pray for you," she sobbed quietly, "I will pray for you."

"And I for you, sweet lady," said Clary kissing the cold cheek.

Clary walked steadily uphill, Lina on her back and Dove at her side, till, on the highest point, she had a clear view of all that lay before her. Great wooded hills and mountains ranged to her west, while to the east, the land fell away to the horizon. There was no break in the forests, no sign of wood smoke denoting man, so with the sun to her back she began walking downhill, veering slightly to the east, for she would have to do a great circle in order to get home. Whenever there was a stream, she drank copiously and washed the baby, hunting down soft moss to line her cloths. Sparingly, she dipped the dried, hard breads into water, and sucked on them, giving a morsel to her dog. As evening fell, she looked desperately for somewhere safe for them to hide. That first night, with the baby and Dove held close for warmth, she sheltered in a great hollow tree, and despite her fear, footsore and weary, slept.

Where and how she did not know, she cut her foot on a stone, so now felt walking ever more painful. Eventually, when she was on her last bread, she came to the edge of the forest and saw at the bottom of a great sweep of meadow, a huddle of roofs nestling at the end of a road. Smoke rose from one, so she hobbled forward, holding Dove on a cord, close to her. It was the poorest little inn, just one room and a barrel of ale on a board. Entering, she surprised a woman who looked half tipsy, drinking from a great wooden mug.

"Good day, mistress," Clary approached her. "Tell me do, what place am I at?" The woman gawped at her, ale dribbling from her toothless mouth. She put her mug down and reaching for another, drew fresh ale and pushed it across to Clary. "Wood End, daughter, Wood End." Clary nodded, sat on the bench at the board and gratefully drank the ale. It was surprisingly good, and stronger than what she had known in the past. "Do you have business here then daughter?" The innwife peered closely at her, then saw the baby and her filthy face broke into a smile. "Ah, a babby!" she exclaimed, "a little beauty too I can see," and suddenly she was all care and concern. "You'll be hungry no doubt, my dearling, nursing that angel. Wait while old Jane gets you a bit to sup on." She fussed about the fire, muttering to herself. A steaming wooden bowl was suddenly put into Clary's hands, and as there was no spoon, she put it to her lips and drank. It was delicious and hot though, and she quickly finished it, while the woman watched her every move.

"Excellent!" she exclaimed, putting the bowl down, then realizing that her word had shocked the innwife she quickly added, "very good, mistress, I can see you have a way with the cooking pot."

Obviously pleased, the bowl was filled again and the old woman went off as usual muttering to herself, leaving Clary to look about her. Full and warm, she put the bowl on the earthen floor for Dove to finish it up.

It seemed that old Jane was alone all day, the woodmen coming in at night for ale and pottage. Obviously pleased with her unexpected company, she produced an ancient little cradle, dusting it down and cooing happily at Lina, lavished love and praise on her while, Clary washed up her pots at the stream, soaking her foot in the cold, fast-running water. It was a relief being with a human being again, yet she had to be careful, and thought quickly of some story to tell the old one. When she got back, sure enough the questioning began. "So what are you doing my girl, out alone in the woods with a babe, and no man to guard you?"

Clary tried to still her heart. It would not do to confide in the old one, for soon the men would arrive and in her cups, she would surely tell all. "My man said he would meet us hereabouts, mistress," she replied. "But I cut my foot so was slow, and I fear that perhaps he came and went already?" ending on a query.

The innwife frowned. Of course no stranger had been by, just the usual woodmen and charcoal burners. "Was this the place he said to meet you, dearling," she asked, still frowning.

Clary looked down at her feet, clean now but sore still. "I don't know mistress, but if I may bide with you for a day or two to rest, maybe he will come. Or, if not, I must go on to find him."

So they stayed, and at night, when the men came in for their ale and pottage, Clary went up to the planks on the smoky rafters so to avoid them, surprisingly with the innwife's approval. It wasn't often such a pretty lass came their way, and old Jane could see that she was not one to truckle with rough woodmen.

The woodmen wisely always brought something in from the woods for the pot. Usually it was wild garlic, greens and strange, early mushrooms, some which Clary did not know and feared but Jane reassured her that no one had ever died at her board. Once they brought conies, so the pottage was rich with meat.

Liking the old woman, Clary helped her how she could, sweeping and swilling out the floor and scrubbing down the board with ashes and a root, then standing it against the wall outside in the sunshine, so it was fresh. Then, opening up a sack of brown, wheaten flour, they baked in a ramshackle beehive oven standing some way off. It was moving how the old one enjoyed the baby too, finding old cloths to bind her in, and while Clary worked, tenderly walking her to sleep.

God must have heard Ursuline's prayers, for one day, the innwife suddenly called to Clary. "Look, my dearling, see, a stranger is coming, could this be your man do you think?" So Clary looked, and there approaching in the distance came a man leading a pony. Clary's heart jumped. Handing the baby to the old one, she picked up her skirts and hurried down the track toward him.

Close now, she saw a tall man, topped with a strange, wide-brimmed, high-crowned hat. Around the braid of the hat were tucked herbs. Ah, Clary understood, he was a green man, collecting herbs for the physicians and salters. Stopping just in front of him she dipped and said breathlessly, "good sir, in the name of the Virgin, I beg you to stop awhile and have some words with me, for I have a great favour to ask of you."

For a moment the man tipped his head back and she saw the whitest face, with white eyebrows and pink eyes staring at her. Coming a little closer, he peered at her. "Well mistress, here I am, speak on," supposing the poor little wench wanted some brew either to remove an unwanted child, or to give to an unwilling lover. They were all the same, these simple girls, believing that he was a magician. Clary moved to the side of the lane and sat down on a hummock. Puzzled, he did the same.

"It is a long story sir, one which I must necessarily make sure you understand most clearly. I hope in your goodness, you will assist me." He inclined his head and pulled his hat down to shade his eyes as a ray of sunlight fell on them from a gap in a passing cloud. Briefly she told him of her abduction and escape. Then she told about coming here, the kindness of the old innwife, and her lie that she was waiting for her man. She paused, then continued.

"Will you, good sir, for the love of God, pretend to be my man, so that I may leave this place safely. For if the outlaws come by, they would soon learn of a single woman and child, but if I was your mistress, 'tis likely they would not."

The odd man listened, then turned to her enquiring. "Child? Do you have a child?" He saw through his poor eyes, a vision of loveliness as he bent forward. A fleeting and sweet smile crossed her face as Clary told him of Lina.

"I am not ignorant in your trade, good sir," she said, "for a forefather of ours was a healer, who left a wonderful book, which we still have and use in our family."

Rising, he held out his hand to help her up.

"That is good, so you can help me for some days. Now," he almost smiled, "mistress mine, what is your name?"

Miraculously it worked. Old Jane received him like a long-lost son telling him how glad she was he had come, and what a beautiful little daughter he had. Then, looking carefully at him she added, "and so like you Master Green, with your pale hair. But her eyes are blue." Which caused the strange man, to cross himself, and thank God.

Lina chortled at the new man, which delighted him, and yes, their hair was the same, very pale. Even Dove accepted him, as he settled for the night in their loft. Prepared for the worst, Clary was surprised by his mating. For first he removed his hat, opened his breeks and entering her was quick as a buck rabbit and swiftly done.

One evening the woodsmen brought a small deer and after skinning it, they set it on a spit and jovially ate their pottage while waiting for it to cook.

The green man bought them ale and spoke with them, showing them herbs and some mushrooms, and they told him where to find them on the morrow.

They stayed for a few days while he searched for what he needed, before leaving satisfied, with tears and entreaties from the innwife to return one day.

The first night after they left the inn, they slept under a canvas hitched to a low tree, and while Clary nursed Lina, the odd man watched her closely.

"You'll not be wanting to get with child too soon again will you, mistress? The little one must grow apace yet." Clary nodded, wondering at his question. After she had laid the baby down to sleep the man showed her a leaf, then, hoisting up her skirt, pressed it gently but deep inside her before taking her, his hat off, with his usual speed. When he had his breath he added. "Wash it out in the morning, it will prevent you from conceiving till the little one is weaned."

Their pace was leisurely, his poor eyes seeking this and that, and Clary was soon a great help to him, so they moved faster. Any village they came to, he tucked the herbs he was searching for in his hat, and if the folk knew of it, he later gave them something small, if he found that it was a worthwhile patch for him to harvest. Often they had to stop to dry his herbs, either paying to stay in a pentice, or even in the open if the days were fine. He attended to her feet and at a larger village bought her wooden-soled shoes, which were too big, but with moss in the toes, she was comfortable and glad of them. It was a strange time, and gradually her anxieties retreated while she interested herself in his work, and helped him. He had a little glass attached to a red string, such as she had never seen before and which he greatly valued. When he was not using it, he tucked it into a little sleeve on his hat. While gathering together, he taught her much, crushing and sniffing the herb, then pressing her to do the same. He showed her how the little glass caused the leaf to look huge, like magic and pointed out little secrets therein. It had, surprisingly, turned out an agreeable union for all of them. Lina and Dove were well-fed and happy and although Clary did not like the mating, she had to endure it, for she knew well, that it could be much worse.

The pony was laden so high that the man now also carried a pack on his back, yet being herbs, it was not heavy. As they walked along, he told her of the men for whom he gathered, happy that he would soon be unloading his goods at the big town they were coming to. It had rained for several days and they stayed at an inn on the far bank, a large inn, comparatively clean and well run which Clary appreciated. They rested for some days and Clary begged a bath tub for herself and the little one. Mr. Green was strangely touched as he watched his little family giggling in the hot water, and was glad they had been unable to arrive earlier because of the flood. Then, as the water fell, he joined the other passengers waiting on the river's edge, piled his bags into the ferry boat, and went with the other folk to cross the river to the town.

"Stay here, lass," he told her, fondly kissing Lina who stretched out her arms to him, warming his heart. "No my angel," he kissed her again," I shall be back by nightfall. It is better you stay here safe, out of the stink and contagion of the town."

They stood on the bank waving, as the little boat shoved off, several others by them. Barely was it into mid-river, when Clary saw a great tree floating towards them, a branch up, out of the water like a claw, going straight at them. She screamed and pointed. Others around her put their hands to their mouths in horror, surely they must avoid it.

Too late, the boatman tried to shove it off with his oar, but the movement caused the boat to tip over, throwing all and everyone into the water. Handing the baby to a bystander and lifting her skirts, Clary ran along the bank, her eyes on the green man, laden down with his back pack, he was obviously in difficulties. It seemed he was no swimmer, for his efforts were futile, yet he saw her running along the bank

With what seemed a great effort, he raised his hat and shouted to her. "My hat, my hat!" and was gone in the dark, swirling waters.

CHAPTER THIRTY

ROM, HANNAH

The little girl gazed upwards into the deep green of the tree. It was too hard. She knew that she couldn't climb up into it. Then she thought of her father. Da had said in his soft voice.

"'Tis a great tree the oak, Hannah mine, a special tree. And if you ever need to hide, this is the best one hereabouts to get into." He had placed his hands stirrup-wise under her foot, and hoisted her up. It was useful to know of good hiding places. She had dug her toes into the rough bark and clung with her fingers for the first stretch, for there was no da here with his stirrup-hands to help her. On the third try, angry, hurting but determined, she reached the first branch and clung to it for a moment, getting her breath.

It surely was a good tree to hide in too, for she lay along a stout branch there most of the day and the many people who passed by on the lane never saw her. She had found the same cradle in the boughs which da had put her into and content, had closed her eyes. It was peaceful there, just the small birds twittering high above her, and there was a rustle of a light breeze. It was comfortable too, and she wondered if she had dropped off to sleep and missed him.

It had started as a bad day, right from the beginning. Her mother was angry about something, she knew not what, and she heard them speaking. The high, indignant voice of her mother, and the soft low replies from her father. Then, he had gone to town, his pack on his back, to try to sell his things. As usual, he never forgot, he swept her up in his arms and roundly kissed her before he went, whispering in her ear. "Be a good girl today, my love," eyes skewing backwards at her mother, "mind her now, for she is in an ill humour." He did not say "as usual", which Hannah would have said, for her mother always grumbled, seemingly constantly dissatisfied with her life. Just once her da had explained to her that it was in her blood. "For her old mam was a right disagreeable woman."

Hannah hated to hear her mother's voice raised, and often ran away, which is how she came to know of this tree.

Their camp, where they had been for some days now, was on the river's edge, just under a scooped out bank which gave some protection from the weather and other folk. Her mother picked herbs and made the sweetest posies and sold them in town on the church steps. Her parents went selling on alternative days; they never went together for some reason, so generally they made enough money to eat, if not much more.

Her da was clever. He caught conies which the townsfolk liked to eat, while she, Hannah, was sick of them, preferring fowl. Mind you, it saddened her to see the little bodies stripped of their pretty feathers, even if the few mouthfuls were tasty. As well as snaring conies to sell, he made wooden things, bowls, bill hooks, scythe handles, anything indeed which he found of the right shape in the forests.

"You stay here," her mother had spoken crossly. "I'm going to town. I need some things. If your da comes back you tell him I'm a picking herbs for a lady."

Hannah wasn't sure what her mother was speaking about, was she picking herbs or going to town? But she nodded, vaguely feeling that something was wrong.

Lying in the cool of the great tree she puzzled, over what she thought she had just seen. Or had it been a dream? Her mother had gone off towards the town, then along the road, two men, town men, not like them, had spoken with her. Her mother had seemed anxious and kept looking this way and that as if she was afraid. Then one of the men had given her some money, for Hannah saw her put it in her hanging purse, and they had left, the men back to town and her mother home. She shifted, suddenly stiff and rearranged herself, unease making her little brow pucker. A sound alerted her, like an owl coughing, and she beamed with delight, da was back.

"How did you know I was here, da?" she asked, her elfin face peering through the branches at her father who was nimbly hoisting himself up.

"Because," he kissed her nose, "I saw a leaf fall, my treasure. So I knew someone was up here, and guess who?" and tickled her, holding on to one skinny arm so that she didn't fall for giggling. "How long have you been up here Hanny? Are you hungry?" and took a sweet, barley bun out of his pack and gave it to her.

Leaning against him she ate it with relish, yet all the while she was thinking of what she saw, or did she dream it? "Da?" he nodded, dark eyes twinkling at her in the green gloom. "Da, I think that I saw mother talking with two men. Not our people, town men." She paused while she finished the bun. "They gave her some money before they went. She looked frightened. Something was wrong."

Han held his daughter close, he looked unseeing through the branches of the great tree, thinking. "Tell me again, Hannah, carefully, everything."

Speaking softly she told him everything which she remembered. Then, "but da, I'm not sure if I did really see it, or if it was a dream."

Han considered his daughter, and wondered if she was going to be one of the very few who really did have the gift. They didn't speak for a time while Han thought. If she had seen it, then he must be off. If she had not, and she had the gift, he must still be off. Either way, he was well aware that Gilly was tired of him and their way of life. Ever since her troublesome mother had died and they had left that broken-down old hovel, she had yearned for a house.

"I'm Rom," he had explained countless times, "we do not have houses. We travel and home is where we stay the night, the day or the week. I only stopped with you because I loved you and because of the babe. It was no life in that hovel and well you know it."

"Why can't we try to find a tiny cottage in the town, then you can go and come and make and sell things as you do now. And I can do the same. But not forever moving on, carrying all we have on our backs!" There had been a silence and Han then sighed deeply. "Gilly flower, if you want to live in a town with a leaking roof over your head I can't stop you. Any man will give you a home, pretty lass that you are. So go if that is what you want, for I cannot."

It was never ending.

"I don't want any man," she'd begin to cry, "it's you I want." So he took her in his arms and loved her and she was content for a day or two. It had, he well knew, been a mistake setting up with her. But then he could not resist her pretty face, fine, fair hair, beautiful pale skin and blue eyes. And she sang like a lark.

"You'll regret the day, Han," the Rom all told him all too often. "If you settle with her they'll be after you, blaming you when their well goes dry, or their cow dies. Stick with your own kind, Han, fair hair and blue eyes are just skin deep. Beware of her people, for they will always be after you." Which was certainly true, for they had. No matter how clean he kept and tried to be respectable for her sake, he was an outsider and sure enough, he got blamed for anything which went wrong or was missing.

Stroking the dark curls of his daughter he sighed again. What of her? How could he leave her? Yet he must for if they got him, what would her fate be? Taking the cord from his neck he opened the tiny leather pocket there and took out a small silver charm. Then taking the cord from her neck he opened her little pocket and pushed the charm in alongside her golden coin. It was silver, a little monkey they thought, very, very old, Han had told her, because it had come from a long way away with his great, great grandfather. He thought it was holy. Hannah watched what he did, eyes wide.

"Why are you giving me your charm, da? You're going, aren't you?" she said surely. He nodded. "Why must you go, da?"

Again he sighed, the pain heavy on his heart where lay his feather-light daughter. "Your ma is tired of me, Hanny, so it is better I go off, for a while anyway. Here", and kissing her, he took some coins from his purse and folded them into her hand, "it seems like she has reported me for some past sin, and if I don't go quickly, they'll find me and hang me in no time."

They backed down the tree, the coins in her mouth for safety, Hannah was carefully lowered to the ground.

"See about, lass, and give me the all clear if no one is around. Otherwise just go home, and I'll stay here till night." Moments latter, an owl coughed and Han lowered himself to the ground. With a swift backward glance and raised palm he slipped across the road into the woods and was gone.

Hannah made her way home slowly by the river bank. At times she stopped to pick the wild raspberries, then washed her face and hands in the river. Her mother did not like her because she wasn't pale and fair like herself, but brown like her da. Well not quite as brown as her da, or the Rom children she sometimes played with. There were times when she wished that she was pale and fair as her mother, but her da always told her that at least she had a beautiful voice like her ma. So she began to sing as she wandered along, for she felt so low in spirits, and singing usually helped.

"Where have you been?" her mother's voice cut into her reverie. "Come here at once, you bad girl."

She tried to make herself small as the evening fell and her father didn't come home. Two men came, she recognized them, so she had not been dreaming. They shouted at her mother and she cried and gave them back their money and then they left.

In the morning they packed up and left, her mother furious, having to leave half their things behind under the overhang for she couldn't carry them all. Hannah humped a bundle on her back and meekly followed till they stopped, it being too dark to go on and slept in a ditch as they were.

There followed many unhappy days of moving on and being hungry and wishing that da would return to them. She was so tired from carrying her bundle, so weary from lack of good food, she could barely go on.

At last they came to a small town where they slept the night in the yard of an old woman. Next day, her mother kissed her, not something she did very often, and pulling her usually down-turned mouth into a smile said, "Now Hannah my love, you are going to stay with Mistress Betty who will teach you lace-making. I've told her what a clever girl you are, and what quick fingers you have, so learn well, and I'll be back for you before long."

Hannah looked up at her mother and knew that she was lying, and that she would not be back. The purse which hung at her side under her apron was heavy, pulling down on the strap, so she guessed that she had been sold to the lace-maker. Well she was tired of moving every day, hungry and miserable. So her mother was going too. It was actually a relief so she raised her hand in the Rom farewell and forced a smile.

It was quite the best thing which had ever happened to her, for Mistress Betty was a good soul, and under her kindly guidance, she learned to make lace. Every kind of lace too, lace with a tatting hook, lace with a cushion and bobbins, and braid lace. Hannah enjoyed it all. Her quick hands and eyes soon picked up what the old lady taught her, and life was suddenly peaceful. Always remembering how her father had skilfully turned the most ordinary piece of wood into something special, she rejoiced in her new work. Da would be so pleased. They fared well at the lace-maker's cottage too, with daily pottage which was filling if not so interesting. Mistress Betty had a little garden, a cat and some hens and Hannah made friends with them all.

It was a very little house, with just one small room which served all their needs. On the front, there was a broad, open lean-to where they usually sat working in the light, if the weather was fine. On the beams just above where they worked, lay some broad wooden planks where the mistress stored her well-wrapped, completed lace, out of sight of folk and away from the smoke of the house. A rickety ladder which was used for placing it there, was brought into the house at night for safety.

Every week her mistress went to the market with their lace and usually sold it all. Sometimes ladies came and placed orders and her mistress was pleased with Hannah for she not only brought in money, she helped with the garden and in keeping the house swept and clean.

Now and again peddlers came and bought their lace too, bargaining fiercely over it, for they had to buy well to make their profit.

Well, all good things must come to an end, so Hannah had heard her da often say, as once again they had had to move on. One day a woman came, bringing her two timid young step-daughters.

"They must learn a trade, mistress," she said in a hard voice. "How are we to keep all these children I know not," and gave them a shove, handing a purse to the lace-maker. "This will pay for their food until they are productive."

Hannah was delighted to have the company of the sweet girls who were fair and pretty like her mother and did her best to help them settle in. Undoubtedly the house was now very cramped, for at night, with three bodies sleeping on the floor, as well as the mistress's bed, there was not much room to move.

Mistress Betty let Hannah guide the girls in their first, easy lessons. It was pleasant having good children about, and she enjoyed her leisure listening to their chatter and watching their heads bowed over their work.

It was inevitable that Hannah was the one to go. For Mistress Betty had paid for her, while the new girls were being paid for. Hannah was deeply upset, an awful ache, heavy in her guts; but she said not a word. What could it do anyway? The worst thing was that her new master was Jack the pedlar. Of all the pedlars who came to their door, she thought him the worst. He was small and skinny with a ragged beard and black, broken teeth. He just looked evil, smelt terrible, or so she thought. He whined and wheedled and bargained ferociously over the lace, and the mistress usually gave in to him more quickly than usual to have him gone.

Undoubtedly the poor woman felt some guilt, for she was very kind to Hannah the day that Jack came for her. While she crowded close to the two sisters in the night, she heard them bargaining away over what she must take in way of materials.

"Now Jack," Mistress Betty raised her voice. "Don't ruin her eyes by making her work too many hours, and don't go buying the cheapest hog-tallow candles when she works in the winter. My girls know to keep their work clean, and hog-tallow might be cheap, yet as you know it makes much black smoke which will cause the lace to be grey. No one wants dirty lace. You just spend a trifle more and get mutton-tallow candles, or bullock, which last and burn better anyway," she lowered her voice but Hannah strove to hear her.

"And if you must use her, Jack, dirty little man that you are, you take her from behind. For I see that she is a very slight, poor little thing not fit for breeding. You put her with child and she will die most likely." She sighed dramatically, "Yes I fear that she is not fit for mothering."

The only good thing about being with Jack was that he had a dog and a pony. Both were desperately rough, poor creatures, who shied away from her until they realized that she would not kick or beat them. Gradually she gained their confidence, for she slept in the stables with them. While in the evenings Jack drank himself senseless in taverns, she crept out and led the pony to good grazing, or fetched it water, and tried, not very successfully to comb out its tangles. The dog took longer to befriend. It was a huge fierce beast, trained to fight and guard the pedlar's packs. Gradually, by scrounging scraps for him at the inns, he understood that she meant well and even let her remove his ugly spiked collar in order to pick off the burrs which nestled there.

At last they came to what Jack called "his home". A broken-down shed, with barely one wall still standing, it was quietly situated outside a village and no one ever came their way, for it was not on the way to anywhere. The first night there he lit a small fire in the middle of the broken floor and angrily unloaded his packs. Fearful of his boot or fist, Hannah took the pony out to tether it on the lee by the stream.

Now poor little Hannah understood Mistress Betty's words to Jack on the last night. For when she returned he roughly caught a hold of her, hoisted up her shift and cruelly took her, like a dog. When he had finished, he threw her aside and went to sleep on his cloak. Hurting and shocked, Hannah went out into the dusk and again made her way back to the stream to wash herself. A cold nose nudged into her face, a wet tongue extravagantly licked her, so Hannah put her arms about the great dog and sobbed into his thick fur.

The following days were happier and of surprising interest to Hannah, for Jack rebuilt their house. Now this, she thought in her child's mind, I can do when da comes back, and then mother will be happy. So she threw herself into the work with enthusiasm, which surprised and pleased the pedlar, so at day's end he took a little red ribbon from his pack and gave it to her. That he used her again was not so good, but Hannah shut her eyes and mouth tightly and tried to forget it.

When the house was finished, they both stood and gazed at it proudly. Jack had cut the willow saplings from the stream edge, split them and roughly woven them between the upright timbers which still stood. Next, he wove twigs in-between till the walls looked like a thin hedge. Then they had collected clay in a basket which the pony carried up from a small beach down-stream and lastly, they mixed it with dung and daubed it over the laths and twigs. Gradually the gaping holes in the walls of the tiny house filled and then they began on the roof. After replacing the roof saplings, he laid withies across and tied them down with twisted reeds. Hannah watched carefully with her bright intelligence and anticipated his needs so they worked relatively fast. At last he took the pony up to the moor, there to cut ling and while Hannah led the pony down and unloaded it, he cut the next lot. It was satisfying if tiring work.

The weather changed just as the ling roof was completed, and Jack went off to the nearest inn, to reappear after two days in a sorry state, but at least Hannah had had time to make their home comfortable. When the ling was tied down to the saplings which were the roof timbers, the one-roomed house seemed to the child a real haven. It did let a little rain in it was true, but not so much, and over the years the ling would compact so to became dryer. There was one small window, which had no shutter, and a south-facing doorway which had a poor skin curtain which barely covered it.

"I'll see to that next time," said Jack, pretty pleased with himself and unconsciously proud that the child was impressed with his efforts. He noted the driest corner and hung a board there on which to place the lace making equipment.

"Wash your hands before you work, girl." Hannah nodded, which of course she had learned from Mistress Betty, who always wrapped her work in a clean kerchief before setting it aside for the night.

One day he returned from the village with a small sack of oats, another of barley, a bit of bacon, some soft soap in a pot, "to keep your hands clean" and a sack of roots. He guessed that the child was Rom from the colour of her, so she must be used to foraging for herself. He considered he had been most generous in leaving her what he had. While he gave her his orders of what she must make, how much, how wide and so on, she realized that he did not know how quickly she could work. It would be a mere few weeks and the yarns would be finished, but her enthusiasm for building did not extend to hours of lace making, so she just nodded.

The only thing she missed when he left, was the company of the pony and the dog. At first, she worked when the light was good, in the doorway of the little house, afraid that he might come back to spy on her. As time went by she worked out a routine, she worked diligently until all the materials he had left were finished, her laces neat and wrapped on the shelf, before running free.

Of course she knew how to snare conies, hadn't da shown her? Of course she also knew which berries and mushrooms to pick and which roots to dig, so her basic stores were augmented by the bountiful fruits of the earth which were there all about her for the gathering.

The hovel, for that is what it was, lay hidden in a fold of land above the stream, where once a mighty glacier had gouged a valley. She knew that a village lay nearby, but for the time being, she did not bother to investigate. Being an only child, she was never lonely. She had realized early on, that being an only was unusual for Rom, but then da said that when Rom married out, it was usually the case. She watched the deer coming down to drink late at night, their delicate young, fitful at their sides. She laughed silently at the hare who played in the early mornings, weird in half mist. A good sized coney did her three days, which was as long as it would keep good hung up above the gentle smoke of her fire. Despite being alone, she was happy, keeping her home swept and clean, every bit the little housewife, singing as she worked.

Then one day she found a friend. Having gone further a-field to lay her snares, she heard a sobbing just outside the wood. A young woman was gathering kindling into her apron and crying bitterly. Hannah stood up and showed herself so as not to frighten the girl.

"Who are you?" said the stranger, sniffing, seeing the odd little child and dropping her wood to lift her apron to blow her nose.

"I'm Hannah," she replied, beginning to gather up the sticks, "why are you crying, mistress?" Which set her off again. It was a calm evening and so they sat on the soft turf on the edge of the wood chattering. They must have been there for some time, the older girl apparently glad to have someone to speak with. Hannah listened, uttering little sounds of sympathy and encouragement till the shadows lengthened and with a start the girl jumped up saying she must get home to give her man his supper. They met often after that, and Hannah took to helping her new friend whose name was Tilly, not so different from her ma's name. In turn, Tilly used to give the skinny little girl bread and cheese, which she loved, and if Hannah had more than one coney, she gave it in exchange.

It was difficult understanding grown-ups, for surely Tilly must be one to have a man. Hannah listened to her friend, saddened by her tale, but sure she would never submit to such treatment. It seemed that an old farmer had wanted a new wife when his woman died. As she had borne him no children, he wanted a young, hale wife, so that his farm and fortune would go to his heirs. Tilly was the youngest of an arrow-smith's five children and, without her consent, of course, had been wed to the old man. When every month her bleeding came, he beat her savagely, then took her, for it seemed the beating gave him courage and energy which at other times he did not have.

"I should like a little one," said Tilly tearfully. "It is lonesome there with that bad-tempered old man. Yet how can I bear him a child when he is only able to bed me once a month?" She sobbed afresh. "Even my own folks, not understanding, are angry with me."

Hannah shuddered, remembering the pain which Jack inflicted on her, and thought it a very hard way to make a babe.

Each time after Jack came back from his rounds, she crept around trying to be invisible while she assessed his mood. Making a gentle show of welcoming him, she made sure he had a good meal while she took the animals down to the stream to wash them and clean them of their tangles. When he left, she felt a great sense of freedom and was happy despite the loss of the animals. She really missed them, except that now she had a friend to talk with sometimes. As time went on, so too did her fear increase of Jack's return. It seemed that she sensed his coming, and became quiet and depressed, staying near the house, making sure it was clean and that there was a coney ready to roast. When the weight lay heavy on her chest so that ordinary breathing seemed difficult, she went to her little hiding-place in the bank above the house, lay there on a bed of dry bracken, and watched. Sometimes she slept, sometimes she just looked up into the feathery branches of the linden tree and listened to the birds there.

A blackbird called his alarm, and Hannah stiffened with renewed fear. Then a great weight of damp fur fell on her, licking, licking, and Hannah had to laugh, for here was the dog, who had found her and was pleased to see her. Accepting his love, she gave in to the ecstatic welcome, giggling until he settled down. Then, knowing that Jack wouldn't be far behind, fear welled up in her again and she wondered what his mood would be as she hastened down to greet him.

Jack was pleased with his purchase, he considered that she had been a good investment, already paid for as the laces sold well, ever in demand. He very gradually brought increasingly more yarn for her to make up, but Hannah was nimble fingered and with experience and practise had no trouble in completing her work in good time.

Gradually she began to tell him about Tilly and the old farmer and Tilly's longing for a child. For a moment she thought that Jack's eyes gleamed. Carefully not looking at her, he pressed her for more information. Here was opportunity, he thought and began calling at the farm, his face clean and his hair slicked down. Tilly told Hannah that he was very nice, very respectful and that her husband enjoyed talking with him and hearing the news of the world outside the village.

Hannah pushed at the embers of the little fire in the centre of the floor and watching the smoke make its way out of the hole in the roof, waiting for Jack to come home. She felt uncomfortable with the strange new manner about him and even her friend Tilly seemed different. It seemed that Jack fancied her, but Tilly still had a man. It was confusing. The unease had grown over time, till now she gazed absently frowning into the gentle flame which flickered on the hearth.

A face appeared, then a hand, and in the hand was a knife, and it was coming at her. Shocked, she fell over backwards onto the sleeping dog who yelped with fright. Hannah comforted it trembling, knowing quite certainly that the face was Jack's and that he was going to kill her.

When he returned she pretended sleep but watched him with slit eyes. He had brought in a bunch of a small plant with shiny blackish berries, a plant which da had told her to leave alone, even if it was pretty. In the dim light she watched the peddler working with it. Then, he took his precious small flagon of brandywine and dealt out a little into his cup, grinding it with a stout stick. When it was done he carefully poured the liquid into another smaller flask, of the ones which he sold elixirs in. Hannah hardly dared to breathe, suddenly understanding.

"Wash out my cup very well," he ordered her in the morning, "use ash and a good root and scour it out thoroughly." He eyed her with distaste, remembering pale skin and soft eyes. Well, the child had certainly served her purpose. He took out a small copper mirror from inside of his many pocketed cloak and trimmed his whiskers. Maybe, if he did this very carefully, this time next year, he smiled at his reflection, he would be a landed farmer. He blandly accepted to himself that he was no longer young, and life on the road had grown wearisome. Unconsciously he put his hand to his knife and glanced at the child. Later, he thought, when his plan was under way. He paused for a moment thinking, then comforted the unusual, tiny pang of conscience with the thought he would kill her so quickly, she would know nothing of it. Then with a cheerful whistle he went off, ducking under the low door. Smiling to himself, his broken black teeth like standing stones in his pinched face, he thought of himself as going a-courting.

When she was sure he had gone, despite being tired, for she had slept badly, Hannah worked swiftly. He had been very late and she needed to do her task well. Fear gripped her heart as she took his cup and the little flagon outside in the sunlight. Having picked the same black berries, she poured a very little brandywine into the cup, she used the same stick he had, and stirred with it. Twice she did this, pouring the wine back into the nearly empty flagon. Then, shivering on bare feet, she took some ash from the cold fire and went down to the stream where she scoured out the cup thoroughly. The dog whined, feeling her unease, and she hugged him, little fingers absently searching for burrs.

All that day Jack was unusually busy. "I'm off tomorrow," he said, his mood surprisingly light while he sorted his wares and re-packed his bundles and pack. He whistled as he worked. "You're a good girl," he gave her a quick smile, "so I'm going to make sure you keep warm, for autumn is coming, and the night's grow chilly."

Hannah watched in disbelief as he made several journeys into the wood with a bill hook and the pony, returning loaded with faggots which he threw down by the fireplace so there was little room in the tiny house to move. "If I leave it here it'll dry out for you, so you need not be cold a-nights."

Trying to still her trembling, Hannah went through her daily chores as normally as she could. "Then if you are off master, I'll make sure you get a good hot meal in you. I'll borrow Tilly's cooking pot and make a fine rabbit stew. I saw a bullace tree yonder, with just a few ripe already, you'll like that. Maybe I'll beg some roots off her too, I know her parsnips are coming up great. If I make a big stew, you can have half tonight and the rest before you set off in the morning." She knew she was babbling, but she was moving about quickly so he wouldn't notice that she was trembling.

Speeding through her snares she found two good conies and squatting by the stream, skinned and gutted them. So he was going to kill her tonight, or early tomorrow, then set fire to the house with her inside before going off.

Tilly welcomed her quietly; her man was sick she said, looking worried. But she gave Hannah some bread, lent her the cooking pot and together they pulled some parsnips and a small turnip. Hannah looked at her friend and saw the unease in her eyes. So he was killing the old farmer so that he could come back to live with Tilly, be her man and take over the land. But first, she realized that she must be killed, for no doubt she would be in the way.

Impulsively she planted a kiss on her friend's cheek, then ran home to wash and cut up the roots. Soon a wonderful smell filled the air. She had found lots of wild garlic leaves, been extravagant with the salty bacon, and the bullace would give the stew a fine tangy taste. Stealthily she added the last of the brandywine from the flagon for extra flavour, and set the small flask beside his ale pot by the fire with their bowls. All the while behind the house Jack whistled happily as he packed and made ready for his departure, till it was too dark to work any more.

It was a very good meal, and Jack ate heartily of it, generous in his praise as he took more, sopping up the gravy with Tilly's good bread. When he had finished and swilled down the last of the ale, he took up the brandy wine flask. Replete and in too good a mood to question such extravagance, he lazed in front of the fire and emptied it.

Hannah took her shawl and made her way to her hiding place and together with the dog, slept surprisingly well. She woke in the early dawn, and realizing that she was still alive, crept furtively down to the house.

At first she thought he was still sleeping, for he lay comfortably on his pile of bracken as usual. Then she realized that he was quite still, and after holding her breath, made sure that he wasn't breathing. Sitting back on her heels by his body, she sighed deeply. Then, looking about her little home she did feel a pang of regret, but he had shown her what to do, and do it she must. Quietly as was her habit, she pulled forward the piles of faggots which he had provided for her cremation and placed them carefully all about his body. Her own few things in the house, she carried outside, opened and put into the packs. Her lace making equipment and materials, her few kitchen utensils and Jack's cloak where she suspected he kept his money, for he always kept it close by him. Then, loading up the pony, she led him down to the stream where she tethered him. Squatting beside him, she spooned up the rest of the stew, from Tilly's pot, handing the dog the meat, till she was full to bursting.

"You clean it out for me," she told the dog, shoving the pot under his surprised nose. Patting him, she looked around carefully before returning to the house.

So I'm on the move again, she thought, as she looked about her home of three years, a house she had grown to love, her first permanent home. Checking that she had left nothing, she re-lit the fire, for the first time in her life, extravagantly piling on the wood to make a great blaze. Then, she unhooked the door curtain to make a draught, and only when she saw the fire was getting a good hold, did she return to the river to wash herself all over. A thick mist carpeted her as she worked on her scrubbing. A good sign she knew, heralding fine weather.

Taking up a familiar root dipped in river sand she scoured out Tilly's pot, rinsed it well and set it upside down on a rock to drain where it would be easily found.

The dog whined, anxiously looking back toward the house and uneasily started to make for the strange sounds of a great fire above them. Hannah looked up, satisfied to see the flames leaping, high above the trees. She called the dog and comforting him, shouldered on Jack's cloak which was really too heavy. Untying the pony, she clicked her tongue and set off downstream just as the sun rose over the hill on a beautiful morn.

It was several days before Tilly came, seeking Hannah and her cooking pot. First of all her man had died, so they had buried him, then the trouble began with his family, and hers. She had finally silenced them by announcing that at last she was with child, so it was understood that she could not be turned out of her home and that the farm would go to her babe. Despite her secret delight, Tilly did feel very vulnerable and frightened by the sudden events so managed to weep abundantly, which was fitting. When at last they had all gone, she decided to find Hannah, although she had never been to her house before, only knowing the general direction of it. At last her wanderings brought her to a still smoking burnt-out ruin, and she frowned, wondering about it. Then she went down to the stream and there, sitting upturned on a stone, was her pot, safe and clean. Sitting beside it her thoughts ran wildly, for now she realized why Hannah had not come all these past days to see her or bring back her pot. Guessing that her little friend had burned to death, for Jack had said he was leaving and there was no sign of the pony, it might easily have happened. So many cottages burnt to the ground, taking their folk with them.

Now, in real sorrow, Tilly put her head in her hands and wept bitterly for her little friend.

CHAPTER THIRTY ONE

MAGNUS WEAVER

Mistress Weaver crept in, her head down so if he was looking, he couldn't see her. Going across to the fire, she lifted the lid of the pot, and carefully tipped in the wild greens she had just been cleaning. Giving the pot a good stir, she then sat on the stool by the fire and blew it up.

The clacking of the loom continued, and she could tell, after so many years of living with the man, that he was angry, which is why his cloth was always so good and close.

She blew again, till a flame flickered and the fire came to life. It was one thing making good cloth with the money it brought in, yet he was mean, and they had always fared badly. Until Odi had come back that is. For even with Annie gone, the boy was expert at foraging, nowadays supplying her with many good things such as the greens which she liked, and rabbit. So she, in turn, did her best for him, poor soul, taking him eggs, milk and bread and occasionally pottage. Well she knew that without Annie, he had grown lazy with his cooking, as all men alone.

Life was always wearisome she thought, yet just having the boy to think about had made it a little more worthwhile. Magnus had always been a disgruntled man from when she first met him. Her father had taken her to the coast to learn stitching, because since her mother had died they were, despite being weavers, pretty ragged. There they had met a sailor from across the sea, who according to him had been ill-treated and thrown off his boat. Then, being young and trusting, she had believed all his sad stories, and complimented by his attentions, their pairing had all come about so easily. They had wed within weeks and soon he was in their home, helping her father, learning to weave, being very much the son about the house. While her father lived, they were happy, and he seemed a kindly sort of man. True, when her monthly courses came, he always grumbled at her, telling her of all the children he had sired, back in his home country, blaming her. Eventually he stopped, realizing that it did little good, and after her father died, he stopped being pleasant. As the man, he took over all that had been hers, put the money away secretly, and was always sullen.

The best time was when he took the bales of cloth to sell, every few months or so. That he came back stinking of strong drink and much else, disgusted her, but she said nothing. While he was away, Mistress Weaver was free to come and go, visit the spinners at leisure, laugh and talk and spend the time of day with them as of old, instead of collecting their wool and running home with it, afraid of his displeasure. The villagers soon grew to dislike Magnus, uneasy, for he had changed so much. For a start, the moment the old weaver died, he began putting on airs, insisting on petty rules, as if he knew everything there was to know about wool and cloth. They knew that he did not, but was an ignorant fool, a simple newcomer to the trade.

When Mistress Weaver had told them, her eyes alight with joy, that she thought she was with child, they were so glad for her. Pressing her belly, thrilling to the leaps and knocks of her unborn child, they had rejoiced with her, sure that it would be a good, strong one. Even Magnus was kind, his eyes proud as she waddled along, holding her huge belly in front of her, like a great shield.

When her birthing began, the women of the village had hurried to the weaver's house, bright with anticipation. For theirs was a small community with its share of losses, and every new birth held hope for all of them. It was a hard birth, they all agreed, for she was old, her bones locked and when the child was born, with its huge head, they had understood. Then, as it opened its mouth and screamed with rage at the cold, bright world, they noticed an eye, surely much bigger than the other, and fell silent, crossing themselves.

Magnus had been furious with her. She had borne him a monster, an ugly odious child, unlike the handsome, fair little children back home whom he remembered. Turning the women out of his house he had started shouting at her, endlessly raging, incoherent, sometimes slipping into his old tongue. Poor Mistress Weaver had lain dry-eyed on the bed, so tired, bewildered and unbelieving.

When the squire and the priest had come up, he had abused them, shutting the door in their faces, cursing them and all who lived in the village.

"From where did you get that child?" he had shouted at her. "Did you consort with the devil, for surely he has nothing of me in him." She had cowered on the bed, too weak to respond or go out. "He looks like Odin, yes, he is Odin's son, not mine, and he has no place in my house," forgetting that it was not his but hers. "Get him out of here, the ugly, noisy brat, devil's spawn."

The pot boiled over and hissed into the fire so she quickly lifted the lid and stirred it, pushing the crane away from the heat. Very carefully, she spooned a good helping of pottage into a bowl which she had sat in a pail beside her. With her ears trained for any change of sound from the loom behind her, she put the lid back on and quietly rose. Without looking at him she took the pail up and went out. Stepping past the wool store, she ducked under the low thatch of the shed where the pony stood. Feeling about in the manger, she found two, still warm eggs and putting them in the pail beside the bowl, covered them with a handful of straw. Now she went down the hill on her bare feet and made for what she still thought of as Annie's house.

She still missed Annie, realizing that she had probably been her only friend, for what with her mean-tempered man and now the strange child, the village were embarrassed with her. Smiling she called out as she approached, to give him warning of her coming. Out he came, a big smile on his face, pulling his cap on to cover his eye, as was his habit. Unconsciously, Mistress Weaver surveyed her son with her usual surprise. He was really a fine lad, not counting the eye of course. His hair was wavy, a rich chestnut colour, and he was tall and strong.

"I've brought you some pottage, James my dear," for she now insisted on calling him his given Christian name, not the ugly Odi, wished on him by his father, and everyone else. "That was a fine coney you brought me, and with the bacon, greens and barley, has made it good and nourishing." For Mistress Weaver was a clever woman, and knew the rudiments of health and diet, learnt from her mother, and her mother before her. "You are such a good lad, what would I do without you."

Odi again smiled at Mistress Weaver who he had grown to like, though he couldn't say he would ever love her as a mother. His dear lost Annie had been that to him, Annie, who had such a beautiful soul, suffering like him from her ugliness. Yet her words pleased him, for he missed Annie's constant loving praise and felt for his birth mother, who suffered because of him, especially from the hands of her man.

Eagle, his cat stretched and yawned on the couch at the back of the shelter and hearing him Mistress Weaver laughed. "I'll bring you some milk next time, Eagle," she said, for she was pleasantly pleased when the boy had told her that she was the only one in the village whom the cat didn't hide from.

Taking out the bowl and eggs from the pail, he dropped his skeins of newly spun wool in their place. "Thank you kindly, mistress," he said, "you make a fine stew always. And for the eggs, you know how I love them." He never forgot that Annie had always told him that he must be polite.

Pleased, she went back to the village, pausing to call through the doorways of the dim little houses, whether any spun wool was ready for her to take.

As she neared the house, she was aware that the loom was silent. Bracing herself, the pail held in front of her, she entered, ready to show him the wool and to make the tallies. He was standing, his back to the fire, and his face was tight and angry.

"So where have you been, mistress?" he shouted loudly. A soft wind carried his voice down to the village and those who heard, stopped their labours for the moment, pity filling their hearts for the weaver's woman. She held out the pail for him to see, and had it dashed from her hand. "A pail! A pail! Since when did you need a heavy, wooden pail to carry wool in. What," he raised his voice even more, "is wrong with your basket?"

Well that was the beginning of it, and in the village, they clearly heard the quarrel on the wind, his outraged, accusing voice, and her high, defensive replies. The gentle squire's wife was just shooing the hens out of her hall again, when she stopped to listen to the screams. She was a nervous woman, afraid of all violence and began to tremble. Never in her life had she experienced such, yet she felt every blow, and shrank with every scream. Running to call the priest, she went on down the hill to call the boy. It had become known that Mistress Weaver often took him food, spending time with him, as she had when Annie was alive. Breathless she arrived at the little shelter and pulled at his sleeve.

"Oh, come, Odi, oh do come, good lad, for I fear that Master Weaver is beating your mother." They hurried up the hill, passing the old priest and several other alarmed villagers also hurrying their way. It was not unusual for a man to beat his wife, but the weaver was a brutal man, and his beatings were becoming more frequent and more violent. They paused at the door looking at each other and then Odi went in.

"Stop!" shouted Odi, in a great voice, seeing the weaver through the gloom, lift his arm holding a stick, ready to once more beat the poor woman on the floor. "Stop!" for Odi could not bear violence of word or deed. "Stop that!"

The weaver stopped for a moment, astonished by the fierce demand from the boy. Then he sneered, and brought his arm down with greater force, silencing the woman, then glared, jubilant at the impertinent, interfering devil's spawn before him.

Slowly, hate rising in him as a fierce tide, Odi approached the weaver and seizing the stick from his hand, suddenly found inhuman strength to beat, and beat the coward who fell wailing and writhing to the floor. On he went, and on, till he had no more strength. Then, lifting the body of the broken woman in his arms, he went out into the light, into a circle of stunned villagers. He was just able to lay her into the squire's arms before he fainted away to the ground before them.

Somehow, the villagers managed to carry the two bodies to the hall. Odi, who was soon stirring, they laid before the fireplace, a blanket over him and under his head. Mistress Weaver, they laid tenderly on the board, then stood back, now clearly seeing her, horrified by her injuries, not knowing where to start. Soon all the women were running for linen bandages and salves, and after washing her and making her as comfortable as they could, they waited. Odi rose to his feet and stood beside his mother.

"I'm sorry," he said, "I am so very sorry," meaning for causing her such pain, for hitting the weaver, for being born, for being himself. Mistress Weaver fluttered a hand and he took it, holding it warmly. She smiled weakly at him and closed her eyes. Blood was leaking in her brain from a tiny ruptured vein in her head, causing her to be drowsy. They stood about, wiped her brow with damp cloths, and prayed.

The weaver lay for awhile, dazed, the ship was rolling, and he had just been flogged for stealing the boy's rations. It wasn't fair, for he had been hungry, and the boy was little and didn't need so much. But the skipper had seen him and as was his way, had vented his fury on him. Magnus hated the skipper, hated the boy, the ship, the sea. In fact he hated everything and everyone. Why did he have to suffer them at all, it wasn't fair.

Slowly the sea calmed and Magnus realized that he was in his own house, not on deck. It came back to him, as he felt his own pain, his beating his stupid, useless wife. Then her son, Odin's son too for sure, actually taking the stick out of his hands and beating him too, just as that old captain had. Ah, but who had had the last laugh then eh? For coming back on board one night, Magnus had quietly slipped his knife into the back of the fool, and gently eased him overboard, first wiping his knife on his breeks. Life had been slightly easier after that, for a while anyway.

He got up stiffly, brushed a drop of blood from his forehead and made to leave. First, he lifted the board of the loom on which he sat and took out his purse, from its hiding place; it was agreeably heavy. Washing, then anointing his wounds with pig's fat, he waited till dusk fell, enjoying the pottage the stupid woman had made. Then he quietly walked the loaded pony past the shuttered cottages and away from the village. He had wasted enough time. Now with money in his purse and a trade, he would go home, north, across the sea to his own country and surprise them all.

The squire insisted that Odi stayed the night, and his mistress brought out a pallet and another large soft blanket to cover him. The women stayed close to Mistress Weaver, and in the dimness of the firelight, Odi could see that they were agitated. When next he woke, he heard the priest praying, and later, recognized the prayers for the dead. Odi lay, staring up at the dawn light from the smoke hole high above, realizing that it had happened again. Another good person in his life was gone. Mistress Weaver must be dead, for they had wrapped her in a shroud, and the women lay about her on the floor, sleeping at last.

No one was surprised to find that the weaver had left. They buried Mistress Weaver, and although, not unexpectedly, no money could be found in her house, her son gave more than enough to the priest, to say masses for her soul.

Odi went back to his shelter, and now and again went to the village for food, or to seek company. A new weaver was found, who agreed to give Odi rent, seeing as how he was the weaver's child. The squire agreed to mind it for him, so the rhythm of the village was soon calm again, and the spinners were once more busy supplying wool for the loom.

One day, about a month after Mistress Weaver had died, Odi disappeared. They were surprised, having got to know him as a good and reliable boy, despite his eye. They questioned each other as to whether he had told any of them that he was going. They looked in his shelter and found everything as it had been while he was living there. Well, they supposed, he'd gone off for awhile and would be back again, as he and Annie always had. There was no sign of his great wild-cat either.

Further away, Hannah began to sing, for they were almost at the place where she was beginning to feel happy. Hearing her, and sensing her mood, the pony and dog quickened their pace till very soon, they could see the roofs through the trees in a hollow. Things had changed since she had first struck out on her own, wearing Jack's hat and cloak and pretending to be his son. The first year had been grim, she'd had no idea that being a pedlar was so hard and fraught with danger. Many was the time when the dog had defended her so viciously, that they had had to slip away in the night.

Gradually it came to her that just selling lace, door to door, farm to holding, castle to keep, was the best plan. In between she rented a room, if the weather was poor usually for a couple of weeks, but longer in the winter. There she worked quietly, having also now learned to spin linen thread, so she didn't have to seek out suppliers. People got to know and welcome her, and she never had to sleep in with the packmen or carters any more, for the inn-wives felt a kindly responsibility towards her and they so admired her lace which she always let them have extra of.

Having often wondered how Mistress Betty, her old teacher fared, she had finally made her way to her town. So much had changed. New buildings stood where meadows had been, and Mistress Betty's little old house was a pile of rubble. Forlorn, she had stood in front of it, hoping that it hadn't fallen down with the old lady inside. But no, the inn-wife had told her that she had died peacefully, from something in her guts. When Hannah asked if there was another lace-maker in town, thinking she might even settle there, she was disappointed to hear there was.

On her third visit, she had asked until she was shown where the lace-maker lived. It was quite a surprise, for it was part of the castle, a grand new building which was being built in fits and starts, wooden scaffolding and stone blocks all over the place. An area which was completed was pointed out to her. Here was the lock up with several small rooms by it for the officers in charge.

The door had been opened showing a pretty young woman, full with child. Hannah gave her most winning smile and told her that she was a lace-maker too, and would like to have words with her, for she travelled, and they might be able to do business together. The young woman had stared at her for a long moment without speaking. Then flushing, she had thrown her arms around her crying, "Hannah!"

It was Daisy, grown so tall and pretty, Daisy, the elder of the two little sisters who had also been at Mistress Betty, to learn lace-making. How they had laughed and hugged and chattered. So she had a friend to visit, and this time, Daisy must surely have her babe, so Hannah hurried on. Daisy had wed with a soldier of the local lord, who having been wounded in a battle was no longer fit for warfare, and had been given the job as a guard of the lock-up. Not that it was a hard job, for he shared it with two others, doing a rota, two on and one off. The pay was modest, but the great advantage was that they had a little house too.

Hannah looked about her and thought that Daisy had done well. The house was merely a room, one of three, with doors going out into a pretty courtyard where there was a well a kitchen and a privy. One front door served them all, opening into a hallway where there was a board and stool for the officer on duty. High above the board was a row of hooks on which hung two great keys.

Daisy was always happy to see Hannah, and made lace for her to sell, bringing extra money in, which obviously impressed her man.

The baby was a girl, a lovely little thing, and Daisy was pleased to see how Hannah loved her. Once more the friends sat and chattered every day while working at their cushions, inventing new designs, and just enjoying each other's company. Daisy's friend became a familiar figure at the castle, smiling at the builders as they toiled at their work, giving them cheer. Hannah had rented a small room above a bakers, where the pony and dog could sleep in the stable in the yard at the back. Every afternoon she took them out, roaming the hills around, calling at the little hamlets and farmhouses, in case there were orders. On her rounds she sometimes laid snares, for meat was expensive in the market, and Daisy and the baker's wife were always glad to accept her conies.

One evening, coming home later than usual, so it was dusk, they clattered up the new cobbled road to the keep. Hannah tied the pony outside, for she had a good sized coney for Daisy, and didn't want to leave it till morning. Just as she was walking up to the door, she heard an owl cough. Stopping suddenly, shocked, her senses alert, she listened, trying to make out where it came from. It had been years since she had heard it, and her heart leapt, maybe it was da? When there was silence for the moment, she tried to remember how to do it, coughed, tried again, and there it was clearly, a coughing owl. Back it came urgently and Hannah suddenly realized that it came from low down. The keep had an underground dungeon which had the smallest window. Trying to remember how to reply, she lowered her call, soft and soothing, just as her da had. Now she sprang two at a time up the steps to Daisy's door, the coney in her hand; Daisy would know something.

It was a lad, Daisy said, who'd murdered someone, so it was said, and was due to hang soon. More she didn't know. Hannah was in a turmoil. She had been called, someone needed help. The next morning she went in to see Daisy, nodding to the officer who lazed at the board, she carefully noted the keys. Then she went home, pleading that her eyes ached and whittled at two pieces of wood, to form rough keys. When the baker was out on his rounds, she opened the oven door and pushed her work about in the embers to blacken them.

“I beg of you, Daisy,” she said. “I do not know who it is, but it has to be Rom, one of us, and it was I who heard the call for help.” Daisy frowned, for this was a Hannah she didn't know. She frowned and shook her head.

"I cannot help you, Hannah, for if I was discovered, my man would lose his job, and then where would we be?" Hannah pursed her lips and sighed.

"Daisy, I promise you that no one will know," she drew out a rag and unwrapping it revealing two, big black keys. Daisy gasped, looked at them, then her.

"How did you get them?" for she had just seen them hanging up, or had she, and the officer on duty always carried the other two.

Hannah smiled for the first time, leaning forward to kiss her friend's rosy cheek. "I made them, silly, they're just wood, blackened in the fire, not real. The real ones are still hanging up. My da was very handy with a whittling knife, I must have the gift from him." Then, eyes deeply serious she took Daisy's hands. "I beg you to help me. All I want you to do is tell me what it is like down there, which way to go. And while I am down, to go walking with the baby, say she is teething and fretful, and talk with the officer on duty, keep his interest, till you hear my pony moving off." She then pulled out the cord from around her neck and opened a tiny, leather purse hanging there. Next moment she was holding up a small, golden coin. "This was given to me when I was a baby," taking Daisy's baby's hand, she pressed the coin into it and folded its fat fingers around it. "Daisy, I beg you to help me." For a moment, her friend hesitated, but very soon, Daisy glowed, and nodded.

Later that night, the alarm bell started ringing, and Daisy urged her husband, one of the officers on watch, to go to see what the trouble was. Then, Hannah arrived, breathless, hung her mantle on the hook on the back of the door and climbed up and changed the keys. For if an officer came in, and they were not there, it would be the first thing that he would notice despite the dimness. On bare feet, she ran silently to open the small door in a great gate into the keep, the huge key, turning terribly slowly in the lock. Pushing it shut, she felt her way through the passageway, then down a stair, in deep darkness underground till she came to another door. On tip-toe, very softly, she coughed as an owl. Immediately there was an answer, so after feeling the door, again struggling with the second key, she drew the shivering creature out as it swung open and as quietly as she could, shut and re-locked it. "Try to be very quiet," she said in Rom. When he didn't react, she paused, tried to see his face but gave up and repeated her words in English, which he did seem to understand. Retracing her steps, pausing at the main door, all the while firmly holding on to her prisoner, she listened and heard Daisy's sweet voice some way off, around the keep.

"Now go," she gave the silent figure a push, "get to my pony which is by the wall and lie flat and still while I put the keys back. Don't move till I come." Fear caused her to run more swiftly and climbing up once more on the board she replaced the keys, putting the wooden ones in her blouse. Then, calming herself, she took up her hooded mantle which hung on the back of the hall door, and went out where the pony stood, with the dog beside it, helped the boy up and made him lie down. Urging it down the cobbles, she saw Daisy walking with the officer, coming slowly towards her. With her body shielding the one lying over the pony, she waved.

"I've taken my cushion Daisy, so I will finish the piece before I see you tomorrow. I hope that the baby lets you sleep now. Good night my friend. Goodnight officer."

Walking steadily, she waited till they were well out of town before she eased her hurrying and it wasn't till they were far away that she stopped. Helping the lad down from the pony, she still could not see him because it was so dark. Steadying him with her hand she thought that apart from being stinking and filthy, he was well built and much taller than she, but bent and cowed, not surprisingly. It crossed her mind that he was injured, from the little noises he made, no doubt beaten, but she had done her bit, so now it was up to him and the saints.

"I don't know who you are, or what crime you have committed, how you know of the coughing owl, or where you are going. But you are free now, and I urge you to go west into the hills, as far as you can, crossing water as often as you can, to put the dogs off your scent. It wouldn't hurt you to bathe either," she added as she pushed a bag into his hand, "here is bread, cheese and a little money, and" she took off her blanket, "you'd better take this too, for it is cold at night." He just stood there, dumb and numb, breathing deeply, unable to say a word. "Go now," she gave him a push, "go with God."

Mounting the pony she turned and hurried off, so that she did not see a stealthy feline run to the boy, or hear the boy weep with happiness because his friend had come to find him.

She was still sleeping when Daisy came up the ladder to her attic room, her face a picture of anxiety, soon to be of laughter. They went over it, step by step, move by move, giggling, rolling about. The baker's wife listened to them through the thin boards and smiled. How good it was that her funny little gypsy tenant had a friend. How good it was that laughter filled the building and warmed her heart. Meanwhile all the town was in uproar, for, it was said, the murderer had flown out of the tiny, dungeon window in the guise of a cat, for how else could he have escaped? And some said they had seen a strange large cat about.

"Never, ever tell another living soul of last night's work, Daisy," Hannah entreated her friend. But she need not have worried, for despite their laughter, they were both fearful, until it was officially agreed that indeed witchcraft had been involved, and none of the officers was suspected of doing anything other than their duty. Daisy even gave evidence, her baby in her arms, before the lord and his assizes that she had spoken with the officer as he did his rounds. And the fire, which had caused the alarm bells to ring, must have been caused by a chimney spark, and only the rotten thatch of old Mistress Betty's old ruined cottage had burnt, none other.

Clary had continued to run down-stream along the river bank, hoping to see the green man emerge from the water, but just his hat sailed on, till at last an eddy brought it to the bank further along, and absently, she picked it up, emptied out the water and held it against her, shocked and suddenly, unexpectedly sad.

The inn folk were all kindness and concern, and some officers from the town came the next day to investigate the drownings.

"It is long overdue that we have a bridge," said the mayor, and the priest agreed. Somehow they would raise the town taxes, even making a levy on all travellers, for this was not the first time a boat had capsized with loss of life. A physician and the salter came to see her, properly sympathetic, having not even known that their supplier had a wife, let alone an enchanting daughter. They mourned the loss of their herbs, for he had been a very trusted herbalist, and entreated Clary to try to replace them if she could.

But Clary was so truly shocked at the drownings, and at being alone again, that she could do nothing, promise no one, for anything. Not that she had even really cared for Master Green, he had happened in her life, a kindly man, who had looked after them and now was gone. She stayed on at the inn, in the same little chamber under the thatch with the pony safely stabled in the yard. Lying on the good bed with Lina and Dove, she spent hours just gazing at the roof timbers, listening to the mice and birds in the thatch, unhearing. So emotionally spent was she, she was almost unable to move.

Then, she thought to look for the little glass which he had kept in his hat, and investigating, she found it and much else. Now she understood just why he had shouted, "my hat, my hat," at her, before the water engulfed him. This was where he kept his money, a lot of it, funny, kind man.

Sending for the mayor, she made a donation in memory of her man, begging him, if his body should come up along their banks, to give him decent burial with masses for his soul.

Eventually she found the courage to move, paid her bill and with a very rested pony, rode out one morning, along the river road. Sometimes she rode with Lina in her arms, other times she walked, leaving the baby asleep hanging from the saddle balancing her meagre bags. It was good to be out again, and there were many travellers along the road so she felt safe enough. Every time she saw a pack train, she stopped and asked them if they knew how far it was to Marsh Newton. None had even heard of it until one day, one man said he did know it, for surely very good cheese came from there? He had once transported some, and would never forget it. Clary actually smiled and gave him an extravagant coin. So it was there somewhere, not just a memory, a dream. He thought that she must go west, but he wasn't sure. The problem was getting across the river which was still high, and bridges were few.

They stopped at inns for food and at first, for a bed, but Clary found that most places were filthy, quite apart from the worrying and usual interest in her, for women travelling alone were not common. Almost without fail before she slept, she heard the awful brawling of drunken men, and clutched her baby and dog close.

Then they came to a busy bridge and she rested there, still asking those who looked like travellers. She bought a good length of canvas and another of thick if rough wool from a peddler, because she thought on the whole she might be happier sleeping out, if she could find quiet places. Having done it before, she remembered that it was far better than bedding down with other snoring travellers, where you had to watch your very shoes. So she turned away from the river road, watching the sunset each day, always going to the west. The country grew wilder, more as she remembered the area around the outlaw's settlement and she grew afraid. So then she veered south, and it became less wild.

When it began to rain, she took out Master Green's wide brimmed hat, and holding Lina close under it, had a modicum of shelter, until they reached a village. This was a turning point in her travels, and she couldn't think why she hadn't thought of it before. For now, as she approached habitation, the simple folk knew that she was a herb gatherer. Gone were the questions and tongue clicking as to her lone state. Now there was sympathy for her, but with their understandable egotism, the poor country folk were more interested in what they could get from her as a result of merely telling her where they had always known a certain herb grew.

Clary felt happier, with more purpose, and bought some simple linen cloth to sew bags, sitting out some wet days in a village, profitably occupied. Now she knew what herbs the physicians and salters needed, she just had to find, dry and carry them. The one great advantage of collecting herbs was that they were very light to carry.

She grew anxious however, for some days there was a touch of autumn in the air and she knew she must get home by winter.

"Yes," said more and more people she passed on the by-ways, Marsh Newton was ahead, somewhere.

They came to a monastery and she stayed there two days, conversing with the healer monk, who being old, his sight failing, was glad of her herbs which she exchanged for bed and board. It had been a long time since she had lost herself in the glorious masses, and attended every one, even the night ones, wishing that she had the courage to have Lina baptized, and have herself blessed, but she did not. Too many questions would result, and she still felt vulnerable and afraid. There would be time enough when she got home with the strength and love of her family all about her. It was there that she learned that Master Green had a name, for on seeing the hat, it had immediately been recognized and they said masses for the soul of Zakarius Green.

There were some very hot days, and Clary tried to keep in the forest, and wherever there was a stream, to bathe in its icy cold water. She found that her daughter had a love for water, providing she was lowered into it very slowly. Then she would splash and crow, frightening herself by wetting her face, then laugh again.

Even the pony and dog stood in the shallows and relished being wet. Knowing that a thunder-storm was coming, Clary looked out for shelter, anything, a rock over-hang if no village lay along the road. As the sky grew darker, the heat more oppressive, she became anxious, and held a tight rein on the pony who sensed the coming storm and was skittish.

Suddenly there was a great flash of lightning and the thunder roared. Hurrying along the merest track, Clary searched desperately for some shelter, but there was none. Another great flash of lightening hit a tree and after the hot days, ignited it, burning, like a brand against the dark sky. Then a new sound seemed to join the sky's roar. Turning onto a small path which led into the woods, Clary dragged the pony on, entreating it to hasten.

A rushing, and crashing, squealing, screaming and breaking of undergrowth seemed to surround her. Just as the rain began to come down in huge, fat drops, blinded, Lina screaming in fright, she forged ahead until, suddenly, on the path in front of her, a wild man appeared, as if from nowhere. Startled, she pushed her hair out of her eyes to see him and gaped at him, and instead of running away he approached her, grabbed her hand

and the pony's halter and began pulling them. Wild noise swirled about them, lightening, thunder, and the ever louder sound of something else nearer and nearer.

A great cave loomed through the pouring rain and once under its roof, dry, clutching the baby, Clary stopped breathless and wild-eyed as a great herd of swine raced past them, crashing through the undergrowth, squealing with fright at the deafening storm. It was shocking, and Clary clutched her daughter tightly, while the tide of screaming animals roared past. After they had gone and the noise abated, slowly and surely, Clary began to laugh. Then it held her and she doubled up, collapsing on the earth floor and soon the wild man began to laugh too, and reaching out, took the baby and they laughed till they could laugh no more.

Drying her eyes on her wet skirt, Clary took the baby who, frightened by the unusual noise about her, had begun to cry again. Weakly Clary held her, and opening her bodice, gave her to suck for comfort. Then, in the lull which followed, there was just the sound of heavy rain pouring down outside and Clary looked at her companion.

He was just a very dirty lad. He was tall and well-built, but had the innocent and clumsy ways of a child. She wondered if he was touched in the head, but soon decided that he was not, that indeed he was highly intelligent if not at all learned. He was fearfully ugly. With his blood, dried hair cropped short matted and wet, his filthy head was full of caked and festering wounds, but worse than everything else, one eye was huge, dominating his face. Clary stilled her fear, realizing that he meant her no harm, on the contrary, he was watching the nursing babe with utmost tenderness.

"Thank you so much, my dear. Oh what a fright wasn't it? I just could not understand what the noise was. First the storm, then the hogs," and she began to laugh again. "What a good thing that you found us, bless you, for otherwise we would most likely be not only soaking wet, but overrun by swine." He did not reply, so intent was he on the child. "What is your name, my boy?" she finished.

Then he looked up at her, kindness in the smaller eye, his mouth in a smile.

"James," he said, "James." Only half realizing that this woman had called him "my boy" as had Annie always.

She nodded and repeated, "James, and I am Clary, and this," she indicated the babe at her breast, "is Lina, and with a hand on the shivering dog, "she is Dove, and the pony?" She had not known if it had a name, so suddenly asked, "Do you have a good name for him?"

The boy looked at the pony whose flanks were still heaving from their dash. He nodded. "Storm?"

Clary smiled delighted. "What a good name, Storm, yes, thank you, I like it and think it is highly suitable." She looked about them, realizing that this must be his home. Then she saw yellow eyes observing her from a rock ledge at the back of the cave, and started.

Seeing her, James smiled and called out, "Do not be afraid, Eagle, for we have kindly company." So he told her how Eagle had come to be his cat and his friend, and that he followed him everywhere.

Although she felt quite safe and glad that they were in the dry, she was wet and cold. "Do you think that we can make a fire my dearling, to get warm, and dry out?"

Now the lad leapt up and ran hither and thither making a fire in the hearth and soon a good blaze burned in the centre of the cave. He then took her wet clothes and hung them on peg branches which were set into crevices in the cave ceiling to dry. The pony was unloaded and put to the side, and Dove went off exploring. After Clary had unpacked the bread and cheese, she sat, cutting it up, wrapped in her blanket, and they ate companionably, to the sound of heavy rain.

Clary was intrigued by her saviour, for he seemed the gentlest soul, despite his horrific looks. It continued to rain heavily for two days, during which time she attended his head, where she saw signs of terrible violence. Then she cut and stitched the woollen cloth she had bought at the bridge, and again saw signs of dreadful, though fading, bruising on his body and wondered how the poor lad had obtained them. She smiled when she had done, for she had made him a sort of flowing monk's shift, with a great hood at the back, which he could cover his head with. But first she urged him to bathe, gave him her little wooden pot of soft soap and obediently he went off, returning blue, shivering but clean. Like a small child, he offered her his finger and toe nails to trim, and warmly thanked her. They stayed at the cave for some days, until the woods had dried a little. Each day he disappeared and returned with something good to cook. While he mostly busied himself caring for them, he did sometimes play a little pipe, which delighted the baby, or sang to her, little baby songs without words.

"It is time to go now, James," she said, carefully packing up and loading the pony, Storm. "We shall go home now, will you come with us?" He gazed at her, and she looked into his small eye, the eye she realized he saw through. There was every emotion in that little eye, fear, sorrow, hope, love. Leaning forward she drew him to her and held him close. She realized that she was only just a little taller than he. "Well my dearling, would you like to come home with me, and be my boy, a brother for Lina. If you will call me mother you will surely be her big brother." Her hand stroked his poor head, and she felt his stiffness quiver. Then he began to weep, silently at first, shaking uncontrollably, then with long drawn out cries, desperate, lonely. Clary held him fast, rocking, murmuring words of comfort, till they became aware that Lina, who had been asleep had heard, and now joined him, raising her little voice bitterly in sympathy. So they began to laugh again and ended up in a huddle on the floor of the cave all together, giving and taking comfort, arms about each other.

They set off, slithering through the mud, the rising steam, and the freshness of a washed earth on a beautiful morning. Clary saw that her new son was suddenly happy, so naturally easing her burdens by leading the pony, carrying the baby, lighting fires and foraging for food as if he had done so all his life. They sang as they walked along, skirting the puddles along the lanes, and sometimes she told him about home, and the family, which he listened to, avidly.

Piers would accept him she knew, Piers who was so kind and understanding. Of course Jessie would make a fuss, but then when did she not. Clary felt a new optimism as they walked on into September and passed bullocks straining the ropes, drawing the timber along the good earth, and heard the woodmen calling, their whips renting the air.

They came out of the forest as evening fell, and finally, there, far below them lay the water-meadows, and just above the silver river stood a huddle of roofs, a wisp of smoke rising from them. Clary stopped and rested a hand on the boy's arm.

"Home!" she said, nodding towards the hall, way below them.

"Home!" he echoed.

And then they began going down the hill.

CHAPTER THIRTY TWO

JAMES

They reached the farm as the last streaks of day were fading. Clary could smell the wood smoke from the chimney, but there seemed to be no light showing from the chinks in the shutters. So if they were still up, they were at the board, sitting by firelight.

Clary's heart quickened, as she led the way unerringly to the stable. The old dog Ned gave one bark; then scenting her, wagged his tail, for this one he remembered was kind, who never kicked him and gave him good scraps to eat.

Smoothing James's healing head, she handed him the baby. "Will you sit here awhile my dearling, for I must go alone to see what is what. It might be too much for me to take you both in at the beginning. Let me tell them I am back first, for having been away a year and more, is a long time." She took her blanket and wrapped it about him covering Lina too. "Rest now, be sure I shall be back shortly, but first I must see how it is with my husband and family."

James obediently sat in the straw, his back against the manger, and cuddled the baby. If she said she would be back shortly, he knew she would, for here at last was another good woman whom he could trust implicitly. Beside him, Storm had his head in the manger and ate noisily. It was obvious that there were other beasts in the byre, but they just shuffled their feet, blew through their noses and let be. No doubt Eagle would be exploring and hunting rats and mice.Clary carefully made her way through the dusk, her heart hammering and her breath coming in little gasps.

"Piers! Oh, Piers!" A great longing for him swept through her body, and she clenched her thighs, trembling for him. Then the old fears assailed her. Would he have already taken another wife? Well who could blame him, with two little boys it was certain he needed one. If so, would he put the new one away, poor wench, and take her back? Or, if she was beautiful, and perhaps with child, would he keep her, and send her, Clary, his first wife and love, home to her parents?

She crept around to the west side of the hall, where there was still a glimmer of light from the setting sun, and felt her way to their window. Well she knew, smiling softly to herself, how often they had climbed down from it so as not to disturb the others, and so down to the river. There Clary had swam, naked as the day she was born, and loving her beauty, Piers had come in after her. He had never learned to swim, but they had laughed and played till, shivering and wet, they had crept in through the window again. Drawing the shutter to behind them, trying to be very quiet, they had dried and held each other giggling, till they were once more warm.

The shutter gave, and, glad that there was no window glass yet, she pulled herself up into the chamber.

"What is it Jessie?" a voice came softly from the bed. "Is the baby sick?"

Clary stood stock still, alert to the familiar voice, but it seemed her breath was coming so fast, she had no voice.

"Jessie? What is it?" again.

Still she could not speak, frozen. What was grandmother doing in their bed? There was the sound of someone sitting up, the creaks of the bed, and again the voice, anxious now, "Who is there, what do you want?" sharp.

"It's Clary, grandmother, not Jessie, I am come home."

Somehow they found each other in the gloom, and Clary rested her head in her grandmother's lap and silently wept while the old hands smoothed, caressed, and the dear familiar voice whispered endearments.

At last, Clary could not bear not to ask, "Grandmother, where are my boys? And where is Piers? What are you doing sleeping in our bed?"

Now it was the turn of the old one to weep, and without knowing why, it was Clary's turn to comfort. Finally, wiping her nose on her night shift, Moya drew her favourite granddaughter into the bed and covered her, to stop her trembling.

"The boys are well my dearling, they are asleep in the loft above with your sister, Fleur, who has been helping me in turn with the other girls since you left." She paused, drew breath and blurted, "Piers is dead, my dearling. They found him in the woods the next day, after he had gone racing after you, when you were abducted. When the horse came back alone, we guessed some ill had befallen him. They must have waited for him, tripped the horse and then when he was down, put an axe in his head. For there was just the one wound, and we understood he had died immediately and suffered no pain. He looked so peaceful when we buried him. Oh my Clary, my sweetest dear, that it should be I who gives you this grievous news!"

Clary heard unbelieving. So, she thought, one of the wretched outlaws had stayed behind to do the deed, and she felt that she would faint with the horror of it. Lina's father had killed Piers, her dearly beloved husband, or at least had ordered it done. Silently the tears began coursing down her cheeks, but then, remembering Lina and James in the stable she stopped them and hardened her heart. Lina was Pier's child, and no one would ever know otherwise.

"I have a beautiful baby daughter, right now in the stable being nursed by my adopted son, James. This is a lad who saved us in time of need, a good lad, sad, lonely, ugly, with the softest heart. Grandmother, I must go to them, so will you make ready a pallet, light a rush, find a little food, while I fetch them?"

Sitting on the pallet with James, she held the little dish of oat cakes and urged him to eat them and drink the milk while she nursed Lina. At least the great cot was still there, and Clary changed her daughter's cloth and laid her to sleep, just as the rush light flickered and died.

After they were settled, Clary lay beside her grandmother and stared into the darkness. Her mind raced, for now everything would be different with Piers gone. She must be very strong. She must keep hold of what she and Piers had for the children. She must see her parents and Father Benjamin and she must sleep.

Moya rose early as was her way and went to blow up the fire at the hearth, and pushed the crane over to heat the kettle. Somehow she had always felt that Clary was not dead, for who could kill such a lovely woman, and she had believed that somehow, one day, she would return. Now she quietly carried the wooden tub to their chamber, and began filling it with cold water, in order to top it with hot for when Clary woke, it was clear, that she needed to bathe.

"Can I help you, grandmother?" James' voice came quietly from the pallet on the other side of the chamber. Moya startled and straightened her back.

"But of course, my dear," it was just getting light and she strained to see the abomination which Clary had brought back. In the night's flickering rush light, he had seemed all eye, but mild mannered, as Clary had assured her. "It will be a tribulation for Clary to meet the family again, so I will bathe her and wash her hair. But first use the piss-pot dear, then yes, a strong arm will help me greatly."

Lucas heard the sounds of activity from his cupboard bed in the hall, but didn't stir. Things were not happy in his house again, so he preferred to stay in bed for as long as he decently could.

Carrying a pitcher of warmed milk, sweetened with honey and more oat cakes, Moya set them by the window which she opened a crack. Then, back in the hall, she stealthily took two of the best tallow candles, lit them in the hearth and carried them back and with the light of them, closed the shutter once more. It would not do to have the room fresh and cold for a bath. Sitting on the bed she stroked Clary's head.

"Clary dearling, I have the bath ready for you. Thankfully your good James has helped me carry the water. If you are to meet the family, my love, I want you to look beautiful and clean. But first, drink," and offered her a cup of milk.

Clary sat in the hot bath while her grandmother poured the water over her head and washed it with soft soap. They spoke quietly, and Clary learned that not only had Jessie a daughter, Rowena, after Luke's mother, just a little older than Lina, she was with child again, hoping of course for a son this time. When Lina heard the soft voices, she made a sound, so deftly Moya unwrapped and wiped her down and handed her to her mother in the bath. While she nursed, they washed her, and Moya cooed with delight over the chubby, fair baby.

"She is an angel," she said. "How Felicia will rejoice having you back and with such a little dear." She surveyed her carefully. "I do believe that she is very fair, just like Fleur, your great grandmother." Then taking the baby she wrapped her in a linen cloth and put her into the still warm bed. "Who as you know," she went on as she now rubbed Clary's hair, "was not only my aunt by marriage, she was my godmother too."

Clary, also wrapped in a linen sheet slid in the bed beside her daughter, feeling unusually clean and light.

"The water is still warm, James my dear," Moya stood over his pallet. "Shall you also be nice and clean to meet your new family?"

Later, she asked Clary about the scars on the boy's head and body, and Clary told her that as yet she knew not his whole story. Yet the one thing that she did know, was that he was the kindest lad, and that she would keep him by her for as long as he wished to stay. "For I fear he was well nigh beaten to death, poor soul, yet he helped me in time of need, and after he joined us, I was never afraid again."

Moya gazed at her granddaughter with compassionate eyes. It would be a long time before her whole story would come out, poor child.

"Where are my clothes, grandmother," said Clary puzzled, looking into her empty dower chest.

Looking at her, Moya anxiously took her hand.

"It has been very difficult since you left, Clary dearling. Jessie was distraught when they could not find you. Of course she found caring for the boys and the household too much, hence we came, although it was too hard for the girls, so they take it in turns. Fleur is here now, but she is due to go home soon and Leah will come in her stead. I felt I must stay, because understandably, old Lukas did not want us to take the twins away. Without you to keep Jessie in her place, old though I am, it seems that I am the next best person to do it."

Clary nodded.

"But my clothes, grandmother?"

Still looking anxious Moya went to some wooden hooks on the wall and unhooked a dress. "You'd better wear Fleur's second dress, for Jessie has taken yours, thinking that you wouldn't be back and needing them."

Her face severe and closed, Clary stepped into her younger sister's dress, wondering what other unpleasant changes she would find. Then she went across to Pier's chest, and gratefully lifted out his clothes, shutting her eyes, suddenly feeling faint with the smell of him. Turning to James she laid them on the bed, and said very gently,

"Well you at least have good clothes to wear my dearling. See," she held them up. "You are so clean and fresh, and you will feel quite a new little man now."

Looking hard at her grandmother, so words were not necessary, she went out of the bed chamber and into the hall. If Piers was dead, he did not need his clothes any more, and the boy certainly did.

Luke was at the board, and with his hand halfway to his mouth, he stopped short, for although it was still dim in there, here surely was not his young sister-in-law Fleur, but Clary.

"I am back, Luke," she said firmly, and also sat at the board. "Much has happened to me over this year and more, but I am home now, alas a widow, as my love, Piers is dead, so grandmother has told me." She paused, watching the myriad emotions on his face. "So when father and Jessie are up, and my parents arrive, for Fleur will send for them, we will have much to discuss as to our future. For," she stared coldly at him, comparing him with the soft, sweet looks of Piers, "I have a little daughter, who sadly Piers will never see, and I adopted a lad along the road, a strange, ugly boy with the best heart. He will help me in what ever I chose to do." She paused, staring directly at him. "I hear I must congratulate you also on a little daughter, with another one on the way." He nodded, dumbfounded and surprised that the gentle Clary of his memory, now seemed firm and strong.

When her sister Fleur came down the ladder from the sleeping loft, on seeing Clary she began to weep so they stood, the sisters, rocking and comforting each other.

"It will be strange for the boys to meet me again who no doubt they have forgotten. So my sweet Fleur, we must be very quiet and careful, till they take to me again in their own time." Clary watched with hungry eyes as her twins came carefully down the ladder backwards, their aunt seeing to their every step. First they used the piss-pot, and Clary watched them proudly, for they were as fine a brace of little lads that she had ever seen.

Having noticed her, they stood while Fleur dressed them. Perhaps something in their memory caused them to look at her again and again. For a start she did look much like their Aunt Jessie, who was to be avoided at all times. Then, she did look like their Aunts Fleur, Leah and Maria of the tower who came to look after them. And she looked like Aunt Joan too, the one at Marsh Newton. Yet, they kept looking at her, a tiny identical frown in their eyes, as they were dressed. Then they took Fleur's hands and went into the hall to break their fast.

Clary smiled across at James, who had watched fascinated from the shadows, for of course Clary had told him all about her sons.

"So there they are my dearling, just as I told you, as peas in a pod, your little brothers, Lucius and Stephen." After helping him to dress in Pier's work clothes, she tried to comb his sparse, chestnut hair over his great eye, but could not. Then, reaching into Pier's chest, she drew out a cap, again feeling an intolerable pain engulf her which she immediately dismissed. "Here then dearling, this was the very first gift which I made for my husband, the softest fleece it was too." she drew the cap down over his eye. "Is that well, James? Does it pain you at all? For poor souls, they have so many shocks coming to them what with me reappearing, and with little Lina, who they know nothing of. If you will wear Pier's cap for the time being, it might help." Then taking his hand, she kissed him and led him into the hall.

Luke had gone and Moya, Fleur and the boys were at the board eating while at the other end, Lucas sat with a babe on his knee. There was no sign of Jessie. As Lucas had no teeth, he held a crust of bread in a bowl of milk and in turns with the child, sucked on it.

Clary looked at her little niece and her heart melted. Not unlike Lina, she was smaller, and when, handing Lina to her grandfather, she took Rowena, she found that she was indeed a light-weight baby. While Lina, some months younger, was plump and a good weight, Rowena was slight, a skinny baby with nervous, huge, grey eyes. Holding her close, understanding, and filled with pity, Clary kissed and crooned to her. After resisting for a moment, the little thing relaxed into her body so it was the most natural thing to, to undo her bodice and put the child to suck.

After watching her for awhile, Lucas got up and pouring a great mug of butter-milk from a pitcher, pushed it across to his daughter-in-law. His eyes were kind, grateful but worried.

"It's alright, father," she said, surprised at the strong, anxious sucking of the child at her breast, "we are born to it. Our family seems to breed twins, so I am used to it, but thank you, for of course you are right, I must drink a lot, and not neglect my own child."

When Rowena had suckled from both sides, she lay full and contentedly sleepy. Lifting her up, which caused a great gust of wind to belch from her, Clary went to the east side of the hall, knocked on the door and went in.

Jessie was lying against the pillows and expecting either Moya or Fleur, looked up sleepily. Then her eyes widened with surprise, for although the dress was Fleur's, it was not she but Clary. Sitting bolt upright, she stared at her twin.

"So I am back Jessie, and I have to congratulate you on this sweet daughter. Grandmother tells me that you are already with child again, which sorrows me, for this little one is too light for her age; you will have to be more careful next time.

Jessie gasped. For was this hard, forthright woman her soft twin, Clary?

"Ah," Clary went across to a handsome new cradle on the far side, Luke's side she noticed, of the bed. "Did Luke make it for you?" as she gently lowered the sleeping child down. "What a fine cradle."

"He did," replied Jessie, finding her voice, "and where have you been this past two years?"

Clary looked at her sister and realized that not only was she with child, but that she was fat. "It is not two years, as well you know Jessie, it is just over a year. I was abducted at the fair at the same time as Joan's wedding. All of which I shall relate to you when mother and father come, for a year is a long time, and I have a great deal to tell, not much of it good." Then going to the hooks on the wall, she sorted through the robes hanging there. "And now I will take my dresses back!" Draping them over her arm, she made for the door. "Don't ever touch or take my things again," she said severely and went out.

By the time Jessie emerged from her bed chamber, the day was well advanced.

The wash tubs were before the fire filled with Clary's dresses, the board and floor were clean and no one was in sight.

Out on the hillside, Lucas stood with his dog Ned, his sheep and cattle, and thought of his unexpected new family, a sweet grey dog and a fine pony. The boy James, walked behind, Piers' cap anchored sideways over his head, was carrying Lina, who obviously loved him, and was leading the pony on which sat the twins. They were waving down towards the river where Clary was seeing off Luke and Fleur.

"Ask mother to bring any old dresses she can spare for me," she entreated, for I have grown so thin, and must stitch mine smaller, which will take time. And," quietly in her ear, "ask her to sort out some soft little pieces of silk so that I can make patches for my new son, to cover his eye comfortably." Kissing her sister warmly, she watched as she picked up her skirts and walked to the flat through the icy water, following behind her brother-in-law.

Then she returned to the little group on the hill and kissed them all, even old Lucas, who flushed with pleasure.

"Oh but, it is lovely to be home again," she said, and they all smiled happily. "But now I must go to prepare a good meal for us," turning to Lucas, "father, how fares the store room?"

Lucas looked at the ground and worked his toe into a tussock. Blinking up at her he sighed. "Poorly, daughter, for with you gone we have not had the good stores put away with diligence." He again avoided her eyes so she frowned, wondering what he meant by "poorly".

"Well, James my dear, if you will lay some snares, look, over there by the bushes in the dip, I remember there being quite a warren there, and I will pluck some greens, so we shall fare well tomorrow, if not today." Taking Lina into her arms, she went back to the hall.

Jessie looked up from the board where she was eating bread and milk. The honey pot was beside her, and Clary thought that it was just as well that Father Byford was a good bee keeper, for she was ladling it on.

"Meet my little daughter Jessie," her tone was kindly, "it is nice for our girls to be so close together, for they will grow up as sisters as we did."

Jessie looked in surprise at the plump, light haired little girl on Clary's arm, and thought that she had never seen such blue eyes before. Truly she was lovely, and the babe, just then, noticing the new, not so unfamiliar face before her, Lina gave her most charming smile.

"She is lovely, Clary," Jessie said, a quiver of discomfort in her stomach, thinking of her own poor little one, "how old is she?"

Clary went to the side board and took down a mug, then filled it from the pitcher by Jessie. Sitting down she undid her bodice and put Lina to suckle. Then, mindful of Father Byford's concern, she drank deep, and was rewarded by the prickling surge of new milk filling her breasts.

"I suppose that she is a month or two younger than your Rowena, Jessie, for I must have been newly, just with child, when I was abducted." She gazed lovingly at her daughter, holding her hand. No one will ever know that you are base-born my dearling, she thought, and, thanks to God and the saints, you are the most bonny lass, bigger than Jessie's poor, under fed little scrap. "The shame is that Piers can not see her, for he would love her so," and her eyes filled with tears.

"But do you really think that she is Piers child?" Jessie spoke in a hard voice, jealousy rising in her like a great tide.

Clary looked straight at her. "Be careful what you say Jessie!"

So Jessie shoved another spoon in her mouth and looked pointedly at Lina. "But look at her eyes, and her hair," she exclaimed loudly, through her mouthful, "None of us have such hair, we are yellow headed, while she is white. We have grey-blue eyes, hers are deep blue."

Unconsciously Clary smoothed the soft white hair on her daughter's head and tried to still the hammering in her heart. "So she must be like our great grandmother Fleur, as grandmother told me just this morning."

She was rudely cut off.

"She is not, our grandmother," her voice raised, "and what she says is not, important, or true."

Now Clary stood up and putting the baby on her shawl on the floor, she did up her bodice.

"She may not be your grandmother, Jessie, but she is mine. She has loved and cared for us since we were babes, and I in turn love her and will care for her as she ages. Who but she would leave the comfort of the manor, giving the money to father, the lovely furnishings to be distributed to us girls. Why did she leave the marsh tower, the love and care of mother and father? She came unselfishly, came to look after my poor little sons when they lost both their parents! She knew, as did all the family, that you could not cope. Which of course they were right in. It was a selfless act of grandmother to leave the comforts of the tower, to come here, and I shall ever be grateful to her."

At the door Moya paused, the basket of eggs on her arm, feeling faint. "Oh girls," she murmured to herself, "oh Clary, my most dear, ssh, ssh."

"Why?" Clary went on, trying not to shout, "you can't even get up of a morn to feed your family. You could not have cared for the boys. And as for your poor little maid, compare her with mine. If she were my Lina, it would not have been surprising, having been born under terrible conditions, lacking all comfort and sustenance. I would have understood her being skinny and fretful, instead of plump and happy." Scooping up her baby again, she glared at her sister. "You are lazy, Jessie, you have always been lazy, and arrogant, and rude. And though I always knew, I tried to ignore your poor manners, to make excuses, because I loved you. Well, love you I still do, for that is a thing of the heart, but like you, I most certainly do not!" So she turned, just as Moya came in, with the egg basket on her arm.

"And don't expect my husband to keep you and your brood," shouted Jessie after her, which surprised Clary, who stopped and gave her sister such a disdainful look, she stopped her tirade immediately.

Early next morning, just as she was clearing out the old strewing from the hall, the hens all about her, busily scratching for scraps, she was alerted by a shout from the river.

"Well did you think that we could wait a moment longer than dawn to see you?" said her father, swinging her around as he had done when she was little. Horrified at how thin she was, he set her down with a great kiss. Then she went joyfully into her mother's arms, both women sobbing with love.

It was a beautiful autumn day, and happiness flowed through the open doors and windows of the Byford hall. They had brought a great flat boat drawn behind them, filled with clothes and stores, for well they knew from their daughters who had taken it in turns to help Moya, that provisions were always low.

James and Lina were introduced, and were well kissed, discussion carefully kept for afterwards as to the strange child which Clary had brought home. Marking their names in his head, James muttered to himself, "Grandfather Woodman and Grandmother Woodman, Aunt Leah, Aunt Maria and James and John".

Both sets of twin boys were led off by the younger girls, and chattering happily, they followed James to the warren. Cries of delight rent the air when they found, oh clever James, that he had caught six fine conies. Clustering close behind Robin and James, they watched as they skinned and cleaned the rabbits on the river's edge, all ready to lay on the hearth embers to roast.

"Oh, my sweetest new granddaughter," said Felicia, feasting her eyes on Lina. "An angel, no less, and as grandmother says, so fair, as was my grandmother, Fleur. Oh Clary," her eyes glinted, "how happy Piers would be if he could see us now."

They left with the evening, and Clary felt so happy, having given her family the pleasure of their return, her pain at Pier's loss eased just a little.

"I have been away more than a year," she addressed her parents as they were about to leave. "It will take time for me to tell you of the misfortunes and adventures which befell me during that time. But for now, I am home, and well, and I must find a way to keep my family, for with my dower land, it should not be so very difficult."

It was several days before Clary felt her home was sufficiently orderly to leave, for she wished to go to Marsh Newton to see Joan and Father Benjamin. It had been a great work and the Byford men had helped her how they could, while Moya and James minded the children. Clary had said that she did not now need Leah to stay, now she was home again. Meanwhile, Jessie was in a great sulk, either from her sister's harsh words or the lack of attention, so she pleaded sickness and stayed abed.

After nursing Rowena, for this she did twice a day at least when Jessie was not about, Clary asked James to saddle up the pony and with Dove alongside, carrying Lina, they walked down to the ford.

Just as they were on the far bank, the river high, but the ford stones still proud and passable, they were alerted by a strange sound. They stopped and listened, looking at each other, eyes wide. Then, looking back to the hall, they saw Moya and old Lukas hurrying down the path, the little boys screaming in their arms. Telling James to wait with Lina and the pony, Clary raced recklessly back across the ford, getting her skirts very wet. On the far bank she fell on her knees and held her arms out for her twins, who, ceasing their noise, fell into them.

Apparently, having seen her leaving, they had suddenly realized that she was their mother, and it was all too much, for she was leaving again. Wiping their noses and her eyes, laughing weakly, she once again kissed her grandmother and she and Lucas crossed the ford again. Then James lifted them up and they happily rode, still hick-upping from their tears, with Lina between them, on the broad back of the pony.

The Innmans were so joyful to see her, and having heard she was back, had prepared a feast, so they sat in the great parlour and feasted on Mol's good cooking, and Clary and Joan could hardly bear to be parted. Clary admired Joan's fine little son, three months old, while everyone sought to hold Lina, the surprise and joy. The Innman boys took James to see around their stable of fine horses, and they played football with an old pig's bladder happily in the courtyards while the adults talked endlessly, catching up on the news of a whole year.

They told her that the Goldsmith family had gone away, due to much good fortune and were now in the castle on the coast, under the protection of the duke and duchess. How her friend Deborah had been devastated by her loss, for her father had died, but that a carter had taken a letter to her from Joan that morning, with news of her return.

"Now," Clary held her chin out, "we must go to Pier's grave, for I must show him our new son and daughter. And afterwards, I would like to visit Father Benjamin."

Mol changed her apron and went along with Clary, carrying the baby, with James holding the hands of his little brothers. As they walked along, they gathered the last wild flowers along the verges, so by the time they arrived at the church yard, they had a pretty posy which Clary laid on her husband's mound. They sat then, all of them around it on the short grass of autumn, and talked about Piers, and of how he had been the sweetest and best man in the world.

Then Clary rose, brushed down her skirts and told them to stay there and make daisy chains while she visited the priest.

"Good day Jessica," Father Benjamin said, seeing the figure enter the church door. "You are too late and too early for mass, but another will come along very soon if you will stay awhile."

"It isn't Jessica, Father," said Clary softly, "It is Clarissa. I am home again."

She didn't know how long she stayed there in the beautiful church, telling him all that had befallen her. Well, almost all, and in her heart she asked God's forgiveness for omitting to tell his servant that her daughter was base-born, Jasper's child, and not Piers. Then, when folk began to arrive for the next mass, and an anxious Mol followed them in with the children, she rose to leave.

"If I may come back tomorrow, Father, and if you will bless me, and baptize my little daughter, Piers and I will be ever grateful to you."

Later that evening, when his congregation had gone to their suppers and bed, Benjamin stood by Piers' grave, looking down at the sweet little posy. It was a miracle that the gentle Clary was back, but so sad that here, under the sod, lay another good soul, who God had thought to take unto himself, so leaving the woman and children alone. He sighed deeply. He could never understand the workings of the Almighty.

That evening Tobias called some friends together to advise Clary as to the best way to use her land advantageously in order to support her children. They knew of course that the Woodman and Jerome families supplied the provisions for the family and royal ships. So they recommended her to buy up the old cows, due for slaughter at Martin Mass, to try to gather a good milking herd together for cheese making in spring.

"It is not too late to plant roots for them to eat, come the harsh weather after Christ Mass," said one. "And if you ask about, there will be many a small holding glad to sell you a flat, loaded high with hay, for the winter months," said another." "If you dry the old cows off quickly," said a third, "they can manage on low commons till the spring flush and calving, only then you may have to seek out milk-maids, and then only will you have to work very hard with cheese making. By then your little one will be on her legs no doubt, and into everything," tickling Lina under the chin, wishing that his plain daughters were half so pretty, "you will be busy."

Clary felt uplifted by the kindly support and advice from Tobias and the town's elders. When she asked about apple, pear, and plum trees, promises came immediately, and she took Master Green's money from her purse and gave it to them in advance. This reminded her of the few walnuts she still had from the outlaw's place, and she knew that Father Byford would plant them for her, for he had a good way with all seeds, so, perhaps they might also one day have fine walnut trees too.

Next day the whole family went to the church in their best clothes, and Father Benjamin blessed Clary, late it was true, but he understood the reason while others did not. Next, taking up the beautiful little girl child, he baptized her Ursuline Molly, and Mol stood proudly as Godmother, while the boy James, and he, Father Benjamin himself, stood Godfathers.

Troubled, Clary went home, and that night, with a frown between her eyes, wondered how she could find the money to buy cows, let alone feed for them. For although the money in her purse seemed plenty, she knew it would not go so far. Knowing that her parents had three more daughters to supply dowries for, she would not approach them. When everyone was abed, taking out Master Green's hat, she went through it, piling the gold and silver into little heaps, quite unaware that Moya was watching her.

"What is troubling you so, my dearling," asked Moya.

Sweeping the coins back into the hat and snuffing the guttering candle, Clary climbed into bed, grateful for her grandmother's warm body.

"It was the suggestion that I buy up old cows at Martin Mass, and feed for the winter, so that next year I can start cheese making to supply the uncle's ships, so to keep us. I will also buy sheep and mix the milk don't you think? That will make a richer cream and better cheese."

Next day, when James had taken the boys out to help grandfather cut the thistles to burn, and Luke was away with the cattle, Moya drew her favourite grandchild into their room and leant a stool up against the door.

"Now my dearling," she heaved at the lid of her great chest. "The time has come for you to see what Mistress Miller kept in her chest, all of which now belongs to me, she having given it to me at her death." When she had taken out many cloths and clothes, she lifted a board at the bottom. "See here, Clary my own," and there, in the space under the board, wrapped in fleeces, were beautiful, gold plate, many pieces, small bowls, goblets, some cups, and a great oval dish, chased and worked with wondrous scenes. "I do not know where the millers found these, but surely they are not only very old, they are very precious." She pointed at the scene on the platter. "See, see, Clary, so fine, so beautiful, a shame to be locked away for so long so that no one could enjoy them."

"Oh, grandmother!" said Clary, breathless, wide eyed, "have you kept these secret for all these years?"

"I was waiting for the right time to show you, for when I am gone my dearling, they are for you and yours. Now is the time, don't you think, to send for good Deborah, who would never cheat you, and show her the smallest piece, and ask her to sell it for you?"

Deborah came with surprising speed, for with the joyful news that her friend was safe and home, she left everything and begged a boat from the castle, not even knowing about the golden cup. Then, when they had finished with their rejoicing and lay, exhausted on the bed that night, Clary showed her the cup, and begged her never to ask her from where it came, asked her to sell it for her and told her what she needed the money for.

Now Deborah was again amazed, and with the light of a tallow candle, she turned the cup, this way and that, marvelling at the workmanship, weighing it in her hand. It was not only of exquisite workmanship, it weighed heavy and surely was pure gold.

"This is way beyond our means, Clary dear," she said, wrapping it up in an old stocking of Piers before putting it in her travelling bag. "It would be a crime to melt it down, for I am almost sure it is pure gold, for it must be very ancient. But the workmanship, oh, Clary, that I could do half as well." She spoke again, as if to herself, "I will offer it to his grace, for he loves beautiful things, and will surely pay well for it. There will not be the need to tell him from where I got it, such is our business."

The days drew in and Clary, James and the children dug holes for the young trees which arrived, their roots well tied in great balls with earth and rough sacking. They made good progress planning out the new orchards with old Lucas telling them where and how. He was pleased, for it showed him that his daughter-in-law intended remaining at the hall, and not returning to her parents taking his grandsons.

As autumn drew in, Clary went out with the children to gather rose hips, for there were plenty and so beautiful. The problem were the thorns, but salve was always to hand.

"You will see my dearlings," said Clary, pounding them in the mortar while they were still soft, "when it is cold and dark we shall have lovely rose coloured drink, laced with a little of grandfather's fine honey, and be sure, not only will it give us good cheer, but it will keep away the sniffles. Unfortunately, the elder berries are over, for they are a good remedy for coughs. Next year, dearlings, yes?" With smiles they nodded in happy agreement. Doing things with mother Clary was always pleasant.

In midwinter, Jessie gave birth to another daughter and wept, but they made much of her, her parents, braving the precarious icy river, stayed some nights to give her cheer.

All the while, Clary did as Tobias and his friends had suggested, and hearing of her needs, folk walked their dry, old cows along to the hall, where Clary paid them, a mite more than what they would have received from the butchers to salt down. Luke, silent but kindly, begged help from the winter wood men, to build more byres, for with so many cattle, space was getting short to house them all.

It had frightened her that there, in their bed chamber stood the old chest, and there, in its depths lay a king's ransom. Even so, Clary felt new hope for her future, but was always careful with money, for come the spring, she would be hiring milk maids. Over the long winter, she and Moya span linen and twisted hemp and worked every spare hour at the loom, for they would need fine cheese cloths and strong hempen cords to wrap the cheeses for survival at sea. Passing the word to the Jeromes that she would need small vats, she also made an order for salt through them. They had all been so pleased with her return, and when she told them of the riverside carter who she had met on her journey, how he had praised their cheese, their merry, open faces creased with delight.

On a rare fine, midwinter's day, she took the children out for a while to escape the boredom of the hall. They stood by the river, their fishing lines slack by the ford, when a tiny, basket shaped boat came downstream, carrying two men. James, forgetting the cold, waded out to help them to shore, for such a frail craft could not cope with the rocks at the ford. They were masons, and all they had at the bottom of their frail craft, were their hammers and chisels. Father and son, they slept that night by the hearth in the hall, and by morning, Moya and Clary had decided to engage them to quarry out the rock bluff, just above the house, to cut stone for a garden wall while making a cool, cheese store. So the masons stayed all winter, and James, ever willing, learned their skill, helping them with his strength and intelligence. So another precious piece was sent to Deborah in order to pay them.

Miraculously, even with the extra mouths, they were never short of provisions. The strange, ugly boy James, with his endless energy, had proved his worth in so many ways. He had quickly become the right hand of both Byford men, besides always helping the women in the hall or playing his pipe to entertain the children. He caught eels in his woven basket traps, snared conies, and helped with the sheep and cattle. It seemed that he had so many gifts and crafts in his hands, added to his constant, good humour, they forgot his looks, and grew to love him.

Every time she went to Marsh Newton, Clary took wild flowers, or a posy of hips and haws for Pier's grave, depending on the seasons and what was available. Leading her children, she sat them in the side of the church to hear the mass. At night, she prayed to God to help her raise her family well. Then, staring up in the darkness, her mind reached for Pier's, and she told him of her day's doings, and of how they fared. Careful not to disturb her grandmother, she lay quite still, missing him with her mind and her body. Hot tears slid down the side of her face and into her ears but she never made a sound.

Life at the farm became calm and ordered and ignorant of the secret new wealth in their hall, the Byford men thought that their comfortable bellies were because Clary had returned, with her adopted son and their fine ability to keep the store cupboard full.

Now they waited for spring and the new grass, and hoped that all the old cows and sheep who had escaped slaughter, would give them heifer calves, good lambs and plenty of milk.

CHAPTER THIRTY THREE

DEBORAH

They sat close to him, each holding a hand. It was very peaceful. Deborah lifted the hand she was holding and kissed it, and was rewarded with a small smile. Louisa sat on the other side of the bed, and used her free hand to quietly wipe her eyes and blow her nose. So he was leaving them, this dear man, who she had lived so happily with for so many years. She glanced up at their child, and her heart filled with gratitude. At least she would not be alone in this foreign land. But, and her brow puckered, it surely was no longer that, for they had lived here so comfortably, so safely, for so long, it was surely home.

"Joseph," she said softly, and leant forward to kiss him, "my sweet Joseph." He smiled again, a reward. For Louisa said his name as no one else did. The J was so soft, a "Sh", the rest a gentle whisper. He pressed her hand.

Life after all, had been kind to him. His mind wandered, back, back, to the mountains, the sea, the heat and dust, the smell of garlic and jasmine.

The Duchess had crept in, a precious spray of jasmine in her hand which she had picked from the sheltered south wall of her little garden. Louisa bowed her head, made a quiet request and the maid brought a tall wine glass in which the Duchess put the spray.

The priest had been, her grace had sent her own Spanish priest and Joseph had felt comforted by his accented Latin, so familiar, so distant. He had no worries now, for his daughter was such a talented goldsmith, her hands would never lay idle. He thought about his son-in-law, and his grandsons. They too would do well in life. He smiled gently with the thought of the boys, Joseph and David, how proud his mother would be of them, his father and grandfather too, that shadowy old man whom he scarcely knew.

To have one physician in the family was a great gift, but two? Although still young, that was their chosen path. And they were clever, Deborah's sons, thinking, seeking young men, not following the numerous mountebanks and charlatans who puffed themselves up with their ridiculous knowledge. He opened his eyes and saw his Donna there standing behind his daughter.

"Donna," he mouthed, and smiled. With a rustle of skirts, she knelt by his bed and bowed her now grey head, the beautiful net veil brushing his hand.

"Dear Joseph," they always spoke in Spanish together, "I am glad that you are still here, sweet friend, for I have just come from the chapel where I was thanking the Virgin for you, and for our years of friendship." Again, there was a slight pressure of her hand and the faintest smile. She rose, nodded to Joseph's women and left silently. A tear started in her eye which she brushed away impatiently as she walked with her ladies back to her rooms. There was no need to weep for Joseph, for there was a saintly man whom God would welcome in his heaven. But she would miss him, his beautiful manners, his humour, and she must help his family, as his had helped hers, so many years before.

"Debbie, mine," Joseph whispered, "Tell your sons that I am very proud of them, tell them that my grandfather was a famous physician." He paused, remembering while Deborah lent forward, afraid to lose any precious word. "Tell them to be especially kind to Jews, for my grandfather was one, do not forget my Debbie?" So he smiled and held their hands and hours later, faded quietly away.

"Perhaps I should take mother away for a little while," Deborah said to their graces after the funeral was over. "She will miss him so, even though he was ill and useless, just being here without him will make her sad."

"Will you go to France then Deborah?" the Duke asked, "no doubt there is a ship in the harbour who will take you, when we have some fair weather." But Deborah shook her head.

"No, Sire," she spoke quietly and surely, "my mother does not yearn for her old country, your castle and England are her home now." She paused, suddenly knowing exactly where they would go. "We will visit our old friends at Byford Hall near Marsh Newton. Grandmother Moya still lives, is very old, as is my mother. We have all been friends since I was born. I always called her grandmother, not having one myself. It is a large farming family, our children are very close, almost as kin." Having made the decision, she smiled. "However, if your grace will lend us a boat, for we must go slowly for mother's health? I want her to rest and enjoy herself, not be exhausted by our journey."

So it was all arranged, with every care and thought to make their little excursion pleasant and easy.

"I have asked my kinsman, Lord of Highclere, to let you rest at his castle which is about half the way. He is an easy man, and I know that he and his family will welcome you."

They set out on a bright morning, Deborah, Louisa and their maid, escorted by two of the castle boatmen, the one, young and strong, with his old father, who was coming for the jaunt. They were as usual drawn by a strong horse who was glad to be out of the stink of the town and looked forward to being turned out for a time in good pasture. When they arrived at the halfway jetty they were pleased to find horses waiting to transport them and a chair for Louisa, for the way up to the castle was steep. Deborah knew the town quite well, having stopped there several times on her way. But, although she had met many of the Duke's kin and friends through her work, she did not know this lord or his lady.

They were given charming rooms, warmed by fires despite the early summer weather, with great bowls of flowers and fruit to delight them. Louisa looked about pleased, impressed by the thoughtfulness of their reception. She stayed quietly in her room the first days, Deborah by her, and when the day came that they were invited to dine in the hall, they put on their best clothes and jewels, and went down.

It was not as formal as the Duke's board, and the family was small, just one son. Deborah looked carefully around. It seemed that the lord's lady mother had died, but his wife, a comely younger lady, sat at the high table and organised everything. Lord Robert was an affable man, plump and smiling, lounging easily in his great chair. His doublet was very fine, and he wore a jewelled chain and many rings, which she tried to look at without being rude. His son Richard was a little younger perhaps than her own sons, a handsome boy, favouring rather his uncle than his father. Certainly Lord Robert's brother, Sir Thomas was the better looking. Quieter, taller, with stunning blue eyes, he was so charming to them, they felt very welcome. Ever observant, Deborah noted that unlike his brother, his clothes were almost severe in cut and colour and he wore no jewellery but a simple finger ring. He seemed none the less the better dressed, indeed elegant, and if she did but know, had always been the delight of the tailors in comparison with his elder brother.

The first evening they sat long at the board in the dim candle light, the silver shining, conversation easy. The meal was good, not too fancy, which Louisa approved of, and a lute played softly somewhere in the shadows. Afterwards the board games were brought out and they played casually, with laughter. Dipping as they left, the duke's lady called that the chair be brought up and two stout fellows carried Louisa up to her bed chamber.

There was not the formality in this smaller castle, as in the Duke's, for mid-morning, the lady sent a message that she would like to show them her garden, if they wished, after they had been to mass. Once more the chair was brought and they wound up and up, through dim corridors and winding stairs, till at a doorway, the bright light of day blinded them for a moment.

"Welcome again, ladies," Karina came forward beaming. She was pleased to do something for the Duke, and his letter had explained their guests' recent bereavement, so now, she strove to make them quietly happy and comfortable.

They walked slowly around the small, flower-filled garden, breathing the dew-fresh scents of numerous plants. Then they looked over the battlements, a never ending fascination, down across the town, the jumble of red tiled and thatched roofs, some with gentle smoking chimneys, to the river, and far, far off to the horizon and to the distant sea. Two trays were brought by a pretty, fair woman called Margaret and a daughter. They sat with the guests under the honey suckle and rose arbour serving the sherbets and cakes and surprisingly called the lady, "mother" and "grandmother". Deborah, with her sharp eye, was perplexed, for these small, bonny women, bore no resemblance to either the lady, or to the two lords they had met the evening before.

Karina smiled at her, reading her thoughts perfectly and explained that Margaret had been born to her by her first husband, who had died.

"Ask your brothers and Richard if they would care to join us up here, Margaret. Make sure to also come yourself with the children, for we must enjoy our guests and the fine days, because well you know how I love being in the garden rather than in that smoky old hall."

Deborah was pleased with their days, noting that her mother had stopped weeping and now had begun to take notice of all which was about her. More, she seemed intrigued by the lady, eager, whenever possible, to speak French with her.

"Did you pack my two old buckles?" she asked her daughter in their room. Deborah opened their jewellery box and brought them out. Despite having had a goldsmith husband, Louisa had few jewels, apparently preferring these two, interesting gem studded buckles.

"As if I would leave them behind mother, your old favourites" she said, pinning them on either side of the neck of her robe, instead of her shoes and her mother wore them thereafter every day.

They were soon to leave, for after some heavy rain, the days were clear again and fit for the rest of their journey, a mere half a day. One of Margaret's daughters knocked, came in and invited them for a last afternoon in the garden. The chair stood as usual outside, waiting for Mistress Louisa. Deborah looked at the girl, not fair as the rest of the children, but with an unusually dark skin, greenish eyes, and dark, red-black hair.

"And what are you called, Margaret's daughter?" she asked. The girl dipped.

"I am Karen, Mistress Scrivener, named for my grandmother, Lady Karina." and dipped again.

Old she was, yet despite her loss of hearing, the familiar name alerted her.

"Is the lady called Karina?" Louisa asked, suddenly finding that she felt just a little faint. Deborah crossed to her mother quickly and drew out a stool for her to sit on. "Is she?" she persevered, ignoring her daughter's concern. The girl nodded with a "Yes, mistress."

"And tell me, Karen," Louisa felt a new, exciting strength course through her, "did she come from over the seas, when she was young, or was she born here?" Holding out her hand she drew the girl closer so that she could see her more clearly.

"She came from far, far away, mistress," Karen held the cold, thin, gnarled old hand firmly. "My grandfather, Thomas, my mother's father, the horse master, brought her back from the crusade with him when she was a little girl. You see," she touched her own cheek, "I have something of her mother's grandmother who was a dark lady; so she tells us."

Now Louisa got up and hurried to the door, Deborah close behind her. In the garden, fresh from the rain, Karina had just picked a bunch of flowers to give her guests. Hands out stretched in greeting, she offered the bunch to Mistress Goldsmith.

Louisa pressed forward, ignoring the flowers, she peered into Karina's face.

"Karina? Is it really you Karina?" There was no sound, just some small birds who living high in the little garden, now rustled in the creepers. Karina looked at Deborah, her eyes wide with enquiry. Perhaps the old lady was losing her wits?

"My name is Karina, Mistress Goldsmith," she replied uncertainty making her hesitate.

"And Thomas, and did you and Doume' rent the room above my father's stable across the sea?"

Now it was Karina's turn to feel her breath going. She nodded as Mistress Goldsmith held her face in her hands. "And mother and I made you dresses, so that you could travel decently to England?" Karina kept nodding. "And taught you to walk like a girl, not a stable boy, and how to curtsey? Then, when you left, you gave my Doume' your stallion, Harran, and a bag of gold?"

By now Karina was unashamedly weeping, so too was Mistress Goldsmith. Madame Doume', Louisa, took her in her arms and somehow they found themselves on the seat under the arbour, weeping and laughing.

Deborah stood with the others present, each one with wet eyes, for to witness the reunion of long-lost old friends, was as a miracle. Of course they did not go on to Byford Hall for several more days, for hadn't they so much to talk about?

Louisa seemed to grow in strength from the encounter, yet, as she tried to explain, touching her precious buckles which the child Karina had given her and her mother, something, some tiny instinct had told her, that she remembered her.

With assurances that they would stop by on the return journey, Deborah and Louisa left for Byford Hall leaving Karina and her family basking in some sort of magical glow. Once more her children and grand children pressured her to tell them of her youth, her journey, of Dummy, dear, good Dummy, and her meeting with Louisa and her parents.

A horn blew, announcing the arrival of a boat below the ford, and because they were expecting their friends the Goldsmiths, everyone dropped their tasks and ran to the landing below the house.

The young boatman drew his craft in while his old father held the tiller. It was a pretty, flower studded landing stage, with a host of even prettier maids standing at the top.

Clustering around, the Byford family stood perilously close to the edge of the wall in huge excitement, helping them up the steps, all laughter and welcome. Deborah was amazed at how the children had grown, and looking around, by the many changes. What had been a gaunt old hall farm was now gracious, with beauty everywhere in the buildings, the orchards and gardens, all, Clary assured her quietly, thanks to her help.

There was still gold plate at the bottom of the chest, but the several pieces which Deborah had sold for Clary, had caused the hall to become a very fine fortified farm. The ford was no more, a handsome stone bridge spanning the river in its stead. The South banks of the river all along the property were built up, but prettily, with saxifrage and mosses tucked into the cavities of the stone work, making a brave show.

"With so many daughters in the house," Clary explained, "we seem to have added beauty to most things. If," she smiled at the six golden heads about them, "we had had all boys, be sure it would all be pure utility."

She showed Deborah around, greeting those who worked here and there, for girls or not, they were obliged to help in all tasks, or there would be poor stores for all of them in the winter.

Deborah was impressed. The cows and sheep were milked twice a day by everyone with hands large enough except Jessie who remained in the hall over the fire. Clary's sons James, Lucius and Stephen, all tall strong lads led the cattle in, saw to the girls milking and then carried the urns into the cheese caves in the bluff for Clary to turn into excellent cheeses. Lina, the fairest head, with the bluest eyes, had developed hay fever during the early summer, to her annoyance, so spent more time in than out. It was she who toiled in the walled garden, packing up seedlings in bundles, and laying them neatly in trugs. The rest of the family planted them out in the small fields opposite the house, over the river, directed by Luke, now grown stooped and grey. It was a cheerful sight, a line of bright, chattering or singing girls, who, bare footed, skirts hoicked up, planted the seedlings in neat rows in the good, alluvial soil. There would never be a shortage of onions, cabbage and roots in the winter.

Clary seemed very stout now, but Deborah soon realized that her stoutness was due to her clothing. For not only did she wear thick skirts over her petticoats, when they undressed at night, Deborah saw that she also wore three aprons. The rough work one on top, her everyday one next, but underneath them both Clary wore a very old, soft apron, of which she had several, and these were for blowing noses. Apparently, all the children kept away from Jessie who was rough, while Clary tenderly told them to "blow hard." Then, she put some salve about their noses. Deborah laughed and Clary made a wry face.

"With so many children and constant colds, it is a solution. Yet strangely, my Lina is the most healthy of them all, despite her poor beginnings. However, she is banished indoors for some weeks every summer," Clary told her friend. "An old wise woman told me to keep her thus, for with her sneezing, her eyes might cross," she made a humorous face of horror so they laughed. "And that would never do for my lovely Lina! Thankfully grandfather has good bees, for the old woman told me too, that she must have a spoon of honey every day. Perhaps," she laughed lightly, "that is why she is so sweet herself."

The fine old spring now had stone channels flowing in several directions, with stoppers or channel changes, forking conveniently to take the water here and there. It all seemed so clever and labour saving, Deborah observed it carefully. Most women had to carry their water from well or river to their kitchens, while here, it ran in, then out and down to the river.

They sat in Clary's herb garden as evening fell, and Stephen played his pipe, and the girls sang, and Deborah thought how wonderful it was to be out of the city and in the good country air once more. They spoke till very late, the two good old friends, while Moya and Louisa talked too, for they had not seen each other for many years. All the while old Lucas, half blind and hard of hearing, was at least aware that his home was a place of laughter and happiness once more.

Felicia and Robin came with the younger children as yet unmarried, and pallets were set about the hall at night, then stacked against the walls during the day.

Louisa told them about meeting her old friend, of her buckles, and of how they had met so many years before. Then Moya told stories about her childhood at Castle Pomeroy, and made them laugh.

Just once The Goldsmiths went to Marsh Newton and stood outside their old house, now a roper's, admired all the new buildings and dined handsomely at the Toby Jug.

After being away for one month, Deborah and Louisa returned home making a short stop to see Karina. The duchess had ordered that their quarters be freshly painted, so they were not so sad to be back, having been uplifted from their weeks away, and from the company of their much loved friends.

Shortly after they left an accident befell James while he was out with the cattle. A young, horned heifer had somehow got herself caught in the roots of an old tree, where she had been scratching her head. While James had struggled to loose her, she had panicked and with a jerk, she was free. As her head came up, a horn entered his great eye, breaking it, and pulling it out of its socket.

It was the dog who brought the cattle home, and hearing their noisy arrival, Clary had looked out for James, then seeing he was not with them, had with all haste ridden the pony out in the direction he had gone, until she had found him, on his knees, holding his head, moaning quietly in agony.

"Oh my dearling," she was sobbing, "what has happened? Oh my dear James, my sweet boy," and through the mists of his agony, James heard her, and took heart.

Somehow, lying on the back of the pony she slowly brought him back to the hall, where she laid him in her room. First she bathed his wound, working around the eye which hung on his cheek like an open and over ripe fruit. Unaware that she was half sobbing while she worked, her hands trembled so, that Moya forced her to sit and calm herself. This was no ordinary wound, and she did not know what to do. Her pain killers were the normal, country cures, and she set chips of dry willow bark to boil, spooning the bitter tea into his mouth with entreaty. Taking Lee's herbal from her chest, she found the stone wrapped in its fine linen bag, so this she pressed to James' temple, in the hope it might help.

At last the next day, it was decided that Lucius and Rowena should go to the Goldsmiths, where their sons were studying under a good physician. He must come! Clary pointed to where Lee had written about severe wounds, and told him to show it to the apothecary. This and money she pressed into her son's hands, and hoped that his sixteen years were sufficient to take him there and back safely.

"Hurry, my dearling, come back quickly, with the physician. Look after the book, and each other."

So began days of waiting and worrying while she regularly bathed James' wound with calendula water, and pressed comfrey poultices around his badly bruised face.

It was easy to lie absolutely still, for any movement jarred him so. James lay, spoke quietly when necessary, and gradually the pain receded.

The castle physician himself came, sent by the duchess. With him were Deborah's two sons, come for the experience. Clary sat in her garden while Moya and Lina stayed close at hand to fetch and carry anything which was needed. The gentle, dark and handsome Scrivener boys, assisted their master with the removal of James' eye. When it was done, Clary sat beside her adopted son, holding his hand, weeping.

"Come mistress," the physician smiled kindly at her, "there is no need for tears now. The work is done, and thanks to your care it was a clean wound and easy enough for me to remove the eye." He asked if he may borrow the herbal, written by their fore-father, for he said, "I would be very grateful to have it copied as it is most excellent, and there is much that with my years of being a physician, I do not know."

Greatly relieved, the family set to entertaining their guests, for it was too dark to make the homeward journey. Having known each other since they were small, the young people talked quietly, learning of each other's lives, and enjoying the company. The boatmen sat with them, enjoying the change and being treated as equals and not being sent to the kitchens which was the way generally, while the horse revelled in his freedom.

The older man, the father of the younger boatman, seemed to watch Lina closely, a worried look on his face, but he didn't speak of his interest for some time when he was home.

They packed up herbs and cheeses for Deborah and the physician, and having paid him handsomely, waved him off, every one of them tired from lack of sleep due to worry and emotion.

Early summer, the fields of grain rustled in the lightest wind, and they prepared for harvest. It would be a good year, and Clary considered that she need not as usual, buy all the grain left over from the corn exchange for her beasts. Over the past years, with her flocks and herd of cows, she had bought up all that was left from the previous year, so that the barns could be cleaned, and made ready for the new harvest.

Perhaps it was due to her anxiety over James, but she did not go to Marsh Newton for many weeks. A message came from the corn merchants, asking her to collect their surplus grain as usual. Exhausted, Clary was irritated by their assumption that she must take it. She was so tired and it was so much work. Each year without fail she had climbed the hill above the hall to the threshing floor and re-winnowed all they sent, to clear the grains of weevils and other insects. She and her children had carted the sacks up the hill and toiled for days, laying the grain out to dry, raking and tossing it, then bagging it up again, always watching the weather. Every year she had spun and woven hemp, to make new bags, to replace those worn or holed by rats. Not that there were many vermin, for Eagle, James' cat, despite being very old, was a fine hunter and his offspring were prolific. When it was all done, they stored it on one side of the grain store, in the hope that it was clean again and would not pollute the new crop. How could she manage just with the twins without James' great energy? So she thanked the messenger for coming, but told him that as they expected a very good harvest, she did not need their grain this year.

To their surprise, the elders arrived the next day, their faces cold, their voices angry. Having given her the surplus every year at a very good price, now she was refusing to take it, and what were the poor small farmers to do? The whole family including Jessie, listened to their indignant tirade. They were shocked, for no contract had ever been made, indeed they had been only too glad to get rid of their dirty old grain which was usually fit only for animals. Could they not change their minds? Must they take the old stock just because they had in the past? The men raged on and on, giving each other courage to continue, buoyed up by old Lucas's fine cider.

Utterly weary, obviously thoroughly reluctant, Clary finally agreed to take it, paid them then and there, on condition that this time, they would be responsible for carting it to the hall. For, she told them, she was too weary to even think about it and her eldest son was not yet well from a grievous accident, so they were short handed.

"I'll be able to help, mother." James said, still pale and weak but sitting up now, a great swathe of linen around his head.

"You will not!" exclaimed Clary crossly. Not cross with him, but with the very thought of the labour which stretched before her, "Though how we shall manage without you, I do not know." For immediately after cleansing the old grain, the harvest would be upon them, and she already felt exhausted.

The heat was dreadful, tiny thunder bugs filled the air, their hair and their clothing. With her twins, Lina and Jessie's four elder daughters, Clary began the arduous task of re-winnowing the grain. There usually was a wind up there at the round, stone-lined threshing floor, on the hill above the hall. Now it was still and sultry, the sun bright and hot and the sky, very blue and cloudless. They worked silently, just in their shifts, and took it in turns to run down to the hall, to plod back, carrying a great jug of small ale, to refresh them.

On the third day, when they were almost done, Clary stood up, holding her back again, pain screaming through every muscle. Homely sounds drifted up from the hall below. Luke she knew, was sharpening the scythes for the harvest, which they would begin perhaps during the next week. A hen joyfully announced her egg, and a sick calf, left alone while its mother was out, lowed mournfully. A small boat paddled way below, down stream, and she guessed it was an eel trapper or fisherman, taking his wares to the town.

Then, she inevitably looked up, west at the far horizon, and there was, clear as clear, a tiny anvil shaped cloud. Clary frowned, suddenly remembering her beloved uncles James and John, who, so many years before had, lying on the lawn at the marsh tower, taught them, about clouds.

Again and again she watched it, growing ever larger, a tiny panic rising in her, a Thor cloud, forecasting heavy rain.

"Come on my dearlings," she appealed to the children around her. "Quickly, let us finish this last bag and be done with it, for we have had enough with this work, and I fear that rain is coming."

As one, they stopped their tasks and looked toward the horizon too. New energy filled them for they too had learned to read the sky. They soon had carted all the sacks down to the empty, clean and newly lime-washed grain store. Then, still in their shifts, they ran down to the river, Clary with them, and bathed in the cool, refreshing water so that the chaff and insects floated off.

"Luke, father," Clary's anxiety seemed catching. "I think we must start cutting the fields tomorrow, for I see rain coming, heavy rain."

They all went out, but being low, their horizon was not so far seeing.

"Are you sure?" asked Luke, observing his weary daughters, worrying that perhaps a day or two would rest them before the cutting and sheaving began.

"Yes, are you quite sure?" echoed Jessie, to be reassured by a clamour of young voices.

"Then we must begin tomorrow," said Luke, resigned.

Clary looked at her brother-in-law from under her head cloth. She liked him well enough, although she thought him a great fool, too weak to cope with Jessie, always cowed and servile towards her. Vaguely, she realized that Luke had lusted for her in the past, but that now he was too weary with his wife and daughters to lust after anything. Clary loved her five nieces, particularly Rowena, the first, who she had breast fed beside Lina, when they were babes. All five were so pretty, fair, with fine, grey eyes and sweet natures. Yet each time Jessie gave birth to another daughter, she wailed with rage, blaming Luke, who just stood there sadly, unable to defend himself. On the other hand, it was he who had backed Clary the several times when Jessie had produced a suitor for her; each one more nasty than the other.

"Leave her be, Jessie," he would say. "Let her choose what to do with her own life, and not be given to some man who likely will not treat her well." So they had left, ghastly, fat, ravenous eyed men, and Jessie had been righteously indignant that her efforts had been thwarted. Even so, Clary had a reluctant gratitude towards Luke. Each time they had presented themselves, she had felt unclean, their eyes raking her body, their flabby mouths wet with anticipation. They hung about, trying to tempt her with extravagant promises, with their hands in their breeks playing with themselves, while she tried to escape, leaving grandmother to fob them off with excuses. There were, she always contemplated when they had gone, all too few men who matched Piers, indeed all the Byford men, including her twins, in manners, looks and physique.

"We won't have time to stook them, Luke", panted Clary as she tied a sheath up expertly. "They won't dry before the rain comes. If we clear the hall and set up hurdles on logs, they can dry off in there. For I smell rain, we will barely have the time to finish cutting. Let us do the wheat first, then the rye and barley."

This harvest, there was no singing, and their bread and cheese was eaten as they worked as if a demon pursued them. Constantly, they looked to the West where great black clouds gathered, then bent their backs to scythe or gather the straw into stooks.

Before dawn they were up and out in the fields, Luke and the twins cutting, Clary and the girls following behind. Gathering up the corn, they tied it with strong twists of straw which Jessie and grandmother made, sitting under a tree on the edge of the field. Jessie's youngest, a little dear of three, ran hither and thither delivering the ties, feeling that she too was helping.

In the hall, James carefully worked, happy to be of use again, yet moving his head with care, for it still pained him. He had swept out all the strewing herbs and laid every hurdle he could find up on logs so there was space and air underneath. Soon Lucius and Stephen brought in the sheaves, piled high on the sledge. Wet from sweat, red faced from exertion, and pulling on their every reserve, they smiled briefly in thanks to their older brother.

They worked till very late, the younger girls being sent in, quite obviously too tired to go on. Next morning, they were out early, despite the sky being dark and sullen, and toiled till, with just half a field of barley left, the rain came down.

"Just let's load what we have cut," shouted Lucius through the roar of the storm, "never mind about making sheaves, pile it on the sledge and girls, get on top to hold it down." So the pony willingly ran, the boys pushing the stacked sledge, and gathering up arms full, they scurried in and out of the hall, till it was unloaded.

Shivering and wet, they grouped in front of the east hearth where the cooking was done. Tutting and fussing Jessie dried and changed her daughters and Lina, while the twins put the pony away and closed all the doors and shutters and the barns. Clary and James tidied the stacked hurdles, pleased with what they had been able to save. Exhausted, they went to their beds early, listening to the storm raging above their heads, the rain beating down on the old thatch.

It rained, and rained and rained. Whenever the sky lightened for a little while, they all rushed out, their waxed bonnets tied firmly on, shawls over their shoulders, to do what chores they could. The hay, high in the barn, ready for winter fodder, went down, and Clary worried, for it was still summer, yet was glad that she had been bullied into buying last year's grain.

They kept both the east and the west hearths burning, night and day, and James quietly saw to the systematic turning of the sheaves on the hurdles. They had cleared a corner at the south end of the hall, and every day, as the straw dried, they re-arranged it so to dry better. All the creatures were as miserable as were the humans, and were kept in their stalls except the hens who found their way in and had a feast. But at least, they consoled themselves, they would have plenty of eggs, if little else.

Having not yet stored up their winter supply of wood, a late summer, after the harvest job, they were low on wood for the hearths. This was incidentally solved by a huge build up of flotsam on the upper side of the bridge. So again, when there was the smallest break in the clouds, the boys went out and salvaged what wood there was, while clearing the jam which threatened to take away the bridge. Not only was there wood, which they stacked in the huge fire places to dry, making it even more cramped, many drowned creatures were entangled in the jam, once even to their surprise, a dead peacock. Not able to eat it, for goodness knew how long it had been in the water, none the less the girls plucked the poor creature, laying its sodden feathers to dry by the hearth on a cloth. Then, glad of something different to do at that dreary time, they happily admired the iridescent beauty of the colours.

Weeks and weeks later, at last the sky lightened and a weak sun filtered through the fitful, shifting clouds. The hall, slowly becoming less cramped as the sheaves were cleared, was opened and aired and the bedraggled hens came out of the barn once more to hunt for spilt grain and what morsels they could.

They looked out onto a desolate world. The fields were water logged, the ditches running still, even after the rain had stopped. Still high and raging, the river had burst its banks and swamped their fields of roots. They all gazed on the ruination of the farm with horror, oh all that work. Unless the weather improved greatly, this would be a desperate winter.

Luke and the boys braved the road to town, often having to pass a long way around, leaving it, in order not to get too wet and muddy. At the Toby Jug, they met with a worried Tobias and Mol, for the whole crop had been destroyed, and everyone in the area was in despair, anxious about the coming winter.

"We managed to get in the bulk of our grain, Toby," said Luke. "Thanks to Clary seeing the anvil cloud from the threshing floor up the hill, we went at it quickly, truly, like mad things, storing our sheaves in the hall instead of leaving them in the field to dry which they never would have."

Tobias was impressed, and hoping, as they were family, that they would be able to supply him. Without grain, how could he keep his ale house going.

"Our root fields are gone," said Lucius gloomily.

"And the saints know how we shall feed the stock, let alone the family, this winter."

It was the same everywhere. The fields lay flat and sodden, the grain rotting, black and foul in the ear. Those who salvaged what they could became ill, for it seemed there was a curse on the land, the rain had ruined a whole summer's harvest.

Where it started, they would never know. Yet it spread swiftly, as a poison, word that Widow Byford was a witch, she who had bought the last year's grain against her will. It was she, they whispered, who had in spite, caused the floods. Yet they were the only people to have brought in their grain harvest. Once again, the town elders came back to Byford Hall, and this time, drinking butter milk, their voices rose high again. Clary sat, eyes downcast, listening to them, astonished at first, then, deeply afraid.

"Did you put a spell on us Mistress?" one shouted. "Because you did not wish to buy the left over grain?" ended another. "Did you think that you could destroy our harvest, saving yours, just because we felt that you owed it to the town's exchange?"

On and on they went, demanding back their grain, which Clary, with Luke supporting her, claimed they had all but used up to feed the beasts already due to the deluge.

So they marched to the Byford grain store, set up on its staddle stones, dry, vermin free, and full. Looking at each other knowingly, they quickly counted the sacks there. No one else had brought in so much grain. Sourly, they noted in one corner, the bagged up few old harvest's grain, and then, without a word, mounted their horses and rode away.

The family gazed at each other in disbelief. What was going on? Why did those usually wise men come here with their accusations, then leave, without a word.

Early next morning, Michael Innman, Joan's husband came, fear in his eyes.

He went straight to Clary. "Aunt Clary," his breathing fast, as if he, not the horse had made a swift journey. "Father says that you must leave here. Go at once to your parents, or to the Jerome's in the forest, there to hide until this madness has all blown over."

Clary looked at him, her face pale but composed.

"This is my home, Michael. I do not know of why I must run to hide, for I have done nothing wrong in any way." The whole family stood about, eyes wide.

"Oh we all know that," Michael went on, "of course you have done nothing wrong. Weather is weather, and haven't we all suffered from it, and we know that this winter will be a bad one for man and beast. But," he wiped his brow, "father is much concerned. You must leave, or they will come and take you to the court as a witch. Foolish folk have to blame someone."

She really wanted to laugh, for it was indeed so very foolish. Yet all the same, she had heard of the dreadful things which they did to poor, old wise women, just to slake their fear and envy.

"Bless you, Michael, go home and tell your father, that as I am totally innocent of anything other than trying to safe guard my family, they need have no fear. Luckily, my seafaring uncles taught us to read the skies, which has stood us all in good stead for many years."

More days passed, and slowly the earth dried out. Their investigation of the root fields was depressing, yet here and there, some brave plants remained.

"We must re-plant what few seeds I have left, and hope that we can save those growing, for next year." said Luke, and led his daughters out to sow them.

Clary stitched the small pieces of silk which her mother had given her, then carefully fitted them over James' empty eye socket. Somehow he looked much better with the great eye gone, quite normal and ordinary. One now focused on the remaining eye, which always smiled, bright with intelligence.

"Mother," he sat still while she fitted the eye patch, "I am afraid for you. Those people will take you away, and we all know that you are no witch, even if you are a healer and a wise woman."

"Do not fear for me, my dearling. Before God, I have done nothing wrong. How can they accuse me of tampering with the weather? That is God's work. And anyway, look how we have suffered from the rain too."

They came of course, three great men from the town, one who Clary knew, a crowd of townsfolk behind them, yammering for her blood. Deathly pale, Clary asked if she might change into a warmer gown and fetch her shawl and a clean apron.

When they tried to tie her hands behind her back her three sons leapt to her defence, eyes blazing, fists at the ready. It was Clary who calmed them.

Dearlings," she soothed, "you know as well as I do, that I have done no wrong. Now these good men have come to do the work they are designated, but indeed," she turned to them, "it is not necessary to tie my hands, for I am just a weak woman, how could I escape you?"

Going to every member of the family, she kissed them, entreating them to watch out for each other.

"Fear not my dears, this is all a sad mistake, of simple people trying to blame me for something which is in God's hands. For well we know that my sea faring uncles taught me to read the sky for the weather, but only God has control of it."

As she left the house, head held high, the crowd surged across the bridge throwing great clods of earth and abuse at her. The clods only hit one of the henchmen which angered him so he roared at them. They went down stream and boarded a boat and sailed away.

"Grandfather, grandmother, uncle," James was white with anger and tight lipped. "I will follow on with the pony. I must see where they take her and make sure they treat her decently. Lucius, go to the marsh tower and tell our grandparents, Stephen, go to town and tell the Innmans and Father Benjamin what has happened, if indeed they don't know already." Turning to Lina he held her close. "Stay at home and pray my dearling," and kissed the top of her head. "I'll send word be sure," he patted Jessie's hand, Jessie who was again large with child, weeping and distraught.

Moya gave James the purse and looked out warm clothes and food for him. How great was her relief that this adopted son would know just the right thing to do.

"God and the saints bless and look over you, my dearling," she reached up and kissed him. "That we are come to this James, thank you my dear boy," and wept.

It was a long time since James had been in a city, but unerringly, he found his way. First he stopped at a decent looking small inn and stabled the pony. Then he enquired of the jail, or keep, where prisoners were kept. With his hair lightly covering his eye patch, no one noticed him as he made his way, passing a coin here and there, till finally he found himself in the under ground prison.

It was the stench which he remembered most. Urine and dung, vomit and despair. With a small jar of wine and some oat cakes in his doublet, he approached the door. A small barred window was set in it, rather high up. Fetid, stinking air came out, and he could hear moans from the suffering. Once there, he simply did not know what to do and just stood while he thought. He handed the guard another coin and told him to move off and rest awhile, which the man did smiling. For with the great key on his belt, no one could escape from there.

James stood eyes closed remembering the horror of it. Now here, his optimism failed, and he simply could not think what to do. The guard would not open the door, for any amount of gold, and Clary was inside with perhaps fifty souls; who knew how many? Then he had a thought, and putting his mouth close to the little window, he coughed as an owl. There was no reply, but a silence, so he coughed again, low and sure, just as Han had taught him. Then it came, surprisingly close, just on the other side of the door, a soft reply.

Of course the Rom were always in trouble, either for stealing, which they certainly did as their God given right, or from some false testament.

"Do you hear me, friend?"

"I hear you."

"I am Odi, child of Annie with the blue eyes and wretched face, do you remember me?" There was a pause.

"I believe so, Odi. Did you not have a wild cat and a goat and did you not make good baskets?"

The breath he had been holding came out of his body in sheer relief. He reached his hand up to the bars and pressed an oatcake through it.

"Is there a new woman in there, friend, a neat woman, who they accuse of witch craft. She would have come last evening."

"Do you have another oat cake lad, for I am hungry?"

"I have," James stretched up again, "and if you help me and my adopted mother, you shall never be hungry in your life again, I swear."

Suddenly a dirty face appeared at the window, somehow she had found a niche for her toes and managed to climb up.

"Yes I remember you," she said, her voice quiet, husky. "I was but a young thing when you came to our camp one time, with my uncle Han."

Alerted, James asked where Han was. There was a ghost of a laugh. "How should I know, he is free as the wind, not as I, in this terrible place."

A paroxysm of coughing broke from her and she dropped down again. After some moments she was up again, gasping for breath. "Tell me what I can do for you, if I can I will."

James passed the little wine jar and the rest of the cakes up.

"Give her half, and be sure to let her drink first, for I fear that you have the lung rot and you will give it to her. But, I shall be back with more as soon as I can, I promise. Just tell her that James is here, for James was my God given name. It will give her heart."

Handing another coin to the guard, James left, glad to be in the stench of the streets, rather than the stink of the prison. Now he made his way to the castle, up hill always, taking the steps in the narrow cobbled lanes, two at a time, he was soon there.

"Direct me to Mistress Scrivener please," he offered a coin to the gateman. Then he was there, in Deborah's apartments, standing before her work bench and she was on her feet coming to greet him. Now he felt, here was help.

CHAPTER THIRTY FOUR

BENJAMIN

"Clarissa?" the quiet voice alerted her but she did not reply or even move. "Clarissa? It is I, Father Benjamin, come to visit you."

Wearily, as if her arm was too heavy to lift, she moved it slowly across the bed, and he grasped her hand.

"It is all over, dear lady. You have been freed of any guilt, your accusers have been condemned as trouble makers. None of that wicked story had any truth to it, none was any of your fault. We all know that."

Clary heard him, but did not reply. Well, what was there to say? She was broken, body and soul, by an injustice too great for her to understand. So she pressed his hand in thanks, and closed her eyes again.

What kind of world was it, that stupid, greedy men could torment an innocent woman so? How could they, knowing that her husband was dead, knowing how she laboured to keep her children? The pain cut through her again and again as she asked herself these questions, for there was never an answer. Men were just bad. Widows were helpless before them. That is how life was.

Then her thoughts changed and James came to mind. He had saved her once before from storm and swine, and this time it had been much the same.

As a hand had felt her in the stinking darkness, she withdrew into the tightest ball, for they had all done that, to see who and what, and if there was anything worth stealing on her person. Then a voice hissed in her ear,

"Here, lass, here is an oat cake and wine, sent by James." Clary started, then asked her shadowy companion in a whisper, to say it again. James! Oh dear James! So he had come, and for sure he would get her out of this place soon. The hand pushed a small jar and an oat cake into her hands. "Drink lass, eat. I'm called Ivy, and when you are done, I shall be glad to drink the rest, for I am drying up."

Another figure loomed over them and tried to grab at Clary's hands but with surprising speed, Ivy had her foot out and the thief was thrown to the floor, howling.

"James will come back soon," Ivy continued as Clary munched the oat cake, wondering which of the girls had made it, for it was very good. Then she drank deeply of the jar, and handed it to her protector.

"I knew him when we were young, but his name was Odi then, not James," she said.

Despite the wretchedness of her situation, Clary was intrigued. The voice at her side was husky and her words were hardly clear. It was impossible to see anything other than the faint shadow of a face, it was so dark in their prison. Yet as she had known James, Clary felt a great bond with the creature who sat close to her, and thereafter for the following few terrible days, protected her fiercely.

Lying in the dimness of her new bed chamber, between clean bed sheets fragrant with lavender, she shivered suddenly, remembering the terrors of prison, and held the long, cool hands of her priest.

Benjamin held her hand firmly. "Try not to think about it, Clarissa dear. It is past now, put it behind you. Justice will be done, I shall see to that, be quite sure."

He was right, of course. It was pointless re-living the nightmare. Yet even so, there had been some good from it. For Ivy had told her what she knew of James' childhood, and when she was taken out, Ivy was let free too, pardoned by the Duke, for what ever minor misdemeanour she had committed.

Although she knew that she was clean, the memory of itching caused her to want to scratch. They had bathed her, in hot scented water, washing her hair, scrubbing her body till she was pink. And all the while, that precious friend Deborah had murmured endearments, as if to a small child. Vaguely, she remembered them asking if she minded if they cut off her hair.

"You are lice-ridden, Clary my child," said Louisa, looking in despair at the minute, pearl like eggs, stuck to the golden strands of her clean hair. "They do not come off, they cling to the hair tightly and the only way to rid you of them is to cut it all off. But you can wear a pretty head cloth, dearling, and with your lovely face, no one will notice. Besides, it will make you feel light and clean again, I promise you."

After she had merely nodded, they hastily cut at her head with scissors, finally taking a great blade to shave it bare. It would be years later, when she could talk about it, that she asked them if they knew then, when her hair had turned snowy white. Deborah had first only been horrified by her condition, but as she washed Clary, she had realized as the hair grew in that the beautiful corn-yellow hair she had envied all her life, was now bleached white from shock. Barely able to hide her tears, she had shown her mother, miming, so not to distress her friend any further. It had been Louisa who had suggested they cut it all off, and in very short time, every flea ridden lock went to burn, straight, hissing onto the fire.

The great door of the prison had opened and her name had been called. Pulling her to her feet Ivy had whispered urgently in her ear, the clamour of the other prisoners drowning her words. After the darkness, the light in the dim hallway was bright, and Clary blinked, automatically trying to tidy herself. Smoothing back her hair, she found that her head-cloth had gone. It was Deborah and James who stood there before her, their faces stiff with shock at her appearance. After they had covered her with a cloak and hood and given her food and drink, they told her that hers being a church matter, they were trying to reach the bishop. As the Duke was away, they could not ask him for help.

Now they moved her, no doubt at great expense, to a tiny cell high up in the keep. Although still miserable, Clary was at least without the stench and despair of her previous companions. Here Deborah visited her daily, brought her blankets to keep herself warm, little bunches of flowers and food, to lift her heart. The days passed, empty and cheerless and she was glad that only Deborah and her mother, being confidants of the Duke and Duchess, were permitted to visit her. The very thought of her children seeing her in such conditions made her weep.

At last she was taken to a court, there to stand accused of the sin of witch craft. A row of stern looking men sat on a high bench along one side of the room. Her accusers were lower down on another bench and she noted their fine, bright clothes and their satisfied faces when she was brought it. Then it began.

Had she asked the devil's help to spite the burgers of Marsh Newton? Had she caused it to rain for weeks on end in retaliation to their insisting that she buy their surplus grain? Was it her intention to destroy their crops and cause hunger and pestilence as revenge? On and on they went, reading out all that she was accused of. Stiff from her confinement, trying not to scratch herself, Clary stood before them, wan and expressionless.

Carefully looking about the court room, she suddenly saw Father Benjamin there and her eyes widened in surprise. Then he winked! A tiny but positive wink. Or did he? His strange, light grey eyes seemed to bore into her.

Answering each question as clearly as she could, the clerics stared at her coldly. Then, Father Benjamin stood up to give evidence. How could she have ever thought him cold? Clever yes, but never so clever as here and now, defending her so skilfully. The court listened, with the occasional nodding of heads. He made it all quite clear.

Mistress Clarissa Byford was a good and devout woman. He had been her priest ever since he had officiated at her wedding to Piers Byford. Never, at any time since, had he seen cause to criticize her, on the contrary. As far as he understood, she had been an excellent wife and mother, even through tragic circumstances. By her natural intelligence she had learned as a child, the art of sky reading from her sea-faring uncles. Well, many country folk knew it, which all present must know. If they could but lift their eyes to the heavens to see, it was there for them to understand. Thus she had known of the storm coming, so she had hastened her family to hurry with the harvest, keeping it in their hall and not leaving it stooked out in the rain. Which is why, he looked pointedly at the burgers, they had their grain in the store, from observation with the eyes the good Lord had given her. With her keen mind, and her ability to work hard, they had fared better than most, although they would also suffer hardship having a big family. Most of their roots were washed away by the flooding river, and they had used up far too much precious hay to feed the stock already. He spoke slowly and clearly, as if to children or simpletons.

She was the victim of slander and lies. It was the greedy burgers of Marsh Newton who should be standing in her place, accused of trying to destroy a good widow who only sought to bring up her children on her own. This was a hard time, when all good neighbours should be helping each other, not giving false accusations. And, he raised his hand, did the rain not fall on other villages, other towns, other farms, all who had no knowledge of Mistress Byford and they poor souls had also lost all their harvest?

Clary watched him carefully. When he had finished, his cool grey eyes met hers. He was trying to tell her something.

He ended, as quietly and firmly as he had begun and there was no sound in the court as everyone strained to hear his words. Lastly, he proposed that the burgers of Marsh Newton be fined for their irreverent act in falsely accusing an innocent, God fearing woman. A fine might teach them not to cause so much trouble and sorrow, as well as bringing worthy clerics to sit at a false witch trial, wasting their time.

Grey heads nodded agreement, and the burgers visibly shrunk in their seats.

His eyes seemed to bore into hers. What? What should she say?

The first judge rose and pronounced her innocence, adding a substantial fine to be collected from the folk of Marsh Newton so they would be more careful in future with their accusations. Then, he nodded at Clary, and asked her if she had anything more to say.

Looking once more at Father Benjamin, it came, suddenly, like a dart.

Curtsying low, she bowed her head to all the holy men and priests assembled.

"Sires, Fathers," she tried to speak clearly, loud enough for all corners of the room to hear, but not as a brazen. "Sires, I thank you for your verdict of innocence, not only for myself, but for my children. We are but a small part of our little community, but I fear there are other innocent wives and children who will suffer in my stead, if you enforce a fine upon my accusers." She gazed at a patch of sunlight on the strewn floor, deliberately not looking at the burgers of Marsh Newton. "They too have suffered gravely from the deluge, and I fear will suffer even more with hunger and pestilence in the coming winter as we shall. Therefore I beg you not to impose any fine on their men-folk, for it was they who made a grave error of judgment, not their families. May God guide you in his mercy, as you have shown mercy to me."

There was a long silence in the court room. Then, the heads turned and they spoke in whispers till finally all nodded to the leader.

"It shall be as you ask, daughter," he rose and took up his staff, beat it three times on the floor, "and may God be with you."

They waited till the court emptied before Deborah put a hooded mantle about Clary, and led her out. How long she stayed with the Goldsmiths, she did not know, for a great lassitude came over her, so that the slightest effort seemed to drag her down.

Father Benjamin came to escort her when Deborah sent word. For Clary was so fearful of everything, even to going home, they needed his help. Once in the boat however, Clary realized how she had missed the river and the fresh air. Watching the great horse walking solidly on the path, pulling them upstream, she wondered what he was thinking, if indeed he was thinking. A new awareness of life possessed her, as if, as a grown woman, she was re-born.

Now she was home, safe and loved, yet even now, fear tugged at her senses. Never in her life had she imagined such cruelty and deprivation as she had experienced in that prison. On the road, she had slept in rough inns, heard bawdy talk and seen much poverty. Yet it had been nothing in comparison to that filthy, vermin infested pit, where humans licked the walls, or the filth on the floor, for life giving moisture. Many was the time she would cry out and Moya's arms would hold her, sweet words soothing, as if to a babe. Perhaps, she thought wryly on good days, as her hair grew, her fears would shrink.

The first thing she did was order the killing or selling of all but two of the cows. The family were aghast, yet she was adamant. Through them, she insisted, they had almost had a great tragedy in their family. To have a mother burnt as a witch was a fearful millstone about the neck and so, just the best cows were kept for milk for the children, and cheese. They would take them to a bull elsewhere when the time came.

Tobias took what he could, her parents and the Jeromes too. The others they killed, salted and what they would not need, they sent down stream to the ships. Only when it was done, did Clary rest. Yet her face was severe with sorrow as she endlessly cleaned, chopped and boiled down the fat to make lard and tallow candles. She had liked her beasts, counting them as family, but the humans came first.

Mid winter was hard along the river, with the ice growing from the sides to the middle, and the icicles hanging from the bridge like a portcullis. They were careful at the hall, as were all folks due to the poor summer. Felicia sent venison and smoked eels, wild boar and capons to help them out over Christmas. The tower had become a quiet place at last, with all but Maria, the youngest Woodman daughter as yet un-wed, left at home. Leah had wed a small landowner the other side of Marsh Newton, the Woodman girls were much in demand, and even the boys, James and John were gone. For the uncles were growing old and delighting in their living reincarnations, had the boys at the coast, learning seamanship.

They came unexpectedly, by horse along the river side, Felicia, Robin and Maria, to give good cheer to Clary, and to be there for the birth of Jessie's sixth child. The larger poor Jessie grew, the more querulous she became. Fearful she would bear another daughter, she tried to hold off the birth, to prevent another disappointment.

It began early in the morning quietly, but very soon the whole house knew that Jessie was in travail. Suddenly, Clary lost her lassitude and ran hither and thither with the women, making everything ready.

"Clary?" Maria stood, head bent as was her way. "Shall I take the children out, for the sun is shining and if we wrap up warm and walk briskly, it will get us out of the house for awhile."

Clary looked fondly at her last sister. Much as Maria looked like the rest of them, her manner was so quiet, her ways so gentle, they often wondered where she came from.

"From your great grandmother, Fleur," said Moya, "she was a quiet one, my word she was." and said no more.

"You are so clever, Maria dear," Clary gave her the warmest smile. "Let us find old Master Miller's bone skates, and the little sledge. I will pack you a lunch box and some ale, so you can go as far as you like and perhaps gather any berries you see to decorate our hearth, which will give us all cheer."

"And will you give me something for the birds, Clary?"

Clary stared at her. Was the girl quite loose in the head? Perhaps she was and that was why they hadn't found her a husband yet. Here they were, a big family and winter not halfway gone with barely enough provisions for themselves, and she wanted to feed the birds! Although she did not reply, and had no intention to give her anything, a great old crust of bread caught her eye in the depths of the bread crock, so smiling to herself, she dropped it into the basket.

Off they went, eyes glowing, well wrapped up with mittens, scarves, shawls and hats, to leave the hall strangely quiet except for Jessie, who never had been quiet with her birthing.

High above on the edge of the woods, the three boys were digging a pit.

"Well at least we are keeping out of the way and warm with your caper, James," said Stephen, resting on his shovel for a moment. The earth was not too hard under the lee of the wood, not frozen solid as it was elsewhere.

"You'd better have some luck this time, old son," said Lucius, who although the eldest by mere moments, had firmly established himself as the heir. "There must be plenty of other work for us to be doing down at the barn, without digging pits for you to catch piglets in." Yet they were amiable, and here, they could not hear the screams which rent the air down at the hall.

They straightened their backs at the sound of girl's voices far below. Each one smiled as they caught sight of them, laughing, skipping, as summer's russet butterflies, unaware that they were being observed.

"That's good," said James, stabbing the earth with his pick, still a little careful of his hurt, "better they are out in the sunshine for a few hours, than about the hall with all that fuss going on."

The pit was getting a goodly size now, and Stephen jumped in to scoop up the soil to throw it out. Although James was much older than they were, the two boys loved him as a brother for he had a simple, ageless nature, as well as being the man of their farm. Grandfather only saw to his bees now, and even in that James helped him for the old man could barely see. Their uncle Luke was bowed with work and sorrow, for his had been a difficult marriage, for their aunt was never an easy woman.

"Now that the cattle have gone," James talked in between neat stabs at the earth, "we have room for more stock. I tell you I've seen the swine up here, and if I could catch a couple of sows, feed them every day so they get tame and come on their own, we shall have fine roast pork regularly."

Lopping off branches from a near by pine tree, he threw them down into the pit so that the piglings wouldn't get hurt when they fell in.

"And what about the Forest Wardens?" said Lucius, jokingly. "Who will swing if we are caught catching pigs?" James ignored him and bent his back to his task. Ever since that day when the wild swine had sent Clary and Lina his way, he'd had a yearning to have some. He'd buy a domestic boar and mate them, let them roam in the woods foraging, but make sure that they had some buttermilk to tempt them home every night.

"Right!" he said smiling, "that's it boys, now let us hope some little pigs come this way."

The sun was dropping down to the horizon and it suddenly began to get cold. The girls were skating on a flooded piece of meadow, so shallow that they were not afraid to fall in should the ice break. They had eaten their bread and cheese and were still warm, but Maria felt the cold creeping into her clogs, and knew they must go back.

"Right!" she called, "who will be first back at the hall? Who will be the first to know if we have a new baby girl," she stopped for effect, "or boy?" she ended cheerfully. With a whoop they began running back the way they came, their warm breath blowing white, in the cold air.

"Come dearling," Maria took the hand of her youngest niece, "see what aunt Clary put at the bottom of the basket? A fine crust of bread. Shall we give it to the poor, cold little birds for their supper?" They walked hand in hand towards the river, where a few birds pecked about on the frozen flats.

John the smith lay under the gnarled little tree whose roots were half exposed. He had almost been warm, sheltered there from the north, the sun giving just a little heat before it slid down to the horizon. Tonight I shall die, he said to himself, not really caring. He felt so weak! From hunger of course, and lugging his hammers which had seemed to get increasingly heavy with every mile. He was so sure that he had come the right way. Yet he had walked for hours, and the town he was making for did not appear. Pulling his cloak tight about him, he drew his head into its folds and glinted at the water. If he got up to drink, he would lose all the heat he had about him. Yet he had kept going by drinking, every few miles, determined somehow to live.

He had heard swans or geese perhaps, and thought about trying to catch one to eat, then laughed at himself. He catch anything? He was so weak he could barely walk now.

A sound above him on the bank alerted him. He'd heard that geese and swans could be vicious, yet his mouth watered at the thought of them roasted. Something fell near him, and there was a flurry of little birds fighting for it. He frowned. Again, something flew through the air and the birds squabbled noisily about it once more. Cautiously, so as not to lose his precious heat, he sat up and looked around. There on the bank above him stood two figures beautifully lit by the setting sun, a young woman and a child. They were busy, tearing at something and tossing it into the air for the birds. Then the child saw him and froze. Tugging the woman's hand, she pointed. For a moment they stared at each other. The woman hesitated, turned to go, then came down the bank to stand in front of him.

"You'll die this night if you stay out here, lad," she said. He noted she had the nicest voice. "It will be the hardest frost. Won't you come and sleep in our barn? The beasts will keep you warmer than if you sleep here." He was looking at her hand in which half a crust was held. Again she hesitated, then, she offered it to him. "It's just a stale crust, fit only for the birds, but if you want it?" and backed away.

He watched them go, turning now and then to look at him. He sucked at the crust which softened and the taste spread through his mouth like nectar. A barn, she said, full of warm hay and beasts. Finishing his crust, he struggled to get up, but his legs gave way and the warmth which he had tried so hard to keep about his body, evaporated as his cloak fell open.

As they hurried towards the hall, the older girls came to meet her, their faces despondent. Mother had just birthed another girl. Maria nodded, pushed the little one inside and ran around to find the boys.

"James, oh James," she collided with him as she hurtled around a corner. Then straightening and getting her breath she said, "Please James, there is a man, lying under the old tree by the river. He is ill, perhaps dying. James, I beg you, for the love of God, go and fetch him and put him in the barn to sleep, where he will at least be warm."

James smiled kindly at Maria, who was his adopted aunt, but was almost the same age as he. He had always liked her, a quiet, soft girl, diligent and kind. But now he hesitated.

"You know that mother is nervous about strangers coming here, Maria. You say he is ill? If he is, do you want us to catch his contagion? Maybe he is a thief, and will murder us in our beds?" His one eye twinkled at her. But she was most serious.

"He is hungry and weak, but from what I saw of him, he is young and otherwise strong." Pulling at his jerkin she implored him again, "Go, I beg you, dear James, please, please, or I shall not be able to sleep for worrying."

Fondly, as with a sister, he put his arm about her. "I will go, but first, you run to the hall, fill a flask with milk and set a hot poker in it. Then, dribble a spoon of honey in and stopper it well. There is nothing better for weakness than milk and honey, I know." With a friendly pat on her well clothed behind, he sent her off while he went to find his cloak. He was quite glad to have a reason not to go into the hall with the lamentations from Jessie, and the long faces of all the family. Besides, he well remembered being cold and hungry; he would go to see Maria's waif. With the flask next to his shirt, on a strange impulse, he drew the sledge out from the barn, and harnessed Storm to it. Pleased with the unexpected outing, Storm trotted along with vigour.

At the tree, James got off the sledge and slid down the slope to the dark shadow which sheltered under it. Night was falling fast and the frost was already deep. Squatting on his hunkers, he drew the warm flask out of his jerkin and offered it to the still figure.

"Drink this, my friend," he said, shoving it at him. "It is good, warm milk, laced with honey, and will do wonders to restore you." But the hand which reached out shook so violently, that James kept hold of the flask, and helped him drink. Just a little spilled but with his hand and the strangers too, the milk went down.

"Did the angel send you? Are you indeed God, come to take me to heaven?" James was not sure whether this was a joke, so he answered honestly.

"No, my name is James and my aunt Maria told me you were here. She asked me to fetch you to sleep in the barn." There was a long silence.

"The trouble is, man, my legs won't obey me," replied the stranger. "I'm not sure that I can get up, let alone walk to your barn." James felt his sympathy flow, for all this was too familiar.

"Come," he put an arm under the others elbow, "up with you, for Storm the pony is here with the sledge, and you shall not have to walk more than a few steps." Somehow they scrambled up the bank and James lifted the stranger on to the sledge. "Hold on now, for we shall run for home, try not to fall off," and Storm began to pull and soon was trotting along the bank, with James at his head.

He took him to the small barn to be with the sheep, because it was lower built and warmer than the big one, now half empty with the cattle gone. Lifting him gently, he helped him inside and felt his way in the darkness to a corner. A dim light alerted him and Maria approached with a horn lantern held high.

"Do you have him James?" she asked, peering in the gloom. "Oh bless you, dearling, now I can rest easy tonight." Carrying a thick cloak and a dish, she went down on her knees beside James. "Will he do, do you think?" anxious, kindly.

John Smith coughed, spat to one side and then looked directly into the woman's face. He saw anxious eyes in a sweet oval face framed by a thick woollen head cloth. Then she smiled, relieved to see that he was well, and John Smith thought, I shall marry this angel, but I trust that she is not wed already, and that the little lass with her is not her own.

"I am John, the blacksmith," he said, "and I thank you most humbly kind lady, for finding me." Maria got up with a rustle, embarrassed by his direct gaze.

"Well I am glad you are not out there freezing to death. Here," she put the hot bowl into his hands, "sup this pottage which will warm you, and cover yourself with this cloak. God give you a good night, and we shall see you in the morning."

James let her go before, making sure John Smith was eating, he felt his way out into the night and drew the door closed behind him. After seeing to Storm, he called his very old friend Eagle, who came from the shadows and after a loving greeting, jumping on the pony's warm back as was his habit, purring and went to sleep.

In the hall, they sat at the board eating the good pottage which Felicia had made. James smiled warmly at his adopted grandparents. He liked them, and grandmother's pottage was always interesting. In the gloom, he spooned up the steaming hot mess, felt a damson stone and deftly spat it to the floor while the sharp taste milled about his mouth. It was strangely quiet and no one spoke. The little girls were already in bed, no doubt tired from their exertions and Jessie must be sleeping too, for her wailing had ceased.

"Where is mother?" he asked. They looked into their bowls and did not answer.

"Perhaps she is tired too," said Felicia, "it was a wearisome day."

For some time now, since the accident to his eye, James had chosen not to sleep in the loft with the boys, but on a pallet in the hall. He was always the last to bed and the first up, and he attended to the hearth, making sure all was ready for Clary in the morning. Sometimes he sat up late and spoke to grandfather Byford, whose work he had almost entirely taken over. Ever hungry for knowledge, he liked the stern old man because of what he taught him. In return Lucas, was as delighted with his extra grandson, to be able pass things on to, now he was well nigh useless at all else.

Over the years, more building had taken place and now there were more chambers on the east side of the hall, Jessie's side. On the west side, which was Clary's, there was the walled garden.

James spoke with Lucas for awhile, telling him about the stranger in the barn, that he was a smith, and perhaps in the morning he could see him. It was good for the old man to speak with this bright young man, for Luke was always silent. His deafness made it hard to understand the children although the women made the effort to speak clearly so that he could hear them. Reaching across he touched James' head with affection, for this one always found some little news of the day's happenings to tell him and clearly, so that he understood.

Later that night, James woke to see Clary, still in her day dress, over the fire.

"What is it, mother?" he asked softly. She looked so terribly tired, yet she came over to sit on a stool by him.

"My dear, it has happened at last. A son, Jessie has a son. It was twins again but one of each." She seemed to rock with fatigue and he sat her down on his pallet, with her back to the wall, his coverlet over her. "After the girl, he slipped out, a tiny little thing, and Jessie was lamenting so loudly she didn't realize it was another one. She must have thought that it was the after birth, which was as well, for thinking him dead, I took him away." She closed her eyes. "But he lives, for the moment. He is so small, his sister having all the strength. We lined a basket with hot stones and covered them well. Luke is with him now, in the rising cupboard where it is warm. Oh!" she covered her face with her hands, "if only he lives, they will be so happy."

It was a fitful night, with furtive comings and goings. Moya, Felicia, Robin and Maria were the only ones privy to the boy's birth. Before the family rose, it was agreed, that whatever the weather, the grandparents Woodman would take all the children to Marsh Newton, on the pretext of going to mass, to see the Christmas play. They would lodge with Joan, at the inn, so to let peace and quiet enable those at the hall to concentrate their love and care on the tiny infant boy.

"You must go too, boys," Luke seemed suddenly very positive, as he told his nephews that they could surely have some days rest over the holy days.

They took it in turns, one always in the rising cupboard, the little warm nook backed onto the chimney where the bread was set to rise. Otherwise they cared for Jessie and the little girl baby, or took their turn to sleep, exhausted, for some hours.

"Ah, Jessie," Clary combed her sister's hair back and gently braided it. "As usual, you have too much milk. Come, let me take some off you to ease your pain." And Jessie, once again bitterly disappointed with her latest daughter, leaned back on the pillows, her eyes shut, and allowed Clary to ease the first, thick good milk from her swollen breasts, without a murmur.

James quietly went about his work and saw that the log pile in the hall was kept high. He and Maria went to the barn in turn to see to John Smith, who had slept and eaten and now was glad to have their company. They saw that he, like James, was a great, well built young man; well he was a blacksmith, so it should not have been unexpected. Having eaten well, his strength seemed to come back and he and James took the cattle and sheep out, and collected his tools which he had left in a sack by the little tree. The days were bright and beautiful, and the earth frozen hard in the iron hand of winter.

On the third day after his birth, Clary decided that the little boy would live, with care, and that spoonfuls of chamomile tea and Jessie's good milk from the pap pot were no longer enough for him. Knowing her sister well, she gathered the remaining family together and united, they stood around her bed, while Luke gave her the news.

"Wife," Luke's voice trembled, whether from tiredness or emotion they couldn't tell. "Wife, we have a precious gift for you for Christ's birthday." He sat on the bed and took her hand. The family stood close around, and Jessie frowned, surprised by their continued loving attention. "When our new little daughter was born, there was another babe with her, a son!" Now her eyes opened and she stared around at their smiling faces.

"He just slipped out, Jessie," Clary spoke now, "and I was only ready for the after birth. A tiny little boy, Jessie, but I thought him dead, for at first he didn't breath, and just lay, like a rag doll in my hands. You were lamenting so, you did not hear my cry as I ran with him to the warmth of the rising cupboard." Luke who had gone out, shortly returned with the smallest bundle on his arm. Tenderly, he laid his son in his wife's arms, while the others quietly went out.

Jessie looked down at her longed son, her face incredulous with rapture. A son, a son! Very carefully she undid her bodice and pressed the great red nipple into his tiny mouth. Somehow, he took it, messily at first, then suckling properly. Luke let his tears fall unashamed, as he watched them.

"His name is Piers," he said. And Jessie merely nodded.

They were surprised, all of them. They had been sure that when they told her, Jessie would rage and abuse them for their actions. Yet she did not, probably realizing their general fatigue and good intentions. Now she took over their vigil, taking her son back to the rising cupboard, only bringing him out to nurse him. For it was bitterly cold, and despite both hearths burning in the hall, they made very little impression. Fearful of running short of wood and charcoal, the brazier in Jessie's chamber was let out so she attended the babies in the hall, close by the fire surrounded by the wooden maidens and blankets.

A well recovered John Smith helped James with all the tasks, taking the beasts out for some hours each day, tossing the hay down from the lofts for them at night. He told them that there had been much hardship and sickness in the village where he came from, and that due to the hard winter after the wet summer, there was little work. He also told how his master and mistress had taken ill with their chests and died, and how, as he had done his seven years apprenticeship, he had decided to try to find a new, busier work place for himself. He and James agreed to go to bring the anvil, which he had buried in the midden, come good weather, and it was accepted that he set up his forge at the farm.

The new twins were well. Both slept in the rising cupboard now to keep warm, and Jessie seemed suddenly soft and kindly to everyone, including her new daughter.

"We must ask Father Benjamin to come to baptize them, as soon as the holy days are over," said Moya. Well wrapped in shawls, she usually sat by a hearth, and did little tasks for Clary and Maria though in cold days, she laid aside her constant knitting of stockings. She had grown so small and bent, her hands like claws, her mouth almost empty of teeth. They did not know how old she was, except that she must be very old. She and Luke were as shadows in the place, agreeable, gentle, yet always willing in their way, to help with what ever small tasks came to hand.

"We are blessed, Luke Byford," said Moya in her thin, old voice, "not many folk live to our age, or to see their great grandchildren born." How much he heard she did not know, but he always nodded.

James rode carefully across the frozen plain to Marsh Newton to tell the family the good news and to return, and to ask Father Benjamin if he would favour them with a visit.

How pleasant it was to receive a letter, beautifully written and an invitation too, not the usual cold directives and orders. Benjamin mulled over Clary's words. So, and the saints be praised, Jessica at last had a son. Deo Gratis. He packed his cup and vestments with his warmest clothes and rode his little mare to join the Byford family at the inn, for their return to the hall.

"Oh mother, mother," the girls clustered about Jessie, thrilled with their new and unexpected brother. "He is so beautiful," they said. "Look, look," and held his tiny hands and kissed them. Jessie smiled on their fair heads and felt a great new tenderness for all her children.

"It is a pity that you don't have a little chapel as we do," said Felicia. "Though small, ours has served many a purpose, marriages and baptisms." They were sitting at the board and the mood was light. Fresh bread and smoked cheese stood on huge platters and bowls, which they ate with Felicia's tasty pottage. James and John Smith had brought in eight good sized conies, and a meaty pie was being planned.

"There is a good piece of leanish bacon which will go with it nicely," Clary said, after the meal, busy with chopping the suet. "James, dearling, will you bring in onions and carrots from the cold store, and Rowena, see to rinsing and soaking a good bowl of peas for me." She poured a measure of flour into the great crock she used for making pastry. "Lina, reach up high, take a stool, and find a bag of mushrooms and set them to soak also."

Benjamin watched the busy domestic scene in quiet admiration. As with every family, he knew they had their problems, yet he saw now, a happy glow and unison as they worked together for the baptismal feast.

"Will you name our daughter for us Father," said Jessie, an unusually quiet, happy woman at last.

Benjamin thought on it, searching in his mind for something beautiful for the little maid to carry all her life.

"Carola?" he suggested, and Jessie and Luke looked at each other, then nodded, smiling. A pretty name, a Christmas name. So Benjamin felt a greater warmth spread through him, and remembered his boyhood love.

It was a joyful celebration. After the babies were baptized in a beautiful old silver bowl which had come from Lady Felicia, fed, changed and returned to their dark, warm cupboard, the family and guests ate and drank, and felt that this seemed the Christmas feast, the other having been fraught with anxiety.

"Master and Mistress Woodman," John the blacksmith stood up and addressed them. "May I ask for the hand of your daughter Maria in marriage?" Felicia and Robin pretended to be surprised, but having observed the growing fondness between the couple, nodded, smiling.

"If Maria will have you, John," Robin said jovially, "then I suppose we must." Maria blushed prettily and John took her hand.

"Father Benjamin, will you wed us right now?" John beamed, still wondering at his good fortune.

So Luke actually hurried to the cold store and brought out a great jar of brandy wine, the cups were filled and toasts were made to the young couple, the new babies, Father Benjamin and back to the couple again.

Replete, warm and happy, they settled about the hearth and Stephen and James took out their pipes and played. A space was cleared and the children danced, glowing with life and warmth, till at last, their hot stones, well wrapped under their arms, they went off to bed.

Clary sat nursing her cup, looking absently into the flames of the fire. This had been a happy time. Providing they kept away from other folk with their coughs and colds, everyone was well. A small wave of anxiety swept over her, but she brushed it aside. The little Piers seemed strong, and Jessie was being more attentive to him than she had been with all her girls together. It was in the hands of God now, and she whispered a prayer, to God, and to her long lost Piers, to help them.

Lina and Rowena stopped by her with a kiss, for they had cleared away the meal, and now, dipping to Father Benjamin and their grandparents, also went to bed.

In the flickering fire light, the hall was unusually quiet. James had discretely laid out the pallets for himself and Father Benjamin, and John Smith had bowed, thanked them all for their hospitality and happily had gone off to his new wife to the corner in the barn where James had made a makeshift temporary room for the newly weds. Here he and Maria, with her gentle smile and her kindly ways, kept each other warm and whispered of the good life the would have together.

Lucius and Stephen then rose, but Clary lifted her hand to them.

"Stay my sons, just for a little, for I have an announcement to make." Nodding across the hearth at her mother, she smiled. "My mother has said what a shame it is that we have no chapel here, and indeed it is." She paused, resuming her intent gaze at the fire. "As you know, since the dreadful events of the autumn, I have not been to Marsh Newton, or to church. I feel such pain from those town's folk who falsely accused me, at this moment, I never wish to set eyes on them again. I wonder if I shall ever return to town." She paused for a moment, remembering the hard eyes of Marsh Newton's burgers at the court. Shaking her head, as if to get rid of the memory, she continued. "Yet I grieve for the peace that the mass gives me, and now, with mother's words, think that perhaps we might have a chapel here."

Intent on her words, the gathering shifted on their seats and looked at her expectantly. Turning to Father Benjamin, she addressed him.

"Father, it must be all of twenty years since we first met. I ask you to advise and assist me with the proper authorities. Up the hill, in a hollow before the woods, there is a small old ruin. My husband Piers told me that he thought it in some way related to our spring here, for the carving on the stone is the same, and there are some words in Latin engraved on one. Perhaps we can re-use the stone, and build the smallest chapel there, for our own use. I will pay for it, in memory of my husband."

No one moved. Her words fell sweetly on their ears and each one saw in his mind's eye, a little stone church, nestled in the dip before the trees, high above the farm. As one they nodded, smiling at each other.

"What a beautiful idea, Clarissa," Benjamin said. "Surely I will assist you in every way I can. I see no reason why it should not be, and our bishop is a man of vision, I am certain we shall have his support." He pondered for a moment, then added. "Maybe, I, in my old age, which is nigh upon me, can come to be your priest, and live quietly there, as a hermit, worshipping God in his pure country air."

Clary smiled, and reaching down, took Moya's hand in hers. The storm was over. A new year was ahead of them. Jessie was happy, thanks be to God and Saint Margaret.

Curtsying to the elders in the company, low, as Lady Felicia had taught her, she then led Moya to bed.

CHAPTER THIRTY FIVE

LINA

It was very hot in the garden. Outside, where there were no walls, no doubt there was a breeze, for the river always seemed to attract coolness. She could hear them singing in the distance, and pursed her mouth.

"You make faces like that," said grandmother Moya, "one day the wind will change and it will set. And you will be ugly for the rest of your life."

Lina sneezed and wiped her nose. "I wish the wind would blow, for I am so hot, grandmother. Oh but!" She stood up straight and tipped back the brim of the huge straw hat she wore, "I am tired with being shut up, and not allowed to go with the others."

"And," persevered Moya, "if you put your hat back like that, you will get brown as a peasant."

Lina grinned. She loved her grandmother, and she had heard it all before.

"I am a peasant." she replied, which drew a sort of strangled kind of howl, from Moya. Lina laughed merrily. "Oh, granny, don't be cross, I am just teasing you," and leaned forward to kiss the incredibly old, wrinkled face.

She sneezed again. It happened every year at hay making. Joseph Scrivener had told her that it might just go, one day, and meanwhile to take a spoon of honey, every single day of the year, which she already did, an old woman having told her mother about it. This she did and much enjoyed, and perhaps the sneezing did grow less. It was mother, with her fear of old wives tales who insisted that she stay within the walls of the farm, especially when they were hay making.

"I cannot imagine how it would be to have a cross-eyed daughter," Clary said when the hay season approached. "We would never be able to find you a husband, dearling, if those beautiful eyes went dither-ways."

So here she was, digging up cabbage seedlings, bunching them into twenties, rolling their roots in little balls of earth, and tying them up, in a broad leaf, ready to plant. This she would participate in, as soon as the hay was in, a back breaking task, not nearly as much fun as hay making.

It was beautiful in the garden though. The walls were high, mellow grey stone, and on the top there were all manner of pretty little plants and mosses growing. Every time they saw something interesting growing wild, they gathered them and tucked them into a crevice. Or sometimes in or on top of the walls, which surrounded the whole farm, or along the river where the boats stopped. Her bare feet pressed the chamomile kindly, and its scent engulfed her. Apart from the seedlings, which James had sown, there were herbs for mother's potions, and flowers, lots of flowers, for joy. After the cabbages, there would be the other vegetables.

Lina considered that all this beauty was marred by the several and peculiar bird scarers which James had insisted on erecting. Funny branches festooned with rags and clappers, but he insisted in order to preserve the garden.

Moya rose to her feet unsteadily but found her cane and walked in the direction of the house.

"Can I fetch something for you, grandmother?" But Moya did not hear. Going to the seat under the bower just vacated, Lina moved the knitting to one side and stretched out. If you saw the bag of knitting and stockings laid about anywhere, granny would be close by. In winter, she said her hands were too cold to knit, but all summer, she never put it down. They had a colour code. Brown, dyed with easy walnut, for the men, creamy for the women, and pretty colours for the little ones. It was not so easy dyeing linen as was wool, and she knew that her mother found it irksome. But as granny saw to it that they all had stockings, it was a small thing to please her. Often, she asked the spinsters to add wool to their flax yarn, to make them warmer and stronger. When holes appeared at heel or toe, she undid the whole stocking and salvaged what yarn she could. They were handsome, comfortable stockings, and goodness knew who would make them if granny did not. Yet she was a crafty old lady, who seemed to drop stitches only when there were granddaughters about. Then she would plead with them, claiming her eyes were no good, to pick up the stitches and maybe do a little of her knitting, so the girls learnt, without knowing it.

Old Dove lay in a shady patch, and snored gently. She was quite grey about her muzzle now, but still very smooth to touch. Her mother said that Dove was just a little older than she was. Fourteen years is very old for a dog, but Dove was special. Not exactly a lap dog, for she was too tall, but her mother loved her, and the dog loved her mother. She was put in the garden for the time being because they had just killed a steer in the yard, and dogs weren't allowed.

The doves swirled overhead and Lina watched them, fascinated by their flight. How lovely it would be to sail like them through the air, it was a soothing sound to hear them billing and cooing in the cotte.Rested from her small idleness, Lina got up and went back to her basket. Sitting on the lawn, she counted the packed seedlings, eighty five, nearly there. The chinking of a bridle alerted her, and she looked up. Who could be close by? They were all out in the hay meadow. The gate scraped, and pushing it open, a boy came in, leading a beautiful horse.

Surprised, Lina frowned, then spoke firmly.

"And what do you think that you are doing in here? Get that thing," she flicked a hand at the horse, "out of the garden."

Richard backed the horse out, but poked his head back around the gate.

"Tell me, little mistress, where can I find a man to see to my horse?"

Still frowning, Lina looked at the intruder more carefully. Find a man, to look to his horse?

"Go around to the river gate," she said shortly, and suddenly embarrassed, bent her head to her work again. Oh, her inner voice cried. Here she was in her shift, half naked. With bare feet! Find a man indeed! Oooh! What did he think this place was anyway, a hostelry?Moya came back, carrying a jug and two cups.

"Here we are, my dear," she set them down carefully on the side of the bench. "Come sweeting, time to slake your thirst."

"Is there anyone at the river gate, grandmother?" she asked. Moya considered for a moment. Surely she had just seen James going in to refill their ale pitcher.

As evening fell, tired, they trooped in, scythes and rakes over their shoulders. When it had begun, they did not know, but every year, instead of walking over the bridge, they stood their implements against the bridge wall and waded into the water. Probably they had done just that before the bridge existed, when there was only a ford. The wondrous coolness revived them, and splashing and laughing, they rinsed the sweat and grass seeds off them, to emerge dripping wet, but cool at last. Lina usually joined them, for she too was hot, but this time she skulked in the garden, then washed down in the bed chamber. There was no sign of the boy and horse, and she felt horribly embarrassed.

"Come along, Lina," Clary came in undoing her apron, sweat beading her lip. "We have company tonight, Lord Richard Highclere from the smaller castle, you remember, Aunt Deborah mentioned him, the only son of Lord Rupert."

Meekly Lina inclined her head, and unhooked her plainest gown.

"Not that one, cuckoo," her mother seemed flustered. "Wear last year's blue linen." Lina watched her mother carefully. She had also taken down her blue gown, the dark blue, from the special dye which James and John sent. "His horse is lame, and he will stay here till they send grooms with another one. No doubt we can get the message to his people, for they will be worrying. Now!" she looked at her daughter properly as she tied a fresh cloth over her hair and noticed some reticence. "What is the matter with you, my girl? You all complain because you never have interesting company, and here we have, and you stand there like a wilting flower. Quickly, child, for I need your help." She hurried out and Clary finished her washing and put on her blue dress, combing her hair without haste.

Rowena, her favourite cousin came rushing in. "Lina, Lina, the nicest, most handsome young man is here and will sit at our board tonight, and perhaps stay too, if he cannot get home." Looking at her cousin, Rowena drew back. "Well! Isn't that good news?" Lina arched a brow and said coolly, "Well, perhaps." Rushing up to her, Rowena felt Lina's brow.

"Are you sick? Why the long face? Didn't you hear me Lina? A handsome young man will join us at the board, a lord too."

At least she was glad that the hall had been cleared that very morning, and been re-strewn. The little ones had, as usual, gathered up the prettiest herbs. Meadow sweet, cranes bill, mallow, sweet sage and even some daisies, just for the floor. Lina cast her eye about her home. It was rare that she did, for it was all so familiar, even if she had not, as the others, been born there. It was, she supposed, handsome. On two sides of the hall, great hearths stood, though in summer only one was lit. Grandmother had brought many of her lovely, carved pieces of furniture from her old manor, and the great dishes from over the seas stood handsome on the side boards. It must be poor compared with a lord's hall, but none the less the girls ran hither and thither, bumping into each other in their haste. He was outside with the boys drying off on the river wall after joining them for a swim. The girls hurried, for they had yet to milk and everything must be all ready by the time they came in.

"Now girls", Clary wiped her face on her apron. "We have cold beef with damson sauce. Salmon. Eels. A parsnip and bacon pie. A great dish of peas pudding. Fresh bread and soft, herby cheese. We have," she thought as the astonished faces of the girls before her registered this wild extravagance. They knew that at haymaking or harvest, the meals were extra good, but not to this extent. "Damson cheese. Rowena, run to the dairy and tip off some cream carefully if you will. Then," she was looking at nothing, her mind's eye skimming the pantry shelves, "perhaps two of you can go to the fig tree, place some leaves on a basket and then lay the fruit, good ones mind, ripe and not waspy, on it." They ran, while Clary bustled about. "And check if any of last year's walnuts are still good, put them in a silver bowl."

Jessie came in, a basket on her hip. Clary looked at her appalled. She really did look like an old washer woman. Poor Jessie, half her teeth were gone and she was too fat. Clary went up to her and took away the basket, putting it in the rising cupboard. "Jessie dear," she pulled at the old, worn head cloth, then wheeled her sister into her bed chamber. "We have company, dearling," she said, racing here and there, sorting through the clothes which hung on the pegs on the wall. "Deborah's acquaintances, at least their relative, from the castle. Ah do come on dear, do your hair and make the best of yourself. Put on your baptismal cross, we don't want him to think we are just poor peasants."

The table looked fine, all laid out with large, brown trenchers, the best bowls and napkins, the glass and silver, quite like Christmas. Clary peeped out of the door down towards the river, then hurried back.

"Rowena, Lina, fetch nine wax candles and put them in the silver sticks will you?" The girls looked at each other, wide eyed. Nine wax candles! The silver candlesticks! Word went around all the girls, wax, wax candles!

"Right, Richard," Lucius led the way to their bedchamber, "we'll have to find you some dry clothing, but you'll need a belt for we are taller than you." Opening a chest he drew out his best shirt and jerkin, then calling across to Stephen he asked, "Have you any hose without holes? And what about those cool, blue braise which mother made you?" They stood back as their guest pulled on their clothes eyeing him with humour. "Well, not quite right, but yours will be clean and dry tomorrow, no doubt the mothers will see to them. So," Lucius slapped their new friend gently on his back, "Will you see about the farm, for I just heard the sheep coming in and until they're milked, we shan't sit at the board."

They went around, showing Richard their home. He was greatly intrigued, for although his grandmother had a farm, this one was quite different. Looking about, he had never been to such a place before. There was no one around, so he supposed that they were all milking. He had seen a huge flock of sheep grazing on the hills as he had walked down. They went through an open courtyard where a spring splashed into a great basin, and they all stopped to drink. It was beautiful, cold water. Richard peered down and ran his finger over the lettering on the stone.

"My uncle would be interested to see this, Lucius. He is a fine Latin scholar. Do you know what it says?" Lucius nodded.

"It is a dedication to an ancient god, we believe, by one Lucius. It is where grandfather and uncle and I get our names, being the first born. Apparently, we have been here a very long time." He wiped his mouth on his sleeve. "We are very lucky to have such a spring, which never, thanks be to God, ever dies, and," he grinned, "it saves us a great deal of work, no hauling water." They walked through some simple cloisters, where washing was hung up under cover, great wooden tubs stood upside down, by what he supposed, was the wash house. It seemed all very organized.

"This is our mother's still room," Stephen held the door open, leading from a dark passage. The smell of herbs filled their nostrils. "She is quite a healer and herbalist." He smiled at the boy, smaller than they were, dark and handsome with bright blue eyes. "No doubt she'll see to your mare after supper. This is," he hesitated, then forged on, "a busy time for us Richard. Excuse us that we did not attend to her immediately, but James is doing what he can. Cold water will surely reduce the swelling, until mother has time to see to her."

Richard brushed away the apology. He could see how busy they were. Next, they went through a gate into a walled garden, and Richard's eyes gleamed with the memory of the gorgeous girl who had been so short with him. Moya still sat in the bower, knitting her endless stockings and kissing her, Stephen took her by the elbow, whispering that as they had grand company, she really must change for the board and walked with her, to her room. Not that she could hear him but she sensed his urgency so went along willingly.

At the top end of the farm, Lucius and Richard stopped and looked down over the assorted mossy thatched roofs, smoke lazily rising from a chimney on the hall. It was one of those glorious summer evenings which imprint on the memory, calm, a haze on the horizon, and very beautiful.

A sudden and terrible, unearthly yell rose from quite close by, and Richard started, automatically clutching his heart. Lucius burst out laughing, doubling up, then straightened and pulling his sleeve, pointed through a narrow slit in the wall, to the edge of the wood. A sudden eruption of life poured from it, a stream of squealing, striped brown piglets raced towards them.

"Come quickly," Lucius tugged at his sleeve. They ran along to a lower place and giving Richard a leg up so he could see over the wall, Lucius had much trouble holding him there for his laughter.

Wide eyed, Richard struggled to perch on it and reached down a hand so that Lucius could pull himself up beside him.

James was there, a little way along the wall by a gate, pouring buttermilk into a trough, shouting endearments to the crowd who bustled about his feet.

How they laughed. With tears pouring down their cheeks, they rocked on the top of the wall, till James saw them, and waved.

"He loves those pigs," Lucius said as he jumped down and offered a hand to his guest. "Yet when the time comes, he manages to kill them very efficiently, and relishes their meat." Almost weak from laughter, they made their way down again, passed the ale house, the corn store, stables and barns. Hearing metal strike on metal, they stopped at the forge where John was mending a scythe.

"Do it in the morning, John," said Lucius, "see we have a guest, and mother is putting on an extra good meal for us tonight." John paused, his hammer in the air. He grinned at them and carried on. The fire was right, so he would finish the job. Any food which Mistress Clary made was good, so what would be new?

Then the little dear Carola came in sniffing, trying not to cry and holding her hands carefully. John Smith looked at her and stopped his work and took the bundled up little sobbing creature into his arms.

"What is it, my angel, why do you weep so?" and took a rag from his pocket and mopped at her face. It came out slowly. Apparently Carola had dropped a needle in the hall and no one could find it, so Jessie had set about her daughter's hands fiercely with her spindle. John kissed the reddened hands and reached for the pot of salve which he always kept by the fire and rubbed it on.

"There now my dearling, you will be better, and John will make you as many fine needles as you want." Mollified, Carola smiled and together they returned to the hall the fire and task abandoned.

No one heard John Smith hiss into Jessie's ear, but Jessie frightened, took note.

"Never hit her hands again, mistress, for hands are precious, she has to use them all her life. And be sure I will make her as many fine needles as you all want. I will start working on them tomorrow but you be sure never, ever to beat those little hands again."

Richard looked about the hall, a little smoky from the fire, surprisingly large for a yeoman's hall, dark and rather mysterious. Along the walls stood fine carved pieces of furniture, a few beautiful hangings and the floor was fresh strewn. His uncle Thomas came to mind. This place would interest him. Slowly, the family members came in and took their places at the board, a very old man at the head, with the old grandmother he had seen earlier at the other end. Through the smoke, he saw so many golden girls, who shyly peeped at him, before quickly looking away as they did their tasks. Stephen served him, bringing a bowl for him to wash his hands, and towel as he had been taught. When they were all seated, Richard between Lucius and Stephen, they began to enjoy their meal.

Never having been a big eater, Richard suddenly felt hungry and the fare was so good, quite unusual, he enjoyed it. When he was feeling comfortable he looked at the faces about the board. There seemed to be two sisters; the younger one, Clary being the mother of his attractive new friends. There were mainly girls, with just one little lad who hung on to his mother's apron. He assumed that she was the elder. It was all quite confusing to one who came from a very small family. Try though he did, he could not make out the girl of the garden. Until he realized that though most of them looked at him openly, just one, at the far end of the table, kept her eyes down.

"Who is that girl?" he asked Stephen. Both brothers looked to where he pointed and broke into laughter.

"That, my friend, is our only sister, Lina. The rest belong to our mother's twin, Aunt Jessie, we seem to have twins in our family." Richard was surprised. For Lucius and Stephen were very alike, just their personalities seemed different. He looked carefully at the aunt. "She has had more children than our mother, who was widowed young," Lucius said softly, "that is why she looks so old." Richard nodded. But it was their sister he wanted to know more about. Watching her in the dim light, he thought her very beautiful, with her hair shining and almost silver.

"I came across her in the garden, when I first arrived," he explained, "I am sorry to say she was not impressed with me and my poor horse, and told us very firmly, to get out."

The twins slapped their knees and rolled on their bench laughing. It seemed that laughter came to them easily. The company stopped and looked at them in enquiry, except Lina.

"That is our girl," Lucius said, "feisty, I think you might call her, quite different from our gentle cousins."

"As we have not been introduced, will you do me the honour later on?"

When they had finished, Clary went to the door leaving the girls to clear up and take the pots to the wash house. Being mid summer, it was still light, and she was anxious for the young lord's family. She would be so worried if one of her boys did not return from a ride. Then she spotted a carter coming from Marsh Newton, and taking up her shawl, she ran down to the bridge, a crusty oat cake in her apron to give him, to ask him to take the message.

At the castle, sure enough there was consternation.

"Do not worry so, mother," Thomas paused in his pacing. "He is a sound boy, as well you know. He will have found somewhere to spend the night. It is, I'm afraid, my fault, I noticed his horse was favouring a leg as he went out, I should have made him change horses. But how he lost his groom, I know not."

Karina did worry. She loved Richard passionately, as her own grandson, and wished for the thousandth time, that Rupert had chosen a good breeding wife to give him a proper brood. One child was not enough. It was so difficult, to spoil or not to spoil, to chase out, or not to? What would become of them if that precious child met with misfortune. Then she looked at Margaret, Rupert and Thomas, her love child. So like him, so tall and handsome, and more, so good and able. Now why hadn't he wed, and given her grandchildren?

"Well I think that we should send out a search party." Thomas didn't reply. The worst thing was that Rupert was away, staying with the duke. Now Jasper had few worries, for he had a fine family. Grown sons, hawk nosed young men, who favoured their mother. Years later, his lady had borne a charming daughter, quite the apple of their eyes. She had nothing of her mother and looked like him, very fair.

It must have been well past midnight when he heard voices at the outer gate. Going to the window he leaned out. There was a half moon and he could just see a figure far below. Then, running surely down the dark passages, he arrived just as the gate was being closed.

"What news?" he said breathlessly. The night watchman greeted him with a salute.

"A carter, Sir Thomas. He brought a message that the young lord is safe and well and biding at one Byford Hall, near to Marsh Newton." Thomas sighed in relief, slapped the watchman on the arm and pushing open the door, ran lightly down the cobbled way until he came to the carter. Taking out a coin, he pressed it into the man's hand.

"So did you see him, Master Carter?" still breathless.

"No sire that I did not. It was Mistress Byford who came running to tell me to bring you the message. Seems the young lord's horse went lame. She said all is well with the lad and they are enjoying his company."

Thomas felt a small warmth settle in his gut at the words.

"And do you know that family, Master Carter? Are they decent folk?"

The carter looked at the lord in the dimness of the night and saw the worry on his face.

"Why bless me, sire," he said kindly, "they is the best folk round about. Gentry they is, or was. You've no need to worry about your lad while he is with them. A big farm it is, with a grand family of youngsters too, and, he'll be having a merry old time, I'll be bound."

Amused by the carter's description, and hoping that Richard was having a merry old time, he went back into the castle. Before going back to his own room, he put his head around his mother's bed chamber door and told her.

"So now I can sleep," said Karina crossly. But she knew she would not, for she was much too upset. She'd have some strong words to mete out when he returned.

At the farm, they sat in the garden in the cool, as the moon rose. Stephen and James played their pipes softly, and Richard thought how beautiful it all was. Clary and Lina came to wish them good night, and now Lina smiled at him. Richard felt his throat constrict, a sudden flurry burst in his heart.

"I am sorry that I was short with you," she said softly, "It was just such a surprise." Her smile was enchanting, and he took her hand and kissed it.

"Next time I come, I'll enter through the river gate and I hope that you will forgive me."

James, Lucius and Stephen looked at each other with big eyes, trying not to grin. Oh my, he kissed her hand, but he was obviously entranced by their Lina, and quite right too.

"Bed," said Lucius. "We have to take some sheep to Marsh Newton tomorrow and will have to leave quite early." Turning to James he added, "will you come? Or shall we take them?"

"I have other work, Lucius, you take them. And don't forget that mother wants Master Potter to stop by, for she has some orders for him."

It seemed unbearably early when Richard felt his shoulder being shaken.

"Come on, old son," Lucius was standing in the middle of the room dragging his clothes on. "You can help us, sheep are fools and our old dog is worse than useless. We must get another soon."

They went on foot across the plain driving the sheep in front of them as the early morning mist was still rising.

"Get behind them, get behind them," Stephen shouted as two made a bid to escape.

Running swiftly behind the sheep, Richard seemed to drive them on faster in the wrong direction. Lucius loomed large and purposeful and they veered back towards the little flock.

"Not behind their rumps, you damn fool boy," he roared, breathless, "behind them, to stop them getting away."

Richard was mortified by his mistake, and stunned at being called a damned fool boy for the first time in his life.

"Sorry!" he shouted.

They waved at him, their faces merry again. "I told you they are stupid." And that was an end to it.

At the Toby Jug, they introduced him to another aunt, and the Innman family. They were royally entertained but left soon enough, for the hay had to be got in, and the sky promised rain in a couple of days. Taking up a rake, he stood in line and after carefully watching the girls, strove to be useful. Lina was no where to be seen, but he was too busy to fret for long. No doubt he'd meet her at the board. When they got home he was exhausted and hungry, and this time he took off most of his clothes before going into the river with the others.

"It was the best time!" he told his uncle and grandmother, wincing at his stiffness from unaccustomed work. "It was such fun! They were so nice." They listened to him, Thomas with a humorous twinkle in his eye, Karina frankly furious.

"You could have been kidnapped!"

"I was not!"

"You might have been killed!"

"Here I am, alive and well!"

"I was so worried, Richard," and took out a kerchief to wipe her eyes.

His heart melted and he hugged her. Then, he whispered in her ear,

"And grandmother, I met the most beautiful girl!"

Now she actually smiled, and from across the room, Thomas wondered at the cause of her sudden change of mood.

"Tell me, dear child." she said, eyes alight. He did, about going into the garden, her reprimand, the hall and all the family. But especially Lina.

"I should like to marry her, grandmother."

Her face serious again, she said. "Perhaps you are a little too young, Richard."

"Perhaps, grandmother, but I will grow up soon."

"It would be good to marry then, for with only one heir, we would be in trouble if anything happens to you. Which is why I was so worried." They sat peacefully for awhile with their thoughts. "It is not good is it, being an only child?" he nodded, remembering the camaraderie of the Byfords. "I was an only," she went on, eyes glazed, remembering, unseeing, "except, well I was not really. For I had so many little brothers, about six, I think, then the last one, a half brother, but they all died." He held her hand, for his uncle had told him something of her story.

"Are you very old, grandmother?"

She planted a lusty kiss on his cheek. "Yes my treasure, I suppose I am, but sometimes, inside, I still feel like a little girl."

"I will try to have lots of children for you then, grandmother, so you need never worry about our line. So I will ask uncle if we may go to visit the Byfords soon, for I wish to take them gifts. For not only were they so kind to me, they did send you some excellent cheese, as well as giving me fine liniment for my horse."

"They did indeed, and yes, take Thomas, he is a wise old owl. Even if he never wed to give me grandchildren, which grieves me. Margaret, thank heaven, has made up for it with her five."

They did go to Byford Hall, he and Thomas with two grooms. When they arrived, it seemed that there was no one there, although a wisp of smoke was lazily drifting from a chimney. Richard told the grooms to wait by the bridge while he and Thomas explored. Right at the top, where James fed his pigs, there was a foothold in the wall, and together they managed to climb up and in.

No one was there, because, it being Sunday, they had all gone to the little church on the hill, now completed. Father Benjamin had come to stay, for he was being replaced by a new, younger priest and had gone up with them.

Delighting in the peace of the deserted farmstead, Clary had half filled the great wooden wash tubs with cold water, and boiled up the kettles to start the wash. The girls would be picking wild greens on their way and she had the pastry ready to make a pie. The pease pudding was setting in the pantry, and a large ham was cooling in its water with the roots. James' project with the swine had been a great success. As they lived in the woods, only coming down for their feed, there was not the mess and stink one would expect about the farm, when keeping pigs.

Well ahead of herself, she quickly stripped off and sank into the luxury of a hot bath. Wetting her hair, which had grown long again, she lathered it with the best soap. Then, as Deborah had advised, she carefully rubbed in the thick, chamomile tea she had prepared. It was true, her silver-white hair did now have a yellow sheen. Not that it mattered, for as she always covered her head with a cloth, no one saw it anyway. Lying there, her eyes closed, she thought about prison and her hair going white. Now she even blessed it, for Lina looked more like her now, than when it was yellow. When she was done, she dropped all the dirty clothes in the tub and trod them down to soak for tomorrow's washing. It was a good feeling to be ahead of herself, and feel so light and clean.

Putting on the silk robe which her uncles had given her years before, a luxury from far lands, she made her way to the garden, Dove at her heels.

"You go that way, uncle," said Richard," and I will go this. I just cannot understand it. There has to be someone here." So silently, almost as thieves, they crept off, going their separate ways.

Thomas looked carefully about as he went through the rambling open yards, passageways and courts. What an unusual place, he thought. It had a touch of simple grandeur, extreme order, which appealed to him, even an ecclesiastical air. Not at all what one would expect of yeoman farmers. At the end of a dim passage set between two buildings, ignoring the doors on either side, he chose the middle way, a gate, through which he saw the green of a garden. Carefully pushing it open, he beheld a miracle. There was an arbour draped with honeysuckle and briar roses, where lay a beautiful woman. A dove-grey dog lay at her side, her robe was bright, flowery, patterned silk, and her hair, silver/gold, lay all about her,

The dog raised its head and he saw from its eyes that it must be almost blind.

"Ssh!" said the woman, her eyes still closed, laying her hand on its head. So it lay down again.

Hardly daring to breathe, Thomas continued to watch the gentle rise and fall of her breast, his pulse quickening. Then, very gently he withdrew, quietly pulling the gate shut behind him.

Leaning against the wall, he stood in the dimness of the passage and wondered at the sight which he had just seen. What a beautiful woman! What an extraordinary and enchanted place!

In the hall, Richard had found old Lucas and grandmother Moya in their usual places by the hearth. It was they who told him where the family were, gone up to the new little church on the hill, with Father Benjamin to celebrate their first mass there.

"Come!" Richard saw his uncle appear. "The grandparents are here, and they told me that the rest of the family are up the hill celebrating mass for the first time at the little church they have just built. Let us go too," and hurried out to the horses.

They were all just coming out when the horsemen rode up. Seeing Richard, as one their faces broke into smiles of welcome. Then, thinking that Thomas was his father for he so favoured him, they all curtseyed low.

Father Benjamin came forward and they all trooped back into the church again.

"It is charming," said Thomas after making his abeyance. "What a privilege to have such a fine little church to worship in, and situated in such a beautiful place." In his mind he thought hastily through the store room at the castle where many, ecclesiastical items were stored. "I hope that we might donate something in way of decoration, in thanks to you for taking in our boy," and made a mock swipe at Richard, which is just what he did to the delight of all the family. "My mother was so worried about him."

Thomas was rather silent when they returned home the next day, his mind milling with his thoughts. It had been such a happy little interlude in their lives. Everything had been perfect. He and Richard had been given a comfortable bed chamber off the hall while the grooms had been provided with pallets. Richard had been so excited and pleased to show him around, with almost a propriety air. Despite being a family of seventeen souls, they managed very well with coping with five extra.

As with Richard, it had taken him time to work out who belonged to whom. He supposed the beauty he had spied in the garden was Mistress Clarissa. He watched her carefully as she sped about, issuing orders to the young people, handsome in a dark blue gown and clean white, lace edged apron. The priest had been most helpful with introducing them all as they hurried about, preparing for the meal. Which, he had found most excellent.

He noted the fine hangings, the old furniture and plate, which Richard had spoken of, not to mention the wax candles in silver sticks.

Handing over the hamper which his mother had sent, he thanked Mistress Clary most warmly for her hospitality to Richard.

"My nephew is an only child, mistress," he said, interested to see a strand of silver hair escaped from her scarf, so like her daughter's. "He does have cousins, my sister's children, but they lead very busy lives and he tends to be rather solitary in the castle."

Clary smiled warmly up at the handsome man. Although dark, he did have a resemblance to her grandfather Stephen. He was so like Richard, with an easy charm, and was elegant, in an austere way.

"As you see, sire," they walked along the river wall, "he gets along marvellously well with our youngsters. I do hope that he will come again, and you too, sire," she added hastily, "if you can manage in our rather humdrum household."

When they had left and the hall was cleared and quiet again, Jessie and Clary unpacked the hamper.

"Oranges!" breathed Jessie, picking one up and jamming it to her nose.

"Oh good," said Clary, piling them onto a great bowl, "I shall dry the skins again, as I did with the others which James and John sent. For they do give a dash to apple pie, mashed pumpkin or fish stew."

"I think I see a budding romance between the young lord and your Lina," Jessie said, her voice odd and squeaky. Clary looked at her sharply.

"Don't be silly, Jessie, they are just children."

"So," Jessie reminded her, "were we!"

Karina carefully unpacked the little basket which Richard, his eyes shining with happiness, had brought her. More little soft cheeses, smoked and wrapped in walnut leaves. Hard cheese, tied and waxed in hempen cloth, which would keep for winter.

"I have decided, grandmother, I truly intend to marry Lina. For not only is she most beautiful, she is so gifted in so many ways. They all speak French," which surprised Karina, "and look," he opened his doublet to expose a narrow braid around his waist, "when I admired her work, she gave this to me." He whirled around, stamping his feet in a mock clog dance which they had taught him. "I shall go down to the town tomorrow and buy her a beautiful present for the next time we go."

Rupert was perplexed by the sudden burst of life which surrounded him. Both his son, brother, and even his mother seemed to be joyful about some new acquaintances they had made in the country. The cheese they had provided was, true, quite excellent, but surely, yeoman farmers?

"What were you thinking about, Thomas. Allowing my son to fraternize with such lowly people? All he talks about is some wench called Lina, his beautiful fair damsel, while I have been busy discussing his nuptials with Jasper."

Thomas concentrated on the quill he was shaving. His pen knife was blunt, he must sharpen it.

"His horse was lame," he said as causally as he could, "they gave him shelter, for which we were most grateful. It wouldn't have done for him to be out in the forest alone all night. Wretched boy," he added, with feeling. "Mother and I were so worried. So tell me, Rupert," happy to change the subject, "What has Jasper to say?"

"Apparently the second, admittedly older man," Rupert told him, "who was betrothed to his daughter Ursuline, has died. The girl is young yet, but it is something which has to be arranged. He is now enquiring with the bishop whether our relationship is too close for Richard to wed with her. I cannot believe it, though I do forget which fore-father of ours was also his." He sighed greatly, his kinsman having alerted him to his responsibilities at last. "He and his lady will be coming to stay shortly, to meet the boy, so we can thrash it out."

The great bed chamber made ready, Karina went up to her garden to pick flowers for it. Pausing for breath every few stairs, she wondered how much longer she would be able to climb up them, perhaps she would soon indulge in a chair. She was getting old and it seemed only yesterday that Jasper was here, when Philippa first came.

Jasper and his duchess liked Richard. His lady was particularly insistent that her last, most precious child, should make a happy marriage. Although of lesser nobility, the Highcleres were kin, having the advantage of living mere miles away, instead of across the sea. It was quite one thing if younger sons married abroad, and another if their only daughter did. The duchess was therefore most gracious to the family, particularly to Richard, but increasingly perplexed by his tales of a farming family with whom he was friends.

"What is all this about?" Jasper asked, when the ladies had retired. "I hear that your son is not only lusting after some lowly wench, but speaks of marrying her!"

Thomas rose and stabbed at the fire, causing a great cloud of sparks to rise up.

"Well yes," Rupert felt most discomfited. "I was away when this accident occurred, his horse went lame and he happened upon them. Puppy love, Jasper, you know how it is, he'll get over it soon enough, as for wedding the girl, certainly not. He shall never have my blessing, indeed, I will not allow it."

They sat moodily, silently gazing into the fire. The dogs were shifty, wanting to go out, so Thomas went to the door and called them.

"Provide the girl with a dowry, enough, but not too much." Jasper was a man of the world, "the family will jump at it, and that will be an end to the matter. And," he shifted in his chair, thinking about his young kinsman, comparing him with his own, tall, well built sons, "send Richard off to sea. The boy has some growing to do, let him see a little of the world, as he is too young to go to court yet. I have some reliable captains in my port, my sons have sailed safely with them, many times. Yes," he slapped his knee feeling he had hit upon the right course, "marry the girl off and send Richard to sea for a year or two. That'll make him forget his passion in no time."

Thomas had returned to the fireplace and heard the last words, his fists bunched. Rupert looked up at him, suddenly feeling positive. Jasper was a good advisor, a reliable man, able to see things clearly and make swift decisions.

"Hear that, Tom?" he called to Thomas. "Now why didn't I think about it myself. Jasper suggests that we offer the girl, Lina, or what ever her name is, a dowry. Her family will no doubt be delighted and marry her off. Richard can go to sea, learn something of the world, and be freed of his obsession. I'll ask the purser to get things organized and as you have been to the girl's place, perhaps you could take what we decide on, and inform her parents of my wishes."

Thomas glared at his brother, his pulse racing. Half brother. There were times when he almost hated him. Send Richard, son of his heart off to sea? Why the lad was barely out of skirts.

"Very well," he eyed them coldly, "we shall talk it over in the morning, sires," He bowed to Duke Jasper and nodded to Rupert. "Sleep well," and left.

CHAPTER THIRTY SIX

THOMAS

There was no more discussion about Richard going away. Thomas kept busy, organising the castle guard, repairs to the water front, alms for soldiers widows and pensions for the older men, and all his usual tasks. He did not, for various reasons, see very much of the family. Even so, the purser came to Thomas with a bag of gold, with word from Lord Rupert, to follow his instructions.

Thomas put the little bag, unopened in his chest, and got on with his life. His father had left his foster daughter Margaret, a farm. As her husband, the horse master was always too busy to attend to it, Thomas and his mother, Karina often went out there, staying a few days perhaps, to organize the harvests. Margaret's dream was that when her man grew too old to continue his work, they would move there to live.

It was a good farm, with some acres of wheat, rye and oats, as well as some orchards of plums and apples. Karina particularly enjoyed their visits, for she said that it reminded her of her childhood home.

Thomas was worried. He could not say why, even to himself, but he felt unsettled. The boy was too, although he tried to hide it. They both thought of the Byford farm most of the day and half the night, or rather the women there.

Thomas knew in his heart that Clarissa would be outraged by the presentation of the gold with its conditions. He would be, if he were in her place. Somehow he had to reach her, but how? It went around his head and he began to lose weight with worry, which of course Karina, with her finely tuned mind, noticed. Her most loved people were is sorrow, Thomas and Richard, and she guessed why. They were in love. Waiting till they were peaceful and alone together in her garden, she suddenly said.

"Do you think my dears, that now the harvests are over, you could take me for a little excursion somewhere. I grow weary of this old place. I feel that before winter sets in, I need a little change of scenery."

They looked at her surprised. She had always been the most contented woman, happy wherever she was, so long as she had her family near by.

"Would you like to visit Mistress Scrivener, mother?"

Karina thought for a moment, or pretended to "No, dear," she tried to smile at him but it didn't work. "Firstly, with Louisa gone, I should be sad. Secondly, Deborah is always so busy. Thirdly, you know how I dislike the city, and if I went there, I would be obliged to stay with Jasper and his family and it would be no rest at all."

They contemplated, silent, surprised by her unusual request.

"Do you think," finally she spoke, "would it be too rude, imposing, if we could ask your friends near Marsh Newton, if we could visit them? They are after all friends of Deborah you know, she and her parents lived at Marsh Newton years ago."

It was as if the sun shone through storm clouds. Both her beloved boys lit up and smiled warmly at her.

"Of course it wouldn't be too much!" Richard burst forth. "They are such a warm people, with their extended family, for sure they could find corners to fit us in, eh, uncle, what do you think?"

Thomas was surprised by the beating of his heart, for yes, it was a grand idea, yet, he was cautious.

"I'll have to write," he said, "tell them that you need a little change before winter and would like to lodge at the inn at Marsh Newton, and could we call to see them. I'd feel embarrassed to ask, outright, if we three, mother's maid and a groom could stay. Then," he paused, pleased with his idea, "they may invite us to stay with them."

"Lina, Lina," Clary broke the seal, her hands trembling, "a letter from Sir Thomas Highclere." Lina stood before her, eyes wide with excitement. "Read it to me, dearling," Clary said, handing her the parchment, "for my eyes are not as good as yours." Lina read it, twice. It was a short, very polite letter.

"Of course they cannot stay at the inn," she said indignantly. "They must stay here." She whirled about in a spin, "Oh mother, how exciting, Richard told me a lot about his grandmother. It seems she is a foreign lady who came here when she was little, and that she had many exciting adventures in her life. And when she was little, Mistress Doume' knew her in France."

Clary rooted in her little chest and drew out a small sheet of vellum. Dusting it she frowned.

"Will this do, do you think? Have we anything fit for ink? My goodness but we have become peasants. I can't remember when I last wrote a letter, what would the, Lady Felicia think of me?" and ended cheerfully, "You'll have to do it."

Lina jumped up and went out. There was an elderberry tree just outside the door leading to the garden. It was to keep the witches away of course, but right now, there were a few ripe berries. Lina took a bowl from her mother's still room and carefully filled it. Then she washed her hands of the red juice, which did not really come off, and sat down at a little table on the window seat. Meanwhile, Clary took up a small pestle and mortar and ground the berries, till there was just a little juice at the bottom to write with.

She was so grateful to her grandmother for teaching the children how to read and write. Not that the boys were as good as Lina, for hers was a clear hand, and she read far better than they did.

Excited, they took their time, doing several rough copies on a slate, till they were satisfied.

"Dear Sir Thomas", she wrote, "we thank you for your letter which finds us all very well, by the Grace of God. My mother will not think of you staying at the inn, although it is comfortable there, and is owned by our kin, who would see to your every need. We however, would like your company here. This is not such a busy time on the farm, with just the cider to be made. We all much look forward to seeing you, Richard and your lady mother, when you can come.

Till then, I am your happy friend,

Ursuline Byford."

"My goodness," said Thomas, "what a fine, clear hand she has." Turning to his mother he smiled warmly at her. She seemed to have shrunk in old age, never having been very tall, she grew smaller as the years passed. "So there you are, mother, we shall wait for the opportunity, and for good weather, and then we can help them with their apple picking."

That none of them mentioned their plans to Rupert didn't bother them at all. For Rupert was often away these days, visiting the Duke in the city.

"We will put the men in my room as before, Lina," Clary stood, looking at her still room. "I will curtain off the two alcoves on either side of the chimney in here, and put Lady Karina in one, and grandmother and I will sleep in the other. It will be a little small, but we shall manage. I am sure that the girls will welcome you to sleep with them. If," she was seeing her arrangements in her mind, "they bring any staff, they will have to sleep in the hall."

James wouldn't think of letting her put up curtains, so he bullied the boys to help him saw thin planks, to make proper divisions with. A great elm had come down on the edge of the wood, and tethering the plough oxen to it, they hauled it down to the saw pit. The wide planks which they cut, showed handsome markings, and they were pleased with their efforts.

"Oh boys," Clary clasped her hands and gazed at their fine work, "you are so, so clever." So they felt it was worth it, and although it was definitely autumn now, went for a swim each day, to get the sawdust out of their hair, nose, ears and eyes. Now, in the swing of wood working, they also made a large bed, to accommodate both Clary and grandmother, and moved it into the alcove before the last sheet of wood partitioning went in place. After stringing it with strong hempen rope, they set to stuffing a huge mattress cover with sweet hay and sheep's wool putting several covers over it to make it comfortable.

Excited by the changes, Clary drew out some of her treasures to decorate the little rooms. "Well, I've had them in my dower chest for so many years," she justified her actions, "it is time to use them to compliment our boy's hard work."

They arrived early afternoon in the castle barge. The little twins Carola and Piers saw them first, and with squeals of excitement, loudly announced the arrival.

Karina brought one of Margaret's daughters, the quiet, dark Karen, to help her. The girls, pleased with their unexpected guest, quickly made space for her in their room, and everyone was happy.

Richard had warned his uncle to bring work clothes, for the previous time, having none, he had borrowed from the twins, and intended to be organized for a change. The boys viewed him with amusement, for if he said they were working clothes, they wondered what theirs might be called.

James had, over the years, made great baskets from willow wands which they stored for regular use. They all carried them together, up to the orchard to gather up the windfalls, and pick the apples off the trees.

"Mind the wasps," came the constant cry, or Clary would be called to anoint a sting with vinegar and her magic healing salve. With the crop picked and carted down to the farm, they began the cider making. It was a long, hot and sticky task chopping up the apples, and they took it in turns to put on old, wooden soled clogs to crush the apples to pulp. With skirts hoicked up, they sang and stamped in time. Soon the golden juice poured from the tub and grandfather stood by to tell the boys what to do, as he did every year. At the end of the day, autumn or no, they rushed down to the river, waded in, gasping at the cold, and at least washed legs and arms.

Karina had made sure that they brought great quantities of special foods, and Clary and Jessie were dumb founded when they opened the hampers. Meals became quite an adventure with all the strange and wonderful foods they had brought.

"Well I knew you had a big family," said Karina, "and we are surely more happy here with you, than at an inn. It quite reminds me of my childhood, and my own grandmother, bringing in the harvest to store for the winter."

In the evenings, they sat in the hall after their meal, played chess, or sang, and it was a gracious and happy time. Karina loved the many, golden haired girls sitting on stools at her feet, demanding stories of her young life. Surprisingly she suddenly found she was remembering so much, after years of being too busy to.

"Tell us about your farm?" the children asked, eagerly, the day done. Thomas half listened as his mother spoke of her childhood, far, far away. He had never tired of listening to her.

"We had a tower," Karina said, using her hands to describe it. "It was the oldest part, which had been there before my grandmother first went to live there."

"Our grandparents live at a tower," piped one of Jessie's younger daughters. Thomas was intrigued and wondered which tower, and who their other grandparents were. But the rest of the children hushed her fiercely. They wanted to hear about the Lady Karina's tower, knowing their own already.

While appearing to enjoy all the children, Karina watched Lina with a quiet eye. She was indeed as Richard said, lovely. Her skin was fair, with a smattering of freckles, so attractive if unladylike, and her deep blue eyes were fascinating, not unlike her son Thomas's. She also watched Clarissa, who, when she thought she was not observed, looking at Thomas. At other times, when she was busy, Karina saw Thomas watching Clarissa. Well!

When the children cleared the hall and took to dancing, Clary led the elders away to her still room for quiet.

Thomas was impressed with it, the new panelling polished and shining, and the ceiling hung with bunches of herbs which when touched, gave off every scent. The glazed windows looked out onto the herb garden where they sometimes also walked, or they sat in the arbour.

Thomas noticed hangings and cushions, oddly all the same and wondered who had worked them. They depicted coats of arms interwoven with each other, and when he touched one, Moya leaned forward and pointed to one part.

"Those are the arms of my husband, Sir Stephen de Elancourt," she said softly.

He heard her, surprised. So he pointed to another part of the cushion with a question on his face. "Those are of my uncle, Clary's great grandfather, Baron Roland Pomeroy." Intrigued, more baffled, Thomas asked.

"If he was your uncle, how was he Clary's great grandfather, Lady Moya?" She looked at him, her old eyes twinkling.

"I am not her real grandmother, that is why. Jessica, Uncle Roland's only child, died young, leaving one daughter and then, I married Stephen, and became mother to her daughter Felicia, Clary's mother. Sadly I had no children of my own. But," she smiled, and he saw that once she had been a lovely woman, "all these are mine now, for the time being anyway."

Thomas was baffled, it seemed too complicated to take in. He pointed to the tiny, yellow fleur de lis,

"And this?" he asked, ""where does this fit in?"

She peered at it frowning.

"There was talk that the first Lady Felicia Elancourt's mother was descended from the king, a great granddaughter, I believe. Sir Nicholas was French, a nobody, just a good business man, but, theirs was a great love match at least."

Now Thomas was greatly interested, for history had always fascinated him.

"Did not the baron and Sir Nicholas have lands then, Lady Moya?" She thought deeply, then her face cleared.

"Yes," she said, patting the de Elancourt arms. "When Lady Felicia and Stephen died in an epidemic, I sold the manor. Much of the furnishings you see here were from there. The rest is at the tower, or the other girls have pieces, here and there." She thought for a moment longer, moving her hand to the Pomeroy arms.

"He chased us out, the brute, after Uncle Roland died. He killed old Agnes too. Lee had gone just before uncle, so we were alone, a group of bereaved, frightened, lonely women. May he rot in hell."

"Who, grandmother, who chased you out?" asked Thomas, intrigued.

"Godfrey, yes that was his given name, and he took Roland's family name, although he was just a stepson. No, I do not recall his birth name. It was from then, that our fortunes fell, but perhaps we have since been happier, after all."

Clary came in and looked concerned at her grandmother.

"Dearling, you look so tired. Come, let me help you to bed, I will read to you for a little, from the Book of Hours, if you like, then you must sleep. For lovely though it is to have guests, I see it tires you." Holding the old lady under the elbow, she aided her gently into the new little room on the side of the chimney piece.

Thomas felt as if his head was spinning. Was the old one telling fairy tales? But no, he stroked the cushion by him, admiring again the lovely colours and the hand work. Did she know what she was saying? He looked at other similar tapestries, then across at the open door where Clary who had left her chores was reading a little book to her grandmother. The mystery deepened by the day. Who were these people?

"May I read to her, Mistress Clary, your grandmother," Thomas asked, "for you are busy as usual, are you not?"

Clary smiled her thanks at him, for yes she was busy, and tired. Looking across to her daughter she said,

"Come dearling, let us run to get tomorrow started."

So it was that Thomas held Lee's Book of Hours in his hands, and admired the exquisite little paintings, the prayers and the fine, sloping writing.

Then turning to the end, he saw the names, the whole family tree with the coats of arms. Goodness!

The journey home was beautiful, and intent on looking at all they passed, gliding effortlessly down stream, contented, they barely spoke. Karina was happy. She had watched her treasures being happy, really and truly happy. She had seen their secret glances of love, to their beloved. Son and grandson, both, had found themselves beautiful, gifted women, so who could ask for more? That they were of lowly stock, worried Karina not one bit. Her own grandmother, and mother indeed, though somewhat differently, had been slaves, when fortune had altered their lives. A fish jumped, perhaps to escape their prow, and Karina watched the sun lit spray fall and wondered at how minute memories were coming back to her, of those long past days of her early childhood.

Autumn really set in, with trees in vivid hues, and a sharp nip in the air, early and late. Thomas and Richard lived in their own worlds of dreams and contentment, and got on with their lives with an absent air.

A great storage barn had collapsed in a storm and Thomas was called to a small town a few miles north. He was the lord's authority to organize the salvage of the grain and the re-building of the barn before the winter came. A certain amount of grain had been stolen by the poor, but the castle henchmen were on guard now, waiting for him.

When the task was done, weary, Thomas came home, glad to be done with the petty squabbles of small town burgers. Late, he put his head around the door of the hall and saw his brother, unusually drunk, lying about, surrounded by some of his bawdier officers. He merely nodded and went to bed.

It was not unusual for him not to see his nephew for a day or two at a time. In a place like theirs, they might cross paths several times without sighting each other.

"How's Richard?" Thomas asked his mother on the third day, strangely worried. Karina looked up from her needlework which she could no longer see very well.

"I was hoping to hear that from you, for I was at the farm, picking cobnuts and haven't seen him for several days. It is not like Richard not to visit me."

"Where?" Thomas called across the heads of the merry officers to his obviously drunken brother, "is Richard?"

Did he or did he not notice unease amongst the gathering? Rupert put his tankard down untidily, slopping it over, wiped his mouth on his sleeve and looked at him with blood shot eyes.

"Eh? Eh?" he said, stupidly. One by one his drinking companions rose and slipped out, leaving the brothers alone together.

"You heard me!" Thomas leaned forward, then hastily backed at the stink of drink and unwashed man. "Where is Richard?" His voice has risen.

Rupert was nodding, dribbling, looking anywhere than at the hard eyes of his brother.

"I knew that you'd be angry. I was sure that you would put a stop to it. Then, what would Jasper say?" He paused, wiped his mouth on his sleeve again and tried to sit up straight. Thomas narrowed his eyes. So Jasper was in this, was he? He waited.

"It is all very well for you," Rupert began to moan now. "You are the younger, you do not have the responsibility. If I went against Jasper's advice, he'd turn his back on us, you don't understand, you never did. Any more than you ever liked me." He began to blubber, wet and snivelling, the drink having made him weak and silly. "Why didn't you like me, Thomas? What did I ever do to hurt you? You were my baby brother, always so handsome, so admired, while I, the elder, the heir, was barely glanced at. They all looked at you, with your sweet face and nice manners but it was no good, try as I might, I could not be like you!" A great howl rose from his ample belly and Thomas took a step back in shock. "Even the tailors complain that I do not have the figure and deportment you have." He wept now, rocking in his chair.

Thomas drew up a stool and sat down on it weary. So he had sent Richard away, on Jasper's advice. Damned be Jasper! With his sons, it wouldn't occur to him how very precious their only chick was to all of them. He gazed into the fire unseeing, remembering the day, so long ago when his little world had shattered.

When his wonderful, older brother Rupert had referred to him as "just one of my father's bastards", how it had hurt, how it even hurt now, even though when their parents had wed, he and Margaret had stood under the marriage canopy and been legitimised.

"So how long has he left?" he had to raise his voice to make Rupert stop with his snivelling. "When did he leave?"

Rupert blew his nose on a napkin he had found down the side of his chair, and red eyed, dared to look up at his brother. "Two, three days. I think. There was a ship going. Jasper said he must leave before the winter storms, and there was an especially fine ship about to sail south," he ended on a pleading note. "I sent Giles, his man with him. He is a good, loyal servant, he will take care of Richard."

"Did he say goodbye to mother?" Hard, Thomas now stood again, his blue eyes ice cold, his fists clenched, furious.

"No, er, she was away, I think, there wasn't time, but," he rose and made his way unsteadily to a small box near the fireplace. "He wrote to both of you, here, here," and returned to his chair, head in hands.

Taking the letter, Thomas strode out of the hall, and two at a time, ran up to his mother's room. Taking her in his arms he told her, whispering the news into her headcloth, then, using his small dagger, prized open the seal and read the letter to her.

It was short, loving, unusually wise for such a young man. He explained that it must be done, to preserve their honour. That their kinsman Jasper would be so offended if his advice was ignored. He would take the greatest care of himself. He would be back, bigger and he hoped better. He fully intended making Lina Byford his lady wife. This was just one step in that direction. Then, he implored his uncle to visit Byford Hall now and again, to offer them any help they might need.

"May God and his saints watch over you both till I return, I shall pray for you till then." he wrote, "your ever loving, Richard."

Karina was sobbing quietly by now, unbelieving, yet knowing that he had gone, and the dear child had written his farewells to them, so loving, so able and wise.

"At least go, Thomas, my love. Go to see if he has gone yet. Make sure he is well provisioned and clothed. That fool Rupert won't have thought of any of that, we can be sure." And fell to weeping once more.

Glad to have something to do, Thomas brightened, and kissing his mother fiercely, he told her, with hope in his voice, "I'll do that, mother. But at least the good Giles is with him, and being Margaret's kinsman, will take extra good care of him. I'll go right now, and if he has changed his mind, I'll bring him home. If not, as you say, I'll make sure, some how or the other, that he is well provisioned." He kissed her again. "Be of good cheer, precious mother. I shall be back as soon as I have seen to it." So he ran, forgetting his weariness, pushed just a few clothes and gold into a saddle bag, and left within the hour.

Karina was not of good cheer. She held Richard's letter, kissed it, and wept again. She felt responsible somehow. She should have guided Rupert more wisely. Yet hadn't she, loving him since his birth, nursing him beside little Margaret, being the best mother she could be to him always. Her distressed maid hovered around her, but she shooed her away. Finally, unable to settle, she rose and made her way downstairs, but Rupert wasn't in the hall. A footman told her that he was in the solar, upstairs. Gathering her skirts, she slowly toiled up, her breath coming in gasps at the effort. Pushing open the solar door, she confronted her foster son.

Later, much later, when Thomas came home, he gleaned the truth of the story from Rupert, a quivering wreck, her maid, and the footman. It seemed that Karina had finally lost her patience with Rupert, and raged unmercifully at him.

All the distress she had ever felt, the shame at his laziness, his sloppiness, his useless marriage, out it poured. Just when Richard had found his own bride, a fine, healthy country girl, a child breeder, he had to interfere. This time he had gone too far. Dishonestly, behind their backs like a sneak-thief, he had sent their precious boy away, without even farewells. Karina felt strong, as at last she told her foster son, sweet Philippa's son, what a fool he was.

"And poor, sweet Philippa," she raged, "who asked me to look after you as she was dying, how disappointed she would be! And Robert my husband, that fine, sensible lord, how he would be ashamed of you! Shame on you, Rupert Highclere, shame."

Then, a pain so great, she knew she could not survive it, rose in her breast, and Karina held her skirts, made her last, deep, elegant curtsey, and slowly sank, dead to the floor.

At the port, Thomas raced toward the one large ship which lay tied there. Meanwhile, his groom ran to the second largest ship. They were greeted cordially, but no, the seamen they spoke to knew nothing, and they were advised to call at a small, tall house on the quay. There, they would find answers.

The door opened to his knock, and Thomas ducked under the low lintel and found himself in a long, low room. Introducing himself to two elderly men sitting on either side of the hearth, they merely nodded him to a seat, and then enquired as to his business.

Thomas found himself being more expansive than was usual. He told them, briefly yet with humour, of his nephew's banishment, the cause being his love of a young lady. They nodded, almost absently. The woman who had opened the door to him came in with a tray, on which stood beautiful wine glasses, and a fine glass jug of wine.

As she set them on a low table near him, Thomas noticed that although her skin was pale, she had dark, slanting eyes. Bending her head, she listened to one of the old men, nodded and went out again. The other old man asked Thomas's groom to pour out the wine for them, then retreated into silence once more.

Holding his glass, savouring the excellent wine, Thomas looked about the room. Though small, it was handsome, filled with beautiful and unusual objects, obviously from over the seas. Above the shelf over the hearth, a tapestry hung, although darkened by smoke. Frowning, Thomas was sure that he recognized it. Just as he had begun to realize that it was the same as several which he had seen in Clary's still room, the door opened.

A young man came in, almost filling the room. Tall and well built, he was obviously a son, for he greatly resembled the two old men. Except his hair was still dark while theirs was white. Thomas wondered if the woman was his mother.

He asked them then, if they knew which ship his nephew Lord Richard Highclere had sailed on, if it was a good ship? Where it was bound?

It had been many years since he had accompanied Rupert as his squire, and he felt an old tingle of excitement. Ports had their own, particular smell. Not only the usual stink of waste and sea, but of tar and foreign lands.

The three men drank their wine, answered his questions briefly, yet seemed somewhat cold and reticent with their friendship.

"Your wine is excellent," he saluted them, noting the rich, ruby red in his glass against the fire light.

"We always have it," one old man said. "Even on our ships." the other continued. "It is our policy to provision well, for we are fortunate in having family who provide us with excellent goods."

"Then tell me," Thomas was puzzled, for they seemed strangely curt, almost threatening towards him, despite their polite front, "will Richard be enjoying this same wine, for it would be good for him to develop a taste for fine wines. At our castle, my mother insists on ale, except at night, and for feast days." They nodded, but said nothing.

Then the young man, more lively than the old, leaned forward.

"What do you and your mother have to say about the lad's choice of lady? Are you as displeased with it as are the Duke and Lord Rupert."

Thomas grimaced.

"On the contrary," he took another sip, and the woman silently appeared at his side and re-filled his glass. He nodded his thanks at her with a smile. "Mother and I like the girl greatly, she is not only lovely, she is clever, writes a very fair hand and is well versed in womanly duties. Who could ask for more? Indeed we found all her family most pleasing. The very best of country folk I think, fine, honest people, for we had the pleasure to stay with them for some days, a short while back."

It was as if a sigh swept through the room, and the three men actually smiled at him. The young one held up his glass and the woman went around re-filling them all.

"Well met then, Sir Thomas, well said too. For we are Clarissa's uncles," and, interrupted the young man, "I am Clarissa's younger brother. We," he pointed to the older men, "are as they, twins. Your nephew is sailing with my brother John. Lina is our niece and great-niece!"

Thomas looked at them astonished, almost lost for words. He glanced at the overmantle tapestry and they laughed again.

"Oh yes, those boring old tapestries," said John, the young one, "made by our grandmother Jessica. They are everywhere. Every member of our large family has one or two pieces. Although I am told that she was a fine embroiderer, she only created one pattern," he lifted his shoulders in amusement. Then serious, he lent forward.

"Do not fear for your nephew, Sir Thomas. He is in good hands. See," he held his glass towards his uncles, "they survived through good seamanship, and we have learnt everything we know from them. He will be kept safe with Captain John, and at next summer's end, shall be home, safe and sound."

Then, very seriously Thomas added, "When I hope we can arrange a marriage between our young people, unless they, themselves, have altered their minds."

It was a delight being with such warm hearted men. It was as if the sun shone after storm, the sudden change in them. Thomas could not believe the coincidence, but was assured that the Duke had always used their ships, whose timbers originated from forests where Clarissa's family came from.

Instead of leaving immediately, he told his man to take the boat and return to the castle to inform the Lady Karina, all the good news, that he would be back soon, and to rest easy. Then he went with his new found friends to a good fish tavern along the quay, and enjoyed himself better than he had in years.

They would not have him leave that night, so he took the absent John's bunk, in the tall house, and slept soundly, till the seagulls woke him early in the morning.

It had rained hard overnight and Thomas stole out, to walk along the quay, fascinated by the craft which lay, tied up there. The cobbles shone, wet and clean, and just a few cats slunk about, hunting for scraps by the fishermen's nets.

"If you will be going to Byford Hall any time soon," an uncle said, now bright eyed and warm, "perhaps you will take some things to them from us. For we always sent our nieces special gifts from over the seas, and now the boys do just the same for their sisters and neices."

They walked along through narrow, cobbled streets, the gulls screaming overhead, till they came to a warehouse. A great basket hamper was brought up, and going to and fro, ordering the warehouse men to this and that, it was soon filled, straw stuffing causing the contents to be safe.

"Clary will know how to divide it," her uncle said surely. "She was always the sensible one." Thomas sucked in his breath then found himself glowing with pleasure at the kind words.

"Tell me," he hesitated, "did you ever give her a beautiful, bright, silken robe?"

They looked at each other, the old men frowning. Muttering to each other for some moments, their faces suddenly cleared.

"With flowers, and birds you mean?" Thomas nodded, and they looked at him astonished. How strange that he should have seen Clary in that, which was hardly decent.

They put him on one of their small boats to take him home, with honest invitations to visit them again, whenever he could. Young James helped him down and clapped him on the back. Thomas left feeling unusually happy, with so much really interesting to tell his mother. His mind was eased too, for now he felt that Richard would surely be well cared for in the hands of these excellent men.

Suddenly feeling younger than their years, the two old men returned to their house, and sat by the hearth, as usual facing each other, but smiling.

The river was running strongly, and they tacked and rowed, until they came to narrow waters and the tow path. There they stopped and harnessed up two great horses, so slowly made their way upstream. When they reached the town, Thomas looked uncertainly at the hamper sent for Clary. Suddenly changing his mind, he told them to pull in and beckoned to a boy who sat with a poor fishing stick.

"Go up to the castle, lad, and tell the Lady Karina that all is well and that Sir Thomas is going to Byford Hall, up river. Tell her that I shall be home tomorrow," and threw him a coin. They drew away, and Thomas watched as the boy stood, his mouth hanging open, and waved his hand at him, shouting, "Go, go!"

As they approached the hall, he thought he could see all the family working out on the water meadows. There was a team of oxen pulling the plough through the thick, black earth, and the girls, their head cloths fluttering, were busy alongside.

He found Jessie and grandmother Moya in the hall, folding linen. Old Lucas sat, head on his chest, by the hearth. Bowing to them all, Thomas took Moya's hand and kissed it. The boatmen came in with the hamper and set it down while Thomas explained that it was from their kinsmen at the port.

"She's in her still room," said Moya quietly, without being asked. He flashed a quick smile at her and she thought again, what a handsome man he was.

Turning to Jessie, he asked if she could give the boatmen some food, for it had been an early start and was cold on the river. Then, he strode off surely, and made his way to Clary's room.

Carefully turning the pages of Lee's herbal, Clary was frowning. Grandfather Lucas was ill and in pain, and it seemed his heart would not stop beating. So he lived on, miserable, and she could do nothing for him. She raised her head at the knock on the door. "Come." she said.

Thomas went in and stood staring at her. Surprised to see him, Clary rose, and he came slowly to stand by her. The scent of her in this room, with its herbs and flowers was intoxicating. First he reached for her hands, and kissed them, his heart beating fast and his breath coming in little gasps. Then, he drew her into his arms and said simply,

"I love you, Clarissa. I do believe that I have always loved you."

Now it was her turn to gasp, and as she tried to pull away, he held her fast.

"What, will you deny me then mistress?" he bent and smiling, peered into her eyes. "Do I not appeal to you? Must I go away, as has my nephew Richard, who loves your daughter?" He held her fast, so she stopped resisting and leaned into his jerkin.

Then, unbidden tears began to fall from her eyes, and she felt as if her heart would burst. Startled, Thomas, lifted her chin and kissed the salt tears away, and lifting her up, carried her to the window seat. How long they sat there they knew not, but he gentled her in his arms as a child, and kissed her with passion as a women. Her cheek, her brow, her neck, her mouth, all the while murmuring sweet words of love. She in turn smiled, wetly, and it seemed the most natural and beautiful thing to do, to reach up and return his kisses.

Serious suddenly, still holding her, he told her of the recent events which had torn at their lives. Of how, unbeknown to his mother and himself, Richard had gone away, but, having met her very own kinfolk at the port, he was certain he would be home again safe in the year or so.

Then it was her turn to tell him of how in the middle of the night, Richard had appeared, having told the boat to come up-stream first, before taking him to the port. How he had asked her, and her sons, for Lina's hand.

"Then," she smiled tremulously up at him. "They sat in the arbour, where he gave her his ring, and they talked, with a warm cover over them till early light, my boys sitting guard." She actually laughed then, burying her face in his damp jerkin. "As if Richard would take liberties with Lina, who he loves."

Amazed, delighted, Thomas gave a great laugh and held her unbearably tight.

"Oh excellent boy," he kissed her fiercely. "Oh well done, Richard!" So they smiled at each other, love radiating from all about them.

Putting her down, absently straightening her robe and apron, he looked at her once more, seriously, deeply loving.

"Will you take me to your husband, Clarissa?"

With the softest smile, her eyes locked to his she replied, "I will."

So they kissed again and somehow back on the window seat, holding hands they talked as lovers do, about this and that and nothing much at all. Such speed, such sure knowledge of their mutual love, a miracle.

"Will your mother mind?" asked Clary, a tiny frown between her eyes. He laughed, a great shout of joy.

"Never! You don't know my mother, mistress, for she is a scheming, designing woman. Why do you suppose that she brought us here to stay with you? She thought that I didn't see her observing you, or me. I saw her! No," serious again, "although she tried over the years to wed me, this time she did it so cleverly, I know, she will be wondrously joyful." Twisting off his one, little finger ring, he took Clary's hand and finding it only fitted her middle finger, pressed it on. Kissing it, looking deep into her eyes, he made her his promise.

"I will wed you as soon as I can. I will love you to my dying day. Will you accept me, my lady, as your husband?"

This time really smiling, Clary reached up to him, kissing him roundly so he lifted her up and whirled her round about. "Well, say it, woman, tell me!"

"I will, Thomas my love, I very happily will."

They went to the hall then, and seeing them, Moya began to weep, clasping their hands, reaching up to kiss them both while Jessie stood dumb founded, not understanding.

A horn sounded, and they turned their heads towards the river. Another boat hove to. It was unusual for two to come up their little stream so soon after each other. A man came in, his eyes anxious, looking about. Then seeing Thomas he strode towards him swiftly and went down on one knee. Recognising him as the castle's head boatman, a fellow who he had gone fishing with many times when they were both striplings, Thomas leaned forward to hold his shoulder.

"What is it Mathew, what is the trouble?"

Taking his lord's hand, his face working, words struggling to come from his quivering mouth he finally said,

"Sire, I bring you grievous bad news. The lady, your mother, the Lady Karina, is dead."

CHAPTER THIRTY SEVEN

KAREN

It was cold in the garden room, for no one had lit a fire there for some days, since the funeral in fact. Now it crackled softly with the logs Karen had just set a light to, it would warm up soon.

Karen sat at the loom, and gazed unseeing, through tear filled eyes at the cloth which her grandmother had been working at. Strange how she had continued her own ways, disregarding title and wealth. She lifted off the cover and saw the deep, deep green cloth, and the basket of wools lay beside her, great hanks of it, and the rod bobbins ready to weave. It was too much to bear, that this piece of cloth, where her hands had lovingly worked, should now lay unfinished. So Karen blew her nose noisily on her apron and picked up a rod. It was going to be hard without Karina, the queen pin of their lives. And she, Karen, the odd one out, who she secretly hoped her grandmother had loved best of all, would no longer have anyone to care for and love. Why, oh why had she left her that night and gone to see her parents? Perhaps if she hadn't, she would not have gone raging to Rupert, and died. Feeling with her feet for the pedals, she inserted the rod, shoved it through and began work.

Rupert stood, breathless at the top of the stairs and listened. Surely he was hearing things, for mother was dead, yet he could hear her loom clacking and thumping from within the garden room. Then, peering through the mottled window panes he saw his niece, Karen, and his heart eased. Taking a breath, he went in, and touched her shoulder.

"Well, my dear. So here we are, those who loved her, searching for her where she would be." Her sob brought a constriction to his throat, so he gently held her, smoothing her head. "Do not weep, sweet Karen. She was an old lady, as you well know, having had a long and eventful life, which few of us could imagine. But you are right to finish her work. It was for you, you know." It was a lie, on the moment, for he really did not know for whom she was weaving this length of cloth. "She told me so." But in his head he thought that he heard Karina saluting him, for once saying the right thing. "You are right to finish it, and to keep her room warm."

He looked about it, the familiarity from his earliest childhood. Happiness, security, beauty, it held all those things for him. Here she had raised them, away from the pomp and draughts of the castle. Again he felt a constriction and tried to control it. Now, even if a little late, he would be the son she had always wanted him to be.

"I do not doubt," he had sat down in his usual chair, "when Richard weds, his lady will also love this place, the garden, the views and this comfortable, homely room. So Karen dear," they exchanged weak smiles, "keep it lived in for the moment. It wouldn't do to let it fall into disuse and decay."

Thomas poked his head around the door, entered and he in turn, sat on his usual chair. It had just happened like that, Margaret had one too.

"So here we are," he said quietly, "trying to find some trace of her." Then turning to his niece he said, "what will you do now, Karen? For you were her right hand in all things, and will be lost for awhile."

Karen looked gratefully at her uncle. She had always liked him better than Rupert, but then they were true kin. It had come about so slowly, her assisting her grandmother, more and more until she was her unofficial, personal maid. Karina had taken the quiet, awkward child into her care very early, for Margaret had not understood her at all, and had looked at her darkish skin, her green eyes and her red/black hair and wondered where she had come from.

"She is like my family," had said Karina. "It is from my blood she gets her colouring, she has nothing of dear Tom, like the rest of you."

Karen had liked her life in the castle. It was more ordered than in her home with its lively comings and goings, where everything it seemed, centred about horses. Not that she didn't like horses, she did, but not being dung smelling for the most part of the day.

"That is good you are completing her piece," Thomas nodded towards the loom. "She'd have been pleased." They sat in silence for a while, just listening to the regular working of the loom. "When you have completed it, and when the days of mourning are over, perhaps you would like to come with me to the Byfords again?"

Now she did really smile and nodded. More than anything she would like that, for her days there had been such a joy to her, and for once she had not felt odd. Apart from just liking the happy place, she had felt a strange, new warmth towards James, the eldest son, who, despite his eye, was a fine man.

Turning to his brother, Thomas said, "Will you come down to the solar with me Rupert, for there are some matters we must attend to."

Once there, Rupert tried not to look at the place where Karina had sunk to her death. Noticing it, Thomas felt a sympathy, something which he had, unexpectedly over these last days. His brother really seemed more quiet and serious, long may it last, he thought. He held out some papers.

"These have just come from the Woodmen captains, at the port. They sent our letters, and expect a reply in a month or so. They say that their ships make a habit of meeting up if at all possible, but they have an agent in each port, where letters are left and passed on."

Rupert was pleased. At least they would have some communication with Richard, if not too regularly. "Good, good," he said.

"Now to another matter Rupert. A delicate one, which I hope, you being closer to Jasper than I am, you will aid me in." Thomas paced the room, his mind flitting to the Byford Hall, Clary, Lina, and the mysteries which surrounded them. "I should like you to invite Jasper to stay with us for awhile, then take him to see the Byfords. He must meet Richard's maid, so that he sees that she is quite suitable for him. Mother was quite right you know, Rupert. We need good breeding women for a change. Our family history with child bearing wives has been sorely lacking. All we have had is only sons, one after the other." Rupert tried to interrupt, but Thomas waved him silent. "Yes I know I would be your second heir if anything happened to Richard. But, I am not wed, and am perhaps too old to father a family. I do not know." The pity was, he thought to himself yet again, that Rupert's wife had not been robust, and then with Richard, the only survivor, being at sea, maybe dying, drowning, being beset by pirates, taking ill, God forbid. "So let us introduce Jasper to Lina, and I vouch that he will be so charmed by her, he won't take exception. And by the way, all this business of our being too closely related is nonsense. The duchess wants her only daughter nearby. That is the crux of the matter."

He stood up and went across to where he knew his mother had died.

"Also, perhaps it would be fitting, for the sake of history, to have a good stone plaque made to set here, what do you think?" He shifted the strewings with his toe. "A memorial to mother. Something like,

In the year of our Lord, and so on, in the reign of our liege lord King Henry, on this spot died Karina, wife of Lord Robert Highclere, a true lady."

Thomas watched as the tears came from Rupert's eyes so he put his arm around his brother's shoulder.

"Now cease your tears, Rupert. It is over, done, she is gone, she was a very old lady, having had a most eventful life. Can you imagine how she would like to see you so distressed, and, how she would scold you now for your nonsense?"

But it was a little too close to the truth, for her scolding had killed her, and Rupert gave a great sob.

He had dreaded Thomas coming home. He had drunk and wept himself into a state of exhaustion, and yes fear. For his brother had every right to rage and accuse him of her death. But Thomas had yet again surprised him, taken him in his arms and comforted him, as if he were the younger brother. Now, now he would show him that he really was a true knight. If Richard came home still wanting to marry the Byford girl, he would bless them, and meanwhile he would invite Jasper, because Thomas wanted it.

"Then we also have the matter of Karen." Thomas went on quietly. "We both know that she was as good as mother's personal maid, attending to her with care and consideration let alone love. We have to look after her, for she is grieving, as we are. I know that mother was scrupulous in filling Karen's dower chest, practically and with gold and that Margaret still has the task of sharing out mother's jewels between all the girls."

He sighed deeply, lovelorn for Clary, missing being able to tell his mother of their glorious new love. But Mother knew, he was sure of that, wherever she was. Now it was the question of making order in the aftermath of her death. Strange that even guessing her age, they had never anticipated it.

"I propose that we ask Mistress Byford to take Karen into her household, for awhile at least. There are two, very elderly people there requiring constant care, and Karen has a gift for caring. Right now she needs to be needed, so what do you say?"

They agreed to put it to the Byfords first, while Karen completed her weaving, and her sorrow lessened. Margaret was relieved, for Karen had always been a difficult child, over conscious of her light, peach coloured skin and dark hair, afraid that she was odd amongst all her very fair siblings.

Clary read the letter pleased, and understood that by their having Karen, so much would be easier, certainly, her life with the old ones. It was so thoughtful for everyone, Karen's being of use and happy amongst her new friends. Not least, for Thomas and herself, a contact, a reason for being in touch. For it had been a bitter blow seeing his shocked face on hearing of his mother's death and his immediate departure. Yet his letters came every week, loving, caring, lifting her spirits and making her feel young again.

The Duke was away at court, so the brothers let their plans idle, while winter closed in on them, and the wind blew fiercely while they worried about Richard, the first Christmas without him and Karina.

"Let us ask Mistress Byford if we may visit them over Christ's Mass, Rupert. We can take Karen with us, settle her in and be back before new year to feast our people. Yes I know they will not expect much, after mother's death, but we have a duty to them, for so many will be missing her and her generosity at this time."

With the wind behind them they made good time. The castle barge was towed by one of the usual great horses, and they sat, well wrapped in their cloaks, gazing at the passing winter-bleached country, eyes alight.

If anyone noticed their love, Clary and Thomas did not care. For at every opportunity they were together. In the hall, the still room, the garden, or even walking to Marsh Newton they stayed as close to each other as they could. The family took it in turns to spend some of the Twelve days at the inn, there to be merry with the Innmans.

James had created a light sledge for the horses to draw up to the church, for the old people could no longer walk, yet still wanted to attend mass. Rupert was his old cheerful self, and, as Thomas had been, was much impressed with the order of the place. In the evenings he played chess with who ever would play with him, and took to drinking with Luke and Jessie. Of course, they were all secretly so proud to have their lord staying in their house, and each one did their best to make it agreeable.

The night before Christmas, they held a feast, and Felicia and Robin came, so the farm was truly filled with friends and family, Rupert pleased to meet the younger brother of his sea captain friends. The girls collected ivy and fir branches from the wood, and draped it over the beams and about the two hearths. A lump of lime was ground up and soaked and splashes of white wash were laid on the green, "as snow" said the girls. For as yet, and thanks be to God, there was none. The boys lined up to be tidied, and Clary took out her sharpest scissors to trim their hair and beards, and their finger nails.

"You have lime wash on your hair," said Clary, as she clipped at James' head, to make him neat for the holy day.

"It is not lime-wash, mother dear," James replied cheerfully, "it is white hair!"

Clary bent to see more clearly.

"Who told you that?" Surprised, for she still thought of James as a boy.

"Carola, of course," James smiled quietly, "who else, the little dear." They laughed, for yes, Carola, Jessie's last daughter, was the forthright one, whose innocence could never hurt.

They cleared the hall, sweeping the rushes to one side, setting the boards and trestles against the wall, so that there would be room for dancing. On either side of the hearths the old people blinked and clapped their hands, and golden cider was poured out, to quench thirsts. Felicia sat beside Moya, marvelling at how her children loved to dance, forcing the men up, cajoling and bullying the unwilling, for they were, even with the two barge men, as always, out numbered. For Karen, all this was new, and she glowed with delight.

"Forward, three, four, turn and curtsy, back and three four, round you go." They pushed and pulled the newcomers who soon learned it, while Robin, the call master, tapped at a copper cooking pot while the pipes played. "Sideways, three four, turn and curtsy, take his hands and move along. Forward, three, four, turn and curtsy, back and three, four, round you go."

The dance, having begun slowly, gathered speed till the second "round you go" became a great lift, the men swinging their partners, up and around. Cheerfully shoving Lucius out of the way, Thomas took a hold of Clary's waist and threw her up in the air, so they all tried to do the same till eventually exhausted, they fell laughing onto stools and benches, happy and warm from the dance. Watching James whenever she could, Karen felt an excitement flicker in her breast.

They went up to the little church on Christmas morning, with Moya, old Luke and the children on the sled, well covered with sheepskins. Father Benjamin now lived there, in a tiny shippon with a single glass pane in the small window, so the sun shine in, from the south side. From there he could see the wondrous view, erect a pennant if in need, and relish his privacy. Clary had given him Master Green's eye glass, and Moya had lent him all the books from the manor. Once a week, the family went up for a mass, taking his provisions and his laundry. The rest of the time he communed with God and nature.

The boys had gone on ahead on Christmas morn and lit charcoal braziers, helping Father Benjamin make ready for the holy day. Jasper was shown the carved stones from the well and the old ruin which they had used to build their little church. He could not remember enjoying himself so much in years and with the good, country fare, the organized running of the place, he was greatly impressed. Pleased that Karen was remaining, he noted with his new found awareness that she often looked at James Byford and sought to please him with her ready help.

After the mass, they closed the church, and took Father Benjamin down to the hall, for Felicia firmly told him that it would be too cold for him to stay up there all winter, and she feared that snow was on the way. Going down was much easier with the elders and the twins on the sledge too, and they all sang, looking down across to the darkening river and water meadows.

The pain of their impending parting was deep. When Clary and Thomas took Moya to the still room, of course she chose to slip into her bed with her hot stone and close the door so that her precious Clary could have some last, sweet moments with her love.

"It may be some weeks till I come again," Thomas held her close. "But I shall think of you, every hour of every day, and wait for your thoughts to reach me."

The sky was heavy and low when they left the next day, and apart from Clary, everyone was glad to run inside to huddle by the fires the moment the barge drew away. Standing alone on the bridge, Clary raised her hand, and Rupert and Thomas waved back till around the bend. If Rupert wondered about his brother and Mistress Byford, he said nothing.

It snowed that night and for two more days, and at the beginning the children enjoyed the novelty of it. Then, it became bitterly cold so that walking in the yards was treacherous so they scattered ashes and sawdust on the paths, and clung to each other for support. Cold hands and toes became chapped, and Clary offered around salve made from the best clarified pig fat, simmered down with calendula, or crushed onions, in a mortar to smear on to chilblains. The one good thing about milking the sheep was holding their small, warm udders.

They all slept in the hall and side bed chambers now, for with the two hearths burning day and night, they were the only warm places. As soon as it was dark and the milking was done, they all went to their beds or pallets, rolled up in their covers, and tried to sleep. It was James who went about shutting doors tightly, often with a second plank along the bottom to prevent the snow from drifting it, for the wind had got up again, and he thought from the sudden mildness of the air that it was snowing again.

Did he hear a cry? James, frowned into his cover, and drew it up closer. Yet it went on, with a scratching at the door, a mite louder than the wind. Knowing that he would never sleep with the worrying of it, he rose, dragged his cover about himself tightly and went to the door. Opening it a fraction, a nose appeared and pushed it open enough for a large dog to come in.

With a sigh, James recognized the dog as belonging to a pedlar, and he didn't much care for pedlars. They all wore the cruel, spiked iron collars, hence were never beaten by opponents. It limped across to a hearth and collapsed with a great sigh. If there was a dog about, thought James, then where was its owner? James resigned himself, so shoved the poker into the fire before going to the dairy to fetch a dish of milk. With a hiss, the poker warmed the milk and James nudged the poor brute to drink it. With the unexpected warmth in its belly, it looked around dazed, then ran to the door and whined.

James opened the door a crack, but it would not go. The hall was so dim, with just the firelight, he could not even see its eyes, just that it was all wet from melted snow. Groaning inwardly, James found his boots, put on all his clothes and borrowed Lucius heavy cloak which was nearest on the rack, took up a strong crook and lit a sound horn lantern and slipped out with the dog.

With new strength, the dog raced ahead, then ran back, and led the way. It was so dark, despite the snow, and James stumbled and fell, totally disorientated, snow swirling wetly about him, but understood that the dog was waiting for him.

Damned be all pedlars, he thought, falling again. The wind was fierce and little icy flakes sliced his face. Then the dog began to bark and James was astonished to bump into a shaggy, wet pony.

"Alright, dog," James cursed under his breath, "so where's the pedlar?" The dog went on barking, digging, snuffing, so at last James got down on his knees and reached into a ditch till he touched cloth. Pulling with all his might, he drew out a body covered with snow, and throwing it over his shoulder, held on to the pony for support and turned for home. At last they got to the barn where he laid the body on the straw, took the load off the pony and led him to a manger, where he hoped there was a little hay. At least it was fairly warm and sheltered in there with the other beasts, better than outside.

Sternly, he told the dog to stay there, and was surprised that it seemed to understand him. Lifting the body, he then made his way unerringly back to the hall. More than anything he wanted to call Clary, for when he had taken off the sodden, snow encrusted cloak, there lay a mere boy, light as a feather and well nigh dead.

Rubbing the wet head, removing the clogs, he finally got the boy down to his damp brais and shirt and hauling him onto his pallet, held him close with the covers tight about to keep them warm.

"Well, what ever next." Clary stood over him, and with a start James realized that he had overslept, for there was just a hint of morning in the hall. He scrambled up and threw the covers back over the boy before pulling on his breeks and jerkin which were still wet. Clary pursed her mouth, looking severely at him. "Well, where did this one come from?"

When he went out to the barn to start feeding the animals, the new pony looked at him with a bright and expectant eye, and the dog dragged itself from out of under the manger and vaguely wagged its tail at him.

By the time he had done his work, Lucius and Stephen with him but all cold and speechless, it was daylight and the girls were milking the sheep.

Clary and Jessie were hanging over James' pallet, looking at the newcomer.

"Well, it lives," said Jessie sourly, "another mouth to feed I suppose." Clary stroked the boy's head and felt it was raging hot, a winter fever or a contagion? Then she lifted and a lid and a dark brown eye flickered at her.

It was like having an infant again. They spooned first, borridge tea into his mouth, which he accepted, not as was usual, fighting the strange taste. He took milk and honey, just the same. Rowena, Karen and Clary carried the pallet near to the fire, and began undressing the limp boy. He made no objection, no sound while they pealed off filthy, wet and verminous rags, throwing them into the fire.

"Perhaps we'd better cut his hair right off too," Clary said, remembering when Deborah had shaved her head. "I know it is cold, but I shall find a warm hat for him. I think that after all, a bath is needed." A tub was brought in and water heated while they cut his hair, having him closely wrapped in a cover against the cold. Then, as they stripped him off, they found that he was a she.

Clary sat down suddenly on a stool by the bath. "Oh sweet Jesus, it's a poor little maid."

So they put the clothes maiden around draped with covers and bathed the poor thing, who neither looked at them or spoke, but at least and at last she was clean, shaved and warm. "Rowena, Karen, will you have her in your bed, dears? I cannot have her sleeping like this in the hall, it isn't right." So she was carried away and put to bed with hot stones at her feet, where she slept, and slept.

The snow was coming down fast and Luke looked out, dubious about taking the animals out. James agreed with him, no point in their getting frozen for nothing to eat. So with worried eyes they tossed down more hay from the loft, hoping that it would last till the spring.

Later, they would say it was the worst winter they could remember, for everything that could go wrong, did. The weight of snow on the barn roof caused it to yaw and groan, and Stephen, the lightest, had to climb up to shovel it off.

Despite the extra care from Karen, Grandfather Lucas suddenly took it into his head to go outside. Slipping out, when the women were busy, and by the time they found him he was dead, sitting apparently sleeping on the log bench along the river path.

"Where did he think he was going," wept Clary, aware that with the newcomer, they might have neglected him. Moya said nothing, just sitting, huddled in front of the fire. "It's all the fault of that new boy James brought in," Jessie wailed, "if you hadn't been fussing over him, you'd have seen grandfather going out." No one replied.

Father Benjamin spoke his prayers over Lucas while the boys made a box from the left over elm planks. He would have to lie somewhere cold until they could get him up to the church.

James remembered what grandfather had told him, and went to the corner of the barn where the bee skeps were stored over winter.

"Your master is dead good bees, so now, I am your master."

Then Luke cut himself with a rusty knife and did not come in to have it cleansed and in three days he was dead too.

The lamentations were terrible, with Jessie putting the blame on James and the stranger, which they now all understood was a girl.

"Stop it, stop it," Clary was near tears. "It had nothing to do with the child. Father went out because he knew it was time. Luke died because he did not come to me to have his wound washed and treated. The girl lies near death too, and you put the blame on James, without whom Lina and I might well be dead also." Then she burst into tears, for it was all too much, this dreadful long winter without Thomas near or even word from him for weeks.

The three boys and Father Benjamin took the two bodies on the sled drawn by the oxen and buried them together in a temporary, shallow grave, for the ground was rock hard. It was too cold and too far, for the girls to go. The men came back silent and exhausted, and after their pottage, went straight to bed.

Everyone felt cold and ill, and now Clary feared for Moya who said barely a word. Every task seemed too much, the milking and the cheese making, feeding and mucking out the beasts. The flour ran out, so, unable to take a sack of wheat to the miller, they got out the quern and at least kept warm taking it in turns grinding the grain, making the flour, oh so slowly.

Shivering in her still room, for she refused a brazier on the principle they might run out of fuel, Clary crushed rose hips in her mortar and made teas, sweetened with honey to give cheer.

It was so unlike all the lovely, golden girls to be so wretched, so Father Benjamin taught them some holy plays, and at last they began to take an interest in something other than their own little woes.

Then a horn sounded on the river, and it was the castle barge with Rupert, all bundled up in furs, bringing food and cheer and letters for Lina from Richard, and for Clary from Thomas. Forgetting their red noses and chapped lips, they welcomed him royally. When Rupert asked Karen if she wished to come home, she quietly declined, saying that she was most happy to stay.

Spring came slowly that year, and they heard that the floods had receded, leaving Marsh Newton stranded, on an oxbow lake, for the river had changed course again, so now the town had lost its water way. For the moment, the town officers had no plans, perhaps they were too shocked, or hoping for a miracle.

Then Clary took James to one side and told him that he must take the poor, strange little lass outside in the sun, and he must make her speak, and be normal. For at first they had thought by her small size she was a girl, but now realized she was a full grown woman. Not that she had been any trouble, she just lay silently. She ate what they gave her, used the piss pot or the privy which they led her to each day, and then she slept again.

James lifted her up in his strong arms, and as a feather, she settled in them, with no objection. Every day she sat in a corner out of wind and if there was sunshine, she sat, with the big dog by her, both non complaining, gazing out across the river to the water meadows. It took some time, but eventually her spirits and reason returned. Clary had cut down old dresses to clothe her, combed her short hair and put a pretty cloth on her head, so she looked so sweet, with all the girls taking it in turns to sit by her, singing, holding her hand and chattering. Karen, feeling some kinship, especially cared for the little stranger, with her dark skin, and lovely eyes.

Eventually, James, squatting beside her, asked her name. She gazed at him, brown eyes in a brown, pixie face, really looking at him, gone the vague, far away look.

"I am Hannah," she said clearly.

James started and he felt his heart quicken.

"And little Hannah, do you remember the name of your father and mother?"

She frowned, just a little, then smiled.

"Da is called Han." She said, the smile wide on her face.

"And your ma was called Gilly Flower." He watched the myriad emotions on the small face before him. She nodded.

"Then we are old, old friends, Hannah girl, for I knew you when I was a little lad, and you were a new born babe. My name was Odi then, from Odin, for I had a great, ugly eye, now gone, thanks to the horn of a silly heifer."

With a delicate hand she lifted his hair which was licked over the silk eye patch Clary always made for him and nodded.

"My foster mother, Annie, gave you a gold coin when you were a babe, your parents were so pleased. Your da was always a very good friend to us, the best." He stopped, remembering, then clearing his throat, coughed as an owl.

So it all came out, there in the lee of the wind, in a nook of the stone bridge, on a sunny spring morning. Hannah told him of her adventures, and finally that it was she who had taken him out of the prison, and paid, with that same gold coin. It was as if they could not smile wider, their joy was incredible.

That evening by firelight in the hall, James and Hannah told their stories to the rapt attention of all the family. Now and again a question was asked, which between them, they answered. The soft lamentations of sorrow, in taken breaths, the light clapping of hands, the shouts of laughter filled the hall and as one, they voiced their gratitude to Hannah for so cleverly saving James.

"Was that how you came to be so sorely beaten, James my son?" asked Clary quietly that night, as she pressed her lips to his head. For well she remembered the poor wild boy of the woods who had saved them from deluge and swine, and his terrible wounds. James sat quietly for some moments.

"It was because of my father, Magnus, the weaver. He must have hired men to catch and beat me, have false accusations made against me and have me put into prison." Clary fought back her tears and held her first son, true, not of her body, but surely of her heart.

Hannah now came to life, searching out her lace making things from the goods taken from the back of the pony. So, she began to teach the girls, enthralled, excited by a new art, their quick minds and nimble fingers worked every spare hour there was. Meanwhile, Hannah found her old speedy rhythm and worked at her lace, while the girls were out in the fields planting, or milking. Even Jessica was impressed, peering at the delicate work, excited that her daughters were learning something new and beautiful and would now have plentiful lace on their garments. Without even being asked, she took out their store of fine linen threads and gave them around, and then sat with them companionably, spinning the flax to make more.

Only when it seemed that all the girls had each learnt a pattern, did Hannah confide in James, that she must leave. Horrified, he told her she must stay, join the family as had he, so many years before. But there seemed a new urgency about her, and her gaze would always stray downriver.

"I must go, Odi", she whispered, "I feel that da is in trouble and he needs me." And James looked at her helplessly wondering how, in that big wide world, she would ever find her da. Sadly, they all realized that they could hold her no longer.

To put aside their disappointment, the little ones began to groom the big dog. If it had been amazed, it sat, subdued and suffered their ministrations, never growling or snapping as they cut away tufts of clotted hair, or prized out burs, all the while crooning and caressing. Finally, combing it, they led it into the river, and Piers, having taken, without asking of course, a small wooden bowl of soft soap, they thoroughly washed the poor creature.

Proud of their handiwork on the dog, which true did look better and happier, they then turned their attention on to the pony, and started all over again, on a larger scale. Clary saw them first, and hid her smile, hoping that Jessie would remain indoors. Eventually, unaccustomed to the quiet, she did emerge and ready to remonstrate, was silenced by Clary who held her hand over her mouth and taking her sister's arm, turned her back into the hall.

"Let them be Jessie," she finally burst out laughing. "Never have I seen those two so busy and happy, oh the kind little dears, but they will miss Hannah."

James took a big horse while Hannah rode her pony, tail and mane trimmed, brushed and burnished, the baskets re-made and filled, secured on its back. The whole family stood and watched them go, and the little twins howled their sorrow till their sisters took them in, cleaned their noses and worked on finding amusement for them.

James booked into the inn below the town and leaving Hannah, went to make enquiries. With his usual handing out of coins, he learned that no Rom were in the keep, but was recommended to go on to the big town by the coast. After resting for the night, they set off and began enquiries again. This was all familiar territory to James, but he tried not to think of when Clary had been incarcerated in that huge and terrible keep. Once again leaving Hannah in an inn where their mounts were well stabled, James climbed up the steps to the keep, but instead of going to the gate, he wandered around, looking for slit windows.

Under each one, pushing through thorn bushes, he stood as high as he could on the rough boulders, determined to be heard. If anyone heard an owl cough, they must only have thought it odd in the light of day. Twice he went around, till, at last, he saw a hand waving from a slit, and what he thought might have been an owl's cough. So he made his way to the gate and passing coins, eventually found a man who told him that for sure, there were Rom inside. More money passed hands so he went to enquire if any Rom there was named Han.

Deborah was not to be found and as evening came, James grew desperate until one of her physician sons came, having heard he was there.

It was as usual, ghastly, stinking and filthy. David, Deborah's son led the way, surely, with authority, till they came to a cold, dark place where the pitiful remains of humanity lay prone, or dead or cringing. Once again James, coughed as an owl, and, after moments, one figure, dim in the horn lamp light, slowly crept towards them.

"Han?" James held the skeletal cold hand. "Han? Is that you, old friend? It is I, Odi." There was no reply, it did not speak, yet small sounds came from it, and James suddenly realized that Han was weeping. Taking off his cloak, he wrapped the bundle of bones carefully and lifted it up. "Thank you David," he said, "Can we go now, I will pay whatever is needed, just let us get out of this place."

David took them to his surgery where he undressed what had been Han, washed him and gave him weak chicken soup, and wrapping him warmly, then left him to sleep.

Back at the inn James demanded a bath and Hannah attended him, forgetting that he was a man and not her kin in her anxiety to hear what he knew.

"He is in poor health, Hannah, very poor health. We must find somewhere warm for you both to live till he is well again." Knowing full well that Han would never be well again.

It was David who organized a convent to take them, a small convent just outside town, who cared for the sick. Hannah went willingly and overjoyed to be with her father again, and didn't care that for the moment he did not know who she was.

Odi though, he did know, held his hand, tried to give thanks but though his voice could not for his weakness, his eyes said much.

James spoke to the sisters and showed them Hannah's lace work which they cried over in delight. So it was agreed they would keep the two of them, and Hannah would care for her father and make lace for them to sell in payment for their keep.Meanwhile, the kindly David, Deborah's son, would visit regularly.

It took a long time for James to tell the family about his latest experiences and because of the bad memories, he kept his story light, with a happy ending.

Han did know his daughter before he died, but warmly, in comfort, and they had time to speak quietly about Odi, what had happened to him, and of Hannah's life.

James did visit again, and before he left, Hannah begged him to take the pony and dog back to the hall.

"They will be happy there, Odi dear, there is work and feed for them, while here, I am not sure they re welcome." Then she smiled, "the little children will be so happy, won't they?" So James took them back and indeed it was the best for them all. Hannah stayed at the convent, which became famous for its delicate lace, and occasionally, James visited her, full of tales of the life at Byford Hall.

CHAPTER THIRTY EIGHT

DUKE JASPER

The duke felt tired, true, he was not young any more, but he suddenly felt the burdens of his life very heavy. Yet what burdens? Compared with the ordinary man, his life was unbelievably good. There was comparative peace in the land, not too high taxes or demands for expensive ships or men to sail them for the king.

His family life was calm, he was even a grandfather, his sons having married well and now were producing charming children. So there was no problem with the inheritance. His good wife was therefore content, except, now this was the trouble. Ursuline. At fifteen she was a balm to his eyes, like him, fair, like his sister, also Ursuline, unlike the boys with their dark handsome looks from their mother. At fifteen she should be betrothed at least. Yet both previous grooms, older men, it was true, had died. For her part, Ursuline seemed not to care, a gentle, happy girl, quite unlike her namesake who he remembered sadly, had always been, according to their nurse, a handful. His Ursuline, was happy to stay home with them, thanks be to God.

He had not thought of his sister for years, well, it was many years since she was lost to them, disappearing in the forests, typical.

It was the name, Lina, which had woken all his morbid thoughts, for of course that is what they had called his wayward, spoilt sister, Lina. Many years his junior, for other babes had died, they had all indulged her hopelessly, and her loss had been bitter, a mystery. He dwelt on the name, Lina, a common enough name, well, wasn't it?

He had planned for the pleasant Highclere boy, Richard, for his daughter's groom, but apparently he had already given his heart, silly pup.

Now Sir Thomas Highclere had come to see him, a good fellow, twice the man of his brother.

Thomas came in and bowed low. They made light conversation over glasses of good red wine, yet Thomas fidgeted till the duke called a page to summon his wife and daughter, who he knew, both liked this distant cousin. They spoke of this and that, the harvests, the state of the country, the usual, man talk. The rustling of skirts announced the arrival of the duchess and her daughter. Rising when they came in, Thomas bowed again.

"Your Grace, Lady Ursuline," he bowed and smiled at the ladies warmly, enquired after their health, the grandchildren. The lady took a chair near the window and brought out her sewing. Finally, niceties over, Thomas stilled his heart and spoke, smiling at the young lady. He must be careful, tactful. "Such a strange thing has come to pass, Lady Ursuline, for I have only ever heard your name in this house, yet now, not only have I met another Ursuline, she looks so very like you, well it seems as if you are sisters."

The duchess paused with her sewing and looked carefully at their guest.

Thomas went on, feeling strangely nervous.

"It is just such a coincidence that the two girls, your young lady, and Lina, the young girl I am recently acquainted with, Ursuline Byford, should look so a like. I thought that my memory was tricking me, but now I see it was not. They are, very, very a like."

The duke frowned and wondered what Thomas was talking about.

"You mean that the girl, Lina is also Ursuline? A most unusual name, for a yeoman's daughter." There was a silence, while both men watched the girl sit herself carefully on a stool near the fireplace.

Thomas coughed, he must find words to interest the duke and not irritate him so he would be dismissed. Knowing that somewhere along the blood lines they were kin was no reason to rub salt in the wounds of the duke, now not too pleased that the stubborn young Richard was apparently, showing another interest.

"This is what I thought, Sire," he was waved to a chair and gratefully took it. "When I received a letter from her, beautifully written I must say, most unusual, as you say, for a yeoman's daughter, signed Ursuline." He drew out the small roll of vellum and handed it to the duke, who then passed it to his wife and daughter.

"I was shocked. For although I was just a lad, I do remember your sister, sire, the child is so like her, fairest hair, bluest eyes and now I wonder, could there be some connection."

The duke frowned, gazing into the fire, what was the man talking about? Connection?

Thomas coughed again and hurried on.

"When I visited Byford Hall with Richard, this to give our thanks for their taking him in when his horse was lame, I was really surprised to see tapestries, denoting the arms of the family. Most interesting, extraordinary, beautifully worked, yet all the same, apparently done by a grandmother. Pomeroy, de Alencourt and even of apparently the first Lady Felicia de Alencourt who was a blood descendant of one of our kings, way back, of course. So," he ended rather lamely, "I wondered if there could be any connection, for yeomen they might be, but astonishing yeomen they certainly are, whose children read and write and", he paused for effect, "they speak French."

Now he had caught the attention of young Ursuline, who leant forward.

"Sir Thomas, is the other Lina really like me? With fair hair and blue eyes, what else can you tell me, for I'd love to meet her."

Thomas did his best, telling of how the Byford Lina had scolded Richard for taking his horse into the walled garden and sent him to the river gate. How she and her many girl cousins danced and sang and what a happy time they had during those few days. He did not of course mention that he had been several times since, careful not to mention his love, Clarissa. The duke was amused. So a yeoman's daughter had scolded his young relative, Richard Highclere, and sent him packing, well, that certainly sounded familiar. Not his gentle daughter, Ursuline, no, most unlike her, but his long lost sister certainly.

"I do not think we are related to the de Alencourts but perhaps to the Pomeroys," he frowned in thought, "but I will send for the secretary who has charge of all our family affairs, he might know."

Meanwhile, his daughter sat on the edge of her stool and smiled at Sir Thomas, who she had always thought so very nice, so distinguished looking, with such a kindly smile. When her parents had suggested his nephew, Richard to her, she hadn't been appalled, as she had been when they had proposed the two old men previously. Young and handsome, he had seemed a kindly young boy who was more like his uncle than his father.

"Sir Thomas," she gave him her most charming smile. "Do you think that I could meet with this other Ursuline? For I have few friends here, and it would be a joy to go into the country and meet happy young people."

The duchess looked sternly at her daughter, what was she talking about? Go into the country to meet yeomen farmers? Tugging at her needle, she spoke quietly in Spanish, to admonish her daughter.

Hearing and at least understanding the gist of what she said, the duke, ever indulgent of this, his last beloved child, disagreed with her.

"Madam", he turned his gaze unusually severely on his wife, "What harm would there be in letting her take some days away in the good country air, away from the stink of the town?"

Ursuline's eyes twinkled, for now she knew she would be going with Sir Thomas for her father's word was law. Careful not to upset her mother, she crossed to her father's chair.

"Oh father," she dimpled at him, "I really would like to go away, just for a few days, if," she turned to her mother, "mother will allow it, and Sir Thomas will safely accompany me."

So it was agreed, and Thomas assured the duchess that a maid would not be necessary as his niece, Karen, was at Byford Hall, and caring for the elderly Lady Moya de Alencourt so she would surely help their daughter with her dressing.

A horn sounded and a fine boat came into view. All the girls dropped their chores for, for sure, here was Sir Thomas again. Combing hair, straightening clothes, putting on clean aprons, for there was not the time to do more, they stood, fluttering their hands, at the river side, beaming at the travellers in welcome.

Then, almost as one, they stopped, for with him, sat a small figure, a girl, finely dressed, pretty, familiar. They moved back as they came up the steps and Ursuline, holding Sir Thomas' hand noticed the myriad colourful flowers growing in the wall.

For a moment, they were unusually silent, then all dipped low, and still slightly astonished, came forward as Sir Thomas introduced his companion.

"Lady Ursuline," he glanced around, then spotting Lina beckoned her closer.

"Let me present you with another Ursuline, such an unusual name, and I see that you truly do look a like." He watched closely as the two girls stared at each other, it was true, they were a like, except Lina was a fraction taller.

Lina dipped low as she had been taught, and surprisingly, Ursuline dipped in return. Then Lina smiled and put out her hand,

"Come, meet my cousins, although you'll never remember all their names."

They trouped into the hall where a flustered Clary had been tidying herself with Moya and Karen trying to assist her but being more nuisance than help. It was unusual for Thomas to just arrive, he usually sent word.

Having presented the visitor, the girls, as butterflies, rushed away, for there was a new calf born, and they wanted their guest to see it.

Clary stood quietly, shocked, for surely the Lady Ursuline did look strikingly like her Lina. She turned her eyes to Thomas, who seeing her distress, quickly took her hands and kissed them. Turning to Moya, he bowed,

"Lady Moya," he said, also kissing her hand. "Will you allow me to take Clary to the still room for quiet talk, and not allow the young to interrupt us?" Moya nodded, but as her sight was dim, she had not noticed the newcomer amongst the golden girls who had caused her dearling to suddenly go silent.

Seated by the window, he took her hands,

"What troubles you, my own?"

Clary sat, her eyes downcast, fearful that she would weep. But she must not. Perhaps it was the time to tell this lovely man her secret, then he would leave her, alone once more. Taking up his hand, she kissed it, and held it near her face.

"I would have told you one day," she said, "but it seems I must tell you now. I am fearful of your disapproval, for I love you greatly. But you surely must know that, now."

Still holding his hand she began to tell him, right from the beginning, of buying the goose and goslings, of being abducted, cruelly raped. Of being taken far, far away, the sheer horror and misery of it, then, finding that she was with child, not by Piers, her husband as she had hoped, but by Jasper. Now he started at the name, but she went on. How Jasper's mother had befriended her.

"His mother, the Lady Ursuline I do believe, told me of how, as a foolish young girl, she had escaped her escort and found herself in the hands of wild men of the hills, outlaws, robbers and horse thieves, and how she had thought it all good sport, believing that she would soon be found. But she was not, and finding herself with child, had tried to escape to run home for a wise woman to remove the child as she was to be married before long."

Clary sat silent for moments, remembering the poor, beautiful, maimed woman. Sighing deeply, she continued. "When she tried to run away," She stopped again, trying to be calm, "her man beat her savagely, breaking her jaw, so she had difficulty in speaking and eating, and her leg, all crooked, so she could not walk, or run away again. A great rough man he was, yet apparently, he loved her deeply." Again Clary paused, remembering. "We became friends, we spoke French together so that we had some privacy, I tried to ease her pain with herbs and tried to feed her nourishing foods. Then one day, after Lina was born, her image, who she adored, I wept, and confessed that I had a gentle husband and two lovely little sons. Dear lady, she was shocked, upset by my news, for having been wed by mother church, it was a sin, taking me and using me so roughly. There were many other women living in those caves, all stolen no doubt, but from poor, probably large families who wouldn't care too much if one girl was taken."

Thomas drew her head onto his shoulder and gently kissed her brow.

"The lady then told me I must leave, take Lina, give her a better life than this we suffered, waiting till the men were away, for Jasper, her only child, would surely do the same to me as his father had done to her, if he caught me. It was she who arranged my escape, knowing the ways of her men and the best route for me to run. Before I left, she gave a little spoon to the baby, which had been her own, loving her as she did."

Clary rose and went to a chest, and opening it found a silk cloth and brought it to Thomas. It was a horn spoon with a silver inset, the letter "U" inscribed on it which Thomas examined closely and nodded.

"Now I understand, my dearest mistress, yet I am deeply sad to hear of how both you and the Lady Ursuline suffered, but glad at least, that for awhile anyway, she had you for comfort."

Now she had begun, Clary felt she must go on with her tale, but thought it politic not to tell him too much of Master Green, just that she had helped him, gathering and selling herbs to the apothecaries, an old man with poor eyes, and that when he had drowned, she had taken his pony and having found James, they had all finally come safely home. Here, to find the tragic tale of how Piers had followed the thieves, only to receive an axe in his head.

They sat silently, holding each other, hearing each other's heartbeats till Clary felt calm again, hugely relieved having told him.

"May I tell the duke, my love?" he asked softly, "for he grieves still for his sister I know. And may I show him Lina's spoon, which he might recognize?"

"If you tell him Thomas, he will know that my beautiful Lina is baseborn, albeit grand daughter of his sister, and this secret which has lain heavily in my heart for so long, will be public."

Thomas thought for awhile. She was right, but somehow he must tell the duke, and have him accept Lina as his great niece, child of Jasper, his namesake.

"Will you trust me, my angel? Will you let me do it my way, for I see your lovely daughter is of his family, just look at those two, as twins, with their almost white hair and bluest eyes."

Again they sat quietly until Thomas jumped up. "Let us go to the little church to speak with Father Benjamin, he will advise us." So kissing her roundly he pulled her hands and they returned to the hall.

But they didn't go up to the church that day, or the next, because Thomas took Lina and her brothers to the side and told them he wished to marry their mother and wished them to stay but preferred it if the other young ones could be sent off somewhere.

It was Lina who decided they must all go to the marsh tower to see the grandparents, so amid huge excitement, two flats were loaded up with provisions. James even killed a fat lamb and sent off three quarters of it and a whole side of pork because Felicia and Robin now lived very quiet lives and would not be expecting such a crowd of visitors. Jessica fussed over her twins, really Piers naturally, Carola was expendable, but was firmly put down by all her daughters. Of course they must go too.

Showing proper reluctance, Lina said she must stay behind to help so even Karen went, happy to have time away from her duties. Ursuline hadn't remembered ever being so joyful, such excitement, so much laughter. Off they went in the early morning with John Smith taking the head of the lead horse, and Maria in the second flat with her baby boy well bundled up, happy to be soon showing him to her parents.

The mist was thick, damp and mysterious but they had wrapped up well, feeling very brave and adventurous. Soon the sun came out which warmed them and they watched the land slowly pass by, the water birds silently fishing and the fish jumping.

Next day, Moya and Jessie put on their finest clothes, much to Clary's surprise and asked James to saddle up the pony to draw the sledge for them.

"Come mother," Lina steered her mother to her own room where she did her herbal work. "You too must dress finely, your blue I think, and so will I. It is a fine day and Sir Thomas is here, why not?"

It was a fine day and after the three boys had barred all the doors and gates, they set off up the hill towards the little church. Lina ran on ahead to warn Father Benjamin, carrying his laundry for he must be clean for the occasion. Meanwhile, Clary walked up on the arm of Sir Thomas, who had been quietly told to dawdle. She laughed afterwards when she thought about it, so much quiet planning and she hadn't guessed a thing.

Father Benjamin met them in the porch of his little church, his face washed by the busy Lina, and a fresh robe on for the occasion. Only then did Clary understand what it was all about and taking Thomas hand, she smiled radiantly during their short marriage ceremony.

After the mass, they went outside into the sunlight and Lina did a strange thing. Approaching Sir Thomas, she curtseyed low and said simply,

"Father."

James, albeit surprised, followed her till all three boys had bowed to their mother's new husband. Thomas felt a great happiness and held them all in his strong arms, tears trying to blush from his eyes. Clary too, amazed, touched, joined the circle so that standing a little way back, the priest, Jessica and Moya, gazed joyful and incredulous.

"Thank you for witnessing our marriage," Thomas kissed the hands of Moya, Jessie and Lina. "But now I ask you to keep it secret for just a little while, until the time is right to tell the world of our great good fortune. I will explain to you why, then, for now, I just thank you for taking me into your family."

To Clary's surprise, Jessica was to make her wedding night perfect. Fat, even somewhat lame from her weight, none the less, Jessie ran and made preparations. She put a small brazier with charcoal to burn in Clary's chamber to warm it, wine and oatcakes, fruit and walnuts. She prepared fresh linen on the big bed, and sprinkled lavender under the plumped up mattress.

Only then did she return to the hall and happily helped prepare a little feast of roasted lamb cutlets, parsnips, fresh bread rolls and soft cheese.

Lina and her brothers refrained from escorting their mother to her bridal chamber as was usually the custom. Instead, they kissed and withdrew, so Clary and Thomas sped quickly to her still room, holding hands, like children.

It was a gentle yet hungry loving by two lonely people, and Clary understood and was grateful for her sister's thoughtfulness in providing a brazier. They loved and talked and loved again, amazed by their mutual understanding of each other.

Thomas told Clary about the woman he had kept for some years, widow of one of their men at arms. How she had become quietly crazed before she died, and how he had brought up her two sons, now in the employ of the castle. Clary had already told Thomas of Lina's father, Jasper, now she told him, giggling, about the rabbit like mating of Master Green, and his care that she should not get with child again in order that she might continue nursing Lina, who he loved as his own.

They did not know who brought trays of food for them, carefully covered with a cloth, and left in the still room, but they enjoyed sitting up in bed eating, talking quietly and marvelling at their happiness.

Until there was an urgent knock on the door,

"Mother, father, rise please, for the boats are come home."

So quickly they dressed all the while stealing kisses, laughing.

"How can I hide my happiness?" asked Clary, now fully dressed, tying on her apron, with Thomas' arms about her interfering.

"The right time will come to tell the world, my dearest love, but, not yet."

They were there to greet the travellers as they stepped off the flats, all trying to speak at once, wonderfully excited by their little holiday. In they came, like a blather of summer butterflies, only more noisy. Running to kiss everyone, they tried to tell of their days, all at once.

"Mother asked to keep two of the girls, Jessie," Maria said. "I fear they sorely need company and help and we must discuss together who should stay there and if it may be a permanent agreement." What she confided in Lina later in their bed, was that two of the Jerome lads had spent much time with them, being extremely helpful in all things, and it looked as if two of her nieces had admirers.

"Although I know we are not blood kin, they are so close to our family in every way for generations," she whispered, "I think the girls would be happy, they are splendid young men and fine workers. Someone has to take over the marsh tower."

Ursuline, looking very bonny with colour in her cheeks spoke enthusiastically to Sir Thomas. Bubbling over, she tried to remember all the exciting things which she had done, but could not. Yet he could see a happy difference in her, quite another young lady from the quiet rather prim girl he had known previously.

Fortunately, as the girls were in such a state of high excitement, they failed to note the happiness which already pervaded Byford Hall.

"Now you gadflies" said Lucius with a mock stern voice, "To work, for we have been sore pressed coping in your absence, smocks and aprons please, for we are so tired without help from your pretty hands."

Order was soon restored, and even Ursuline tried to help, but was not of much use.

"Send her up to check over the apples," said Stephen. "No, I'll take her. Come", he held out a hand, "I will fetch the ladder and you can go up and see if there are any left worth keeping. And I will help you."

So it was that Stephen and Ursuline spent time together, and she thought him the nicest boy, did her best, but at the same time favoured him with her most charming smiles. Stephen, so used to girls, saw this one differently, and felt a tremor in his heart. Despite looking very like his sister, this Ursuline had a different air, yes definitely, he looked at her with new eyes.

Eventually, Sir Thomas saw that he must leave and after serious consultation with the sisters, it was agreed that if Ursuline was happy, she might stay a little longer, if Sir Thomas would inform her parents.

One last blissful night the newly weds had together, Lina somehow preventing her cousins from interrupting their happiness.

The duke looked over Sir Thomas and was pleased to see him looking better. The letter from his daughter made him smile, and he gave it to a page to take it immediately to the duchess.

"It has been a merry time, sire," Thomas smiled broadly at his kinsman, "oh but what a cheerful group of young people, your sweet daughter, right happily in the middle of it."

He went on to tell the duke of their little journey, up river, to the Woodman grandparents at the Marsh Tower, apparently a great success.

"I understand that Robert Woodman is the younger brother of the Woodmen at the port, and father of the young Woodman twins who now take over. They who build and sail ships, you know them of course. These are as charming and decent folk and they, with others round about, supply the ships from their land."

Jasper looked at Sir Thomas in faint surprise. So, these people were related to the ship men who he knew well, with whom his sons had sailed far and safely.

Perhaps now is the time, thought Thomas, now he is interested and pleased that all is well with his daughter.

"Now sire," he rose and shut and locked the door of the small room where they sat, "I need to speak to you very privily, without audience of any kind. You might well wish to confide in what I tell you to your lady, but for now, I feel my news is just for your ears." He leant forward in his chair. "I hope I do right in relating this story, I feel that I am, and hope not to cause you too much distress."

Very quietly, he began, first telling of the astonishing likeness the duke's daughter with Ursuline Byford, of how shocked Mistress Clary had been, on seeing them together, and how, when the children were visiting the Marsh Tower, she had, in deepest sorrow, confided her whole tragic story in him.

Everything, from the murder of her husband Piers Byford, the abduction to the caves by Jasper, his name sake, of cruel raping and beating. Of meeting a beautiful but maimed lady, woman of the leader of the outlaws with whom she spoke French. Then later, the eventual birth of her daughter, named by the Lady Ursuline, for herself, and her ultimate escape, aided by the lady.

The duke sat and stared, and began trembling. Then Thomas took a piece of silk from his purse and handed it the duke, who opening it, finally broke, and began weeping.

Thomas sucked in his breath and tried to keep a hold on his own emotions, for the sobbing was that of a broken man.

Holding the duke's hand, he went on quietly, elaborating, explaining what Clary had told him, the rash young lady, spirited, unworldly as to the true roughness of life, and how she had suffered for it.

"Now sire," Thomas had waited for a lull in the other's distress, "let us talk to practicalities. We can send out a search party with information from Mistress Clary. It is almost sixteen years since she left that place, so I believe, and I do not expect to find anything. But for your comfort, this is something which should be done, and sire," he pressed the ringed hand, "I will go with a good troupe of men, and hope to find something, anything, though I seriously doubt we will find your sister alive for Clary said she was very frail." The duke nodded, wiping his eyes and nose, for this was not a man to be driven to tears yet he was grievously distressed.

"One last thing, Sire, I beg it as a favour to Mistress Clary, who shamed by her terrible experiences, has lied all these years as to the paternity of her daughter to protect her. More than anything, she is fearful that the label of bastard, be put on her innocent and lovely daughter. I entreat you, somehow, to aid me in this, to protect this young girl, more than likely your great niece, for I think very highly of Clarissa and indeed of all her large family." Again the duke nodded, gathering himself together once more.

"You always were a good man, Thomas, I am honoured to be your relative and friend. I will do everything you say, for of course not only must I aid you in protecting those good people, I do not wish shame to be brought upon my own sister."

They talked late into the night, the duchess finally insisting that they unlock the door, with a meal and wine brought in. Kneeling beside her husband, the duchess saw his sorrow and understood something was amiss. He patted her hand and kissed it.

"I will tell you everything, my dear lady, eventually. But now I can tell you, in the strictest confidence, that at last, I have word of my lost sister, Ursuline, be content with that." He lay awake for hours, worrying, then, stole to his wife's chamber and got into bed with her. "I can not sleep my lady, I ask for your warmth and company. Tomorrow I will request that the box of jewels belonging to my sister be brought to me, for by rights, they belong to Ursuline Byford. I will not rest easy until some justice is done."

The duchess having been surprised by her lord's visit to her bed chamber, listened, and pursed her mouth. Give jewels to a farm girl? Certainly not. So while the duke finally slept his lady did not, because she was so angry.

Late into the night Thomas wrote letters. To his brother, and to Clary, and finally he slept, deeply, for the past hours had been draining and his emotions were raw. He just hoped that the duke would honour his word and not fail his Clary. He must trust him, it was all he could do now.

In the morning, quietly, the two men spoke again and it was agreed that the duke would accompany Thomas to Byford Hall to collect his daughter, so to meet her likeness and Mistress Clary.

While preparations were being made, Thomas went to see Deborah, begging her help in choosing bolts of cloth to take, for now it seemed that his beloved in her homespun clothes, must become a lady in fine fabrics.

The horn blew several times from far away so everyone at the hall had time to gather themselves, rushing hither and thither and made neat and respectable. Thomas pressed the dukes' arm and spoke quietly to urge him courage.

Ursuline was on the steps as the barge drew in and threw herself into her father's arms amidst laughter and clapping while Thomas had eyes only for his lovely wife. Somewhat amazed by his reception, the duke came into the hall just as Jessie and Rowena had completed tidying it. It was undoubtedly, impressive, lofty, spacious, and he understood later that the Woodmen at the port had built it years previously. Well that accounted for it of course.

Firstly all the girls were introduced and dipped low, and the duke gazed in fascination at Lina Byford who surely was just the image of his lost sister. Such blue eyes, such pale hair, he resisted the urge to caress her, but still, kissed her hand laughing, saying that she must be the long lost twin of his daughter. Then Clary and Jessie came forward and curtseyed low, but Ursuline was in such high excitement, she dragged her father about, her new friends all about them, till he had seen all of Byford Hall.

The sisters unpacked the generous hampers once again and Clary quickly put the bales of cloth onto a high shelf in her still room to look at later.

When the boys came in early evening, having brought the sheep and cattle, Clary introduced them, and they in turn, bowed low. It had been one thing to have yet another girl in the place, but a duke! The boards were set up and the best of everything put out. No longer were the wax candles considered unusual, and James was wryly thankful that the bees were doing well. While preparations were being made for a good meal, James carried Moya to the walled garden and sat her carefully on the bench in the arbour, under which now lay buried, Clary's gentle dog, Dove. Moya, now so old and small, watched the activities with rheumy eyes, felt Clary's hand trembling, and wondered why.

"My grandmother, your grace, Lady de Alencourt." The duke took the cold wrinkled hand and kissed it. Taking a deep breath, he raised his voice as he had been warned the lady was short of hearing.

"Lady de Alencourt," he gently chaffed the hand in his. "What a wonderful big family you have, my daughter has never been so happy," then putting a mock scold face at his daughter, "or so loud!" They laughed, all of them, a joyful sound.

"I do believe that somewhere along the line, we are related, for your great granddaughter, Lina, is the spitting image of my sister and indeed my daughter. Strange they even have the same name." And Thomas standing to one side, let his breath out in relief.

Moya looked closely at the Duke and nodded.

"Yes perhaps, you do have something of my uncle, Baron Pomeroy. Clary, bring the Book of Hours please dearling, it is all there in the back."

Together they looked at the family tree, beautifully written first by Lee, of the Pomeroys, then on to the de Alencourt, who had royal blood. Quietly, Moya told of Godfrey turning them out of Castle Pomeroy, that they still kept safe two copies of Baron Roland's will but how since then, their fortunes had fallen. Shortly after they had moved to the marsh tower her cousin, Jessica, the Barons' daughter, had married Sir Stephen, and of how after the baroness' death, she had married Sir Stephen. Then, Felicia, her step-daughter, had married a good man, Robert Woodman, and how they had prospered.

"I have an able secretary who is very knowledgeable as to our blood lines, something stirs in my memory on the Pomeroy line," said the duke after some moments, "he will seek it out, for I am quite certain we have a connection."

Thomas looked at Clary and gave her the lightest smile, grateful that this clever cousin was restored in humour, and was handling the situation superbly.

CHAPTER THIRTY NINE

LUCIUS

Lucius lent his tall stick against the stone troughs where the sheep were drinking. He watched them absently, then realized the main trough was over flowing, shifted the wooden sluice and ran quickly up to the well to replace the others. He remembered when the mason had lived with them for a long winter, cutting into the rock above the old well, making a fine, cold cave room which his mother used for her cheese storing. He also remembered how they had carefully shifted the troughs down the slope, so the animals would have pure drinking water.

It had all been due to James, of course, his older brother, although he knew he wasn't a brother at all, but, he had been there for as long as Lucius remembered. It had been James who had worked out the wooden sluices, cut them from logs into channels and set them usefully all over the farm.

The system was quite the envy of all who saw them, for it meant no one had to carry heavy buckets of water to house or barn. His mother said that this had helped them all in health, saving bent limbs and hurting backs.

The sheep jostled and pushed till they were all satisfied, then, the lead sheep, an old one, set off at a pace towards the milking shed where no doubt the girls would be waiting, for they would have heard the sound of the myriad little bronze sheep bells approaching.

He wasn't sure if he was happy with their visitors, yet he could not find a reason not to be. The girl, so like their own Lina was a delight, and seemed to love their simple country ways. Her father, the duke too, seemed amazingly content. But he worried that their presence would somehow make a difference to their orderly lives. Already he watched his twin, Stephen, covertly gaze at the Lady Ursuline. What was he thinking of? These were grand, wealthy people, just visiting for a few days, would Stephen break his heart for such?

Then he thought of his own sore heart, how he daily fought and railed against his instincts, how could he criticise Stephen, the gentle one, for wanting such a beauty, even if she were just a shadow of their sister.

Following the sheep he arrived at the low milking shed as the girls gathered, their pails in their hands, their faces as ever, wreathed with smiles.

"Oh Lucius," Jessie's second daughter, Fleur ran beside him, shoving the sheep towards their places where they stuck their heads into the mangers to search about for the chopped roots. "We are going to teach Ursuline how to milk!"

Lucius cast his eyes to heaven then caught those of his love, Rowena. His heart turned over. How long could they keep this up? How soon would someone discover them? He gave her the faintest smile and returned to Fleur.

"No doubt my dearling, she will find it a most useful art in the castle at the city!" A chorus of gentle laughter greeted his remark.

After he had washed, he went from the hall to the bedchamber he now shared with Stephen and James, there being visitors, sleeping on pallets in the hall was not deemed correct by his mother. Even the two bargemen had been moved to an attic so that the hall would be free and tidy. He noticed his mother had laid out his best clean clothes for them, for tonight there was to be a farewell feast, as the guests would be leaving in the morning.

James had brought in some old apple roots for the fireplaces, and already the scented smoke gently filled the hall. It did look lovely and Lucius was filled with a strange pride of this, his home. Perhaps he could just go on living here, take Rowena for his woman, if not his wife, blessed by the church. For he knew, wretchedly, their dreams were impossible, that not only were they cousins, they were double cousins, and it would not do.

Ursuline had begun to teach the girls some sedate dances from the city which they loved. Poor Stephen and James were bullied into playing their pipes for them, and the golden heads swept and dipped and now the older people got up to join them. Even the little twins, Carola and Piers, danced, behaved and did not fight, so their mother watched on in pride. The duke, taking Clary's hand bowed low, and off they went, behind the row of girls, then Sir Thomas took his turn, and Lucius wondered how they managed to be so outwardly polite to each other, when at night, they were in each other's arms. He winced with pain and Rowena seeing it, raised her brows.

Now if his mother and new father could manage to hide their marriage as well as they did, why couldn't he and Rowena? He brushed away the thought and took her hand.

"Just an ache in my heart, my dearling," he said quietly into her hair as they turned. And saw with a smile the colour rise up her neck into her face.

"You will come to stay with us, won't you" cried Ursuline, going down the steps to the barge. "I shall miss you so gravely. Thank you, thank you!" And after kissing them all, then she kissed her hands at them, when she was seated.

Thomas put Moya's hand to his lips and murmured, hoping she could hear him.

"Be sure I will love her all my life, Lady Moya, just I must wait till the time is right, before announcing it."

"Look after her, my dear son Thomas, for she is so precious, I could not bear to have her hurt."

"Never, my dear lady, be easy, never." Then onto Jessie outside, who dimpled at having her hand kissed, and was happier than she had ever been, what a compliment they had, with such nobility in the hall.

Lina, James, Lucius and Stephen he drew to one side and spoke quiet words of affection and reassurance.

"You will hear from me shortly, but I fear the duke has a task for me which may take me away for perhaps a month. Take care of your precious mother for me, my beautiful wife."

Quiet returned to Byford Hall yet something joyful remained for the girls insisted on dancing most evenings, while the brothers were ever indulgent of them, playing their pipes or even getting up to dance. Quite different from the hurly burly of their own country dances, which, none the less, their noble friends had also enjoyed.

The bargemen steered with the tide of the river, and soon they were away from the hall and friends. Old Matthew, who had been with the duke since they were boys watched the Lady Ursuline. The other one, taller, fairer and just a little prettier with the bluest eyes had constantly caught his attention.

"Sire," he said, and because of his age and long service, even his son at the tiller did not interrupt him. "For sure I think that those people must be kin of yours, for the Lady Ursuline, your lady sister, surely has a double there at Byford Hall?"

The duke heard, pursed his lip and thought not to answer but Thomas had heard it too, so he replied.

"Matthew, old friend, I think you are right, for you knew my sister as did Sir Thomas who brought me here with the same thought, and now I will get the secretary to search to see if we are indeed related."

They dropped off Thomas at his landing place, so he could run up to the castle and get clothes and some horses and a groom to come with him to do the duke's task, as soon as possible. Holding the Lady Ursuline's hand he whispered to her,

"Be careful not to irritate your lady mother, my dear, with all you have seen and done, she might not appreciate it," which gave the young, Ursuline something to think about, during the last miles downriver to her home.

The duke called his officers to choose reliable men at arms, telling them that Sir Thomas Highclere would go with them, to track down horse thieves and outlaws, in the mountains to the West. A troupe of thirty were soon assembled, well armed, and excited to be doing something.

Thomas arrived shortly and with the rough map given to him by Clary, and instructions clearly in his mind, he told the men it might be too late to find those they sought, but they would try. Rupert was at court, so the chamberlain was in charge of the castle, and Margaret and her family had provisioned him and sent him off with warm, clean clothes. Happily, two of her sons came as his grooms. Before he left, he took Margaret to the garden room, Karina's room, at the top of the castle and told her his news, that he was wed at last. So Margaret wept into her apron and held him close.

Ursuline had taken heed of what Sir Thomas had whispered to her before leaving them, and suddenly, at nearly sixteen, she felt grown up and aware of other people. Nothing would erase her happiness from her stay at Byford Hall and the Marsh Tower, so slowly, she did tell her mother, tactfully, little incidents. Yet oh but she missed them, her joyful new friends and wondered how she kept on thinking of Stephen, with whom she had sorted apples in the loft, and danced, and how he had held her so tenderly and smiled into her eyes so gently.

Thomas led the troupe off early morning, and soon they were well away, along the river road, and being on horseback, much faster than Clary had travelled. Eventually, there still stood the inn where Clary had stayed where they put up for the night. Now a fine new stone bridge spanned the river, where previously the only way across had been with a ferry man. Thomas enquired about a drowning some sixteen years before, which was well remembered, even to Master Green who, who had been a regular and sadly had left a pretty widow and dearling baby daughter. Satisfied, he forged on, the way increasingly more difficult, yet Clary had remembered some of the villages and so they climbed ever higher into the hills. His enquiries about the outlaws drew a blank, but at last, one old woman told of how, yes there had been such, so it was told, but higher up in some caves by a river, brutes who stole innocent daughters from their parent's hearths. They hadn't been seen for many a year, spitting into the dust she thanked the Virgin, and was rewarded by the jubilant Thomas who gave her a coin, the like of which she had never seen in her whole life.

It was wild country, and using long handled axes they made a slow way for themselves through wild woods along a river which thankfully, was not too high. At night they put up rough tentage against the constant drizzle and laid about fires and talked about their exploits during wars and skirmishes. Two were always on watch, but they met no man. Each day they toiled up, till at last, the surroundings seemed right. Thomas felt that they had found the entrance to the place, which, albeit very over grown, resembled the cave area, a river running through, which Clary had told him about. Taking the officer in charge to one side, he suggested that the men be divided into groups, and sent off to investigate, and if possible to hunt, for they were low on food.

"Tell them that I understand that there are some fine walnut trees about here, and as it is the time of year, they might like to gather some to take home to their families."

It was suddenly quiet when the men dispersed, and after tethering their horses, Thomas led the three, the officer and Margaret's two sons, cutting their way through the brambles and saplings which tore at their clothes, up past the dark caves. The officer made a torch and lit it, so carefully they went in, brushing aside the half grown trees which barred the entrances. It seemed as if the first cave was empty, but, soon they became aware of white bones scattered on the floor, and the officer held up a skull.

"A little child, I think sire, many more in here too. Perhaps a contagion, the plague maybe, but, I think it is many years since their souls were taken." He crossed himself and laid the skull down gently.

Clary had told him of a clearing on a small hilltop above the complex, away from the river, where the sunlight had warmed the poor maimed lady. His face stern, he made his way up, slashing with his sword at the thorns which caught him. It was a surprise, yet it was not. Somehow he had expected to find something of worth. A pile of stones stood in the middle of a clearing, a great cairn indeed, surprisingly free of vegetation and the men set to shift the stones. Only when they had come to a slate topped grave, did Thomas ask them to leave. This he must do alone.

Carefully he lifted the white bones, placing all them in his spare cloak, he went down and washed them gently in a side pool of the river. Sure enough, the skull had a great break on its jaw, and a leg bone had mended itself all crooked. Thomas felt deep sorrow for the long lost lady, carefully wrapping all the bones up again in his cloak which he tied up securely.

The men returned that night, one group with a wild piglet, another with a deer, so they made a great fire and feasted, glad that now they could return home. With gentle understanding, Margaret's sons took Thomas a little way from the noisy men, making him a slight cover from the drizzle, so he sat with his thoughts, watching the sparks fly high in the air, while the rain came again, hissing into the glowing embers.

On the way home, much easier now they knew their way, a young soldier came to Thomas and handing him a small bag said,

"We did collect walnuts, sire, and have picked out the finest for you to take home for Christmas." Which so touched and amused Thomas, who knew immediately who he would give them to, he thanked him profusely.

As they rode into the castle, word flew to the duke who waited in the same small room where he and Thomas could be alone together. A guard at the door saluted Thomas and as he knocked and entered, an elderly scribe shuffled his papers together and went out leaving the duke with his cousin, Thomas.

It was moving, sorrowful yet joyful. Thomas laid his carefully wrapped cloak into the Duke's hands.

"I am sure that it is she, sire, the broken jaw, the crooked leg, all as Mistress Byford told me." He then went on quietly, telling of the apparent care in which her body had been laid in a slate bed, a great cairn above it. Obvious evidence, that she had indeed been loved, and revered by those wild people.

Once again the duke wept, cradling the bone filled cloak and once again the duchess came insisting on entrance and gave him comfort.

"How can we ever thank you, Sir Thomas. His grace will rest easy now his sister is found, for now she can be buried in the family crypt, with the blessing of Mother Church."

Rupert stopped by as was his way, in great good spirits from his time at court, but quickly subdued his enthusiasm on learning the news of the first Lady Ursuline. Yet it was a good thing he was there, for a quiet family but grand funeral was made for the Lady, her bones now in a fine casket, with at last, masses sung for her soul.

At Byford Hall, the women were busy sewing the bolts of cloth given them by Sir Thomas, for they hoped that Ursuline would remember her promise to invite them. Joan Innman had sent sewing women and a proper tailor to help them. That they made their own lace for ruffles and trimmings was as a miracle, and Clary thought they must make some lengths to give to Ursuline and her lady mother. Lucius watched as they laboured, heads bent, so happy with their work and dreams. Fortunately, he knew they could not all go, for there was work to do, even now, in the autumn, so they had decided that should they be invited, Clary, Lina and Fleur would go. John Smith said he might go along too, for he needed iron, as the smith at Marsh Newton had left owing to the changes of the river, so John had much work. Lucius knew that Stephen longed to go with them too, but he said nothing, throwing himself into his labours with extra zeal, so nothing was said.

A letter came for Clary, telling her all about the expedition, the finding of the place she had so carefully described, and finally, how they had found the grave and bones of the Lady Ursuline. Clary quietly put the letter with the others she had received from her husband, merely telling the family that as the duke's family were in mourning, they would not be invited just yet.

They watched her, their mother, and knew that something had come in the letter to distress her, yet she said nothing and tried to go on with her busy life as usual. Moya too noticed, by now so very old and frail, James had to carry her from bed to hall where she was put close to the fire and cosseted by one and all. Her blessing was Karen, Thomas' niece, who seemed ever at her side despite being now involved with all the work of the hall and farm. Occasionally she found strength on her good days, to tell them stories of her young life at the castle or Marsh Tower. Then they all sat close and very still to catch her words. One evening, holding Karen's warm hand in hers, she told them of her parent's marriage.

"My mother Joan, was the natural daughter of Baron Pomeroy, and when the baron married, he had one son, Roland, who as her little brother, she adored. Sadly Roland made a poor marriage, an older lady already with grown sons, one, you will remember, the dreadful Godfrey, who threw us out. The lady hated my mother who was young and quite fair, but mostly because my uncle, the baron loved her so, and of course, she was the chatelaine of the castle, which she ran beautifully. It came to my mother's notice that the lady was planning a marriage for her, and she was greatly a-feared. Around that time, a visiting groom had his foot stood on, and my mother, knowing the good healing country ways, cared for him. His name was Anders, a handsome lad, and seeing goodness and kindness to beasts in him, one day my mother invited him into the lady garden," she stopped and gazed into the fire for a moment. "Oh children, you can not imagine how lovely that little garden was." Then paused again and remembered that she was telling a story. "So she asked Anders to wed with her," Moya actually laughed, a low husky laugh in which they all joined. "He was astonished, so he told me, for he was just a groom, and albeit baseborn, she was the daughter of the old baron. I was very much their last child, and my three older brother's many children, the Andersons, still live round and about and care for the old castle." She pressed Karen's hand. "My mother was very wise you know, but it was brave of her to ask Anders to be her husband and go against the lady's wishes. It was a good union. I believe that my father's father was from over the sea to the East, and he gave my mother the lump of amber, which of course you have all seen on Felicia, for it came to me, and I gave it to her."

Happily, kissing their great-grandmother, who was not, but still was, they went to bed thinking about the story and the lady garden, which of course they knew about, for hadn't they all seen the lovely little paintings of it in their forefather Lee's beautiful Book of Hours?

Finally, the following spring, the summons came for them to go to visit Ursuline and her family. But James, Lucius and Stephen were invited too. John said that he and Maria would see to everything providing the rest of the family gave extra help. With the three brothers away, they would just do the minimum work.

It was an exciting time, and even if he did not want to go, Lucius could not help but feeling intrigued. Fleur was to go too, as she and Ursuline seemed to have formed a happy friendship, and the extravagant new clothes were carefully folded and packed in fine baskets which James had made in anticipation.

Little packets of home made lace were carefully folded in linen pouches, and the best cheeses were packed into a small barrel. Clary seemed overly nervous as Lucius handed her into the flat and the two laden vessels pushed off to cries of farewell from all the family.

Yet there were great surprises at the castle, for there were again three Highcleres there to greet them.

Thomas stood with his brother and newly returned nephew at the top of the imposing staircase of the Dukes' castle. He kept on glancing at Richard, who had grown taller, broader and more ruddy skinned from his voyages. It had been a wondrous surprise when he had suddenly arrived unexpectedly, and although they had not had the opportunity to speak privately, he had informed Richard, that all the Byford family were due shortly.

Of course the foolish castle steward was trying to make a great occasion of it, and the Duke and all his family were all standing ready to greet their guests when the trumpeters held forth, not too much out of tune. Colourful banners hung, liveried men at arms stood to attention, at least to the country folk, it was very impressive.

Having been led to the foot of the stairs, the steward arranged the family as if it were some sort of pageant. Lina went ahead with Lucius and Stephen on either side, the three handsome Byfords, blonde, well dressed and the twins with hair and beards trimmed and washed neatly. Several steps below, Clary and Fleur were put on either side of James. They walked slowly up the great wide stairs, rather intimidated by the grandeur and the crowds of people on either side. Trumpets blew and the girls carefully carried their very long skirts for fear of tripping.

When they were half way up, a sudden interruption alerted them. A tiny old woman scuttled with surprising speed out from the crowd and ran to Lina, took her hands and kissing her, babbled in a high voice that she had grown, and where, oh naughty girl, had she been all this time? Lina looked shocked while her hands and face were kissed many times over, and all the while the old lady was weeping and stroking Lina's face. Time seemed to stand still, for no one moved, then people on the side began to murmur and one came forward to try to remove the old one.

Lucius and Stephen looked on in horror, took their sister's arms while James ran up to support them. At last, the hosts at the top of the stairs came to life and Thomas and Richard ran down and gently taking the old one, handed her over to others who had come after her.

"You will see her later, nanny," Thomas patted her hand, "first, she must see the duke, you understand dearie, don't you?" So it was that the poor old thing was led away, still craning her neck to look at Lina who was now weeping, Richard holding her close.

Below them, generally un-noticed, another little tragedy was happening, for Clary had fainted, something she had never in her life done before. Fleur was trying to support her when the boys, turned, saw what was happening, they then rushed to their mother's aid. Thomas then saw what had happened and ran to his wife. It was somehow all shocking and he and James carried Clary to a small office off the stairs, and the whole, beautifully arranged presentation was a total shambles.

The duchess was furious, these yeomen coming to their castle, such a fuss being made over their arrival, like royalty. How dare they cause such a commotion? But the duke was otherwise shocked, understanding that his sister's ancient nursemaid had been the cause of all the trouble, poor old dear, thinking that the Lady Ursuline had returned. Any doubts which lingered in his mind were swept away. First old Matthew, having had his say, now old nanny recognising her charge, and causing havoc. He was deeply touched and felt his heart beating too fast.

The duchess swept into the small guard's office on the stair. Country women did not faint, all this was for attention. Being already furious with her husband over his intention to give the girl his sister's jewels, her face was cold as she gazed at the scene.

The woman was lying on a low bed, ashen faced with her children and Richard Highclere kneeling beside her. The two girls were weeping, others fanning the pale woman, at least the eldest boy had asked for wine.

"You will all leave this room now," said the duchess, hard voiced, stumbling over her words in English in her rage. "So much fuss, go now," she pushed them, "you have caused so much trouble, I and my ladies will see to your mother."

Clary breathed in deeply, and was grateful when the wine arrived and sipped it, trembling, the colour slowly returning to her cheeks. She was unaware that the richly gowned and jewelled lady was the duchess and took her hand.

"Thank you lady," she pressed the hand, "Truly it is nothing. Well at least nothing serious. I am with child, and all this has perhaps been too much, or perhaps my gown is too tight."

The duchess heard the quiet voice and was shocked.

"But Mistress Byford, I understood that you were widowed?"

Clary nodded and smiled weakly.

"And so I was, for sixteen years, but I am now wed to Sir Thomas, and I was hoping to tell him this joyous news over these days, for, he does not yet know. He had hoped to keep our marriage a secret for the time being."

It took moments to understand, and being a kindly woman, the duchess melted, and suddenly her anger evaporated. A blessed little child, and good Sir Thomas did not yet know. Gently, Magdalena's women escorted Clary to her own sumptuous chamber where she was laid to rest herself, while the duchess sent for Sir Thomas while she herself went to find the Byford children.

What might have been a disastrous occasion, now turned into a joyful one. Somehow, the happy news was out, and Thomas could feel his smile almost splitting his mouth.

Finally, through the crush of people, Thomas made his way to the duchess' chamber, where she shoed out all the hovering and fluttering, smiling ladies.

"Is it true? My Clarissa," he held out his arms for Clary and shut his eyes, taking in the sweet country scent of her, camomile and lavender. So Clary told him that indeed it was true but that she had felt she wanted to tell him privately. At which they both laughed, for now the whole castle knew, and there was an air of joy all about them.

Deborah came with David, one of her physician sons, but there were no anxieties, she was well, just perhaps the new too tight clothes, the whole journey and the reception had been too much.

It was an auspicious beginning to their visit, and soon everyone relaxed and enjoyed each other's company and made much of Clary. Ursuline and Fleur ran all over the castle together and explored as they had at the Hall and the Marsh Tower.

The duke took Clary and Thomas to the chapel where they heard mass and Clary went to the place where the Lady Ursuline now lay together with her parents in a fine tomb. There she knelt for some moments, eyes closed, resting her hands on it, quietly thanking her, and saying her farewells.

Thomas, always the tactful one who smoothed ruffled feelings, commiserated yet congratulated the steward on the fine reception and sympathised with him for the regrettable incident of the old nursemaid.

How they arranged it, goodness knows, but the young people asked if they might do a dance for the assembled guests and family. It was to take place in the very old hall, all built in fine stone with three great, round pillars at one end.

James and Lucius appeared to be in charge, if not exhibiting, and they arranged lamps near the pillars, with the audience, at the other in the other end, in shadow.

Stephen came out first, dressed in a plain, soft blue doublet and hose. Very casually, he leaned against the centre pillar and began to sweetly play on his pipe. Then one of the girls, in that light, it was impossible to see if it were Lina or Ursuline, again dressed all in blue, came out and tripped past Stephen prettily, turning her head to see him before going behind the next pillar.

Stephen stopped playing, and peered towards her. Then he began to play again. Where upon another lovely girl in blue, appeared from the first pillar. Or was it the same maiden? It was such a simple little play, with the court minstrels taking up Stephen's tune, and the girls ran behind Stephen's back, dipped and disappeared behind one or other of the great round pillars.

By now the audience were enjoying themselves with laughter and clapping, so that the three were encouraged, and when one girl appeared unexpectedly from a pillar, Stephen jumped as high as he could, as if in fright. Which brought much laughter.

He then crept towards a pillar, placed his arms around it and shuffled right around it slowly, walking his fingers on the stone. Having gone all around and finding no girl, he looked properly perplexed. More laughter. So he returned to the middle pillar and began to play his pipe again. From one side came a dainty hand and plucked his sleeve but no, there was no one there. Then from the other side came a hand and again, there was no one, finally he began to play again and before him ran the two girls laughing as they ran, around one pillar across to the other like a cat's cradle, so once again, Stephen made, to catch one, only to see another appear so again, he leapt up into the air as if in fright. So their little act ended with their bowing and curtseying while the minstrels played prettily and James and Lucius laughed doubled up and everyone clapped and laughed but of course, wondered at the two girls in blue.

Even the duchess had been amused, for it had been innocent fun and everyone seemed to enjoy it. Whereas the duke was delighted with his pretty daughter and Ursuline introduced her "cousin" Lina, as her companion, and it was noted how very a like the two girls were. Afterwards, there was some dancing with all the young people joining in. It was Fleur who quietly thanked David Scrivener for caring for her aunt, then tugged his hand to join in. The elders, seated on a dais, watched with pleasure as the youngsters turned and twisted, and even did some merry country dancing, with Stephen and James accompanying the castle musicians.

So despite the unfortunate beginning of their stay, it all ended happily and they went home, laughing with much to tell.

CHAPTER FORTY

KARINA, THE NEW LADY HIGNCLERE

Life would never be the same after that grand and chaotic occasion. Thomas and Clary went to live at the castle downriver and Clary settled into the top rooms of the old Tower, where the old Lady Karina had made her garden. Thomas, Robert and Margaret often sat with her and told her tales of their childhood, but Thomas insisted that Clary always used a chair for going up and down, as this was a most unexpected and precious child, and it was Robert who arranged for two stout lads to be ever available for her needs.

Richard of course spent as much of his time as he could at the Hall and the day came when James announced he would be killing the hogs and needed all the help he could get. Richard was alarmed, for much as he had enjoyed hunting, this was different. Yet he realized that all the good things which he had taken for granted must be a great amount of work, donning the smock and thick apron Lina gave him, he watched in trepidation as the preparations began.

A sack of salt was produced and some of the girls took to pounding the rough grains in two mortars. James went off and cut some elder branches and hollowed them out to fix on to a horn funnel so that the intestines might be well cleansed. A great jar of apple vinegar came next, followed by a smaller one of honey. Bags of dried herbs and garlic were set on a board and another pestle and mortar were put beside them for special use. It seemed endless and Richard wondered when the killing would begin.

That night, he lay in James' bed while poor exhausted James slept deeply on a pallet having refused to let their guest sleep so low. He heard the deep breathing of the three Byford brothers, while he, his mind still racing, could not sleep. Of course having been a city boy, how could he have known of the huge and horrible work entailed by country folk to provide such good things which seemed automatically to come to their castle table. Thoughts still milling in his head, he felt nothing but admiration for these new friends, who he knew would soon be his relatives. They were so skilled, and even the killing, which he had dreaded had been quiet, the great beasts brought in one at a time to feast on their last and specially good meal. Then, after James had taken one of John Smith's heavy hammers to its head, even he had been called to drag the heavy senseless creature, where with its back legs tied, they hauled it up onto a strong, specially built frame where James skilfully had cut its throat and two girls swiftly caught the blood in buckets. On and on it had gone, task after task and he was running like the rest of them carrying, cutting, fine chopping, setting the lard to clarify. The steam and the stink were horrible, but they toiled on, every one even the little twins, doing their bit.

Apparently even the larger bones they cleansed to hand to the miller down stream where he would set them just touching the millstones when making animal feed. For James told him, now things were becoming more prosperous in the land, they were growing common beans to grind up for feed should they be short, as so often in the past they were. So the powder of the bones would add more goodness to the bean-meal, and the stock would prosper.

At the evening meal, James announced his plan to take John Smith to the town to buy iron, for he wanted to make a large spit to put over the fireplace.

"I have early childhood memories of monasteries, and maybe castle kitchens where my foster mother took me to sell her baskets. They had great long iron spits with the whole beast turning on it. Delicious." Everyone listened closely, for it was not often that James spoke about his early life.

They let Richard sleep next morning to his shame, and by the time he had woken, the worst was done. Just the black pudding and the sausage mix, sitting in the cold cheese cave, were waiting to be put into their casings all the while the good herbs, garlic and salt were soaking into the mess to give good flavour.

Downriver at the castle, thankfully, she was feeling marvellously well, so Clary begged to go up river to see her grandmother and parents as well as all the family. It seemed an easy ride, well wrapped up, slowly going up and down stream so it was agreed that she would go once a month. After the killing of the hogs, Clary praised her family for their great successes, and asked her grandmother with gentle humour, how Richard had fared. For although very old, Grandmother Moya was still able to understand what was going on, even if she couldn't see or hear very well. And the parents from the Marsh Tower always came, delighted to see their daughter so happily re-married.

Clary was amused, for obviously they had been told not to be too noisy, to be very careful of her, and Clary smiled to herself. If they had seen the conditions she had lived in while she had been carrying Lina! Yet she did realize that they were all concerned for her good health, now she was sixteen years older.

Clary worried that both her parents had aged, her father's hair almost white, her mother stooped, yet it was always a joyful time.

Grandmother Moya was finally fading. It was as if she knew the beloved granddaughter of her soul was happy, settled, well married again. Clary held her icy cold hands and kissed them, and one day Moya took her little purse from her girdle and gave Clary her ring which Sir Stephen had given her. In the softest voice, for she had so little strength left in her, Moya said,

"It is de Alencourt Clary, given to the great great, perhaps, great grandmother by the king who was her grandfather, so I believe. Wear it please, for we have a proud heritage and though our family has gone down since, I believe it may well go up again now, as families do."

Clary looked at the little gold ring, worn and light, but just discernable on it, a coat of arms. She closed her eyes and remembered Grandmother Felicia wearing it proudly, so she tried it, but it would only fit her smallest finger, for unlike those other women, she had toiled hard all her life, and her hands were not slim and beautiful as theirs had been. None the less, she was greatly pleased and leaned down and caressed the wrinkled old face.

"I shall make sure that Lina has it one day, grandmother. Thank you for giving it to me, I am proud of it, and I know that Thomas will be intrigued by it. Thank you, sweetest dearling".

"And what is left in Mistress Miller's chest, is yours, my most dear child," whispered Moya, feeling that time was running out for her. "The great dish, and the last two goblets, dearling, a dowry for Lina?" And Clary bent her head and tried to hide her tears, nodding, kissing the soft old face, gently holding her in her arms.

So it was that Moya died, at peace, in her sleep, and they took her up to the little church on the hill, covered with wild flowers, and wept a few tears, but rejoiced in her life, which had been such a long and very useful one.

At the Highclere castle, another very aged lady was carried up to see Clary. Mistress Chamberlain, with no teeth at all now, came and sat in the garden and lisped her stories of the first Lady Karina, the lady mother of Thomas, Robert and Margaret. And she told Clary of the great shared secret of Thomas' birth and how overjoyed the tired lord was to see his double with those blue, blue eyes, when he returned from service with the king. Then she told of the time when Karina married her lord and Thomas and Margaret both stood under the marriage awning so to be legitimised.

At Byford Hall, for that was what it was called now although, with the stone bridge, there was no ford any more, the girls were finding admirers and all busy making their dowries and filling their fine chests. There were two great looms as well as a small braid loom now set up in the hall, and there was always a girl sitting at one or the other when tasks were done. For weaving was pleasant work, a reward for all the hours of spinning. Sitting down, working out new patterns, weaving in the exciting new colours from the dye pot, the girls kept busy and happy and were proud to show their handiwork to their visitors. On fine days, if there was little farm work to be done, they took their lace cushions or tatting out to the walled garden and worked and sang. The men of the hall listened, wherever they laboured, their moods light, for it seemed there was joy everywhere.

Since Clary had moved away, the girls had quietly taken over the running of the cheese making and the domestic cooking. For Jessie was a poor cook, her mind always elsewhere and her potage was always sloppy, over cooked and tasteless.

Ever since James had introduced pork to their diet, their stews and roasts were infinitely more delicious than before, and they all seemed to benefit from the extra good food.

The girls took it in turns to visit their grandparents up river and their Aunt Clary downriver and while in town learned of new fashions and fripperies.

"Rowena," Jessie demanded her older daughter who she had never really liked, "I want you to go up to Father Benjamin with his clothes and food." Rowena loved her mother, not as much as she loved her secret foster mother, Aunt Clary, who had nursed her at her breast along with Lina, so many years ago. But she knew of her mother's dislike and that she always got given the unpleasant tasks, "Well you are the eldest" would say Jessie, when she saw her first born's downcast face.

Lucius came in and quickly volunteered to take the things up to the little church. But Jessie would have none of it.

"You have other work to do Lucius, don't indulge her. I have told Rowena she must go, thank you Lucius, I am afraid Father Benjamin is not too well and Clary will be angry with me if he is neglected. I want Rowena to see him and if there is anything we can do for him." Having put the bundle of clean clothes and the hamper on the board, she went off, mumbling to herself. "Difficult old man, persisting on living up there, all alone."

Lucius smiled at his cousin, his love, and put his finger to his lips spoke very quietly.

"I will meet you by the forest gate my angel, just in a short time," and went off as if on some other errand.

It was a beautiful evening and the river glinted far below them as they toiled up the hill, Lucius insisting on carrying everything on his broad shoulders. He had waited for this opportunity, for it was so difficult with so many people about to have any time alone with Rowena. His aunt was now producing suitors for her, for she was sixteen and ready to be wed. The sorrow they both felt was intense, for they knew that the law would not allow them to marry.

Father Benjamin was sitting outside his little church on the stout wooden bench James had made for him. Afraid to startle him, the young people called their greetings as they approached, but the old priest smiled at them.

"I knew you'd be coming, for you are late, things are not as punctual as when your mother was in charge, Lucius. No offence my child," he took Rowena's hand, not remembering which of the seven lovely maidens she was, but guessing she belonged to Jessica. "I was hoping someone would come, for see, I have a thorn in my finger and need help to remove it."

Luckily Rowena had a pin in her dress, so carefully she worked at the thorn till it popped out.

"I must press it awhile, Father, to make it bleed as it might have gone bad, I hope that I do not hurt you?" Lucius went around the little garden which he knew his mother had planted and found a plantain leaf so pulled it and rubbed it on the tiny wound for healing.

They sat beside the old man and marvelled at the familiar view, at peace together for once without prying eyes and gossipy tongues. There, across the plain, lay the smudge of the small town, Marsh Newton, a drift of smoke rising from most houses, the church, on higher ground, the tower proud in the evening light. It was impossible to pick out anything else, although they tried to see the inn, where their Aunt Joan lived with her large family.

Benjamin watched them sideways, for his eyes were no longer sharp but he could see if he didn't look straight ahead. He frowned, a small patter in his heart alarming him.

"Are you well, my children, are you content? What ails you, for I sense that something does, you may tell me, for I am old and hopefully wise, at last." They sat silently, then Lucius took Rowena's hand and held it.

"Father Benjamin, you have known us all our lives. You know our parents, our people, our ways. Father, is it such a sin to love ones cousin? For truly, I have loved Rowena since she was but a little maid, and now her mother plans to wed her to some stranger. I am bereft, Father. The pain I feel is so deep, it is almost as a stab wound. What can I do, what can we do?"

They sat for some time, half watching the old man who appeared to have his eyes closed. Eventually he sighed deeply.

"Yes, I see that you have a problem my dears, but understand, that laws like this were made for the good of the people, not just for the power of the church. Small, isolated villages would intermarry, for generations, and children would eventually inherit weaknesses. Often this would be a calamity, producing idiots, or maimed bodies. Not, of course that just the simple people intermarried. I have read ancient books where kings married their sisters, thinking to keep their blood line pure, with disastrous results. At the same time, I have observed the creatures of the earth totally disregard relationships, for they have no memory, no education, as we do, and they survive well enough."

There was another long silence.

"If, my dear children, you could leave this place, go far away where no one knows you, then you could be safe from the wrath of the church." As if changing his line of thought, the old priest smiled at Lucius.

"Did you know that I officiated at the marriage of your parents, and sadly, and all too soon, dear Lucius, I buried your father. What a charming, gentle boy he was, so in love with your mother, it warmed the heart. So let me say this. As I am old, it matters not to me the laws of the church or the land. Your family, mainly your mother, Lady Clarissa, was always more than good to me. If, you can find a way to leave, without incurring suspicion, it will be my honour to perform the marriage for you two, quietly, in memory and gratitude to your parents."

Rowena and Lucius sat, eyes round, hearts hammering and said not a word, thoughts whirling about their heads like a mill race.

"Now, before you go, dear children, let us spend some moments in our precious little House of God to pray, and later, we will speak again. Thank you for your visit and take heart. Nothing is impossible when it is pure and good." After they had knelt and been blessed and said some prayers the old priest saw them to the door. "God be with you. Be of good cheer, remember, that which is hardest to obtain, often is the most blessed in the end. I hope to see you all on Sunday."

They ran down the hill hand in hand, pulled into the shelter of some bushes and held each other tightly. A blackbird sang his evening song with gusto, so for a moment, delighted, they listened to him.

"We will find a way, there my dearling," said Lucius dragging his thoughts away from the happy bird, his own heart bursting with joy too. "Father Benjamin said he would marry us, so we must look for a way and the only one we can trust is James. He will help I know, Stephen is too soft and afraid and your mother will smell him out and that will be that." He kissed her deeply and held her very close. "Now we have hope, let us quietly go about our lives until the opportunity comes and above all, you must not marry any one else."

Giggling at the thought, Rowena, lighter in spirit ran the rest of the way home and at the board told about the thorn in Father Benjamin's finger and of how wise he was and how beautiful the view was, on and on until Lucius' raised eye brow caused her to stop her babbling. Yet still she smiled.

The day came when it was decided that Lina should go to attend Clary whose time was near. As usual, with the flat loaded with good country provisions, they set off down stream well muffled up against the spring drizzle.

All was prepared. The great cradle and bedding were aired. The binding sheets were neatly folded in the press and Clary welcomed her daughter gratefully as time hung heavily and she was becoming bored by her inactivity. At least she had insisted on being taken to the garden every day when it was fine, or to the hall if wet. Never had she been locked up in a darkened room as some of the ladies seemed to think necessary. She had always been too busy, but she didn't tell of her previous life for they might well be shocked by it.

The first pain came gently in the early hours, just before dawn and she lay still, just touching her lord for comfort.

"I feel lazy, my lord," she smiled up at him as he rose and watched as his man helped him to dress. "Maybe today I will stay in bed and hold court like a great lady, but do please visit me some time?"

Thomas looked down at his beloved lady, pleased that she would rest, for her inactivity had irked her so much lately, it had been difficult to know just who to listen to for advice.

"Lie there, my Clary, be as lazy as you can be, for surely you will be busy soon with a little one and the castle to run as you want. I will send Lina." Kissing her hand, he left, quite unaware that his child was getting ready to enter the world.

The hours passed, the days passed. Clary could not imagine that she would take so long in birthing a child. She became tired, of everything, but mostly of hearing the words,

"It is your age, lady, it often takes longer when you are older."

But then she just became too tired, tired of the waiting, tired of the intermittent pain which wrenched her body, tired of even living.

Lina watched her mother fearfully, seemingly to grow weaker each hour. Was this how child birth was, and Clary seeing her daughter's anxiety took her hand.

"It is not always so," she said in the softest voice, "My other children gave me pain but they did not keep us waiting like this. Lina my child, send for Jessie, and James, tell James to bring Lee's healing book. I recall something like this in it." Then she turned her head to the side and rested, unaware of the fearful anxiety of all her loved ones.

They came, Jessie, breathless from the stairs, frantic that the sister who had cared for her for every one of her birthings, should now be in trouble. James came, hastily kissed his mother but sat near the window to read Lee's book. If she said something in there might help, he would find it. Fear gripped his heart, for he loved his foster mother, his life's mother, with a fierce, deep love.

Midwives came from the town, from the Duchess, all with their own herbals remedies which Clary obediently drank, shuddering with the distaste of them. On it went, Thomas frantic in his pleadings with the physicians, wishing that Joseph or David, Deborah's sons were not away with the duke.

Jessie clung close to her twin sister, at last, realizing how precious she was, how she had always aided her in all matters. The only time she left her side was to find a privy, and on that occasion poor Jessie learned that she was no longer a lovely slim woman as her sister, for as she approached the end of one of the endless corridors, she saw a fat, jowly woman and beckoned to her, for she was lost in that maze. The figure beckoned back, but did not speak, and it took a little time for Jessie to realize that the fat, toothless woman she was trying to speak with, was herself in a great looking glass. Shocked, she looked more carefully and began to weep, for where had gone her youth and beauty which it seemed Clary even now still had.

On the fourth day, James thought he had found what he was looking for. In Lee's neat hand, there it was, how to urge the lazy birth to progress.

He looked at his hands, huge, gnarled, creased with years of hard work and dirt. No, they would not do. Then he suddenly thought of Karen and surprisingly for him, he took control, and ordered a boat to go at all speed to Byford Hall to bring Karen and calendula oil.

When she arrived, James took her to a small anti room and held her hands. They were small and neat, yes, they would do. So he took the little scissors from his pouch and trimmed her nails very short, then set her hands in a bowl of hot calendula water and cleansed them till she thought he would remove the skin. Only then did he read from Lee's book, what she must do.

Her hands in her lap folded in a clean white napkin, Karen carefully observed the man she had grown to love. She too would do anything to help the Lady Clarissa, but then who wouldn't, she had always been the kindest woman to everyone.

"Of course I will do it, and then will you wed with me, James Clarysson?"

James stared at her astonished for a moment.

"Oh I will do what you ask, James," said Karen, her heart beating faster, "But I should like to be wed with you so that one day I might have children too and time passes by and no one offers for me." Only then, her face flaming, did she look down at her hands, grateful to the Lady Moya for telling them the story of how her parents had wed.

"I will wed you gladly, Karen, and be sure mother will be greatly pleased. But come now, quickly, or we will lose her, as did Lee, which he wrote about of a past mother, a Fleur, with such sorrow."

James turned everyone out of the room, his one eye glinting in anger at any objections.

"We will get this babe be sure, but go!" He shouted which made Clary take notice then James sat close to her, held Lee's book, told her what it said what they would do, Karen with the slim fingers, and her own good calendula oil.

Suddenly it seemed that Clary's body answered to the delicate probing finger, for very soon, a tiny head appeared, face up, not as usual, face down, and now James shouted joyfully for the midwives and Jessie and so at last they delivered a tiny, dark haired daughter, whose thin cry caused Clary to smile despite her exhaustion. Thomas was ushered in, his brother weeping beside him and suddenly all was joy as the baby was washed and swaddled and laid in the cradle to rest while they quietly fed Clary chicken soup, spoon by spoon and sighed with gratitude and relief.

"She is just like Karina," said Robert, peering at the tiny thing in the huge cradle. "Thomas, won't you name her thus? For I do believe she will have curls just as did mother."

James took Karen by the hand and pulled her along until they came to a quiet corner where he kissed her roundly to her surprise and laughed at her.

"Now I will take you to your father to ask for your hand, that precious, clever hand which saved two lives." Suddenly serious he tipped her chin so he could see her face. Strange green eyes surveyed him, unusual, beautiful. Gently now, he kissed her again and pulling her by the hand, ran down the castle steps his heart light, happy after days of fear. Suddenly the realization came to him that when he married Karen, he would surely be KIN. No more the adopted son, the poor bruised and beaten son Clary had found, but kin, real kin.

So at the same time that the precious new child of Clary and Thomas was baptised, James and Karen stood in the church porch and Karen's mother Margaret wept tears of joy. So much good had come about, so much joy. Carefully she sorted through her mother Karina's jewels and gave some to Karen for her wedding and to the little Lady Highclere for her baptism.

They saw rather little of Richard, for he seemed to spend much time at the Hall, and surprisingly, Jessie was the one to watch, and to raise a finger if she thought that he and Lina were being too familiar.

Richard either came by boat, or if the day was fine, on his horse. He had learned that one of the grooms had family in Marsh Newton so he always chose to bring him and sent him off to be with them for a few days.

"Oh good, Richard," said James, "I am glad you are come for we are to kill some pigs again and we'll need all the help we can get." Then seeing Richard's face, and smiling inside, he added, "Oh don't worry, we will find you suitable really old clothes." Richard was shocked, for he knew he would be no help at all, yet the family just got on with their preparations, apparently not noticing his discomfort, sharpening knives, dragging out rough old aprons and head cloths. The truth was that no one enjoyed this work, even if they did enjoy the results.

Lina watched Richard and felt very sorry for him. She knew that the boys were testing his nerve and determined to help him.

"Stay near me," she told him, as if he needed telling, "It is a messy business, but it must be done. The first time is surely the worst, you now have some experience, but since James got the pigs from the forest, we have enjoyed a better life and we send much to the ships for provisions which helps in other ways. Of course we will miss mother, for she was very efficient, and Aunt Jessie is so slow."

The preparations seemed endless. Strong wooden boxes, well caulked by Robin were set with water in them to swell. These were for the hams Richard learned. Every kind of receptacle was scoured and set, upside down to drain, to hold the precious lard which would be clarified and poured in, well sealed and kept up high on shelves in the store room away from any vermin. The best fat was to be kept for salves and creams, more work, but for later as the clarified and cleansed fat could be safely stored till needed.

CHAPTER FORTY ONE

THE UNCLES

They sat, as usual, on either side of the fireplace facing each other. Not that they looked at each other much, for, being twins, and very similar, it was as if they were looking at themselves, in a looking glass.

It had been very quiet of late, steady work in the ship yard, just two small merchant ships being built, and few visitors, which suited them. The winter storms nearly over, they considered whether to pay a visit to Clary, now at Highclere and with a beautiful little daughter. They were inordinately pleased, for it seemed that their favourite niece, who they had known from the very moment of her birth, had not had an easy life. And now with Sir Thomas, a man they greatly respected, she was happy and a lady indeed.

The fact that her family had come from grand roots had never seemed to bother her, or indeed them. Perhaps Jessica regretted losing their lands, well she did have many daughters true, lovely girls all and gifted housewives so a dowry might not be so very important. But, securely, in the monk's seats on which both uncles sat, was all their gold so if there was need, it was there for them, this is what one did for true kin. United in thought, they nodded agreeably to each other.

A fearful clatter interrupted their peaceful reveries, and the tall narrow house shook with the weight of which ever nephew was thundering down the stairs more noisily that usual. It was John.

"Come uncles, come quickly to look," he said breathlessly, "there is a ship coming in, one of ours, listing badly, we must go to the yard to attend to it."

The uncles looked at him wryly.

"What ship? How do you know it is one of ours?" John held out his new telescope and his urgency reached them, so they rose and wearily followed him right up to the top of the house to an open window and looked. He was right! Their amiable faces looked serious. For sure it was listing heavily. Running as fast as they could, no longer boys, they followed John down and dragged their cloaks off the racks in the narrow hall calling to their housekeeper that they were going to the yard.

Behind the house the stable boy was cleaning tack. He had been on a ship until he lost his leg and these good seamen had taken him on, so he worked diligently to please them.

"Never mind the cleaning," said one of the young masters, breathlessly, "there is a ship coming in, listing badly, one of ours, quickly, let us saddle up the horses". And by the time the uncles arrived the horses were ready for them and up they went and off with a clatter. So the boy dropped his cleaning rags and took up his crutch and hobbled through the covered gateway to the sea wall where before long, several other old sailors joined him.

"Tis one of ours," he said glowing, "but listing badly, must have been caught in that last storm." And felt his pulse racing. Even if he could not go to sea any more, this was the next best thing. He leaned into the salt laden wind and watched as in the distance the great ship limped in.

John arrived at the yard first in a flurry of anxiety and slipped from his horse, throwing the bridle over a post.

"James!" he called, "where is James?" Frowns on their brows, something was a miss, the men near him pointed to where his twin was leaning over a parchment with the overseer. "James", he reached him in great strides and shoved him unceremoniously towards the stout little stone tower which acted as look out, and in bad times, as a beacon. "Up man, up and fast!" and shoved him up the single wooden ladder which went to the top. Astonished, James kept looking down at his brother and muttering "whys" and "wherefores" but John had his head firmly under his twin's buttocks and shoved him up, without ceremony till they reached the top. Breathless, he took out his precious little telescope, scanned the sea for a moment, grunted, then passed it to his twin.

"Oh Sweet Jesus," said James, shocked, "it is one of ours, but", he looked more carefully, "What is the pennant?" John took the telescope for a moment but impatiently stuck it back in his jacket.

"Never mind whose pennant brother, let us get them in, that is the main thing." And from the little tower he hollered for all his worth to gather all the men together by the two boats they kept for hauling ships out of the yard, or occasionally, for hauling them in as today.

By the time the uncles had stiffly climbed down from their horses, the yard was a hive of activity.

"Extra oars!" roared one. The men watched one master, then the other and ran.

"Extra ropes!" called the other. And the men, who hadn't seen the crippled ship because of the high shingle bank obeyed because of the urgency in their employer's voices, and guessed a ship was in trouble.

"You go in one and I'll take the other," yelled John, and with a full contingent of strong men, they rowed out through the narrow river mouth into the open sea.

The tide was just on the turn both men realized immediately, so they must move, and fast, or otherwise they would find it well nigh impossible to bring the big ship in.

On the ship, Captain Martin raised his telescope once again trying to find the narrow entrance to the little river on which the yard was situated.

"They've seen us!" his voice loud and full of relief, "Here they come, two boats and they will lead us in." Then he handed his telescope to the king who stood beside him who took it up and gazed in awe at the two small boats churning through the water towards them.

After that it was all shouting and chaos with ropes being flung and tied fast and men calling to each other oblivious of the royalty on board. About turn, then, and the men heaved even more mightily at their oars and slowly, slowly the great ship which dwarfed them, followed meekly until through the river mouth, they veered into a dock used to repair damaged vessels.

Then, chests heaving, they all lent on their oars and rested, greatly satisfied, while their fellows made good and tied up till eventually, great grins on every face, they stepped out of their boats and made to the dockside where the uncles were already greeting the captain. Letting out huge breaths the twins winked at each other.

"How did you know it was coming?" called James.

"I was up at the top of the house when something told me to use my telescope," called back John, "Oh my, but what a fright, one of our best ships, I tell you brother, I thought my heart would pop out of my mouth I was so shocked." And all the men about smiled broadly, for they liked their young masters.

"Well done, Martin," the uncles shook his hands beaming. "Grief man, what happened? How did you get holed so?" and Captain Martin greatly relieved to be safe especially with his precious passenger, tried to skew his eyes around to the deck behind him, to tell them where the king stood.

Shortly, they were all presented and there was much bowing and the men took off their caps and cheered so it was a greatly relieved captain who quietly asked if there was any place of comfort for his majesty to rest while the ship was repaired.

"Go, my boy, find Duke Jasper and tell him we have a most special guest. Explain accommodation will be needed. Bring decent horses. GO boy, as fast as you can."

So it was that James rode furiously to the duke's castle, for the tide was running out fast now, and a horse was better than a boat. Arriving at the castle, breathless he handed his heaving horse to a groom asked for the duke and ran up to the hall. Sensing his urgency, armed guards ran to tell the duke there was an emergency. So it was that James Woodman asked the duke to accept His Majesty, the King with a small entourage, which delighted the duke but threw the duchess into a frenzy of anxiety. Word was sent urgently to the horse master, the best horses, but quickly.

By happy chance, Sir Thomas and Lady Highclere were visiting, so Clary found herself advising the flustered duchess and messengers were sent down into the town to purchase every extravagance in quantity. On impulse, Clary asked Thomas if he would send Richard to go to the hall and bring her children, what good meat they had, cheeses, anything to help the frantic duchess. So off Richard raced happily.

"You understand my love," said Clary, "I am so proud of my children, I wish them to have the opportunity to meet the king." Thomas smiled at his wife and drew her close whispering in her ear, yet soon he was up on a good horse and off they rode, all leading another for the unexpected party. Meanwhile at the yard, the king was fascinated to watch the speedy and expert work begun on his ship. The two masters called the carpenters and overseer and with help from all the men, the ship was righted slowly with stout poles in the mud as the water was pumped out by hand and the damage could be seen.

"How did this happen friend, Martin?" said an uncle. The captain shook his head in disbelief and shame.

"I was entertaining His Majesty below and the wind was so fluky, wicked it was, and the helmsman, who is a good lad, could not hold her. So here we are. And I must say Masters Woodman, never have I been so pleased to see help arrive so speedily as today."

"Ah well" said one uncle, "It was John who spotted you from an upstairs window and came like a bat from hell to tell us, thanks be to God."

The king was listening to all this while watching the experts work on the vessel and he was amused,

"It seems sires, that you are a good family team, which is all to our benefit, most exciting I have to say, seeing your little boats and fine fellows run out to meet us and then, bring us safely home. I shall ever be indebted to you." Pleased, they all bowed all the while watching the start of repairs begin with the many good men slithering in the black ooze trying to set the supports safely.

"It will be a few days Sire before the hull is dried and we can make good repairs, it is not a bad hole, but we must wait. Meanwhile one of our nephews has ridden to Duke Jasper at the castle to tell him of your arrival and to bring horses so we must unload your belongings for transport. With the tide running out now, we could not manage to take a boat upstream."

Despite their tiredness, the oarsmen ran hither and thither to make a place for the king and his entourage to sit comfortably under a canopy of sail cloth although the weather was fair. Others carried His Majesty's goods from the ship and loaded them carefully on the dock side there to await a dray to fetch them in due course. It was a hive of industry, in fact a splendid change for the men who would have plenty to tell their families, and meanwhile the king was pleased with the speed and efficiency of the whole operation. The trauma of their arrival was soon forgotten, accompanied with good wine and fellowship certainly helped when each man in the yard was given a coin for his efforts.

Then Duke Jasper arrived with his kinsman Sir Thomas Highclere and after much bowing and gasping at the tale, they mounted their horses and rode along the river road to the castle, the king with them.

By the time the king arrived, the whole town knew he was coming and they had hung cloths and pennants from their windows and all the burgers dressed in their best, stood in their doorways with trays of their best cups brimming with their finest ale to offer the guests.

What had almost ended in tragedy, now was a joyful time with his majesty delighted to be on solid earth again and receiving such a welcome from an area he barely knew. They rode up to the castle where Duke Jasper and his lady strove to entertain him and his party until a new party arrived with many fair young people, obviously all related somehow, and delightfully charming and bright. The weather turned fair so there was plenty to do, and in the evenings, the young entertained their guests with singing and dancing.

The two Ursulina's and Stephen were persuaded to put on their silly act, which they did somehow with more energy and nonsense to the delight of the gathering.

"This has been a good time Jasper," said his majesty. "I can't remember enjoying myself so well for many a year. But I must be off home to work, for you know, kings do work, even if their ministers do most of the preliminaries. May I return sire, bring my lady wife, perhaps next year, for I think there is some knighting to do, so many good men who saved us must not be forgotten."

So it was the town went back to normal but with the promise of another visit, there was plenty to talk about and plan for.

It seemed so quiet back at the hall even if the family found themselves secretly smiling, remembering some odd occasion. As usual there was plenty of work to do with the waning of the year, stores to be put up, with thought of the long winter ahead goading everyone to do their best. Without Clary there to guide them, Lina and Rowena took up the reigns of housewifely duties always united and efficient.

James and John Smith took a flat to the town to buy metal for the forge for the winter months and James had decided that now with plenty of porkers, they must make a fine spit, a fearful extravagance, all that iron, but he insisted, and John was entirely in agreement. Inevitably they also had a long list of orders from the girls and Jessie. Well the winter needed brightening up and they must prepare for months being cut off and missing the fun of the past months.

Then they must be sure to have enough wood for the fires and cooking. Lucius and Stephen were high above the hall dragging timber down from the edge of the forest with the oxen and horses when even there, they heard the screams. Fearful and endless screaming, so shocked, looking at each other they abandoned their task, mounted the horses and sped down the hill to be met by the sight of the girls who were either all rushing about or seemed to be standing in agitation in the cattle yard, gazing up at the barn roof, their mouths open.

"Stop screaming!" ordered Lucius, so sudden quiet fell and aprons were twisted in anxious hands instead. Jessie was sobbing and no amount of comfort would stop her.

There they were, the twins of course, Piers right at the end of the apex with Carola not far behind weeping bitterly. The cause of their efforts, was clear to see. A kitten stood right at the end of the roof, where Piers was seated astride the roof crown, reaching out to it.

The brothers ran for the longest ladder and Stephen, being the lighter, started up, Lucius holding it steady. Grasping Carola by her skirts, he handed her down to reaching hands and then went back up for Piers. But Piers, ever spoilt by his mother, had other ideas. Having got so far, he was determined to catch the kitten so edged forward even further, to all their consternation.

At last Stephen caught a hold of Piers shirt and dragging him kicking and screaming. Then he carefully let him slip down the roof onto a pile of dung which was conveniently piled up below.

Stephen realized now that his own position was precarious for the thatch was old and rotting and he could not get a purchase on it any way. While Piers was being angrily taken into the hall, only Lucius was there to watch his twin and understood immediately that he was in trouble.

How it happened they did not know or indeed ever remember, for Lucius ran to break the fall of his brother and they both landed on the cobbled yard and pain shot through Lucius shoulder while Stephen lay seemingly unconscious. The kitten meanwhile bounded down safely to return to its mother in the byre.

When the girls came out to give their thanks they were shocked to see the brothers lying on the hard cobbles, Lucius ashen faced clutching his shoulder while Stephen lay apparently lifeless beside him.

Running back into the hall Lina gasped out the fearful news, told Rowena what to do, then ran with James who had just come in with the animals, to the river to hurry into the flat moored there. A good river was running but all the same, James pulled mightily on the oars while Lina wept quietly holding the tiller oar.

Stopping briefly at the first town, James gave a good coin to a boatman to send word with all haste to Lady Highclere that her sons had fallen off a barn roof and she must go to them immediately.

On they went, this time in another boat with two good oarsmen, leaving the flat for Clary and James was able to sit in the stern holding Lina tight, his cloak wrapped about her, and consoling her as best he could. Lucius he was sure had either broken an arm or collar bone, but Stephen? He closed his eyes remembering the ashen face of his second brother lying there on the cobbles. He would thrash that spoilt little lad when he got back, see if he didn't.

As soon as they arrived James ordered a large horse and taking Lina up in front of him, rode with speed to the castle. They must find the doctors, Deborah's sons and return to the hall as soon as possible.

Meanwhile back at the hall Rowena gently threw covers over Stephen still lying on the cobbles and ascertained that yes, Lucius had broken his collar bone so tied a soft scarf tightly around him to support the arm and took him in to sit by the fire and into the care of her sisters. Now she took his head into her breast and held him, not caring who saw, but if they did, they would just understand it was for comfort, which it was.

John meanwhile had somehow managed to draw the covers around and under Stephen and gently, inch by inch eased him onto a broad plank and was drawing him into the hall. Everyone whispered. John's wife, Maria took out great grand father Lee's book and poured over it close to a candle flame. Stephen remained deathly silent but they saw he was breathing so drew him close to the fire well covered, hot stones at his feet and waited. It seemed eternity and finally the younger girls lit horn lanterns and placed them on the bridge to give courage to those returning home. The waiting was so painful it was a small task to keep them busy.

Then Rowena realized she had not prepared the meal so they scurried about chopping vegetables quickly and silently, and she took a good lump of bacon from the store and set the younger girls to make little herb dumplings to drop into the pot. Karen then thought sensibly to go to Clary's old room where she lit a brazier so at least when they came in from the chill river, they might be warm.

At last they heard the horn and several of the girls, pulling shawls about their shoulders, ran out, oh so grateful to see Clary and Sir Thomas who came in quickly, and Clary fell on her knees beside her sons.

"I am not gravely hurt," said Lucius, "and see, the girls have read in great-grandfather Lee's book what to do so I am bound up and not in a lot of pain." He paused and looked down at his brother. "I tried to break his fall, mother, but could not. I am hoping the Scrivener boys will come soon for it is Stephen who needs them, not I."

Clary held his head in her hands and kissed him, then felt Stephen's head, and dropped a light kiss on it. She was shocked and cold with fear, how had this happened, her wonderful, handsome healthy sons? Never before had they such an accident, at least since James had his eye put out by that silly heifer.

They all began speaking at once, and somehow between the babble, Clary understood that young Piers had been the cause, spoilt, disobedient child he was. With a scathing look at Jessica, she took up a candle and together with Rowena and Maria went to her old still room. There the two girls lit more lights then sat, watching sister and aunt with her hands in head thinking.

"Fetch "The Stone", please, Rowena, I am sure Deborah's sons will have medicines, for James will tell them the problem, but at least let us make some strong willow bark tea for Lucius."

They worked well together as of old, quickly snipping the tough bark into the heating water while Clary searched through her small pots of salve, more to keep busy than with any thought of doing good. Rowena assured her that they had kept up the stores of salves and teas since she left, and Clary felt warmly towards these good young women who so resembled her in every way.

Another horn sounded and the younger Scrivener son strode in behind James and tossing his cloak to one side, fell to his knees beside Stephen. He was a good doctor and liked this family enormously but his experienced eye told him that Stephen Byford was gravely ill, with possibly many broken bones. Quietly and quickly he instructed everyone what to do. Swiftly, on felt slippers they ran about and drew the great clothes maidens around Stephen and hung blankets on them to make a small private room in front of the big open fireplace. Even Fleur who felt a warm love for David Scrivener could not even smile at him, the situation was so grave. Lina, desperate to have word of Richard finally asked her new father, who taking her hands explained quietly that Lord Rupert had taken Richard to court and, he dug into his jerkin, here was a letter, asking forgiveness for not giving it sooner. So Lina ran lightly and took a wax candle stump and lit it in the girl's room where she gratefully read it and tucked it next to her heart under her bodice.

Then most of them retreated to the second hearth, now lit, where the big pot was bubbling gently. Quietly they drew up stools and sat cupping their bowls, all staring into the fire, so afraid.

James would never forget that night. Carefully stripping the clothes off Stephen so that his wounds could be seen, David Scrivener straightened the bent legs and assessed his task, perhaps some broken ribs? Certainly two broken legs.

"Some bendy withies please, James, but strong. Split and smoothed please. Rowena, ask your Aunt Clary for good linen bands, I have some but fear I might need extra."

Both James and John went out into the evening gloom to the stack of hurdle withies and took them into the hall where they could see better and began work as swiftly and quietly as they could with their two sharp adze. At one moment James looked up to see Jessie clutching her son with a fearfully worried look on her face, but held his tongue.

"Do you have any soft felt, ladies?" David sat back on his knees and appealed to the girls. Off they went to search in their many chests and returned with odd lengths of felt, eyes huge with anxiety. Gratefully David took the felt, assessed it and put it to warm on the maiden. Smearing good comfrey salve on the shattered legs, he gently bound the legs with the felt before reaching for the withies. After bending them he chose the smoothest and more flexible then bound the leg with soft bands of linen. Now David took a hold of one of Stephen's legs and telling James to hold him carefully under his arms, pulled, till a snap told him the broken bones were in place. Then he did the same with the second leg and everyone winced at the sound. Listening to Stephen's breath, David thought it better to get on with the painful task while his patient was in a faint. When both legs were firmly strapped together with more withies, David then went over Stephen's body. Bruises had begun to show and he feared for sure that some ribs were broken, but they would mend in time. Again smearing comfrey salve on Stephen's chest, he laid on more felt and many soft blankets, then he listened again and felt he could do no more for now.

Worse, privately, he feared that Stephen had hit his head on the cobbles, for a small trickle of blood seeped through his fair hair and he earnestly wished his brother were here to give an opinion and help. Having carefully sponged the wound clean he loosely wrapped Stephen's head in a clean linen cloth. Then he tried to make the unconscious boy as comfortable as he could, tucking sheepskins under his head and buttocks for when he woke.

"Now we must wait, and I smell willow bark tea, Lady Clary, keep some by while I attend to Lucius."

It was a very quiet family who absently ate their pottage and bread and dared not to look at each other. Karen organized two pallets by the fire to be made up for David with James beside Stephen should any help be needed and silently the young ones went to bed, not to sleep but to worry and Clary held her son's hands and kissed them and tried not to weep. Jessie had taken her twins to their room and was not to be seen or heard.

Night had fallen but James ran up the hill carrying a big horn lantern to the forgotten oxen and brought them home.

CHAPTER FORTY TWO

DAVID

Having not been to Byford Hall before, David was impressed. His work with the injured brothers done, he sat back on his heels and surveyed the tall building with its blackened beams and its fine proportions. While ministering to his patients, he had been aware of quiet activity all about him.

He knew his mother was deeply attached to the family, having known them since she was a small child. He had of course met them, at least some of them, at the duke's for great events. Somehow he had been too busy to notice them carefully, except one perhaps, Fleur, who he had danced with and enjoyed her fair beauty.

Night had fallen and it seemed most in the place had gone to their beds. David heard James, the eldest son, speaking quietly to his mother, then leading her away, Sir Thomas with them. Then, stoking up both fires, James rolled into his blanket and watched his brothers.

Lucius was propped up in a cupboard bed close by, great bolsters supporting his back and his injured shoulder. David went across to him with a cup of willow bark tea and he drank it, barely making a face, for it was very bitter.

Stephen was another matter, he was still unconscious, his breathing shallow, there was nothing to do but wait so David too rolled himself up and stretched out on his pallet facing his patient. Through the night, James rose many times to keep the fires going and twice he changed the wrapped heated stones to tuck about Stephen's broken body.

David finally fell asleep as dawn came and with it the family, quietly going about, doing their tasks.

"Sir Thomas, perhaps you can go to the Duke and ask if Joseph Scrivener can come, I have a feeling that David would like his help." James, always the first up, never seeming to need very much sleep, woke John and pushed the flat off with the two men in it.

Deborah wrung her hands in sorrow for her friend's sons, and hastily sent off a boy to find her elder son, Joseph. Of course he must go, for David would need his help. She quickly packed up a bag for her sons with clean clothes and bandages, should they be needed. They had a good apprentice, a distant cousin of her husband, he could cope in the absence of the two physicians.

It was a fair day when the mist had lifted, and for autumn, it was mild and when the sun broke through, it became warm. They opened all the shutters at the hall to let the air and sunlight in, which made everything somehow seem more cheerful.

Everyone was alerted to the horn and ran to greet the boat from the duke's castle. There was Joseph and a small well wrapped figure, it was the Lady Ursuline.

"My dear child," Clary reached to help her up. "What are you doing abroad so early? And does your mother know you are here?" Ursuline hung her head, she looked very tired.

"I could not sleep lady, I was so worried about Stephen, so I persuaded Joseph to bring me. But I did leave word, so they know where I am."

Clary was exasperated, another anxiety. She pursed her mouth and gave Joseph a fierce look but he only raised his shoulders as if to say, I tried!

They trouped into the hall and Joseph went to speak with his brother quietly. Then they both knelt beside Stephen and Joseph examined him. After looking at the leg splints over which he nodded, he removed the cloth on Stephen's head. Karen was close by and ran to do his bidding of fetching boiled water. Gently, he wiped away the crusted blood and looked at the wound. Speaking softly to his brother they put some comfrey salve on and re-wrapped it. Only then he went to the cupboard bed to speak gently to Lucius and saw his arm was bound to his body so would mend in time.

At last the anxious family drew the two doctors close to the fire where they were given hot milk with honey and oat cakes and then they waited.

David looked to Joseph who was the elder and probably more experienced and nodded. Joseph gazed into the fire and began to speak quietly.

"Lucius will do," he said, "A broken collar bone will mend but he must simply not work to allow it to break again. Thankfully he is a strong young man and has been well nurtured." He paused. "Stephen is more gravely ill, and David has done a good job on his legs which will take longer to mend. It was the blow to his head which worries us. Perhaps the best thing is that he is unconscious, so he is obliged to rest. I would very much like to take him home with us but not yet. We really do not know the extent of his injuries so he must keep still."

The family listened quietly, Thomas holding Clary's hand very tightly.

"I would like to show you how to move him just a little each day till he wakens. If he gets sore, it will not do. By chance you have any more sheepskins?"

To which James jumped up and ran out to return before long with several skins over his arm, glad he had made more than enough.

"Luckily, David, we had worked on these when we killed the lambs, and they are soft and clean, will they do?"

David gave a rare smile to James who he much respected and taking Clary, Karen and Rowena, behind the screens around Stephen, they heard him quietly giving instructions.

"Use the sheet to tip him to the side very slowly. Push the sheepskin under but put salve on his back and buttocks first, rub gently, about four times a day, then clean linen before resting him on the sheepskins and place cloths between his legs in case he soils himself."

The rest of the family stood by the other fireplace and held their breath, Lina and Ursuline clutching at each other in anxiety.

"Now," said David, sure that these good women would do their very best, "I have a task for you all." As one they brightened, a task, thanks be to the Virgin, now they could do something. "One at a time, with intervals, for he must rest in his sleep, I want you to speak with him. Quietly, gently, simple things, which he might be glad to hear. For very often people who are as he, unconscious, can hear, and later when they wake, tell of it. So take it in turns. Do not tire him out, perhaps you have an hour glass?" So this treasure was quickly brought from one of the court cupboards which came from the manor. "Oh excellent. Now, every hour for just a tenth of the glass, one must speak to Stephen, one at a time, make a rota, domestic things, what is going on about the farm, nothing taxing or serious please. Who will be in charge?"

Lina stepped forward.

"I will Doctor Scrivener, and we thank you for your time and care of my brother." She was near to weeping but Joseph gave her a little hug for courage, so she gave him a watery smile instead.

Once more the Scrivener brothers spoke quietly together and David announced he would like to stay for a few more days while his brother returned home.

"And, if you please, Joseph, you will take the Lady Ursuline, as I am quite sure her mother will be displeased by her sudden departure." Yet looking around, Ursuline had disappeared and once again Clary set her mouth and rounded on her daughter and nieces, unusually for her, raising her voice. Here she was for her sons, having left her baby daughter at the castle, and troubles seem to pile up, she could barely prevent herself from weeping.

"It will not do, girls," she hissed at them to their astonishment, "she is naughty and self willed and we will be the ones in trouble when her parents come to fetch her." Yet Ursuline could not be found and no one seemed to know where she had hidden, so exasperated, Clary wrote to the duchess, trying not to sound too indignant, and gave the letter to Joseph to give her.

In her still room she put her arms about Thomas and leant into his jerkin.

"Oh my love, you see, another naughty Ursuline, determined to have her own way, we must find her and return her home." And Thomas held her firmly and comforted her as only he could.

But Ursuline was in the apple store which was where she and Stephen had sorted apples the year before, and she hid behind a great cross beam and ate apples and waited. Then, in the night, she crept down and oh so quietly crept to Stephen's side, just James seeing her but he shut his eye and pretended he was a sleep. So she whispered to Stephen, holding his hand, told him where she was hiding, and that she loved him and wanted him to get well so that he would wed with her. On and on she whispered in his ear, the firelight flickering over them, until she felt she must not tire him as had said Joseph and she crept away back to her hiding place with James behind her.

James, being the good soul that he was, said not a word to anyone, but watched her and shortly afterwards, went up to the apple store with a blanket and a dish of food and assured the stubborn girl he would not tell, yet. And kindly, as was his way, told her that he thought she was doing Stephen much good with her night time visits, but that sooner or later her parents would come for her and that she, and indeed all of them, would be in dire trouble.

The duchess was furious. She raged and stamped at her cowering husband, her English quite deserting her for her mother tongue. The duke in turn was distraught, but probably more so than his wife, because hadn't he been through all this before years ago with his sister.

"This is what comes of mixing with low people," she raged at him, "irresponsible, only thinking of their own sons, not of our daughter. Goodness knows what will befall her in that place."

Suddenly, the duke brightened and wiped his eyes for he had been weeping remembering the last time. He rang the bell by his chair to summon a page.

"I will send for the two Woodman nephews to come, they must go to the hall to their relatives. No doubt they will be of use now they are short handed with two young men injured. They will find and bring Ursuline home." This at least quietened the duchess somewhat.

So it was that John and James Woodman, Clary's young brothers, were summoned from the port, where indeed there was not so much work. The duke met them in his solar which he thought best, so as not to have his lady rage at them, who were innocent of everything. In no time they were going upstream, more anxious to hear that their young nephews had fallen and were hurt, than the disappearance of the young Lady Ursuline.

They passed the boat with Joseph Scrivener in and stopped, holding tightly to each other's craft for a few moments talk. Sorrow filled their faces at news of Stephen, who still lay silently, while Lucius was thankfully not so hurt. As they pushed off waving, they realized they had not enquired about the duke's daughter, but well, they'd know soon enough.

The horn summoned those who were not involved in busy tasks, and ran out to greet the two young uncles who were joyfully welcomed. Clary held her brothers both close and wept, for she had not seen them for some time and surely this was a most excellent moment to appear.

"The duke sent us, Clary, Sir Thomas" one said. "We will stay and be of help as you are short handed," said the other. "But we must not forget that perhaps the main reason we were sent was to find and return their daughter, the Lady Ursuline. They are most anxious to have her home."

Faces clouded, and James busied himself helping tying up the boat securely, averting his face. But he too was glad to see these handsome twins, all so a-like the rest of the family if dark haired instead of fair and rather more ruddy faced from sea and wind. To take the attention away from his guilt, he suggested to everyone's pleasure, that he take a horse and go to fetch Felicia and Robin who would also be delighted to see their sons.

In they trouped in where the atmosphere was suddenly more happy while the girls ran about fetching chairs and stools and James and John Smith brought in more wood for the fires.

The young uncles then looked at their poor silent nephew and felt his brow. Somehow this was quite the worst accident they could remember in the family, apart from James eye, which in the end seemed a Godsend. Lucius was more than glad to see them, and more, to hear that it being autumn, neither would be captaining a ship till spring, and therefore would be able to stay, and help. Lucius felt half his anxieties disappear as he had worried gravely how James and John Smith would manage to run the place without them. All that remained now to be solved was Stephen's health, but he had great faith in David who kept close, quietly and carefully watching over him.

"Where have you hidden the young lady?" one twin asked. The sea of innocent and surprised faces looked up at them and heads shook.

"Truly, lads, we do not know, for she slipped away and hid herself knowing that she would be ordered home," said Clary quietly, "I am afraid," she hesitated, "what a silly thing to say." She laughed a gentle laugh. "I think that Ursuline cares for Stephen, I have been watching them, and worrying, of course." Now the older girls looked down at their feet and did not dare to catch each other's eye.

"You see," Clary waved her hand at them, "I was not the only one who noticed. Look at them, guilty girls. But," she raised her voice, "it will NOT do! Just because Lina and Richard are betrothed, does not mean that the duke will accept a yeoman farmer for his daughter." There was silence in the hall, except for the crackling of the fire.

The family came from the marsh tower and quietly rejoiced in each other despite their anxiety over Stephen. They only stayed one night, but Felicia insisted on taking Jessie and her twins with her, for the hall was suddenly so crowded and Jessie looked very cowed and downcast. Not a word was said about the cause of the accident, but Felicia learned of it privily from Clary yet promised not to speak of it. Young Piers was spoilt, no routine, no discipline, well she would see that he had both at the marsh tower despite his foolish mother.

On the third night after his fall, Ursuline came again, held his hand, kissed it sweetly and wept silent tears and begged him to get well. Somewhere in the mists of his being Stephen heard her, and knew who it was, and in the darkness smiled. Without much strength, but all the same he knew he must tell her that he felt the same, he pressed her hand and with a cry, she realized what had happened.

David jumped up from his pallet on hearing, and James ran to light a candle so they could see.

"He pressed my hand," Ursuline wept, "He pressed my hand."

James always knew what to do and ran to push a poker into the hot embers, worrying up the fire to a good blaze and then to fetch milk and honey and he gave the cup to David and together they very gently lifted Stephen's head up and spooned the warm drink into his mouth. Now his eyes opened, and the first thing he saw was a sweet, tear lined face before him, so he smiled again.

In the night, the weather changed suddenly and the sky was black in the morning very soon to deluge with heavy rain. Once again more wood was brought in, the fires were well lit and candles were brought out and all the shutters were closed tight. Yet despite the darkness in the hall, the mood was light for they all now had hope that Stephen was getting better. Even so, David asked them to be quiet for him and to continue speaking with him in shifts which of course delighted them. And each one sought in their minds something new and exciting to tell him of their day, giving him a sip of chamomile tea, or milk with honey to sustain him.

Even so, it was a grim time with everyone always wet and a new leak in the hall roof which the twins and James saw to with many anxious eyes watching as they climbed up high and stuffed the cracks in the thatch with moss, which had been gathered in summer and was kept in great sacks in the barn specially for such emergencies.

This was an opportunity to weave despite the dimness of the hall, nothing fancy, just plain linen cloth which would make smocks and cloak lining for the coming year. Any spare hand was set to carding and spinning the wool and it was amazing how much they achieved and even Ursuline learnt, to her great satisfaction. Then out came the lace cushions and the better linen thread was miraculously changed into lengths of beautiful lace.

"Well, Ursuline," said Lina. "You must take a gift for your mother, she will be greatly impressed." Which made the young lady, toil ever more diligently.

Every day, come rain or shine, milking done, Rowena took the younger girls to the cheese cave to put the lamb rennet in the great copper pans for the morrow when the curds would be cut and hung up in stout cloths to drain. It was good to be busy and the young ones had to learn, so with the emergency, everyone was more willing to help. But, tasks done, they ran back to the hall, cast their shawls on hooks to dry and took up new ones and huddled near to the fires.

To their surprise, a great knocking came on the outer door and they all looked up surprised, who would be out on such a night? And who was it, but Aunt Joan from the inn, wet through but joyful to see her brothers and sisters, and nieces. A tinker had stopped by to tell her that Jessie was at the marsh tower with her parents and the little twins, and something of the tragedy, so she thought it the moment to come. Yet how she laughed, as they took off her sodden clothing and re-dressed her as best they could. Aunt Joan was a great one for laughter, which was just what was needed and they clustered about to hear all her news.

Now that Ursuline had been discovered, she did her best to be helpful in all ways, yet it seemed the best thing she could do, was to sit with Stephen, who although weak, had began to be reasonable, but sadly, was feeling the pain in his legs.

David undid the outer binding and looked to see if all was well, no rubbing or sore places, and then re-bound the legs on the splints, changing the linen and gave him the good pain killing willow tea. At least with the extra hands, they could take turns to lift him and James set to making some sort of carrying bed with handles, in the hope the weather would improve.

On the whole, the mood was lighter at the hall, yet Clary fretted which caused Sir Thomas to decide he must return to be with their little daughter as well as take news to the duke.

Again, James set to bending withies into the flat boat and covering the hood with a large piece of thick felt they had made from all the scraps of wool and dag ends of many shearings.

"Will you come with me Lady Ursuline?" asked Sir Thomas, but when she began to weep he gave up and simply got into the flat, grateful for the modicum of cover, for the rain was relentless and more for the excellent James who rowed them swiftly downstream with the flow.

Having ascertained that his precious daughter was all too well, he continued with James downriver to see the duke. Both men were silent for they knew their arrival would bring recriminations from the duchess if not from the duke. Soaking wet, they were announced, and at least were given some dry clothes, hot wine and a good fire to warm up.

"How?" said Sir Thomas, "could we bring her in this terrible weather?"

James studied his feet. What a clever man was his new father, he would never have thought of saying that, for he and his siblings had always been used to be out in all weathers.

"She would have caught her death of cold, Sire, far better she stay at the hall till the weather improves. My lady would not hear of it, too great a risk for such a young girl, although the Lady Ursuline wanted to come with us."

And a useful liar too, thought James, trying not to smile. But later, in the chamber they shared, he teased his father who grinned in the dark.

"Ah but James, my son, if you had lived with this type of person all your life, you too would have learned how to handle them."

The sun shone again and Ursuline boarded a flat with Lady Clary, David, James and John Smith and suddenly the hall seemed so quiet and empty. Clary tenderly kissed her sons and promised she would return soon, just she missed her baby daughter. Smiling, they understood.

Yet Stephen was definitely better, furious with his inactivity and desperate to be up and about. The contraption which James had devised was a boon, for Stephen could be carried about, oh so carefully, but always within the hall for fear of tripping and undoing David's good work.

Lucius went with his twin uncles about the land to see if any damage had occurred during the foul weather, but apart from being very wet, all was well.

Suddenly the girls came to life with their washing, and hanging their linen up in the little cloisters beyond the hall towards Clary's still room. The autumn was well advanced but they joyfully went out in search of berries to dry for their wool dying, and went up to the little church to see if the poor abandoned Father Benjamin was well.

Life resumed a sort of normality with the pleasure of having their sea faring young uncles with them. They learnt more songs, and James and Stephen played their pipes so evenings were a pleasure. Then James gave Stephen a small sharp knife and some soft wood and told him to make a doll for Carola who would be back soon, and this gave him hours of concentration with not too bad a result.

Attention moved from Stephen to Karen, who was large with child and all the family were filled with anticipation, a baby, a new baby. James had built an oak cradle himself and carved it finely but hidden it away so Karen did not see it. Maria's little son was just walking now and was the doll of the hall, ever willing hands to take his, so many gentle girls eager to play with him.

Karen birthed easily with no fuss and was gratefully praised by everyone, well remembering the noise which Jessie had made.

James had asked his mother Clary if he could name the child, if a girl, for her. So there she was, another Clarissa, with pale skin and rich chestnut hair like her father. It was a time to rejoice and James truly felt he had never been so happy in all his life.

CHAPTER FORTY THREE

THE KING

It was a mild winter with practically no snow. Lucius healed well and began taking over his old tasks. The uncles stayed on, actually enjoying the space of the hall compared with their tall narrow house which they shared with the uncles, or indeed, the cramped quarters on board. Not least, they enjoyed the company of their young relatives and getting to know them. Stephen too was healing with monthly visits from David or Joseph who removed the splints from his legs and then began oiling and exercising the poor thin limbs. Poor Stephen, he was horrified looking down on his stick legs, but in time they would get better he was most earnestly assured. His strength took so long to return, he felt so weak and was furious by his inaction.

"You must rest," said David. "Do not try to run before you can walk. You had two broken legs and you must give them time to heal. Eat very well, which I know you will in this place." He laughed. Truly it was a pleasure to visit this family, and more and more he spent time with Fleur, Jessie's second daughter and confided in his brother that he wished to ask for her hand.

With spring, Ursuline came with Clary and her enchanting little daughter, Karina. What delight, another baby to play with, to walk holding hands, to sing to and to wonder at her dark curls, and bluest eyes. Then they had the exciting news that the king was, as he had promised, coming in the summer. Such excitement, so much chattering, and with Stephen now walking albeit with two crutches, beaming with delight and quite unable to hide his pleasure at seeing the young lady. Due to his inability to go far, and Ursuline's inability to be useful, they were spending much time together. Clary quietly scolded her son for his behaviour, telling him that in the long run Ursuline would suffer for her parent's disapproval and she would be lovelorn, as no doubt he would be too. Then when she had the opportunity, she spoke with Ursuline, and told her gently that Stephen must find a strong, hard working country girl for his wife, especially now when perhaps his legs would never be the same again, and that they must stop seeing each other so they would leave on the morrow.

Everyone at the hall sadly understood more or less why their lovely guests were leaving so soon and Ursuline wept and made herself look quite plain with swollen eyes and red nose. Stephen meanwhile was put onto a flat boat and taken to the marsh tower to visit his grandparents so there would be no sad farewells and no more trysts. It was a distressing time and there were few smiles in a home normally full of joy.

Lina packed some of her lengths of lace to send to the duchess. And little Carola, worried that her home seemed so sad went to John the smith and begged he made some fine sewing needles for her to send.

Just recently, while out with the animals, James had discovered a bank of the whitest chalk, and he had brought some home, rasped it finely, and placed it in a fine linen cloth.

"Now my dearlings," pulling each girl towards him he gently tapped their noses with the little chalk bag. "I think that this is much better than the flour which Aunt Jessie uses. Now if we put some lavender in with it, surely it will also smell nicely."

Suddenly everyone was collecting little lumps of white chalk and rasping and grinding it finely in a mortar, and certainly, the lavender made it smell wonderful. Here was another gift to send, a new thing, which pleased them all greatly, such excitement. Little bags of fine, yet strong linen trimmed with a border of lace, they were pleased with themselves and James for finding such treasure. Even Jessie was impressed and asked for one to powder her nose. Each soul at the hall prepared little gifts, wrapped in linen, for the desolate Ursuline to take. Of course they did not leave on the morrow with Stephen out of the way, and by the time she left, burdened down with gifts, Ursuline had regained her sweet face although it seemed she had stopped eating and looked thinner which alarmed Clary.

"We will have to support the duke in the catering of the king's retinue which I believe will be at least two hundred, if not more," said James, "so many hangers-on going for a holiday, no doubt most of them quite useless." The family were surprised, for James didn't normally speak badly about anyone.

"We must write lists girls, Lucius, of what we can provide. Perhaps when the Scriveners come again, we can ask them to consult with the castle staff."

So quite apart from their own needs, providing the ships, the Innmans, and of course old Father Benjamin, they began planning to grow more, breed more and gather more. Instead of eating the eggs, they set them under broody hens for chicks and soon the place was full of irate mother hens jealously guarding their young against any four legged creatures who might come too near. The springtime work was the hardest, with sowing and planting out, yet high summer was easier, provided it rained in moderation. They missed their young uncles who had livened up their days and lent some good strong arms to every task. But they were both sea captains and were needed by the senior uncles, now becoming old, to take ships, cargoes and passengers all over the world.

They were all out in the fields in front of the hall on the other side of the river planting a second crop of parsnips when Fleur straightened up, easing her back, and looked to the East where a small group of horsemen were approaching. Quickly she pointed them out to James whose sight was not as good as hers.

"Run," he called to Rowena who was the nearest to the bridge, "Run and shut the main gate quickly, for we do not know who these people are." Then he in turn ran to be there to meet them, carrying his hoe, whoever they were. It was unusual for horsemen to ride along the towpath, for local people always travelled by boat. Anxious, the girls stopped their planting and stood up and watched and the group stop before James, dismount and then shake his hands. With relief the girls bent back to this the most wearing and boring work, yet they all loved roasted parsnips, and Clary had taught them a wonderful new pie, bacon, onions and parsnips in pastry. Yet they hurried for they saw the visitors going into the hall with James and were eager to join them to see who and what.

Such a surprise, for they were two Jeromes and three Andersons, so it was a merry evening after the girls had hurriedly washed their legs in the river and run into the hall. The familiar Jeromes were as always, big and blonde and brimming with life and fun, while the Andersons were rather quiet, strangers, albeit kin. Of course it was Lina and Rowena who introduced everybody to them, and took out the Book of Hours to trace their relationship.

Never had the milking been done so swiftly or the pans set for cheese done with such haste, for here were visitors with news to tell of other places.

All aches and pains of the working day forgotten the girls ran around and laid the board as beautifully as they knew how and lit the silver candlesticks with wax candles. James pulled great jars of ale and cider and they lit the two fires for although it was not cold at all, it was heartening and cheerful. Despite not expecting guests, the girl's managed to lay on a fair repast of cold, thick, minty peas pudding, two pigs chaps, which they had intended for Sunday, and cut into thin slices to lay on the bread and three cheeses, followed by wild berries which the youngsters had proudly picked and even opened their mouths for examination to check they had not tasted any on the way.

After the young ones had gone to bed, it was the Andersons who explained just why they had come, having been sent by Master Woodman and his lady from the marsh tower.

They were square set men with fine faces and light hair. Well dressed for yeomen, they spoke with a different accent which took the hall people some time to get accustomed to.

"We went to see cousin Felicia because Castle Pomeroy is now abandoned, Sir Godfrey having died ages ago, without issue. Of course we thought that someone of that usurper family might come to claim the castle and land, but no one did, and we and ours have cared for it, using the land for grazing and so forth, collecting the tithes safely, until we decided what we should do. We felt it time for the family to come back, for it is needed and we are there, to offer every assistance."

The whole family fell silent at this news. Of course they knew the story of how Sir Godfrey had ill used their women folk, and driven them out with extreme roughness. And how, being a party of women, they had left, realizing that they were no match for such a vitriolic man. Even so, it was all a long time ago, and life had changed.

"We shall have to speak to my mother, Clarissa about this," said Lucius, "her good husband, Sir Thomas Highclere will know what to do," and left it at that for the moment.

It was a jolly evening, getting to know the old and new friends or indeed kin and they spoke long into the dusk.

"I am impressed with the work you have done in the marshes opposite" said one Jerome, "it is some years since we were by here to see our mill relations." The other took it up. "We were not even sure if we had come to the right place, for it was so changed. Your dykes and your willows have dried out the land marvellously, we remember it as a great waste of marsh and now it seems it is all fine, viable land."

The three Byford men laughed, for of course they had forgotten the years of toil which had gone into digging the drains to take off the surplus water to run into the river. Or the endless planting of willow slips, and the eternal moving of stones, to the edges of the fields.

"It was mainly our brother, James you know, for he is the elder and stronger, and seems to have boundless energy." They laughed lightly.

"Well," said James, "I was the lucky one, for I was adopted into this family and was so happy, for the first time since my childhood when my foster mother, Annie died, it was easy. For when Mother Clarissa brought me here it was a paradise compared to what I had before. Father Lucas taught me so much, which as a seeking boy, was wonderful. I was fed good food, well, you see how well we do," he laughed his soft, kind laugh, "I belong to a beautiful and ever increasing family. Who could ask for more?" He reached out and caressed his wife Karen absently. The guests noted the small girl asleep on her lap and that she was with child again. Surely this was a good place.

They smiled, everyone. Even if they knew the story, coming from James, the man of the hall now, it was sweet music to their ears. Carola gently wrapped her arms about his neck, kissing him extravagantly as was her way, and he drew her onto his lap and cuddled her, for she treated him as her father. James' wonderful chestnut hair and beard were now filled with white, yet he was just the same as always.

The following day the Jeromes made their way to the mill downriver while the Andersons stayed awhile, and saw what a fine, well run farm Byford Hall was. They were impressed and hoped that some of these excellent young people, would come back to Castle Pomeroy with their energy and knowledge.

It was Lina, of course, who wrote to her mother. It had to be small writing for they had very little vellum left so she told her parents the minimum. Yet this had a fine result for her when absently mourning her lack of writing materials, the Jeromes brightened, for one of their large family still made vellum, the gift passed down from their grandfather and great grandfather.

"We have orders from the churches and monasteries, and even pay some of our taxes, albeit reluctantly, with vellum."

The hall family looked carefully yet surreptitiously at these long lost relatives, the descendants of Anders and Joan. There was no sign of the heavy features of the old baron, whose small picture was painted in the Book of Hours. It had been his natural daughter, Joan who had been mother to their own precious dead grandmother, Moya. These kin were different, with features rather fine, and their countenance although quiet, was pleasant.

"If you could stay a few more days," Lina took the roll of hostess for although Jessie was there, her mind had wandered and she was so deaf, there was no point in consulting her. It was a constant surprise to all of them how very different the twin sisters had grown. Yet they were kind to Jessie, and tried to care for the younger children who were definitely rather wild, as she certainly did not. "We can send word to my mother and Sir Thomas her husband to come to meet you, they would like that. And of course you must visit our little church and Grandmother Moya's grave, for she would be greatly pleased that you are here."

"Meanwhile you may care to visit Marsh Newton, our small town, I believe that we have some small tasks to do there and some of us can take you, and meet Aunt Joan and her family, more relatives." said Lucius with a twinkle.

Very carefully, they all looked at each other. This was the first time they had heard of a visit to town, but they held their peace, guessing that Lucius was merely being polite. Yet, sure enough, some small tasks were arranged and two of the older girls happily went with their guests and stayed the night at the Innmans which was good because there they met even more kin.

So the Andersons stayed, and a message was sent to Clary and three days later, a horn sounded and the whole family ran to greet the boat which pulled up at the bridge and Clary was joyfully relieved of her daughter and Sir Thomas met the Andersons and so once again there was a happy evening meal but this time with more planning.

The men stayed up late speaking, and Sir Thomas noted every detail in his fine brain and began to make a plan, one which he would not divulge yet, for it needed much thought.

Clary also brought word for Lina that Richard was with the king in France, which made her lovely eyes grow round, yet at night she could not help shed some tears.

It had been some months since she had seen him, and although he did write, it seemed the letters took so long to come, with old news. She even began to wonder if perhaps her dreams of being his wife were just that, dreams. So, heavy eyed next day, Lina went about her chores, giving herself put-by and unpleasant work so she could look miserable with foundation. Even if her new father was a Highclere, and even if her mother assured her that she had a dowry fit for a prince, Lina knew doubts in her heart, which was heavy.

The Sciveners had written so at least Fleur was joyful and they made many suggestions as to what the constable at the duke's castle would need for the king's arrival.

Thankfully with the long, light days, they had much time to finish weaving beautiful lengths and to stitch their new clothes, for Clary had brought much finery for trimmings. In some ways they were fearful of not being splendid enough, but Clary consoled them.

"You are all lovely to look on, with beautiful hair, and with simple clothes yet well trimmed, you can compete with everyone. Far better not to be over dressed and an embarrassment as alas, most of the burgers wives will be." Of course they would not all be going, it was not possible, so for the moment it was decided that Lina and Fleur and the three boys would go. If His Majesty stayed long, then they could change places, "For," Clary assured them, "It is really not so pleasant being in such a crowd, although you will mostly stay with us up river and visit daily."

The invitation came at last, written by Ursuline. In a flurry of excitement the girls completed their sewing, collected up more little gifts of lace, John's fine needles and powder bags should they meet agreeable people to give them to, and the day finally dawned.

Lina looking serene in blue and Fleur in green, with cloaks, not shawls on their shoulders, the girls stepped into the flat amongst the veritable pile of goods which James had insisted they must take. Next came the men, hair cut and beards short trimmed and looking every bit as fine as the girls. The cries of farewell followed them way down stream and the ones left behind went in to mope but hope that perhaps they would be sent for, eventually.

Sir Thomas had sent chairs for the girls and horses for the men and soon they were at Highclere Castle playing with the enchanting toddler, Karina, and talking non stop to Clary who smiled at their excitement.

All the goods sent from the hall were carefully itemised and sent on to the duke's constable and Thomas told them that they had even lent three quarters of their boards and benches from the hall, in order that there would be enough to seat the multitude.

Deborah and her two sons came to visit briefly and David spoke to the brothers about his wish to wed Fleur. Happy though they were, they felt that he must visit Jessie who was her surviving parent, but they were sure she would agree.

Now, with a smile, Deborah handed out jewels to the girls, all made for them from the last of the Lady Karina's horde which she had brought from oh, so far away and so long ago. Light and pretty they were, earrings and necklaces which would set off their fair good looks and add to their new clothes. Clary simply smiled all the time, for life was good and here were her young people happy and so lovely, life had after all, been kind to them.

They took a large boat well adorned with pennants and greenery and the excitement was tangible. People along the way gazed at them, waved and blew kisses with their hands, for surely they were a sight to see. James for once was not pulling an oar, as he had done so many times in the past whenever there had been a crisis. He was a handsome, broad man, a fraction shorter than his brothers, and wore a silken eye patch licked over with a slick of hair so it was barely noticeable. As he sat idle, his thoughts flew back over his life, dearest Annie, Han, little Hannah.

There was a great jostling at the Duke's mooring stage with many boats vying for space and people shouting and they had to wait their turn, but even that was pleasurable, with so much to see. Suddenly a great and beautiful craft came up river, ten men rowing, and who was at the helm, but one of the twin uncles, the other, though they could not tell which one, standing at the prow. Lord Rupert and Richard were there too, having returned from France with the king.

And there sat the king, magnificently dressed and all smiles, with his lady and many courtiers looking very fine in velvets and satins and with jewels flashing in the morning sunlight.

It just happened that the hall folk's boat was near to the king's, and when the twins saw their sister and nieces and nephews, they waved mightily, so the king recognising them as kin, asked to be presented again.

What a scramble, amidst laughter, climbing up and out onto the stage and there he was, the king, bowing to them while the family bowed too and curtseyed low.

"So here you are, family of our friends who saved me from the sea?" said the king, and Clary curtseyed and said loud enough for all to hear,

"And we thank God that they did so, your Majesty." Which raised a cheer and a light clapping of hands which delighted everyone and then horses were brought for the royal party and off they went amidst much rejoicing.

At the hall, Rowena and Maria were making bread. This was a twice weekly task but they made less this time due to the fewer numbers. Maria's little son sat in an empty basket and kneaded some dough happily while the girls worked in their wooden troughs. It was such a regular thing to bake, no one thought of it as a chore, and generally they all took turns. Right now Karen was with child again so she could not help, for it was known that women with child did not make good bread. The younger girls were out with John, stringing up peas, a new art which caused the peas to be so fresh and green and easier to pick than when lying on the earth.

"They'll be back soon," said Maria, turning and pummelling her dough with grave concentration, "Do not look so downcast Rowena."

Rowena looked surprised, for she thought she was making a good show of being cheerful.

"You are right, Maria, you notice too much of course. But they will be back soon."

They worked on silently, each with their own thoughts. Although Maria was aunt to Rowena, they were close in age, and Rowena remembered Grandmother Moya saying that Maria was very like their fore mother, the quiet Fleur.

"I do hope that they are having a merry time," she said, just to break the silence. Yet in her heart she also hoped that Lucius was thinking of her as she was always thinking of him.

The days stretched and the duke and duchess were hosts to so many people while there were joists and wrestling competitions for the masses and the bowmen showed off their prowess, while the king and his party enjoyed it all immensely. One or other of the Scrivener doctors was always about to see to wounds, however great or slight.

In the evenings the minstrels played and those who wished danced. The duke smiled proudly at his daughter who was looking so beautiful. Yet the duchess, whose eyes were sharper, saw the reason for her beauty and gaiety, it was because of the handsome yeoman Stephen, and pursed her mouth. Fleur, Lina and Ursuline were a delight to watch in their happiness with their young men. Not one in the gathering could help but notice them, and how similar they looked too. Even so, the kindly Richard was appalled by the story of Stephen's serious fall and offered his arm on going up and down the endless stairs for despite being mended, Stephen's legs were stiff, and still painful.

"You must not leave till I tell you," said Sir Thomas, somewhat sternly, ever busy entertaining, hunting, organizing and all too rarely seeing his family at home at Highclere Castle where they returned with some of the overflow guests for the occasional nights. "I have important words to have with the king and you will stay, if you please."

Inevitably it rained, and hard for several days so the entertainment came inside. Now those with petitions to the king came forward and disputes were settled and some folk left smiling while others left with their mouths turned down.

His Majesty sought out a few noblemen with their families for good company and conversation in the evenings after dining and listened to the minstrels. Amongst them were the Highclere brothers, with Lady Clarissa and her handsome children. Two sons played pipes rather well and joined the duke's men making fine music together. Even the queen who did not speak very good English was charmed by the fair good looks and simplicity of Lady Clarissa's family. She was indeed happy to be there, in the country, near the sea.

At last Thomas had the opportunity to speak with the king about Castle Pomeroy, and he told of how the old baron had built a fine church there, which with all else, was surely suffering neglect. Quietly, with few yet sound words, he told the king the origin of the family, and of how the sea captains he knew, were all bound up in the story. He then held Clary's hand out to show the king her small ring. "It came from the de Alencourt, sire, or rather from Lady de Alencourt, the Grand-daughter of the king of the time." Intrigued the king looked closely at it, nodded, smiled and kissed her hand.

"So my Lady Highclere, perhaps way back we are related? I shall investigate be sure."

CHAPTER FORTY FOUR

THE NEW POMEROYS

A secretary was called the next day, an ancient and worthy old man who wore eye glasses, which the family had never seen before. He was filled with knowledge of his Majesty's subjects, past and present and carried many scrolls and his servant carried even more and heavy books. Sure enough, he had found out about Baron Roland Pomeroy and that the scribe of the day had written kindly of him, "Trustworthy" it was written.

"So, Sir Thomas," the king said. "I like your idea, that at last this family should re-gain what is rightfully theirs after many hardships. I see from the two wills, that all is in order and correct as you say. Poor ladies, to suffer so shameful a story. But, it must be done properly and from what you tell me, the first heirs are indeed the Woodman sea captains. They are the only sons of the line, they must be offered the title and lands."

Thomas lowered his head in thought, he actually had not thought of them, and now he somehow felt that John and James Woodman would not care to leave their seafaring life.

"I will send for them, majesty, only they can reply."

But he was right, for when they arrived the next day they laughed merrily at the idea of being landlocked, and came grinning, their weatherworn faces quite a delight to see as they knelt before their king.

"Not us," said one, "we have our lives mapped out," said the other." Offer it to nephew Lucius Sire, he is a fine man, a good country squire and is our sister Clarissa's eldest son, because you know, James was adopted and anyway, he would refuse point blank." Their grey eyes smiled and they looked to their brother-in-law Thomas.

"What do you think then, brother Thomas?"

Thomas was thinking, and asked the king if they could send for Lucius.

By the time Lucius came, the conversation had turned inevitably to ships and it was awhile before he was noticed.

"Lucius," said the king, beckoning him closer. "What say you to going back to Castle Pomeroy as baron, bring the area back to prosperity and send me fine bowmen? Your Uncles James and John have refused!"

Lucius gazed astonished at his king, so they all laughed at him. He then began to stutter which made them laugh more, but Lucius was serious.

"Sire, it would greatly please me to go back to our roots. But there is something which is forgotten. My Aunt Jessica was the elder, and her first daughter should have some entitlement. My aunt's only little son Piers, will take on Byford Hall in time, but if you will agree for Rowena and myself to share the baronetcy, that might be agreeable to everyone, especially my aunt. Rowena is a very sound young woman and I should know having grown up with her as a sister. If she could come with me, we could share all responsibilities. I understand from other kin living near there, the place is dire and seriously in need of much care."

There was a long silence, but it sounded good, and the king clapped his hands for attention.

"We shall have a ceremony, now, yes now. Summon my old secretary again. Call your brothers Lucius, your uncles are here already, I shall make some new knights this day, and you will see, the sun will shine again tomorrow," which by the way it did. They hurried to do his bidding.

"Sir James Woodman, oh Sweet Jesus," laughed the king, "which is which?" looking at first one, then the other, and liking what he saw, laughed again, so they all laughed with him.

"Sir John Woodman, now have I got it right?" and they laughed more. "Master Seamen to His Majesty, yes?" They bowed low. Turning to the others he went on, suddenly feeling a glow of goodwill in his heart.

"Lucius, Baron Pomeroy, and to have returned all lands originally taken by stealth by an unworthy.

Sir Stephen de Alencourt, a valiant knight, yes," he smiled kindly, having noted Stephen's limp, "I heard that you rescued your rascal nephew and niece from a barn roof, hence your unfortunate accident." He turned to James.

"Sir James Byford. Valiant adopted son of my kinswoman, Lady Highclere, I understand that I have many reasons to thank you for your love and loyalty to this sweet lady."

Eyes wide, the three brothers gazed at each other, and grinned, bowed low.

The king then turned to Sir Thomas and asked,

"There my friend, are you happy now?" So Thomas knelt down and kissed the king's hand and a tear fell on it, so surprisingly the king laid his hand on his loyal subject's head. "Enough my lords," the king seemed in high good spirits, "Tomorrow is another day and we will celebrate properly. Baron Pomeroy, send for the Baroness if you please, I should like to make her acquaintance. Now, let us to the mass and thank the good Lord for our many blessings."

At the hall, Rowena felt herself grow nervous, for she felt that Lucius would be home soon so she washed her hair with chamomile, combed it long and carefully and put on her second best gown and prettiest apron.

A horn sounded downriver and as one, the household ran, except Jessie who was happy sitting in her chair by the great fireplace knitting stockings, for now with Grandmother Moya gone, this endless task had been left to her.

It was James and Lucius.

Oh the delight, the hugging and kissing, sweet slender arms were wound around their two necks as if to choke them.

They told them, about the king, the happy times, the dancing and feasting and the music. Last, as if it were a joke, they told what the king had done, and although the family believed them, they did not.

"Come Rowena," Lucius felt his heart hammering. "James you and I will go to tell Father Benjamin, while you," he glowered at the gaggle of girls around them, "will make a feast. Perhaps we will take the pony and bring Father Benjamin down to bless us. What do you think?" They chorused their agreement and ran to their duties while the three went up the hill leading the old pony to the church.

So it was that Lucius and Rowena were married by Father Benjamin while the all seeing James, smiled on.

"But keep it secret for now," said Father Benjamin, "go to your lands and prosper and no one will know you are kin being so far from here. Wait till I am dead if there is any trouble, blame it on me. But be discrete." They held his icy hands in theirs and took him out to the pony and walked on either side to hold him steady till they reached the gate of Byford Hall at the bottom of the hill.

At the hall the girls had laid what flowers they could find on the table so it looked glorious and festive and Rowena caressed her mother and told her the news, shouting in her better ear, that now she was a baroness and would soon be going to Castle Pomeroy.

In their chamber, James held his wife and felt the miracle of his new child move against him.

"Well my Lady Byford," he stroked her hair, "your mother will be pleased don't you think?" But Karen was so full of emotion that she just sobbed into James' fine jerkin, her lovely green eyes which came from her fore mother, Adina brimming. Pleased? Of course she would be pleased, that her odd daughter, the strange looking, plain one, had made such a good and fruitful marriage. Finally she smiled and lifted her wet face to be kissed.

The girls came back from their many days away and at the same time a messenger arrived with a stout package of beautiful vellum from the Jeromes. Lina sat down immediately and wrote with her fair hand to their kin at Castle Pomeroy all that had taken place and that they now had a new baron of the old blood line.

Clary came too, with a barge of fine furniture and many rolls of cloth for of course she could imagine how desolate the old place would be, as indeed it had been when she had just once seen it as a child.

"You must also take a loom and some of Fleur's tapestries, but, Rowena, do remember to hang them in the sun, at least twice a year, and put bay and lavender behind them against the moths." She wrung her hands. "Oh my dearlings," tears in her eyes, "but what a huge task you have before you, although I know that our Anderson cousins will give you every help. Indeed the village and church people will be overjoyed to once again have a lord and lady to care for them. I am just so very sorry, my dearlings, that I am not younger so to come and help you."

They gently reassured her, and in their hearts they rejoiced that they were wed by mother church and that soon, they would be a proper man and wife, baron and baroness of their own domain.

At the marsh tower, Robin and Felicia, despite their age, were invigorated by all the good news so too were gathering many things to send off to Castle Pomeroy and the Jeromes, happy to be involved, organized great bullock drawn drays to take it all.

Before they left, Richard came and begged them to come once more to the Highclere Castle where he and Lina would wed.

"You must be there with us," he entreated. "I know we are young but we have made up our minds and father and uncle have agreed. Ursuline and her lady mother are coming, all the Scriveners too, but sadly, the long festivities with the royal party have taken their toll and his grace is not too well."

It was a charming wedding with Lina the most beautiful bride and Clary had taken out the last of the gold plate from Mistress Miller's chest, which was set on the high table for the feast and proudly displayed.

"I inherited it from my grandmother, Lady Moya." She told anyone who asked and they were greatly impressed.

When Lina left the hall, then Rowena, the younger girls, Maria and Karen took over all domestic tasks but it did seem very quiet without them.

James and Karen moved into Clary's rooms where Karen seemed to have a gift with herbs too so the tradition went on.

John and Maria took the boy's room and Stephen slept downstairs in Grandfather Luke's cupboard bed for it pained his legs to climb. So much change, but life went on and autumn came with wind and rain, Martin Mass and the cull of the beasts and the arduous work it involved.

The Jeromes stopped by on their way with their sacks of grain to have milled and left their stout barrels to be filled for the Woodman's ships. Nothing changed, but everything did, yet new babes were born, and James was happy to have another daughter who he named Annie, and two years later, another he called Hannah. Who would grow up at Byford Hall, and there learn to be useful women with hard work and happiness.

"I would like to bear you a son, my James," said Karen when the third daughter was born. James kissed her brow and stroked the head of the new baby.

"Not if you knew what men I have in my family my dearling." He replied, thinking of the violent Magnus. "These dearlings are perfect. Fret not for a son for we have been thrice blessed with these angels."

Word came from Ursuline that her father the duke was ailing, and seemed not to have any courage, although he was greatly satisfied with the honour paid him by the King's visit which had been such a success. He drew his eldest son to his ear and whispered some last instructions, then just lay quietly, listening to masses or music or to lady wife.

The duke died that winter, and his duchess was desolate and lent heavily on her daughter, while her eldest son, whose silly wife she did not like, took over, making many changes mostly not to her liking.

"How am I to grow old, the dowager here?" she would weep and go to their chapel where her lord lay now beside his sister. There she would kneel, touching their tomb and pray to the Virgin for guidance. At least Ursuline was being the perfect daughter, she thanked the saints for that.

If she seemed perfect on the surface, Ursuline was very definitely her own woman. Each week she wrote to Sir Stephen de Alencourt, her lovely yoeman, Stephen, and every week he would reply, albeit not so tidily, as he had never worried about book learning, leaving it all to his sister.

Ursuline determined to be friends with her sister-in-law and whenever possible visited her brother's quarters in the castle.

"In my heart," she told them one day in a light voice, "I believe my mother would like to return to her own home, to the warmth of Spain." The seed sown, the duke's wife spoke quietly to her husband on the subject, for she thought that a wonderful idea, having two duchess in one place, was too much. Finally, it was he, in turn, who lightly suggested it to his mother.

Duchess Magdalena listened appalled, for that journey? And the countries in between always at war, could she face it? It had been bad enough when she was young, but now? Days upon weeks of uncomfortable travel in the heat with fear of bandits and capture for hostage despite their great armed guard. Yet she thought and remembered, childhood memories, of a palace on a hillside with wonderful views over the sea to Africa, of warm winds, and cool water coming down the mountainside. Her memories of the city were not so happy, for her brothers and she had been tutored by harsh men and women and forced to wear tight and too hot clothing. It had been a relief when she had met and fallen deeply in love with the English Lord, even if at that time he was merely a third son. War and pestilence took the older two, so suddenly, he was a Duke and it was not so difficult to persuade her dowager mother's permission and to come with her to his far off island in the mist. It was terrible to be widowed and helpless, yet in the small hours of the night, she thought, and with the light of one small lamp watched her beautiful daughter sleeping peacefully by her side. Of course she must be found a husband, yet her son did nothing about it, as indeed neither had her duke. Well he had tried, but old men, who had died, and anyway despite their titles and lands, she had not really cared for them. The winter passed and spring came slowly, and Ursuline asked if they could visit Lady Clarissa and her new son, Robert, another wonderful surprise, this time as his mother, blonde, a gift of God indeed. When they arrived at Castle Highclere, Ursuline saw that her closest friend and cousin, Lina was also with child, and shed some tears in the night, making sure her mother would notice.

When Clary suggested that the day being extraordinarily fine and warm, perhaps they could even spend the night, they take a barge to Byford Hall, somehow the duchess was swept along with enthusiasm and off they went. The children well wrapped up, Clary anxious to show her family her new son, they were drawn by a great horse along the towpath and enjoyed the beauty of the passing country.

It had been a long, wearisome winter, and the duchess had felt the loss of her lord deeply. So many years had passed since they had met in the court of her brother, and while she mourned, she had begun to remember the tall, rather rough young foreigner with his chestnut hair and blue eyes who had smiled secretly at her. And yes, she even smiled at wondering at her boldness, in insisting that he was her man, even to persuading her mother, the old Donna, the dowager, to come with her to his country. After that long and dreadful journey, they had been happy and theirs had been a remarkably good marriage.

She remembered the unexpected. Indeed miraculous delight in meeting with David Goldsmith, who she barely remembered as a small boy, although she did remember his sister, her first real friend. It had been as a miracle to her mother, once more wearing her precious crucifix. So life had been good, even if she had lost three children in infancy, taken by God for angels.

Magdalena now felt a curious optimism and the relief, to further explore this country and agreed to go with her new, good fiend, Clarissa Highclere, who was a true lady, so natural and unaffected. Her years with the duke had been good, but now she realized that she had been tied to the castle and her family. Here was an opportunity to explore the countryside and meet the charming relatives of Clarissa in their home.

Such a frantic rearranging of quarters there was, and poor Karen had to leave her still room and return it to Clary who took the duchess with her. Ursuline of course, remembering her several happy previous visits was rarely to be seen, just at the board, and surprisingly, she made herself useful, collecting eggs, picking vegetables, sorting apples and sitting in the sun with the girls, sorting and pealing. Naturally whenever possible she accompanied Stephen and they both glowed with happiness despite being tactfully distant when the duchess was about.

"Let us go to the marsh tower, now we have come this far," said Clary, "I would like to show my little Robert to my parents." So another upheaval came about with stores and bedding being loaded on to the flats amidst much laughter. They sent back to the castles for more clothing and bedding which arrived soon enough.

Felicia and Robin Woodman had been warned of their visitors' arrival and the tower had been swept and burnished for them. The marsh tower now stood some way from the marshes, willows and fields filled the landscape where in the early years it had all been water.

The duchess was quietly impressed and openly delighted with this new excursion and the fine, country hospitality they received.

"I was born in this bed, Magdalena," said Clary, patting the beautiful quilt which covered it. "My seafaring uncles, twin elder brothers to my father who of course are known to you, were here as my father had gone to take the village midwife to another woman in travail. And I just arrived, perhaps an hour after my sister, Jessica." She laughed, remembering the story of how they had named her. "The uncles, who actually never wed, had at that time a lady each, one called Clara and the other Isabelle. They quarrelled happily until my astonished father returned to find they had another brace of babies, and it was he who settled the matter, by naming me, Clarissa."

Gone were the raw days of old, when the old hunting lodge had been broken and unlived in. Now, with the fine house skirting the tower, its windows shining in the sun, all the woodwork which Grandfather Stephen had made was now silver and mellowed, it was indeed a gracious home.

They spent many days there, and the duchess felt her sorrow lift with the spring which was extraordinarily good. Even Ursuline, who having left her Stephen at the hall, was agreeable, secretly pleased that her mother should meet his kin, and able to observe their fine homes.

By now, the little church in the village was quite substantial, for the local people had brought stones from round about, and built up the wood and sod walls of old. Every day, the new young priest, fearfully impressed with the new gentry, would come to the tower and give a mass in the tiny chapel built into the massive walls or they would go to his church which was a fraction larger.

Magdalena asked to be taught to spin, and was delighted with her success. Next as a host of birds, they scoured the surrounding fields for dye plants, and Felicia showed them the book filled with dye recipes written by Grandmother Moya when she was young, and they again all admired the exquisite tapestries done by Fleur, and later, the repetitive coats of arms done by the long dead true grandmother, Jessica.

"It is a little confusing, your grace, so many names the same, each generation taking them from the past." Felicia was enjoying her guests and daily the village people came and she told them what she would like them to obtain for her and sure enough, they would return with plentiful and good provisions for her to offer her guests and family.

In the evenings, they either sat in the long, low kitchen and talked, the younger ones enthralled by the stories. Even Magdalena drew on her childhood memories of her distant country, and told of heat and sunshine, figs and grapes growing abundantly, and the palace over looking the bluest sea.

Occasionally they would go to the tower and Robin would, as of old, beat a copper pot and set the girls dancing.

On an impulse, Clary called for the Jeromes to visit, and tried, somehow, to explain their relationship, which was not, but never mind.

"Dearlings," she was ever amazed at how alike they all were, big, robust, very fair and always agreeable. "Do you think it possible? Do I ask too much? Can you advise me, would it be safe for us to visit Castle Pomeroy?"

They considered, looking at each other, for this was a responsible quest.

"We will enquire," one said shortly, they had never been great talkers. "If we get parties of family to meet you at stages," said the other. "It will be safe." They pondered, looking at the floor. "And perhaps you did not know Aunt Clarissa that one of our lads is now smith at Castle Pomeroy so we will send word." Yet not one remembered that Joany, true mother of Jerome, had been daughter of the blacksmith at Castle Pomeroy.

Once again they packed up but this time great drays came to take them and Felicia and Robin waved and suddenly thought how empty their home was, until they settled in again.

"Mother, may I take Rowena one of your kittens, for they originate from James's Eagle, do they not?" After much indecision one was chosen, the most like Eagle thought Clary, for he was quite willing to dig his little teeth into any careless hand. "Be sure they won't have any trouble with rats and mice from now onwards." The kitten, securely put in a comfortable basket soon forgot his mother and enjoyed the constant attention of the girls.

It was an exciting journey, albeit slow, the oxen lumbering along pulling the heavy drays, yet there always seemed something to point to and wonder at. Each day, they stopped at a small woodsman clearing where apparently they were expected, fed fine meats grilled on open fires, country bread and ale and made their beds in the drays covered with stout cloths. Ah but, such an adventure. Even when it rained, the thick forest canopy shielded them, and the days passed happily.

On the third day, horsemen approached, but the leading Jerome waved and drew up his beasts, for it was Lucius with a groom. Such a joyful meeting, he embraced his mother, gazed in fascination at his small new half brother, bowed to her grace and kissed her hand and hugged the other girls, including Ursuline fondly.

The forest thinned out as they approached Castle Pomeroy, showing many, small timber built, lath and mud houses along the way. Clary was astonished, for the village was now indeed a town. Dominated by the fine stone church which Roland had built, so the first thing they did was to step inside, greet the priest, and kneel to say prayers in thanks for their safe journey and to pray for their ancestors. They passed down the main street where many people bowed and curtseyed to them, obviously delighted to have the old family visiting, past the moot hall which Lee had insisted was necessary, then on up to the old castle where a beautiful Rowena welcomed them.

"What a mercy you did not come three months ago," she said, pulling her aunt along. "Oh but you have never seen such a sad place, despite the attentions of our cousins, the Andersons." They wandered, or ran through the dim halls and corridors and at last settled in the solar where two little maids, obviously Jeromes, brought, cakes and wine.

The duchess was once more impressed and sat back observing this extraordinary family whom they had befriended. Lucius, ever hungry for news, pressed Clary for anything she could think of to tell him.

"I, we, Rowena and I, are greatly happy to be here, but we miss our family and the noise and chatter of the girls," he caught a hold of a passing cousin and drew her on to his knee. "So tell me miss, have you missed me?" To which she extravagantly embraced him ensuring he knew full well just how much.

They ate in the great hall with a huge blaze in the long chimney piece to cut into the chill which was inevitable in such an old, stone-built building. The kitten's basket was put to the side of the great fireplace and sure enough, thereafter, he became a fine mouser.

"The first Fleur was born here, so too Jerome," Clary told the duchess, "it is all written down in forefather Lee's book, who was an excellent healer, and their father. Perhaps Magdalena, you have heard of his healing book, for I know the Scriveners have a copy?"

After their repast Lucius showed them where they had restored the old well which obviously had a good, clean spring running under it, for the water was icy and sweet.

"Such a task that was too mother," he said, holding her hand, "so neglected and full of waste. But look," he led them to the buttery where a fine new solid oak door stood. "We found the key at the bottom of the well, where the wicked Sir Godfrey had thrown it, after killing poor old Agnes and locking all the staff inside the buttery." The guests were properly shocked and then impressed when Lucius put the great old key into the wonderful new lock which had been made by their new blacksmith, John Jerome. "We were fortunate indeed your grace, that all this was written down by our step-grandmother, the Lady de Alencourt. She was daughter to Joan, who was the natural daughter of the baron and to our foremother, Lady Felicia de Alencourt, who insisted that we all learned to read and write and every summer we took turns to visit her manor to learn book work as well as for the girls to be good housewives and embroiderers. You will understand, it was a joyful time for everyone."

Some of the girls were put to sleep in the gatehouse, and perhaps the shades of Lee, Fleur and Jerome smiled over them in their old home.

The following days they went to the fine church and the girls picked wild flowers to lay on the crypt of Baron Roland and his family, while the duchess took in everything with a shrewd eye. So they were not true yeomen stock at all, she wished that she could tell her duke.

People came to the castle, from courtesy and duty, and the few knights who lived round about were welcomed to the board so it was all very agreeable and many more days passed.

The happiest times were when they all sat doing small tasks in the lady garden, shelling peas, sorting wools and just chattering.

"It was very overgrown when we came," said Rowena, "it seemed much smaller with the bushes and creepers falling into the centre, but now," she spread her hands, "you see, it is just like in the Book of Hours."

They returned to their castles by mid summer, refreshed, renewed and content. Sir Thomas came with horses to meet them, lifting his wife off the dray and roundly kissing her and delighted in his little son, now not so little, indeed a big and bonny boy.

After they had left, Rowena gratefully let out her tight apron strings, for she was with child, and had thought it politic to not yet let it be known. Yet it had been such a joyful and unexpected time, and she was so grateful to her Aunt Clary, who was indeed, her mother-in-law, if she did but know, for it had been just what they needed, an interruption in toil.

"If it is a boy, we'll call him Roland, yes?" Lucius hugged his wife, disregarding the servant girls who were tidying up. But then, they were Jeromes, and kin, they smiled shyly from under their head cloths. They liked this family and it was well they were there for their brother was the blacksmith, and they were minding him.

"And if it is a girl, we'll call her Fleur. Yes?" Lucius replied, Rowena laughed.

"No more Jessicas, please, right?" They laughed merrily and went to help with the work, for they were truly blessed, and the visit had put them all in high good spirits.

"You keep well my dearling wife, eat well and sleep well and maybe we'll even have a brace again!"

CHAPTER FORTY FIVE

THE DREAM

The duchess found herself vaguely dissatisfied with herself and her life when she returned to the familiar comfort of her old home. Without a doubt it had been an excellent change, especially so since her lord had died. Not only had she found the company of Clarissa's family very easy, they had all been such a happy, busy family and now, she seemed to yearn towards a more simple way of life as theirs.

In the mists of her memory, it seemed familiar, and her mind kept going back to the possibility of returning to her childhood home. It might not be such a bad idea to write to her brother, or her nephews, to broach the subject. Picking up the silver bell beside her chair, she rang it firmly.

"There you are," she smiled at the page who had darted in. "Now, listen carefully, I want you to find Master Scrivener and ask him to come with his writing materials. You understand?" The boy nodded and sped away. So she had made one small decision, and would work on that.

Master Scrivener came with all speed, his satchel and his box of quills at the ready, he bowed. She noted sadly for a moment how stooped and old he was getting.

"Donna?" for they spoke in Spanish when they were alone and had business to do. He placed his vellums, slate and quills on a table close to the window, for the day was dull and it was rather dark. There was a comfortable silence between them, now, old friends as well as being lady and scribe.

"I would like you to write to my brother in Spain," she said, unconsciously twisting her crucifix, the one inherited from her mother which Deborah had given to her that first amazing meeting. "This was a good summer for me Jonathan, and my courage is higher than since my lord died. I begin to dream of returning to my old home, and wish to ask my brother if he thinks it possible."

As a good scribe, he listened and waited.

"It is the journey which frightens me, and I wonder if my daughter will accompany me." Of course she was thinking aloud. "I saw that her affection for Stephen de Alencourt lasts, and it is in my mind, that poor boy, with his injuries, the warmer climate might be advantageous to his health. As she seems determined to wed with him, this might be a good solution for all of us."

Still Jonathan listened and bowed his head. He too had been thinking along these lines, but more extensively than his donna, he cleared his throat.

"If I may make another suggestion my, donna?" she raised her hand, nodded, so he went on. "I have carefully watched all these young people, and I see that my son David is very close to Fleur Byford. Now you know that Fleur and the Lady Ursuline are devoted friends. Forgive me for suggesting to you that you will need a physician for your journey, let me say I would be happy if you had one. David tells his brother that he has asked for Fleur, so if the young people travelled with you, it might be a merry and useful party. Whether or not he returns here is another matter, but if he weds Fleur, it could be very agreeable." Magdalena looked directly at her scribe, a man she trusted, who was married to her dear Joseph's clever daughter. For a moment she did not reply, then smiled. Now that had been a marriage, which she had arranged, which had worked well for all of them.

"And Jonathan, please go in person to the port with the letters, and speak with the captains. It is now late summer, and I wonder if two," she raised two fingers in emphasis, "two ships could be arranged for our use for early next summer?"

So the dream was beginning and Magdalena and her scribe Jonathan felt a small excitement in their hearts.

The four Woodman captains listened to the quiet voice of their duchess's scribe. Well, a major journey, carrying special people, two ships, and some of their young relatives going. Not, they were assured, that any of them knew of the lady's plan, yet, for she wanted to know if it were feasible.

The two old and the two young captains looked at each other, their thoughts milling in their heads. To make two ships comfortable for the ladies, would be quite a challenge, for life on board was pretty cramped, it would take the carpenters all winter to re-fit. As one they nodded.

"Come," said Sir John Woodman, "let us go to the port and we will explain something of the problems such a journey would create."

"Yes," said Sir James Woodman, "much depends on how far they wish to sail, if just to the North of Iberia, or around it to the South. It would necessarily have to be a leisurely voyage, with many convenient moorings for the lady and her party. But come, you can see what we are up against. What ever the voyage, it would not be without its dangers."

So Jonathan went with the two young Woodman captains and enjoyed going on board a fine vessel and listening to the brothers discussing possible alterations. The smell and the sounds of creaking wood as the ship lay idly in low water was soothing. It was obvious that they much enjoyed their lives and work, and he knew from experience that they were very careful in all their dealings. Undoubtedly his donna would find the accommodation very cramped, but, if as the twins hinted, they made land frequently, they could even stay in convents along the way occasionally, or go for little pilgrimages. He had heard a little of his donna's journey when she and her mother had come to this green island. They had travelled by horse, and wagon when the roads were possible for the dowager but it had been a slow and painful journey, seemingly full of fear and hardship despite their escort of a small army.

On his return he went to see the duchess and told her his findings. Magdalena felt a new happiness and optimism and decided it was time to encourage the relationship of her beloved daughter and her non yeoman. First she asked her scribe to write to Lady Clarissa Highclere, for she missed her company and would like to speak privily with her on all these dreams. Clary was sound, Magdalena knew that, but how would she feel to have a son sent far away, even if it would help his health. When the letter arrived, Clary called for Lina, for she was near her time, and had told her mother that she did not want her gone visiting. This Clary understood, so again, it was Lina who wrote and explained the problem, inviting the duchess to come to see them instead, if possible.

On receiving the letter, the duchess brightened, another little journey, and as she so enjoyed the company of Clarissa Highclere, she made herself and her maid hurry with their preparations. This travelling had greatly cheered her and she was glad to have at least another little journey before the autumn storms came.

The two ladies sat in the garden house at the very top of the old tower having been carried by chair to save their legs. Magdalena looked about her with pleasure. The Martin-mass daisies were out and the little garden was neat and being prepared for winter.

"How clever you are, Clarissa, to have this dear garden, so private, so pretty." Clary smiled at her friend, wondering how she had ever thought of her as being pompous.

"Not me, my friend," she put down her sewing, "it was Thomas' mother who made this little house, the Lady Karina, using her own gold for the glass and how clever she was to make a kitchen and a sluice. It is a solace and now I become rather tired and stiff, I, as she, indulge in being carried up those dreadful stairs." They laughed lightly, for indeed the stairs were endless and winding. "It is a joy to have your company again, your grace." A hand was raised.

"While we are friends alone, there is no ceremony between us dear Clary, please?" They sat in companionable silence as do compatible women. "You will wonder why I wanted to see you again so soon? Of course for the pleasure of it, but also because I have a dream and it is good to speak to a good friend about such. I need to hear your views, I wish to have your opinion, yet I am concerned that I might distress you, and that would never do."

Clary listened to the beautiful still accented voice. Certainly she realized that the duchess had something of import to discuss, so she waited, and hoped the nurses would not bring her little children up just yet. She smiled her encouragement at the other woman.

"Our little journey Clary, to your old home, to your parent's tower, to Castle Pomeroy, I have re-gained my courage for life, a new optimism, and I am so very grateful to you for those delightful weeks. They will always be in my memory, an England which I barely knew, ever being cooped up in that great castle."

Clary waited.

"I begin to feel the need to return to my old home, to my old country. It seems such an ambition at my age, yet my mother did it coming here with me, so many years ago. But then, she was made of sterner stuff than I, having lived in an old palace above the sea so many miles from what we might call, civilization."

Clary listened, a thread of excitement reaching her.

"Then my sweet friend, you must go, even if I will be desolate without you. What is there to stop you?"

Now Magdalena did a strange thing, she sank on her knees in front of Clary and took her hands, pressing them.

"My daughter, Clarissa, my daughter, Ursuline, we are so close, and since my lord died, I tend to need her company ever more."

Again, Clary listened and nodded.

"My sons are fine men, grown with their own families, I have no worries for them. But Ursuline?" The silence stretched. "You know that originally I did not approve of Ursuline's choice of husband," she rushed on. "I was ignorant about you and your family and proud, yet now I see that you are indeed the finest friends I have ever had. If," she squeezed Clary's hands ever tighter, "if Ursuline and Stephen wish to marry, would you be agreeable to his coming with us. Believe me sweet friend, I have thought long and hard on all this, if Stephen came, the warm climate would help his injuries, only how could you part with him?" A tear fell from the corner of her eye and Clary wiped it away tenderly.

"Rise please, Magdalena, if the maids come in and find us thus, what will they think?" They laughed lightly and the duchess arranged herself on a seat beside Clary. "With so many sisters, yes, even a twin sister, I have never had such a closeness in thought with any of them as I do with you. I guessed what you were thinking, for I saw the yearning in your eyes when you spoke of your old home."

Then almost in a hurry they did speak, and the duchess told Clary what her good scribe had said, about Fleur and his physician son, and how he had already been to the port to see her relatives.

Their peace was broken with a whoop and laughter, two little children came running in followed by their breathless nurses. Karina, so dark haired with curls in front and Robert, with his very straight fair hair, close behind. The two women embraced them and the duchess sang them a little song in Spanish which delighted them.

"But Clarissa, God and his Holy Mother have blessed you greatly." and everyone smiled for indeed these little Highclere children were very attractive.

When they were led off, protesting of course, the two ladies continued talking till a maid came to light the candles and the fire.

"Lucius is gone," said Clary, "very happily taking the reigns of Castle Pomeroy into his sound hands. James, bless him, will stay at the hall to train young Piers to take over, and Stephen. Well my sweet friend, I shall miss him of course, but he has loved your daughter with a strong passion for a very long time. I think you are right, a warmer climate will help him whereas here with all his broken bones, his old age could be quite problematical. Now," she lent forward and kissed her friend, "send for your daughter and I will send for my son and let them see that they are not, disapproved of anymore, but even have our blessing. It will make waiting for Lina's lying in pass more agreeably."

Jonathan the scribe wrote letters to his duchess' brothers, and several more and dispatched them to the Woodman captains for the next ship going South. It was as if there was an urgency in all their actions, for now the duchess had made up her mind, she rejoiced in making plans. But she determined to be moderate, not easy for her who had always had so much. One maid, who would sleep with her, two cooks. Her mind flew from one task to the other. She ordered chests filled with old clothes to be brought out and saw to much sorting, laundering, giving away to the poor. It was a good feeling to be doing something so positive.

Ursuline stayed on at Highclere and kept her friend and kin, Lina company the last boring and uncomfortable days of her pregnancy. They played lutes and harps and sang and Lina was carried up to the top of the old tower where they relaxed in the comfort of Karina's old house. Richard too was loathe to stray too far and what ever he was doing, he returned by nightfall, to be with his wife and held her hard belly and laughed at the little heals which pushed up her ribs.

Thomas could not remember a better or happier time at Castle Highclere for with Rupert calm and relishing the thought that his one child would now produce an heir, all was very well between them.

Lina slipped from her bed and went to find Ursuline, although it was still night.

"Dearling," she held her hand, "I think my time has come, and I want you for company these early hours of waiting. Do come with me please, we will go up to the garden and be peaceful together."

If Lina was calm, Ursuline certainly was not and Lina had to sqeeze her hand very tightly to stop her from crying "Just we two, sweet cousin, for now, things will change, and your friendship is so precious to me, I need you a little longer just to myself."

So they crept up, step by step, Lina stopping, leaning against the stone walls of the stairs whenever a wave of pain overcame her.

At last they were at the top and Ursuline, who had learned much over the past times spent with the Byfords, now lit the fire and fussed over Lina who she helped into the most comfortable chair, a warm shawl over her.

Foolishly, the maids went into a rare panic until Clary calmed them knowing full well where the two girls would be. While she dressed, Clary could not help remembering Lina's birth. How she had run away and now she was grateful that Lina had a friend, indeed kin, to be with her.

"Leave them awhile," she said. "A first usually takes its time, andwe can make everything ready while they are at peace together."

Two hours later, Clary and a maid went up to the garden room carrying a tray. She smiled kindly at the girls.

"My but you have thrown the maids into a rare panic, disappearing like that. How goes it my dearling?" she spoke to Lina, "Not too severe yet?"

Lina looked at her mother with new eyes, she who had born five children, without, had said Grandmother Moya, uttering a sound.

On her knees beside her daughter, Clary put her hand on the hard belly.

"We are all ready for you my precious dearling, so when you are ready to come down, you will be carried in a chair," she smiled wryly. Oh but if anyone knew, she thought, perhaps one day she would tell her, running away from the squalor and cold of that cave, to give birth alone in the forest.

Lina looked at her mother gratefully.

"I think perhaps mother, I am ready now. The pains were not bad at first and it has been lovely having Ursuline with me this dawn."

So the chair was called for and the young men aware of what was happening, of their precious cargo, were extra slow, counting each step as they went down feeling important and just a little nervous.

Ursuline called a page to send word to the duchess to come, at all speed, for she felt that her mother would be pleased.

It was as if a wind blew through the castle, down the steps to the town, through all the little alleyways and paths. For the page, excited with the task of telling the duchess to come, threw his message to anyone he passed,

"The Lady Richard is in travail!" Each and every one receiving the news cast their eyes up, towards the castle, crossed themselves making a blessing, and hurried on, to pass on the news with glowing eyes, perhaps fingering their rosaries.

Even if they had not yet been summoned, the midwives gathered their baskets again, checking what was in there, and began the toil, up, up yet not minding, because another babe was coming and they surely wanted some of the glory of it. All day people watched the castle, for a maidservant had told her family, who had told everyone else, that she would hang a red coverlet on the battlements facing the town, for a boy, or a white one, for a girl.

By night, they were all weary and did not see the white cloth till they rose in the dawn. A girl child, ah well they were young, there was plenty of time for boys in the future.

Tired but happy, Lina looked at her little daughter in awe. A perfect little child with a white fuzz for hair and so far, having not opened her eyes, they had no idea what colour they were. She had been born in the early hours, a good sign said the duchess, an easy temperament for sure. Richard just gazed at this his first offspring, and smoothed back the wet hair from Lina's brow.

"Oh but you are so clever, my love," he whispered, "another angel, as you I think." So she slept then, sorry she had not given her lord an heir, but smiling at his words, was amazed at the perfection of their little daughter, and glad it was all over.

"Ursuline, my sweetest friend, we wish you to be Godmother and I hope you will approve if we name her for your mother?"

Both the duchess and Ursuline were delighted and on the third day, a small ceremony was held in the castle chapel.

"My gift to her is my crucifix," said Ursuline, taking it off and laying it on the little form, "for one day my mother will leave me hers, of which this is a smaller copy."

"And mine," said the duchess, "is the gold plate which my husband bought for me years ago."

Clary felt herself grow faint, for of course this was from Mistress Miller, left to Grandmother Moya and sold in days of need. How wonderful and strange life was.

When the excitement of the new arrival calmed, life resumed, yet with an urgency and Richard went to the port, sometimes collecting the duchess, ostentatiously just for an outing. Meanwhile, Ursuline went to visit Lina and the baby, Magdalena, always hoping that Stephen would be there as increasingly he was.

It had come as a shock to Stephen, his inability to work as hard and long as he had in the past. With Lucius gone, the bulk of the work fell on James, yet, now the farm was organized, it ran smoothly and James was clever in his training of young Piers who had grown into a sturdy and surprisingly willing lad.

True, the girls still helped with the planting out and helping at harvests, but altogether, there being fewer mouths to feed, life seemed easier. Whenever there was extra work, James went to Marsh Newton and brought hands from the church steps.

It did not matter which salve he put on his legs, in the cold of winter, he was full of pain and any exertion caused him anxiety. How could he make a life for himself and Ursuline? As handsome as were all the by-the-ford young, Stephen grew thin with worry, something which those close to him did not notice, but, the duchess did.

When they met at Clary and Thomas' home, Stephen stood in the background well aware that her grace did not consider him good enough for her daughter. Then one day she beckoned him with a jewelled hand.

"Sit with me, Sir Stephen, tell me some news of your life and doings." Stephen was shocked, well what to tell her? That he was as a broken reed, little help to his family and without any hope for the future?

"Your Grace," he hesitated, "I must be honest with you. I do little due to my poor condition. It is a shock and horror to me not to be able to help my elder brother, James, as I used. Indeed, all I seem to do now is the accounts for him, because you see, mother adopted him rather late and he had little education. Now with Lucius gone to Castle Pomeroy, he is the man of the hall."

Magdalena heard him and felt sorrow that she had not been more friendly to him in the past.

"Do you think that it is the cold climate then, Sir Stephen? For although I am much older than you, and never had as grievous an accident as you had, I must tell you, that the aches and pains of age are a trial to me. This is between us, for daily I find that I yearn for my old country, where the sun shines, indeed sometimes too hot, but now I think to return as my lord is dead and two duchesses in one castle is not so clever."

Stephen held his breath, surely, oh surely not. His heart pumped fast and he tried to steady his breathing. Was she indicating that she was going to take his beloved with her? So he had no reply and just looked at the floor, at the fine great decorated tiles which he had never noticed before.

"It seems to me Stephen," he did notice she had left off the Sir. "That you and my daughter have an affection for each other, and although in the beginning I was against the match, now I see that you are indeed a fine young man, from a most interesting and noble family." She rested her hand on his arm. "If my dear Stephen, you wish to wed with my daughter, Ursuline, you have my blessing."

Stephen turned to the duchess and gave her the warmest smile. Then taking up her hand, he kissed, it, hard, as a boy.

"Your Grace, thank you a thousand times, now may I go to Ursuline to tell her?" She smiled, such a charming smile but held on to his hand,

"I am not finished yet my boy, do not be in such a hurry, you must hear more." She then confessed her plans and his captain uncles' involvement and how, all being well, they could sail early summer the coming year.

Incredulous, Stephen again kissed the hand, tried to jump up and grimaced in pain at his foolishness.

"Lady," his grey eyes smiled down at her, "I will be the best husband to your daughter, and the kindest son to you. To give such happiness I surely know, you will have your reward."

It was out, the dream, which looked as if it might become reality. So much to do, so many letters to write, with wings on their heels, the young couple basked in their happiness, and helped where and how they could.

"You are not upset with me, my dear friend Clary?" asked the duchess just a little tearfully. "For you will lose your son, perhaps never to see him again."

Now it was Clary who took up the jewelled hand and absently gazed at the great cabochon ruby set there.

"Magdalena, my dearling, your news is wonderful, just wonderful. You will return to your own land with your precious daughter, and by your goodness, will take my dear son, Stephen with you. Don't think that I have not been deeply anxious for him. That accident was critical, so many bones broken, and I have watched him trying to hide the pain. Thomas, who has travelled far, assures me that warmer climes will suit him, ease his hurts, for of course, the uncles and brothers are so involved in their secret enterprise, someone let it slip out. Let us hope he can be usefully employed somewhere, somehow in your country when he is better, for as you know, we are a working family, despite," she smiled at her companion, "our recent elevation, or should I say re-elevation in life." They sat then, two friends idly speaking, both aware that this was precious time, which would not last forever.

CHAPTER FORTY SIX

THE PARTING

"So you knew all along," Stephen chided Richard, "and you never even hinted it to me, some friend." Richard smiled casually at his brother-in-law.

"I was told in great confidence not to divulge it, Stephen. I never even told my wife! For you know how those girls do chatter and it would be out in no time!"

They were on the way to the port with the tide running out so their passage was swift and effortless.

"The captains have asked us to go along and advise them on the new accommodation for the ladies. When I went on my voyage, there were many things I thought to do to make life more comfortable. But I must be tactful," he grinned, "not one of my gifts."

They were met at the port with horses which sped their way to the inlet where the ships lay. There was a busy sound of hammering and sawing, so they could see that some work had begun already.

When inside the ships, they saw that much had been removed and what had seemed a pokey little ship, now looked large and airy.

Together with his uncles James and John, they toured the gutted insides of the ships.

"We had spoken idly for some time to do such," said James, "but it is always good to have other opinions and we after all are accustomed to pretty cramped quarters. We must try to make things more comfortable for the ladies."

The four men wandered about the strangely emptied hull each with his own thoughts.

"As we will be travelling South, it does not much matter which side their cabins are, except being ladies, I do not doubt they will want to look landwards, for it is our intention to make port as often as possible, for their sakes."

Slates were brought out and they sketched their ideas, arguing, agreeing, changing their minds, rubbing out, until they had some sort of plan.

"Now," said Sir James, "if you can bring Her Grace the next fine day, we can discuss it with her. They must understand that we will do our best for their comfort, but, none the less, their quarters will be small, especially in comparison with their present accommodation."

"When will you and, Ursuline wed then, Stephen?" they were riding back as the tide was not yet turned and Stephen was anxious to get back.

"It is not in my hands," his words were whipped away by the wind which drove them along. "The duchess has her plans, and I for one will most gratefully go along with them. That she has accepted me for my Ursuline's husband is enough. Meanwhile I must get fit for the journey, indeed I have an appointment this evening with David Scrivener who has been teaching me how to cope with my disabilities."

Richard nodded, he was glad that the couple would at last be properly united. Well he remembered the pain of separation from his Lina, and now, he smiled to himself, he had a beautiful wife and daughter, and there was another little one on the way so she had confided in him. His life was good, and more than anything, he wanted his friends to be happy too, even if he would indeed miss them sorely.

Over the winter months, any bright day, despite the piercing cold wind, parties rode from the castles to the port to examine and admire the work going on. Slowly, slowly order was made. Fine thick mattresses were made to put into the complete cabins, and hangings to line the walls to please the duchess although later, the sailors looked wryly to the deck while they were being put up. If extra space had been given to the gentry, it meant less for them. Yet this was a new venture and they all looked forward to it.

"James, my clever brother, I need your advice and ideas," said Stephen when next James came to Highclere to visit his mother. "I am wondering if you and John can work out the smallest cooker at the smithy, an oven indeed, for charcoal, safe and strong for them to have on board? It was Richard who suggested it, with memories of his sailings."

James looked at his brother, his quick mind running.

"Let me think on it, Stephen, and discuss the possibilities with John." But he saw it in his mind's eye, sheets of iron formed into a box with slabs of stone cut to fit around and under it for safety. A drawer underneath to hold the charcoal, easily pulled out, to be filled and emptied. Yes surely, they would work something out.

He spoke with John about it, slate in hand, and together they worked out the smallest charcoal cooker which would be used by the personal staff of the duchess. In no time, one was made. They laughed as they carefully carried it on a board to the hall, there to press Maria and Fleur to use it. The second was better, neater, with a small pipe going out of the top which could be put out of a porthole. They were highly amused and pleased with their efforts and waited for a fine day to take them to the ships.

Now the slow packing began, sorting, discarding, re-packing.

Fleur was now officially betrothed to David Scrivener and he had agreed to go to Spain with his duchess at least for the journey. Whether they would stay or not, remained to be seen.

Clary left her family and went to the hall where she gathered, dried and packed up the herbs she thought they might need. On the one hand she was really happy for her son Stephen, for his marriage, for the fact he would be more comfortable in a warmer country. But oh the pain of loss, hastily, she brushed it aside. To never see him again? Oh my gentle Stephen.

With Lucius away but not so far, and Lina actually at the castle with her little one, and her own two dear little children, she realized how fortunate she was. But Stephen, so like Piers in every way, how she would miss him.

So the women all worked and tried to smile but tears were not so far from falling, and often they would hurry off on a sudden errand and lift their aprons to wipe their eyes.

Carola came to Clary, her little face anxious. "Aunt Clary, what can I give to Fleur to take on the ship? I do want to give her something."

Clary thought watching the sweet face pucker. She was stripping the dried leaves off mint which when really dry she would later pound in a mortar. Then she suddenly had an idea. Holding a strong stalk from the mint, she held it out to Carola.

"Dearling, how about going through this basket of waste mint stalks. Find the fattest and strongest, and we will cut them into equal lengths, then lay them to thoroughly dry out. Then you can use your own spun wool and tie them in bundles. So my little love, you can give them to Fleur, and indeed for all the travellers, for cleaning their teeth. She will be so pleased as mint tastes nice?" Carola beamed at her aunt and sat down immediately and began sorting the stalks.

Small baskets were collected and the gifts were placed in, all marked, providing the two ships equally. Little packets of sewing needles wrapped in greased cloth, so they would not rust, bundles of lace, funny small bags of powdered chalk scented with lavender. It went on, many different kinds of herbs for every small indisposition, herbs to add flavour to their meals, mint tooth sticks, all together a surprising number of small yet useful gifts.

"Essential I would say," said Clary. "A loving reminder of home comforts. You are a kind and loving girly my Carola, so thoughtful," and kissed her roundly.

Deborah held her friend's hands, eyes glistening.

"It is wonderful for me to know that Fleur, your niece, of your family, will be wed with my David. Then at last we shall be related, although you have always been sister of my heart. My parents would be overjoyed if they knew. And my father," she paused for a moment seeing in her mind's eye that frail, grey old man with milky eyes, "He would be more than joyful to know that one of ours is going back to his birth country."

They held hands thinking, and as all mothers, worrying.

"Her Grace has written about the old palace above the sea, and about my father's lands and old home, if it is vacant still. The house would be ideal for Fleur and David and that little village would greatly benefit from a physician. I know her brother will organize everything for they are amazed and full of joy that she is going home after all these years. Perhaps she will prefer to stay in the city, but perhaps at her age, not. It would be far more agreeable and healthy to be in the old palace which she remembers acutely. It can be very hot there of course, but those old buildings were built so strong and thick so to keep cool. And of course there is often a good sea breeze."

Deborah knew she was talking too much, but felt she must to reassure her friend. "For myself, I am torn between delight that my son, such an able physician, should be going back, to his roots as it were, but a good Christian boy so he will have no troubles as did my father's family." She pulled Clary close and wept a little. "This saying farewell and parting will almost be too much, we must keep close my sweet friend." Wetly laughing, the two women lifted their aprons and dried their eyes and got on with their tasks, packing medical herbs and weaving bindings and generally trying to anticipate every need.

Baskets and small trunks were made and filled with fine cloth for it might take time to settle in their new home and country and if there were plenty of available stores, life would be easier for them all. Lavender and bay leaves were put in fine bags between the cloth, and with the advice of the duchess, they did not put heavy woollen cloth, just a few rolls of fine warm stuff for shawls for the cool winter evenings.

They stood there, the two of them, eyes pleading. Carola, the prettiest little maid, and her twin, Piers, now a tall young man, handsome and earnest. Of course it was Carola who came out with it, her voice gentle, beseeching, eyes wide with appeal.

"Dearest James, will you teach us how to make some little wooden bowls so we can fill them with soap for their journey?"

James looked at the two, who he had known from birth. Carola who he had always loved, and now Piers, becoming a fine young man, so willing to learn all and everything he could teach him. Just as well for Piers would one day be master of Byford Hall. He pondered, thinking over his wood store, wondering the best technique to make bowls. The best and most handsome bowls would be made on a lathe, and he could set one up easily with a sapling.

"If I teach you," he began, "can you then manage on your own for you know that I am most busy also making preparations for our people for their journey. And once made, Carola, can you make really good, hard-ish soap to fill them?" They nodded eagerly, beaming.

"Then tomorrow we start, Carola, you begin to organize the best lard, check out the lavender too, and Piers, you gather up the chisels to sharpen them while I search out a sapling. Now that is a really fine idea my dearlings, why none of us even thought of it before I know not."

Having started them off, with occasional visits to check their remarkable progress, James returned to his making of good barrels for food for the journey, and all the friends and relations contributed so they were set ready in the cool cheese room waiting for nearer the time for departure. This was a purpose to their lives, not just for existence, for the winter to come, but for a future for their loved ones, and the niggle of pain which twisted every heart occasionally, was hastily dismissed.

Weeks and months passed and the days grew warmer and surreptitiously the hall men took the goods downstream to the port where they were carefully packed, each marked with its contents and well sealed.

Eventually, the evenings grown long, the duchess summoned the travellers and all their families and they gathered at the great castle for feasting and farewells.

Felicia and Robin came, claiming this to be their very last excursion, for said Felicia,

"This is the parting of the ways, so much to talk about, so much to imprint on young minds. Never to forget."

"Perhaps my dears, now is the time to have weddings?" suggested the duchess. "So all our people can rejoice and wish you well."

So it was that Ursuline and Stephen and Fleur and David were wed together and it was a great feast for a great many people, families and friends from far and wide.

Then one evening, they were surprised to have James appear with a small, neat person, dressed almost as a nun, head bowed.

"I have one more passenger for you, your grace, friends, so small she will not take much room, but perhaps her lace cushions and spun flax might take more space. My very old friend, as kin, Hannah, wishes to accompany you."

They were for a moment silent, then the Byford women ran to the newcomer and kissed her, holding her hands and laughing with joy. They had never imagined Hannah would leave the convent where she had lived for years, first nursing her father Han till his death, then staying peacefully and teaching the nuns lace making, so their convent had some little fame for their beautiful work.

"May I come with you, Lady?" Hannah said, curtsying deep before the duchess. "I am a useful sort of person and will make lace for my living, so will be no burden to anyone," she said in a quiet clear voice. "It could be that I might teach your people also?"

Having seen the welcome given to the strange little woman, of course the duchess agreed.

So Hannah was the reason for more and new stories to be told that evening about the great fireplace. First James, then she, making the best of their memories of how he had as a young boy, met her as a tiny babe. Years later, not knowing who he was, of how she had saved his life, and the story of the supposed cat flying out of the prison window. Now the girls clapped their hands, incredulous, having not heard of it before. Then the wicked winter night when they were all a-bed and the great dog had insisted that James came with him to find her buried deep in the snow. It was all a marvellous story, and both James and Hannah were badgered to give more facts till it was dark despite being mid summer.

"You all realize," said Felicia, somehow in a strong voice, so she held their attention, "we have all come from many roots and branches to be one big family. Our ways were far and foreign," she smiled at Thomas, Margaret and Rupert. "Your lady mother came from a-far, your grace, David, we not so far, yet we are all here, intermingled, so many roots, so many branches, I bless you all from my heart, for now we come to the parting of the ways, some to return to old homes, some to new. Yet part we must, which grieves us all yet, it is life my dearlings, life." A tear shone in her eye and she brushed it aside. "I will now go to my bed, come dear Robin, let us leave the young to say their farewells, for the morrow will be so busy."

Curtseying to the duchess, kissing her young relatives all, she went out, and for a while they were silent, thinking on her words.

Somehow, uplifted by the arrival of Hannah and the new stories, their mother, grandmother, kinswoman, courage filled their hearts so when they gathered in the morning on fine horses to ride at last to the port and their ships, it was a happy group, with shining eyes and ready smiles.

The uncles and the twin captains bustled about and settled everyone in. Apart from their small personal bags, the luggage had been stowed on board over the days, zealously guarded.

It seemed as if the entire two towns had come to see them off, such a throng, good natured, but, some, with a certain sadness. All the burgers came, dressed in their finest, the castle people who could be spared, with the priests in their vestments, holding their great crosses. The poorest of the poor came too, in their new clothes, recently given them by the duchess. Horses stamped, their harnesses jingling, seagulls wheeling overhead cried in alarm, at the jostling crowd. It was not every day that their duchess, her lovely lady daughter with her handsome new husband, and their entourage left, but this time, for good.

The family who had just come, to say farewell, were impressed with the fine arrangements of the small, but practical cabins and felt a strange longing to be going too. A Mass was said on the quay by the several priests, united for once, and the scent of incense floated in wafts of white across the little port mingling with the fish smells, the tar, and now the inevitable stink of the throng.

Faces were set in determined smiles, for certainly there would be time for tears in privacy later on.

"We will see how the way ahead lies," said Sir John Woodman.

"If we hear of any trouble, we will simply take the long route. But be sure our passengers will have as comfortable a voyage as we can arrange for them," said Sir James Woodman.

Each would captain one of the two ships, having gathered together a good crew with promises of fine rewards if all went well. The return journey would be different, with wine filling the holds and every spare cranny unless of course they happened to hear of new passengers wishing to go North.

"Be sure, my dear sister," said Sir James, taking Clary's hands, "we will not take any risks. We will watch the skies for foul weather and run to port so that our people can go ashore and see new places, so avoid discomfort on board."

What they had not told anyone was that they had sent a small and fast ship to survey the way ahead, and she could turn about, come to meet them to tell them the news. It was not every day they carried such a precious cargo and they were taking every precaution against trouble.

Lucius held his brother in his arms and said not a word. For they had always been so close, words were not necessary. Without a backward glance, he turned and mounted his horse to ride back to Castle Pomeroy and his sweet wife and children.

Clary then held Stephen, tears escaping despite her good intentions, but all she managed to say was, "Write, and I will."

Each member of the family had their own way to caress and say farewell, for God alone knew if they would meet on this earth again.

The ships looked wonderful, bright, clean, with pennants flying, the Duchess' arms as well as the Woodman, fluttering from on high and while the captains shouted and the crews shouted to each other, the wind whisked away their cries which mingled with that of the seagulls.

A good wind rose and first one ship, then the other put up sails and they were away with their passengers on the sunlit deck waving and their loved ones on the dock holding napkins to the air for as long as they could be seen. The crowd cheered and waved till the ships were far out to sea.

"Let the throng return home first, while you rest awhile with us," said one of the uncles.

"Yes indeed," said the other, "come to our humble home and take some refreshment and let us speak awhile about the marvellous way our families have come together so miraculously."

So they trouped into the tall narrow house and drank excellent wine from beautiful glass and laughed at the smoke dimmed tapestry above the fireplace, so familiar to them all.

It was a silent group who mounted their horses and slowly made their way back to the castle.

"Come and take wine with us," said the young duke, "to wish them a fair journey."

"Or let us go to say a mass for their safe arrival," said the young duchess.

But the Highcleres and the Byfords declined, sorrow in their hearts, knowing it was very possible they would never see their people again in this life and somehow they must learn to bear it.

"Forgive us," said James, knowing how they all felt. "We must go to our homes, where be sure we will say our prayers this night and every night for their safety."

On arrival at Highclere Castle, they found a flat just arrived from Byford Hall with John Smith tying up.

"James, my friend, go quickly to the hall where your lady is in travail these past two days. I am come to fetch Doctor Joseph for her, as the girls and the midwife are concerned. Go, go!" he said, roughly pushing James into the flat, "I will follow on with the doctor."

So it was that the day really did end badly, with Clary and Sir Thomas insisting they travelled with him, for Karen was a niece and precious to all of them.

CHAPTER FORTY SEVEN

CLARISSA

It was a whole year since the ships had sailed away on that beautiful morning and Clarissa was sitting in Karina's room high up on the castle battlements. They had heard several times, precious letters, and in her mind she blessed her younger brothers for their thoughtful arrangements to make sure letters went and came.

She was spinning flax on the new wheel which Thomas had bought her, via her brothers, of course, because these wondrous little machines were not yet well known in England. There was no need for her to spin, she knew that, but this was a pleasant, easy past-time, quicker than with a spindle, and Karina's loom still stood by a window so when she had enough yarn spun, she could call the warper and then weave some good cloth. She paused awhile, happy with her dream, and then went on to think of the family now so far away, and settled, and her dearest Stephen a father, a lovely boy called Jasper after Ursuline's father, the duke. The next boy, he assured her, his writing so much improved, would be named Piers, for his own father.

So the names went on, so many forefathers and foremothers, with so many fine names to give them. Fleur too had a child with her good David and they had named her Deborah, and Clary carefully wrote them all into the back of Lee's book. Soon she would have to insert another page of vellum.

Taking up and wetting the flax, Clary's mind then went to the Hall, where her dear James was running everything perfectly. Even young Piers was turning into a fine young man who did what he was told and was not a shadow of the spoilt child he had been.

Father Benjamin had finally come down the hill to live at the hall and slept in the old cupboard bed of grandfather Lucus. They never knew how old he was, but he became very quiet and slept most of the time. Then he became ill, so the girls told her, some deep pain in him which they could not ease.

"Carolla, come and help me please," called Karen. The old man started and called out.

"Carolla, is it you?"

Mystified, the girl took his hands and stroked them.

"I am here, Father Benjamin, here are my hands." Which he held fiercely, then eased.

"Stay with me then, my dearling, if you please, do not go away and leave me again." Carolla worried, looked at her aunt and got a nod.

"Of course I will stay with you always." So the old priest thought of his long lost love and believing it was she, held the young hands of the babe he had named for her, and slowly faded away over the next days.

So another old one had gone to his maker, and Clarissa's face unconsciously fell when she heard the news, for Jessie had died, quietly in her sleep too, and being the same age, Clary felt her own immortality.

They had always been so blessed, even Jessie who was not the most caring mother, regretting her many daughters, only having time for the longed for son when he finally arrived. Most people lost babies or indeed their young children, yet perhaps being somewhat isolated, away from the stink and stews of towns, the only child to be born dead, had been poor Karen's.

She thought over that fateful evening when they had left the port only a year ago, sad already to have seen their loved ones sail away, then speeding to the Hall where Karen was birthing her fourth child.

It had been a long, agonising birth, and James was frantic. He had told her later when it was all over, he had not wanted more children, let alone a son, for his memories of his father still stayed deep in his soul, his wickedness and violence. When finally they dragged the poor mite from his mother, he was dead, and James was shocked, for, he had turned away from her so she would not see his tears, sure enough, here was a son of Magnus.

The men stayed up late making the little box and lining it, and apparently very early in the morning, James had walked up to the church and buried it, an unsanctified child. Poor Karen, the son she wanted so much, and she took a long time to re-gain her strength so it was hard on the rest of the family coping.

A sudden smile crossed Clary's gentle face, for now she thought of the Pomeroys, her son and her niece, forbidden by the church to wed, yet, wed indeed by the church. Old Castle Pomeroy was once again a thriving and lively place, with four fine, healthy children racing about, making the old hallways and staircases ring with their noise.

She re-called stories of Lee, her mind flitting through images of his precious Book or Hours, that early forefather and his children, gentle Fleur who created such fine tapestries, and Jerome, patriarch of a great brood, who had almost killed some visiting pages for some misdemeanour.

"What do you think about my sweet lady wife?" a beloved voice cut into her reveries. "I have been watching you through the window, and I would love to know."

Clary turned and lifted her face to be kissed. Thomas was always the one who sensed her feelings, so now she smiled warmly at him.

"I was thinking about family, Thomas. All those past forebears of ours, our roots and branches, so many of them, mostly thankfully good people, and I was thinking of our dears across the seas."

He lent across and tucked a stray, pure white hair into her coif. Not a day passed when he didn't thank God and his sweet Mother, for giving him this treasure.

"So why dear lady, did you think that I toiled up those wicked and endless stairs?" He undid the pouch hanging from his belt and grinning, watched her smile ever broader. "Letters my own, just come, your good brother sent them hastily up river for us." Almost reverently, he drew them out and handed them to her. For after all, they had travelled so many miles.

"I have sent a message to Lina to come, for surely her eyes are so good, and she shall read them out to us." He had hardly finished speaking when it seemed a great rushing wind arrived, for Lina lead the way, skirts rustling, followed by a veritable entourage of people. Her two charming children, their nursemaids, two pages and last but not least, Rupert, puffing mightily.

"Sit, sit, brother," said Thomas drawing his familiar chair up, "letters from the family across the sea, a precious day indeed, despite this foul day of mist and rain."

There was much scuffling, settling of chairs, and Clary took the little Magdalena on to her lap.

"Read!" she said, handing the letters to Lina, "and do not run up those stairs any more please, remember your condition."

Lina gave a slightly impertinent look at her mother, who had by now told her everything, (except the truth of her paternity) of her own birth.

"Mother dear," her face softened. "Well you know that I am in body and soul a country woman, do stop worrying. Now!" She accepted Sir Thomas's small dagger and cut the seals of the four letters, "Be quiet my dear children or you will be sent down."

So firstly, she opened the duchess' letter, written she guessed by Ursuline, for the writing was small and neat.

To my families at my old home and at Highclere. May this letter find you by the Grace of God and his Sweet Mother, all in good health, as are we.

All is very well with us, the old palace is wondrously cool in the heat of the day, and Ursuline is directing the gardeners to make a fine herb bed for our own use. So to my first request, seeds please, the yellow daisies which we do have here, but only very small. Ursuline is making a tall hedge to protect the delicate herbs, so at least in spring, with the North wind from the mountains, they will do well.

Our next news is that at last, our palace being thoroughly restored by the goodness of my brother and nephews, I am considering building a proper church in the village. Fleur tells me about the churches her family built in the past, and this will give me joy in my old age with the knowledge that my body shall lie peacefully, and pray God, my soul will go to Heaven. No doubt by the time we write again, we will have begun this Holy work.

My very dear family, and my friend Clarissa, may the good Lord watch over all of you and keep you ever in good health.

Your loving Magdalena, dowager Duchess and now Donna of her own palace.

Lina beamed at everyone and carefully folded the letter. She had taken to copying them for all the family, an arduous task, but at least her life was one of total leisure now, she had plenty of time to do so.

"Now to open," she looked carefully at the next roll of vellum, "Stephen and Ursuline's," for the writing was the same. There was a re-settling in chairs, the maids and page extra careful to remain unobtrusive, for this was news from abroad, and they would proudly pass it on to everyone.

To my mother Lady Highclere and Sir Thomas, sister Lina, cousins and dear friends, may God be with you as he is with us. May you have good health and joy in your lives as have we.

Our dear David Scrivener is taking Stephen down to the sea very often on a great mule, to bathe his legs in the warm sea water where he gives him exercises and the warmth of the sun has great benefit to him and he is well, thanks be to God, his Holy Mother, and David.

Our lives are pleasant, and our little son is a happy child and growing apace. The only sorrow we have is that you are unable to see him, and that he is unable to play with all his cousins.

Both my Stephen and I, do sometimes find the heat tiring, so we retreat to our inner rooms of the palace, open the windows to the North, so ensuring a breeze, especially at night. Yet I am grateful to be close to my mother, and to know that my husband is benefiting from this climate. Only we wish, we could see your dear faces, and laugh with you.

For my dearly loved husband Stephen, I Ursuline, send this letter with our dearest love in the hope that God will watch over you, while we wait for your next letters. Ursuline.

That letter was carefully put away and another drawn out.

"Oh," cried Lina, "it is from Hannah, how lovely!"

My dearest ladies, indeed, all my adopted family, especially James, my Odi of our past, I send you so many good wishes from this lovely land where I am always warm.

You will be pleased to learn that I am now living in the village with Fleur and David which enables me to teach the local women to make lace. In this they are quick and deft handed, and their lace is now in demand and giving them a richer life. It has been a struggle, I confess, teaching them firstly to spin, and to keep their hands clean. I see you laugh my very dear ones, but lace must be clean. My teacher, oh so many years ago, taught me that.

Please, if any of you have contact with the convent who gave me and my father succour, send them my warmest greetings and tell them my news.

Fleur is writing this for me, for as a simple Rom woman, I cannot write but remember you all with greatest affection, Your own Hannah.

A warm glow filled the hearts of all who sat listening and now they did not speak for awhile, remembering the little Rom girl of that terrible winter night, who was warm at last.

"One last one," said Lina, breaking the silence, a strange deep contentment filling her heart. Taking out the last letter she smoothed it on her knee.

"To our dearest Families, Scriveners, Highcleres and Byfords, we greet you with heartfelt love in the hope that Our Lord is watching over you, as he does us.

We are living in the charming old house which had been David's great-grandmother's. We look out from the terrace at the sea and to Afrika and are deeply content with our lives. Hannah helps me with my daughter, and I can tell you that soon I will write to you about our next child.

David is busy, he has taken over the work of his forefather physician and is much in demand, even by the foreign sailors and their families who come to our small port. It is they who provide David with many medical herbs, for our herb gardens are not yet well established to harvest.

He also cares for our Donna who is too busy with building her fine church to care for her own health.

There is a man in our village who is clever with paint and he will make some small portraits of us all to send to you so you do not forget us.

May Our Lady and Our Lord take care of you all, your loving, Fleur."

They all sat silently thinking about the letters, seeing in their mind's eye, the view across the sea, then Lina took up the first letter and read them all again.

"I must write to my uncles, James and John with our gratitude, and indeed ask after the health of the great uncles who are certainly of a goodly age." Satisfied, contented, the party drifted away, small smiles on their mouths, for the news was all good.

Clarissa pressed her husband's hand.

"Dear husband, I suddenly have the need to go to the Marsh Tower, for although I know the girls are more than capable, I wish to see my parents, for they grow old too and the journey here will tire them."

Ever the agreeable man, Sir Thomas nodded and set off to organise a flat with provisions. He had a great respect for his wife's instincts and if she felt she must go to visit her parents, then go she must.

Little had changed on the river, the cranes sitting, watching bright eyed for their dinner. The reeds swaying in the wind, the great horse placidly plodding along, Matthew leading him, his wide hooves making a solid sound on the tow path. A pleasant breeze helping the flat along, making a gentle spray from the river.

Of course they stopped briefly at Byford Hall, and when Thomas and Matthew had helped Clary up the stone steps, she ran like a girl into her old home.

"Lady Byford," she called, a smile on her face, and Karen ran in breathless, a child under her arm and embraced her kinswoman.

"We could not pass by without seeing you dearling," she said, "but my son James, where is he?" After a little time and much calling, James appeared, wiping his hands on a cloth and hugged his mother till she appealed to be let down. Thomas then assured them they would call by on their return in a day or two, with all the news, but dusk would soon fall and they must be off to reach the Marsh Tower by nightfall.

At last, there it was, the Marsh Tower, like a sentinel, and Clary held Thomas' hand and her secret smile told him of her happiness to be here again. Oh and the joy she would give her parents with all the news from the family now so far away. Lifting Thomas' hand she kissed it, life was kind, how blessed they were, and kissed the hand again.

"Perhaps I am a little nervous of asking you this, dear Thomas," Clary said still holding his hand tightly. "As Magdalena went back to her country, so do I feel a great yearning to move back to the Marsh Tower. A place of such happiness, peace and memories, with my beloved husband and dearling little children. There," she rushed on, "to care for my parents in their old age, to be between Lucius and Lina, not too far from either. Thomas," she strained to see him in the dusk, "tell me what you think?"

Thomas smiled, for this good woman he would do anything, so he leant down and kissed her again.

"Shall we put it to your parents then, for if they are willing, so am I." Which brought about a crow of delight from Clary and she held him close.

At the prow of the flat, Matthew lifted the horn and blew hard. There it stood, a dark sentinel against a deep, dark blue sky. Lights began to show that they were heard, and eagerly they floated forward, voices calling. They were home, all was well.

19253473R00363

Made in the USA
Charleston, SC
14 May 2013